SWEENEY TODD.

VOL. I.

MARK INGESTRIE AND JOHANNA OAKLEY.

SWEENEY TODD,

THE BARBER *of* FLEET-STREET.

(Original Title: The String of Pearls)

VOL. I

By

JAMES MALCOLM RYMER

With George MacFarren and Thomas Preskett Prest

Edited and Annotated by Finn J.D. John

Pulp-Lit
PRODUCTIONS
CORVALLIS, OREGON

Dustjacket and book cover by Natalie Conaway.

First edition, softcover

ISBN: 978-1-63591-682-9

Pulp-Lit Productions
Corvallis, Oregon

http://pulp-lit.com

INTRODUCTION.

The notorious tale of Sweeney Todd and Sarah* Lovett first reached the reading public of London in the form of a serial novel published in Edward Lloyd's *People's Periodical and Family Library* starting in November of 1846.

It was one of those narratives that instantly catalyzes something in the reading public. English literature would never be quite the same.

The story deftly adopted and expanded on urban legendry and mixed it into what you might call a "hyper-local" story. Its atmosphere, still today, evokes old London. The character types were familiar ones to mid-1800s Londoners: the big, boisterous, not-too-smart beefeater, the uppity law clerk, the shamelessly hypocritical nonconformist parson, the self-important church beadle. The locations where the action played out were real places — most of which you can still visit today.

The moral world of Sweeney Todd and Mrs. Lovett was familiar to lower-class Londoners too. The story's narrator never shrinks from a full description of brutality and injustice.

Moreover, although *The String of Pearls* obviously owes a lot to Charles Dickens, in some ways it runs just opposite Dickens' approach. Dickens, although he had considerable personal

---

* *Mrs. Lovett's first name is different in several other versions of this story; however, since she's referred to as Sarah in this one, we're using it here.*

experience of lower-class London life, functioned in most ways as the eyes and conscience of middle-class London. Terrible things happen in Dickens stories, but there is some end that they are moving toward. If we spend enough time with a character to get to know her, to learn her story, and to start rooting for her to overcome the odds against her, we can be pretty sure that our investment in her will be rewarded by either a triumphant ending or a meaningful death. We can usually be pretty sure that our emotional investment will not end up at the bottom of an old dry well, the victim of a brutal and senseless murder by a pair of corrupt madhouse-keepers, and nothing more said upon the subject until her skeleton is casually mentioned at the very end of the story.

Some of that is no doubt an effect of sloppy craftsmanship; Lloyd's writers were banging out copy in a terrible hurry, and many narrative threads were left unpicked. But at least some of it is clearly a deliberate artistic decision to match the brutality of early-Victorian Londoners' world with equally brutal storytelling. Life was like that, real life, as an old London chimney sweep or a poor widow or a hack driver. And lower-class London found more in common with the rough-hewn, charming, occasionally savage work of Edward Lloyd's writers than it did with the middle-class sensibilities of Dickens. (It certainly found the price of a Lloyd publication more congenial. One could buy twelve installments of Sweeney Todd's saga for the price of one from Dickens.)

All of which is to say that one could almost consider *The String of*

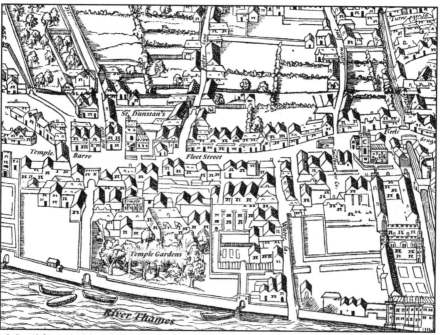

A detail from the "Agas Map" of London in the 16th–17th century, showing the neighbourhood where most of this story takes place.

The old St. Dunstan's Church as it appeared circa 1814, as seen from Fleet Street. Bell Yard, the narrow alley-like street on which Mrs. Lovett's pie shop fronted, was a building or two to the left. Sweeney Todd's barber shop would have been just opposite, across Fleet Street from St. Dunstan's.

Pearls as an early version of a *roman noir* — the "hard-boiled" books that became popular in the years just after the Second World War.

Whether for that reason, or another, the story of Sweeney Todd turned out to be so compelling that Lloyd promptly took the relatively short original serial novel and turned it into one of the "penny dreadful" or "penny blood-and-thunder" serials that he was so well known for: basically eight-page magazines, each with a woodcut illustration and a chapter or two of the story. These he subsequently combined into a single enormous hardcover volume, published in 1850.

It is this "penny-dreadful" version of the Sweeney Todd story that is presented in this collection.

Although the shorter version hangs together better as a novel — being tighter and having a much more coherent story arc — the "penny dreadful" magazines were not experienced that way. Readers got them in short bursts, each of which had to deliver some kind of narrative payload to keep readers engaged. The difference is roughly analogous to the modern difference between a blockbuster movie and a two-season-long serial television show.

Moreover, because much of the audience for "penny dreadfuls" was illiterate, they were made to be read out loud. Cues like phonetic spelling for characters with professional or regional accents, and deliberately mispronounced words (set in italic type so that they would not be overlooked by the aloud-reader) aided the back-street dramatist as he read the story to an audience of friends and relatives.

It's also loaded with witty asides as well as inside jokes and pop-culture references. Many of these have disappeared completely from popular consciousness over the nearly 200 years that have intervened between then and now; but those that can still be identified, along with literary references to popular plays, poems, and novels, are briefly footnoted in this edition.

The goal of these notes, and of this introduction, is not to delve into serious scholarship. That has already been done, rather masterfully, by many others over the years. Rather, we seek to make this remarkably compelling tale more meaningful and enjoyable for a modern reader by contextualizing it as much as possible, and to deliver to you, experiencing this classic "penny blood-and-thunder" in the twenty-first century, an experience as similar as possible to that of one of the original readers who eagerly devoured each subsequent installment in his or her spare moments on the dirty and harried streets of Victorian London.

PREFACE.

THE ROMANCE OF THE STRING OF PEARLS having excited in the Literary world an almost unprecedented interest, it behooves the author to say a few words to his readers upon the completion of his labours.

In answer to the many inquiries that have been, from time to time, made regarding the fact of whether there ever was such a person as Sweeney Todd in existence, we can unhesitatingly say, that there certainly was such a man; and the record of his crimes is still to be found in the chronicles of criminality of this country.

The house in Fleet-street, which was the scene of Todd's crimes, is no more. A fire, which destroyed some half-dozen buildings on that side of the way, involved Todd's in destruction; but the secret passage, although, no doubt, partially blocked up with the re-building of St. Dunstan's Church, connecting the vaults of that edifice with the cellars of what was Todd's house in Fleet-street, still remains.

From the great patronage which this work has received from the reading public, the author has to express his deep and earnest thanks; and he begs to state, that if anything more than another could stimulate him to renewed exertion to please his numerous patrons, it is their kind and liberal appreciation of his past labours.

LONDON, 1850.

THE
STRING OF PEARLS;

or,

THE BARBER OF FLEET-STREET.

A DOMESTIC ROMANCE.

"And now, Tobias, listen to me, and treasure up every word I say." — *"Yes, sir."* — *"I'll cut your throat from ear to ear, if you repeat one word of what passes in this shop, or dare to make any supposition, or draw any conclusion from anything you may see, or hear, or fancy you see or hear."*

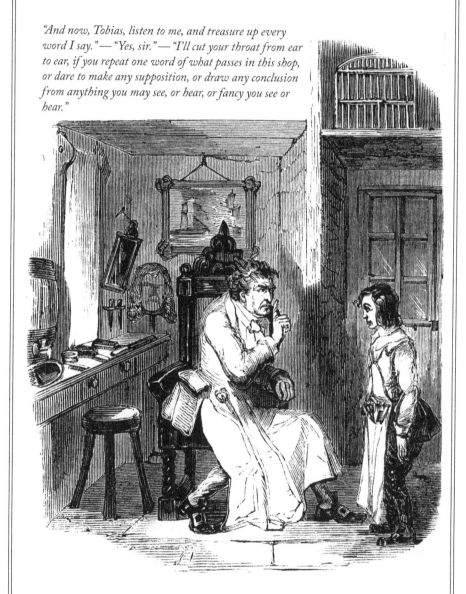

THE BARBER'S LESSON TO HIS APPRENTICE.

CHAPTER I.

BEFORE FLEET-STREET HAD REACHED its present importance, and when George the Third was young, and the two figures who used to strike the chimes at old St. Dunstan's church were in all their glory* — being a great impediment to errand-boys on their progress, and a matter of gaping curiosity to country people — there stood close to the sacred edifice a small barber's shop, which was kept by a man of the name of Sweeney Todd.

How it was that he came by the name of Sweeney, as a Christian appellation, we are at a loss to conceive, but such was his name, as might be seen in extremely corpulent yellow letters over his shop window, by any who chose there to look for it.

Barbers by that time in Fleet-street had not become fashionable, and no more dreamt of calling themselves artists than of taking the Tower by storm; moreover they were not, as they are now, constantly slaughtering fine fat bears,† and yet, somehow people had hair on their heads just the same as they have at present, without the aid of that unctuous auxiliary. Moreover, Sweeney Todd, in common with those really primitive sort of times, did not think it at all necessary to have any waxen effigies of humanity in his window. There was no languishing young lady looking over the left shoulder in order that a profusion of auburn tresses might repose upon her lily neck, and great conquerors and great statesmen were not then, as they are now, held up to public ridicule with dabs of rouge upon their cheeks, a quantity of gunpowder scattered in for beard, and some bristles sticking on end for eyebrows.

No. Sweeney Todd was a barber of the old school, and he never thought

---

* This is a reference to the two clockwork giants who strike the hours and quarter-hours at St. Dunstan's church with their clubs. The clock was removed to the Marquess of Hertford's residence when the church was rebuilt in 1828, and Londoners still remembered and missed them in 1847 when The String of Pearls was published. The clock was not returned to St. Dunstan's until 1935.

† For bear's-grease, a popular hair-and-whisker dressing and treatment for hair loss in the Victorian period. Barbers sometimes displayed captive bears which they claimed were about to be slaughtered to furnish fresh bear's-grease, as an advertisement; but the vast majority of "bear's-grease" sold was really made from pigs.

of glorifying himself on account of any extraneous circumstance. If he had lived in Henry the Eighth's palace, it would be all the same as Henry the Eighth's dog-kennel, and he would scarcely have believed human nature to be so green as to pay an extra sixpence to be shaven and shorn in any particular locality.

A long pole painted white, with a red stripe curling spirally round it, projected into the street from his doorway, and on one of the panes of glass in his window, was presented the following couplet: —

Easy shaving for a penny,
As good as you will find any.

We do not put these lines forth as a specimen of the poetry of the age; they may have been the production of some young Templar; but if they were a little wanting in poetic fire, that was amply made up by the clear and precise manner in which they set forth what they intended.

The barber himself, was a long, low-jointed, ill-put-together sort of fellow, with an immense mouth, and such huge hands and feet, that he was, in his way, quite a natural curiosity; and, what was more wonderful, considering his trade, there never was seen such a head of hair as Sweeney Todd's. We know not what to compare it to; probably it came nearest to what one might suppose to be the appearance of a thick-set hedge, in which a quantity of small wire had got entangled. In truth, it was a most terrific head of hair; and as Sweeney Todd kept all his combs in it — some people said his scissors likewise — when he put his head out of the shop-door to see what sort of weather it was, he might have been mistaken for an Indian warrior with a very remarkable head-dress.

He had a short disagreeable kind of unmirthful laugh, which came in at all sorts of odd times when nobody else saw anything to laugh at at all, and which sometimes made people start again, especially when they were being shaved, and Sweeney Todd would stop short in that operation to indulge in one of those cachinatory effusions. It was evident that the remembrance of some very strange and out-of-the-way joke must occasionally flit across him, and then he gave his hyena-like laugh, but it was so short, so sudden, striking upon the ear for a moment, and then gone, that people have been known to look up to the ceiling, and on the floor, and all round them, to know from whence it had come, scarcely supposing it possible that it proceeded from mortal lips.

Mr. Todd squinted a little, to add to his charms; and so we think that by this time the reader may, in his mind's eye, see the individual whom we wish to present to him. Some thought him a careless enough, harmless fellow, with not much sense in him, and at times they almost considered he was a little cracked; but there were others who shook their heads when they spoke of him; and while they could say nothing to his prejudice, except that they certainly considered he was odd, yet, when they came to consider what a great crime and misdemeanour it really is in this world, to be odd, we shall not be surprised at the ill-odour in which Sweeney Todd was held.

But for all that he did a most thriving business, and was considered by his neighbours to be a very well-to-do sort of man, and decidedly, in city phraseology, warm.

It was so handy for the young students in the Temple to pop over to Sweeney Todd's to get their chins new rasped; so that from morning to night he drove a good business, and was evidently a thriving man.*

There was only one thing that seemed in any way to detract from the great prudence of Sweeney Todd's character, and that was that he rented a large house, of which he occupied nothing but the shop and parlour, leaving the upper part entirely useless, and obstinately refusing to let it on any terms whatever.

Such was the state of things, A.D. 1785, as regarded Sweeney Todd.

THE DAY IS DRAWING TO A CLOSE, and a small drizzling kind of rain is falling, so that there are not many passengers in the streets, and Sweeney Todd is sitting in his shop looking keenly in the face of a boy, who stands in an attitude of trembling subjection before him.

"You will remember," said Sweeney Todd, and he gave his countenance a most horrible twist as he spoke, "you will remember, Tobias Ragg, that you are now my apprentice, that you have of me had board, washing, and lodging, with the exception that you don't sleep here, that you take your meals at home, and that your mother, Mrs. Ragg, does your washing, which she may very well do, being a laundress in the Temple, and making no end of money; as for lodging, you lodge here, you know, very comfortably in the shop all day. Now, are you not a happy dog?"

"Yes, sir," said the boy timidly.

"You will acquire a first-rate profession, quite as good as the law, which your mother tells me she would have put you to, only that a little weakness of the head-piece unqualified you. And now, Tobias, listen to me, and treasure up every word I say."

"Yes, sir."

"I'll cut your throat from ear to ear, if you repeat one word of what passes in this shop, or dare to make any supposition, or draw any conclusion from anything you may see, or hear, or fancy you see or hear. Now you understand me, — I'll cut your throat from ear to ear, — do you understand me?"

---

*The Temple was originally a church and campus of the Knights Templar, established during the Crusades. By the time of this story it had long been a center of London's legal profession, featuring offices, courts, and residences for lawyers, law students, and clerks.

"Yes, sir, I won't say nothing. I wish, sir, as I may be made into veal pies at Lovett's in Bell-yard if I as much as says a word."

Sweeney Todd rose from his seat; and opening his huge mouth, he looked at the boy for a minute or two in silence, as if he fully intended swallowing him, but had not quite made up his mind where to begin.

"Very good," at length he said, "I am satisfied, I am quite satisfied; and mark me — the shop, and the shop only, is your place."

"Yes, sir."

"And if any customer gives you a penny, you can keep it, so that if you get enough of them you will become a rich man; only I will take care of them for you, and when I think you want them I will let you have them. Run out and see what's o'clock by St. Dunstan's."

THERE WAS A SMALL CROWD COLLECTED opposite the church, for the figures were about to strike three-quarters past six; and among that crowd was one man who gazed with as much curiosity as anybody at the exhibition.

"Now for it!" he said, "they are going to begin; well, that is ingenious. Look at the fellow lifting up his club, and down it comes bang upon the old bell."

The three-quarters were struck by the figures; and then the people who had loitered to see it done, many of whom had day by day looked at the same exhibition for years past, walked away, with the exception of the man who seemed so deeply interested.

He remained, and crouching at his feet was a noble-looking dog, who looked likewise up at the figures; and who, observing his master's attention to be closely fixed upon them, endeavoured to show as great an appearance of interest as he possibly could.

"What do you think of that, Hector?" said the man.

The dog gave a short low whine, and then his master proceeded, —

"There is a barber's shop opposite, so before I go any farther, as I have got to see the ladies, although it's on a very melancholy errand, for I have got to tell them that poor Mark Ingestrie is no more, and Heaven knows what poor Johanna will say — I think I should know her by his description of her, poor fellow! It grieves me to think how he used to talk about her in the long night-watches, when all was still, and not a breath of air touched a curl upon his cheek. I could almost think I saw her sometimes, as he used to tell me of her soft beaming eyes, her little gentle pouting lips, and the dimples that played about her mouth. Well, well, it's of no use grieving; he is dead and gone, poor fellow, and the salt water washes over as brave a heart as ever beat. His sweetheart, Johanna, though, shall have the string of pearls for all that; and if she cannot be Mark Ingestrie's wife in this world, she shall be rich and happy, poor young thing, while she stays in it, that is to say as happy as she can be; and she must just look forward to meeting him aloft, where there are no squalls or tempests.—And so I'll go and get shaved at once."

He crossed the road towards Sweeney Todd's shop, and, stepping down the low doorway, he stood face to face with the odd-looking barber.

The dog gave a low growl and sniffed the air.

"Why Hector," said his master, "what's the matter? Down, sir, down!"

"I have a mortal fear of dogs," said Sweeney Todd. "Would you mind him, sir, sitting outside the door and waiting for you, if it's all the same? Only look at him, he is going to fly at me!"

"Then you are the first person he ever touched without provocation," said the man; "but I suppose he don't like your looks, and I must confess I ain't much surprised at that. I have seen a few rum-looking guys in my time, but hang me if ever I saw such a figure-head as yours. What the devil noise was that?"

"It was only me," said Sweeney Todd; "I laughed."

"Laughed! do you call that a laugh? I suppose you caught it of somebody who died of it. If that's your way of laughing, I beg you won't do it any more."

"Stop the dog! stop the dog! I can't have dogs running into my back parlour."

"Here, Hector, here!" cried his master; "get out!"

Most unwillingly the dog left the shop, and crouched down close to the outer door, which the barber took care to close, muttering something about a draught of air coming in, and then, turning to the apprentice boy, who was screwed up in a corner, he said,—

"Tobias, my lad, go to Leadenhall-street, and bring a small bag of the thick biscuits from Mr. Peterson's; say they are for me. Now, sir, I suppose you want to be shaved, and it is well you have come here, for there ain't a shaving-shop, although I say it, in the city of London that ever thinks of polishing anybody off as I do."

"I tell you what it is, master barber: if you come that laugh again, I will get up and go. I don't like it, and there is an end of it."

"Very good," said Sweeney Todd, as he mixed up a lather. "Who are you? where did you come from? and where are you going?"

"That's cool, at all events. Damn it! what do you mean by putting the brush in my mouth? Now, don't laugh; and since you are so fond of asking questions, just answer me one."

"Oh, yes, of course: what is it, sir?"

"Do you know a Mr. Oakley, who lives somewhere in London, and is a spectacle-maker?"

"Yes, to be sure I do—John Oakley, the spectacle-maker, in Fore-street, and he has got a daughter named Johanna, that the young bloods call the Flower of Fore-street."

"Ah, poor thing! do they? Now, confound you! what are you laughing at now? What do you mean by it?"

"Didn't you say, 'Ah, poor thing?' Just turn your head a little a one side; that will do. You have been to sea, sir?"

"Yes, I have, and have only now lately come up the river from an Indian voyage."

"Indeed! where can my strop be? I had it this minute; I must have laid it down somewhere. What an odd thing that I can't see it! It's very extraordinary; what can have become of it? Oh, I recollect, I took it into the parlour. Sit still, sir, I shall not be gone a moment; sit still, sir, if you please. By the by, you can amuse yourself with the *Courier*, sir, for a moment."

Sweeney Todd walked into the back parlour and closed the door.

There was a strange sound suddenly, compounded of a rushing noise and then a heavy blow, immediately after which Sweeney Todd emerged from his parlour, and folding his arms, he looked upon *the vacant chair* where his customer had been seated, but the customer was *gone*, leaving not the slightest trace of his presence behind except his hat, and that Sweeney Todd immediately seized and thrust into a cupboard that was at one corner of the shop.

"What's that?" he said, "what's that? I thought I heard a noise."

"If you please, sir, I have forgot the money, and have run all the way back from St. Paul's churchyard."

In two strides Todd reached Tobias, and clutching him by the arm he dragged him into the farther corner of the shop, and then he stood opposite to him, glaring him full in the face with such a demoniac expression that the boy was frightfully terrified.

"Speak!" cried Todd, "speak! and speak the truth, or your last hour has come. How long were you peeping through the door before you came in?"

"Peeping, sir?"

"Yes, peeping; don't repeat my words, but answer me at once, you will find it better for you in the end."

"I wasn't peeping, sir, at all."

Sweeney Todd drew a long breath as he then said, in a strange, shrieking sort of manner, which he intended, no doubt, should be jocose, —

"Well, well, very well; if you did peep, what then? it's no matter; I only wanted to know, that's all; it was quite a joke, wasn't it — quite funny, though rather odd, eh? Why don't you laugh, you dog? Come, now, there is no harm done. Tell me what you thought about it at once, and we will be merry over it — very merry."

"I don't know what you mean, sir," said the boy, who was quite as much alarmed at Mr. Todd's mirth as he was at his anger. "I don't know what you mean, sir; I only just come back because I hadn't any money to pay for the biscuits at Peterson's."

"I mean nothing at all," said Todd, suddenly turning upon his heel; "what's that scratching at the door?"

Tobias opened the shop-door, and there stood the dog, who looked wistfully round the place, and then gave a howl which seriously alarmed the barber.

"It's the gentleman's dog, sir," said Tobias, "it's the gentleman's dog, sir, that was looking at old St. Dunstan's clock, and came in here to be shaved. It's funny, ain't it, sir, that the dog didn't go away with his master?"

"Why don't you laugh if it's funny? Turn out the dog, Tobias; we'll have no dogs here; I hate the sight of them; turn him out — turn him out."

"I would, sir, in a minute; but I'm afraid he wouldn't let me, somehow. Only look, sir — look; see what he is at now! did you ever see such a violent fellow, sir? why he will have down the cupboard door."

"Stop him — stop him! the devil is in the animal! stop him I say!"

The dog was certainly getting the door open, when Sweeney Todd rushed forward to "stop him!" — but that he was soon admonished of the danger of doing, for the dog gave him a grip of the leg, which made him give such a howl, that he precipitately retreated, and left the animal to do its pleasure. This consisted in forcing open the cupboard door, and seizing upon the hat which Sweeney Todd had thrust therein, and dashing out of the shop with it in triumph.

"The devil's in the beast," muttered Todd, "he's off! Tobias, you said you saw the man who owned that fiend of a cur looking at St. Dunstan's church."

"Yes, sir, I did see him there. If you recollect, you sent me to see the time, and the figures were just going to strike three quarters past six; and before I came away, I heard him say that Mark Ingestrie was dead, and Johanna should have the string of pearls. Then I came in, and then, if you recollect, sir, he came in, and the odd thing, you know, to me, sir, is that he didn't take his dog with him, because you know, sir —"

"Because what?" shouted Todd.

"Because people generally do take their dogs with them, you know, sir; and may I be made into one of Mrs. Lovett's pies, if I don't —"

"Hush, some one comes; it's old Mr. Grant, from the Temple. How do you do, Mr. Grant? Glad to see you looking so well, sir. It does one's heart good to see a gentlemen of your years looking so fresh and hearty. Sit down, sir; a little this way, if you please. Shaved, I suppose?"

"Yes, Todd, yes. Any news?"

"No, sir, nothing stirring. Everything very quiet, sir, except the high wind. They say it blew the king's hat off yesterday, sir, and he borrowed Lord North's. Trade is dull too, sir. I suppose people won't come out to be cleaned and dressed in a mizzling rain. We haven't had anybody in the shop for an hour and a half."

"Lor' sir," said Tobias, "you forget the sea-faring gentleman with the dog, you know, sir."

"Ah! so I do," said Todd. "He went away, and I saw him get into some disturbance, I think, just at the corner of the market."

"I wonder I didn't meet him, sir," said Tobias, "for I came that way; and then it's so very odd leaving his dog behind him."

"Yes, very," said Todd. "Will you excuse me a moment, Mr. Grant? Tobias, my lad, I just want you to lend me a hand in the parlour."

Tobias followed Todd very unsuspectingly into the parlour; but when they got there and the door was closed, the barber sprang upon him like an enraged tiger, and, grappling him by the throat, he gave his head such a succession of knocks against the wainscot, that Mr. Grant must have thought that some carpenter was at work. Then he tore a handful of his hair out, after which he twisted him round, and dealt him such a kick, that he was flung sprawling into a corner of the room, and then, without a word, the barber walked out again to his customer, and bolted his parlour door on the outside, leaving Tobias to digest the usage he had received at his leisure, and in the best way he could.

When he came back to Mr. Grant, he apologised for keeping him waiting, by saying,—

"It became necessary, sir, to teach my new apprentice a little bit of his business. I have left him studying it now. There is nothing like teaching young folks at once."

"Ah!" said Mr. Grant, with a sigh, "I know what it is to let young folks grow wild; for although I have neither chick nor child of my own, I had a sister's son to look to — a handsome, wild, harum-scarum sort of fellow, as like me as one pea is like another. I tried to make a lawyer of him, but it wouldn't do, and it's now more than two years ago he left me altogether; and yet there were some good traits about Mark."

"Mark, sir! Did you say Mark?"

"Yes, that was his name, Mark Ingestrie. God knows what's become of him."

"Oh!" said Sweeney Todd; he went on lathering the chin of Mr. Grant.

CHAPTER II.

THE SPECTACLE-MAKER'S DAUGHTER.

"Johanna, Johanna, my dear, do you know what time it is? Johanna, I say, my dear, are you going to get up? Here's your mother has trotted out to Parson Lupin's, and you know I have got to go to Alderman Judd's house, in

Cripplegate, the first thing, and I haven't had a morsel of breakfast yet. Johanna, my dear, do you hear me?"

These observations were made by Mr. Oakley, the spectacle-maker, at the door of his daughter Johanna's chamber, on the morning after the events we have just recorded at Sweeney Todd's; and presently, a soft sweet voice answered him, saying, —

"I am coming, father, I am coming: in a moment, father, I shall be down."

"Don't hurry yourself, my darling, I can wait."

The little old spectacle-maker descended the staircase again, and sat down in the parlour at the back of the shop, where, in a few moments, he was joined by Johanna, his only and his much-loved child.

She was indeed a creature of the rarest grace and beauty. Her age was eighteen, but she looked rather younger, and upon her face she had that sweetness and intelligence of expression which almost bids defiance to the march of time. Her hair was of a glossy blackness, and what was rare in conjunction with such a feature, her eyes were of a deep and heavenly blue. There was nothing of the commanding or of the severe style of beauty about her, but the expression of her face was all grace and sweetness. It was one of those countenances which one could look at for a long summer's day, as upon the pages of some deeply interesting volume, which furnished the most abundant food for pleasant and delightful reflection.

There was a touch of sadness about her voice, which, perhaps, only tended to make it the more musical, although mournfully so, and which seemed to indicate that at the bottom of her heart there lay some grief which had not yet been spoken — some cherished aspiration of her pure soul, which looked hopeless as regards completion — some remembrance of a former joy, which had been turned to bitterness and grief; it was the cloud in the sunny sky — the shadow through which there still gleamed bright and beautiful sunshine, but which still proclaimed its presence.

"I have kept you waiting, father," she said, as she flung her arms about the old man's neck, "I have kept you waiting."

"Never mind, my dear, never mind. Your mother is so taken up with Mr. Lupin, that you know, this being Wednesday morning, she is off to his prayer meeting, and so I have had no breakfast; and really I think I must discharge Sam."

"Indeed, father! what has he done?"

"Nothing at all, and that's the very reason. I had to take down the shutters myself this morning, and what do you think for? He had the coolness to tell me he couldn't take down the shutters this morning, or sweep out the shop, because his aunt had the toothache."

"A poor excuse, father," said Johanna, as she bustled about and got the breakfast ready; "a very poor excuse."

"Poor indeed! but his month is up to-day, and I must get rid of him. But I suppose I shall have no end of bother with your mother, because his aunt belongs to Mr. Lupin's congregation; but as sure as this is the 20th day of August —"

"It is the 20th day of August," said Johanna, as she sunk into a chair and burst into tears. "It is, it is! I thought I could have controlled this, but I cannot, father, I cannot. It was that which made me late. I knew mother was out; I knew that I ought to be down attending upon you, and I was praying to Heaven for strength to do so because this was the 20th of August."

Johanna spoke these words incoherently, and amidst sobs, and when she had finished them, she leant her sweet face upon her small hands, and wept like a child.

The astonishment, not unmingled with positive dismay, of the old spectacle-maker, was vividly depicted on his countenance, and for some minutes he sat perfectly aghast, with his hands resting on his knees, and looking in the face of his beautiful child — that is to say, as much as he could see of it between those little taper fingers that were spread upon it — as if he were newly awakened from some dream.

"Good God, Johanna!" he said at length, "what is this? My dear child, what has happened? Tell me, my dear, unless you wish to kill me with grief."

"You shall know, father," she said. "I did not think to say a word about it, but considered I had strength enough of mind to keep my sorrows in my own breast, but the effort has been too much for me, and I have been compelled to yield. If you had not looked so kindly on me — if I did not know that you loved me as you do, I should easily have kept my secret, but, knowing that much, I cannot."

"My darling," said the old man, "you are right, there; I do love you. What would the world be to me without you? There was a time, twenty years ago, when your mother made up much of my happiness, but of late, what with Mr. Lupin, and psalm-singing, and tea-drinking, I see very little of her, and what little I do see is not very satisfactory. Tell me, my darling, what it is that vexes you, and I'll soon put it to rights. I don't belong to the city trainbands* for nothing."

"Father, I know that your affection would do all for me that it is possible to do, but you cannot recall the dead to life; and if this day passes over and I see him not, nor hear from him, I know that, instead of finding a home for me whom he loved, he has in the effort to do so found a grave for himself. He said he would, he said he would."

Here she wrung her hands, and wept again, and with such a bitterness of anguish that the old spectacle-maker was at his wit's end, and knew not what on earth to do or say.

---

* *A trainband was a sort of home-guard militia company.*

"My dear, my dear," he cried, "who is he? I hope you don't mean —"

"Hush, father, hush! I know the name that is hovering on your lips, but something seems even now to whisper to me he is no more, and, being so, speak nothing of him, father, but that which is good."

"You mean Mark Ingestrie."

"I do, and if he had a thousand faults, he at least loved me; he loved me truly and most sincerely."

"My dear," said the old spectacle-maker, "you know that I wouldn't for all the world say anything to vex you, nor will I; but tell me what it is that makes this day more than any other so gloomy to you."

"I will, father; you shall hear. It was on this day two years ago that we last met; it was in the Temple-garden, and he had just had a stormy interview with his uncle, Mr. Grant, and you will understand, father, that Mark Ingestrie was not to blame, because —"

"Well, well, my dear, you needn't say anything more upon that point. Girls very seldom admit their lovers are to blame, but there are two ways, you know, Johanna, of telling a story."

"Yes; but, father, why should Mr. Grant seek to force him to the study of a profession he so much disliked?"

"My dear, one would have thought that if Mark Ingestrie really loved you, and found that he might make you his wife, and acquire an honourable subsistence for you and himself — it seems a very wonderful thing to me that he did not do so. You see, my dear, he should have liked you well enough to do something else that he did not like."

"Yes, but father, you know it is hard, when disagreements once arise, for a young ardent spirit to give in entirely; and so from one word, poor Mark, in his disputes with his uncle, got to another, when perhaps one touch of kindness or conciliation from Mr. Grant would have made him quite pliant in his hands."

"Yes, that's the way," said Mr. Oakley; "there is no end of excuses: but go on, my dear, go on, and tell me exactly how this affair now stands."

"I will, father. It was this day two years ago then that we met, and he told me that he and his uncle had at last quarrelled irreconcilably, and that nothing could possibly now patch up the difference between them. We had a long talk."

"Ah! no doubt of that."

"And at length he told me that he must go and seek his fortune — that fortune which he hoped to share with me. He said that he had an opportunity of undertaking a voyage to India, and that if he were successful he should have sufficient to return with, and commence some pursuit in London more congenial to his thoughts and habits than the law."

"Ah, well! what next?"

"He told me that he loved me."

"And you believed him."

"Father, you would have believed him had you heard him speak. His tones were those of such deep sincerity that no actor who ever charmed an audience with an unreal existence could have reached them. There are times and seasons when we know that we are listening to the majestic voice of truth, and there are tones which sink at once into the heart, carrying with them a conviction of their sincerity, which neither time nor circumstance can alter; and such were the tones in which Mark Ingestrie spoke to me."

"And so you suppose, Johanna, that it is easy for a young man who has not patience or energy enough to be respectable at home, to go abroad and make his fortune. Is idleness so much in request in other countries, that it receives such a rich reward, my dear?"

"You judge him harshly, father; you do not know him."

"Heaven forbid that I should judge any one harshly! and I will freely admit that you may know more of his real character than I can, who of course have only seen its surface; but go on, my dear, and tell me all."

"We made an agreement, father, that on that day two years he was to come to me or send me some news of his whereabouts; if I heard nothing of him I was to conclude he was no more, and I cannot help so concluding now."

"But the day has not yet passed."

"I know it has not, and yet I rest upon but a slender hope, father. Do you believe that dreams ever really shadow forth-coming events?"

"I cannot say, my child; I am not disposed to yield credence to any supposed fact because I have dreamt it, but I must confess to having heard some strange instances where these visions of the night have come strictly true."

"Heaven knows but this may be one of them! I had a dream last night. I thought that I was sitting upon the sea-shore, and that all before me was nothing but a fathomless waste of waters. I heard the roar and the dash of the waves distinctly, and each moment the wind grew more furious and fierce, and I saw in the distance a ship — it was battling with the waves, which at one moment lifted it mountains high, and at another plunged it far down into such an abyss, that not a vestige of it could be seen but the topmost spars of the tall mast. And still the storm increased each moment in its fury, and ever and anon there came a strange sullen sound across the waters, and I saw a flash of fire, and knew that those in the ill-fated vessel were thus endeavouring to attract attention and some friendly aid. Father, from the first to the last I knew that Mark Ingestrie was there — my heart told me so: I was certain he was there, and I was helpless — utterly helpless, utterly and entirely unable to lend the slightest aid. I could only gaze upon what was going forward as a silent and terrified spectator of the scene. And at last I heard a cry come over the deep — a strange, loud, wailing cry — which proclaimed to me the fate of the vessel. I saw its mass shiver for a moment in the blackened air, and then all was still for a few seconds, until there arose a strange, wild shriek, that I knew was the despairing cry of those who sank, never to rise again, in that vessel. Oh! that was a frightful sound — it was a sound to linger on the ears, and haunt the memory of sleep — it was a sound never to be forgotten when once heard, but such as might again and again be remembered with horror and affright."

"And all this was in your dream?"

"It was, father, it was."

"And you were helpless?"

"I was — utterly and entirely helpless."

"It was very sad."

"It was, as you shall hear. The ship went down, and that cry that I had heard was the last despairing one given by those who clung to the wreck with scarce a hope, and yet because it was their only refuge, for where else had they to look for the smallest ray of consolation? where else, save in the surging waters, were they to turn for safety? Nowhere! all was lost! all was despair! I tried to scream — I tried to cry aloud to Heaven to have mercy upon those brave and gallant souls who had trusted their dearest possession — life itself — to the mercy of the deep; and while I so tried to render so inefficient succour, I saw a small speck in the sea, and my straining eyes perceived that it was a man floating and clinging to a piece of the wreck, and I knew it was Mark Ingestrie."

"But, my dear, surely you are not annoyed at a dream?"

"It saddened me. I stretched out my arms to save him — I heard him pronounce my name, and call upon me for help. 'Twas all in vain; he battled with the waves as long as human nature could battle with them. He could do no more, and I saw him disappear before my anxious eyes."

"Don't say you saw him, my dear, say you fancy you saw him."

"It was such a fancy as I shall not lose the remembrance of for many a day."

"Well, well, after all, my dear, it's only a dream; and it seems to me, without at all adverting to anything that should give you pain as regards Mark Ingestrie, that you made a very foolish bargain; for only consider how many difficulties might arise in the way of his keeping faith with you. You know I have your happiness so much at heart that, if Mark had been a worthy man and an industrious one, I should not have opposed myself to your union; but, believe me, my dear Johanna, that a young man with great facilities for spending money, and none whatever for earning any, is just about the worst husband you could choose, and such a man was Mark Ingestrie. But come, we will say nothing of this to your mother; let the secret, if we may call it such, rest with me; and if you can inform me in what capacity and in what vessel he left England, I will not carry my prejudice so far against him as to hesitate about making what inquiry I can concerning his fate."

"I know nothing more, father; we parted, and never met again."

"Well, well! dry your eyes, Johanna, and, as I go to Alderman Judd's, I'll think over the matter, which, after all, may not be so bad as you think. The lad is a good-enough looking lad, and has, I believe, a good ability, if he would put it to some useful purpose; but if he goes scampering about the world in an unsettled manner, you are well rid of him, and as for his being dead, you must not conclude that by any means, for somehow or another, like a bad penny, these fellows always come back."

There was more consolation in the kindly tone of the spectacle-maker than in the words he used; but, upon the whole, Johanna was well enough pleased that she had communicated the secret to her father, for now, at all events, she had some one to whom she could mention the name of Mark Ingestrie, without the necessity of concealing the sentiment with which she did so; and when her father had gone, she felt that, by the mere relation of it to him, some of the terrors of her dream had vanished.

She sat for some time in a pleasing reverie, till she was interrupted by Sam, the shop-boy, who came into the parlour and said,—

"Please, Miss Johanna, suppose I was to go down to the docks and try and find out for you Mr. Mark Ingestrie. I say, suppose I was to do that. I heard it all, and if I do find him I'll soon settle him."

"What do you mean?"

"I means that I won't stand it; didn't I tell you, more than three weeks ago, as you was the object of my infections? Didn't I tell you that when aunt died, I should come in for the soap and candle business, and make you my missus?"

The only reply which Johanna gave to this was to rise and leave the room, for her heart was too full of grief and sad speculation to enable her to do now as she had often been in the habit of doing — viz., laugh at Sam's protestations of affection; so he was left to chew the cud of sweet and bitter fancy by himself.

"A thousand d—s!" said he, when he entered the shop: "I always suspected there was some other fellow, and now I know it I am ready to gnaw my head off that ever I consented to come here. Confound him! I hope he is at the bottom of the sea, and eat up by this time. Oh! I should like to smash everybody. If I had my way now I'd just walk into society at large, as they calls it, and let it know what one, two, three, slap in the eye, is — and down it would go."

Mr. Sam, in his rage, did upset a case of spectacles, which went down with a tremendous crash, and which, however good imitation of the manner in which society at large was to be knocked down, was not likely to be at all pleasing to Mr. Oakley.

"I have done it now," he said; "but never mind; I'll try the old dodge whenever I break anything; that is, I'll place it in old Oakley's way, and swear he did it. I never knew such an old goose; you may persuade him into anything; the idea, now, of his pulling down all the shutters this morning because I told him my aunt had the tooth-ache; that was a go, to be sure. But I'll be revenged of that fellow who has took away, I consider, Johanna from me; I'll let him know what a blighted heart is capable of. He won't live long enough to want a pair spectacles, I'll be bound, or else my name ain't Sam Bolt."

CHAPTER III.

A MAN IS LOST.

THE EARLIEST DAWN OF MORNING was glistening upon the masts, the cordage, and the sails of a fleet of vessels lying below Sheerness.

The crews were rousing themselves from their night's repose, and to make their appearance on the decks of the vessels, from which the night-watch had just been relieved.

A man-of-war, which had been the convoy of the fleet of merchantmen through the channel, fired a gun as the first glimpse of the morning sun fell upon her tapering masts. Then from a battery in the neighbourhood came another booming report, and that was answered by another farther off, and then another, until the whole chain of batteries that girded the coast, for it was a time of war, had proclaimed the dawn of another day.

The effect was very fine, in the stillness of the early morn, of this succession of reports; and as they died away in the distance like mimic thunder, some order was given on board the man-of-war, and, in a moment, the masts and cordage seemed perfectly alive with human beings clinging to them in various directions. Then, as if by magic, or as if the ship had been a living thing itself, and had possessed wings, which at the mere instigation of a wish, could be spread far and wide, there fluttered out such sheets of canvas as was wonderful to see; and, as they caught the morning light, and the ship moved from the slight breeze that sprang up from the shore, she looked, indeed, as if she —

"Walked the waters like a thing of life". *

The various crews of the merchantmen stood upon the decks of their respective vessels, gazing after the ship-of-war, as she proceeded upon another mission similar to the one she had just performed in protecting the commerce of the country.

As she passed one vessel, which had been, in point of fact, actually rescued from the enemy, the crew, who had been saved from a foreign prison, cheered lustily.

A line from The Corsair *by Lord Byron (1814)*

There wanted but such an impulse as this, and then every merchant-vessel that the man-of-war passed took up the gladsome shout, and the crew of the huge vessel were not slow in their answer, for three deafening cheers — such as had frequently struck terror into the hearts of England's enemies — awakened many an echo from the shore.

It was a proud and a delightful sight — such a sight as none but an Englishman can thoroughly enjoy — to see that vessel so proudly stemming the waste of waters. We say none but an Englishman can enjoy it, because no other nation has ever attempted to achieve a great maritime existence without being most signally defeated, and leaving us still, as we shall ever be, masters of the seas.

These proceedings were amply sufficient to arouse the crews of all the vessels, and over the taffrail of one in particular, a large-sized merchantman, which had been trading in the Indian seas, two men were leaning. One of them was the captain of the vessel, and the other a passenger, who intended leaving that morning. They were engaged in earnest conversation, and the captain, as he shaded his eyes with his hand, and looked along the surface of the river, said, in reply to some observation from his companion, —

"I'll order my boat the moment Lieutenant Thornhill comes on board; I call him Lieutenant, although I have no right to do so, because he has held that rank in the king's service, but when quite a young man was cashiered for fighting a duel with his superior officer."

"The service has lost a good officer," said the other.

"It has, indeed, a braver man never stepped, nor a better officer; but you see they have certain rules in the service, and everything is sacrificed to maintain them. I can't think what keeps him; he went last night and said he would pull up to the Temple stairs, because he wanted to call upon somebody by the water-side, and after that he was going to the city to transact some business of his own, and that would have brought him nearer here, you see; and there are plenty of things coming down the river."

"He's coming," cried the other; "don't be impatient; you will see him in a few minutes."

"What makes you think that?"

"Because I see his dog — there, don't you see, swimming in the water, and coming towards the ship."

"I cannot imagine — I can see the dog, certainly; but I can't see Thornhill, nor is there any boat at hand. I know not what to make of it. Do you know my mind misgives me that something has happened amiss? The dog seem exhausted. Lend a hand there to Mr. Thornhill's dog, some of you. Why, it's a hat he has in his mouth."

The dog made towards the vessel; but without the assistance of the seamen — with the whole of whom he was an immense favourite — he certainly could not have boarded the vessel; and when he reached the deck, he sank down upon it in a state of complete exhaustion, with the hat still in his grasp.

As the animal lay, panting, upon the deck, the sailors looked at each other in amazement, and there was but one opinion among them all now, and that was that something very serious had unquestionably happened to Mr. Thornhill.

"I dread," said the captain, "an explanation of this occurrence. What on earth can it mean? That's Thornhill's hat, and here is Hector. Give the dog some meat and drink directly — he seems thoroughly exhausted."

The dog ate sparingly of some food that was put before him; and then, seizing the hat again in his mouth, he stood by the side of the ship and howled piteously; then he put down the hat for a moment, and, walking up to the captain, he pulled him by the skirt of the coat.

"You understand him," said the captain to the passenger; "something has happened to Thornhill, I'll be bound; and you see the object of the dog is to get me to follow him to see what it's about."

"Think you so? It is a warning, if it be such at all, that I should not be inclined to neglect; and if you will follow the dog, I will accompany you; there may be more in it than we think of, and we ought not to allow Mr. Thornhill to be in want of any assistance that we can render him, when we consider what great assistance he has been to us. Look how anxious the poor beast is."

The captain ordered a boat to be launched at once, and manned by four stout rowers. He then sprang into it, followed by the passenger, who was a Colonel Jeffery, of the Indian army, and the dog immediately followed them, testifying by his manner great pleasure at the expedition they were undertaking, and carrying the hat with him, which he evidently showed an immense disinclination to part with.

The captain had ordered the boat to proceed up the river towards the Temple stairs, where Hector's master had expressed his intention of proceeding, and, when the faithful animal saw the direction in which they were going, he lay down in the bottom of the boat perfectly satisfied, and gave himself up to that repose, of which he was evidently so much in need.

It cannot be said that Colonel Jeffery suspected that anything of a very serious nature had happened; indeed, their principal anticipation, when they came to talk it over, consisted in the probability that Thornhill had, with an impetuosity of character they knew very well he possessed, interfered to redress what he considered some street grievance, and had got himself into the custody of the civil power in consequence.

"Of course," said the captain, "Master Hector would view that as a very serious affair, and finding himself denied access to his master, you see he has come off to us, which was certainly the most prudent thing he could do, and I should not be at all surprised if he takes us to the door of some watch-house, where we shall find our friend snug enough."

The tide was running up; and that Thornhill had not saved the turn of it, by dropping down earlier to the vessel, was one of the things that surprised the captain. However, they got up quickly, and as at that hour there was not much on the river to impede their progress, and as at that time the Thames was not a thoroughfare for little stinking steam-boats, they soon reached the ancient Temple stairs.

The dog, who had until then seemed to be asleep, suddenly sprung up, and seizing the hat again in his mouth, rushed again on shore, and was closely followed by the captain and colonel.

He led them through the temple with great rapidity, pursuing with admirable tact the precise path that his master had taken towards the entrance to the Temple, in Fleet-street, opposite Chancery-lane. Darting across the road then, he stopped with a low growl at the shop of Sweeney Todd — a proceeding which very much surprised those who followed him, and caused them to pause to hold a consultation ere they proceeded further. While this was proceeding, Todd suddenly opened the door, and aimed a blow at the dog with an iron bar, but the latter dexterously avoided it, and, but that the door was suddenly closed again, he would have made Sweeney Todd regret such an interference.

"We must inquire into this," said the captain; "there seems to be mutual ill-will between that man and the dog."

They both tried to enter the barber's shop, but it was fast on the inside; and, after repeated knockings, Todd called from within, saying, —

"I won't open the door while that dog is there. He is mad, or has a spite against me — I don't know nor care which — it's a fact, that's all I am aware of."

"I will undertake," said the captain, "that the dog shall do you no harm; but open the door, for in we must come, and will."

"I will take your promise," said Sweeney Todd; "but mind you keep it, or I shall protect myself, and take the creature's life; so if you value it, you had better hold it fast."

The captain pacified Hector as well as he could, and likewise tied one end of a silk handkerchief round his neck, and held the other firmly in his grasp, after which Todd, who seemed to have some means from within of seeing what was going on, opened the door, and admitted his visitors.

"Well, gentlemen, shaved, or cut, or dressed, I am at your service; which shall I begin with?"

The dog never took his eyes off Todd, but kept up a low growl from the first moment of his entrance.

"It's rather a remarkable circumstance," said the captain, "but this is a very sagacious dog, you see, and he belongs to a friend of ours, who has most unaccountably disappeared."

"Has he really?" said Todd. "Tobias! Tobias!"

"Yes, sir."

"Run to Mr. Phillips's, in Cateaton-street, and get me six-pennyworth of figs, and don't say that I don't give you the money this time when you go a message. I think I did before, but you swallowed it; and when you come back, just please to remember the insight into business I gave you yesterday."

"Yes," said the boy, with a shudder, for he had a great horror of Sweeney Todd, as well he might, after the severe discipline he had received at his hands, and away he went.

"Well, gentlemen," said Todd, "what is it you require of me?"

"We want to know if any one having the appearance of an officer in the Navy came to your house?"

"Yes — a rather good-looking man, weather-beaten, with a bright blue eye, and rather fair hair."

"Yes, yes! the same."

"Oh! to be sure, he came here, and I shaved him and polished him off."

"What do you mean by polishing him off?"

"Brushing him up a bit, and making him tidy; he said he had got somewhere to go in the city, and asked me the address of a Mr. Oakley, a spectacle-maker. I gave it him, and then he went away; but as I was standing at my door about five minutes afterwards, it seemed to me, as well as I could see the distance, that he got into some row near the market."

"Did this dog come with him?"

"A dog came with him, but whether it was that dog or not I don't know."

"And that's all you know of him?"

"You never spoke a truer word in your life," said Sweeney Todd, as he diligently stropped a razor upon his great horny hand.

This seemed something like a complete fix; and the captain looked at Colonel Jeffery, and the colonel at the captain, for some moments, in complete silence. At length the latter said, —

"It's a very extraordinary thing that the dog should come here if he missed his master somewhere else. I never heard of such a thing."

"Nor I either," said Todd. "It is extraordinary; so extraordinary that if I had not seen it, I would not have believed. I dare say you will find him in the next watch-house."

The dog had watched the countenance of all parties during this brief dialogue, and twice or thrice he had interrupted it by a strange howling cry.

"I'll tell you what it is," said the barber; "if that beast stays here, I'll be the death of him. I hate dogs — detest them; and I tell you, as I told you before, if you value him at all, keep him away from me."

"You say you directed the person you describe to us where to find a spectacle maker named Oakley. We happen to know that he was going in search of such

a person, and as he had property of value about him, we will go there and
ascertain if he reached his destination."

"It is in Fore-street — a little shop with two windows; you cannot miss it."

The dog when he saw they were about to leave, grew furious; and it was
with the greatest difficulty they succeeded, by main force, in getting him out
of the shop, and dragging him some short distance with them, but then he
contrived to get free of the handkerchief that held him, and darting back, he

The dog never took his eyes off Todd, but kept up a low growl from the moment of his entrance. — "It's rather a remarkable circumstance," said the Captain, "but this is a very sagacious dog, you see, and he belongs to a friend of ours, who has most unaccountably disappeared."

sat down at Sweeney Todd's door, howling most piteously.

They had no resource but to leave him, intending fully to call as they came back from Mr. Oakley's; and, as they looked behind them, they saw that Hector was collecting a crowd round the barber's door, and it was a singular thing to see a number of persons surrounding the dog, while he to all appearance, appeared to be making efforts to explain something to the assemblage.

They walked on until they reached the spectacle-maker's. There they paused; for they all of a sudden recollected that the mission that Mr. Thornhill had to execute there was of a very delicate nature, and one by no means to be lightly executed, or even so much as mentioned, probably, in the hearing of Mr. Oakley himself.

"We must not be so hasty," said the colonel.

"But what am I to do? I sail to-night; at least I have to go round to Liverpool with my vessel."

"Do not then call at Mr. Oakley's at all at present; but leave me to ascertain the fact quietly and secretly."

"My anxiety for Thornhill will scarcely permit me to do so; but I suppose I must, and if you write me a letter to the Royal Oak Hotel, at Liverpool, it will be sure to reach me, that is to say, unless you find Mr. Thornhill himself, in which case I need not by any means give you so much trouble."

"You may depend upon me. My friendship for Mr. Thornhill, and gratitude, as you know, for the great service he has rendered to us all, will induce me to do my utmost to discover him; and, but that I know he set his heart upon performing the message he had to deliver accurately and well, I should recommend that we at once go into this house of Mr. Oakley's, only that the fear of compromising the young lady — who is in the case, and who will have quite enough to bear, poor thing, of her own grief — restrains me."

After some more conversation of a similar nature, they decided that this should be the plan adopted. They made an unavailing call at the watch-house of the district, being informed there that no such person, nor any one answering the description of Mr. Thornhill had been engaged in any disturbance, or apprehended by any of the constables; and this only involved the thing in greater mystery than ever, so they went back to try and recover the dog, but that was a matter easier to be desired and determined upon than executed, for threats and persuasions were alike ineffectual.

Hector would not stir an inch from the barber's door. There he sat with the hat by his side, a most melancholy and strange-looking spectacle, and a most efficient guard was he for that hat, and it was evident, that while he chose to exhibit the formidable row of teeth he did occasionally, when anybody showed a disposition to touch it, it would remain sacred. Some people, too, had thrown a few copper coins into the hat, so that Hector, if his mind had been that way inclined, was making a very good thing of it; but who shall describe the anger of Sweeney Todd, when he found that he was so likely to be so beleaguered?

He doubted, if, upon the arrival of the first customer to his shop, the dog might dart in and take him by storm; but that apprehension went off at last, when a young gallant came from the Temple to have his hair dressed, and the dog allowed him to pass in and out unmolested, without making any attempt to follow him. This was something, at all events; but whether or not it insured

Sweeney Todd's personal safety, when he himself should come out, was quite another matter.

It was an experiment, however, which he must try. It was quite out of the question that he should remain a prisoner much longer in his own place, so, after a time, he thought he might try the experiment, and that it would be best done when there were plenty of people there, because if the dog assaulted him, he would have an excuse for any amount of violence he might think proper to use upon the occasion.

It took some time, however, to screw his courage to the sticking-place; but at length, muttering deep curses between his clenched teeth, he made his way to the door, and carried in his hand a long knife, which he thought a more efficient weapon against the dog's teeth than the iron bludgeon he had formerly used.

"I hope he will attack me," said Todd, to himself as he thought; but Tobias, who had come back from the place where they sold the preserved figs, heard him, and after devoutly in his own mind wishing that the dog would actually devour Sweeney, said aloud —

"Oh dear, sir; you don't wish that, I'm sure!"

"Who told you what I wished, or what I did not? Remember, Tobias, and keep your own counsel, or it will be the worse for you, and your mother too — remember that."

The boy shrunk back. How had Sweeney Todd terrified the boy about his mother! He must have done so, or Tobias would never have shrunk as he did.

Then that rascally barber, who we begin to suspect of more crimes than fall ordinarily to the share of man, went cautiously out of his shop door: we cannot pretend to account for why it was so, but, as faithful recorders of facts, we have to state that Hector did not fly at him, but with a melancholy and subdued expression of countenance he looked up in the face of Sweeney Todd; then he whined piteously, as if he would have said, "Give me my master, and I will forgive you all that you have done; give me back my beloved master, and you shall see that I am neither revengeful nor ferocious."

This kind of expression was as legibly written in the poor creature's countenance as if he had actually been endowed with speech, and uttered the words themselves.

This was what Sweeney Todd certainly did not expect, and, to tell the truth, it staggered and astonished him a little. He would have been glad of an excuse to commit some act of violence, but he had now none, and as he looked in the faces of the people who were around, he felt quite convinced that it would not be the most prudent thing in the world to interfere with the dog in any way that savoured of violence.

"Where's the dog's master?" said one.

"Ah, where indeed?" said Todd; "I should not wonder if he had come to some foul end!"

"But I say, old soap-suds," cried a boy; "the dog says you did it."

There was a general laugh, but the barber was by no means disconcerted, and he shortly replied.

"Does he? he is wrong then."

Sweeney Todd had no desire to enter into anything like a controversy with the people, so he turned again and entered his own shop, in a distant corner of which he sat down, and folding his great gaunt-looking arms over his chest, he gave himself up to thought, and if we may judge from the expression of his countenance, those thoughts were of a pleasant anticipatory character, for now and then he gave such a grim sort of smile as might well have sat upon the features of some ogre.

And now we will turn to another scene, of a widely different character.

CHAPTER IV.

THE PIE-SHOP, BELL-YARD.

Hark! twelve o'clock at mid-day is cheerily proclaimed by St. Dunstan's church, and scarcely have the sounds done echoing throughout the neighbourhood, and scarce has the clock of Lincoln's-inn done chiming in with its announcement of the same hour, when Bell-yard, Temple-bar, becomes a scene of commotion.

What a scampering of feet is there, what a laughing and talking, what a jostling to be first; and what an immense number of manoeuvres are resorted to by some of the throng to distance others!

And mostly from Lincoln's-inn do these persons, young and old, but most certainly a majority of the former, come bustling and striving, although from the neighbouring legal establishments likewise there came not a few; the Temple contributes its numbers, and from the more distant Gray's-inn there came a goodly lot.

Now Bell-yard is almost choked up, and a stranger would wonder what could be the matter, and most probably stand in some doorway until the commotion was over.

Is it a fire? is it a fight? or anything else sufficiently alarming and extraordinary to excite the junior members of the legal profession to such a species of madness? No, it is none of these, nor is there a fat cause to be run for, which, in the hands of some clever practitioner, might become quite a vested interest. No, the enjoyment is purely one of a physical character, and all the pacing and racing — all this turmoil and trouble — all this pushing, jostling, laughing, and shouting, is to see who will get first to Lovett's pie-shop.

Yes, on the left-hand side of Bell-yard, going down from Carey-street, was, at the time we write of, one of the most celebrated shops for the sale of veal and pork pies that ever London produced. High and low, rich and poor, resorted to it; its fame had spread far and wide; it was because the first batch of these pies came up at twelve o'clock that there was such a rush of the legal profession to obtain them.

Their fame had spread even to great distances, and many persons carried them to the suburbs of the city as quite a treat to friends and relations there residing. And well did they deserve their reputation, those delicious pies! There was about them a flavour never surpassed, and rarely equalled; the paste was of the most delicate construction, and impregnated with the aroma of a delicious gravy that defies description. Then the small portions of meat which they contained were so tender, and the fat and the lean so artistically mixed up, that to eat one of Lovett's pies was such a provocative to eat another, that many persons who came to lunch stayed to dine, wasting more than an hour, perhaps, of precious time, and endangering — who knows to the contrary? — the success of some law-suit thereby.

The counter in Lovett's shop was in the shape of a horseshoe, and it was the custom of the young bloods from the Temple and Lincoln's-inn to sit in a row upon its edge while they partook of the delicious pies, and chatted gaily about one concern and another.

Many an appointment for the evening was made at Lovett's pie shop, and many a piece of gossiping scandal was there first circulated. The din of tongues was prodigious. The ringing laugh of the boy who looked upon the quarter of an hour he spent at Lovett's as the brightest of the whole twenty-four, mingled gaily with the more boisterous mirth of his seniors; and, oh! with what rapidity the pies disappeared.

They were brought up on large trays, each of which contained about a hundred, and from these trays they were so speedily transferred to the mouths of Mrs. Lovett's customers that it looked quite like a work of magic.

And now we have let out some portion of the secret. There was a Mistress Lovett; but possibly our reader guessed as much, for what but a female hand, and that female buxom, young, and good-looking, could have ventured upon the production of those pies. Yes, Mrs. Lovett was all that; and every enamoured young scion of the law, as he devoured his pie, pleased himself with the idea that the charming Mrs. Lovett had made that pie especially for him, and that fate or predestination had placed it in his hands.

And it was astonishing to see with what impartiality and with what tact the fair pastry-cook bestowed her smiles upon her admirers, so that none could say he was neglected, while it was extremely difficult for any one to say he was preferred.

This was pleasant, but at the same time it was provoking to all except Mrs. Lovett, in whose favour it got up a kind of excitement that paid extraordinarily well, because some of the young fellows thought, that he who consumed the most pies, would be in the most likely way to receive the greatest number of smiles from the lady.

Acting upon this supposition, some of her more enthusiastic admirers went on consuming the pies until they were almost ready to burst. But there were others, again, of a more philosophic turn of mind, who went for the pies only, and did not care one jot for Mrs. Lovett.

These declared that her smile was cold and uncomfortable — that it was upon her lips, but had no place in her heart — that it was the set smile of a ballet-dancer, which is about one of the most unmirthful things in existence.*

Then there were some who went even beyond this, and, while they admitted the excellence of the pies, and went every day to partake of them, swore that Mrs. Lovett had quite a sinister aspect, and that they could see what a merely superficial affair her blandishments were, and that there was —

"A lurking devil in her eye,"†

— that, if once roused, would be capable of achieving some serious things, and might not be so easily quelled again.

By five minutes past twelve Mrs. Lovett's counter was full, and the savoury steam of the hot pies went out in fragrant clouds into Bell-yard, being sniffed up by many a poor wretch passing by who lacked the means of making one in the throng that were devouring the dainty morsels within.

"Why, Tobias Ragg," said a young man, with his mouth full of pie, "where have you been since you left Mr. Snow's in Paper-buildings? I have not seen you for some days."

"No," said Tobias, "I have gone into another line; instead of being a lawyer, and helping to shave the clients, I am going to shave the lawyers now. A twopenny pork, if you please, Mrs. Lovett. Ah! who would be an emperor, if he couldn't get pies like these? — eh, Master Clift?"

"Well, they are good; of course we know that, Tobias; but do you mean to say you are going to be a barber?"

Throughout the Regency period and well into the early Victorian era, ballet was considered a debased art form, and ballet dancers were widely regarded as little more than prostitutes at the service of wealthy patrons.

† *From "The Honey Moon," an 1805 comedic play by John Tobin.*

"Yes, I am with Sweeney Todd, the barber of Fleet-street, close to St. Dunstan's."

"The deuce you are! well, I am going to a party to-night, and I'll drop in and get dressed and shaved, and patronise your master."

Tobias put his mouth close to the ear of the young lawyer, and in a fearful sort of whisper said the one word — "Don't."

"Don't! what for?"

Tobias made no answer; and, throwing down his twopence, scampered out of the shop as fast as he could. He had only sent a message by Sweeney Todd in the neighbourhood; but, as he heard the clock strike twelve, and two penny pieces were lying at the bottom of his pocket, it was not in human nature to resist running into Lovett's and converting them into a pork pie.

"What an odd thing!" thought the young lawyer. "I'll just drop in at Sweeney Todd's now on purpose, and ask Tobias what he means. I quite forgot, too, while he was here, to ask him what all that riot was about a dog at Todd's door."

"A veal!" said a young man, rushing in; "a twopenny veal, Mrs. Lovett." When he got it he consumed it with voracity, and then noticing an acquaintance in the shop, he whispered to him, —

"I can't stand it any more. I have cut the spectacle-maker — Johanna is faithless, and I know not what to do."

"Have another pie."

"But what's a pie to Johanna Oakley? You know, Dilki, that I only went there to be near the charmer. Damn the shutters and curse the spectacles! She loves another, and I'm a desperate individual! I should like to do some horrible and desperate act. Oh, Johanna, Johanna! you have driven me to the verge of what do you call it — I'll take another veal, if you please, Mrs. Lovett."

"Well, I was wondering how you got on," said his friend Dilki, "and thinking of calling upon you."

"Oh! it was all right — it was all right at first; she smiled upon me."

"You are quite sure she didn't laugh at you?"

"Sir! Mr. Dilki!"

"I say, are you sure that instead of smiling upon you she was not laughing at you!"

"Am I sure? Do you wish to insult me, Mr. Dilki? I look upon you as a puppy, sir — a horrid puppy."

"Very good; now I am convinced that the girl has been having a bit of fun at your expense. — Are you not aware, Sam, that your nose turns up so much that it's enough to pitch you head over heels. How do you suppose that any girl under forty-five would waste a word upon you? Mind, I don't say this to offend you in any way, but just quietly, by way of asking a question."

Sam looked daggers, and probably he might have attempted some desperate act in the pie-shop, if at the moment he had not caught the eye of Mrs. Lovett, and he saw by the expression of that lady's face, that anything in the shape of a riot would be speedily suppressed, so he darted out of the place at once to carry his sorrows and his bitterness elsewhere.

It was only between twelve and one o'clock that such a tremendous rush and influx of visitors came to the pie-shop, for although there was a good custom the whole day, and the concern was a money-making one from morning till night, it was at that hour principally that the great consumption of pies took place.

Tobias knew from experience that Sweeney Todd was a skilful calculator of the time it ought to take to go to different places, and accordingly since he had occupied some portion of that most valuable of all commodities at Mrs. Lovett's, he arrived quite breathless at his master's shop.

There sat the mysterious dog with the hat, and Tobias lingered for a moment to speak to the animal. Dogs are great physiognomists; and as the creature looked into Tobias's face he seemed to draw a favourable conclusion regarding him, for he submitted to a caress.

"Poor fellow!" said Tobias. "I wish I knew what had become of your master, but it made me shake like a leaf to wake up last night and ask myself the question. You shan't starve, though, if I can help it. I haven't much for myself, but you shall have some of it."

As he spoke, Tobias took from his pocket some not very tempting cold meat, which was intended for his own dinner, and which he had wrapped up in not the cleanest of cloths. He gave a piece to the dog, who took it with a dejected air, and then crouched down at Sweeney Todd's door again.

Just then, as Tobias was about to enter the shop, he thought he heard from within, a strange shrieking sort of sound. On the impulse of the moment he recoiled a step or two, and then, from some other impulse, he dashed forward at once, and entered the shop.

The first object that presented itself to his attention, lying upon a side table, was a hat with a handsome gold-headed walking cane lying across it.

The arm-chair in which customers usually sat to be shaved was vacant, and Sweeney Todd's face was just projected into the shop from the back parlour, and wearing a most singular and hideous expression.

"Well, Tobias," he said, as he advanced, rubbing his great hands together, "well, Tobias! so you could not resist the pie-shop?"

"How does he know?" thought Tobias. "Yes, sir, I have been to the pie-shop, but I didn't stay a minute."

"Hark ye, Tobias! the only thing I can excuse in the way of delay upon an errand is, for you to get one of Mrs. Lovett's pies; that I can look over, so think no more about it. Are they not delicious, Tobias?"

"Yes, sir, they are; but some gentleman seems to have left his hat and stick."

"Yes," said Sweeney Todd, "he has;" and lifting the stick he struck Tobias a blow with it that felled him to the ground. "Lesson the second to Tobias Ragg, which teaches him to make no remarks about what does not concern him. You may think what you like, Tobias Ragg, but you shall say only what I like."

"I won't endure it," cried the boy; "I won't be knocked about in this way, I tell you, Sweeney Todd, I won't."

"You won't! have you forgotten your mother?"

"You say you have a power over my mother; but I don't know what it is, and I cannot and will not believe it; I'll leave you, and, come of it what may, I'll go to sea or anywhere rather than stay in such a place as this."

"Oh, you will, will you? Then, Tobias, you and I must come to some explanation. I'll tell you what power I have over your mother, and then perhaps you will be satisfied. Last winter, when the frost had continued eighteen weeks, and you and your mother were starving, she was employed to clean out the chambers of a Mr. King, in the Temple, a cold-hearted, severe man, who never forgave anything in all his life, and never will."

"I remember," said Tobias; "we were starving and owed a whole guinea* for rent; but mother borrowed it and paid it, and after that got a situation where she now is."

"Ah, you think so. The rent was paid; but, Tobias, my boy, a word in your ear — she took a silver candlestick from Mr. King's chambers to pay it. I know it. I can prove it. Think of that, Tobias, and be discreet."

"Have mercy upon us," said the boy; "they would take her life!"

"Her life!" screamed Sweeney Todd; "aye, to be sure they would; they would hang her — hang her, I say; and now mind, if you force me by any conduct of your own, to mention this thing, you are your mother's executioner. I had better go and be deputy hangman at once, and turn her off."

"Horrible, horrible!"

"Oh, you don't like that? Indeed, that don't suit you, Master Tobias? Be discreet then, and you have nothing to fear. Do not force me to show a power which will be as complete as it is terrific."

"I will say nothing — I will think nothing."

" 'Tis well; now go and put that hat and stick in yonder cupboard. I shall be absent for a short time; and if any one comes, tell them I am called out, and shall not return for an hour or perhaps longer, and mind you take good care of the shop."

Sweeney Todd took off his apron, and put on an immense coat with huge lapels, and then, clapping a three-cornered hat on his head, and casting a strange withering kind of look at Tobias, he sallied forth into the street.

---

* A quarter-ounce gold coin. By the 1840s it was no longer in common use, but a "guinea" was a popular reference to 21 shillings (there were 20 shillings to the pound).

CHAPTER V.

THE MEETING IN THE TEMPLE.

ALAS! POOR JOHANNA OAKLEY — thy day has passed away and brought with it no tidings of him you love; and oh! what a weary day, full of fearful doubts and anxieties, has it been!

Tortured by doubts, hopes, and fears, that day was one of the most wretched that poor Johanna had ever passed. Not even two years before, when she had parted with her lover, had she felt such an exquisite pang of anguish as now filled her heart, when she saw the day gliding away and the evening creeping on apace, without word or token from Mark Ingestrie.

She did not herself know, until all the agony of disappointment had come across her, how much she had counted upon hearing something from him on that occasion; and when the evening deepened into night, and hope grew so slender that she could no longer rely upon it for the least support, she was compelled to proceed to her own chamber, and, feigning indisposition to avoid her mother's questions — for Mrs. Oakley was at home, and making herself and everybody else as uncomfortable as possible — she flung herself on her humble couch and gave way to a perfect passion of tears.

"Oh, Mark, Mark!" she said, "why do you thus desert me, when I have relied so abundantly upon your true affection? Oh, why have you not sent me some token of your existence, and of your continued love? the merest slightest word would have been sufficient, and I should have been happy."

She wept then such bitter tears as only such a heart as hers can know, when it feels the deep and bitter anguish of desertion, and when the rock, upon which it supposed it had built its fondest hopes, resolves itself to a mere quicksand, in which becomes engulfed all of good that this world can afford to the just and the beautiful.

Oh, it is heartrending to think that such a one as she, Johanna Oakley, a being so full of all those holy and gentle emotions which should constitute the truest felicity, should thus feel that life to her had lost its greatest charms, and that nothing but despair remained.

"I will wait until midnight," she said; "and even then it will be a mockery to seek repose, and to-morrow I must myself make some exertion to discover some tidings of him."

Then she began to ask herself what that exertion could be, and in what manner a young and inexperienced girl, such as she was, could hope to succeed in her inquiries. And the midnight hour came at last, telling her that, giving the utmost latitude to the word day, it had gone at last, and she was left despairing.

She lay the whole of that night sobbing, and only at times dropping into an unquiet slumber, during which painful images were presented to her, all, however, having the same tendency, and pointing towards the presumed fact that Mark Ingestrie was no more.

But the weariest night to the weariest waker will pass away, and at length the soft and beautiful dawn stole into the chamber of Johanna Oakley, chasing away some of the more horrible visions of the night, but having little effect in subduing the sadness that had taken possession of her.

She felt that it would be better for her to make her appearance below, than to hazard the remarks and conjectures that her not doing so would give rise to, so all unfitted as she was to engage in the most ordinary intercourse, she crept down to the breakfast-parlour, looking more like the ghost of her former self than the bright and beautiful being we have represented her to the reader.

Her father understood what it was that robbed her cheeks of their bloom; and although he saw it with much distress, yet he fortified himself with what he considered were some substantial reasons for future hopefulness.

It had become part of his philosophy — it generally is a part of the philosophy of the old — to consider that those sensations of the mind that arise from disappointed affection are of the most evanescent character; and that, although for a time they exhibit themselves with violence, they, like grief for the dead, soon pass away, scarcely leaving a trace behind of their former existence.

And perhaps he was right as regards the greater number of those passions; but he was certainly wrong when he applied that sort of worldly-wise knowledge to his daughter Johanna. She was one of those rare beings whose hearts are not won by every gaudy flutterer who may buzz the accents of admiration in their ears. No; she was qualified, eminently qualified, to love once, but only once; and, like the passion-flower, that blooms into abundant beauty once, and never afterwards puts forth a blossom, she allowed her heart to expand to the soft influence of affection, which, when crushed by adversity, was gone for ever.

"Really, Johanna," said Mrs. Oakley, in the true conventicle twang, "you look so pale and ill that I must positively speak to Mr. Lupin about you."

"Mr. Lupin, my dear," said the spectacle-maker, "may be all very well in his way, as a parson; but I don't see what he can have to do with Johanna looking pale."

"A pious man, Mr. Oakley, has to do with everything and everybody."

"Then he must be the most intolerable bore in existence; and I don't wonder at his being kicked out of some people's houses, as I have heard Mr. Lupin has been."

"And if he has, Mr. Oakley, I can tell you he glories in it. Mr. Lupin likes to suffer for the faith; and if he were to be made a martyr of to-morrow, I am quite certain it would give him a deal of pleasure."

"My dear, I am quite sure it would not give him half the pleasure it would me."

"I understand your insinuation, Mr. Oakley: you would like to have him murdered on account of his holiness; but, though you can say these kind of things at your own breakfast-table, you won't say as much to him when he comes to tea this afternoon."

"To tea, Mrs. Oakley! haven't I told you over and over again, that I will not have that man in my house?"

"And haven't I told you, Mr. Oakley, twice that number of times that he shall come to tea? and I have asked him now, and it can't be altered."

"But, Mrs. Oakley—"

"It's of no use, Mr. Oakley, your talking. Mr. Lupin is coming to tea, and come he shall; and if you don't like it, you can go out. There now, I am sure you can't complain, now you have actually the liberty of going out; but you are like the dog in the manger, Mr. Oakley, I know that well enough, and nothing will please you."

"A fine liberty, indeed, the liberty of going out of my own house to let somebody else into it that I don't like!"

"Johanna, my dear," said Mrs. Oakley, "I think my old complaint is coming on, of the beating of the heart, and the hysterics. I know what produces it — it's your father's brutality; and, just because Dr. Fungus said over and over again that I was to be perfectly quiet, your father seizes upon the opportunity like a wild beast, or a raving maniac, to try and make me ill."

Mr. Oakley jumped up, stamped his feet upon the floor and uttering something about the probability of his becoming a maniac in a very short time, rushed into his shop, and set to polishing the spectacles as if he were doing it for a wager.

This little affair between her father and mother, certainly had had the effect, for a time, of diverting attention from Johanna, and she was able to assume a cheerfulness she did not feel; but she had something of her father's spirit in her as regarded Mr. Lupin, and most decidedly objected to sitting down to any meal whatever with that individual, so that Mrs. Oakley was left in a minority of one upon the occasion, which perhaps, as she fully expected it, was no great matter after all.

Johanna went up stairs to her own room, which commanded a view of the street. It was an old-fashioned house, with a balcony in front, and as she looked listlessly out into Fore-street, which was far then from being the thoroughfare it is now, she saw standing in a doorway on the opposite side of the way a stranger, who was looking intently at the house, and who, when he caught her eye, walked instantly across to it, and cast something into the balcony of the first floor. Then he touched his cap, and walked rapidly from the street.

The thought immediately occurred to Johanna that this might possibly be some messenger from him concerning whose existence and welfare she was so deeply anxious. It was not to be wondered at, therefore, that with the name of Mark Ingestrie upon her lips she should rush down to the balcony in intense anxiety to hear, and see if such was really the case.

When she reached the balcony she found lying in it a scrap of paper, in which a stone was wrapped up, in order to give it weight, so that it might be cast with a certainty into the balcony. With trembling eagerness she opened the paper, and read upon it the following words: —

"For news of Mark Ingestrie, come to the Temple-gardens one hour before sunset, and do not fear addressing a man who will be holding a white rose in his hand."

"He lives! he lives!" she cried. "He lives, and joy again becomes the inhabitant of my bosom! Oh, it is daylight now and sunshine compared to the black midnight of despair. Mark Ingestrie lives, and I shall be happy yet."

She placed the little scrap of paper carefully in her bosom, and then, with clasped hands and a delighted expression of countenance, she repeated the brief and expressive words it contained, adding, —

"Yes, yes, I will be there; the white rose is an emblem of his purity and affection, his spotless love, and that is why his messenger carries it. I will be there. One hour, aye, two hours before sunset, I will be there. Joy, joy! he lives, he lives! Mark Ingestrie lives! Perchance, too, successful in his object, he returns to tell me that he can make me his, and that no obstacle can now interfere to frustrate our union. Time, time, float onwards on your fleetest pinions!"

She went to her own apartment, but it was not, as she had last gone to it, to weep; on the contrary, it was to smile at her former fears, and to admit the philosophy of the assertion that we suffer much more from a dread of those things that never happen than we do for actual calamities which occur in their full force to us.

"Oh, that this messenger," she said, "had come but yesterday! What hours of anguish I should have been spared! But I will not complain; it shall not be said that I repine at present joy because it did not come before. I will be happy when I can; and, in the consciousness that I shall soon hear blissful tidings of Mark Ingestrie, I will banish every fear."

The impatience which she now felt brought its pains and its penalties with it, and yet it was quite a different description of feeling to any she had formerly endured, and certainly far more desirable than the absolute anguish that had taken possession of her upon hearing nothing of Mark Ingestrie.

It was strange, very strange, that the thought never crossed her that the tidings she had to hear in the Temple-gardens from the stranger might be evil ones, but certainly such a thought did not occur to her, and she looked forward with joy and satisfaction to a meeting which she certainly had no evidence to know, might not be of the most disastrous character.

She asked herself over and over again if she should tell her father what had occurred, but as often as she thought of doing so she shrank from carrying out the mental suggestion, and all the natural disposition again to keep to herself the secret of her happiness returned to her in full force.

But yet she was not so unjust as not to feel that it was treating her father but slightingly to throw all her sorrows into his lap, as it were, and then to keep from him everything of joy appertaining to the same circumstances.

This was a thing that she was not likely to continue doing, and so she made up her mind to relieve her conscience from the pang it would otherwise have had, by determining to tell him, after the interview in the Temple-gardens, what was its result; but she could not make up her mind to do so beforehand; it was so pleasant and so delicious to keep the secret all to herself, and to feel that she alone knew that her lover had so closely kept faith with her as to be only one day behind his time in sending to her, and that day, perhaps, far from being his fault.

And so she reasoned to herself and tried to while away the anxious hours, sometimes succeeding in forgetting how long it was still to sunset, and at others feeling as if each minute was perversely swelling itself out into ten times its usual proportion of time in order to become wearisome to her.

She had said that she would be at the Temple-gardens two hours before sunset instead of one, and she kept her word, for, looking happier than she had done for weeks, she tripped down the stairs of her father's house, and was about to leave it by the private staircase, when a strange gaunt-looking figure attracted her attention.

This was no other than the Rev. Mr. Lupin: he was a long strange-looking man, and upon this occasion he came upon what he called horseback, that is to say, he was mounted upon a very small pony, which seemed quite unequal to support his weight, and was so short that, if the reverend gentleman had not poked his legs out at an angle, they must inevitably have touched the ground.

"Praise the Lord!" he said: "I have intercepted the evil one. Maiden, I have come here at thy mother's bidding, and thou shalt remain and partake of the mixture called tea."

Johanna scarcely condescended to glance at him, but drawing her mantle close around her, which he actually had the impertinence to endeavour to lay hold of, she walked on, so that the reverend gentleman was left to make the best he could of the matter.

"Stop," he cried, "stop! I can well perceive that the devil has a strong hold of you: I can well perceive — the lord have mercy upon me! this animal hath some design against me as sure as fate."

This last ejaculation arose from the fact that the pony had flung up his heels behind in a most mysterious manner.

"I am afraid, sir," said a lad who was no more than our old acquaintance, Sam — "I am afraid, sir, that there is something the matter with the pony."

Up went the pony's heels again in the same unaccountable manner.

"God bless me!" said the reverend gentleman; "he never did such a thing before. I — there he goes again — murder! Young man, I pray you to help me to get down; I think I know you; you are the nephew of the goodly Mrs. Pump — truly this animal wishes to be the death of me."

At this moment the pony gave such a vigorous kick up behind, that Mr. Lupin was fairly pitched upon his head, and made a complete summerset, alighting with his heels in the spectacle-maker's passage; and it unfortunately happened that Mrs. Oakley at that moment, hearing the altercation, came rushing out, and the first thing she did was to fall sprawling over Mr. Lupin's feet.

Sam now felt it time to go; and as we dislike useless mysteries, we may as well explain that these extraordinary circumstances arose from the fact that Sam had brought from the haberdasher's opposite a halfpenny-worth of pins, and had amused himself by making a pincushion of the hind quarters of the Reverend Mr. Lupin's pony, which, not being accustomed to that sort of thing, had kicked out vigorously in opposition to the same, and produced the results we have recorded.

Johanna Oakley was some distance upon her road before the reverend gentleman was pitched into her father's house in the manner we have described, so that she knew nothing of it, nor would she have cared if she had, for her mind was wholly bent upon the expedition she was proceeding on.

As she walked upon that side of the way of Fleet-street where Sweeney Todd's house and shop were situated, a feeling of curiosity prompted her to stop for a moment and look at the melancholy-looking dog that stood watching a hat at his door.

The appearance of grief upon the creature's face could not be mistaken, and, as she gazed, she saw the shop-door gently opened and a piece of meat thrown out.

"These are kind people," she said, "be they whom they may;" but when she saw the dog turn away with loathing, and herself observed that there was a white powder upon it, the idea that it was poisoned, and only intended for the poor creature's destruction, came instantly across her mind.

And when she saw the horrible-looking face of Sweeney Todd glaring at her from the partially-opened door, she could not doubt any further the fact, for that face was quite enough to give a warrant for any amount of villany whatever.

She passed on with a shudder, little suspecting, however, that that dog had anything to do with her fate, or the circumstances which made up the sum of her destiny.

IT WANTED A FULL HOUR to the appointed time of meeting when she reached the Temple-gardens, and partly blaming herself that she was so soon, while at the same time she would not for worlds have been away, she sat down on one of the garden-seats to think over the past, and to recall to her memory with all the vivid freshness of young Love's devotion, the many gentle words which from time to time had been spoken to her two summers since by him whose faith she had never doubted, and whose image was enshrined at the bottom of her heart.

CHAPTER VI.

THE CONFERENCE, AND THE FEARFUL NARRATION IN THE GARDEN.

THE TEMPLE CLOCK STRUCK THE HOUR of meeting, and Johanna looked anxiously around her for any one who should seem to her to bear the appearance of being such a person as she might suppose Mark Ingestrie would choose for his messenger.

She turned her eyes towards the gate, for she thought she heard it close, and then she saw a gentlemanly-looking man, attired in a cloak, and who was looking around him, apparently in search of some one.

When his eye fell upon her he immediately produced from beneath his cloak a white rose, and in another minute they met.

"I have the honour," he said, "of speaking to Miss Johanna Oakley?"

"Yes, sir; and you are Mark Ingestrie's messenger?"

"I am; that is to say, I am he who comes to bring you news of Mark Ingestrie, although I grieve to say I am not the messenger that was expressly deputed by him so to do."

"Oh! sir, your looks are sad and serious; you seem as if you would announce that some misfortune had occurred. Tell me that it is not so; speak to me at once, or my heart will break!"

"Compose yourself, lady, I pray you."

"I cannot — dare not do so, unless you tell me he lives. Tell me that Mark Ingestrie lives, and then I shall be all patience: tell me that, and you shall not hear a murmur from me. Speak the word at once — at once! It is cruel, believe me, it is cruel to keep me in this suspense."

"This is one of the saddest errands I ever came upon," said the stranger, as he led Johanna to a seat. "Recollect, lady, what creatures of accident and chance we are — recollect how the slightest circumstances will affect us, in driving us to the confines of despair, and remember by how frail a tenure the best of us hold existence."

"No more — no more!" shrieked Johanna, as she clasped her hands — "I know all now, and am desolate."

She let her face drop upon her hands, and shook as with a convulsion of grief.

"Mark, Mark!" she cried, "you have gone from me! I thought not this — I thought not this. Oh, Heaven! why have I lived so long as to have the capacity to listen to such fearful tidings? Lost — lost — all lost! God of Heaven! what a wilderness the world is now to me!"

"Let me pray you, lady, to subdue this passion of grief, and listen truly to what I shall unfold to you. There is much to hear and much to speculate upon; and if, from all that I have learnt, I cannot, dare not tell you that Mark Ingestrie lives, I likewise shrink from telling you he is no more."

"Speak again — say those words again! There is hope, then — oh, there is a hope!"

"There is a hope; and better is it that your mind should receive the first shock of the probability of the death of him whom you have so anxiously expected, and then afterwards, from what I shall relate to you, gather hope that it may not be so, than that from the first you should expect too much, and then have those expectations rudely destroyed."

"It is so — it is so; this is kind of you, and if I cannot thank you as I ought, you will know that it is because I am in a state of too great affliction so to do, and not from want of will; you will understand that — I am sure you will understand that."

"Make no excuses to me. Believe me, I can fully appreciate all that you would say, and all that you must feel. I ought to tell you who I am, that you may have confidence in what I have to relate to you. My name is Jeffery, and I am a colonel in the Indian army."

"I am much beholden to you, sir; but you bring with you a passport to my confidence, in the name of Mark Ingestrie, which is at once sufficient. I live again in the hope that you have given me of his continued existence, and in that hope I will maintain a cheerful resignation that shall enable me to bear up against all you have to tell me, be it what it may, and with a feeling that through much suffering there may come joy at last. You shall find me very patient, aye, extremely patient — so patient that you shall scarcely see the havoc that grief has already made here."

She pressed her hands upon her breast as she spoke, and looked in his face with such an expression of tearful melancholy that it was quite heart-rending to witness it; and he, although not used to the melting mood, was

compelled to pause for a few moments ere he could proceed in the task he had set himself.

"I will be as brief," he said, "as possible, consistent with stating all that is requisite for me to state, and I must commence by asking you if you are aware under what circumstances it was that Mark Ingestrie was abroad?"

"I am aware of so much, that a quarrel with his uncle, Mr. Grant, was the great cause, and that his main endeavour was to better his fortunes, so that we might be happy, and independent of those who looked not with an eye of favour upon our projected union."

"Yes, but, what I meant was, were you aware of the sort of adventure he

"She turned her eyes towards the gate, and saw a gentlemanly-looking man attired in a cloak, apparently in search of some one."

embarked in to the Indian seas?"

"No, I know nothing further; we met here on this spot, we parted at yonder gate, and we have never met again."

"Then I have something to tell you, in order to make the narrative clear and explicit."

They both sat upon the garden seat; and while Johanna fixed her eyes upon her companion's face, expressive as it was of the most generous emotions and noble feelings, he commenced relating to her the incidents which never left her memory, and in which she took so deep an interest.

"You must know," he said, "that what it was which so much inflamed the imagination of Mark Ingestrie, consisted in this. There came to London a man with a well-authenticated and extremely well put together report, that there had been discovered, in one of the small islands near the Indian seas, a river which deposited an enormous quantity of gold-dust in its progress to the ocean. He told his story so well, and seemed to be such a perfect master of all the circumstances connected with it, that there was scarcely room for a doubt upon the subject. The thing was kept quiet and secret; and a meeting was held of some influential men — influential on account of the money they possessed, among whom was one who had towards Mark Ingestrie most friendly feelings; so Mark attended the meeting with this friend of his, although he felt his utter incapacity, from want of resources, to take any part in the affair. But he was not aware of what his friend's generous intentions were in the matter until they were explained to him, and they consisted in this: — He, the friend, was to provide the necessary means for embarking in the adventure, so far as regarded taking a share in it, and he told Mark Ingestrie that, if he would go personally on the expedition, he should share in the proceeds with him, be they what they might. Now, to a young man like Ingestrie, totally destitute of personal resources, but of ardent and enthusiastic temperament, you can imagine how extremely tempting such an offer was likely to be. He embraced it at once with the greatest pleasure, and from that moment he took an interest in the affair of the closest and most powerful description. It seized completely hold of his imagination, presenting itself to him in the most tempting colours; and from the description that has been given me of his enthusiastic disposition, I can well imagine with what kindness and impetuosity he would enter into such an affair."

"You know him well?" said Johanna, gently.

"No, I never saw him. All that I say concerning him is from the description of another who did know him well, and who sailed with him in the vessel that ultimately left the port of London on the vague and wild adventure I have mentioned."

"That one, be he who he may, must have known Mark Ingestrie well, and have enjoyed much of his confidence to be able to describe him so accurately."

"I believe that such was the case; and it is from the lips of that one, instead of from mine, that you ought to have heard what I am now relating. That gentleman, whose name was Thornhill, ought to have made to you this communication; but by some strange accident it seems he has been prevented, or you would not be here listening to me upon a subject which would have come better from his lips."

"And was he to have come yesterday to me?"

"He was."

"Then Mark Ingestrie kept his word; and but for the adverse circumstances which delayed his messenger, I should yesterday have heard what you are now relating to me. I pray you go on, sir, and pardon this interruption."

"I need not trouble you with all the negotiations, the trouble, and the difficulty that arose before the expedition could be started fairly — suffice it to say, that at length, after much annoyance and trouble, it was started, and a vessel was duly chartered and manned for the purpose of proceeding to the Indian seas in search of the treasure, which was reported to be there for the first adventurer who had the boldness to seek it.

"It was a gallant vessel. I saw it many a mile from England ere it sunk beneath the waves, never to rise again."

"Sunk!"

"Yes; it was an ill-fated ship, and it did sink; but I must not anticipate — let me proceed in my narrative with regularity. The ship was called the *Star*; and if those who went with it looked upon it as the star of their destiny, they were correct enough, and it might be considered an evil star for them, inasmuch as nothing but disappointment and bitterness became their ultimate portion. And Mark Ingestrie, I am told, was the most hopeful man on board. Already in imagination he could fancy himself homeward-bound with the vessel, ballasted and crammed with the rich produce of that shining river. Already he fancied what he could do with his abundant wealth, and I have not a doubt but that, in common with many who went on that adventure, he enjoyed to the full the spending of the wealth he should obtain in imagination — perhaps, indeed, more than if he had obtained it in reality. Among the adventurers was one Thornhill, who had been a lieutenant in the Royal Navy, and between him and young Ingestrie there arose a remarkable friendship — a friendship so strong and powerful, that there can be no doubt that they communicated to each other all their hopes and fears; and if anything could materially tend to beguile the tedium of such a weary voyage as those adventurers had undertaken, it certainly would be the free communication and confidential intercourse between two such kindred spirits as Thornhill and Mark Ingestrie. You will bear in mind, Miss Oakley, that in making this communication to you, I am putting together what I myself heard at different times, so as to make it for you a distinct narrative, which you can have no difficulty in comprehending, because, as I before stated, I never saw Mark Ingestrie, and it was only once, for about five minutes, that I saw the vessel in which he went upon his perilous adventure — for perilous it turned out to be — to the Indian seas. It was from Thornhill I got my information during the many weary and monotonous hours consumed in a home-bound voyage from India. It appears that without accident or cross of any description the *Star* reached the Indian ocean, and the supposed immediate locality of the spot where the treasure was to be found, and there she was spoken with by a vessel homeward-bound from India, called the *Neptune*. It was evening, and the sun had sunk in the horizon with some appearances that betokened a storm. I was on board that Indian vessel; we did not expect anything serious, although we made every preparation for rough weather, and as it turned out, it was well indeed we did, for never within the memory of the oldest seamen, had such a storm ravished the coast. A furious gale, which it was impossible to withstand, drove us southward; and but for the utmost precautions, aided by courage and temerity on the part of the seamen, such as I had never before witnessed in the merchant-service, we escaped with trifling damage, but we were driven at least 200 miles out of our course; and instead of getting, as we ought to have done, to the Cape by a certain time, we were an immense distance eastward of it. It was just as the storm, which lasted three nights and two days, began to abate, that towards the horizon we saw a dull red light; and as it was not in a quarter of the sky where any such appearance might be imagined, nor were we in a latitude where electro-phenomena might be expected, we steered toward it, surmising what turned out afterwards to be fully correct."

"It was a ship on fire!" said Johanna.

"It was."

"Alas! alas! I guessed it. A frightful suspicion from the first crossed my mind. It was a ship on fire, and that ship was —"

"The *Star* was bound upon its adventurous course, although driven far out of it by adverse winds and waves. After about half an hour's sailing we came within sight distinctly of a blazing vessel. We could hear the roar of the flames, and through our glasses we could see them curling up the cordage, and dancing from mast to mast, like fiery serpents, exulting in the destruction they were making. We made all sail, and strained every inch of canvas to reach the ill-fated vessel, for distances at sea that look small are in reality very great, and an hour's hard sailing in a fair wind, with every stitch of canvas set, would not do more than enable us to reach that ill-fated bark; but fancy in an hour what ravages the flames might make! The vessel was doomed. The fiat had gone forth that it was to be among the things that had been; and long before we could reach the spot upon which it floated idly on the now comparatively calm waters, we saw a bright shower of sparks rush up into the air. Then came a loud roaring sound over the surface of the deep, and all was still — the ship had disappeared, and the water closed over it for ever."

"But how knew you," said Johanna, as she clasped her hands, and the pallid expression of her countenance betrayed the deep interest she took in the narration, "how knew you that the ship was the *Star*? might it not have been some other ill-fated vessel that met with so dreadful a fate?"

"I will tell you: although we had seen the ship go down, we kept on our course, straining every effort to reach the spot, with the hope of picking up some of the crew, who surely had made an effort by the boats to leave the burning vessel. The captain of the Indiaman kept his glass at his eye, and presently he said to me, — 'There is a floating piece of wreck, and something clinging to it; I know not if there be a man, but what I can perceive seems to me to be the head of a dog.' I looked through the glass myself, and saw the same object; but as we neared it, we found it was a large piece of the wreck, with a dog and a man supported by it, who were clinging with all the energy of desperation.

"In ten minutes more we had them on board the vessel — the man was the Lieutenant Thornhill I have before mentioned, and the dog belonged to him. He related to us that the ship, we had seen burning was the *Star*, and that it had never reached its destination, and that he believed all had perished but himself and the dog; for, although one of the boats had been launched, so desperate a rush was made into it by the crew that it had swamped, and all perished. Such was his own state of exhaustion, that, after he had made this short statement, it was some days before he left his hammock; but when he did, and began to mingle with us, we found an intelligent, cheerful companion — such a one, indeed, as we were glad to have on board, and in confidence he related to the captain and myself the object of the voyage of the *Star*, and the previous particulars with which I have made you acquainted. And then, during a night-watch, when the soft and beautiful moonlight was more than usually inviting, and he and I were on the deck, enjoying the coolness of the night, after the intense heat of the day in the tropics, he said to me, — 'I have a very sad mission to perform when I get to London. On board our vessel was a young man named Mark Ingestrie; and some short time before the vessel in which we were went down, he begged of me to call upon a young lady named Johanna Oakley, the daughter of a spectacle-maker in London, providing I should be saved and he perish; and of the latter event, he felt so strong a presentiment that he gave me a string of pearls, which I was to present to her in his name; but where he got them I have not the least idea, for they are of immense value.' Mr. Thornhill showed me the pearls, which were of different sizes, roughly strung together, but of great value; and when we reached the river Thames, which was only three days since, he left us with his dog, carrying his string of pearls with him, to find out where you reside."

"Alas! he never came."

"No; from all the inquiries we can make, and all the information we can learn, it seems he disappeared somewhere about Fleet-street."

"Disappeared!"

"Yes; we can trace him to the Temple-stairs, and from thence to the barber' shop, kept by a man named Sweeney Todd; but beyond there no information of him can be obtained."

"Sweeney Todd!"

"Yes; and what makes the affair more extraordinary, is, that neither force nor persuasion will induce Thornhill's dog to leave the place."

"I saw it — I saw the creature, and it looked imploringly, although kindly, in my face; but little did I think, when I paused a moment to look upon that melancholy but faithful animal, that it held a part in my destiny. Oh! Mark Ingestrie, Mark Ingestrie, dare I hope that you live when all else have perished?"

"I have told you all that I can tell you, and, according as your own judgment may dictate to you, you can encourage hope, or extinguish it for ever. I have kept back nothing from you which can make the affair worse or better — I have added nothing; but you have it simply as it was told to me."

"He is lost — he is lost."

"I am one, lady, who always thinks certainty of any sort preferable to suspense; and although, while there is no positive news of death, the continuance of life ought fairly to be assumed, yet you must perceive, from a review of all the circumstances, upon how very slender a foundation all our hopes must rest."

"I have no hope — I have no hope — he is lost to me for ever! It were madness to think he lived. Oh, Mark, Mark! and is this the end of all our fond affection? did I indeed look my last upon that face, when on this spot we parted?"

"The uncertainty," said Colonel Jeffery, wishing to withdraw as much as possible from a consideration of her own sorrows, "the uncertainty, too, that prevails with regard to the fate of poor Mr. Thornhill, is a sad thing. I much fear that those precious pearls he had, have been seen by some one who has not scrupled to obtain possession of them by his death."

"Yes, it would seem so indeed; but what are pearls to me? Oh! would that they had sunk to the bottom of that Indian sea, from whence they had been plucked. Alas, alas! it has been their thirst for gain that has produced all these evils. We might have been poor here, but we should have been happy. Rich we ought to have been, in contentment; but now all is lost, and the world to me can present nothing that is to be desired, but one small spot large enough to be my grave."

She leant upon the arm of the garden-seat, and gave herself up to such a passion of tears that Colonel Jeffery felt he dared not interrupt her. There is something exceeding sacred about real grief which awes the beholder, and it was with an involuntary feeling of respect that Colonel Jeffery stepped a few paces off, and waited until that burst of agony had passed away. It was during those brief moments that he overheard some words uttered by one who seemed likewise to be suffering from that prolific source of all affliction, disappointed affection. Seated at some short distance was a maiden, and one not young enough to be called a youth, but still not far enough advanced in existence to have had all his better feelings crushed by an admixture with the cold world, and he was listening while the maiden spoke.

"It is the neglect," she said, "which touched me to the heart. But one word spoken or written, one message of affection, to tell me that the memory of a love I thought would be eternal, still lingered in your heart, would have been a world of consolation; but it came not, and all was despair."

"Listen to me," said her companion, "and if ever in this world you can believe that one who truly loves can be cruel to be kind, believe that I am that one. I yielded for a time to the fascination of a passion which should never have found a home within my heart; but yet it was far more of a sentiment than a passion, inasmuch as never for one moment did an evil thought mingle with its pure aspirations.

"It was a dream of joy, which for a time obliterated a remembrance that ought never to have been forgotten; but when I was rudely awakened to the fact that those whose opinions were of importance to your welfare and your happiness knew nothing of love, but in its grossest aspect, it became necessary at once to crush a feeling, which, in its continuance, could shadow forth nothing but evil."

"You may not imagine, and you may never know — for I cannot tell the heart-pangs that it has cost me to persevere in a line of conduct which I felt was due to you — whatever heart-pangs it might cost me. I have been content to imagine that your affection would turn to indifference, perchance to hatred; that a consciousness of being slighted would arouse in your defence all a woman's pride, and that thus you would be lifted above regret. Farewell for ever! I dare not love you honestly and truly; and better is it thus to part than to persevere in a delusive dream that can but terminate in degradation and sadness."

"Do you hear those words?" whispered Colonel Jeffery to Johanna. "You perceive that others suffer, and from the same cause, the perils of affection."

"I do. I will go home, and pray for strength to maintain my heart against this sad affliction."

"The course of true love never yet ran smooth; wonder not, therefore, Johanna Oakley, that yours has suffered such a blight. It is the great curse of the highest and noblest feelings of which humanity is capable, that while, under felicitous circumstances, they produce to us an extraordinary amount of happiness; when anything adverse occurs, they are most prolific sources of misery. Shall I accompany you?"

Johanna felt grateful for the support of the colonel's arm towards her own home, and as they passed the barber's shop they were surprised to see that the dog and the hat were gone.

CHAPTER VII.

THE BARBER AND THE LAPIDARY.

IT IS NIGHT; AND A MAN, one of the most celebrated lapidaries in London, but yet a man frugal withal, although rich, is putting up the shutters of his shop.

This lapidary is an old man; his scanty hair is white, and his hands shake as he secures the fastenings, and then, over and over again, feels and shakes each shutter, to be assured that his shop is well secured.

This shop of his is in Moorfields, then a place very much frequented by dealers in bullion and precious stones. He was about entering his door, just having cast a satisfied look upon the fastening of his shop, when a tall, ungainly-looking man stepped up to him. This man had a three-cornered hat, much too small for him, perched upon the top of his great hideous-looking head, while the coat he wore had ample skirts enough to have made another of ordinary dimensions.

Our readers will have no difficulty in recognising Sweeney Todd, and well might the little old lapidary start as such a very unprepossessing-looking personage addressed him.

"You deal," he said, "in precious stones."

"Yes, I do," was the reply; "but it's rather late. Do you want to buy or sell?"

"To sell."

"Humph! Ah, I dare say it's something not in my line; the only order I get is for pearls, and they are not in the market."

"And I have nothing but pearls to sell," said Sweeney Todd; "I mean to keep all my diamonds, my garnets, topazes, brilliants, emeralds, and rubies."

"The deuce you do! Why, you don't mean to say you have any of them? Be off with you! I am too old to joke with, and am waiting for my supper."

"Will you look at the pearls I have?"

"Little seed pearls, I suppose; they are of no value, and I don't want them, we have plenty of those. It's real, genuine, large pearls we want. Pearls worth thousands."

"Will you look at mine?"

"No; good night!"

"Very good; then I will take them to Mr. Coventry up the street. He will, perhaps, deal with me for them if you cannot."

The lapidary hesitated. "Stop," he said; "what's the use of going to Mr.

Coventry? he has not the means of purchasing what I can pay present cash for. Come in, come in; I will, at all events, look at what you have for sale."

Thus encouraged, Sweeney Todd entered the little, low, dusky shop, and the lapidary having procured a light, and taken care to keep his customer outside the counter, put on his spectacles, and said —

"Now, sir, where are your pearls?"

"There," said Sweeney Todd, as he laid a string of twenty-four pearls before the lapidary.

The old man's eyes opened to an enormous width, and he pushed his spectacles right upon his forehead as he glared in the face of Sweeney Todd with undisguised astonishment. Then down came his spectacles again, and taking up the string of pearls he rapidly examined every one of them, after which, he exclaimed, —

"Real, real, by Heaven! All real!"

Then he pushed his spectacles up again to the top of his head, and took another long stare at Sweeney Todd.

"I know they are real," said the latter. "Will you deal with me or will you not?"

"Will I deal with you? Yes; I am not quite sure they are real. Let me look again. Oh, I see, counterfeits; but so well done, that really for the curiosity of the thing, I will give fifty pounds for them."

"I am fond of curiosities," said Sweeney Todd, "and as they are not real, I will keep them; they will do for a present to some child or another."

"What, give those to a child? you must be mad — that is to say, not mad, but certainly indiscreet. Come, now, at a word, I'll give you one hundred pounds for them."

"Hark ye," said Sweeney Todd, "it neither suits my inclination nor my time to stand here chaffing with you. I know the value of the pearls, and, as a matter of ordinary and every-day business, I will sell them to you so that you may get a handsome profit."

"What do you call a handsome profit?"

"The pearls are worth twelve thousand pounds, and I will let you have them for ten. What do you think of that for an offer?"

"What odd noise was that?"

"Oh, it was only I who laughed. Come, what do you say, at once; are we to do business or are we not?"

"Hark ye, my friend; since you do know the value of your pearls, and this is to be a downright business transaction, I think I can find a customer who will give eleven thousand pounds for them, and if so, I have no objection to give you eight thousand pounds."

"Give me the eight thousand pounds," said Sweeney Todd, "and let me go. I hate bargaining."

"Stop a bit; there are some rather important things to consider. You must know, my friend, that a string of pearls of this value are not be bought like a few ounces of old silver of anybody who might come with it. Such a string of pearls as these are like a house, or an estate, and when they change hands, the vendor must give every satisfaction as to how he came by them, and prove how he can give to the purchaser a good right and title to them."

"Pshaw!" said Sweeney Todd, "who will question you, you are well known to be in the trade, and to be continually dealing in such things?"

"That's all very fine; but I don't see why I should give you the full value of an article without evidence as to how you came by it."

"In other words you mean, you don't care how I came by them, provided I sell them to you at a thief's price, but if I want their value you mean to be particular."

"My good sir, you may conclude what you like. Show me that you have a right to dispose of the pearls, and you need go no further than my shop for a customer."

"I am no disposed to take that trouble, so I shall bid you good night, and if you want any pearls again, I would certainly advise you not to be so wonderfully particular where you get them."

Sweeney Todd strode towards the door, but the lapidary was not going to part with him so easy, so springing over his counter with an agility one would not have expected from so old a man, he was at the door in a moment, and shouted at the top of his lungs —

"Stop thief! Stop thief! Stop him! There he goes! The big fellow with the three-cornered hat! Stop thief! Stop thief!"

These cries, uttered with great vehemence as they were, could not be totally ineffectual, but they roused the whole neighbourhood, and before Sweeney Todd had proceeded many yards a man made an attempt to collar him, but was repulsed by such a terrific blow in the face, that another person, who had run half-way across the road with a similar object, turned and went back again, thinking it scarcely prudent to risk his own safety in apprehending a criminal for the good of the public.

Having got rid thus of one of his foes, Sweeney Todd, with an inward determination to come back some day and be the death of the old lapidary, looked anxiously about for some court down which he could plunge, and so get out of sight of the many pursuers who were sure to attack him in the public streets. His ignorance of the locality, however, was a great bar to such a proceeding, for the great dread he had was, that he might get down some blind alley, and so be completely caged, and at the mercy of those who followed him.

He pelted on at a tremendous speed, but it was quite astonishing to see how the little old lapidary ran after him, falling down every now and then, and never stopping to pick himself up, as people say, but rolling on and getting on his feet in some miraculous manner, that was quite wonderful to behold, particularly in one so aged and so apparently unable to undertake any active exertion. There was one thing, however, he could not continue doing, and that was to cry "stop thief!" for he had lost his wind, and was quite incapable of uttering a word. How long he would have continued the chase is doubtful, but his career was suddenly put an end to, as regards that, by tripping his foot over a projecting stone in the pavement, and shooting headlong down a cellar which was open.

But abler persons than the little old lapidary had taken up the chase, and Sweeney Todd was hard pressed; and, although he ran very fast, the provoking thing was, that in consequence of the cries and shouts of his pursuers, new people took up the chase, who were fresh and vigorous and close to him. There is something awful in seeing a human being thus hunted by his fellows; and although we can have no sympathy with such a man as Sweeney Todd, because, from all that has happened, we begin to have some very horrible suspicion concerning him, still, as a general principle, it does not decrease the fact, that it is a dreadful thing to see a human being hunted through the streets. On he flew at the top of his speed, striking down whoever opposed him, until at last many who could have outrun him gave up the chase, not liking to encounter the knock-down blow which such a hand as his seemed capable of inflicting. His teeth were set, and his breathing became short and laborious, just as a man sprung out at a shop-door and succeeded in laying hold of him.

"I have got you, have I?" he said.

Sweeney Todd uttered not a word, but, putting forth an amount of strength that was perfectly prodigious, he seized the man by a great handful of his hair, and by his clothes behind, and flung him through a shop-window, smashing glass, framework, and everything in its progress. The man gave a shriek, for it was his own shop, and he was a dealer in fancy goods of the most flimsy texture, so that the smash with which he came down among his stock-in-trade, produced at once what the haberdashers are so delighted with in the present day, namely, a ruinous sacrifice. This occurrence had a great effect upon Sweeney Todd's pursuers; it taught them the practical wisdom of not interfering with a man possessed evidently of such tremendous powers of mischief, and consequently, as just about this period the defeat of the little lapidary took place, he got considerably the start of his pursuers. He was by no means safe. The cry of "stop thief!" still sounded in his ears, and on he flew, panting with the exertion he made, till he heard a man behind him, say,—

"Turn into the second court on your right, and you will be safe — I'll follow you. They shan't nab you, if I can help it."

Sweeney Todd had not much confidence in human nature — it was not likely he would; but, panting and exhausted as he was, the voice of any one speaking in friendly accents was welcome, and, rather impulsively than from reflection, he darted down the second court to his right.

CHAPTER VIII.

THE THIEVES' HOME.

IN A VERY FEW MINUTES Sweeney Todd found that this court had no thoroughfare, and therefore there was no outlet or escape, but he immediately concluded that something more was to be found than was at first sight to be seen, and casting a furtive glance beside him in the direction in which he had come, rested his hand upon a door which stood close by. The door gave way, and Sweeney Todd, hearing, as he imagined, a noise in the street, dashed in, and closed the door, and then he, heedless of all consequences, walked to the end of a long dirty passage, and, pushing open a door, descended a short flight of steps, to the bottom of which he had scarcely got, when the door which faced him at the bottom of the steps opened by some hand, and he suddenly found himself in the presence of a number of men seated round a large table. In an instant all eyes were turned towards Sweeney Todd, who was quite unprepared for such a scene, and for a minute he knew not what to say; but, as indecision was not Sweeney Todd's characteristic, he at once advanced to the table and sat down. There was some surprise evinced by the persons who were seated in that room, of whom there were many more than a score, and much talking was going on among them, which did not appear to cease on his entrance. Those who were near him looked hard at him, but nothing was said for some minutes, and Sweeney Todd looked about to understand, if he could, how he was placed, though it could not be much a matter of doubt as to the character of the individuals present.*

Their looks were often an index to their vocations, for all grades of the worst of characters were there, and some of them were by no means complimentary to human nature, for there were some of the most desperate characters that were to be found in London. Sweeney Todd gave a glance around him, and at once satisfied himself of the desperate nature of the assembly into which he had thrust himself. They were dressed in various fashions, some after the manner of the city — some more gay, and some half military, while not a few wore the garb of countrymen; but there was in all that an air of scampish, off-hand behaviour, not unmixed with brutality.

---

* *It was well known, or at least widely believed, that robbers, thieves, and highwaymen had "safe houses" tucked away here and there among London's more respectable neighborhoods, in which criminals could lay low before or after a job. They were referred to as "rookeries."*

"Friend," said one, who sat near him, "how came you here; are you known here?"

"I came here, because I found the door open, and I was told by some one to come here, as I was pursued."

"Pursued?"

"Aye, some one running after me, you know."

"I know what being pursued is," replied the man, "and yet I know nothing of you."

"That is not at all astonishing," said Sweeney, "seeing that I never saw you before, nor you me; but that makes no difference. I'm in difficulties, and I suppose a man may do his best to escape the consequences?"

"Yes, he may, yet that is no reason why he should come here; this is the place for free friends, who know and aid one another."

"And such I am willing to be; but at the same time I must have a beginning. I cannot be initiated without some one introducing me. I have sought protection, and I have found it; if there be any objection to my remaining here any longer, I will leave."

"No, no," said a tall man on the other side of the table, "I have heard what you have said, and we do not usually allow any such things; you have come here unasked, and now we must have a little explanation — our own safety may demand it; at all events we have our customs, and they must be complied with."

"And what are your customs?" demanded Todd.

"This: you must answer the question which we shall propound unto you; now answer truly what we shall ask of you."

"Speak," said Todd, "and I will answer all that you propose to me, if possible."

"We will not tax you too hardly, depend upon it: who are you?"

"Candidly, then," said Todd, "that's a question I do not like to answer, nor do I think it is one that you ought to ask. It is an inconvenient thing to name oneself — you must pass by that inquiry."

"Shall we do so?" inquired the interrogator of those around him, and gathering his cue from their looks, he, after a brief space, continued —

"Well, we will pass over that, seeing it is not necessary, but you must tell us what you are — cutpurse, footpad, or what not?"

"I am neither."

"Then tell us in your own words," said the man, "and be candid with us. What are you?"

"I am an artificial pearl-maker — or sham pearl-maker, whichever way you please to call it."

"A sham pearl-maker! that may be an honest trade for all we know, and that will hardly be your passport to our house, friend sham pearl-maker!"

"That may be as you say," replied Todd, "but I will challenge any man to equal me in my calling. I have made pearls that would pass with almost a lapidary, and which would pass with nearly all the nobility."

"I begin to understand you, friend; but I would wish to have some proof of what you say; we may hear a very good tale, and yet none of it shall be true; we are not men to be made dupes of, besides, there are enough to take vengeance, if we desire it."

"Ay, to be sure there is," said a gruff voice from the other end of the table, which was echoed from one to the other, till it came to the top of the table.

"Proof! proof! proof!" now resounded from one end of the room to the other.

"My friends," said Sweeney Todd, rising up, and advancing to the table, and thrusting his hand into his bosom and drawing out the string of twenty-four pearls, "I challenge you, or any one, to make a set of artificial pearls equal to these; they are my make, and I'll stand to it in any reasonable sum, that you cannot bring a man who shall beat me in my calling."

"Just hand them to me," said the man who had made himself interrogator.

Sweeney Todd threw the pearls on the table carelessly, and then said—

"There, look at them well, they'll bear it, and I reckon, though there may be some good judges amongst you, that you cannot any of you tell them from real pearls, if you had not been told so."

"Oh, yes, we know pretty well," said the man, "what these things are, we have now and then a good string in our possession, and that helps us to judge of them. Well, this is certainly a good imitation."

"Let me see it," said a fat man: "I was bred a jeweller, and I might say born, only I couldn't stick to it; nobody likes working for years upon little pay, and no fun with the gals. I say, hand it here!"

"Well," said Todd, "if you or anybody ever produced as good an imitation, I'll swallow the whole string; and knowing there's poison in the composition, it would not be a comfortable thing to think of."

"Certainly not," said the big man, "certainly not, but hand them over, and I'll tell you all about it."

The pearls were given into his hands; and Sweeney Todd felt some misgivings about his precious charge, and yet he showed it not, for he turned to the man who sat beside him, saying—

"If he can tell true pearls from them, he knows more than I think he does, for I am a maker, and have often had the true pearl in my hand."

"And I suppose," said the man, "you have tried your hand at putting the one for the other, and so doing your confiding customers."

"Yes, yes, that is the dodge, I can see very well," said another man, winking at the first; "and a good one too, I have known them do so with diamonds."

"Yes, but never with pearls; however, there are some trades that it is desirable to know."

"You're right."

The fat man now carefully examined the pearls, set them down on the table, and looked hard at them.

"There now, I told you I could bother you. You are not so good a judge that you would not have known, if you had not been told they were sham pearls, but what they were real."

"I must say, you have produced the best imitations I have ever seen. Why you ought to make your fortune in a few years — a handsome fortune!"

"So I should, but for one thing."

"And what is that?"

"The difficulty," said Todd, "of getting rid of them; if you ask anything below their value, you are suspected, and you run the chance of being stopped and losing them at the least, and perhaps entail a prosecution."

"Very true; but there is risk in everything; we all run risks; but then the harvest!"

"That may be," said Todd, "but this is peculiarly dangerous. I have not the means of getting introduction to the nobility themselves, and if I had I should be doubted, for they would say a working man cannot come honestly by such valuable things, and then I must concoct a tale to escape the Mayor of London."

"Ha! — ha! — ha!"

"Well, then, you can take them to a goldsmith."

"There are not many of them who would do so: they would not deal in them; and, moreover, I have been to one or two of them; as for a lapidary, why, he is not so easily cheated."

"Have you tried?"

"I did, and had to make the best of my way out, pursued as quickly as they could run, and I thought at one time I must have been stopped, but a few lucky turns brought me clear, when I was told to turn up this court; and I came in here."

"Well," said one man, who had been examining the pearls, "and did the lapidary find out they were not real?"

"Yes, he did; and he wanted to stop me and the string together, for trying to impose upon him; however, I made a rush at the door, which he tried to shut, but I was the stronger man, and here I am."

"It has been a close chance for you," said one.

"Yes, it just has," replied Sweeney, taking up the string of pearls, which he replaced in his clothes, and continued to converse with some of those around him.

Things now subsided into their general course; and little notice was taken of Sweeney. There was some drink on the board, of which all partook. Sweeney had some, too, and took the precaution of emptying his pockets before them all, and gave them a share of his money to pay his footing. This was policy, and they all drank to his success, and were very good companions. Sweeney, however, was desirous of getting out as soon as he could, and more than once cast his eyes towards the door; but he saw there were eyes upon him, and dared not excite suspicion, for he might undo all that he had done. To lose the precious treasure he possessed would be maddening; he had succeeded to admiration in inducing the belief that what he showed them was merely a counterfeit; but he knew so well that they were real, and that a latent feeling that they were humbugged might be hanging about; and that the first suspicious movement he would be watched, and some desperate attempt made to make him give them up. It was with no small violence to his own feelings that he listened to their conversation, and appeared to take an interest in their proceedings.

"Well," said one, who sat next him, "I'm just off for the north-road."

"Any fortune there?"

"Not much; and yet I mustn't complain: these last three weeks, the best I have had has been two sixties."

"Well, that would do very well."

"Yes, the last man I stopped was a regular looby Londoner; he appeared like a don, complete tip-top man of fashion; but, Lord! when I came to look over him, he hadn't as much as would carry me twenty-four miles on the road."

"Indeed! don't you think he had any hidden about him? — they do do so now."

"Ah, ah!" returned another, "well said, old fellow; 'tis a true remark, that we can't always judge a man from appearances. Lor! bless me, now, who'd 'a thought your swell cove proved to be out o' luck? Well, I'm sorry for you; but you know 'tis a long lane that has no turning, as Mr. Somebody says — so, perhaps, you'll be more fortunate another time. But come, cheer up, whilst I relate an adventure that occurred a little time ago; 'twas a slice of good luck, I assure you, for I had no difficulty in bouncing my victim, out of a good swag of tin; for you know farmers returning from market are not always too wary and careful, especially as the lots of wine they take at the market dinners make the cosy old boys ripe and mellow for sleep. Well, I met one of these jolly gentlemen, mounted on horseback, who declared he had nothing but a few paltry guineas about him; however, that would not do — I searched him, and found a hundred and four pounds secreted about his person."

"Where did you find it?"

"About him. I tore his clothes to ribands. A pretty figure he looked upon horseback, I assure you. By Jove, I could hardly help laughing; in fact, I did laugh at him, which so enraged him, that he immediately threatened to horse-whip me, and yet he dared not defend his money; but I threatened to shoot him, and that soon brought him to his senses."

"I should imagine so. Did you ever have a fight for it?" inquired Sweeney Todd.

"Yes, several times. Ah! it's by no means an easy life, you may depend. It is free, but dangerous. I have been fired at six or seven times."

"So many?"

"Yes. I was near York once, when I stopped a gentleman; I thought him an easy conquest, but not as he turned out, for he was a regular devil."

"Resisted you?"

"Yes, he did. I was coming along when I met him, and I demanded his money. 'I can keep it myself,' he said, 'and do not want any assistance to take care of it.'

"'But I want it,' said I; 'your money or your life.'

"'You must have both, for we are not to be parted,' he said, presenting his pistol at me; and then I had only time to escape from the effect of the shot. I struck the pistol up with my riding-whip, and the bullet passed by my temples, and almost stunned me. I cocked and fired; he did the same, but I hit him, and he fell. He fired, however, but missed me. I was down upon him; he begged hard for life."

"Did you give it him?"

"Yes; I dragged him to the side of the road, and then left him. Having done so much, I mounted my horse and came away as fast as I could, and then I made for London, and spent a merry day or two there."

"I can imagine you must enjoy your trips into the country, and then you must have still greater relish for the change when you come to London — the change is so great and so entire."

"So it is; but have you never any run of luck in your line? I should think you must at times succeed in tricking the public."

"Yes, yes," said Todd, "now and then we do — but I tell you it is only now and then; and I have been afraid of doing too much. In small sums I have been a gainer; but I want to do something grand. I tried it on, but at the same time I have failed."

"That is bad; but you may have more opportunities by and by. Luck is all chance."

"Yes," said Todd, "that is true, but the sooner the better, for I am growing impatient."

Conversation now went on; each man speaking of his exploits, which were always some species of rascality and robbery, accompanied by violence generally; some were midnight robbers and breakers into people's houses; in fact, all the crimes that could be imagined. This place was, in fact, a complete house of rendezvous for thieves, cutpurses, highwaymen, footpads, and burglars of every grade and description — a formidable set of men of the most determined and desperate appearance. Sweeney Todd hardly knew how to rise and leave the place, though it was now growing very late, and he was most anxious to get safe out of the den he was in; but how to do that, was a problem yet to be solved.

"What is the time?" he muttered to the man next to him.

"Past midnight," was the reply.

"Then I must leave here," he answered, "for I have work that I must be at in a very short time, and I shall not have too much time."

So saying he watched his opportunity, and rising, walked up to the door, which he opened and went out; after that he walked up the five steps that led to the passage, and this latter had hardly been gained when the street-door opened, and another man came in at the same moment, and met him face to face.

"What do you do here?"

"I am going out," said Sweeney Todd.

"You are going back; come back with me."

"I will not," said Todd. "You must be a better man than I am, if you make me; I'll do my best to resist your attack, if you intend one."

"That I do," replied the man; and he made a determined rush upon Sweeney, who was scarcely prepared for such a sudden onslaught, and was pushed back till he came to the head of the stairs, where a struggle took place, and both rolled down the steps. The door was thrown open, and every one rushed out to see what was the matter, but it was some moments before they could make it out.

"What does he do here?" said the first, as soon as he could speak, and pointing to Sweeney Todd.

"It's all right."

"All wrong, I say."

"He's a sham-pearl maker, and has shown us a string of sham pearls that are beautiful."

"Psha!"

"I will insist upon seeing them; give them to me," he said, "or you do not leave this place."

"I will not," said Sweeney.

"You must. Here, help me — but I don't want help, I can do it by myself."

As he spoke, he made a desperate attempt to collar Sweeney and pull him to the earth, but he had miscalculated his strength when he imagined that he was superior to Todd, who was by far the more powerful man of the two, and resisted the attack with success. Suddenly, by an Herculean effort, he caught his adversary below the waist, and lifting him up, he threw him upon the floor with great force; and then, not wishing to see how the gang would take this — whether they would take the part of their companion or of himself he knew not — he thought he had an advantage in the distance, and he rushed up stairs as fast as he could, and reached the door before they could overtake him to prevent him. Indeed, for more than a minute they were irresolute what to do; but they were somehow prejudicial in favour of their companion, and they rushed up after Sweeney just as he had got to the door. He would have had time to escape them, but, by some means, the door became fast, and he could not open it, exert himself how he would. There was no time to lose; they were coming to the head of the stairs, and Sweeney had hardly time to reach the stairs, to fly upwards, when he felt himself grasped by the throat. This he soon released himself from; for he struck the man who seized him a heavy blow, and he fell backwards, and Todd found his way up to the first floor, but he was closely pursued. Here was another struggle; and again Sweeney Todd was the victor, but he was hard pressed by those who followed him — fortunately for him there was a mop left in a pail of water, this he seized hold of, and, swinging it over his head, he brought it full on the head of the first man who came near him. Dab it came, soft and wet, and splashed over some others who were close at hand.

It is astonishing what an effect a new weapon will sometimes have. There was not a man among them, who would not have faced danger in more ways than one, that would not have rushed headlong upon deadly and destructive weapons, but who were quite awed when a heavy wet mop was dashed into their faces. They were completely paralysed for a moment; indeed, they began to look upon it as something between a joke and a serious matter and either would have been taken just as they might be termed.

"Get the pearls!" shouted the man who had first stopped him; "seize the spy! seize him — secure him — rush at him! You are men enough to hold one man!"

Sweeney Todd saw matters were growing serious, and he plied his mop most vigorously upon those who were ascending, but they had become somewhat used to the mop, and it had lost much of its novelty, and was by no means a dangerous weapon. They rushed on, despite the heavy blows showered by Sweeney, and he was compelled to give way stair after stair. The head of the mop came off, and then there remained but the handle, which formed an efficient weapon, and which made fearful havoc on the heads of the assailants; and despite all that their slouched hats could do in the way of protecting them, yet the staff came with a crushing effect. The best fight in the world cannot last for ever; and Sweeney again found numbers were not to be resisted for long; indeed, he could not have physical energy enough to sustain his own efforts, supposing he had received no blows in return. He turned and fled as he was forced back to the landing, and then came to the next stair-head, and again he made a desperate stand. This went on for stair after stair, and continued for more than two or three hours. There were moments of cessation when they all stood still and looked at each other.

"Fire upon him!" said one.

"No, no; we shall have the authorities down upon us, and then all will go wrong."

"I think we had much better have let it alone in the first place, as he was in, for you may be sure this won't make him keep a secret; we shall all be split upon as sure as fate."

"Well, then, rush upon him, and down with him. Never let him out! On to him! Hurrah!"

Away they went, but they were resolutely met by the staff of Sweeney Todd, who had gained new strength by the short rest he had had.

"Down with the spy!"

This was shouted out by the men, but as each of them approached, they were struck down, and at length, finding himself on the second floor landing, and being fearful that some one was descending from above, he rushed into one of the inner rooms. In an instant he had locked the doors, which were strong and powerful.

"Now," he muttered, "for means to escape."

He waited a moment to wipe the sweat from his brow, and then he crossed the floor to the windows, which were open. They were the old-fashioned bay-windows, with the heavy ornamental work which some houses possessed, and overhung the low door-ways, and protected them from the weather.

"This will do," he said, as he looked down to the pavement — "this will do. I will try this descent, if I fall."

The people on the other side of the door were exerting all their force to break it open, and it had already given one or two ominous creaks, and a few minutes more would probably let them into the room. The streets were clear — no human being was moving about, and there were faint signs of the approach of morning. He paused a moment to inhale the fresh air, and then he got outside of the window. By means of the sound oaken ornaments, he contrived to get down to the drawing-room balcony, and then he soon got down into the street. As he walked slowly away, he could hear the crash of the door, and a slight cheer, as they entered the room; and he could imagine to himself the appearance of the faces of those who entered, when they found the bird had flown, and the room was empty.

Sweeney Todd had not far to go; he soon turned into Fleet-street, and made for his own house. He looked about him, but there were none near him; he was tired and exhausted, and right glad was he when he found himself at his own door. Then stealthily he put the key into the door, and slowly entered the house.

CHAPTER IX.

JOHANNA AT HOME, AND THE RESOLUTION.

JOHANNA OAKLEY WOULD NOT ALLOW Colonel Jeffery to accompany her all the way home, and he, appreciating the scruples of the young girl, did not press his attention upon her, but left her at the corner of Fore-street, after getting from her a half promise that she would meet him again on that day week, at the same hour, in the Temple-gardens.

"I ask this of you, Johanna Oakley," he said, "because I have resolved to make all the exertion in my power to discover what has become of Mr. Thornhill, in whose fate I am sure I have succeeded in interesting you, although you care so little for the string of pearls which he has in trust for you."

"I do, indeed, care little for them," said Johanna, "so little, that it may be said to amount to nothing."

"But still they are yours, and you ought to have the option of disposing of them as you please. It is not well to despise such gifts of fortune; for if you can yourself do nothing with them, there are surely some others whom you may know, upon whom they would bestow great happiness."

"A string of pearls, great happiness?" said Johanna, inquiringly.

"Your mind is so occupied by your grief that you quite forget such strings are of great value. I have seen those pearls, Johanna, and can assure you that they are in themselves a fortune."

"I suppose," she said sadly, "it is too much for human nature to expect two blessings at once. I had the fond, warm heart that loved me without the fortune, that would have enabled us to live in comfort and affluence; and now, when that is perchance within my grasp, the heart, that was by far the more costly possession, and the richest jewel of them all, lies beneath the wave with its bright influences, and its glorious and romantic aspirations, quenched for ever."

"You will meet me then, as I request of you, to hear if I have any news for you?"

"I will endeavour so to do. I have all the will; but Heaven knows if I may have the power."

"What mean you, Johanna?"

"I cannot tell what a week's anxiety may do; I know not but a sick bed may be my resting-place, until I exchange it for the tomb. I feel even now my strength fail me, and that I am scarcely able to totter to my home. Farewell, sir! I owe you my best thanks, as well for the trouble you have taken, as for the kindly manner in which you have detailed to me what has passed."

"Remember," said Colonel Jeffery, "that I bid you *adieu*, with the hope of meeting you again."

It was thus they parted, and Johanna proceeded to her father's house. Who now that had met her and had chanced not to see that sweet face, which could never be forgotten, would have supposed her to be the once gay and sprightly Johanna Oakley? Her steps were sad and solemn, and all the juvenile elasticity of her frame seemed like one prepared for death; and she hoped that she would be able to glide, silently and unobserved, to her own little bed-chamber — that chamber where she had slept since she was a child, and on the little couch, on which she had so often laid down to sleep that holy and calm slumber which such hearts as hers can only know.

But she was doomed to be disappointed, for the Rev. Mr. Lupin was still there, and as Mrs. Oakley had placed before that pious individual a great assortment of creature comforts, and among the rest some mulled wine, which seemed particularly to agree with him, he showed no disposition to depart. It unfortunately happened that this wine, of which the reverend gentleman partook with such a holy relish, was kept in a cellar, and Mrs. Oakley had had occasion twice to go down to procure a fresh supply, and it was on a third journey for the same purpose that she encountered poor Johanna, who had just let herself in at the private door.

"Oh! you have come home, have you?" said Mrs. Oakley; "I wonder where you have been to, gallivanting; but I suppose I may wonder long enough before you will tell me. Go into the parlour, I want to speak to you."

Now poor Johanna had quite forgotten the very existence of Mr. Lupin — so, rather than explain to her mother, which she knew would beget more questions, she wished to go to bed at once, notwithstanding it was an hour before the usual time for so doing, she walked unsuspectingly into the parlour; and as Mr. Lupin was sitting, the slightest movement of his chair closed the door, so she could not escape.

Under any other circumstances probably Johanna would have insisted upon leaving the apartment; but a glance at the countenance of the pious individual was quite sufficient to convince her that he had been sacrificing sufficiently to Bacchus to be capable of any amount of effrontery, so that she dreaded passing him, more especially as he swayed his arms about like the sails of a windmill. She thought at least that when her mother returned she would rescue her; but in that hope she was mistaken, and Johanna had no more idea of the extent to which religious fanaticism will carry its victim, than she had of the manners and customs of the inhabitants of the moon. When Mrs. Oakley did return, she had some difficulty in getting into the apartment, inasmuch as Mr. Lupin's chair occupied so large a portion of it; but when she did obtain admission, and Johanna said —

"Mother, I beg of you to protect me against this man, and allow me a free passage from the apartment!"

Mrs. Oakley affected to lift up her hands in amazement, as she said —

"How dare you speak so disrespectfully of a chosen vessel? How dare you, I say, do such a thing — it's enough to drive any one mad to see the young girls now-a-days!"

"Don't snub her — don't snub the virgin," said Mr. Lupin; "she don't know the honour yet that's intended her."

"She don't deserve it," said Mrs. Oakley, "she don't deserve it."

"Never mind, madam — never mind; we — we — we don't get all what we deserve in this world."

"Take a drop of something, Mr. Lupin; you have got the hiccups."

"Yes; I — I rather think I have a little. Isn't it a shame that anybody so intimate with the Lord should have the hiccups? What a lot of lights you have got burning, Mrs. Oakley!"

"A lot of lights, Mr. Lupin! Why, there is only one; but perhaps you allude to the lights of the gospel?"

"No; I — I don't, just at present; damn the lights of the gospel — that is to say, I mean damn all backsliders! But there is a lot of lights, and no mistake, Mrs. Oakley. Give me a drop of something, I'm as dry as dust."

"There is some more mulled wine, Mr. Lupin; but I am surprised that you think there is more than one light."

"It's a miracle madam, in consequence of my great faith. I have faith in s — s — s — six lights, and here they are."

"Do you see that, Johanna?" exclaimed Mrs. Oakley, "are you not convinced now of the holiness of Mr. Lupin?"

"I am convinced of his drunkenness, mother, and entreat of you to let me leave the room at once."

"Tell her of the honour," said Mr. Lupin — "tell her of the honour."

"I don't know, Mr. Lupin; but don't you think it would be better to take some other opportunity?"

"Very well, then, this is the opportunity."

"If it's your pleasure, Mr. Lupin, I will. You must know, then, Johanna, that Mr. Lupin has been kind enough to consent to save my soul, on condition that you marry him, and I am quite sure you can have no reasonable objection; indeed, I think it's the least you can do, whether you have any objection or not."

"Well put," said Mr. Lupin, "excellently well put."

"Mother," said Johanna, "if you are so far gone in superstition, as to believe this miserable drunkard ought to come between you and heaven, I am so lost as not to be able to reject the offer with more scorn and contempt than ever

I thought I could have entertained for any human being; but hypocrisy never, to my mind, wears so disgusting a garb as when it attires itself in the outward show of religion."

"This conduct is unbearable," cried Mrs. Oakley; "am I to have one of the Lord's saints under my own roof?"

"If he were ten times a saint, mother, instead of being nothing but a miserable, drunken profligate, it would be better that he should be insulted ten times over, than that you should permit your own child to have passed through the indignity of having to reject such a proposition as that which has just been made. I must claim the protection of my father; he will not suffer one, towards whom he has ever shown an affection, the remembrance of which sinks deep into my heart, to meet with so cruel an insult beneath his roof."

"That's right, my dear," cried Mr. Oakley, at that moment pushing open the parlour-door. "That's right, my dear; you never spoke truer words in all your life."

A faint scream came from Mrs. Oakley, and the Rev. Mr. Lupin immediately seized upon the fresh jug of mulled wine, and finished it at a draught.

"Get behind me, Satan," he said. "Mr. Oakley, you will be damned if you say a word to me."

"It's all the same, then," said Mr. Oakley; "for I'll be damned if I don't. Then, Ben! Ben! come — come in, Ben."

"I'm a coming," said a deep voice, and a man about six feet four inches in height, and nearly two-thirds of that amount in width, entered the parlour. "I'm a coming, Oakley, my boy. Put on your blessed spectacles, and tell me which is the fellow."

"I could have sworn it," said Mrs. Oakley, as she gave the table a knock with her fist,—"I could have sworn when you came in, Oakley—I could have sworn, you little snivelling, shrivelled-up wretch, you'd no more have dared to come into this parlour as never was with those words in your mouth, than you'd have dared to have flown, if you hadn't had your cousin, Big Ben, the beef-eater, from the Tower, with you."

"Take it easy, ma'am," said Ben, as he sat down in a chair, which immediately broke all to pieces with his weight. "Take it easy, ma'am; the devil—what's this?"

"Never mind, Ben," said Mr. Oakley, "it's only a chair; get up."

"A cheer," said Ben; "do you call that a cheer? but never mind—take it easy."

"Why, you big, bullying, idle, swilling and guttling ruffian!"

"Go on, marm, go on."

"You good-for-nothing lump of carrion; a dog wears his own coat, but you wear your master's, you great stupid, overgrown, lurking hound. You parish-brought-up wild beast, go and mind your lions and elephants in the

Tower,* and don't come into honest people's houses, you cut-throat, bullying, pickpocketing wretch."

"Go on, marm, go on."

This was a kind of dialogue that could not last, and Mrs. Oakley sank down exhausted, and then Ben said—

"I tell you what, marm, I considers you—I looks upon you, marm, as a female wariety of that 'ere animal as is very useful and sagacious, marm."

There was no mistake in this allusion, and Mrs. Oakley was about to make some reply, when the Rev. Mr. Lupin rose from his chair, saying—

"Bless you all! I think I'll go home."

"Not yet, Mr. Tulip," said Ben; "you had better sit down again—we've got something to say to you."

"Young man, young man, let me pass. If you do not, you will endanger your soul."

"I ain't got none," said Ben; "I'm only a beef-eater, and don't pretend to such luxuries."

"The heathen!" exclaimed Mrs. Oakley, "the horrid heathen! but there's one consolation, and that is, that he will be fried in his own fat for everlasting."

"Oh, that's nothing," said Ben; "I think I shall like it, especially if it's any pleasure to you. I suppose that's what you call a Christian consolation. Will you sit down, Mr. Tulip?"

"My name ain't Tulip, but Lupin; but if you wish it, I don't mind sitting down, of course."

The beef-eater, with a movement of his foot, kicked away the reverend gentleman's chair, and down he sat with a dab upon the floor.

"My dear," said Mr. Oakley to Johanna, "you go to bed, and then your mother can't say you have anything to do with this affair. I intend to rid my house of this man. Good night, my dear, good night."

Johanna kissed her father on the cheek, and then left the room, not at all sorry that so vigorous a movement was about being made for the suppression of Mr. Lupin.

When she was gone, Mrs. Oakley spoke, saying—

"Mr. Lupin, I bid you good night, and, of course, after the rough treatment of these wretches, I can hardly expect you to come again. Good night, Mr. Lupin, good night."

"That's all very well, marm," said Ben, "but before this 'ere wild beast of a parson goes away, I want to admonish him. He don't seem to be wide awake, and I must rouse him up."

Ben took hold of the reverend gentleman's nose, and gave it such an awful pinch, that when he took his finger and thumb away, it was perfectly blue.

---

* The Royal menagerie was then housed in the Tower of London.

"Murder! oh, murder! my nose! my nose!" shrieked Mr. Lupin, and at that moment Mrs. Oakley, who was afraid to attack Ben, gave her husband such an open-handed whack on the side of his head, that the little man reeled again, and saw a great many more lights than the Rev. Mr. Lupin had done under the influence of the mulled wine.

"Very good," said Ben; "now we are getting into the thick of it."

With this Ben took from his pocket a coil of rope, one end of which was a noose, and that he dexterously threw over Mrs. Oakley's head.

"Murder!" she shrieked. "Oakley, are you going to see me murdered before your eyes?"

"There is such a singing in my ears," said Mr. Oakley, "that I can't see anything."

"This is the way," said Ben, "we manages the wild beastesses when they shuts their ears to all sorts of argument. Now, marm, if you please, a little this way."

Ben looked about until he found a strong hook in the wall, over which, in consequence of his great height, he was enabled to draw the rope, and then the other end of it he tied securely to the leg of a heavy secretaire that was in the room, so that Mrs. Oakley was well secured.

"Murder!" she cried. "Oakley, are you a man, that you stand by and see me treated in this way by this big brute?"

"I can't see anything," said Mr. Oakley; "there is such a singing in my ears; I told you so before — I can't see anything."

"Now, ma'am, you may just say what you like," said Ben; "it won't matter a bit, any more than the grumbling of a bear with a sore head; and as for you, Mr. Tulip, you'll just get down on your knees, and beg Mr. Oakley's pardon for coming and drinking his tea without his leave, and having the infernal impudence to speak to his daughter."

"Don't do it, Mr. Lupin," cried Mrs. Oakley — "don't do it."

"You hear," said Ben, "what the lady advises. Now, I am quite different; I advise you to do it — for, if you don't, I shan't hurt you, but it strikes me I shall be obliged to fall on you and crush you."

"I think I will," said Mr. Lupin: "the saints were always forced to yield to the Philistines."

"If you call me any names," said Ben, "I'll just wring your neck,"

"Young man, young man, let me exhort you. Allow me to go, and I will put up prayers for your conversion."

"Confound your impudence! what do you suppose the beasts in the Tower would do, if I was converted? Why, that 'ere tiger, we have had lately, would eat his own tail, to think as I had turned out such an ass. Come, I can't waste any more of my precious time; and if you don't get down on your knees directly, we'll see what we can do."

BIG BEN COMPELS MR. LUPIN TO DO PENANCE.

"I must," said Mr. Lupin, "I must, I suppose;" and down he flopped on his knees.

"Very good; now repeat after me. — I am a wolf that stole sheeps' clothing."

"Yes; 'I am a wolf that stole sheeps' clothing'— the Lord forgive me."

"Perhaps he may, and perhaps he mayn't. Now go on — all that's wirtuous is my loathing."

"Oh dear, yes — 'all that's wirtuous is my loathing.'"

"Mr. Oakley, I have offended."

"Yes; I am a miserable sinner, Mr. Oakley, I have offended."

"And asks his pardon, on my bended—"

"Oh dear, yes—I asks his pardon on my bended—The Lord have mercy upon us, miserable sinners!"

"Knees—I won't do so no more."

"Yes,—knees, I won't do so no more."

"As sure as I lies on this floor."

"Yes,—as sure as I lies on this floor.—Death and the devil, you've killed me!"

Ben took hold of the reverend gentleman by the back of the neck, and pressed his head down upon the floor, until his nose, which had before been such a sufferer, was nearly completely flattened with his face.

"Now you may go," said Ben.

Mr. Lupin scrambled to his feet; but Ben followed him into the passage, and did not yet let him go, until he had accelerated his movements by two hearty kicks. And then the victorious beef-eater returned to the parlour.

"Why, Ben," said Mr. Oakley, "you are quite a poet."

"I believe you, Oakley, my boy," said Ben, "and now let us be off, and have a pint round the corner."

"What!" exclaimed Mrs. Oakley, "and leave me here, you wretches?"

"Yes," said Ben, "unless you promises never to be a female variety of a useful animal again, and begs pardon of Mr. Oakley, for giving him all this trouble; as for me, I'll let you off cheap, you shall only give me a kiss, and say you loves me."

"If I do, may I be—"

"Damned, you mean."

"No, I don't; choked I was going to say."

"Then you may be choked, for you have nothing to do but to let your legs go from under you, and you will be hung as comfortable as possible—come along, Oakley."

"Mr. Oakley—stop, stop—don't leave me here. I am sorry."

"That's enough," said Mr. Oakley; "and now, my dear, bear in mind one thing from me—I intend from this time forward to be master in my own house. If you and I are to live together, we must do so on very different terms to what we have been living, and if you won't make yourself agreeable, Lawyer Hutchins tells me that I can turn you out and give you a maintenance; and, in that case, I'll have my sister Rachel home to mind house for me; so now you know my determination, and what you have to expect. If you wish to begin, well, do so at once, by getting something nice and tasty for Ben's supper."

Mrs. Oakley made the required promise, and being released, she set about preparations for the supper in real earnest, but whether was really subdued or not we shall, in due time, see.

CHAPTER X.

THE COLONEL AND HIS FRIEND.

COLONEL JEFFERY WAS NOT AT ALL satisfied with the state of affairs, as regarded the disappointment of Mr. Thornhill, for whom he entertained a sincere regard, both on account of the private estimation in which he held him, and on account of actual services rendered to Thornhill by him. Not to detain Johanna Oakley in the Temple-gardens, he had stopped his narrative completely at the point when what concerned her had ceased, and had said nothing of much danger which the ship *Neptune* and its crew and passengers had gone through, after Mr. Thornhill had been taken on board with his dog. The fact is, the storm which he had mentioned was only the first of a series of gales of wind that buffeted the ship about for some weeks, doing it much damage, and enforcing almost the necessity of putting in somewhere for repairs. But a glance at the map will be sufficient to show that, situated as the *Neptune* was, the nearest port at which they could at all expect assistance, was the British Colony, at the Cape of Good Hope; but such was the contrary nature of the winds and waves, that just upon the evening of a tempestuous day, they found themselves bearing down close in shore, on the eastern coast of Madagascar. There was much apprehension that the vessel would strike on a rocky shore; but the water was deep, and the vessel rode well; there was a squall, and they let go both anchors to secure the vessel, as they were so close in shore, lest they should be driven in and stranded. It was fortunate they had so secured themselves, for the gale while it lasted blew half a hurricane, and the ship lost some of her mast, and some other trifling damage, which, however, entailed upon them the necessity of remaining there a few days, to cut timber to repair their masts, and to obtain a few supplies.

There is but little to interest a general reader in the description of a gale. Order after order was given until the masts and spars went one by one, and then the orders for clearing the wreck were given. There was much work to be done, and but little pleasure in doing it, for it was wet and miserable while it lasted, and there was the danger of being driven upon a lee shore, and knocked to pieces upon the rocks. This danger was averted, and they anchored safe at a very short distance from the shore in comparative security.

"We are safe now," remarked the captain, as he gave his second in command charge of the deck, and approached Mr. Thornhill and Colonel Jeffery.

"I am happy it is so," replied Jeffery.

"Well, captain," said Mr. Thornhill, "I am glad we have done with being knocked about; we are anchored, and the water here appears smooth enough."

"It is so, and I dare say it will remain so; it is a beautiful basin of water — deep and good anchorage; but you see it is not large enough to make a fine harbour."

"True; but it is rocky."

"It is, and that may make it sometimes dangerous, though I don't know that it would be so in some gales. The sea may beat in at the opening, which is deep enough for anything to enter — even Noah's ark would enter easily enough."

"What will you do now?"

"Stay here a day or so, and send boats ashore to cut some pine trees, to refit the ship with masts."

"You have no staves, then?"

"Not enough for such a purpose; and we never do go out stored with such things."

"You obtain them wherever you may go to."

"Yes, any part of the world will furnish them in some shape or other."

"When you send ashore, will you permit me to accompany the boat's crew?" said Jeffery.

"Certainly; but the natives of this country are violent and intractable, and should you get into any row with them, there is every probability of your being captured, or some bodily injury done you."

"But I will take care to avoid all that."

"Very well, colonel, you shall be welcome to go."

"I must beg the same permission," said Mr. Thornhill, "for I should much like to see the country, as well as to have some acquaintance with the natives themselves."

"By no means trust yourself alone with them," said the captain, "for if you live you will have cause to repent it — depend upon what I say."

"I will," said Thornhill; "I will go nowhere but where the boat's company goes."

"You will be safe then."

"But do you apprehend any hostile attack from the natives?" inquired Colonel Jeffery.

"No, I do not expect it; but such things have happened before to-day, and I have seen them when least expected, though I have been on this coast before, and yet I never met with any ill-treatment; but there have been many who have touched on this coast, who have had a brush with the natives and come off second best, the natives generally retiring when the ship's company muster strong in number, and calling out the chiefs, who come down in great force, that we may not conquer them."

THE NEXT MORNING THE BOATS were ordered out to go ashore with crews, prepared for cutting timber, and obtaining such staves as the ship was in want of. With these boats old Thornhill and Colonel Jeffery went both of them on board, and after a short ride they reached the shore of Madagascar. It was a beautiful country, and one in which vegetables appear luxuriant and abundant, and the party in search of timber for shipbuilding purposes soon came to some lordly monarchs of the forest, which would have made vessels of themselves. But this was not what was wanted; but where the trees grew thicker and taller, they began to cut some tall pine-trees down. This was the wood they most desired; in fact, it was exactly what they wanted; but they hardly got through a few such trees, when the natives came down upon them, apparently to reconnoitre. At first they were quiet and tractable enough, but anxious to see and inspect everything, being very inquisitive and curious. However, that was easily borne, but at length they became more numerous, and began to pilfer all they could lay their hands upon, which, of course brought resentment, and, after some time, a blow or two was exchanged. Colonel Jeffery was forward, and endeavouring to prevent some violence being offered to one of the wood-cutters; in fact, he was interposing himself between the two contending parties, and tried to restore order and peace, but several armed natives rushed suddenly upon him, secured him, and were hurrying him away to death before any one could stir in his behalf. His doom appeared certain, for, had they succeeded, they would have cruelly and brutally murdered him. However, just at that moment aid was at hand, and Mr. Thornhill, seeing how matters stood, seized a musket from one of the sailors, and rushed after the natives who had Colonel Jeffery. There were three of them, two others had gone on to apprise, it was presumed, the chiefs. When Mr. Thornhill arrived, they had thrown a blanket over the head of Jeffery; but Mr. Thornhill in an instant hurled one down with a blow from the butt-end of his musket, and the second met the same fate, as he turned to see what was the matter. The third, seeing the colonel free, and the musket levelled at his own head, immediately ran after the other two, to avoid any serious consequences to himself.

"Thornhill, you have saved my life," said Colonel Jeffery, excitedly.

"Come away, don't stop here — to the ship! — to the ship!" And as he spoke, they hurried after the crew and they succeeded in reaching the boats and the ship in safety; congratulating themselves not a little upon so lucky an escape from a people quite warlike enough to do mischief, but not civilized enough to distinguish when to do it.

When men are far away from home, and in foreign lands with the skies of other climes above them, their hearts become more closely knit together in those ties of brotherhood which certainly ought to actuate the whole universe, but which as certainly do not do so, except in very rare instances. One of these instances, however, would be found in the conduct of Colonel Jeffery and Mr. Thornhill, even under any circumstances, for they were most emphatically what might be termed kindred spirits; but when we come to unite to that fact the remarkable manner in which they had been thrown together, and the mutual services that they had it in their power to render to each other, we should not be surprised at the almost romantic friendship that arose between them. It was then that Thornhill made the colonel's breast the depository of all his thoughts and all his wishes, and a freedom of intercourse and a community of feeling ensued between them, which when it does take place between persons of really congenial dispositions, produces the most delightful results of human companionship.

No one who has not endured the tedium of a sea voyage, can at all be aware of what a pleasant thing it is to have some one on board, in the rich stores of whose intellect and fancy one can find a never-ending amusement. The winds might now whistle through the cordage, and the waves toss the great ship on their foaming crests; still Thornhill and Jeffery were together, finding, in the midst of danger, solace in each other's society, and each animating the other to the performance of deeds of daring that astonished the crew. The whole voyage was one of the greatest peril, and some of the oldest seamen on board did not scruple, during the continuance of their night watches, to intimate to their companions that the ship, in their opinion, would never reach England, and that she would founder somewhere along the long stretch of the African coast. The captain, of course, made every possible exertion to put a stop to such prophetic sayings, but when once they commenced, in a short time there was no such thing as completely eradicating them; and they, of course, produced the most injurious effect, paralysing the exertions of the crew in times of danger, and making them believe that they were in a doomed ship, and consequently all they could do was useless. Sailors are extremely superstitious on such matters, and there cannot be any reasonable doubt but that some of the disasters that befell the *Neptune* on her homeward voyage from India, may be attributed to this feeling of fatality getting hold of the seamen, and inducing them to think that, let them try what they might, they could not save the ship.

It happened that after they had rounded the Cape, a dense fog came on, such as had not been known on that coast for many a year, although the western shore of Africa at some seasons of the year is rather subject to such a species of vaporous exhalation. Every object was wrapped in the most profound gloom, and yet there was a strong eddy or current of the ocean, flowing parallel with the land, and, as the captain hoped, rather off than on the shore. Still there was a suspicion that the ship was making lee-way, which must eventually bring it on shore, by some of the low promontories that were by the maps indicated to be upon the coast. In consequence of this fear, the greatest anxiety prevailed on board the vessel, and lights were left burning on all parts of the deck, while two men were continually engaged making soundings.

It was about half-an-hour after midnight, as the chronometer indicated a storm, that suddenly the men, who were on watch on the deck, raised a loud

THORNHILL RESCUES COLONEL JEFFERY FROM THE SAVAGES.

cry of dismay. They had suddenly seen, close on to the larboard bow, lights which must belong to some vessel that, like the *Neptune*, was encompassed in the fog, and a collision was quite inevitable, for neither ship had time to put about. The only doubt, which was a fearful and an agonising one to have solved, was whether the stronger vessel was of sufficient bulk and power to run them down, or they it; and that fearful question was one which a few moments must settle. In fact, almost before the echo of that cry of horror which had come from the men, had died away, the vessels met. There was a hideous crash — one shriek of dismay and horror, and then all was still. The *Neptune*, with considerable damage, and some of her bulwarks stove in, sailed on; but the other ship went, with a surging sound, to the bottom of the sea. Alas! nothing could be done. The fog was so dense, that coupled, too, as it was with the darkness of the night, there could be no hope of rescuing one of the ill-fated crew of the ship; and the officers and seamen of the Neptune, although they shouted for some time, and then listened, to hear if any survivors of the ship that had been run down were swimming, no answer came to them; and when in about six hours more, they sailed out of the fog into a clear sunshine, where there was not so much as a cloud to be seen, they looked at each other like men newly awakened from some strange and fearful dream. They never discovered the name of the ship they had run down, and the whole affair remained a profound mystery.

When the Neptune reached the port of London, the affair was repeated, and every exertion was made to obtain some information concerning the ill-fated ship that had met with so fearful a doom. Such were the circumstances which awakened all the liveliest feelings of gratitude on the part of Colonel Jeffery towards Mr. Thornhill; and hence was it that he considered it a sacred duty, now that he was in London, and had the necessary leisure to do so, to leave no stone unturned to discover what had become of him.

After deep and anxious thought, and feeling convinced that there was some mystery which it was beyond his power to discover, he resolved upon asking the opinion of a friend, likewise in the army, a Captain Rathbone, concerning the whole of the facts. This gentleman, and a gentleman he was in the fullest acceptance of the term, was in London; in fact, he had retired from active service, and inhabited a small but pleasant house in the outskirts of the metropolis. It was one of those old-fashioned cottage residences, with all sorts of odd places and corners about it, and a thriving garden full of fine old wood, such as are rather rare near to London, and which are daily becoming more rare, in consequence of the value of land immediately contiguous to the metropolis not permitting large pieces to remain attached to small residences. Captain Rathbone had an amiable family about him, such as he was and might well be proud of, and was living in as great a state of domestic felicity as this world could very well afford him. It was to this gentleman, then, that Colonel Jeffery resolved upon going to lay all the circumstances before him concerning the probable fate of poor Thornhill.

This distance was not so great but that he could walk it conveniently, and he did so, arriving, towards the dusk of the evening, on the following day to that which had witnessed his deeply interesting interview with Johanna Oakley in the Temple-gardens. There is nothing on earth so delightfully refreshing, after a dusty and rather a long country walk, as to suddenly enter a well-kept and extremely verdant garden; and this was the case especially to the feelings of Colonel Jeffery, when he arrived at Lime Tree Lodge, the residence of Captain Rathbone.

He met him with a most cordial and frank welcome — a welcome which he expected, but which was none the less delightful on that account; and, after sitting awhile with the family in the house, he and the captain strolled into the garden, and then Colonel Jeffery commenced his revelation. The captain, with very few interruptions, heard him to an end; and, when he concluded by saying —

"And now I am come to ask your advice upon all these matters;" the captain immediately replied, in his warm, off-hand manner —

"I am afraid you won't find my advice of much importance; but I offer you my active co-operation in anything you think ought to be done or can be done in this affair, which, I assure you deeply interests me, and gives me the greatest possible impulse to exertion. You have but to command me in the matter, and I am completely at your disposal."

"I was quite certain you would say as much. But, notwithstanding the manner in which you shrink from giving an opinion, I am anxious to know what you really think with regard to what are, you will allow, most extraordinary circumstances."

"The most natural thing in the world," said Captain Rathbone, "at the first flush of the affair, seemed to be, that we ought to look for your friend Thornhill at the point where he disappeared."

"At the barber's in Fleet-street?"

"Precisely. Did he leave the barber, or did he not?"

"Sweeney Todd says that he left him, and proceeded down the street towards the city, in pursuance of a direction he had given him to Mr. Oakley, the spectacle-maker, and that he saw him get into some sort of disturbance at the end of the market; but to put against that, we have the fact of the dog remaining by the barber's door, and his refusing to leave it on any amount of solicitation. Now the very fact that a dog could act in such a way proclaims an amount of sagacity that seems to tell loudly against the presumption that such a creature could make any mistake."

"It does. What say you, now, to go into town to-morrow morning, and making a call at the barber's, without proclaiming we have any special errand, except to be shaved and dressed? Do you think he would know you again?"

"Scarcely, in plain clothes. I was in my undress uniform when I called with the captain of the *Neptune*, so that his impression of me must be of decidedly a military character; and the probability is, that he would not know me at all in the clothes of a civilian. I like the idea of giving a call at the barber's."

"Do you think your friend Thornhill was a man likely to talk about the valuable pearls he had in his possession?"

"Certainly not."

"I merely ask you, because they might have offered a great temptation; and if he has experienced any foul play at the hands of the barber, the idea of becoming possessed of such a valuable treasure might have been the inducement."

"I do not think it probable, but it has struck me that, if we obtain any information whatever of Thornhill, it will be in consequence of these very pearls. They are of great value, and not likely to be overlooked; and yet, unless a customer be found for them, they are of no value at all; and nobody buys jewels of that character but from the personal vanity of making, of course, some public display of them."

"That is true; and so, from hand to hand, we might trace those pearls until we come to the individual who must have had them from Thornhill himself, and who might be forced to account most strictly for the manner in which they came into his possession."

After some more desultory conversation upon the subject, it was agreed that Colonel Jeffery should take a bed for the night at Lime Tree Lodge, and that, in the morning, they should both start for London, and, disguising themselves as respectable citizens, make some attempts, by talking about jewels and precious stones, to draw out the barber into a confession that he had something of the sort to dispose of; and, moreover, they fully intended to take away the dog, with the care of which Captain Rathbone charged himself.

We may pass over the pleasant, social evening which the colonel passed with the amiable family of the Rathbones, and, skipping likewise a conversation of some strange and confused dreams which Jeffery had during the night concerning his friend Thornhill, we will presume that both the colonel and the captain have breakfasted, and that they have proceeded to London and are at the shop of a clothier in the neighbourhood of the Strand, in order to procure coats, wigs, and hats, that should disguise them for their visit to Sweeney Todd. Then, arm in arm, they walked towards Fleet-street, and soon arrived opposite the little shop within which there appears to be so much mystery.

"The dog, you perceive, is not here," said the colonel; "I had my suspicions, however, when I passed with Johanna Oakley that something was amiss with him, and I have no doubt but that the rascally barber has fairly compassed his destruction."

"If the barber be innocent," said Captain Rathbone, "you must admit that it would be one of the most confoundedly annoying things in the world to have a dog continually at his door assuming such an aspect of accusation, and in that case I can scarcely wonder at his putting the creature out of the way."

"No, presuming upon his innocence, certainly; but we will say nothing about all that, and remember we must come in as perfect strangers, knowing nothing of the affair of the dog, and presuming nothing about the disappearance of any one in this locality."

"Agreed, come on; if he should see us through the window, hanging about at all or hesitating, his suspicions will be at once awakened, and we shall do no good."

They both entered the shop and found Sweeney Todd wearing an extraordinary singular appearance, for there was a black patch over one of his eyes, which was kept in its place by a green riband that went round his head, so that he looked more fierce and diabolical than ever; and having shaved off a small whisker that he used to wear, his countenance, although to the full as hideous as ever, certainly had a different character of ugliness to that which had before characterised it, and attracted the attention of the colonel. That gentleman would hardly have known him again any where but in his own shop, and when we come to consider Sweeney Todd's adventures of the preceding evening, we shall feel not surprised that he saw the necessity of endeavouring to make as much change in his appearance as possible, for fear he should come across any of the parties who had chased him, and who, for all he knew to the contrary, might, quite unsuspectingly, drop in to be shaved in the course of the morning, perhaps to retail at that acknowledged mart for all sorts of gossip — a barber's shop — some of the very incidents which he has so well qualified himself to relate.

"Shaved and dressed, gentlemen?" said Sweeney Todd, as his customers made their appearance.

"Shaved only," said Captain Rathbone, who had agreed to be principal spokesman, in case Sweeney Todd should have any remembrance of the colonel's voice, and so suspect him.

"Pray be seated," said Sweeney Todd to Colonel Jeffery. "I'll soon polish off your friend, sir, and then I'll begin upon you. Would you like to see the morning paper, sir? it's at your service. I was just looking myself, sir, at a most mysterious circumstance, if it's true, but you can't believe, you know, sir, all that is put in newspapers."

"Thank you — thank you," said the colonel.

Captain Rathbone sat down to be shaved, for he had purposely omitted that operation at home, in order that it should not appear a mere excuse to get into Sweeney Todd's shop.

"Why, sir," continued Sweeney Todd, "as I was saying, it is a most remarkable circumstance."

"Indeed!"

"Yes, sir, an old gentleman of the name of Fidler had been to receive a sum of money at the west-end of the town, and has never been heard of since; that was yesterday, sir, and here is a description of him in the papers of to-day. 'A snuff-coloured coat, and velvet smalls — black velvet, I should have said — silk stockings, and silver shoe-buckles, and a gold-headed cane, with W. D. F. upon it, meaning "William Dumpledown Fidler"—a most mysterious affair, gentlemen.'"

A sort of groan came from the corner of the shop, and, on the impulse of the moment, Colonel Jeffery sprang to his feet, exclaiming—

"What's that — what's that?"

"Oh, it's only my apprentice, Tobias Ragg. He has got a pain in his stomach from eating too many of Lovett's pork pies. Ain't that it, Tobias, my bud?"

"Yes, sir," said Tobias with another groan.

"Oh, indeed," said the colonel, "it ought to make him more careful for the future."

"It's to be hoped it will, sir; Tobias, do you hear what this gentleman says: it ought to make you more careful in future. I am too indulgent to you, that's the fact. Now, sir, I believe you are as clean shaved as ever you were in your life."

"Why, yes," said Captain Rathbone, "I think that will do very well; and now, Mr. Green"—addressing the colonel by that assumed named—"and now, Mr. Green, be quick, or we shall be too late for the duke, and so lose the sale of some of our jewels."

"We shall indeed," said the colonel, "if we don't mind. We sat too long over our breakfast at the inn, and his grace is too rich and too good a customer to lose—he don't mind what price he gives for things that take his fancy, or the fancy of his duchess."

"Jewel merchants, gentlemen, I presume," said Sweeney Todd.

"Yes, we have been in that line for some time; and by one of us trading in one direction, and the other in another, we manage extremely well, because we exchange what suits our different customers, and keep up two distinct connexions."

"A very good plan," said Sweeney Todd. "I'll be as quick as I can with you, sir. Dealing in jewels is better than shaving."

"I dare say it is."

"Of course, it is, sir; here have I been slaving for some years in this shop, and not done much good—that is to say, when I talk of not having done much good, I admit I have made enough to retire upon quietly and comfortably, and I mean to do so very shortly. There you are, sir, shaved with celerity you seldom meet with, and as clean as possible, for the small charge of one penny. Thank you, gentlemen—there's your change; good morning."

They had no resource but to leave the shop; and when they had gone Sweeney Todd, as he stropped the razor he had been using upon his hand, gave a most diabolical grin, muttering—

"Clever—very ingenious—but it won't do. Oh dear, no, not at all! I am not so easily taken in—diamond merchants, ah! ah! and no objection, of course, to deal in pearls—a good jest that, truly, a capital jest. If I had been accustomed to be so easily defeated, I had not now been here a living man. Tobias, Tobias, I say."

"Yes, sir," said the lad, dejectedly.

"Have you forgotten your mother's danger in case you breathe a syllable of anything that has occurred here, or that you think has occurred here, or so much as dream of?"

"No," said the boy, "indeed I have not. I never can forget it, if I were to live a hundred years."

"That's well, prudent, excellent, Tobias. Go out now, and if those two persons who were here last, waylay you in the street, let them say what they will, and do you reply to them as shortly as possible; but be sure you come back to me quickly and report what they do say. They turned to the left, towards the city — now be off with you."

"It's of no use," said Colonel Jeffery to the captain; "the barber is either too cunning for me, or he is really innocent of all participation in the disappearance of Thornhill."

"And yet there are suspicious circumstances. I watched his countenance when the subject of jewels was mentioned, and I saw a sudden change come over it; it was but momentary, but still it gave me a suspicion that he knew something which caution alone kept within the recesses of his breast. The conduct of the boy, too, was strange; and then again, if he has the string of pearls, their value would give him all the power to do what he says he is about to do — viz., to retire from business with an independence."

"Hush! There, did you see that lad?"

"Yes; why it's the barber's boy."

"It is the same lad he called Tobias — shall we speak to him?"

"Let's make a bolder push, and offer him an ample reward for any information he may give us."

"Agreed, agreed."

They both walked up to Tobias, who was listlessly walking along the streets, and when they reached him, they were both struck with the appearance of care and sadness that was upon the boy's face. He looked perfectly haggard and careworn — an expression sad to see upon the face of one so young; and, when the colonel accosted him in a kindly tone, he seemed so unnerved that tears immediately darted to his eyes, although at the same time he shrank back as if alarmed.

"My lad," said the colonel, "you reside, I think, with Sweeney Todd, the barber. Is he not a kind master to you, that you seem so unhappy?"

"No, no — that is, I mean yes, I have nothing to tell. Let me pass on."

"What is the meaning of this confusion?"

"Nothing, nothing."

"I say, my lad, here is a guinea for you, if you will tell us what became of the man of a sea-faring appearance, who came with a dog to your master's house, some days since, to be shaved."

"I cannot tell you," said the boy, "I cannot tell you what I do not know."

"But, you have some idea, probably. Come, we will make it worth your while, and thereby protect you from Sweeney Todd. We have the power to do so, and all the inclination; but you must be quite explicit with us, and tell us frankly what you think, and what you know concerning the man in whose fate we are interested."

"I know nothing, I think nothing," said Tobias. "Let me go, I have nothing to say, except that he was shaved, and went away."

"But how came he to leave his dog behind him?"

"I cannot tell. I know nothing."

"It is evident that you do know something, but hesitate either from fear or some other motive to tell it; as you are inaccessible to fair means, we must resort to others, and you shall at once come before a magistrate, who will force you to speak out."

"Do with me what you will," said Tobias, "I cannot help it. I have nothing to say to you, nothing whatever. Oh, my poor mother, if it were not for you —"

"What then?"

"Nothing! nothing! nothing!"

It was but a threat of the colonel to take the boy before a magistrate, for he had really no grounds for so doing; and if the boy chose to keep a secret, if he had one, not all the magistrates in the world could force words from his lips that he felt not inclined to utter; and so, after one more effort, they felt that they must leave him.

"Boy," said the colonel, "you are young, and cannot well judge of the consequences of particular lines of conduct; you ought to weigh well what you are about, and hesitate long before you determine keeping dangerous secrets: we can convince you that we have the power of completely protecting you from all that Sweeney Todd could possibly attempt. Think again, for this is an opportunity of saving yourself perhaps from much future misery, that may never arise again."

"I have nothing to say," said the boy, "I have nothing to say."

He uttered these words with such an agonized expression of countenance, that they were both convinced he had something to say, and that, too, of the first importance — a something which would be valuable to them in the way of information, extremely valuable probably, and yet which they felt the utter impossibility of wringing from him. They were compelled to leave him, and likewise with the additional mortification, that, far from making any advance in the matter, they had placed themselves and their cause in a much worse position, in so far as they had awakened all Sweeney Todd's suspicions if he were guilty, and yet advanced not one step in the transaction. And then, to make the matter all the more perplexing, there was still the possibility that they might be altogether upon a wrong scent, and that the barber of Fleet-street had no more to do with the disappearance of Mr. Thornhill than they had themselves.

CHAPTER XI.

THE STRANGER AT LOVETT'S.

TOWARDS THE DUSK OF THE EVENING of that day, after the last batch of pies at Lovett's had been disposed of, there walked into the shop a man most miserably clad, and who stood for a few moments staring with weakness and hunger at the counter before he spoke. Mrs. Lovett was there, but she had no smile for him, and instead of its usual bland expression, her countenance wore an aspect of anger, as she forestalled what the man had to say, by exclaiming —

"Go away, we never give anything to beggars."

There came a flush of colour for the moment across the features of the stranger, and then he replied —

"Mistress Lovett, I do not come to ask alms of you, but to know if you can recommend me to any employment?"

"Recommend you! recommend a ragged wretch like you?"

"I am a ragged wretch, and, moreover, quite destitute. In better times I have sat at your counter, and paid cheerfully for what I wanted, and then one of your softest smiles has ever been at my disposal. I do not say this as a reproach to you, because the cause of your smile was well known to be a self-interested one, and when that cause had passed away, I can no longer expect it; but I am so situated, that I am willing to do anything for a mere subsistence."

"Oh, yes, and then when you get into a better case again, I have no doubt but you have quite sufficient insolence to make you unbearable; besides, what employment can we have but pie-making, and we have a man already who suits us very well with the exception that he, as you would do if we were to exchange him, has grown insolent, and fancies himself master of the place."

"Well, well," said the stranger, "of course, there is always sufficient argument against the poor and destitute to keep them so. If you will assert that my conduct will be the nature you describe, it is quite impossible for me to prove the contrary."

He turned and was about to leave the shop, but Mrs. Lovett called after him saying —

"Come in again in two hours."

He paused a moment or two, and then, turning his emaciated countenance upon her, said —

"I will if my strength permit me — water from the pumps in the street is but a poor thing for a man to subsist upon for twenty-four hours."

"You may take one pie."

The half-famished, miserable-looking man seized upon a pie, and devoured it in an instant.

THE STRANGER AT MRS. LOVETT'S PIE SHOP.

"My name," he said, "is Jarvis Williams; I'll be here, never fear, Mrs. Lovett, in two hours; and, notwithstanding all you have said, you shall find no change in my behaviour because I may be well kept and better clothed; but if I should feel dissatisfied with my situation, I will leave it, and no harm done."

So saying, he walked from the shop, and when he was gone, a strange expression came across the countenance of Mrs. Lovett, and she said in a low tone to herself—

"He might suit for a few months, like the rest, and it is clear that we must get rid of the one we have; I must think of it."

THERE IS A CELLAR OF VAST EXTENT, and of dim and sepulchral aspect — some rough red tiles are laid upon the floor, and pieces of flint and large jagged stones have been hammered into the earthen walls to strengthen them; while here and there rough huge pillars made by beams of timber rise perpendicularly from the floor, and prop large flat pieces of wood against the ceiling, to support it. Here and there gleaming lights seem to be peeping out from furnaces, and there is a strange hissing, simmering sound going on, while the whole air is impregnated with a rich and savoury vapour. This is Lovett's pie manufactory beneath the pavement of Bell-yard and at this time a night-batch of some thousands is being made for the purpose of being sent by carts the first thing in the morning all over the suburbs of London. By the earliest dawn of day a crowd of itinerant hawkers of pies would make their appearance, carrying off a large quantity to regular customers who had them daily, and no more thought of being without them, than of forbidding the milkman or the baker to call at their residences. It will be seen and understood, therefore, that the retail part of Mrs. Lovett's business, which took place principally between the hours of twelve and one, was by no means the most important or profitable portion of a concern which was really of immense magnitude, and which brought in a large yearly income. To stand in the cellar when this immense manufacture of what, at first sight, would appear such a trivial article was carried on, and to look about as far as the eye could reach, was by no means to have a sufficient idea of the extent of the place; for there were as many doors in different directions and singular low-arched entrances to different vaults, which all appeared as black as midnight, that one might almost suppose the inhabitants of all the surrounding neighbourhood had, by common consent given up their cellars to Lovett's pie factory. There is but one miserable light, except the occasional fitful glare that comes from the ovens where the pies are stewing, hissing, and spluttering in their own luscious gravy. There is but one man, too, throughout all the place, and he is sitting on a low three-legged stool in one corner, with his head resting upon his hands, and gently rocking to and fro, as he utters scarcely audible moans. He is but lightly clad; in fact, he seems to have but little on him except a shirt and a pair of loose canvas trousers. The sleeves of the former are turned up beyond his elbows, and on his head he has a white night-cap. It seems astonishing that such a man, even with the assistance of Mrs. Lovett, could make so many pies as are required in a day; but then, system does wonders, and in those cellars there are various mechanical contrivances for kneading the dough, chopping up the meat, &c., which greatly reduced the labour.

But what a miserable object is that man — what a sad and soul-stricken wretch he looks! His face is pale and haggard, his eyes deeply sunken; and, as he removes his hands from before his visage, and looks about him, a more perfect picture of horror could not have been found.

"I must leave to-night," he said, in coarse accents — "I must leave to-night. I know too much — my brain is full of horrors. I have not slept now for five nights, nor dare I eat anything but the raw flour. I will leave to-night if they do not watch me too closely. Oh! if I could but get into the streets — if I could but once again breathe the fresh air! Hush! what's that? I thought I heard a noise."

He rose, and stood trembling and listening; but all was still, save the simmering and hissing of the pies, and then he resumed his seat with a deep sigh.

"All the doors fastened upon me," he said, "what can it mean? It's very horrible, and my heart dies within me. Six weeks only have I been here — only six weeks. I was starving before I came. Alas, alas! how much better to have starved! I should have been dead before now, and spared all this agony."

"Skinner!" cried a voice, and it was a female one — "Skinner, how long will the ovens be?"

"A quarter of an hour — a quarter of an hour, Mrs. Lovett. God help me!"

"What is that you say?"

"I said, God help me! — surely a man may say that without offence."

A door slammed shut, and the miserable man was alone again.

"How strangely," he said, "on this night my thoughts go back to early days, and to what I once was. The pleasant scenes of my youth recur to me. I see again the ivy-mantled porch, and the pleasant village green. I hear again the merry ringing laughter of my playmates, and there, in my mind's eye, appears

THE STRANGER IN MRS. LOVETT'S BAKEHOUSE.

to me the bubbling stream, and the ancient mill, the old mansion-house, with its tall turrets, and its air of silent grandeur. I hear the music of the birds, and the winds making rough melody among the trees. 'Tis very strange that all those sights and sounds should come back to me at such a time as this, as if just to remind me what a wretch I am."

He was silent for a few moments, during which he trembled with emotion; then he spoke again, saying —

"Thus the forms of those whom I once knew, and many of whom have gone already to the silent tomb, appear to come thronging round me. They bend their eyes momentarily upon me, and, with settled expressions, show acutely the sympathy they feel for me. I see her, too, who first, in my bosom, lit up the flame of soft affection. I see her gliding past me like the dim vision of a dream, indistinct, but beautiful; no more than a shadow — and yet to me most palpable. What am I now — what am I now?"

He resumed his former position, with his head resting upon his hands; he rocked himself slowly to and fro, uttering those moans of a tortured spirit, which we have before noticed.

But see, one of the small arch doors open, in the gloom of those vaults, and a man, in a stooping posture, creeps in — a half-mask is upon his face, and he wears a cloak; but both his hands are at liberty. In one of them he carries a double-headed hammer, with a powerful handle, of about ten inches in length. He has probably come out of a darker place than the one into which he now so cautiously creeps, for he shades the light from his eyes, as if it were suddenly rather too much for him, and then he looks cautiously round the vault, until he sees the crouched-up figure of the man whose duty it is to attend the ovens. From that moment he looks at nothing else; but advances towards him, steadily and cautiously. It is evident that great secrecy is his object, for he is walking on his stocking soles only; and it is impossible to hear the slightest sounds of his foot-steps. Nearer and nearer he comes, so slowly, and yet so surely, towards him, who still keeps up the low moaning sound, indicative of mental anguish. Now he is close to him, and he bends over him for a moment, with a look of fiendish malice. It is a look which, despite his mask, glances full from his eyes, and then grasping the hammer tightly, in both hands, he raises it slowly above his head, and gives it a swinging motion through the air.

There is no knowing what induced the man that was crouching on the stool to rise at that moment; but he did so, and paced about with great quickness. A sudden shriek burst from his lips, as he beheld so terrific an apparition before him; but, before he could repeat the word, the hammer descended, crushing into his skull, and he fell lifeless, without a moan.

"And so, Mr. Jarvis Williams, you have kept your word," said Mrs. Lovett to the emaciated, care-worn stranger, who had solicited employment of her, "and so, Jarvis Williams, you have kept your word, and come for employment?"

"I have, madam, and hope that you can give it to me: I frankly tell you that I would seek for something better, and more congenial to my disposition, if I could; but who would employ one presenting such a wretched appearance as I do? You see that I am all in rags, and I have told you that I have been half starved, and therefore it is only some common and ordinary employment that I can hope to get, and that made me come to you."

"Well, I don't see why we should not make a trial of you, at all events, so if you like to go down into the bakehouse, I will follow you, and show you what you have to do. You remember that you have to live entirely upon the pies, unless you like to purchase for yourself anything else, which you may do if you can get the money. We give none, and you must likewise agree never to leave the bakehouse."

"Never to leave it?"

"Never, unless you leave it for good, and for all; if upon those conditions you choose to accept the situation, you may, and if not, you can go about your business at once, and leave it alone."

"Alas, madam, I have no resource; but you spoke of having a man already."

"Yes; but he has gone to his friends; he has gone to some of his very oldest friends, who will be quite glad to see him, so now say the word: — are you willing or are you not, to take the situation?"

"My poverty and my destitution consent, if my will be averse, Mrs. Lovett; but, of course, I quite understand that I leave when I please."

"Oh, of course, we never think of keeping anybody many hours after they begin to feel uncomfortable. If you be ready, follow me."

"I am quite ready, and thankful for a shelter. All the brightest visions of my early life have long since faded away, and it matters little or indeed nothing what now becomes of me; I will follow you, madam, freely, upon the conditions you have mentioned."

Mrs. Lovett lifted up a portion of the counter which permitted him to pass behind it, and then he followed her into a small room, which was at the back of the shop. She then took a key from her pocket, and opened an old door which was in the wainscoting, and immediately behind which was a flight of stairs. These she descended, and Jarvis Williams followed her, to a considerable depth, after which she took an iron bar from behind another door, and flung it open, showing her new assistant the interior of that vault which we have already very briefly described.

"These," she said, "are the ovens, and I will proceed to show you how you can manufacture the pies, feed the furnaces, and make yourself generally useful. Flour will be always let down through a trap-door from the upper shop, as well as everything required for making the pies but the meat, and that you will always find ranged upon shelves either in lumps or steaks, in a small room through this door, but it is only at particular times you will find the door open; and whenever you do so, you had better always take out what meat you think you will require for the next batch."

"I understand all that, madam," said Williams, "but how does it get there?"

"That's no business of yours; so long as you are supplied with it, that is sufficient for you; and now I will go through the process of making one pie, so that you may know how to proceed, and you will find with what amazing quickness they can be manufactured if you set about them in the proper manner."

She then showed him how a piece of meat thrown into a machine became finely minced up, by merely turning a handle; and then how flour and water and lard were mixed up together, to make the crust of the pies, by another machine, which threw out the paste thus manufactured in small pieces, each just large enough for a pie. Lastly, she showed him how a tray, which just held a hundred, could be filled, and, by turning a windlass, sent up to the shop, through a square trap-door, which went right up to the very counter.

"And now," she said, "I must leave you. As long as you are industrious you will go on very well, but as soon as you begin to be idle, and neglect the orders which are sent to you by me, you will get a piece of information which will be useful, and which if you be a prudent man will enable you to know what you are about."

"What is that? you may as well give it to me now."

"No; we seldom find there is occasion for it at first, but, after a time, when you get well fed, you are pretty sure to want it."

So saying she left the place, and he heard the door by which he had entered, carefully barred after her. Suddenly then he heard her voice again, and so clearly and distinctly, too, that he thought she must have come back again; but upon looking up at the door, he found that that arose from her speaking through a small grating at the upper part of it, to which her mouth was closely placed.

"Remember your duty," she said, "and I warn you, that any attempt to leave here will be as futile as it will be dangerous."

"Except with your consent, when I relinquish the situation."

"Oh, certainly — certainly, you are quite right there, everybody who relinquishes the situation goes to his old friends, whom he has not seen for many years, perhaps."

"WHAT A STRANGE MANNER OF TALKING she has!" said Jarvis Williams to himself, when he found he was alone. "There seems to be some singular and hidden meaning in every word she utters. What can she mean by a communication being made to me, if I neglect my duty! It is very strange; and what a singular looking place this is! I think it would be quite unbearable if it were not for the delightful odour of the pies, and they are indeed delicious — perhaps more delicious to me, who has been famished so long, and have gone through so much wretchedness; there is no one here but myself, and I am hungry now — frightfully hungry, and whether the pies be done or not, I'll have half a dozen of them at any rate, so here goes."

He opened one of the ovens, and the fragrant steam that came out was perfectly delicious, and he sniffed it up with a satisfaction such as he had never felt before, as regards anything that was eatable.

"Is it possible," he said "that I shall be able to make such delicious pies? At all events one can't starve here, and if it be a kind of imprisonment, it's a pleasant one. Upon my soul, they are nice, even half-cooked — delicious! I'll have another half-dozen, there are lots of them — delightful! I can't keep the gravy from running out of the corners of my mouth. Upon my soul, Mrs. Lovett, I don't know where you get your meat, but it's all as tender as young chickens, and the fat actually melts away in one's mouth. Ah, these are pies, something like pies! — they are positively fit for the gods!"

Mrs. Lovett's new man ate twelve threepenny pies, and then he thought of leaving off. It was a little drawback not to have anything to wash them down with but cold water; but he reconciled himself to this.

"For," as he said, "after all it would be a pity to take the flavour of such pies out of one's mouth — indeed it would be a thousand pities, so I won't think of it, but just put up with what I have got and not complain. I might have gone further and fared worse with a vengeance, and I cannot help looking upon it as a singular piece of good fortune that made me think of coming here in my deep distress to try and get something to do. I have no friends and no money; she whom I loved is faithless, and here I am, master of as many pies as I like, and to all appearance monarch of all I survey; for there really seems to be no one to dispute my supremacy. To be sure my kingdom is rather a gloomy one; but then I can abdicate it when I like, and when I am tired of those delicious pies, if such a thing be possible, which I really very much doubt, I can give up my situation, and think of something else. If I do that, I will leave England for ever; it's no place for me after the many disappointments I have had. No friend left me — my girl false — not a relation but who would turn his back upon me! I will go somewhere where I am unknown and can form new connexions, and perhaps make new friendships of a more permanent and stable character than the old ones, which have all proved so false to me; and, in the meantime, I'll make and eat pies as fast as I can."

CHAPTER XII.

THE RESOLUTION COME TO BY JOHANNA OAKLEY.

THE BEAUTIFUL JOHANNA — WHEN in obedience to the command of her father she left him, and begged him (the beef-eater) to manage matters with the Rev. Mr. Lupin — did not proceed directly up stairs to her apartment, but lingered on the staircase to hear what ensued; and if anything in her dejected state of mind could have given her amusement, it would certainly have been the way in which the beef-eater exacted a retribution from the reverend personage, who was not likely again to intrude himself into the house of the spectacle-maker. But when he was gone, and she heard that a sort of peace had been patched up with her mother — a peace which, from her knowledge of the high contracting parties, she conjectured would not last long — she returned to her room, and locked herself in; so that if any attempt were made to get her down to partake of the supper, it might be supposed she was asleep, for she felt herself totally unequal to the task of making one in any party, however much she might respect the individual members that composed it. And she did respect Ben the beef-eater; for she had a lively recollection of much kindness from him during her early years, and she knew that he had never come to the house when she was a child without bringing her some token of his regard in the shape of a plaything, or some little article of doll's finery, which at that time was very precious. She was not wrong in her conjectures that Ben would make an attempt to get her down stairs, for her father came up at the beef-eater's request, and tapped at her door. She thought the best plan, as indeed it was, would be to make no answer, so that the old spectacle-maker concluded at once what she wished him to conclude, namely, that she had gone to sleep; and he walked quietly down the stairs again, glad that he had not disturbed her, and told Ben as much.

Now, feeling herself quite secure from interruption for the night, Johanna did not attempt to seek repose, but set herself seriously to reflect upon what had occurred. She almost repeated to herself, word for word, what Colonel Jeffery had told her; and, as she revolved the matter over and over again in her brain, a strange thought took possession of her, which she could not banish, and which, when once it found a home within her breast, began to gather probability from every slight circumstance that was in any way connected with it. This thought, strange as it may appear, was, that the Mr. Thornhill, of whom Colonel Jeffery spoke in terms of such high eulogium, was no other than Mark Ingestrie himself.

It is astonishing, when once a thought occurs to the mind, that makes a strong impression, how, with immense rapidity, a rush of evidence will appear to come to support it. And thus it was with regard to this supposition of Johanna Oakley. She immediately remembered a host of little things which favoured the idea, and among the rest, she fully recollected that Mark Ingestrie had told her he meant to change his name when he left England; for that he wished her and her only to know anything of him, or what had become of him; and that his intention was to baffle inquiry, in case it should be made, particularly by Mr. Grant, towards whom he felt a far greater amount of indignation than the circumstances at all warranted him in feeling. Then she recollected all that Colonel Jeffery had said with regard to the gallant and noble conduct of this Mr. Thornhill, and, girl-like, she thought that those high and noble qualities could surely belong to no one but her own lover, to such an extent; and that, therefore, Mr. Thornhill and Mark Ingestrie must be one and the same person. Over and over again, she regretted she had not asked Colonel Jeffery for a personal description of Mr. Thornhill, for that would have settled all her doubts at once, and the idea that she had it still in her power to do so, in consequence of the appointment he had made with her for that day week brought her some consolation.

"It must have been he," she said; "his anxiety to leave the ship, and get here by the day he mentions, proves it; besides, how improbable it is, that at the burning of the ill-fated vessel, Ingestrie should place in the hands of another what he intended for me, when that other was quite as likely, and perhaps more so, to meet with death as Mark himself."

Thus she reasoned, forcing herself each moment into a stronger belief of the identity of Thornhill with Mark Ingestrie, and so certainly narrowing her anxieties to a consideration of the fate of one person instead of two.

"I will meet Colonel Jeffery," she said, "and ask him if this Mr. Thornhill had fair hair, and a soft and pleasing expression about the eyes, that could not fail to be remembered. I will ask him how he spoke, and how he looked; and get him, if he can, to describe to me even the very tones of his voice; and then I shall be sure, without the shadow of a doubt, that it is Mark. But then, oh! then comes the anxious question, of what has been his fate?"

When poor Johanna began to consider the multitude of things that might have happened to her lover during his progress from Sweeney Todd's, in Fleet-street, to her father's house, she became quite lost in a perfect maze of conjecture, and then her thoughts always painfully reverted back to the barber's shop where the dog had been stationed; and she trembled to reflect for a moment upon the frightful danger to which that string of pearls might have subjected him.

"Alas! alas!" she cried, "I can well conceive that the man whom I saw attempting to poison the dog would be capable of any enormity. I saw his face but for a moment, and yet it was one never again to be forgotten. It was a face in which might be read cruelty and evil passions; besides, the man who would put an unoffending animal to a cruel death, shows an absence of feeling, and a baseness of mind, which make him capable of any crime he thinks he can commit with impunity. What can I do — oh! what can I do to unravel this mystery?"

No one could have been more tenderly and gently brought up than Johanna Oakley, but yet, inhabitive of her heart, was a spirit and a determination which few indeed could have given her credit for, by merely looking on the gentle and affectionate countenance which she ordinarily presented. But it is no new phenomenon in the history of the human heart to find that some of the most gentle and loveliest of human creatures are capable of the highest efforts of perversion; and when Johanna Oakley told herself, which she did, she was determined to devote her existence to a discovery of the mystery that enveloped the fate of Mark Ingestrie, she likewise made up her mind that the most likely man for accomplishing that object should not be rejected by her on the score of danger, and she at once set to work considering what those means should be. This seemed an endless task, but still she thought that if, by any means whatever, she could get admittance to the barber's house, she might be able to come to some conclusion as to whether or not it was there where Thornhill, whom she believed to be Ingestrie, had been stayed in his progress.

"Aid me Heaven," she cried, "in the adoption of some means of action on the occasion. Is there any one with whom I dare advise? Alas! I fear not, for the only person in whom I have put my whole heart is my father, and his affection for me would prompt him at once to interpose every possible obstacle to my proceeding, for fear danger should come of it. To be sure, there is Arabella Wilmot, my old school-fellow and bosom friend; she would advise me to the best of her ability, but I much fear she is too romantic and full of odd, strange actions, that she has taken from books, to be a good adviser; and yet what can I do? I must speak to some one, if it be but in case any accident happening to me, my father may get news of it, and I know of no one else whom I can trust but Arabella."

After some little more consideration, Johanna made up her mind that on the following morning she would go to the house of her old school friend, which was in the immediate vicinity, and hold a conversation with her.

"I shall hear something," she said, "at least of a kindly and a consoling character; for what Arabella may want in calm and steady judgment, she fully compensates for in actual feeling, and what is most of all, I know I can trust her word implicitly, and that my secret will remain as safely locked in her breast as if it were in my own."

It was something to come to a conclusion to ask advice, and she felt that some portion of her anxiety was lifted from her mind by the mere fact that she had made so firm a mental resolution, that neither danger nor difficulty should deter her from seeking to know the fate of her lover. She retired to rest now with a greater hope, and while she is courting repose, notwithstanding the chance of the discovered images that fancy may present to her in her slumbers, we will take a glance at the parlour below, and see how far Mrs. Oakley is conveying out the pacific intention she had so tacitly expressed, and how the supper is going forward, which, with not the best grace in the world, she is preparing for her husband, who for the first time in his life had begun to assert his rights, and for big Ben, the beef-eater, whom she as cordially disliked as it was possible for any woman to detest any man. Mrs. Oakley by no means preserved her taciturn demeanour, for after a little she spoke, saying —

"There's nothing tasty in the house; suppose I run over the way to

Waggarge's, and get some of those Epping sausages with the peculiar flavour."*

"Ah, do," said Mr. Oakley, "they are beautiful, Ben, I can assure you."

"Well, I don't know," said Ben the beef-eater, "sausages are all very well in their way, but you need such a plaguey lot of them; for if you only eat them one at a time, how soon will you get through a dozen or two."

"A dozen or two," said Mrs. Oakley; "why, there are only five to a pound."

"Then," said Ben, making a mental calculation, "then, I think, ma'am, that you ought not to get more than nine pounds of them, and that will be a matter of forty-five mouthfuls for us."

"Get nine pounds of them," said Mr. Oakley, "if they be wanted; I know Ben has an appetite."

"Indeed," said Ben, "but I have fell off lately, and don't take to my wittals as I used; you can order, missus, if you please, a gallon of half-and-half† as you go along. One must have a drain of drink of some sort; and mind you don't be going to any expense on my account, and getting anything but the little snack I have mentioned, for ten to one I shall take supper when I get to the Tower; only human nature is weak, you know, missus, and requires something to be a continually a holding of it up."

"Certainly," said Mr. Oakley, "certainly, have what you like, Ben; just say the word before Mrs. Oakley goes out; is there anything else?"

"No, no," said Ben, "oh dear no, nothing to speak of; but if you should pass a shop where they sells fat bacon, about four or five pounds, cut into rashers, you'll find, missus, will help down the blessed sausages."

"Gracious Providence," said Mrs. Oakley, "who is to cook it?"

"Who is to cook it, ma'am? why the kitchen fire, I suppose; but mind ye if the man ain't got any sausages, there's a shop where they sells biled beef at the corner, and I shall be quite satisfied if you brings in about ten or twelve pounds of that. You can make it up into about half a dozen sandwiches."

"Go, my dear, go at once," said Mr. Oakley, "and get Ben his supper. I am quite sure he wants it, and be as quick as you can."

"Ah," said Ben, when Mrs. Oakley was gone, "I didn't tell you how I was sarved last week at Mrs. Harveys. You know they are so precious genteel there that they don't speak above their blessed breaths for fear of wearing themselves out; and they sits down in a chair as if it were balanced only on one leg, and a little more one way or t'other would upset them. Then, if they sees a crumb a laying on the floor they rings the bell, and a poor half-starved devil of a servant comes and says, 'Did you ring, ma'am?' and then they says 'Yes, bring a dust-shovel and a broom, there is a crumb a laying there,' and then says I —'Damn

---

* A particular type of sausage made with pork and beef, seasoned with sage, lemon and nutmeg.

† A mixture of mild and bitter ale.

you all,' says I, 'bring a scavenger's cart, and half-dozen birch brooms, there's a cinder just fell out of the fire.' Then in course they gets shocked, and looks as blue as possible, and arter that, when they see as I ain't agoing, one of them says 'Mr. Benjamin Blumergutts, would you like to take a glass of wine?' 'I should think so,' says I. Then he says, says he, 'which would you prefer, red or white?' says he. 'White,' says I, 'while you are screwing up your courage to pull out the red,' so out they pull it; and as soon as I got hold of the bottle, I knocked the neck of it off over the top bar of the fire-place, and then drank it all up. 'Now, damn ye,' says I, 'you thinks all this is mighty genteel and fine, but I don't, and consider you to be the blessedest set of humbugs ever I set my eyes on; and, if ever you catch me here again, I'll be genteel too, and I can't say more than that. Go to the devil, all of ye.' So out I went, only I met with a little accident in the hall, for they had got a sort of lamp hanging there, and somehow or 'nother, my head went bang into it, and I carried it out round my neck; but when I did get out, I took it off, and shied it slap in at the parlour window. You never heard such a smash in all your life. I dare say they all fainted away for about a week, the blessed humbugs."

"Well, I should not wonder," said Mr. Oakley, "I never go near them, because I don't like their foolish pomposity and pride, which, upon very slender resources, tries to ape what it don't at all understand; but here is Mrs. Oakley with the sausages, and I hope you will make yourself comfortable, Ben."

"Comfortable! I believe ye, I rather shall. I means it, and no mistake."

"I have brought three pounds," said Mrs. Oakley, "and told the man to call in a quarter of an hour, in case there is any more wanted."

"The devil you have; and the bacon, Mrs. Oakley, the bacon!"

"I could not get any—the man had nothing but hams."

"Lor', ma'am, I'd put up with a ham cut thick, and never have said a word about it. I am a angel of a temper, and if you did but know it. Hilloa, look, is that the fellow with the half-and half?"

"Yes, here it is—a pot."

"A what?"

"A pot, to be sure."

"Well, I never; you are getting genteel, Mrs. Oakley. Then give us a hold of it."

Ben took the pot, and emptied it at a draught, and then he gave a tap at the bottom of it with his knuckles, to signify that he had accomplished that feat, and then he said, "I tells you what, ma'am, if you takes me for a baby, it's a great mistake, and any one would think you did, to see you offering me a pot merely; it's an insult, ma'am."

"Fiddle-de-dee," said Mrs. Oakley; "it's a much greater insult to drink it all up, and give nobody a drop."

"Is it? I wants to know how you are to stop it, ma'am, when you gets it to your mouth? that's what I axes you — how are you to stop it, ma'am? You didn't want me to spew it back again, did you, eh, ma'am?"

"You vile, low wretch!"

"Come, come, my dear," said Mr. Oakley, "you know our cousin. Ben don't live among the most refined society, and so you ought to be able to look over a little of — of — his — I may say, I am sure, without offence, roughness now and then; — come, come, there is no harm done, I'm sure. Forget and forgive say I. That's my maxim, and has always been, and will always be."

"Well," said the beef-eater, "it's a good one to get through the world with, and so there's an end of it. I forgives you, Mother Oakley."

"You forgive —"

"Yes, to be sure. Though I am only a beaf-eater, I suppose as I may forgive people for all that — eh, Cousin Oakley?"

"Oh, of course, Ben, of course. Come, come, wife, you know as well as I that Ben has many good qualities, and that take him for all in all, as the man in the play says, we shan't in a hurry look upon his like again."

"And I'm sure I don't want to look upon his like again," said Mrs. Oakley; "I'd rather by a good deal keep him a week than a fortnight. He's enough to breed a famine in the land, that he is."

"Oh, bless you, no," said Ben, "that's amongst your little mistakes, ma'am, I can assure you. By the bye, what a blessed long time that fellow is coming with the rest of the beer and the other sausages — why, what's the matter with you, cousin Oakley — eh, old chap, you look out of sorts?"

"I don't feel just the thing, do you know, Ben."

"Not — the thing — why — why, now you come to mention it, I somehow feel as if all my blessed inside was on a turn and a twist. The devil — I — don't feel comfortable at all I don't."

"And I'm getting very ill," gasped Mr. Oakley.

"And I'm getting iller," said the beef-eater, manufacturing a word for the occasion. "Bless my soul! there's something gone wrong in my inside. I know there's murder — there's a go — oh, Lord! it's a doubling me up, it is."

"I feel as if my last hour had come," said Mr. Oakley — "I'm a — a — dying man — I am — oh, good gracious! there was a twinge!"

Mrs. Oakley, with all the coolness in the world, took down her bonnet from behind the parlour-door where it hung, and, as she put it on said, —

"I told you both that some judgment would come over you, and now you see it has. How do you like it? Providence is good, of course, to its own, and I have —"

"What — what — ?"

"*Pisoned* the half-and-half."

Big Ben, the beef-eater, fell off his chair with a deep groan, and poor Mr. Oakley sat glaring at his wife, and shivering with apprehension, quite unable to speak, while she placed a shawl over her shoulders, as she added in the same tone of calmness she had made the terrific announcement concerning the poisoning —

"Now, you wretches, you see what a woman can do when she makes up her mind for vengeance. As long as you all live, you'll recollect me; but, if you don't, that won't much matter, for you won't live long, I can tell you, and now I'm going to my sister's, Mrs. Tiddiblow."

So saying, Mrs. Oakley turned quickly round, and, with an insulting toss of her head, and not at all caring for the pangs and sufferings of her poor victims, she left the place, and proceeded to her sister's house, where she slept as comfortably as if she had not by any means committed two diabolical murders.

But has she done so, or shall we, for the honour of human nature, discover that she went to a neighbouring chemist's, and only purchased some dreadfully powerful medicinal compound*, which she placed in the half-and-half, and which began to give those pangs to Big Ben, the beef-eater, and to Mr. Oakley, concerning which they were both so eloquent? This must have been the case; for Mrs. Oakley could not have been such a fiend in a human guise as to laugh as she passed the chemist's shop. Oh no! she might not have felt remorse, but that is a very different thing, indeed, from laughing at the matter, unless it were really laughable and not serious, at all. Big Ben and Mr. Oakley must have at length found out how they had been hoaxed, and the most probable thing was that the before-mentioned chemist himself told them; for they sent for him in order to know if anything could be done to save their lives.

Ben from that day forthwith made a determination that he would not visit Mr. Oakley, and the next time they met he said —

"I tell you what it is, that old hag, your wife, is one too many for us, that's a fact; she gets the better of me altogether — so, whenever you feels a little inclined for a gossip about old times, just you come down to the Tower."

"I will, Ben."

"Do; we can always find something to drink, and you can amuse yourself, too, by looking at the animals. Remember, feeding time is two o'clock; so, now and then, I shall expect to see you, and, above all, be sure you let me know if that canting parson, Lupin, comes any more to your house."

"I will, Ben."

"Ah, do; and I'll give him another lesson if he should, and I tell you how I'll do it. I'll get a free admission to the wild beastesses in the Tower, and when he comes to see 'em, for them 'ere sort of fellows always goes everywhere they can go for nothing, I'll just manage to pop him into a cage along of some of the most cantankerous creatures as we have."

"But would not that be dangerous?"

Almost certainly an emetic or purgative of some type — ipecac or similar.

"Oh dear no! we has a laughing hyaena as would frighten him out of his wits; but I don't think as he'd bite him much, do you know. He's as playful as a kitten, and very fond of standing on his head."

"Well, then, Ben, I have, of course, no objection, although I do think that the lesson you have already given to the reverend gentleman will and ought to be fully sufficient for all purposes, and I don't expect we shall see him again."

"But how does Mrs. O. behave to you?" asked Ben.

"Well, Ben, I don't think there's much difference; sometimes she's a little civil, and sometimes she ain't; it's just as she takes it into her head."

"Ah! that all comes of marrying."

"I have often wondered, though, Ben, that you never married."

Ben gave a chuckle as he replied —

"Have you though, really? Well, Cousin Oakley, I don't mind telling you, but the real fact is, once I was very near being served out in that sort of way."

"Indeed!"

"Yes. I'll tell you how it was; there was a girl called Angelina Day, and a nice-looking enough creature she was as you'd wish to see, and didn't seem as if she'd got any claws at all; leastways she kept them in, like a cat at meal times."

"Upon my word, Ben, you have a great knowledge of the world."

"I believe you, I have! Haven't I been brought up among the wild beasts in the Tower all my life? That's the place to get a knowledge of the world in, my boy. I ought to know a thing or two, and in course I does."

"Well, but how was it, Ben, that you did not marry this Angelina you speak of?"

"I'll tell you; she thought she had me as safe as a hare in a trap, and she was as amiable as a lump of cotton. You'd have thought, to look at her, that she did nothing but smile; and, to hear her, that she said nothing but nice, mild, pleasant things, and I really began to think as I had found out the proper sort of animal."

"But you were mistaken?"

"I believe you, I was. One day I'd been there to see her, I mean, at her father's house, and she'd been as amiable as she could be; I got up to go away, with a determination that the next time I got there I would ask her to say yes, and when I had got a little way out of the garden of the house where they lived — it was out of town some distance — I found I had left my little walking-cane behind me, so I goes back to get it, and when I got into the garden I heard a voice."

"Whose voice?"

"Why Angelina's, to be sure; she was speaking to a poor little dab of a servant they had; and oh, my eye! how she did rap out, to be sure! Such a speech as I never heard in all my life. She went on a matter of ten minutes without stopping, and every other word was some ill name or another; and her voice — oh, gracious! it was like a bundle of wire all of a tangle — it was."

"And what did you do, then, upon making such a discovery as that in so very odd and unexpected a manner?"

"Do! What do you suppose I did?"

"I really cannot say, as you are rather an eccentric fellow."

"Well then, I'll tell you. I went up to the house, and just popped in my head, and says I, 'Angelina, I find out that all cats have claws after all; good evening, and no more from your humble servant, who don't mind the job of taming any wild animal but a woman;' and then off I walked, and I never heard of her afterwards."

"Ah, Ben, it's true enough! You never know them beforehand; but after a little time, as you say, then out come the claws."

"They does — they does."

"And I suppose you since, then, made up your mind to be a bachelor for the rest of your life, Ben?"

"Of course I did. After such experience as that, I should have deserved all I got, and no mistake, I can tell you; and if ever you catches me paying any attention to a female woman, just put me in mind of Angelina Day, and you'll see how I shall be off at once like a shot."

"Ah!" said Mr. Oakley, with a sigh, "everybody, Ben, ain't born with your good luck, I can tell you. You are a most fortunate man, Ben, and that's a fact. You must have been born under some lucky planet I think, Ben, or else you never would have had such a warning as you have had about the claws. I found 'em out, Ben, but it was a deal too late; so I had only to put up with my fate, and put the best face I could upon the matter."

"Yes, that's what learned folks call — what's its name — fill — fill — something."

"Philosophy, I suppose you mean, Ben."

"Ah, that's it — you must put up with what you can't help, it means, I take it. It's a fine name for saying you must grin and bear it."

"I suppose that is about the truth, Ben."

IT CANNOT, HOWEVER, BE EXACTLY SAID that the little incident connected with Mr. Lupin had no good effect upon Mrs. Oakley, for it certainly shook most alarmingly her confidence in that pious individual. In the first place, it was quite clear that he shrank from the horrors of martyrdom; and, indeed, to escape any bodily inconvenience, was perfectly willing to put up with any amount of degradation or humiliation that he could be subjected to; and that was, to the apprehension of Mrs. Oakley, a great departure from what a saint ought to be. Then again, her faith in the fact that Mr. Lupin was such a chosen morsel as he had represented himself, was shaken from the circumstance that no miracle in the shape of a judgment had taken place to save him from the malevolence of Big Ben, the beef-eater; so that, taking one thing in connexion with another, Mrs. Oakley was not near so religious a character after that evening as she had been before it, and that was something gained. Then circumstances soon occurred, of which the reader will very shortly be fully aware, which were calculated to awaken all the feelings of Mrs. Oakley, if she had really any feelings to awaken, and to force her to make common cause with her husband in an affair that touched him to the very soul, and did succeed in awakening some feelings in her heart that had lain dormant for a long time, but which were still far from being completely destroyed. These circumstances were closely connected with the fate of one in whom we hope, that by this time, the reader has taken a deep and kindly interest — we mean Johanna — that young and beautiful, and gentle, creature, who seemed to have been created with all the capacity to be so very happy, and yet whose fate had become so clouded by misfortune, and who appears now to be doomed through her best affections to suffer so great an amount of sorrow, and to go through so many sad difficulties. Alas, poor Johanna Oakley! Better had you loved some one of less aspiring feelings, and of less ardent imagination, than he possessed to whom you have given your heart's young affections. It is true that Mark Ingestrie possessed genius, and perhaps it was the glorious light that hovers around that fatal gift which prompted you to love him. But genius is not only a blight and a desolation to its possessor, but it is so to all who are bound to the gifted being by the ties of fond affection. It brings with it that unhappy restlessness of intellect which is ever straining after the unattainable, and which is never content to know the end and ultimatum of earthly hopes and wishes; no, the whole life of such persons is spent in one long struggle for a fancied happiness, which like the *ignis-fatuus* of the swamp* glitters but to betray those who trust to its delusive and flickering beams.

CHAPTER XIII.

JOHANNA'S INTERVIEW WITH ARABELLA WILMOT, AND THE ADVICE.

ALAS! POOR JOHANNA, THOU HAST chosen but an indifferent confidante in the person of that young and inexperienced girl to whom it seems good to thee to impart thy griefs. Not for one moment do we mean to say, that the young creature to whom the spectacle-maker's daughter made up her mind to unbosom

---

* Will-o'-the-wisp, or ghost light of the swamp, in English folklore.

THE SCHOOLFELLOWS, JOHANNA AND ARABELLA.

herself, was not all that any one could wish as regards honour, goodness, and friendship. But she was one of those creatures who yet look upon the world as a fresh green garden, and have not yet lost that romance of existence which the world and its ways soon banish from the breasts of all.

She was young, even almost to girlhood, and, having been the idol of her family circle, she knew just about as little of the great world as a child. But while we cannot but to some extent regret that Johanna should have chosen such a confidant and admirer, we with feelings of great freshness and pleasure proceed to accompany her to that young girl's house.

Now, a visit from Johanna Oakley to the Wilmots was not so rare a thing, that it should excite any unusual surprise, but in this case it did excite unusual pleasure, because they had not been there for some time. And the reason that she had not, may well be found in the peculiar circumstances that had for a considerable period environed her. She had a secret to keep which, although it might not proclaim what it was most legibly upon her countenance, yet proclaimed that it had an existence, and as she had not made Arabella a confidant, she dreaded the other's friendly questions of the young creature. It may seem surprising that Johanna Oakley had kept from one whom she so much esteemed, and with whom she had made such a friendship, the secret of her affections; but that must be accounted for by a difference of ages between them to a sufficient extent in that early period of life to show itself palpably. That difference was not quite two years, but when we likewise state, that Arabella was of that small, delicate style of beauty, which makes her look like a child, when even upon the very verge of womanhood, we shall not be surprised that the girl of seventeen hesitated to confide a secret of the heart to what seemed but a beautiful child.

The last year, however, had made a great difference in the appearance of Arabella, for, although she still looked a year or so younger than she really was, a more staid and thoughtful expression had come over her face, and she no longer presented, at times when she laughed, that child-like expression, which had been as remarkable in her as it was delightful. She was as different looking from Johanna as she could be, for whereas Johanna's hair was of a rich and glossy brown, so nearly allied to black that it was commonly called such; the long waving ringlets that shaded the sweet countenance of Arabella Wilmot were like amber silk blended to a pale beauty. Her eyes were nearly blue, and not that pale grey, which courtesy calls of that celestial colour, and their long, fringing lashes hung upon a cheek of the most delicate and exquisite hue that nature could produce.

Such was the young, loveable, and amiable creature who had made one of those girlish friendships with Johanna Oakley that, when they do endure beyond the period of almost mere childhood, endure for ever, and become one among the most dear and cherished sensations of the heart. The acquaintance had commenced at school, and might have been of that evanescent character of so many school friendships, which, in after life, are scarcely so much remembered as the most dim visions of a dream; but it happened that they were congenial spirits, which, let them be thrown together under any circumstances whatever, would have come together with a perfect and a most endearing confidence in each other's affections. That they were school companions was the mere accident that brought them together, and not the cause of their friendship.

Such, then, was the being to whom Johanna Oakley looked for counsel and assistance; and notwithstanding all that we have said respecting the likelihood of that counsel being of an inactive and girlish character, we cannot withhold our meed of approbation to Johanna, that she had selected one so much in every way worthy of her honest esteem.

The hour at which she called was such as to ensure Arabella being within, and the pleasure which showed itself upon the countenance of the young girl, as she welcomed her old playmate, was a feeling of the most delightful and unaffecting character.

"Why, Johanna," she said, "you so seldom call upon me now, that I suppose I must esteem it as a very special act of grace and favour to see you."

"Arabella," said Johanna, "I do not know what you will say to me when I tell you that my present visit is because I am in a difficulty, and want your advice."

"Then you could not have come to a better person, for I have read all the novels in London, and know all the difficulties that anybody can possibly get into, and, what is more important, too, I know all the means of getting out of them, let them be what they may."

"And yet, Arabella, scarcely in all your novel reading will you find anything so strange and so eventful as the circumstances, I grieve to say, it is in my power to record to you. Sit down, and listen to me, dear Arabella, and you shall know all."

"You surprise and alarm me by that serious countenance, Johanna."

"The subject is a serious one. I love."

"Oh! is that all? So do I; there's a young Captain Desbrook in the King's Guards. He comes here to buy his gloves; and if you did but hear him sigh as he leans over the counter, you would be astonished."

"Ah! but, Arabella, I know you well. Yours is one of those fleeting passions that, like the forked lightning, appear for a moment, and ere you can say behold, is gone again. Mine is deeper in my heart, so deep, that to divorce it from it would be to destroy its home for ever."

"But, why so serious, Johanna? You do not mean to tell me that it is possible for you to love any man without his loving you in return?"

"You are right there, Arabella. I do not come to speak to you of a hopeless passion — far from it; but you shall hear. Lend me, my dear friend, your serious attention, and you shall hear of such mysterious matters."

"Mysterious! — then I shall be in my very element. For know that I quite live and exult in mystery, and you could not possibly have come to any one who would more welcomely receive such a commission from you; I am all impatience."

Johanna then, with great earnestness, related to her friend the whole of the particulars connected with her deep and sincere attachment to Mark Ingestrie. She told her how, in spite of all circumstances which appeared to have a tendency to cast a shadow and blight upon their young affection, they had loved, and loved truly; how Ingestrie, disliking, both from principle and distaste, the study of the law, had quarrelled with his uncle, Mr. Grant, and then how, as a bold adventurer, he had gone to seek his fortunes in the Indian seas; fortunes which promised to be splendid, but which might end in disappointment and defeat, and that they had ended in such calamities most deeply and truly did she mourn to be compelled to state. And she concluded by saying —

"And now, Arabella, you know all I have to tell you. You know how truly I have loved, and how, after teaching myself to expect happiness, I have met with nothing but despair; and you may judge for yourself, how sadly the fate, or rather the mystery, which hangs over Mark Ingestrie, must deeply affect me, and how lost my mind must be in all kinds of conjecture concerning him."

The hilarity of spirits which had characterised Arabella in the earlier part of their interview, entirely left her as Johanna proceeded in her mournful narration, and by the time she had concluded, tears of the most genuine sympathy stood in her eyes. She took the hands of Johanna in both her own, and said to her —

"Why, my poor Johanna, I never expected to hear from your lips so sad a tale. This is most mournful, indeed very mournful; and, although I was half inclined before to quarrel with you for this tardy confidence — for you must recollect that it is the first I have heard of this whole affair — but now the misfortunes that oppress you are quite sufficient, Heaven knows, without me adding to them by the shadow of a reproach."

"They are indeed, Arabella, and believe me, if the course of my love ran smoothly, instead of being, as it has been, full of misadventures, you should have had nothing to complain of on the score of want of confidence; but I will own I did hesitate to inflict on you my miseries, for miseries they have been, and, alas! miseries they seem destined to remain."

"Johanna, you could not have used an argument more delusive than that. It is not one which should have come from your lips to me."

"But surely it was a good motive to spare you pain?"

"And did you think so lightly of my friendship that it was to be entrusted with nothing but what wore a pleasant aspect? True friendship surely is best shown in the encounter of difficulty and distress. I grieve, Johanna, indeed, that you have so much mistaken me."

"Nay, now you do me an injustice: it was not that I doubted your friendship for one moment, but that I did indeed shrink from casting the shadow of my sorrows over what should be, and what I hope is, the sunshine of your heart. That was the respect which deterred me from making you a confidant of, what I suppose I must call, this ill-fated passion."

"No, not ill-fated, Johanna. Let us still believe that the time will come when it will be far otherwise than ill-fated."

"But what do you think of all that I have told you? Can you gather from it any hope?"

"Abundance of hope, Johanna. You have no certainty of the death of Ingestrie."

"I certainly have not, as far as regards the loss of him in the Indian seas; but, Arabella, there is one supposition which, from the first moment that it found a home in my breast, has been growing stronger and stronger, and that supposition is, that this Mr. Thornhill was no other than Mark Ingestrie himself."

"Indeed! Think you so? That would be a strange supposition. Have you any special reasons for such a thought?"

"None — further than a something which seemed ever to tell my heart from the first moment that such was the case, and a consideration of the improbability of the story related by Thornhill. Why should Mark Ingestrie have given him the string of pearls and the message to me, trusting to the preservation of this Thornhill, and assuming, for some strange reason, that he himself must fall?"

"There is good argument in that, Johanna."

"And, moreover, Mark Ingestrie told me he intended altering his name upon the expedition."

"It is strange; but now you mention such a supposition, it appears, do you know, Johanna, each moment more probable to me. Oh, that fatal string of pearls!"

"Fatal, indeed! for if Mark Ingestrie and Thornhill be one and the same person, the possession of those pearls has been the temptation to destroy him."

"There cannot be a doubt upon that point, Johanna, and so you will find in all tales of love and of romance, that jealousy and wealth have been the sources of all the abundant evils which fond and attached hearts have from time to time suffered."

"It is so; I believe, it is so, Arabella; but advise me what to do, for truly I am myself incapable of action. Tell me what you think it is possible to do, under those disastrous circumstances, for there is nothing which I will not dare attempt."

"Why, my dear Johanna, you must perceive that all the evidence you have regarding this Thornhill, follows him up to that barber's shop in Fleet-street, and no farther."

"It does, indeed."

"Can you not imagine, then, that there lies the mystery of his fate; and, from what you have yourself seen of this man, Todd, do you think he is one who would hesitate even at murder?"

"Oh, horror! my own thoughts have taken that dreadful turn, but I dreaded to pronounce the word which would embody them. If, indeed, that fearful-looking man fancied that, by any deed of blood, he could become possessed of such a treasure as that which belonged to Mark Ingestrie, unchristian and illiberal as it may sound, the belief clings to me that he would not hesitate to do it."

"Do not, however, conclude, Johanna, that such is the case. It would appear from all you have heard and seen of these circumstances, that there is some fearful mystery; but do not, Johanna, conclude hastily that that mystery is one of death."

"Be it so, or not," said Johanna, "I must solve it, or go distracted. Heaven have mercy upon me! — for even now I feel a fever in my brain that precludes almost the possibility of rational thought."

"Be calm, be calm — we will think the matter over calmly and seriously; and who knows but that, mere girls as we are, we may think of some adventitious mode of arriving at a knowledge of the truth; and now I am going to tell you something, which your narrative has recalled to my mind."

"Say on, Arabella, I shall listen to you with deep attention."

"A short time since, about six months, I think, an apprentice of my father, in the last week of his servitude, was sent to the west-end of the town, to take a considerable sum of money; but he never came back with it, and from that day to this we have heard nothing of him, although, from inquiry that my father made, he ascertained that he received the money, and that he met an acquaintance in the Strand, who parted from him at the corner of Milford-lane, and to whom he said that he intended to call at Sweeney Todd's, the barber, in Fleet-street, to have his hair dressed, because there was to be a regatta on the Thames, and he was determined to go to it whether my father liked or not."

"And he was never heard of?"

"Never. Of course, my father made every inquiry upon the subject, and called upon Sweeney Todd for the purpose; but, as he declared that no such person had ever called at his shop, the inquiry there terminated."

" 'Tis very strange."

"And most mysterious; for the friends of the youth were indeed indefatigable in their searches for him; and, by subscribing together for the purpose, they offered a large reward to any one who could or would give them information regarding his fate."

"And was it all in vain?"

"All; nothing could be learned whatever. Not even the remotest clue was obtained, and there the affair has rested, in the most profound of mysteries."

Johanna shuddered, and for some few moments the two young girls were silent. It was Johanna who broke that silence, by exclaiming —

"Arabella, assist me with what advice you can, so that I may set about what I purpose with the best prospect of success and the least danger; not that I shrink on my own account from risk, but if any misadventure were to occur to me, I might thereby be incapacitated from pursuing that object, to which I will now devote the remainder of my life."

"But what can you do, my dear Johanna? It was but a short time since there was a placard in the barber's window to say that he wanted a lad as an assistant in his business, but that has been removed, or we might have procured some one to take the situation for the express purpose of playing the spy upon the barber's proceedings."

"But, perchance, still there may be an opportunity of accomplishing something in that way, if you knew of any one that would undertake the adventure."

"There will be no difficulty, Johanna, in discovering one willing to do so, although we might be long in finding one of sufficient capacity that we could trust; but I am adventurous, Johanna, as you know, and I think I could have got my cousin Albert to personate the character, only that I think he's rather a giddy youth, and scarcely to be trusted with a mission of so much importance."

"Yes, and a mission likewise, Arabella, which, by a single false step, might be made frightfully dangerous."

"It might indeed."

"Then it will be unfair to place it upon any one but those who feel most deeply for its success."

"Johanna, the enthusiasm with which you speak awakens in me a thought which I shrink from expressing to you, and which, I fear, perhaps more originates from a certain feeling of romance, which, I believe, is a besetting sin, than from any other cause."

"Name it, Arabella; name it."

"It would be possible for you or I to accomplish the object, by going disguised to the barber's, and accepting such a situation, if it were vacant, for a period of about twenty-four hours, in order that during that time an opportunity might be taken of searching in his house for some evidence upon the subject nearest to your heart."

"It is a happy thought," said Johanna, "and why should I hesitate at encountering any risk, or toil, or difficulty, for him who has risked so much for me? What is there to hinder me from carrying out such a resolution? At any moment, if great danger should beset me, I can rush into the street, and claim protection from the passers-by."

"And moreover, Johanna, if you went on such a mission, remember you go with my knowledge, and that consequently I would bring you assistance, if you appeared not in the specified time for your return."

"Each moment, Arabella, the plan assumes to my mind a better shape. If Sweeney Todd be innocent of contriving anything against the life and liberty of those who seek his shop, I have nothing to fear; but if, on the contrary, he be guilty, danger to me would be the proof of such guilt, and that is a proof which I am willing to chance encountering for the sake of the great object I have in view; but how am I to provide myself with the necessary means?"

"Be at rest upon that score. My cousin Albert and you are as nearly of a size as possible. He will be staying here shortly, and I will secure from his wardrobe a suit of clothes, which I am certain will answer your purpose. But let me implore you to wait until you have had your second interview with Colonel Jeffery."

"That is well thought of; I will meet him, and question him closely as to the personal appearance of this Mr. Thornhill; beside, I shall hear if he has any confirmed suspicion on the subject."

"That is well, you will soon meet him, for the week is running on; and let me implore you, Johanna, to come to me the morning after you have so met him, and then we will again consult upon this plan of operations, which appears to us feasible and desirable."

Some more conversation of a similar character ensued between these young girls; and upon the whole, Johanna Oakley felt much comforted by her visit, and more able to think calmly as well as seriously upon the subject which engrossed her whole thoughts and feelings; and when she returned to her own home, she found that much of the excitement of despair which had formerly had possession of her, had given way to hope; and with that natural feeling of joyousness, and that elasticity of mind which belongs to the young, she began to build in her imagination some airy fabrics of future happiness. Certainly, these suppositions went upon the fact that Mark Ingestrie was a prisoner, and not that his life had been taken by the mysterious barber; for although the possibility of his having been murdered had found a home in her imagination, still to her pure spirit it seemed by far too hideous to be true, and she scarcely could be said really and truly to entertain it as a matter which was likely to be true.

CHAPTER XIV.

TOBIAS'S THREAT, AND ITS CONSEQUENCES.

PERHAPS ONE OF THE MOST PITIABLE objects now in our history is poor Tobias, Sweeney Todd's boy, who certainly had his suspicions aroused in the most terrific manner, but who was terrified, by the threats of what the barber was capable of doing against his mother, from making any disclosures. The effect upon his personal appearance of this wear and tear of his intellect was

striking and manifest. The hue of youth and health entirely departed from his
cheeks, and he looked so sad and careworn, that it was quite a terrible thing to
look upon a young lad so, as it were, upon the threshold of existence, and in
whom anxious thoughts were making such war upon the physical energies. His
cheeks were pale and sunken; his eyes had an unnatural brightness about them,
and, to look upon his lips, one would think they had never parted in a smile for
many a day, so sadly were they compressed together. He seemed ever to be
watching likewise for something fearful, and even as he walked the streets he
would frequently turn and look inquiringly around him with a shudder; and in
his brief interview with Colonel Jeffery and his friend the captain, we can have
a tolerably good comprehension of the state of his mind. Oppressed with fears,
and all sorts of dreadful thoughts, panting to give utterance to what he knew
and to what he suspected, yet terrified into silence for his mother's sake, we
cannot but view him as signally entitled to the sympathy of the reader, and as,
in all respects, one sincerely to be pitied for the cruel circumstances in which
he was placed. The sun is shining brightly, and even that busy region of trade
and commerce, Fleet-street, is looking gay and beautiful; but not for that poor
spirit-stricken lad are any of the sights and sounds which used to make up the
delight of his existence, reaching his eyes or ears now with their accustomed
force. He sits moody and alone, and in the position which he always assumes
when Sweeney Todd is from home — that is to say, with his head resting on his
hands, and looking the picture of melancholy abstraction.

"What shall I do?" he said to himself, "what will become of me? I think if
I live here any longer, I shall go out of my senses. Sweeney Todd is a murderer — I
am quite certain of it, and I wish to say so, but I dare not for my mother's sake.
Alas! alas! the end of it will be, that he will kill me, or that I shall go out of my
senses, and then I shall die in some mad-house, and no one will care what I say."

The boy wept bitterly after he had uttered these melancholy reflections,
and he felt his tears something of a relief to him, so that he looked up after a
little time, and glanced around him.

"What a strange thing," he said, "that people should come into this shop,
to my certain knowledge, who never go out of it again, and yet what becomes
of them I cannot tell."

He looked with a shuddering anxiety towards the parlour, the door of
which Sweeney Todd took care to lock always when he left the place, and he
thought that he should like much to have a thorough examination of that room.

"I have been in it," he said, "and it seems full of cupboards and strange
holes and corners, such as I never saw before, and there is an odd stench in it
that I cannot make out at all; but it's out of the question thinking of ever being
in it above a few minutes at a time, for Sweeney Todd takes good care of that."

The boy rose, and opened a small cupboard that was in the shop. It was
perfectly empty.

TOBIAS ALARMED AT THE MYSTERIOUS APPEARANCE OF TODD.

"Now, that's strange," he said, "there was a walking-stick with an ivory top to it here just before he went out, and I could swear it belonged to a man who came in to be shaved. More than once — ah! and more than twice, too, when I have come in suddenly, I have seen people's hats, and Sweeney Todd would try and make me believe that people go away after being shaved, and leave their hats behind them."

He walked up to the shaving chair as it was called, which was a large, old-fashioned piece of furniture, made of oak, and carved; and, as the boy threw himself into it, he said —

"What an odd thing it is that this chair is screwed so tight to the floor!

Here is a complete fixture, and Sweeney Todd says it is so because it's in the best possible light, and if he were not to make it fast in such a way, the customers would shift it about from place to place, so that he could not conveniently shave them; it may be true, but I don't know."

"And you have your doubts," said the voice of Sweeney Todd, as that individual, with a noiseless step, walked into the shop — "you have your doubts, Tobias? I shall have to cut your throat, that is quite clear."

"No, no, have mercy upon me; I did not mean what I said."

"Then it's uncommonly imprudent to say it, Tobias. Do you remember our last conversation? Do you remember that I can hang your mother when I please, because, if you do not, I beg to put you in mind of that pleasant little circumstance?"

"I cannot forget — I do not forget."

" 'Tis well; and mark me, I will not have you assume such an aspect as you wear when I am not here. You don't look cheerful, Tobias; and, notwithstanding your excellent situation, with little to do, and the number of Lovett's pies you eat, you fall away."

"I cannot help it," said Tobias, "since you told me what you did concerning my mother. I have been so anxious that I cannot help —"

"Why should you be anxious? Her preservation depends upon yourself, and upon yourself wholly. You have but to keep silent, and she is safe; but if you utter one word that shall be displeasing to me about my affairs, mark me, Tobias, she comes to the scaffold; and if I cannot conveniently place you in the same mad-house where the last boy I had was placed, I shall certainly be under the troublesome necessity of cutting your throat."

"I will be silent — I will say nothing, Mr. Todd. I know I shall die soon, and then you will get rid of me altogether, and I don't care how soon that may be, for I am quite weary of my life — I shall be glad when it is over."

"Very good," said the barber; "that's all a matter of taste. And now, Tobias, I desire that you look cheerful and smile, for a gentleman is outside feeling his chin with his hand, and thinking he may as well come in and be shaved. I may want you, Tobias, to go to Billingsgate, and bring me a pennyworth of shrimps."

"Yes," thought Tobias, with a groan — "yes, while you murder him."

CHAPTER XV.

THE SECOND INTERVIEW BETWEEN JOHANNA AND THE COLONEL
IN THE TEMPLE-GARDENS.

NOW THAT THERE WAS A GREAT object to gain by a second interview with Colonel Jeffery, the anxiety of Johanna Oakley to have it became extremely great, and she counted the very hours until the period should arrive when she could again proceed to the Temple-gardens with something like a certainty of finding him.

The object, of course, was to ask him for a description of Mr. Thornhill, sufficiently accurate to enable her to come to something like a positive conclusion as to whether she ought to call him to her own mind as Mark Ingestrie or not. And Colonel Jeffery was not a bit the less anxious to see her than she was to look upon him; for although in divers lands he had looked upon many a fair face, and heard many a voice that had sounded soft and musical in his ears, he had seen none that, to his mind, was so fair, and had heard no voice that he had considered really so musical and charming to listen to, as Johanna Oakley's. A man of more honourable and strict sense of honour than Colonel Jeffery could not have been found, and, therefore it was that he allowed himself to admire the beautiful under any circumstances, because he knew that his admiration was of no dangerous quality, but that, on the contrary, it was one of those feelings which might exist in a bosom such as his, quite undebased by a meaner influence.

We think it necessary, however, before he has his second meeting with Johanna Oakley, to give such an explanation of his thoughts and feelings as it is in our power.

When first he met her, the purity of her mind, and the genuine and beautiful candour of all she said, struck him most forcibly, as well as her great beauty, which could not fail to be extremely manifest. After that he began to reason with himself as to what ought to be his feelings with regard to her — namely, what portion of these ought to be suppressed, and what ought to be encouraged. If Mark Ingestrie were dead, there was not a shadow of interference or dishonour in him, Colonel Jeffery, loving the beautiful girl, who was surely not to be shut out of the pale of all affection because the first person to whom her heart had warmed with a pure and holy passion, was no more.

"It may be," he thought, "that she is incapable of feeling a sentiment which can at all approach that which once she has felt; but still she may be happy and serene, and may pass many joyous hours as the wife of another."

He did not positively make these reflections as applicable to himself, although they had a tendency that way, and he was fast verging to a state of mind which might induce him to give them a more actual application. He did not tell himself that he loved her — no, the word "admiration" took the place of the more powerful term; but then, can we not doubt that, at this time, the germ of a very pure and holy affection was lighted up in the heart of Colonel Jeffery for the beautiful creature who suffered the pangs of so much disappointment, and who loved one so well who, we almost fear, if he were living, was scarcely the sort of person fully to requite such an affection. But we know so little of Mark Ingestrie, and there appears to be so much doubt as to whether he be alive or dead, that we should not prejudge him upon such very insufficient evidence.

Johanna Oakley did think of taking Arabella Wilmot with her to this meeting with Colonel Jeffery, but she abandoned the idea, because it really looked as if she was either afraid of him or afraid of herself, so she resolved to go alone; and when the hour of appointment came, she was then walking upon that broad gravelled path, which has been trodden by some of the best and some of the most eminent, as well as some of the worst of human beings.

It was not likely that with the feelings of Colonel Jeffery towards her, he would keep her waiting. Indeed, he was then a good hour before the time, and his only great dread was, that she might not come. He had some reason for this dread, because it will be readily recollected by the reader, that she had not positively promised to come; so that all he had was a hope that way tending and nothing further. As minute after minute had passed away, she came not, although the time had not yet really arrived; his apprehension that she would not give him the meeting had grown in his mind almost to a certainty, when he saw her timidly advancing along the garden walk. He rose to meet her at once, and for a few moments after he had greeted her with kind civility she could do nothing but look inquiringly in his face, to know if he had any news to tell her of the object of her anxious solicitude.

"I have heard nothing, Miss Oakley," he said, "that can give you any satisfaction concerning the fate of Mr. Thornhill, but we have much suspicion — I say we, because I have taken a friend into my confidence — that something serious must have happened to him, and that the barber, Sweeney Todd, in Fleet-street, at whose door the dog so mysteriously took his post, knows something of that circumstance, be it what it may."

He led her to a seat as she spoke, and when she had recovered sufficiently the agitation of her feelings to speak, she said in a timid, hesitating voice —

"Had Mr. Thornhill fair hair, and large, clear, grey eyes?"

"Yes, he had such; and, I think, his smile was the most singularly beautiful I ever beheld in a man."

"Heaven help me!" said Johanna.

"Have you any reason for asking that question concerning Thornhill?"

"God grant I had not; but, alas! I have indeed. I feel that in Thornhill, I must recognise Mark Ingestrie himself."

"You astonish me."

"It must be so, it must be so; you have described him to me, and I cannot doubt it; Mark Ingestrie and Thornhill are one! I knew that he was going to change his name, when he went out upon that wild adventure to the Indian Sea. I was well aware of that fact."

"I cannot think, Miss Oakley, that you are correct in that supposition. There are many things which induce me to think otherwise; and the first and foremost of them is, that the ingenuous character of Mr. Thornhill forbids the likelihood of such a thing occurring. You may depend it is not — cannot be, as you suppose."

"The proofs are too strong for me, and I find I dare not doubt them. It is so, Colonel Jeffery, as time, perchance, may show; it is sad, very sad, to think that it is so, but I dare not doubt it, now that you have described him to me exactly as he lived."

"I must own, that in giving an opinion on such a point to you, I may be accused of arrogance and presumption, for I have had no description of Mark Ingestrie, and never saw him; and although you never saw certainly Mr. Thornhill, yet I have described him to you, and therefore you are able to judge from that description something of him."

"I am indeed, and I cannot — dare not doubt. It is horrible to be positive on this point to me, because I do fear with you that something dreadful has occurred, and that the barber in Fleet-street could unravel a frightful secret, if he chose, connected with Mark Ingestrie's fate."

"I do sincerely hope from my heart that you are wrong; I hope it, because I tell you frankly, dim and obscure as the hope that Mark Ingestrie may have been picked up from the wreck of his vessel, it is yet stronger than the supposition that Thornhill has escaped the murderous hands of Sweeney Todd, the barber."

Johanna looked in his face so imploringly, and with such an expression of hopelessness, that it was most sad indeed to see her, and quite involuntarily he exclaimed —

"If the sacrifice of my life would be to you a relief, and save you from the pangs you suffer, believe me, it should be made."

She started as she said —

"No, no: Heaven knows enough has been sacrificed already — more than enough, much more than enough. But do not suppose that I am ungrateful for the generous interest you have taken in me. Do not suppose that I think any the less of the generosity and nobility of soul that would offer a sacrifice, because it is one that I would hesitate to accept. No, believe me, Colonel Jeffery, that among the few names that are enrolled in my breast — and such to me will ever be honoured — remember yours will be found while I live, but that will not be long — but that will not be long."

"Nay, do not speak so despairingly."

"Have I not cause for despair?"

"Cause have you for great grief, but yet scarcely for despair. You are young yet, and let me entertain a hope that even if a feeling of regret may mingle with your future thoughts, time will achieve something in tempering your sorrow; and if not great happiness, you may know yet great serenity."

"I dare not hope it, but I know your words are kindly spoken, and most kindly meant."

"You may well assure yourself that they are so."

"I will ascertain his fate, or perish."

"You alarm me by those words, as well as by your manner of uttering them. Let me implore you, Miss Oakley, to attempt nothing rash; remember how weak and inefficient must be the exertions of a young girl like yourself, one who knows so little of the world, and can really understand so little of its wickedness."

"Affection conquers all obstacles, and the weakest and most inefficient girl that ever stepped, if she have strong within her that love which, in all its sacred intensity, knows no fear, shall indeed accomplish much. I feel that, in such a cause, I could shake off all girlish terrors and ordinary alarms; and if there be danger, I would ask, what is life to me without all that could adorn it and make it beautiful?"

"This, indeed, is the very enthusiasm of affection, when, believe me, it will lead you to some excess — to some romantic exercise of feeling, such as will bring great danger in its train, to the unhappiness of those who love you."

"Those who love me — who is there to love me now?"

"Johanna Oakley, I dare not and will not utter words that come thronging to my lips, but which I fear might be unwelcome to your ears; I will not say that I can answer the question that you have asked, because it would sound ungenerous at such a time as this, when you have met me to talk about the fate of another. Oh! forgive me, that, hurried away by the feeling of a moment, I have uttered these words, for I meant not to utter them."

Johanna looked at him in silence, and it might be that there was the slightest possible tinge of reproach in her look, but it was very slight, for one glance at that ingenuous countenance would be sufficient to convince the most sceptical of the truth and single-mindedness of its owner: of this there could be no doubt whatever, and if anything in the shape of a reproach was upon the point of coming from her lips, she forbore to utter it.

"May I hope," he added, "that I have not lowered myself in your esteem, Miss Oakley, by what I have said?"

"I hope," she said gently, "that you will continue to be my friend."

He laid an emphasis on the word "friend," and he fully understood what she meant to imply thereby, and after a moment's pause said —

"Heaven forbid that ever, by word or by action, Johanna, I should do aught to deprive myself of that privilege. Let me be yet your friend, since —"

He left the sentence unfinished, but if he had added the words — "Since I can do no more," he could not have made it more evident to Johanna that those were the words he intended to utter.

"And now," he added, "that I hope and trust we understand each other better than we did, and you are willing to call me by the name of friend, let me once more ask of you, by the privilege of such a title, to be careful of yourself, and not to risk much in order that you may, perhaps, have some remote chance of achieving very little."

"But can I endure this dreadful suspense?"

"It is, alas! too common an infliction on human nature, Johanna. Pardon me for addressing you as Johanna."

"Nay, it requires no excuse. I am accustomed so to be addressed by all who feel a kindly interest for me. Call me Johanna if you will, and I shall feel a greater assurance of your friendship and your esteem."

"I will then avail myself of that permission, and again and again I will entreat you to leave to me the task of making what attempts may be made to discover the fate of Mr. Thornhill. There must be danger even in inquiring for him, if he has met with any foul play, and therefore I ask you to let that danger be mine."

Johanna asked herself if she should or not tell him of the scheme of operations that had been suggested by Arabella Wilmot, but, somehow or another, she shrank most wonderfully from so doing, both on account of the censure which she concluded he would be likely to cast upon it, and the romantic, strange nature of the plan itself, so she said, gently and quickly —

"I will attempt nothing that shall not have some possibility of success attending it. I will be careful, you may depend, for many considerations. My father, I know, centres all his affections in me, and for his sake I will be careful."

"I shall be content then, and now may I hope that this day next week I may see you here again, in order that I may tell you if I have made any discovery, and that you may tell me the same; for my interest in Thornhill is that of a sincere friend, to say nothing of the deep interest in your happiness which I feel, and which now has become an element in the transaction of the highest value?"

"I will come," said Johanna, "if I can come."

"You do not doubt?"

"No, no. I will come, and I hope to bring you some news of him in whom you are so much interested. It shall be no fault of mine if I come not."

He walked with her from the gardens, and together they passed the shop of Sweeney Todd, but the door was close shut, and they saw nothing of the barber, or of that poor boy, his apprentice, who was so much to be pitied. He parted with Johanna near to her father's house, and he walked slowly away with his mind so fully impressed with the excellence and beauty of the spectacle-maker's daughter, that it was quite clear, as long as he lived, he would not be able to rid himself of the favourable impression she had made upon him.

"I love her," he said; "I love her, but she seems in no respect willing to enchain her affections. Alas! alas! how sad it is for me, that the being who above all others I could wish to call my own, instead of a joy to me, I have only encountered that she might impart a pang to my heart. Beautiful and excellent Johanna, I love you, but I can see that your own affections are withered for ever."

CHAPTER XVI.

THE BARBER MAKES ANOTHER ATTEMPT TO SELL THE STRING OF PEARLS.

IT WOULD SEEM AS IF SWEENEY TODD, after his adventure in already trying to dispose of the string of pearls which he possessed, began to feel little doubtful about his chances of success in that matter, for he waited patiently for a considerable period before he again made the attempt, and then he made it after a totally different fashion. Towards the close of night on that same evening when Johanna Oakley had met Colonel Jeffery, for the second time, in the Temple-garden, and while Tobias sat alone in the shop in his usual deep dejection, a stranger entered the place, with a large blue bag in his hand, and looked inquiringly about him.

"Hilloa, my lad!" said he, "is this Mr. Todd's?"

"Yes," said Tobias; "but he is not at home. What do you want?"

"Well, I'll be hanged," said the man, "if this don't beat everything; you don't mean to tell me he is a barber, do you?"

"Indeed I do; don't you see?"

"Yes, I see to be sure; but I'll be shot if I thought of it beforehand. What do you think he has been doing?"

"Doing," said Tobias, with animation; "do you think he will be hung?"

"Why, no, I don't say it is a hanging matter, although you seem as if you wished it was; but I'll just tell you now we are artists at the west-end of the town."

"Artists! Do you mean to say you draw pictures?"

"No, no, we make clothes; but we call ourselves artists now, because tailors are out of fashion."

"Oh, that's it, is it?"

"Yes, that's it; and you would scarcely believe it, but he came to our shop actually, and ordered a suit of clothes, which were to come to no less a sum than thirty pounds, and told us to make them up in such a style that they were to do for any nobleman, and he gave his name and address, as Mr. Todd, at this number in Fleet-street, but I hadn't the least idea that he was a barber; if I had, I am quite certain the clothes would not have been finished in the style they are, but quite the reverse."

"Well," said Tobias, "I can't think what he wants such clothing for, but I suppose it's all right. Was he a tall, ugly-looking fellow?"

"As ugly as the very devil. I'll just show you the things, as he is not at home. The coat is of the finest velvet, lined with silk, and trimmed with lace. Did you ever, in all your life, see such a coat for a barber?"

"Indeed, I never did; but it is some scheme of his, of course. It is a superb coat."

"Yes, and all the rest of the dress is of the same style; what on earth he can be going to do with it I can't think, for it's only fit to go to court in."

"Oh, well, I know nothing about it," said Tobias, with a sigh, "you can leave it or not as you like, it is all one to me."

"Well, you do seem the most melancholy wretch ever I came near; what's the matter with you?"

"The matter with me? Oh, nothing. Of course, I am as happy as I can be. Ain't I Sweeney Todd's apprentice, and ain't that enough to make anybody sing all day long?"

"It may be for all I know, but certainly you don't seem to be in a singing humour; but, however, we artists cannot waste our time, so just be so good as to take care of the clothes, and be sure you give them to your master; and so I wash my hands of the transaction."

"Very good, he shall have them; but do you mean to leave such valuable clothes without getting the money for them?"

"Not exactly, for they are paid for."

"Oh! that makes all the difference — he shall have them."

Scarcely had this tailor left the place, when a boy arrived with a parcel, and, looking around him with undisguised astonishment, said —

"Isn't there some other Mr. Todd, in Fleet-street?"

"Not that I know of," said Tobias. "What have you got there?"

"Silk stockings, gloves, lace, cravats, ruffles, and so on."

"The deuce you have; I dare say it's all right."

"I shall leave them — they are paid for. This is the name, and this is the number. — Now, stupid!"

This last exclamation arose from the fact that this boy, in going out, ran up against another who was coming in.

"Can't you see where you are going?" said the new arrival.

"What's that to you? I have a good mind to punch your head."

"Do it, and then come down our court, and see what a licking I'll give you."

"Will you? Why don't you? Only let me catch you, that's all."

They stood for some moments so closely together that their noses very nearly touched; and then, after mutual assertions of what they would do if they caught each other — although, in either case, to stretch out an arm would have been quite sufficient to have accomplished that object — they separated, and the last comer said to Tobias, in a tone of irritation, probably consequent upon the misunderstanding he had just had with the hosier's boy —

"You can tell Mr. Todd that the carriage will be ready at half-past seven precisely."

And then he went away, leaving Tobias in a state of great bewilderment as to what Sweeney Todd could possibly be about to do with such an amount of finery as that which was evidently coming home for him.

"I can't make it out," he said. "It's some villany, of course, but I can't make out what it is — I wish I knew; I might thwart him in it. He is a villain, and neither could nor would project anything good; but what can I do? I am quite helpless in this, and will just let it take its course. I can only wish for a power of action I shall never possess. Alas, alas! I am very sad, and know not what will become of me. I wish that I was in my grave, and there I am sure I shall be soon, unless something happens to turn the tide of all this wretched evil fortune that has come upon me."

It was in vain for Tobias to think of vexing himself with conjectures as to what Sweeney Todd was about to do with so much finery, for he had not the remotest foundation to go upon in the matter, and could not for the life of him imagine any possible contingency or chance which should make it necessary for the barber to deck himself in such gaudy apparel. All he could do was to lay down in his own mind a general principle as regarded Sweeney Todd's conduct, and that consisted in the fact, that whatever might be his plans, and whatever might be his objects, they were for no good purpose; but, on the contrary, were most certainly intended for the accomplishment of some great evil which that most villanous person intended to perpetrate.

"I will observe all I can," thought Tobias to himself, "and do what I can to put a stop to his mischiefs; but I fear it will be very little he will allow me to observe, and perhaps still less that he will allow me to do; but I can but try, and do my best."

Poor Tobias's best, as regarded achieving anything against Sweeney Todd, we may well suppose would be little indeed, for that individual was not the man to give anybody an opportunity of doing much; and, possessed as he was of the most consummate art, as well as the greatest possible amount of unscrupulousness, there can be very little doubt but that any attempt poor Tobias might make would recoil upon himself.

In about half an hour the barber returned, and his first question was —

"Have any things been left for me?"

"Yes, sir," said Tobias, "here are two parcels, and a boy has been to say that the carriage will be ready at half-past seven precisely."

" 'Tis well," said the barber, "that will do; and Tobias, you will be careful, whilst I am gone, of the shop. I shall be back in half an hour, mind you, and not later; and be sure that I find you here at your post. But you may say, if any one comes here on business, there will be neither shaving nor dressing to-night. You understand me?"

"Yes, sir, certainly."

Sweeney Todd then took the bundles which contained the costly apparel, and retired into the parlour with them; and, as it was then seven o'clock, Tobias correctly enough supposed that he had gone to dress himself, and he waited with a considerable amount of curiosity to see what sort of an appearance the barber would cut in his fine apparel.

Tobias had not to control his impatience long, for in less than twenty minutes, out came Sweeney Todd, attired in the very height of fashion for the period. His waistcoat was something positively gorgeous, and his fingers were loaded with such costly rings, that they quite dazzled the sight of Tobias to look upon; then, moreover, he wore a sword with a jewelled hilt, but it was one which Tobias really thought he had seen before, for he had a recollection that a gentleman had come to have his hair dressed, and had taken it off, and laid just such a sword across his hat during the operation.

"Remember," said Sweeney Todd, "remember your instructions; obey them to the letter, and no doubt you will ultimately become happy and independent."

With these words, Sweeney Todd left the place, and poor Tobias looked after him with a frown, as he repeated the words —

"Happy and independent. Alas! what a mockery it is of this man to speak to me in such a way — I only wish that I were dead!"

But we will leave Tobias to his own reflections, and follow the more interesting progress of Sweeney Todd, who, for some reason best known to himself, was then playing so grand a part, and casting away so large a sum of money. He made his way to a livery-stables in the immediate neighbourhood, and there, sure enough, the horses were being placed to a handsome carriage; and all being very soon in readiness, Sweeney Todd gave some whispered directions to the driver, and the vehicle started off westward.

At that time Hyde Park Corner was very nearly out of town, and it looked as if you were getting a glimpse of the country, and actually seeing something of the peasantry of England, when you got another couple of miles off, and that was the direction in which Sweeney Todd went; and as he goes, we may as well introduce to the reader the sort of individual whom he was going to visit in so much state, and for whom he thought it necessary to go to such great expense.

At that period the follies and vices of the nobility were somewhere about as great as they are now, and consequently extravagance induced on many occasions tremendous sacrifice of money, and it was found extremely convenient on many occasions for them to apply to a man of the name of John Mundel, an exceedingly wealthy person, a Dutchman by extraction, who was reported to make immense sums of money by lending to the nobility and others what they required on emergencies, at enormous rates of interest. But it must not be supposed that John Mundel was so confiding as to lend his money without security. It was quite the reverse, for he took care to have the jewels, some costly plate, or the title-deeds of an estate, perchance, as security, before he would part with a single shilling of his cash. In point of fact, John Mundel was nothing more than a pawnbroker on a very extensive scale, and, although he had an office in town, he usually received his more aristocratic customers at his private residence, which was about two miles off, on the Uxbridge Road.

After this explanation, it can very easily be imagined what was the scheme of Sweeney Todd, and that he considered, if he borrowed from John Mundel a sum equal in amount to half the real value of the pearls, he should be well rid of a property which he certainly could not sufficiently well account for the possession of, to enable him to dispose of it openly to the highest bidder.

We give Sweeney Todd great credit for the scheme he proposed. It was eminently calculated to succeed, and one which, in the way he undertook it, was certainly set about in the best possible style. During the ride, he revolved in his mind exactly what he should say to John Mundel, and, from what we know of him, we may be well convinced that Sweeney Todd was not likely to fail from any amount of bashfulness in the transaction; but that, on the contrary, he was just the man to succeed in any scheme which required great assurance to carry it through; for he was most certainly master of great assurance, and possessed of a kind of diplomatic skill, which, had fortune placed him in a more elevated position of life, would no doubt have made a great man of him, and gained him great political reputation.

John Mundel's villa, which was called, by-the-bye, Mundel House, was a large, handsome, and modern structure, surrounded by a few acres of plea-sure-gardens, which, however, the money-lender never looked at, for his whole soul was too much engrossed by his love for cash to enable him to do so; and, if he derived any satisfaction at all from it, that satisfaction must have been entirely owing to the fact, that he had wrung mansion, grounds, and all the costly furnishing of the former, from an improvident debtor, who had been forced to fly the country, and leave his property wholly in the hands of the money-lender and usurer.

It was but a short drive with the really handsome horses that Sweeney Todd had succeeded in hiring for the occasion, and he soon found himself opposite the entrance gates of the residence of John Mundel. His great object now was that the usurer should see the equipage which he had brought down; and he accordingly desired the footman who accompanied him at once to ring the bell at the entrance-gate, and to say that a gentleman was waiting in his carriage to see Mr. Mundel. This was done; and when the money-lender's servant reported to him that the equipage was a costly one, and that, in his opinion, the visitor must be some nobleman of great rank, John Mundel made no difficulty about the matter, but walked down to the gate at once, where he immediately mentally subscribed to the opinion of his servant, by admitting to himself that the equipage was faultless, and presumed at once that it did belong to some person of great rank. He was proportionally humble, as such men always are, and, advancing to the side of the carriage, he begged to know what commands his lordship — for so he called him at once — had for him?

"I wish to know," said Sweeney Todd, "Mr. Mundel, if you are inclined to lay under an obligation a rather illustrious lady, by helping her out of a little pecuniary difficulty?"

John Mundel glanced again at the equipage, and he likewise saw something of the rich dress of his visitor, who had not disputed the title which had been applied to him, of lord; and he made up his mind accordingly that it was just one of the transactions that would suit him, provided the security that would be offered was of a tangible nature. That was the only point upon which John Mundel had the remotest doubt; but, at all events, he urgently pressed his visitor to alight and walk in.

CHAPTER XIV.

THE GREAT CHANGE IN THE PROSPECTS OF SWEENEY TODD.

As SWEENEY TODD'S OBJECT, so far as regarded the money-lender having seen the carriage, was fully answered, he had no objection to enter the house, which he accordingly did at once, being preceded by John Mundel, who became each moment more and more impressed with the fact, as he considered it, that his guest was some person of very great rank and importance in society. He ushered him into a splendidly-furnished apartment, and after offering him refreshments, which Sweeney Todd politely declined, he waited with no small degree of impatience for his visitor to be more explicit with regard to the object of his visit.

"I should," said Sweeney Todd, "have myself accommodated the illustrious lady with the sum of money she requires, but as I could not do so without incumbering some estates, she positively forbade me to think of it."

"Certainly," said Mr. Mundel, "she is a very illustrious lady, I presume?"

"Very illustrious indeed, but it must be a condition of this transaction, if you at all enter into it, that you are not to inquire precisely who she is, nor are you to inquire precisely who I am."

"It's not my usual way of conducting business, but if everything else be satisfactory, I shall not cavil at that."

"Very good; by everything else being satisfactory, I presume you mean the security offered?"

"Why, yes, that is of great importance, my lord."

"I informed the illustrious lady, that, as the affair was to be wrapped up in something of a mystery, the security must be extremely ample."

"That's a very proper view to take of the matter, my lord." — "I wonder," thought John Mundel, "if he is a duke; I'll call him 'your grace' next time, and see if he objects to it."

"Therefore," continued Sweeney Todd, "the illustrious lady placed in my hands security to a third greater amount than she required."

"Certainly, certainly, a very proper arrangement, your grace; may I ask the nature of the proffered security?"

"Jewels."

"Highly satisfactory and unexceptionable security; they go into a small space, and do not deteriorate in value."

"And if they do," said the barber, "deteriorate in value, it would make no difference to you, for the illustrious person's honour would be committed to your redemption."

"I don't doubt that, your grace, in the least; I merely made the remark incidentally, quite incidentally."

"Of course, of course; and I trust, before going further, that you are quite in a position to enter into this subject."

"Certainly I am, and, I am proud to say, to any amount. Show me the money's worth, your grace, and I will show you the money — that's my way of doing business; and no one can say that John Mundel ever shrunk from a matter that was brought fairly before him, and that he considered worth his going into."

THE BARBER ACTS THE DUKE TO PAWN THE JEWELS.

"It was by hearing such a character of you that I was induced to come to you. What do you think of that?"

Sweeney Todd took from his pocket, with a careless air, the string of pearls, and cast them down before the eyes of the money-lender, who took them up and ran them rapidly through his fingers for a few seconds before he said —

"I thought there was but one string like this in the kingdom, and those belonged to the Queen."

"Well," said Sweeney Todd.

"I humbly beg your grace's pardon. How much money does your grace require on these pearls?"

"Twelve thousand pounds is their current value, if a sale of them was enforced; eight thousand pounds are required of you on their security."

"Eight thousand is a large sum. As a general thing I lend but half the value upon anything; but in this case, to oblige your grace and the illustrious personage, I do not, of course, hesitate for one moment but shall for one month lend you the required amount."

"That will do," said Sweeney Todd, scarcely concealing the exultation he felt at getting so much more from John Mundel than he expected, and which he certainly would not have got if the money-lender had not been most fully and completely impressed with the idea that the pearls belonged to the Queen, and that he had actually at length majesty itself for a customer. He did not suppose for one moment that it was the queen who wanted the money; but his view of the case was, that she had lent the pearls to this nobleman to meet some exigency of his own, and that, of course, they would be redeemed very shortly. Altogether a more pleasant transaction for John Mundel could not have been imagined. It was just the sort of thing he would have looked out for, and had the greatest satisfaction in bringing to a conclusion, and he considered it was opening the door to the highest class of business in his way that he was capable of doing.

"In what name, your grace," he said, "shall I draw a cheque upon my banker?"

"In the name of Colonel George."

"Certainly, certainly; and if your grace will give me an acknowledgment for eight thousand pounds, and please to understand that at the end of a month from this time the transaction will be renewed if necessary, I will give you a cheque for seven thousand five hundred pounds."

"Why seven thousand five hundred only, when you mentioned eight thousand pounds?"

"The five hundred pounds is my little commission upon the transaction. Your grace will perceive that I appreciate highly the honour of your grace's custom, and consequently charge the lowest possible price. I can assure your grace I could get more for my money by a great deal, but the pleasure of being able to meet your grace's views is so great, that I am willing to make a sacrifice, and therefore it is that I say five hundred, when I really ought to say one thousand pounds, taking into consideration the great scarcity of money at the present juncture; and I can assure your grace that—"

"Peace, peace," said Sweeney Todd; "and if it be not convenient to redeem the jewels at the end of a month from this time, you will hear from me most assuredly."

"I am quite satisfied of that," said John Mundel, and he accordingly drew a cheque for seven thousand five hundred pounds, which he handed to Sweeney

Todd, who put it in his pocket, not a little delighted that at last he had got rid of his pearls, even at a price so far beneath their real value.

"I need scarcely urge upon you, Mr. Mundel," he said, "the propriety of keeping this affair profoundly secret."

"Indeed you need not, your grace, for it is part of my business to be discreet and cautious. I should very soon have nothing to do in my line, your grace may depend, if I were to talk about it. No, this transaction will for ever remain locked up in my own breast, and no living soul but your grace and I need know what has occurred."

With this, John Mundel showed Sweeney Todd to his carriage, with abundance of respect, and in two minutes more he was travelling along towards town with what might be considered a small fortune in his pocket.

We should have noticed earlier that Sweeney Todd had, upon the occasion of his going to sell the pearls to the lapidary, in the city, made some great alterations in his appearance, so that it was not likely he should be recognised again to a positive certainly. For example — having no whiskers whatever of his own, he had put on a large black pair of false ones, as well as moustachios, and he had given some colour to his cheeks likewise which had so completely altered his appearance, that those who were most intimate with him would not have known him except by his voice, and that he took good care to alter in his intercourse with John Mundel, so that it should not become a future means of detection.

"I thought that this would succeed," he muttered to himself, as he went towards town, "and I have not been deceived. For three months longer, and only three, I will carry on the business in Fleet-street, so that any sudden alteration in my fortunes may not give rise to suspicion."

He was then silent for some minutes, during which he appeared to be revolving some very knotty question in his brain, and then he said, suddenly —

"Well, well, as regards Tobias, I think it will be safer, unquestionably, to put him out of the way by taking his life, than to try to dispose of him in a mad-house, and I think there are one or two more persons whom it will be highly necessary to prevent being mischievous, at all events at present. I must think — I must think."

When such a man as Sweeney Todd set about thinking, there could be no possible doubt but that some serious mischief was meditated, and any one who could have watched his face during that ride home from the money-lender's, would have seen by its expression that the thoughts which agitated him were of a dark and desperate character, and such as anybody but himself would have shrunk from aghast. But he was not a man to shrink from anything, and, on the contrary, the more a set of circumstances presented themselves in a gloomy and a terrific aspect, the better they seemed to suit him, and the peculiar constitution of his mind. There can be no doubt but that the love of money was the predominant feeling in Sweeney Todd's intellectual organization, and that, by the amount it would bring him, or the amount it would deprive him of, he measured everything. With such a man, then, no question of morality or ordinary feeling could arise, and there can be no doubt that he would quite willingly have sacrificed the whole human race, if, by so doing, he could have achieved any of the objects of his ambition. And so, on his road homeward, he probably made up his mind to plunge still deeper into criminality, and perchance to indulge in acts that a man not already so deeply versed in iniquity would have shrunk from with the most positive terror.

And by a strange style of reasoning, such men as Sweeney Todd reconcile themselves to the most heinous crimes upon the ground of what they call policy. That is to say, that having committed some serious offence, they are compelled to commit a great number more for the purpose of endeavouring to avoid the consequences of the first lot, and hence the continuance of criminality becomes a matter necessary to self-defence, and an essential ingredient in their consideration of self-preservation. Probably Sweeney Todd had been for the greater part of his life, aiming at the possession of extensive pecuniary resources, and, no doubt, by the aid of a superior intellect, and a mind full of craft and design, he had managed to make others subservient to his views; and now that those views were answered, and that his underlings and accomplices were no longer required, they became positively dangerous. He was well aware of that cold-blooded policy which teaches that it is far safer to destroy than to cast away the tools by which a man carves his way to power and fortune.

"They shall die," said Sweeney Todd — "dead men tell no tales, nor women nor boys either, and they shall all die; after which there will, I think, be a serious fire in Fleet-street. Ha! ha! it may spread to what mischief it likes, always provided it stops not short of the entire destruction of my house and premises. Rare sport — rare sport will it be to me, for then I will at once commence a new career, in which the barber will be forgotten, and the man of fashion only seen and remembered, for with this sad addition to my means, I am fully capable of vying with the highest and the noblest, let them be whom they may."

This seemed a pleasant train of reflections to Sweeney Todd, and as the coach entered Fleet-street, there sat such a grim smile upon his countenance that he looked like some fiend in human shape, who had just completed the destruction of a human soul.

When he reached the livery stables to which he directed them to drive, instead of his own shop, he rewarded all who had gone with him most liberally, so that the coachman and footman, who were both servants out of place, would have had no objection for Sweeney Todd every day to have gone on some such an expedition, so that they should receive as liberal wages for the small part they enacted in it as they did upon that occasion. He then walked from the stables toward his own house, but upon reaching there a little disappointment awaited him, for he found to his surprise that no light was burning; and when he placed his hand upon the shop-door, it opened, but there was no trace of Tobias, although he, Sweeney Todd, called loudly upon him the moment he set foot within the shop. Then a feeling of apprehension crept across the barber, and he groped anxiously about for some matches, by the aid of which he hoped to procure a light, and then an explanation of the mysterious absence of Tobias.

But in order that we may, in its proper form, relate how it was that Tobias had had the daring thus, in open contradiction of his master, to be away from the shop, we must devote to Tobias a chapter, which will plead his extenuation.

CHAPTER XV.

TOBIAS'S ADVENTURES DURING THE ABSENCE OF SWEENEY TODD.

TOBIAS GUESSED, AND GUESSED RIGHTLY too, that when Sweeney Todd said he would be away half an hour, he only mentioned that short period of time, in order to keep the lad's vigilance on the alert, and to prevent him from taking any advantage of a more protracted absence. The very style and manner in which he had gone out, precluded the likelihood of it being for so short a period of time; and that circumstance set Tobias seriously thinking over a situation which was becoming more intolerable every day. The lad had the sense to feel that he could not go on much longer as he was going on, and that in a short time such a life would destroy him.

"It is beyond endurance," he said, "and I know not what to do; and since Sweeney Todd has told me that the boy he had before went out of his senses, and is now in the cell of a mad-house, I feel that such will be my fate, and that I too shall come to that dreadful end, and then no one will believe a word I utter, but consider everything to be mere raving."

After a time, as the darkness increased, he lit the lamp which hung in the shop, and which, until it was closed for the night, usually shed a dim ray from the window. Then he sat down to think again, and he said to himself—

"If I could now but summon courage to ask my mother about this robbery which Sweeney Todd imputes to her, she might assure me it was false, and that she never did such a deed; but then it is dreadful for me to ask her such a question, because it may be true; and then, how shocking it would be for her to be forced to confess to me, her own son, such a circumstance."

These were the honourable feelings which prevented Tobias from questioning his mother as regarded Todd's accusation of her—an accusation too dreadful to believe implicitly, and yet sufficiently probable for him to have a strong suspicion that it might be true after all. It is to be deeply regretted that Tobias's philosophy did not carry him a little further, and make him see, the moment the charge was made, that he ought unquestionably to investigate it to the very utmost. But still we could hardly expect, from a mere boy, that acute reasoning and power of action, which depend so much upon the knowledge of the world and an extensive practice in the usages of society. It was sufficient if he felt correctly—we could scarcely expect him to reason so.

But upon this occasion, above all others, he seemed completely overcome by the circumstances which surrounded him; and from his excited manner, one might have almost imagined that the insanity he himself predicted at the close of his career was really not far off. He wrung his hands, and he wept, every now and then, in sad speech, bitterly bemoaning his situation, until at length, with a sudden resolution, he sprang to his feet, exclaiming—

"This night shall end it. I can endure it no more. I will fly from this place, and seek my fortune elsewhere. Any amount of distress, danger, or death itself even, is preferable to the dreadful life I lead."

He walked some paces towards the door, and then he paused, as he said to himself in a low tone—

"Todd will surely not be home yet awhile, and why should I then neglect the only opportunity I may ever have of searching this house to satisfy my mind as regards any of the mysteries that it contains?"

He paused over this thought, and considered well its danger, for dangerous indeed it was to no small extent, but he was desperate; and with a resolution that scarcely could have been expected from him, he determined upon taking that step, above all others, which Todd was almost sure to punish with death. He closed the shop door, and bolted it upon the inside, so that he could not be suddenly interrupted, and then he looked round him carefully for some weapon, by the aid of which he should be able to break his way into the parlour, which the barber always kept closed and locked in his absence. A weapon that would answer the purpose of breaking any lock, if he, Tobias, chose to proceed so roughly to work, was close at hand in the iron bar, which, when the place was closed at night, secured a shutter to the door. Wrought up as he was to almost frenzy, Tobias seized this bar, and, advancing towards the parlour door, he with one blow smashed the lock to atoms, and the door yielded. The moment it did so, there was a crash of glass, and when Tobias entered the room he saw that upon its threshold lay a wine-glass shattered to atoms, and he felt certain that it had been placed in some artful position by Sweeney Todd as a detector, when he should return, of any attempt that had been made upon the door of the parlour.

And now Tobias felt that he was so far committed that he might as well go on with his work, and accordingly he lit a candle, which he found upon the parlour table, and then proceeded to make what discoveries he could.

Several of the cupboards in the room yielded at once to his hands, and in them he found nothing remarkable; but there was one that he could not open; so, without a moment's hesitation, he had recourse to the bar of iron again, and broke its lock, when the door swung open,—and to his astonishment there tumbled out of this cupboard such a volley of hats of all sorts and descriptions, some looped with silver, some three-cornered, and some square, that they formed quite a museum of that article of attire, and excited the greatest surprise in the mind of Tobias, at the same time that they tended very greatly to confirm some other thoughts and feelings which he had concerning Sweeney Todd. This was the only cupboard which was fast, although there was another door which looked as if it opened into one, but when Tobias broke that down with the bar of iron, he found it was the door which led to the staircase conducting to the upper part of the house — that upper part which Sweeney Todd, with all his avarice, would never let, and of which the shutters were kept continually closed, so that the opposite neighbours never caught a glimpse into any of the apartments. With cautious and slow steps, which he adopted instantaneously, although he knew that there was no one in the house but himself, Tobias ascended the staircase.

"I will go to the very top rooms first," he said to himself, "and so examine them all as I come down, and then if Todd should return suddenly, I shall have a better chance of hearing him, than as if I began below and went upwards."

Acting upon this prudent scheme, he went up to the attics, all the doors of which were swinging open, and there was nothing in any of them whatever. He descended to the second floor with the like result, and a feeling of great disappointment began to creep over him at the thought that, after all, the barber's house might not repay the trouble of examination. But when he reached the first floor he soon found abundant reason to alter his opinion. The doors were fast, and he had to burst them open; and, when he got in, he found that those rooms were partially furnished, and that they contained a great quantity of miscellaneous property of all kinds and descriptions. In one corner was an enormous quantity of walking-sticks, some of which were of a very costly and expensive character, with gold and silver chased tops to them, and in another corner was a great number of umbrellas — in fact, at least a hundred of them. Then there were boots and shoes lying upon the floor, partially covered up, as if to keep them from dirt; there were thirty or forty swords of different styles and patterns, many of them appearing to be very firm blades, and in one or two cases the scabbards were richly ornamented. At one end of the front and larger of these two rooms, was an old-fashioned-looking bureau of great size, and with as much wood-work in it as seemed required to make at least a couple of such articles of furniture. This was very securely locked, and presented more difficulties in the way of opening it than any of the doors had done, for the lock was of great strength and apparent durability. Moreover it was not so easily got at, but at length by using the bar as a sort of lever, instead of as a mere machine to strike with, Tobias succeeded in forcing this bureau open, and then his eyes were perfectly dazzled with the amount of jewellery and trinkets of all kinds and descriptions that were exhibited to his gaze. There was a great number of watches, gold chains, silver and gold snuff-boxes, and a large assortment of rings, shoe-buckles, and brooches. These articles must have been of great value, and Tobias could not help exclaiming aloud —

"How could Sweeney Todd come by these articles, except by the murder of their owners?"

This, indeed, seemed but too probable a supposition, and the more especially so, as in a further part of this bureau a great quantity of apparel was found by Tobias. He stood with a candle in his hand, looking upon these various objects for more than a quarter of an hour, and then as a sudden and a natural thought came across him of how completely a few of them even would satisfy his wants and his mother's for a long time to come, he stretched forth his hand towards the glittering mass, but he drew it back again with a shudder, saying —

"No — no, these things are the plunder of the dead. Let Sweeney Todd keep them to himself, and look upon them, if he can, with eyes of enjoyment. I will have none of them; they would bring misfortune along with every guinea that they might be turned into."

As he spoke, he heard St. Dunstan's clock strike nine, and he started at the sound, for it let him know that already Sweeney Todd had been away an hour beyond the time he said he would be absent, so that there was a probability of his quick return now, and it would scarcely be safe to linger longer in his house.

"I must be gone — I must be gone. I should like to look upon my mother's face once more before I leave London for ever perhaps. I may tell her of the danger she is in from Todd's knowledge of her secret; no — no, I cannot speak to her of that; I must go, and leave her to those chances which I hope and trust will work favourably for her."

Flinging down the iron bar which had done him such good service, Tobias stopped not to close any of those receptacles which contained the plunder that Sweeney Todd had taken most probably from murdered persons, but he rushed down stairs into the parlour again, where the boots that had fallen out of the cupboard still lay upon the floor in wild disorder.

It was a strange and sudden whim that took him, rather than a matter of reflection, that induced him, instead of his own hat, to take one of those which were lying so indiscriminately at his feet; and he did so. By mere accident it turned out to be an exceedingly handsome hat, of rich workmanship and material, and then Tobias, feeling terrified lest Sweeney Todd should return

TOBIAS DISCOVERS THE BARBER'S HIDDEN PLUNDER.

before he could leave the place, paid no attention to anything, but turned from the shop, merely pulling the door after him, and then darting over the road towards the Temple like a hunted hare; for his great wish was to see his mother, and then he had an undefined notion that his best plan for escaping the clutches of Sweeney Todd would be to go to sea.

In common with all boys of his age, who know nothing whatever of the life of a sailor, it presented itself in the most fascinating colours. A sailor ashore and a sailor afloat, are about as two different things as the world can present;

but, to the imagination of Tobias Ragg, a sailor was somebody who was always dancing hornpipes, spending money, and telling wonderful stories. No wonder, then, that the profession presented itself under such fascinating colours to all such persons as Tobias; and as it seemed, and seems still, to be a sort of general understanding that the real condition of a sailor should be mystified in every possible way and shape by both novelist and dramatist, it is no wonder that it requires actual experience to enable those parties who are in the habit of being carried away by just what they hear, to come to a correct conclusion.

"I will go to sea!" ejaculated Tobias. "Yes, I will go to sea!"

As he spoke these words he passed out of the gate of the Temple leading into Whitefriars, in which ancient vicinity his mother dwelt, endeavouring to eke out a living as best she might. She was very much surprised (for she happened to be at home) at the unexpected visit of her son, Tobias, and uttered a faint scream as she let fall a flat-iron very nearly upon his toes.

"Mother," he said, "I cannot stay with Sweeney Todd any longer, so do not ask me."

"Not stay with such a respectable man?"

"A respectable man, mother! Alas, alas, how little you know of him! But what am I saying? I dare not speak! Oh, that fatal, fatal candlestick!"

"But how are you to live, and what do you mean by a fatal candlestick?"

"Forgive me — I did not mean to say that! Farewell, mother! I am going to sea."

"To see what, my dear?" said Mrs. Ragg, who was much more difficult to talk to, than even Hamlet's grave-digger. "You don't know how much I am obliged to Sweeney Todd."

"Yes, I do, and that's what drives me mad to think of. Farewell, mother, perhaps for ever! If I can, of course I will communicate with you, but now I dare not stay."

"Oh! what have you done, Tobias — what have you done?"

"Nothing — nothing! but Sweeney Todd is —"

"What — what?"

"No matter — no matter! Nothing — nothing! And yet at this last moment I am almost tempted to ask you concerning a candlestick."

"Don't mention that," said Mrs. Ragg; "I don't want to hear anything said about it."

"It is true, then?"

"Yes; but did Mr. Todd tell you?"

"He did — he did. I have now asked the question I never thought could have passed my lips. Farewell, mother; for ever farewell!"

Tobias rushed out of the place, leaving old Mrs. Ragg astonished at his behaviour, and with a strong suspicion that some accession of insanity had come over him.

"The Lord have mercy upon us!" she said, "what shall I do? I am astonished at Mr. Todd telling him about the candlestick; it's true enough, though, for all that. I recollect it as well as though it were yesterday; it was a very hard winter, and I was minding a set of chambers, when Todd came to shave the gentleman, and I saw him with my own eyes put a silver candlestick in his pocket. Then I went over to his shop and reasoned with him about it, and he gave it me back again, and I brought it to the chambers, and laid it down exactly on the spot where he took it from."

"To be sure," said Mrs. Ragg, after a pause of a few moments, "to be sure, he has been a very good friend to me ever since, but that I suppose is for fear I should tell, and get him hung or transported. But, however, we must take the good with the bad, and when Tobias comes to think of it, he will go back again to his work, I dare say; for, after all, it's a very foolish thing for him to trouble his head whether Mr. Todd stole a silver candlestick or not."

CHAPTER XVI.

THE STRANGE ODOUR IN OLD ST. DUNSTAN'S CHURCH.

ABOUT THIS TIME, AND WHILE the incidents of our most strange and eventful narrative were taking place, the pious frequenters of old St. Dunstan's church began to perceive a strange and most abominable odour throughout that sacred edifice. It was in vain that old women who came to hear the sermons, although they were too deaf to catch a third part of them, brought smelling bottles and other means of stifling their noses; still that dreadful charnel-house sort of smell would make itself most painfully and most disagreeably apparent. And the Rev. Joseph Stillingport, who was the regular preacher, smelt it in the pulpit; and had been seen to sneeze in the midst of a most pious discourse indeed, and to hold to his pious mouth a handkerchief, in which was some strong and pungent essence, for the purpose of trying to overcome the horrible effluvia. The organ-blower and the organ-player were both nearly stifled, for the horrible odour seemed to ascend to the upper part of the church; although those who sat in what may be called the pit, by no means escaped it. The churchwardens looked at each other in their pews with contorted countenances, and were almost afraid to breathe; and the only person who did not complain bitterly of the dreadful odour in St. Dunstan's church, was an old woman who had been a pew-opener for many years; but then she had lost the faculties of her nose, which, perhaps, accounted satisfactorily for that circumstance. At length, however, the nuisance became so intolerable, that the beadle, whose duty it was in the morning to open the church doors, used to come up to them with the massive key in one hand, and a cloth soaked in vinegar in the other, just as the people used to do in the time of the great plague of London; and when he had opened the doors, he used to run over to the other side of the way.

"Ah, Mr. Blunt!" he used to say to the bookseller, who lived opposite — "ah! Mr. Blunt, I is obligated to cut over here, leastways till the *atymouspheric* air is mixed up all along with the *stinkifications* which come from the church."

By this it will be seen that the beadle was rather a learned man, and no doubt went to some mechanics' institution of those days, where he learned something of everything but what was calculated to be of some service to him.

As might be supposed, from the fact that this sort of thing had gone on for a few months, it began to excite some attention with a view to a remedy; for, in the great city of London, a nuisance of any sort or description requires to become venerable by age before any one thinks of removing it; and after that, it is quite clear that that becomes a good argument against removing it at all. But at last, the churchwardens began to have a fear that some pestilential disease would be the result if they for any longer period of time put up with the horrible stench, and that they might be among its first victims, so they began to ask each other what could be done to obviate it.

Probably, if this frightful stench, being suggestive, as it was, of all sorts of horrors, had been graciously pleased to confine itself to some poor locality, nothing would have been heard of it; but when it became actually offensive to a gentleman in a metropolitan pulpit, and when it began to make itself perceptible to the sleepy faculties of the churchwardens of St. Dunstan's church, Fleet-street, so as to prevent them even from dozing through the afternoon sermon, it became a very serious matter indeed.

But what was it, what could it be, and what was to be done to get rid of it? These were the anxious questions that were asked right and left, as regarded the serious nuisance, without the fates graciously acceding any reply.

But yet one thing seemed to be generally agreed, and that was, that it did come, and must come, somehow or other, out of the vaults from beneath the church.

But then, as the pious and hypocritical Mr. Butterwick, who lived opposite, said —

"How could that be, when it was satisfactorily proved by the present books that nobody had been buried in the vaults for some time, and therefore it was a very odd thing that dead people, after leaving off smelling and being disagreeable, should all of a sudden burst out again in that line, and be twice as bad as ever they were at first."

And on Wednesdays sometimes, too, when pious people were not satisfied with the Sunday's devotion, but began again in the middle of the week, that stench was positively terrific. Indeed, so bad was it, that some of the congregation were forced to leave, and have been seen to slink into Bell-yard, where Lovett's pie-shop was situated, and then and there solace themselves with a pork or a veal pie, in order that their mouths and noses should be full of a delightful and agreeable flavour, instead of one most peculiarly and decidedly the reverse.

At last there was a confirmation to be held at St. Dunstan's church, and a great concourse of persons assembled, for a sermon was to be preached by the bishop after the confirmation; and a very great fuss indeed was to be made about really nobody knew exactly what. Preparations, as newspapers say, upon an extensive scale, and regardless of expense, were made for the purpose of adding lustre to the ceremony, and surprising the bishop, when he came, with a good idea that the people who attended St. Dunstan's church were somebodies, and really worth confirming.

The confirmation was to take place at twelve o'clock, and the bells ushered in the morning with their most pious tones, for it was not every day that the authorities of St. Dunstan succeeded in catching a bishop, and when they did so, they were determined to make the most of him. And the numerous authorities, including churchwardens, and even the very beadle, were in an uncommon fluster, and running about, and impeding each other, as authorities always do upon public occasions.

But, to those who only look to the surface of things, and who came to admire what was grand and magnificent in the preparations, the beadle certainly carried away the palm, for that functionary was attired in a completely new cocked hat and coat, and certainly looked very splendid and showy upon the occasion. Moreover, that beadle had been well and judiciously selected, and the parish authorities made no secret of it, when there was an election for beadle, that they threw all their influence into the scale of that candidate who happened to be the biggest, and consequently, who was calculated to wear the official costume with an air that no smaller man could have possibly aspired to on any account.

At half-past eleven o'clock the bishop made his gracious appearance, and was duly ushered into the vestry, where there was a comfortable fire, and on the table in which, likewise, were certain cold chickens and bottles of rare wines; for confirming a number of people, and preaching a sermon besides, was considered no joke, and might, for all they knew, be provocative of a great appetite in the bishop.

And with what a bland and courtly air the bishop smiled as he ascended the steps of St. Dunstan's Church. How affable he was to the churchwardens, and he actually smiled upon a poor miserable charity boy, who, his eyes glaring wide open, and his muffin cap in his hand, was taking his first stare at a real live bishop. To be sure, the beadle knocked him down directly the bishop had passed, for having the presumption to look at such a great personage; but then that was to be expected fully and completely, and only proved that the proverb which permits a cat to look at a king is not equally applicable to charity boys and bishops.

When the bishop got to the vestry, some very complimentary words were uttered to him by the usual officiating clergyman, but, somehow or other, the bland smile had left the lips of the great personage, and, interrupting the vicar in the midst of a fine flowing speech, he said —

"That's all very well, but what a terrible stink there is here!"

The churchwardens gave a groan, for they had flattered themselves that perhaps the bishop would not notice the dreadful smell, or that, if he did, he would think it was accidental, and say nothing about it; but now, when he really did mention it, they found all their hopes scattered to the winds, and that it was necessary to say something.

"Is this horrid charnel-house sort of smell always here?"

"I am afraid it is," said one of the churchwardens.

"Afraid!" said the bishop, "surely you know; you seem to me to have a nose."

"Yes," said the churchwarden, in great confusion, "I have that honour, and I have the pleasure of informing you, my Lord Bishop — I mean I have the honour of informing you that this smell is always here."

The bishop sniffed several times, and then he said —

"It is very dreadful; and I hope that by the next time I come to St. Dunstan's, you will have the pleasure and the honour, both, of informing me that it has gone away."

The churchwarden bowed, and got into an extreme corner, saying to himself —

"This is the bishop's last visit here, and I don't wonder at it, for, as if out of pure spite, the smell is ten times worse than ever to-day."

And so it was, for it seemed to come up through all the crevices of the flooring of the church, with a power and perseverance that was positively dreadful.

The people coughed, and held their handkerchiefs to their noses, remarking to each other —

"Isn't it dreadful? — did you ever know the smell in St. Dunstan's so bad before," and everybody agreed that they never had known it anything like so bad, for that it was positively awful — and so indeed it was.

The anxiety of the bishop to get away was quite manifest, and, if he could have decently taken his departure without confirming anybody at all, there is no doubt but that he would have willingly done so, and left all the congregation to die and be — something or another. But this he could not do, but he could cut it short, and he did so. The people found themselves confirmed before they almost knew where they were, and the bishop would not go into the vestry again on any account, but hurried down the steps of the church, and into his carriage, with the greatest precipitation in the world, thus proving that holiness is no proof against a most abominable stench.

As MAY BE WELL SUPPOSED, after this, the subject assumed a much more serious aspect, and on the following day a solemn meeting was held of all the church authorities, at which it was determined that men should be employed to make a thorough and searching examination of the vaults of St. Dunstan's, with the view of discovering, if possible, from whence particularly the abominable stench emanated. And then it was decided that the stench was to be put down, and that the bishop was to be apprized it was put down, and that he might visit the church in perfect safety.

CHAPTER XVII.

SWEENEY TODD'S PROCEEDINGS CONSEQUENT UPON THE DEPARTURE OF TOBIAS.

WE LEFT THE BARBER IN HIS OWN SHOP, much wondering that Tobias had not responded to the call which he had made upon him, but yet scarcely believing it possible that he could have ventured upon the height of iniquity, which we know Tobias had really been guilty of. He paused for a few moments, and held up the light which he had procured, and gazed around him with inquiring eyes, for he could, indeed, scarcely believe it possible that Tobias had sufficiently cast off his dread of him, Sweeney Todd, to be enabled to achieve any act for his liberation. But when he saw that the lock of the parlour-door was open, positive rage obtained precedence over every other feeling.

"The villain!" he cried, "has he dared really to consummate an act I thought he could not have dreamt of for a moment? Is it possible that he can have presumed so far as to have searched the house?"

That Tobias, however, had presumed so far, the barber soon discovered, and when he went into his parlour and saw what had actually occurred, and that not only was every cupboard door broken open, but that likewise the door which led to the staircase and the upper part of the house had not escaped, he got perfectly furious, and it was some time before he could sufficiently calm himself to reflect upon the probable and possible amount of danger he might run in consequence of these proceedings. When he did, his active mind at once told him that there was not much to be dreaded immediately, for that most probably Tobias, still having the fear before his eyes of what he might do as regarded his mother, had actually run away; and, "in all likelihood," muttered the barber, "he has taken with him something which would allow me to fix upon him the stigma of robbery, but that I must see to."

Having fastened the shop-door securely, he took the light in his hands, and ascended to the upper part of his house — that is to say, the first floor, where alone anything was to be found. He saw at once the open bureau, with all its glittering display of jewels, and as he gazed upon the heap, he muttered —

"I have not so accurate a knowledge of what is here as to be able to say if anything be extracted or not, but I know the amount of money, if I do not know the precise number of jewels which this bureau contains."

He opened a small drawer which had entirely escaped the scrutiny of Tobias, and proceeded to count a large number of guineas which were there.

"These are correct," he said, when he had finished his examination — "these are correct, and he has touched none of them."

He then opened another drawer, in which were a great many packets of silver done up in paper, and these likewise he carefully counted, and was satisfied they were right.

"It is strange," he said, "that he has taken nothing, but yet perhaps it is better that it should be so, inasmuch as it shows a wholesome fear of me. The slightest examination would have shown him these hoards of money; and since he has not made that slight examination, nor discovered any of them, it seems to my mind decisive upon the subject, that he has taken nothing, and perchance I shall discover him easier than I imagine."

He repaired to the parlour again, and carefully divested himself of everything which had enabled him so successfully to impose upon John Mundel, and replaced them by his ordinary costume, after which he fastened up his house and sallied forth, taking his way direct to Mrs. Ragg's humble home, in the expectation that there he would hear something of Tobias, which would give him a clue where to search for him, for search for him he fully intended; but what were his precise intentions perhaps he could hardly have told himself, until he actually found him.

When he reached Mrs. Ragg's house, and made his appearance abruptly before that lady, who seemed somehow or another to be always ironing and always to drop the iron when any one came in, very near their toes, he said —

"Where did your son Tobias go after he left you to-night?"

"Lor! Mr. Todd, is it you? You are as good as a conjuror, sir, for he was here; but bless you, sir, I know no more where he is gone to, than the man in the moon. He said he was going to sea, but I am sure I should not have thought it, that I should not."

"To sea! — then the probability is that he would go down to the docks, but surely not to-night. Do you not expect him back here to sleep?"

"Well, sir, that's a very good thought of yours; and he may come back here to sleep, for all I know to the contrary."

"But you do not know it for a fact?"

"He didn't say so; but he may come, you know, sir, for all that."

"Did he tell you his reason for leaving me?"

"Indeed no, sir; he really did not, and he seemed to me to be a little bit out of his senses."

"Ah! Mrs. Ragg," said Sweeney Todd, "there you have it. From the first moment that he came into my service, I knew and felt confident that he was out of his senses. There was a strangeness of behaviour about him, which soon convinced me of that fact, and I am only anxious about him, in order that some effort may be made to cure him of such a malady, for it is a serious, and a dreadful one, and one which, unless taken in time, will be yet the death of Tobias."

These words were spoken with such solemn seriousness, that they had a wonderful effect upon Mrs. Ragg, who, like most ignorant persons, began immediately to confirm that which she most dreaded.

"Oh, it's too true," she said, "it's too true. He did say some extraordinary things to-night, Mr. Todd, and he said he had something to tell, which was too horrid to speak of. Now the idea, you know, Mr. Todd, of anybody having anything at all to tell, and not telling it at once, is quite singular."

"It is! — and I am sure that his conduct is such you never would be guilty of, Mrs. Ragg; — but hark! what's that?"

"It's a knock, Mr. Todd."

"Hush, stop a moment — what if it be Tobias?"

"Gracious goodness! it can't be him, for he would have come in at once."

"No; I slipped the bolt of the door, because I wished to talk to you without observation; so it may be Tobias, you perceive, after all. But let me hide somewhere, so that I may hear what he says, and be able to judge how his mind is affected. I will not hesitate to do something for him, let it cost what it may."

"There's the cupboard, Mr. Todd. To be sure there is some dirty saucepans and a frying-pan in it, and of course it ain't a fit place to ask you to go into."

"Never mind that — never mind that; only you be careful, for the sake of Tobias's very life, to keep secret that I am here."

The knocking at the door increased each moment in vehemence, and scarcely had Sweeney Todd succeeded in getting into the cupboard along with Mrs. Ragg's pots and pans, and thoroughly concealed himself, when she opened the door; and, sure enough — Tobias, heated, tired, and looking ghastly pale — staggered into the room.

"Mother," he said, "I have taken a new thought, and have come back to you."

"Well, I thought you would, Tobias; and a very good thing it is that you have."

"Listen to me: I thought of flying from England for ever, and of never again setting foot upon its shores. I have altered that determination completely, and I feel now that it is my duty to do something else."

"To do what, Tobias?"

"To tell all I know — to make a clean breast, mother, and, let the conse-quences be what they may, to let justice take its course."

"What do you mean, Tobias?"

"Mother, I have come to a conclusion, that what I have to tell is of such vast importance, compared with any consequences that may arise from the petty robbery of the candlestick, which you know of, that I ought not to hesitate a moment in revealing everything."

"But, my dear Tobias, remember that that is a dreadful secret, and one that must be kept."

"It cannot matter — it cannot matter; and, besides, it is more than probable that by revealing what I actually know, and which is of such great magnitude, I may, mother, in a manner of speaking, perchance completely exonerate you from the consequences of that transaction. Besides, it was long ago, and the prosecutor may have mercy; but, be all that how it may, and be the consequences what they may, I must and will tell what I now know."

"But what is it Tobias, that you know?"

"Something too dreadful for me to utter to you alone. Go into the Temple, mother, to some of the chambers you attend to, and ask them to come to me, and listen to what I have got to say. They will be amply repaid for their trouble, for they will hear that which may, perhaps, save their own lives."

"He is quite gone," thought Mrs. Ragg, "and Mr. Todd is correct; poor Tobias is as mad as he can be!" — "Alas, alas, Tobias, why don't you try to reason yourself into a better state of mind! You don't know a bit what you are saying, any more than the man in the moon."

"I know I am half mad, mother, but yet I know what I am saying well; so do not fancy that it is not to be relied upon, but go and fetch some one at once to listen to what I have to relate."

"Perhaps," thought Mrs. Ragg, "if I were to pretend to humour him, it would be as well, and, while I am gone, Mr. Todd can speak to him."

This was a bright idea of Mrs. Ragg's, and she forthwith proceeded to carry it into execution, saying —

"Well, my dear, if it must be, it must be — and I will go; but I hope while I have gone, somebody will speak to you, and convince you that you ought to try to quiet yourself."

These words Mrs. Ragg uttered aloud, for the special benefit of Sweeney Todd, who, she considered, would have been there to take the hint accordingly. It is needless to say he did hear them, and how far he profited by them, we shall quickly perceive. As for poor Tobias, he had not the remotest idea of the close proximity of his arch enemy; if he had, he would quickly have left that spot, where he might well to conjecture so much danger awaited him; for although Sweeney Todd, under the circumstances, probably felt that he dared not take Tobias's life, still he might exchange something that could place it in his power to do so shortly, with the least personal danger to himself. The door closed after the retreating form of Mrs. Ragg, and as, considering the mission she was gone upon, it was very clear some minutes must elapse before she could return, Sweeney Todd did not feel that there was any very particular hurry in the transaction.

"What shall I do?" he said to himself. "Shall I await his mother's coming again, and get her to aid me, or shall I of myself adopt some means which will put an end to trouble on this boy's account?"

Sweeney Todd was a man tolerably rapid in thought, and he contrived to make up his mind that the best plan, unquestionably, would be to lay hold of Tobias at once, and so prevent the possibility of any appeal to his mother becoming effective. Tobias, when his mother left the place, as he imagined, for the purpose of procuring some one to listen to what he considered to be Sweeney Todd's delinquencies, rested his face upon his hands, and gave himself up to painful and deep thought. He felt that he had arrived at quite a crisis in his history, and that the next few hours could not surely but be very important to him in their results; and so they were indeed, but not certainly exactly in the way that he all along anticipated, for he thought of nothing but of the arrest and discomfiture of Todd, little expecting how close was his proximity to that formidable personage.

"Surely," thought Tobias, "I shall, by disclosing all that I know about Todd, gain some consideration for my mother, and after all, she may not be prosecuted for the robbery of the candlestick, for how very trifling is that affair compared to the much more dreadful things which I more than suspect Sweeney Todd to be guilty of. He is and must be, from all that I have seen and heard, a murderer, although how he disposes of his victims is involved in the most complete mystery, and is to me a matter past all human power of comprehension. I have no idea even upon that subject whatever."

This, indeed, was a great mystery; for, even admitting that Sweeney Todd was a murderer, and it must be allowed that as yet we have only circumstantial evidence of that fact, we can form no conclusion from such evidence as to how he perpetrated the deed, or how afterwards he disposed of the body of his victim. This grand and principal difficulty in the way of committing murder with impunity, namely, the disposal of a corpse, certainly did not seem at all to have any effect upon Sweeney Todd; for if he made corpses, he had some means of getting rid of them with the most wonderful expedition as well as secrecy.

"He is a murderer," thought Tobias. "I know he is, although I have never seen him do the deed, or seen any appearances in the shop of a deed of blood having been committed. Yet why is it that occasionally, when a better dressed person than usual comes into the shop, that he sends me out on some errand to a distant part of the town?"

Tobias did not forget, too, that on more than one occasion he had come back quicker than he had been expected, and that he had caught Sweeney Todd in some little confusion, and seen the hat, the stick, or perhaps the umbrella of the last customer quietly waiting there, although the customer had gone; and even if the glaring improbability of a man leaving his hat behind him in a barber's shop was got over, why did he not come back for it?

This was a circumstance which was entitled to all the weight which Tobias, during his mental cogitations, could give to it, and there could be but one possible explanation of a man not coming back for his hat, and that was that he had not the power to do so.

"This house will be searched," thought Tobias, "and all those things, which of course must have belonged to so many different people, will be found, and then they will be identified, and he will be required to say how he came by them, which, I think, will be a difficult task indeed for Sweeney Todd to accomplish. What a relief it will be to me, to be sure, when he is hanged, as I think he is tolerably sure to be!"

"What a relief," muttered Sweeney Todd, as he slowly opened the door, unseen by Tobias — "what a relief it will be to me when this boy is in his grave, as he will be soon, or else I have forgotten all my moral learning, and turned chicken-hearted — neither of them very likely circumstances."

CHAPTER XVIII.

THE MISADVENTURE OF TOBIAS. — THE MAD-HOUSE ON PECKHAM-RYE.

SWEENEY TODD PAUSED FOR A MOMENT at the cupboard door, before he made up his mind as to whether he should pounce upon poor Tobias at once, or adopt a more creeping, cautious mode of operation. The latter course was by far the most congenial to his mind, and so he adopted it in a moment or so, and stole quietly from his place of concealment, and with so little noise, that Tobias could not have the least suspicion that any one was in the room but himself. Treading, as if each step might involve some serious consequences, he thus at length got completely behind the chair on which Tobias was sitting, and stood with folded arms, and such a hideous smile upon his face, that they together formed no inapt representation of the Mephistopheles of the German drama.

"I shall at length," murmured Tobias, "be free from my present dreadful state of mind, by thus accusing Todd. He is a murderer — of that I have no doubt: it is but a duty of mine to stand forward as his accuser."

Sweeney Todd stretched out his two brawny hands, and clutched Tobias by the head, which he turned round till the boy could see him, and then he said —

"Indeed, Tobias; and did it never strike you that Todd was not so easily to be overcome as you would wish him, eh, Tobias?"

The shock of this astonishing and sudden appearance of Sweeney Todd was so great, that for a few moments Tobias was deprived of all power of speech or action, and with his head so strangely twisted as to seem to threaten the destruction of his neck. He glared into the triumphant and malignant countenance of his persecutor, as he would into that of the arch enemy of all mankind, which probably he now began to think the barber really was. If one thing more than another was calculated to delight such a man as Todd, it certainly was to perceive what a dreadful effect his presence had upon Tobias, who remained for about a minute and a half in this state before he ventured upon uttering a shriek, which, however, when it did come, almost frightened Todd himself. It was one of those cries which can only come from a heart in its utmost agony — a cry which might have heralded the spirit to another world, and proclaimed, as it very nearly did the destruction of the intellect for ever. The barber staggered back a pace or two as he heard it, for it was too terrific even for him, but it was for a very brief period that it had that stunning effect upon him, and then, with a full consciousness of the danger to which it subjected him, he sprang upon poor Tobias as a tiger might be supposed to do upon a lamb, and clutched him by the throat, exclaiming —

"Such another cry, and it is the last you ever live to utter, although it cover me with difficulties to escape the charge of killing you. Peace! I say, peace!"

This exhortation was quite needless, for Tobias could not have uttered a word, had he been ever so much inclined to do so; the barber held his throat with such an iron clutch, as if it had been in a vise.

"Villain," growled Todd, "villain; so this is the way in which you have dared to disregard my injunctions. But no matter, no matter! — you shall have plenty of leisure to reflect upon what you have done for yourself. Fool! to think that you could cope with me — Sweeney Todd! Ha! ha!"

He burst into a laugh, so much more hideous, than his ordinary efforts in that way, that, had Tobias heard it — which he did not, for his head had dropped upon his breast, and he had become insensible — it would have terrified him almost as much as Sweeney Todd's sudden appearance had done.

"So," muttered the barber, "he has fainted, has he? Dull child, that is all the better. For once in a way, Tobias, I will carry you — not to oblige you, but to oblige myself. By all that's damnable, it was a lively thought that brought me here to-night, or else I might, by the dawn of the morning, have had some very troublesome inquiries made of me."

He took Tobias up as easily as if he had been an infant, and strode from the chambers with him, leaving Mrs. Ragg to draw whatever inference she chose from his absence; but feeling convinced that she was too much under his control, to take any steps of a nature to give him the smallest amount of uneasiness.

"The woman," he muttered to himself, "is a double-distilled ass, and can be made to believe anything, so that I have no fear whatever of her. I dare not kill Tobias, because it is necessary, in case of the matter being at any other period mentioned, that his mother shall be in a position to swear that she saw him after this night alive and well."

The barber strode through the Temple, carrying the boy, who seemed not at all in a hurry to recover from the nervous and partial state of suffocation into which he had fallen. As they passed through the gate opening into Fleet-street, the porter, who knew the barber well by sight, said—

"Hilloa, Mr. Todd, is that you? Why, who are you carrying?"

"Yes, it's I," said Todd, "and I am carrying my apprentice boy, Tobias Ragg, poor fellow."

"Poor fellow! — why, what's the matter with him?"

"I can hardly tell you, but he seems to me and to his mother to have gone out of his senses. Good night to you, good night. I'm looking for a coach."

"Good night, Mr. Todd; I don't think you'll get one nearer than the market — what a kind thing now of him to carry the boy! It ain't every master would do that; but we must not judge of people by their looks, and even Sweeney Todd, though he has a face that one would not like to meet in a lonely place on a dark night, may be a kind-hearted man."

Sweeney Todd walked rapidly down Fleet-street, towards old Fleet Market, which was then in all its glory, if that could be called glory which consisted in all sorts of filth, enough to produce a pestilence within the city of London. When there, he addressed a large bundle of great coats, in the middle of which was supposed to be a hackney coachman of the regular old school, and who was lounging over his vehicle, which was as long and lumbering as a city barge.

"Jarvey," he said, "what will you take me to Peckham Rye for?"

"Peckham Rye — you and the boy — there ain't any more of you waiting round the corner, are there —'cos, you know, that won't be fair?"

"No, no, no."

"Well, don't be in a passion, master. I only asked, you know, so you need not be put out about it; I will take you for twelve shillings, and that's what I call remarkably cheap, all things considered."

"I'll give half the amount," said Sweeney Todd, "and you may consider yourself well paid."

"Half, master? — that is cutting it low; but, howsomdever, I suppose I must put up with it, and take you. Get in, I must try and make it up by some better fare out of somebody else."

The barber paid no heed to these renewed remonstrances of the coachman, but got into the vehicle, carrying Tobias with him, apparently with great care

THE BARBER CARRIES OFF TOBIAS TO A PRIVATE MAD-HOUSE.

and consideration; but when the coach door closed, and no one was observing him, he flung him down among the straw that was at the bottom of the vehicle, and resting his immense feet upon him, he gave one of his disagreeable laughs, as he said—

"Well, I think I have you now, Master Tobias; your troubles will soon be over. I am really very much afraid that you will die suddenly, and then there will be an end of you altogether, which will be a very sad thing, though I don't think I shall go into mourning, because I have an opinion that that only keeps alive the bitterness of regret, and that it's a great deal better done without, Master Tobias."

The hackney coach swung about from side to side, in the proper approved manner of hackney coaches in the olden time, when they used to be called "bone setters," and to be thought wonderful if they made a progress of three miles and a half an hour. This was the sort of vehicle, then, in which poor Tobias, still perfectly insensible, was rumbled over Blackfriars-bridge, and so on towards Peckham, which Sweeney Todd had announced to be his place of destination. Going at the rate they did, it was nearly two hours before they arrived upon Peckham Rye; and any one acquainted with that locality is well aware that there are two roads, the one to the left, and the other to the right, both of which are pleasantly enough studded with villa residences. Sweeney Todd directed the coachman to take the road to the left, which he accordingly did, and they pursued it for a distance of about a mile and a half. It must not be supposed that this pleasant district of country was then in the state it is now, as regards inhabitants or cultivation. On the contrary, it was rather a wild spot, on which now and then a serious robbery had been committed; and which had witnessed some of the exploits of those highwaymen, whose adventures, in the present day, if one may judge from the public patronage they may receive, are viewed with such a great amount of interest.* There was a lonely, large, rambling, old-looking house by the way side, on the left. A high wall surrounded it, which only allowed the topmost portion of it to be visible, and that presented great symptoms of decay, in the dilapidated character of the chimney-pot, and the general appearance of discomfort which pervaded it. There Sweeney Todd directed the coachman to stop, and when the vehicle, after swinging to and fro for several minutes, did indeed at last resolve itself into a state of repose, Sweeney Todd got out himself, and rang a bell, the handle of which hung invitingly at the gate. He had to wait several minutes before an answer was given to this summons, but at length a noise proceeded from within, as if several bars and bolts were being withdrawn; and presently the door was opened, and a huge, rough-looking man made his appearance on the threshold.

"Well! what is it now?" he cried.

"I have a patient for Mr. Fogg," said Sweeney Todd. "I want to see him immediately."

"Oh! well, the more the merrier: it don't matter to me a bit. Have you got him with you — and is he tolerably quiet?"

"It's a mere boy, and he is not violently mad, but very decidedly so as regards what he says."

---

* *A reference to the popularity of highway robbers as subjects for other "penny dreadfuls" and broadsheet ballads.*

"Oh! that's it, is it? He can say what he likes here, it can make no difference in the world to us. Bring him in — Mr. Fogg is in his own room."

"I know the way: you take charge of the lad, and I will go and speak to Mr. Fogg about him. But stay, give the coachman these six shillings, and discharge him."

The doorkeeper of the lunatic asylum, for such it was, went out to obey the injunctions of Sweeney Todd, while that rascally individual himself walked along a wide passage to a door which was at the further extremity of it.

CHAPTER XIX.

THE MADHOUSE CELL.

WHEN THE PORTER OF THE MADHOUSE went out to the coach, his first impression was, that the boy, who was said to be insane, was dead — for not even the jolting ride to Peckham had been sufficient to arouse him to a consciousness of how he was situated; and there he lay still at the bottom of the coach alike insensible to joy or sorrow.

"Is he dead?" said the man to the coachman.

"How should I know?" was the reply; "he may be or he may not, but I want to know how long I am to wait here for my fare?"

"There is your money, be off with you. I can see now that the boy is all right, for he breathes, although it's after an odd fashion that he does so. I should rather think he has had a knock on the head, or something of that kind."

As he spoke, he conveyed Tobias within the building, and the coachman, since he had got his six shillings, feeling that he had no further interest in the matter, drove away at once, and paid no more attention to it whatever.

When Sweeney Todd reached the door at the end of the passage, he tapped at it with his knuckles, and a voice cried —

"Who knocks — who knocks? Curses on you all! Who knocks?"

Sweeney Todd did not make any verbal reply to this polite request, but opening the door he walked into the apartment, which is one that really deserves some description. It was a large room with a vaulted roof, and in the centre was a superior oaken table, at which sat a man considerably advanced in years, as was proclaimed by his grizzled locks that graced the sides of his head, but whose herculean frame and robust constitution had otherwise successfully resisted the assaults of time. A lamp swung from the ceiling, which had a shade over the top of it, so that it cast a tolerably bright glow upon the table below, which was

TOBIAS IN THE HANDS OF THE MAD-HOUSE KEEPERS.

covered with books and papers, as well as glasses and bottles of different kinds, which showed that the madhouse-keeper was, at all events, as far as himself was concerned, not at all indifferent to personal comfort. The walls, however, presented the most curious aspect, for they were hung with a variety of tools and implements, which would have puzzled any one not initiated into the matter even to guess at their uses. These were, however, in point of fact, specimens of the different kinds of machinery which were used for the purpose of coercing the unhappy persons whose evil destiny made them members of that establishment.

Those were what is "called the good old times," when all sorts of abuses flourished in perfection, and when the unhappy insane were actually punished as if they were guilty of some great offence. Yes, and worse than that were they punished, for a criminal who might have injustice done to him by any who were in authority over him, could complain, and if he got hold of a person of higher power, his complaints might be listened to; but no one heeded what was said by the poor maniac, whose bitterest accusations of his keepers, let their conduct be what it might, was only listened to and set down as a further proof of his mental disorder. This was indeed a most awful and sad state of things, and, to the disgrace of this country, it is a social evil allowed until very late years to continue in full force. *

Mr. Fogg, the madhouse-keeper, fixed his keen eyes from beneath his shaggy brows, upon Sweeney Todd, as the latter entered his apartment, and then he said —

"Mr. Todd, I think, unless my memory deceives me."

"The same," said the barber, making a hideous face, "I believe I am not easily forgotten."

"True," said Mr. Fogg, as he reached a book, the edge of which was cut into a lot of little slips, on each of which was a capital letter, in the order of the alphabet — "true, you are not easily forgotten, Mr. Todd."

He then opened the book at the letter T, and read from it: —

"Mr. Sweeney Todd, Fleet-street, London, paid one year's keep and burial of Thomas Simkins, aged 15, found dead in his bed, after a residence in the asylum of 10 months and 4 days. I think, Mr. Todd, that was our last little transaction; what can I do now for you, sir?"

"I am rather unfortunate," said Todd, "with my boys. I have got another here, who has shown such decided symptoms of insanity, that it becomes absolutely necessary to place him under your care."

"Indeed! — does he rave?"

"Why, yes he does, and it's the most absurd nonsense in the world that he raves about; for, to hear him, one would really think that, instead of being one of the most humane of men, I was, in point of fact, an absolute murderer."

"A murderer, Mr. Todd!"

"Yes, a murderer — a murderer to all intents and purposes; could anything be more absurd than such an accusation? — I, that have the milk of human kindness flowing in every vein, and whose very appearance ought to be sufficient to convince anybody at once of my kindness of disposition."

Sweeney Todd finished his speech by making such a hideous face, that the madhouse-keeper could not for the life of him tell what to say to it; and then

---

* Abuses in madhouses were a hot topic in the late 1840s, as Parliament had just passed the Lunacy Act of 1845 to curb them, and updated it in 1846 and 1847. The worst abuses occurred in private madhouses, as opposed to county-run ones.

there came one of those short, disagreeable laughs which Todd would at times utter, which, somehow or other, never appeared exactly to come from his mouth, but always made people look up at the walls and ceiling of the apartment in which they were, in great doubt as to whence the remarkable sound came.

"For how long," said the madhouse-keeper, "do you think this malady will continue?"

"I will pay," said Sweeney Todd, as he leaned over the table, and looked in the face of his questioner, "I will pay for twelve months; but I don't think between you and I, that the case will last anything like so long — I think he will die suddenly."

"I shouldn't wonder if he did. Some of our patients do die very suddenly, and, somehow or other, we never know exactly how it happens; but it must be some sort of fit, for they are found dead in the morning in their beds, and then we bury them privately and quietly, without troubling anybody about it at all, which is decidedly the best way, because it saves a great annoyance to friends and relations, as well as prevents any extra expense which otherwise might be foolishly gone to."

"You are wonderfully correct and considerate," said Todd, "and it's no more than what I expected from you, or what any one might expect from a person of your great experience, knowledge, and acquirements. I must confess I am quite delighted to hear you talk in so elevated a strain."

"Why," said Mr. Fogg, with a strange leer upon his face, "we are forced to make ourselves useful, like the rest of the community; and we could not expect people to send their mad friends and relatives here, unless we took good care that their ends and views were answered by so doing. We make no remarks, and we ask no questions. Those are the principles upon which we have conducted business so successfully and so long; those are the principles upon which we shall continue to conduct it, and to merit, we hope, the patronage of the British public."

"Unquestionably — most unquestionably."

"You may as well introduce me to your patient at once, Mr. Todd, for I suppose, by this time, he has been brought into this house."

"Certainly, certainly — I shall have great pleasure in showing him to you."

The madhouse-keeper rose, and so did Mr. Todd, and the former, pointing to the bottles and glasses on the table, said —

"When this business is settled, we can have a friendly glass together."

To this proposition Sweeney Todd assented with a nod, and then they both proceeded to what was called a reception-room in the asylum, and where poor Tobias had been conveyed and laid upon a table, when he showed slight symptoms of recovering from the state of insensibility into which he had fallen, and a man was sluicing water on his face by the assistance of a hearth broom occasionally dipped into a pailful of that fluid.

"Quite young," said the madhouse-keeper, as he looked upon the pale and interesting face of Tobias.

"Yes," said Sweeney Todd, "he is young — more's the pity — and, of course, we deeply regret his present situation."

"Oh, of course, of course; but see, he opens his eyes, and will speak directly."

"Rave, you mean, rave!" said Todd; "don't call it speaking, it is not entitled to the name. Hush! listen to him."

"Where am I?" said Tobias, "where am I? Todd is a murderer — I denounce him."

"You hear — you hear?" said Todd.

"Mad indeed," said the keeper.

"Oh, save me from him — save me from him!" said Tobias, fixing his eyes upon Mr. Fogg. "Save me from him; it is my life he seeks because I know his secrets. He is a murderer — and many a person comes into his shop, who never leaves it again in life, if at all."

"You hear him?" said Todd. "Was there ever anybody so mad?"

"Desperately mad," said the keeper. "Come, come, young fellow, we shall be under the necessity of putting you in a strait waistcoat if you go on in that way. We must do it, for there is no help in such cases if we don't."

Todd slunk back into the dark of the apartment, so that he was not seen, and Tobias continued, in an imploring tone —

"I do not know who you are, sir, or where I am; but let me beg of you to cause the house of Sweeney Todd, the barber, in Fleet-street, near St. Dunstan's church, to be searched, and you will find that he is a murderer. There are at least a hundred hats, quantities of walking sticks, umbrellas, watches, and rings, all belonging to unfortunate persons who, from time to time, have met with their deaths through him."

"How uncommonly mad!" said Mr. Fogg.

"No, no," said Tobias, "I am not mad. Why call me mad, when the truth or falsehood of what I say can be ascertained so easily? Search his house, and if those things be not found there, say that I am mad, and have but dreamed of them. I do not know how he kills the people. That is a great mystery to me yet; but that he does kill them, I have no doubt — I cannot have a doubt."

"Watson!" cried the mad-house keeper. "Hilloa! here, Watson."

"I am here, sir," said the man, who had been dashing water upon poor Tobias's face.

"You will take this lad, Watson, as he seems extremely feverish and unsettled. You will take him and shave his head, Watson, and put a strait waistcoat upon him, and let him be put in one of the dark, damp cells. We must be careful of him, and too much light encourages delirium and fever."

"Oh! no, no!" cried Tobias; "What have I done that I should be subjected to such cruel treatment? what have I done that I should be placed in a cell? If this be a madhouse, I am not mad. Oh! have mercy upon me! — have mercy upon me!"

"You will give him nothing but bread and water, Watson; and the first symptom of his recovery, which will produce better treatment, will be his exonerating his master from what he has said about him; for he must be mad so long as he continues to accuse such a gentleman as Mr. Todd of such things; nobody but a mad man or a mad boy would think of it."

"Then," said Tobias, "I shall continue mad; for if it be madness to know and aver that Sweeney Todd, the barber, of Fleet-street, is a murderer, mad am I, for I know it, and aver it. It is true — it is true."

"Take him away, Watson, and do as I desired you. I begin to find that the boy is a very dangerous character, and more viciously mad than anybody we have had here for a considerable time."

The man named Watson seized upon Tobias, who again uttered a shriek something similar to the one which had come from his lips when Sweeney Todd clutched hold of him in his mother's room. But they were used to such things in that madhouse, and cared little for them, so no one heeded the cry in the least; but poor Tobias was carried to the door half maddened in reality by the horrors that surrounded him. Just as he was being conveyed out, Sweeney Todd stepped up to him, and putting his mouth close to his ear, he whispered —

"Ha! ha! Tobias! how do you feel now? Do you think Sweeney Todd will be hung, or will you die in the cell of a madhouse?"

CHAPTER XX.

THE NEW COOK TO MRS. LOVETT GETS TIRED OF HIS SITUATION.

FROM WHAT WE HAVE ALREADY HAD occasion to record about Mrs. Lovett's new cook, who ate so voraciously in the cellar, our readers will no doubt be induced to believe that he was a gentleman likely enough soon to be tired of his situation. To a starving man, and one who seemed completely abandoned even by hope, Lovett's bake-house, with an unlimited leave to eat as much as possible, must of course present itself in the most desirable and lively colours: and no wonder, therefore, that, banishing all scruple, a man so placed, would take the situation with very little inquiry. But people will tire of good things; and it is a remarkable well-authenticated fact that human nature is prone to be discontented. And those persons who are well acquainted with the human mind, and who know well how little value people set upon things which they possess, while those which they are pursuing, and which seem to be beyond their reach, assume the liveliest colours imaginable, adopt various means of turning this to account. Napoleon took good care that the meanest of his soldiers should see in perspective the possibility of grasping a marshal's baton. Confectioners at the present day, when they take a new apprentice, tell him to eat as much as he likes of those tempting tarts and sweetmeats, one or two of which before had been a most delicious treat. The soldier goes on fighting away, and never gets the marshal's baton. The confectioner's boy crams himself with Banbury cakes, gets dreadfully sick, and never touches one afterwards. And now, to revert to our friend in Mrs. Lovett's bakehouse. At first everything was delightful, and, by the aid of the machinery, he found that it was no difficult matter to keep up the supply of pies by really a very small amount of manual labour. And that labour also was such a labour of love, for the pies were delicious; there could be no mistake about that. He tasted them half cooked, he tasted them wholly, and he tasted them over-done; hot and cold; pork and veal with seasoning, and without seasoning, until at last he had had them in every possible way and shape; and when the fourth day came after his arrival in the cellar, he might have been sitting in rather a contemplative attitude with a pie before him. It was twelve o'clock: he had heard that sound come from the shop. Yes, it was twelve o'clock, and he had eaten nothing yet; but he kept his eye fixed upon the pie that lay untouched before him.

"The pies are all very well," he said; "in fact, of course they are capital pies; and now that I see how they are made, and know that there is nothing wrong in them, I, of course, relish them more than ever; but one can't always live upon pies; it's quite impossible one can subsist upon pies from one end of the year to the other, if they were the finest pies the world ever saw, or ever will see. I don't say anything against the pies — I know they are made of the finest flour, the best possible butter, and that the meat, which comes from God knows where, is the most delicate looking and tender I ever ate in all my life."

He stretched out his hand and broke a small portion of the crust from the pie that was before him, and he tried to eat it. He certainly did succeed; but it was a great effort; and when he had done, he shook his head, saying —

"No, no! — d — n it! I cannot eat it, and that's the fact — one cannot be continually eating pies: it is out of the question, quite out the question; and all I have to remark is — d — n the pies! I really don't think I shall be able to let another one pass my lips."

He rose and paced with rapid strides the place in which he was, and then suddenly he heard a noise; and, looking up, he saw a trap door in the roof open, and a sack of flour begin gradually to come down.

"Hilloa, hilloa!" he cried, "Mrs. Lovett — Mrs. Lovett!"

Down came the flour, and the trap door was closed.

"Oh, I can't stand this sort of thing," he exclaimed; "I cannot be made into a mere machine for the manufacture of pies. I cannot and will not endure it — it is past all bearing."

For the first time almost since his incarceration, for such it really was, he began to think that he would take an accurate survey of the place where this tempting manufacture was carried on. The fact was, his mind had been so intensely occupied during the time he had been there in providing merely for his physical wants, that he had scarcely had time to think or reason upon the probabilities of an uncomfortable termination of his career; but now, when he had really become quite surfeited with the pies, and tired of the darkness and gloom of the place, many unknown fears began to creep across him, and he really trembled, as he asked himself what was to be the end of all. It was with such a feeling as this that he now set about a careful and accurate survey of the place; and taking a little lamp in his hand, he resolved upon peering into every corner of it, with a hope that surely he should find some means by which he should effect an escape from what otherwise threatened to be an intolerable imprisonment.

The vault in which the ovens were situated was the largest; and although a number of smaller ones communicated with it, containing the different mechanical contrivances for pie-making, he could not from any one of them discover an outlet. But it was to the vault where the meat was deposited upon stone shelves that he paid the greatest share of attention, for to that vault he felt convinced there must be some hidden and secret means of ingress, and therefore of egress likewise, or else how came the shelves always so well stocked with meat as they were? This vault was larger than any of the other subsidiary ones, and the roof was very high, and, come into it when he would, it always happened that he found meat enough upon the shelves, cut into large lumps, and sometimes into slices, to make a batch of pies with. When it got there, was not so much a mystery to him as how it got there; for, of course, as he must sleep sometimes, he concluded, naturally enough, that it was brought in by some means during the period that he devoted to repose. He stood in the centre of this vault with the lamp in his hand, and he turned slowly round, surveying the walls and the ceilings with the most critical and marked attention, but not the smallest appearance of an outlet was observable. In fact, the walls were so entirely filled up with the stone shelves, that there was no space left for a door; and as for the ceiling, it seemed perfectly entire. Then the floor was of earth; so that the idea of a trap door opening in it was out of the question, because there was no one on his side of it to place the earth again over it, and give it its compact and usual appearance.

"This is most mysterious," he said; "and if ever I could have been brought to believe that any one had the assistance of the devil himself in conducting human affairs, I should say that by some means Mrs. Lovett had made it worth the while of that elderly individual to assist her; for, unless the meat gets here by some supernatural agency, I really cannot see how it can get here at all. And yet here it is — so fresh, and pure, and white-looking, although I never could tell the pork from the veal myself, for they seemed to me both alike."

He now made a still narrower examination of this vault, but he gained nothing by that. He found that the walls at the back of the shelves were composed of flat pieces of stone, which, no doubt, were necessary for the support of the shelves themselves; but beyond that he made no further discovery, and he was about leaving the place, when he fancied he saw some writing on the inner side of the door. A closer inspection convinced him that there were a number of lines written with lead pencil, and after some difficulty he decyphered them as follows: —

Whatever unhappy wretch reads these lines may bid adieu to the world and all hope, for he is a doomed man! He will never emerge from these vaults with life, for there is a secret connected with them so awful and so hideous, that to write it makes one's blood curdle, and the flesh to creep upon my bones. That secret is this — and you may be assured, whoever is reading these lines, that I write the truth, and that it is as impossible to make that awful truth worse by any exaggeration, as it would be by a candle at mid-day to attempt to add any new lustre to the sunbeams.

Here, most unfortunately, the writing broke off, and our friend, who, up to this point, had perused the lines with the most intense interest, felt great bitterness of disappointment, from the fact that enough should have been written to stimulate his curiosity to the highest possible point, but not enough to gratify it.

"This is, indeed, most provoking," he exclaimed. "What can this most dreadful secret be, which it is impossible to exaggerate? I cannot, for a moment, divine to what it can allude."

In vain he searched over the door for some more writing — there was none to be found, and from the long straggling pencil-mark, which followed the last word, it seemed as if he who had been then writing had been interrupted, and possibly met the fate that he had predicted, and was about to explain the reason of.

"This is worse than no information. I had better have remained in ignorance than have received so indistinct a warning; but they shall not find me an easy victim, and, besides, what power on earth can force me to make pies unless I like, I should wish to know?"

As he stepped out of the place in which the meat was kept into the large vault where the ovens were, he trod upon a piece of paper that was lying upon the ground, and which he was quite certain he had not observed before. It was fresh and white, and clean too, so that it could not have been long there, and he picked it up with some curiosity. That curiosity was, however, soon turned to dismay when he saw what was written upon it, which was to the following effect, and well calculated to produce a considerable amount of alarm in the breast of any one situated as he was, so entirely friendless and so entirely hopeless of any extraneous aid in those dismal vaults, which he began, with a shudder, to suspect would be his tomb: —

You are getting dissatisfied, and therefore it becomes necessary to explain to you your real position, which is simply this: — You are a prisoner, and were such from the first moment that you set foot where you now are; and you will find, unless you are resolved upon sacrificing your life, that your best plan will be to quietly give into the circumstances in which you find yourself placed. Without going into any argument or details upon the subject, it is sufficient to inform you that so long as you continue to make the pies, you will be safe; but if you refuse, then the first time you are caught asleep your throat will be cut.

This document was so much to the purpose, and really had so little of verbosity about it, that it was extremely difficult to doubt its sincerity. It dropped from the half-paralysed hands of that man, who, in the depth of his distress, and urged on by great necessity, had accepted a situation that he would have given worlds to escape from, had he been possessed of them.

"Gracious Heaven!" he exclaimed, "and am I then indeed condemned to such a slavery? Is it possible, that even in the heart of London, I am a prisoner, and without the means of resisting the most frightful threats that are uttered against me? Surely, surely this must be all a dream! It is too terrific to be true!"

He sat down upon that low stool where his predecessor had sat before, receiving his death-wound from the assassin who had glided in behind him, and dealt him that crashing blow, whose only mercy was that it had at once deprived the victim of existence. He could have wept bitterly, wept as he there sat, for he thought over days long passed away, of opportunities let go by with the heedless laugh of youth; he thought over all the chances and fortunes of his life, and now to find himself the miserable inhabitant of a cellar, condemned to a mean and troublesome employment, without even the liberty of leaving that, to starve if he chose, upon pain of death — a frightful death, which had been threatened him, was indeed torment! No wonder that at times he felt himself unnerved, and that a child might have conquered him, while at other moments such a feeling of despair would come across him, that he called aloud upon his enemies to make their appearance, and give him at least the chance of a struggle for his life.

"If I am to die," he cried, "let me die with some weapon in my hand, as a brave man ought, and I will not complain, for there is little indeed in life now which should induce me to cling to it; but I will not be murdered in the dark."

He sprang to his feet, and rushing up to the door, which opened from the house into the vaults, he made a violent and desperate effort to shake it. But such a contingency as this had surely been looked forward to and provided against, for the door was of amazing strength, and most effectually resisted all his efforts, so that the result of his endeavours was but to exhaust himself, and he staggered back, panting and despairing, to the seat he had so recently left. Then he heard a voice, and upon looking up he saw that the small square opening in the upper part of the door, through which he had been before addressed, was open, and a face there appeared; but it was not the face of Mrs. Lovett. On the contrary, it was a large and hideous male physiognomy, and the voice that came from it was croaking and harsh, sounding most unmusically upon the ears of the unfortunate man who was thus made a victim to Mrs. Lovett's pie popularity.

"Continue at your work," said the voice, "or death will be your portion as soon as sleep overcomes you, and you sink exhausted to that repose which you will never awaken from, except to feel the pangs of death, and to be conscious that you are weltering in your blood. Continue at your work, and you will escape all this — neglect it, and your doom is sealed."

"What have I done that I should be made such a victim of? Let me go, and I will swear never to divulge the fact that I have been in these vaults, so I cannot disclose any of their secrets, even if knew them."

"Make pies," said the voice, "eat them, and be happy. How many a man would envy your position — withdrawn from all the struggles of existence, amply provided with board and lodging, and engaged in a pleasant and delightful occupation; it is astonishing how you can be dissatisfied!"

Bang! went the little square orifice at the top of the door, and the voice was heard no more. The jeering mockery of those tones, however, still lingered upon the ear of the unhappy prisoner, and he clasped his head in his hands with a fearful impression upon his brain that he surely must be going mad.

"He will drive me to insanity," he cried; "already I feel a sort of slumber stealing over me for want of exercise, and the confined air of these vaults hinder me from taking regular repose; but now, if I close an eye, I shall expect to find the assassin's knife at my throat."

He sat for some time longer, and not even the dread he had of sleep could prevent a drowsiness creeping across his faculties, and this weariness would not be shaken off by any ordinary means, until at length he sprang to his feet, and shaking himself roughly, like one determined to be wide awake, he said to himself, mournfully —

"I must do their bidding or die; hope may be a delusion here, but I cannot altogether abandon it, and not until its faintest image has departed from my breast can I lie down to sleep and say — Let death come in any shape it may, it is welcome."

With a desperate and despairing energy he set about replenishing the furnaces of the oven, and, when he had got them all in a good state, he commenced manufacturing a batch of one hundred pies, which, when he had finished and placed upon the tray, and set the machine in motion which conducted them up to the shop, he considered to be a sort of price paid for his continued existence, and flinging himself upon the ground, he fell into a deep slumber.

––––––––

CHAPTER XXI.

THE NIGHT AT THE MADHOUSE.

WHEN SWEENEY TODD HAD, WITH SUCH diabolical want of feeling, whispered the few words of mockery which we have recorded in Tobias's ear, when he was carried out of Mr. Fogg's reception-room to be taken to a cell, the villanous barber drew back and indulged in rather a longer laugh than usual.

"Mr. Todd," said Fogg, "I find that you still retain your habit of merriment; but yours ain't the most comfortable laugh in the world, and we seldom hear anything equal to it, even from one of our cells."

"No!" said Sweeney Todd, "I don't suppose you do, and for my part I never heard of a cell laughing yet."

"Oh! you know what I mean, Mr. Todd, well enough."

"That may be," said Todd, "but it would be just as well to say it for all that. I think, however, as I came in you said something about refreshment?"

"I certainly did; and, if you will honour me by stepping back to my room, I think I can offer you, Mr. Todd, a glass of as nice wine as the king himself could put on his table, if he were any judge of that commodity, which I am inclined to think he is not."

"What do you expect," said Sweeney Todd, "that such an idiot should be a judge of? — but I shall have great pleasure in tasting your wine, for I have no hesitation in saying that my work to-night has made me thirsty."

At this moment a shriek was heard, and Sweeney Todd shrank away from the door.

"Oh! it's nothing, it's nothing," said Mr. Fogg; "if you had resided here as long as I have, you would get accustomed to now and then hearing a slight noise. The worst of it is, when half a dozen of the mad fellows get shrieking against each other in the middle of the night. Then, I grant, it is a little annoying."

"What do you do with them?"

"We send in one of the keepers with the lash, and soon put a stop to that. We are forced to keep the upper hand of them, or else we should have no rest. Hark! do you not hear that fellow now? — he is generally pretty quiet, but he has taken it into his head to be outrageous to-day; but one of my men will soon put a stop to that. This way, Mr. Todd, if you please, and as we don't often meet, I think when we do we ought to have a social glass."

Sweeney Todd made several horrible faces as he followed the madhouse-keeper, and he looked as if it would have given him quite as much pleasure, and no doubt it would, to brain that individual, as to drink his wine, although probably he would have preferred doing the latter process first, and executing the former afterwards, and at his leisure. They soon reached the room which was devoted to the use of Mr. Fogg and his friends, and which contained the many little curiosities in the way of madhouse discipline that were in that age considered indispensable in such establishments. Mr. Fogg moved away with his hands a great number of the books and papers which were on the table, so as to leave a vacant space, and then drawing the cork of a bottle, he filled himself a large glass of its contents, and invited Sweeney Todd to do the same, who was by no means slow in following his example.

While these two villains are carousing, and caring nothing for the scenes of misery with which they are surrounded, poor Tobias, in conformity with the orders that had been issued with regard to him, was conveyed along a number of winding passages, and down several staircases, towards the cells of the establishment. In vain he struggled to get free from his captor — as well might a hare have struggled in the fangs of a wolf — nor were his cries at all heeded; although, now and then, the shrieks he uttered were terrible to hear, and enough to fill any one with dismay.

"I am not mad," said he, "indeed I am not mad — let me go, and I will say nothing — not one word shall ever pass my lips regarding Mr. Todd — let me go, oh, let me go, and I will pray for you as long as I live."

Mr. Watson whistled a lively tune.

"If I promise — if I swear to tell nothing, Mr. Todd will not wish me kept here — all he wants is my silence, and I will take any oath he likes. Speak to him for me, I implore you, and let me go."

Mr. Watson commenced the second part of his lively tune, and by that time he reached a door, which he unlocked, and then, setting down Tobias upon the threshold, he gave him a violent kick, which flung him down two steps on to the stone floor of a miserable cell, from the roof of which continual moisture was dripping, the only accommodation it possessed being a truss of damp straw flung into one corner.

"There," said Mr. Watson, "my lad, you can stay there and make yourself comfortable till somebody comes to shave your head, and after that you will find yourself quite a gentleman."

"Mercy! mercy — have mercy upon me!"

"Mercy! — what the devil do you mean by mercy? Well, that's a good joke; but I can tell you, you have come to the wrong shop for that; we don't keep it in stock here, and if we wanted ever so little of it, we should have to go somewhere else for it."

Mr. Watson laughed so much at his own joke, that he felt quite amiable, and told Tobias that if he were perfectly quiet, and said "thank you" for everything, he wouldn't put him on the strait waistcoat, although Mr. Fogg had ordered it; "for," added Mr. Watson, "so far as that goes, I don't care a straw what Mr. Fogg says, or what he does; he can't do without me, damn him! because I know too many of his secrets."

Tobias made no answer to this promise, but he lay upon his back on the floor of the cell wringing his hands despairingly, and feeling that almost already the very atmosphere of that place seemed pregnant with insanity, and giving himself up for lost entirely.

"I shall never — never," he said, "look upon the bright sky and the green fields again. I shall be murdered here, because I know too much; what can save me now? Oh, what an evil chance it was that brought me back again to my mother, when I ought to have been far, far away by this time, instead of being, as I know I am, condemned to death in this frightful place. Despair seizes upon me! What noise is that — a shriek? Yes, yes, there is some other blighted heart beside mine in this dreadful house. Oh, Heaven! what will become of me? I feel already stifled and sick, and faint with the air of this dreadful cell. Help, help, help! have mercy upon me, and I will do anything, promise anything, swear anything."

If poor Tobias had uttered his complaints on the most desolate shore that ever a shipwrecked mariner was cast upon, they could not have been more unheeded than they were in that house of terror. He screamed and shrieked for aid. He called upon all the friends he had ever known in early life, and at that moment he seemed to remember the name of every one who had ever uttered a kind word to him; and to those persons who, alas! could not hear him, but were far enough removed away from his cries, he called for aid in that hour of his deep distress. At length, faint, wearied and exhausted, he lay a mere living wreck in that damp, unwholesome cell, and felt almost willing that death should come and relieve him, at least from the pang of constantly expecting it! His cries, however, had had the effect of summoning up all the wild spirits in that building; and, as he now lay in the quiet of absolute exhaustion, he heard from far and near smothered cries and shrieks and groans, such as one might expect would fill the air of the infernal regions with dismal echoes. A cold and clammy perspiration broke out upon him, as these sounds each moment more plainly fell upon his ear, and as he gazed upon the profound darkness of the cell, his excited fancy began to people it with strange unearthly beings, and he could suppose that he saw hideous faces grinning at him, and huge mis-shapen creatures crawling on the walls, and floating in the damp, pestiferous atmosphere of the wretched cell. In vain he covered his eyes with his hands; those creatures of his imagination were not to be shut out from the mind, and he saw them, if possible, more vividly than before, and presenting themselves in more frightfully tangible shapes. Truly, if such visions should continue to haunt him, poor Tobias was likely enough to follow the fate of many others who had been placed in that establishment perfectly sane, but in a short time exhibited in it as raving lunatics.

"A NICE CLEAR COOL GLASS OF WINE," SAID Sweeney Todd, as he held up his glass between him and the light, "and pleasant drinking; so soft and mild in the mouth, and yet gliding down the throat with a pleasant strength of flavour!"

"Yes," said Mr. Fogg, "it might be worse. You see some patients, who are low and melancholy mad, require stimulants, and their friends send them wine. This is some that was so sent."

"Then you don't trouble the patients with it?"

"What! give a madman wine, while I am here in my senses to drink it? Oh, dear no! that won't do on any account."

"I should certainly, Mr. Fogg, not expect such an act of indiscretion from you, knowing you as I do to be quite a man of the world."

"Thank you for the compliment. This wine, now, was sent for an old gentleman who had turned so melancholy, that he not only would not take food enough to keep life and soul together, but he really terrified his friends so by threatening suicide that they sent him here for a few months; and, as stimulants were recommended for him, they sent this wine, you see; but I stimulated him without it quite as well, for I drink the wine myself and give him an infernal good kick or two every day, and that stimulates him, for it puts him in such a devil of a passion that I am quite sure he doesn't want any wine."

"A good plan," said Sweeney Todd, "but I wonder you don't contrive that your own private room should be free from the annoyance of hearing such sounds as those that have been coming upon my ears for the last five or ten minutes."

"It's impossible; you cannot get out of the way if you live in the house at all; and you see, as regards these mad fellows, they are quite like a pack of wolves, and when once one of them begins howling and shouting, the others are sure to chime in, in full chorus, and make no end of disturbance till we stop them, as I have already told you we do, with a strong hand."

"While I think of it," said Sweeney Todd, as he drew from his pocket a leathern bag, "while I think of it, I may as well pay you the year's money for the lad I have now brought you; you see I have not forgot the excellent rule you have of being paid in advance. There is the amount."

"Ah, Mr. Todd," said the madhouse-keeper as he counted the money, and then placed it in his pocket, "it's a pleasure to do business with a thorough business man like yourself. The bottle stands with you, Mr. Todd, and I beg you will not spare it. Do you know, Mr. Todd, this is a line of life which I have often thought would have suited you; I am certain you have a genius for such things."

"Not equal to you," said Todd; "but as I am fond, certainly, of what is strange and out of the way, some of the scenes and characters you come across would, I have no doubt, be highly entertaining to me."

"Scenes and characters — I believe you! During the course of a business like ours, we come across all sorts of strange things; and if I choose to do it, which of course I don't, I could tell a few tales which would make some people shake in their shoes; but I have no right to tell them, for I have been paid, and what the deuce is it to me?"

"Oh, nothing, of course nothing. But just while we are sipping our wine, now, couldn't you tell me something that would not be betraying anybody's confidence?"

"I could, I could; I don't mean to say that I could not, and I don't care much if I do to you."

CHAPTER XXII.

MR. FOGG'S STORY AT THE MADHOUSE TO SWEENEY TODD.

AFTER A SHORT PAUSE, DURING WHICH MR. FOGG appeared to be referring to the cells of memory, with the view of being refreshed in a matter that had long since been a by-gone, but which he desired to place as clearly before his listener as he could, in fact, to make, if possible, the relation real to him, and to omit nothing during its progress that should be told; or possibly, that amiable individual was engaged in considering if there were any salient point that might criminate himself, or give even a friend a handle to make use of against him; but apparently there was nothing of the kind, for, after a loud "hem!" he filled the glasses, saying —

"Well, now, as you are a friend, I don't mind telling you how we do business here — things that have been done, you know, by others; but I have had my share as well as others — I have known a thing or two, Mr. Todd, and I may say I have done a thing or two, too."

"Well, we must live and let live," said Sweeney Todd, "there's no going against that, you know; if all I have done could speak, why — but no matter, I am listening to you — however, if deeds could speak, one or two clever things would come out rather, I think."

"Ay, 'tis well they don't," said Mr. Fogg, with much solemnity, "if they did they would be constantly speaking at times when it would be very inconvenient to hear them, and dangerous besides."

"So it would," said Sweeney, "a still tongue makes a wise head — but then the silent system would bring no grist to the mill, and we must speak when we know we are right and among friends."

"Of course," said Fogg, "of course, that's the right use of speech, and one may as well be without it, as to have it and not use it; but come — drink, and fill again before I begin, and then to my tale. But we may as well have a sentiment. Sentiment, you know," continued Fogg, "is the very soul of friendship. What do you say to 'The heart that can feel for another?'"*

"With all my soul," said Sweeney Todd; "it's very touching — very touching, indeed. 'The heart that can feel for another!'" and as he spoke, he emptied the glass, which he pushed towards Fogg to refill.

"Well," said Fogg, as he complied, "we have had the sentiment, we may as well have the exemplification."

"Ha! ha! ha!" said Todd, "very good, very good indeed; pray go on, that will do capitally."

"I may as well tell you the whole matter, as it occurred; I will then let you know all I know, and in the same manner. None of the parties are now living, or, at least, they are not in this country, which is just the same thing, so far as I am concerned."

"Then that is an affair settled and done with," remarked Sweeney Todd, parenthetically.

"Yes, quite. — Well, it was one night — such a one as this, and pretty well about the same hour, perhaps somewhat earlier than this. However, it doesn't signify a straw about the hour, but it was quite night, a dark and wet night too, when a knock came at the street-door — a sharp double knock — it was. I was sitting alone, as I might have been now, drinking a glass or two of wine; I was startled, for I was thinking about an affair I had on hand at that very moment, of which there was a little stir. However, I went to the door, and peeped through a grating that I had there, and saw only a man; he had drawn his horse inside the gate, and secured him. He wore a large Whitney riding-coat, with a nap that would have thrown off a deluge. I fancied, or thought I could tell, that he meant no mischief; so I opened the door at once

---

* *A reference to* Jack Steadfast; or, The Heart that Can Feel for Another, *a then-well known broadsheet ballad, copies of which were sold in illustrated form by the same street hawkers who distributed each weekly episode of* Sweeney Todd.

and saw a tall, gentlemanly man, but wrapped up so, that you could not tell who or what he was; but my eyes are sharp, you know, Mr. Todd. We haven't seen so much of the world without learning to distinguish what kind of person one has to deal with?"

"I should think not," said Todd.

" 'Well,' said I, 'what is your pleasure, sir?'

"The stranger paused a moment or two before he made any reply to me.

" 'Is your name Fogg?' he said.

" 'Yes, it is,' said I; 'my name is Fogg — what is your pleasure with me, sir?'

" 'Why,' said he, after another pause, during which he fixed his keen eye very hard upon me — 'why, I wish to have a little private conversation with you, if you can spare so much time, upon a very important matter which I have in hand.'

" 'Walk in, sir,' said I, as soon as I heard what it was he wanted, and he followed me in. 'It is a very unpleasant night, and it's coming on to rain harder. I think it is fortunate you have got housed.'

" 'Yes,' he replied; 'but I am tolerably well protected against the rain, at all events.'

"He came into this very parlour, and took a seat before the fire, with his back to the light, so that I couldn't see his face very well. However, I was determined that I would be satisfied in these particulars, and so, when he had taken off his hat, I stirred up the fire, and had a blaze that illuminated the whole room, and which showed me the sharp, thin visage of my visitor, who was a dark man, with keen grey eyes that were very restless —'

" 'Will you have a glass of wine?' said I; 'the night is cold as well as wet.'

" 'Yes, I will,' he replied; 'I am cold with riding. You have a lonely place about here; your house, I see, stands alone too. You have not many neighbours.'

" 'No, sir,' said I, 'we hadn't need, for when any of the poor things set to screaming, it would make them feel very uncomfortable indeed.'

" 'So it would, there is an advantage in that to yourself as well as to them. It would be disagreeable to you to know that you were disturbing your neighbours, and they would feel equally uncomfortable in being disturbed, and yet you must do your duty.'

" 'Ay! to be sure,' said I; 'I must do my duty, and people won't pay me for letting madmen go, though they may for keeping them; and besides that, I think some on 'em would get their throats cut, if I did.'

" 'You are right — quite right,' said he; 'I am glad to find you of that mind, for I came to you concerning an affair that requires some delicacy about it, since it is a female patient.'

" 'Ah!' said I, 'I always pay great attention, very great attention; and I don't recollect a case, however violent it may be, but what I can overcome. I always make 'em acknowledge me, and there's much art in that.'

"'To be sure, there must be.'

"'And, moreover, they wouldn't so soon crouch and shrink away from me, and do what I tell 'em, if I did not treat them with kindness, that is, as far as is consistent with one's duty, for I mustn't forget that.'

"'Exactly,' he replied; 'those are my sentiments exactly.'

"'And now, sir, will you inform me in what way I can serve you?'

"'Why I have a relative, a female relative, who is unhappily affected with a brain disease; we have tried all we can do, without any effect. Do what we will, it comes to the same thing in the end.'

"'Ah!' said I; 'poor thing — what a dreadful thing it must be to you or any of her friends, who have the charge of her, to see her day by day an incurable maniac. Why, it is just as bad as when a friend or relative is dead, and you are obliged to have the dead body constantly in your house, and before your eyes.'

"'Exactly, my friend,' said the stranger; 'exactly, you are a man of discernment, Mr. Fogg. I see, that is truly the state of the case. You may then guess at the state of our feelings, when we have to part with one beloved by us.'

"As he spoke, he turned right round, and faced me, looking very hard into my face.

"'Well,' said I, 'yours is a hard case; but to have one afflicted about you in the manner the young lady is, is truly distressing; it's like having a perpetual lumbago in your back.'

"'Exactly,' said the stranger. 'I tell you what, you are the very man to do this thing for me.'

"'I am sure of it,' said I.

"'Then we understand each other, eh?' said the stranger. 'I must say I like your appearance, it is not often such people as you and I meet.'

"'I hope it will be to our mutual advantage,' said I, 'because such people don't meet every day, and we oughtn't to meet to no purpose; so, in anything delicate and confidential you may command me.'

"'I see, you are a clever man,' said he; 'well, well, I must pay you in proportion to your talents. How do you do business — by the job, or by the year?'

"'Well,' said I, 'where it's a matter of some nicety, it may be both — but it entirely depends upon circumstances. I had better know exactly what it is I have to do.'

"'Why, you see, it is a young female about eighteen, and she is somewhat troublesome — takes to screaming, and all that kind of thing. I want her taken care of, though you must be very careful she neither runs away nor suddenly commits any mischief, as her madness does not appear to me to have any particular form, and would at times completely deceive the best of us, and then suddenly she will break out violently, and snap or fly at anybody with her teeth.'

"'Is she so bad as that?'

"'Yes, quite. So it is quite impossible to keep her at home; and I expect it will be a devil of a job to get her here. I tell you what you shall have; I'll pay you your yearly charge for board and care, and I'll give you a ten-pound note for your trouble, if you'll come and assist me in securing her, and bringing her down. It will take some trouble.'

"'Very well,' said I, 'that will do, but you must double the note and make it twenty, if you please; it will cost something to come and do the thing well.'

"'I see — very well — we won't disagree about a ten-pound note; but you'll know how to dispose of her if she comes here.'

"'Oh, yes — very healthy place.'

"'But I don't know that health is a very great blessing to any one under such circumstances; indeed, who could regret an early grave to one so severely afflicted?'

"'Nobody ought,' said I; 'if they knew what mad people went through, they would not, I'm sure.'

"'That is very true again, but the fact is, they don't, and they only look at one side of the picture; for my own part, I think that it ought to be so ordained, that when people are so afflicted, nature ought to sink under the affliction, and so insensibly to revert to the former state of nonentity.'

"'Well,' said I, 'that may be as you please, I don't understand all that; but I tell you what, I hope if she were to die much sooner than you expect, you would not think it too much trouble to afford me some compensation for my loss.'

"'Oh dear no! and to show you that I shall entertain no such illiberal feeling, I will give you two hundred pounds, when the certificate of her burial can be produced. You understand me?'

"'Certainly.'

"'Her death will be of little value to me, without the legal proof,' said the stranger; 'so she must die at her own pleasure, or live while she can.'

"'Certainly,' said I.

"'But what terrifies me,' continued the stranger, 'most is, her terror-stricken countenance, always staring us in our faces; and it arose from her being terrified; indeed I think if she were thoroughly frightened, she would fall dead. I am sure, if any wickedly-disposed person were to do so, death would no doubt result.'

"'Ah!' said I, 'it would be a bad job; now tell me where I am to see you, and how about the particulars.'

"'Oh, I will tell you; now, can you be at the corner of Grosvenor-street, near Park-lane?'

"'Yes,' I replied, 'I will.'

"'With a coach too. I wish you to have a coach, and one that you can depend upon, because there may be a little noise. I will try to avoid it, if possible, but we cannot always do what we desire; but you must have good horses.'

"'Now, I tell you what is my plan; that is, if you don't mind the damages, if any happen.'

"'What are they?'

"'This:—suppose a horse falls, and is hurt, or an upset—would you stand the racket?'

"'I would, of course.'

"'Then listen to me; I have had more of these affairs than you have, no doubt. Well, then, I have had experience, which you have not. Now, I'll get a trotting-horse, and a covered cart or chaise—one that will go along well at ten miles an hour, and no mistake about it.'

"'But will it hold enough?'

"'Yes, four or five or six, and, upon a push, I have known eight to cram in it; but then you know we were not particular how we were placed; but still it will hold as many as a hackney coach, only not so conveniently; but then we have nobody in the affair to drive us, and there can't be too few.'

"'Well, that is perhaps best; but have you a man on whom you can depend?—because if you have, why, I would not be in the affair at all.'

"'You must,' said I; 'in the first place, I can depend upon one man best; him I must leave here to mind the place; so if you can manage the girl, I will drive, and I know the road as well as the way to my own mouth—I would rather have as few in it as possible.'

"'Your precaution is very good, and I think I will try and so manage it, that there shall be only you and I acquainted with the transaction; at all events, should it become necessary, it will be time enough to let some other person into the secret at the moment their services are required. That, I think, will be the best arrangement that I can come to—what do you say?'

"'That will do very well—when we get her here, and when I have seen her a few days, I can tell what to do with her.'

"'Exactly; and now, good night—there is the money I promised, and now again, good night! I shall see you at the appointed time.'

"'You will,' said I—'one glass more, it will do you good, and keep the rain out.'

"He took off a glass of wine, and then pulled his hat over his face, and left the house. It was a dark, wet night, and the wind blew, and we heard the sound of his horse's hoofs for some time; however, I shut the door and went in, thinking over in my own mind what would be the gain of my own exertions.

"WELL, AT THE APPOINTED HOUR, I BORROWED a chaise cart, a covered one, with what you call a head to it, and I trotted to town in it. At the appointed time I was at the corner of Grosvenor-street; it was late, and yet I waited there an hour or more before I saw any one. I walked into a little house to get a glass of spirits to keep up the warmth of the body, and when I came out again, I saw some one standing at my horse's head. I immediately went up.

"'Oh, you are here,' he said.

"'Yes I am,' said I, 'I have been here the Lord knows how long. Are you ready?'

"'Yes, I am; come,' said he, as he got into the cart — 'come to the place I shall tell you — I shall only get her into the cart, and you must do the rest.'

"'You'll come back with me; I shall want help on the road, and I have no one with me.'

"'Yes, I will come with you, and manage the girl, but you must drive, and take all the casualties of the road, for I shall have enough to do to hold her and keep her from screaming when she does awake.'

"'What! is she asleep?'

"'I have given her a small dose of laudanum, which will cause her to sleep comfortably for an hour or two, but the cold air and disturbance will most probably awaken her at first.'

"'Throw something over her, and keep her warm, and have something ready to thrust into her mouth, in case she takes to screaming, and then you are all right.'

"'Good,' he replied: 'now wait here. I am going to yon house. When I have entered, and disappeared several minutes, you may quietly drive up, and take your station on the other side of the lamp-post.'

"As he spoke he got out, and walked to a large house, which he entered softly, and left the door ajar; and after he had gone in, I walked the horse quietly up to the lamp-post, and as I placed it, the horse and front of the cart were completely in the dark. I had scarcely got up to the spot, when the door opened, and he looked out to see if anybody was passing. I gave him the word, and out he came, leaving the door, and came with what looked like a bundle of clothes, but which was the young girl and some clothes he had brought with him.

"'Give her to me,' said I, 'and jump up and take the reins; go on as quickly as you can.'

"I took the girl into my arms, and handed her into the back part of the chaise, while he jumped up, and drove away. I placed the young girl in an easy position upon some hay, and stuffed the clothes under her, so as to prevent the jolting from hurting her.

"'Well,' said I, 'you may as well come back here, and sit beside her: she is all right. You seem rather in a stew.'

"'Well, I have run with her in my arms, and altogether it has flurried me.'

"'You had better have some brandy,' said I.

"'No, no! don't stop.'

"'Pooh, pooh!' I replied, pulling up, 'here is the last house we shall come to, to have a good stiff tumbler of hot brandy and water.* Come, have you any change — about a sovereign† will do, because I shall want change on the road? Come, be quick.'

"He handed me a sovereign, saying —

"'Don't you think it's dangerous to stop — we may be watched, or she may wake.'

"'Not a bit of it. She snores too loudly to wake just now, and you'll faint without the cordial; so keep a good look-out upon the wench, and you will recover your nerves again.'

"As I spoke I jumped out, and got two glasses of brandy and water, hot, strong, and sweet, I had in about two minutes made, out of the house.

"'Here,' said I, 'drink — drink it all up — it will make your eyes start out of your head.'

"I spoke the truth, for what with my recommendations, and his nervousness and haste, he drank nearly half of it at a gulp.

"I shall never forget his countenance. Ha! ha! ha! I can't keep my mirth to myself. Just imagine the girl inside a covered cart, all dark, so dark that you could hardly see the outline of the shadow of a man, and then imagine, if you can, a pair of keen eyes, that shone in the dark like cat's eyes, suddenly give out a flash of light, and then turn round in their sockets, showing the whites awfully, and then listen to the fall of the glass, and see him grasp his throat with one hand, and thrust the other hand into his stomach. There was a queer kind of voice came from his throat, and then something like a curse and a groan escaped him.

"'Damn it,' said I, 'what is the matter now? — you've upset all the liquor — you are very nervous — you had better have another dose.'

"'No more — no more,' he said faintly and huskily, 'no more — for God's sake no more. I am almost choked — my throat is scalded, and my entrails on fire!'

"'I told you it was hot,' said I.

"'Yes, hot, boiling hot — go on. I'm mad with pain — push on.'

"'Will you have any water, or anything to cool your throat?' said I.

"'No, no — go on.'

"'Yes,' said I, 'but the brandy and water is hot; however, it's going down very fast now — very fast indeed, here is the last mouthful;' and as I said so, I gulped it down, returned with the one glass, and then paid for the damage.

---

* *Brandy was commonly taken mixed about half-and-half with boiling water, with several spoonfuls of sugar mixed in — like a hot toddy.*

† *Probably an error. The sovereign was a gold coin worth 20 shillings (one pound sterling), first issued to replace the guinea, in the mid-1810s, a good 30 years after the time of this story.*

"This did not occupy five minutes, and away we came along the road at a devil of a pace, and we were all right enough; my friend behind me got over his scald, though he had a very sore gullet, and his intestines were in a very uncomfortable state; but he was better. Away we rattled, the ground rattling to the horse's hoofs and the wheels of the vehicle, the young girl still remaining in the same state of insensibility in which she had first been brought out. No doubt she had taken a stronger dose of the opium than she was willing to admit. That was nothing to me, but made it all the better, because she gave the less trouble, and made it safer. We got here easy enough, drove slap up to the door, which was opened in an instant, jumped out, took the girl, and carried her in. When once these doors are shut upon any one, they may rest assured that it is quite a settled thing, and they don't get out very easy, save in a wooden surtout; indeed, I never lost a boarder by any other means; we always keep one connection, and they are usually so well satisfied, that they never take any one away from us. Well, well! I carried her indoors, and left her in a room by herself on a bed. She was a nice girl — a handsome girl, I suppose people would call her, and had a low, sweet, and plaintive voice. But enough of this.

" 'She's all right,' said I, when I returned to this room, 'It's all right — I have left her.'

" 'She isn't dead,' he inquired, with much terror.

" 'Oh! no, no! she is only asleep, and has not woke up yet from the effects of the laudanum. Will you now give me one year's pay in advance?'

" 'Yes,' he replied, as he handed the money, and the remainder of the bonds. 'Now, how am I to do about getting back to London to-night?'

" 'You had better remain here.'

" 'Oh, no! I should go mad too, if I were to remain here; I must leave here soon.'

" 'Well, will you go to the village inn?'

" 'How far is that off?'

" 'About a mile — you'll reach it easy enough; I'll drive you over for the matter of that, and leave you there. I shall take the cart there.'

" 'Very well, let it be so; I will go. Well, well, I am glad it is all over, and the sooner it is over for ever, the better. I am truly sorry for her, but it cannot be helped. It will kill her, I have no doubt; but that is all the better: she will escape the misery consequent upon her departure, and release us from a weight of care.'

" 'So it will,' said I 'but come, we must go at once, if going you are.'

" 'Yes, yes,' he said hurriedly.

" 'Well then, come along; the horse is not yet unharnessed, and if we do not make haste, we shall be too late to obtain a lodging for the night.'

" 'That is very good,' he said, somewhat wildly: 'I am quite ready — quite.'

"We left the house, and trotted off to the inn at a good rate, where we arrived in about ten minutes or less, and then I put up the horse, and saw him to the inn, and came back as quick as I could on foot. 'Well, well,' I thought, 'this will do, I have had a good day of it — paid well for business, and haven't wanted for sport on the road.'

"Well, I came to the conclusion that if the whole affair was to speedily end, it would be more in my pocket than if she were living, and she would be far happier in heaven than here, Mr. Todd."

"Undoubtedly," said Mr. Sweeney Todd, "undoubtedly, that is a very just observation of yours."

"Well, then, I set to work to find out how the matter could be managed, and I watched her until she awoke. She looked around her, and seemed much surprised and confused, and did not seem to understand her position, while I remained at hand."

"She sighed deeply, and put her hand to her head, and appeared for a time to be quite unable to comprehend what had happened to her, or where she was. I sent some tea to her, as I was not prepared to execute my purpose, and she seemed to recover, and asked some questions, but my man was dumb for the occasion, and would not speak, and the result was, she was very much frightened. I left her so for a week or two, and then, one day, I went into her cell. She had greatly altered in her appearance, and looked very pale.

" 'Well,' said I, 'how do you find yourself, now?'

"She looked up into my face, and shuddered; but she said in a calm voice, looking round her —

" 'Where am I?'

" 'You are here!' said I, 'and you'll be very comfortable if you only take on kindly, but you will have a strait waistcoat put on you if you do not.'

" 'Good God!' she exclaimed, clasping her hands, 'have they put me here — in — in —'

"She could not finish the sentence, and I supplied the word which she did not utter, and then she screamed loudly —

" 'Come,' said I, 'this will never do; you must learn to be quiet, or you'll have fearful consequences.'

" 'Oh mercy, mercy! I will do no wrong! What have I done that I should be brought here? — what have I done? They may take all I have if they will let me live in freedom. I care not where or how poor I may be. Oh, Henry! Henry! — if you knew where I was, would you not fly to my rescue? Yes, you would, you would!'

" 'Ah,' said I, 'there is no Henry here, and you must be content to do without one.'

" 'I could not have believed that my brother would have acted such a base part. I did not think him wicked, although I knew him to be selfish, mean, and stern, yet I did not think he intended such wickedness; but he thinks to rob me of all my property; yes, that is the object he has in sending me here.'

" 'No doubt,' said I.

" 'Shall I ever get out?' she inquired, in a pitiful tone; 'do not say my life is to be spent here!'

" 'Indeed it is,' said I; 'while he lives, you will never leave these walls.'

" 'He shall not attain his end, for I have deeds about me that he will never be able to obtain; indeed, he may kill me, but he cannot benefit by my death.'

" 'Well,' said I, 'it serves him right. And how did you manage that matter? how did you contrive to get the deeds away?'

" 'Never mind that; it is a small deed, and I have secured it. I did not think he would have done this thing; but he may yet relent. Will you aid me? I shall be rich, and can pay you well.'

" 'But your brother,' said I.

" 'Oh, he is rich without mine, but he is over-avaricious; but say you will help me — only help me to get out, and you shall be no loser by the affair.'

" 'Very well,' said I. 'Will you give me this deed as a security that you will keep your word?'

" 'Yes,' she replied, drawing forth the deed — a small parchment — from her bosom. 'Take it; and now let me out. You shall be handsomely rewarded.'

" 'Ah!' said I; 'but you must allow me first to settle this matter with my employers. You must really be mad. We do not hear of young ladies carrying deeds and parchments about them when they are in their senses.'

" 'You do not mean to betray me?' she said, springing up wildly and rushing towards the deed, which I carefully placed in my breast coat-pocket.

" 'Oh dear no! but I shall retain the deed, and speak to your brother about this matter.'

" 'My God! my God!' she exclaimed, and then she sank back on her bed, and in another moment she was covered with blood. She had burst a blood-vessel. I sent for a surgeon and physician, and they both gave it as their opinion that she could not be saved, and that a few hours would see the last of her. This was the fact. She was dead before another half hour, and then I sent to the authorities for the purpose of burial; and, producing the certificate of the medical men, I had no difficulty, and she was buried all comfortably without any trouble.

" 'WELL,' THOUGHT I, 'THIS IS A VERY comfortable affair; but it will be more profitable than I had any idea of, and I must get my first reward first, and if there should be any difficulty, I have the deed to fall back upon. He came down next day, and appeared with rather a long face.

" 'Well,' said he, 'how do matters go on here?'

" 'Very well,' said I, 'how is your throat?'

"I thought he cast a malicious look at me, as much as to imply he laid it all to my charge.

"'Pretty well,' he replied; 'but I was ill for three days. How is the patient?'

"'As well as you could possibly wish,' said I.

"'She takes it kindly, eh? Well, I hardly expected it — but no matter. She'll be a long while on hand, I perceive. You haven't tried the frightening system yet, then?'

"'Hadn't any need,' I replied, putting the certificate of her burial in his hand, and he jumped as if he had been stung by an adder, and turned pale; but he soon recovered, and smiled complaisantly as he said —

"'Ah! well, I see you have been diligent, but I should have liked to have seen her, to have asked her about a missing deed; but no matter.'

"'Now about the two hundred pounds,' said I.

"'Why,' said he, 'I think one will do when you come to consider what you have received, and the short space of time and all: you had a year's board in advance.'

"'I know I had; but because I have done more than you expected, and in a shorter time, instead of giving me more, you have the conscience to offer me less.'

"'No, no, not the — the — what did you call it? — we'll have nothing said about that, — but here is a hundred pounds, and you are well paid.'

"'Well,' said I, taking the money, 'I must have five hundred pounds at any rate, and unless you give it me, I will tell other parties where a certain deed is to be found.'

"'What deed?'

"'The one you were alluding to. Give me four hundred more, and you shall have the deeds.'

"After much conversation and trouble he gave it to me, and I gave him the deed, with which he was well pleased, but looked hard at the money, and seemed to grieve at it very much.

"Since that time I have heard that he was challenged by his sister's lover, and they went out to fight a duel, and he fell — and died. The lover went to the continent, where he has since lived.

"Ah," said Sweeney Todd, "you have had decidedly the best of this affair: nobody gained anything but you."

"Nobody at all that I know of, save distant relations, and I did very well; but then, you know, I can't live upon nothing: it costs me something to keep my house and cellar, but I stick to business, and so I shall as long as business sticks to me."

CHAPTER XXIV.

COLONEL JEFFERY MAKES ANOTHER EFFORT TO COME AT SWEENEY TODD'S SECRET.

IF WE WERE TO SAY THAT COLONEL JEFFERY was satisfied with the state of affairs as regarded the disappearance of his friend Thornhill, or that he made up his mind now contentedly to wait until chance, or the mere progress of time, blew something of a more defined nature in his way, we should be doing that gentleman a very great injustice indeed. On the contrary, he was one of those chivalrous persons who when they do commence anything, take the most ample means to bring it to a conclusion, and are not satisfied that they have made one great effort, which, having failed, is sufficient to satisfy them. Far from this, he was a man who, when he commenced any enterprise, looked forward to but one circumstance that could possibly end it, and that was its full and complete accomplishment in every respect; so that in this affair of Mr. Thornhill, he certainly did not intend by any means to abandon it. But he was not precipitate. His habits of military discipline, and the long life he had led in camps, where anything in the shape of hurry and confusion is much reprobated, made him pause before he decided upon any particular course of action; and this pause was not one contingent upon a belief, or even a surmise in the danger of the course that suggested itself, for such a consideration had no effect whatever upon him; and if some other mode had suddenly suggested itself, which, while it placed his life in the most imminent peril, would have seemed more likely to accomplish his object, it would have been at once most gladly welcomed. And now, therefore, he set about thinking deeply over what could possibly be done further in a matter that as yet appeared to be involved in the most profound of possible mysteries. That the barber's boy, who had been addressed by him, and by his friend, the captain, knew something of an extraordinary character, which fear prevented him from disclosing, he had no doubt, and, as the colonel remarked —

"If fear keeps that lad silent upon the subject, fear may make him speak; and I do not see why we should not endeavour to make ourselves a match for Sweeney Todd in such a matter."

"What do you propose then?" said the captain.

"I should say that the best plan would be, to watch the barber's shop, and take possession of the boy, as we may chance to find an opportunity of so doing."

"Carry him off?"

"Yes, certainly; and as in all likelihood his fear of the barber is but a visionary affair after all, it can easily, when we have him to ourselves, be dispelled; and then, when he finds that we can and will protect him, we shall hear all he has to say."

After some further conversation, the plan was resolved upon; and the captain and the colonel, after making a careful "reconnoissance," as they called it, of Fleet-street, found that by taking up a station at the window of a tavern, which was nearly opposite to the barber's shop, they should be able to take such effectual notice of whoever went in and came out, that they would be sure to see the boy some time during the course of the day. This plan of operations would no doubt have been greatly successful, and Tobias would have fallen into their hands, had he not, alas! for him, poor fellow, already been treated by Sweeney Todd as we have described by being incarcerated in that fearful madhouse on Peckham Rye, which was kept by so unscrupulous a personage as Fogg. And we cannot but consider that it was most unfortunate for the happiness of all those persons in whose fate we take so deep an interest — and in whom we hope, as regards the reader, we have likewise awakened a feeling of great sympathy — if Tobias had not been so infatuated as to make the search he did of the barber's house, but had waited even for twenty-four hours before doing so; in that case, not only would he have escaped the dreadful doom which had awaited him, but Johanna Oakley would have been saved from much danger which afterwards befell her.

But we must not anticipate; and the fearful adventures which it was her doom to pass through, before she met with the reward of her great virtue, and her noble perseverance will speak for themselves, trumpet-tongued indeed.

It was at a very early hour in the morning that the two friends took up their station at the public-house so nearly opposite to Sweeney Todd's, in Fleet-street; and then, having made an arrangement with the landlord of the house, that they were to have undisturbed possession of the room as long as they liked, they both sat at the window, and kept an eye upon Todd's house. It was during the period of time there spent, that Colonel Jeffery first made the captain acquainted with the fact of his great affection for Johanna, and that in her he thought he had at length fixed his wandering fancy, and found, really, the only being with whom he thought he could, in this world taste the sweets of domestic life, and know no regret.

"She is all," he said, "in beauty that the warmest imagination can possibly picture, and along with these personal charms, which certainly are most peerless, I have seen enough of her to feel convinced that she has a mind of the purest order that ever belonged to any human being in the world."

"With such sentiments and feelings towards her, the wonder would be," said the captain, "if you did not love her, as you now avow you do."

"I could not be insensible to her attractions. But, understand me, my dear friend, I do not, on account of my own suddenly-conceived partiality for this young and beautiful creature, intend to commit the injustice of not trying might and main, and with heart and hand, to discover if, as she supposes, it be true that Thornhill and Mark Ingestrie be one and the same person; and when I say that I love her with a depth and a sincerity of affection that makes her happiness of greater importance to me than my own — you know, I think, enough of me to feel convinced that I am speaking only what I really feel."

"I can," said the captain, "and I do give you credit for the greatest possible amount of sincerity, and I feel sufficiently interested myself in the future fate of this fair young creature to wish that she may be convinced her lover is no more, and may so much better herself, as I am quite certain she would, by becoming your wife; for all we can hear of this Ingestrie seems to prove that he is not the most stable-minded of individuals the world ever produced, and perhaps not exactly the sort of man — however, of course, she may think to the contrary, and he may in all sincerity think so likewise — to make such a girl as Johanna Oakley happy."

"I thank you for the kind feeling towards me, my friend, which has dictated that speech, but —"

"Hush!" said the captain, suddenly, "hush! look at the barber!"

"The barber? Sweeney Todd?"

"Yes, yes, there he is; do you not see him? There he is, and he looks as if he had come off a long journey. What can he have been about, I wonder? He is draggled in mud!"

Yes, there was Sweeney Todd, opening his shop from the outside with a key, that after a vast amount of fumbling, he took from his pocket; and, as the captain said, he did indeed look as if he had come off a long journey, for he was draggled with mud, and his appearance altogether was such as to convince any one that he must have been out in most of the heavy rain which had fallen during the early part of the morning upon London and its suburbs. And this was just the fact, for after staying with the madhouse-keeper in the hope that the bad weather which had set in would be alleviated, he had been compelled to give up all chance of such a thing, and as no conveyance of any description was to be had, he enjoyed the pleasure, if it could be called such, of walking home up to his knees in the mud of that dirty neighbourhood. It was, however, some satisfaction to him to feel that he had got rid of Tobias, who, from what he had done as regarded the examination of the house, had become extremely troublesome indeed, and perhaps the most serious enemy that Sweeney Todd had ever had.

"Ha!" he said, as he came within sight of his shop in Fleet-street, — "ha! Master Tobias is safe enough; he will give me no more trouble, that is quite clear. What a wonderfully convenient thing it is to have such a friend as Fogg, who for a consideration will do so much towards ridding one of an uncomfortable encumbrance. It is possible enough that that boy might have compassed my destruction. I wish I dared now chance, with the means I have for the sale of the string of pearls, joined to my other resources, leaving business, and so not be obliged to run the risk and have the trouble of another boy."

Yes, Sweeney Todd would have been glad now to shut up his shop in Fleet-street at once and for ever, but he dreaded that when John Mundel found that his customer did not come back to him to redeem the pearls, that he (John Mundel) would proceed to sell them, and that then their beauty and great worth would excite much attention, and some one might come forward who knew more about their early history than he did.

"I must keep quiet," he thought,—"I must keep quiet; for although I think I was pretty well disguised, and it is not at all likely that any one—no, not even the acute John Mundel himself—would recognise in Sweeney Todd, the poor barber of Fleet-street, the nobleman who came from the queen to borrow £8,000 upon a string of pearls; yet there is a remote possibility of danger; and should there be a disturbance about the precious stones, it is better that I should remain in obscurity until that disturbance is completely over."

This was no doubt admirable policy on the part of Todd, who, although he found himself a rich man, had not, as many people do when they make that most gratifying and interesting discovery, forgotten all the prudence and tact that made him one of that most envied class of personages. He was some few minutes before he could get the key to turn in the lock of his street door, but at length he effected that object and disappeared from before the eyes of the colonel and his friend into his own house, and the door was instantly again closed upon him.

"Well," said Colonel Jeffery, "what do you think of that?"

"I don't know what to think, further than that your friend Todd has been out of town, as the state of his boots abundantly testifies."

"They do, indeed, and he has the appearance of having been a considerable distance, for the mud that is upon his boots is not London mud."

"Certainly not; it is quite of a different character altogether. But see, he is coming out again."

Sweeney Todd strode out of his house, bareheaded now, and proceeded to take down the shutters of his shop, which, there being but three, he accomplished in a few seconds of time, and walked in again with them in his hand, along with the iron bar which had secured them, and which he had released from the inside. This was all the ceremony that took place at the opening of Sweeney Todd's shop, and the only surprise our friends, who were at the public-house window, had upon the subject was, that having a boy, he, Todd, should condescend to make himself so useful as to open his own shop. And nothing could be seen of the lad, although the hour, surely, for his attendance must have arrived; and Todd, equally surely, was not the sort of man to be so indulgent to a boy, whom he employed to make himself generally useful, as to allow him to come when all the dirty work of the early morning was over. But yet such to all appearance would seem to be the case, for presently Todd appeared with a broom in his hand, sweeping out his shop with a rapidity and a vengeance which seemed to say, that he did not perform that operation with the very best grace in the world.

"Where can the boy be?" said the captain. "Do you know, little reason as I may really appear to have for such a supposition, I cannot help in my own mind connecting Todd's having been out of town somehow with the fact of that boy's non-appearance this morning."

"Indeed! — the coincidence is curious, for such was my own thought likewise upon the occasion; and the more I do think of it, the more I feel convinced that such must be the case, and that our watch will be a fruitless one completely. Is it likely — for possible enough it is — that the villain has found out that we have been asking some questions of the boy, and has thought proper to take his life?"

"Do not let us go too far," said the captain, "in mere conjecture; recollect that as yet, let us suspect what we may, we know nothing, and that the mere facts of our not being able to trace Thornhill beyond the shop of this man, will not be sufficient to found an action upon."

"I know all that, and I feel how very cautious we must be; and yet to my mind the whole of the circumstances have been day by day assuming a most hideous air of probability, and I look upon Todd as a murderer already."

"Shall we continue our watch?"

"I scarcely see its utility. Perchance we may see some proceedings which may interest us; but I have a powerful impression that we certainly shall not see the boy we want. But, at all events, the barber, you perceive, has a customer already."

As they looked across the way, they saw a well dressed looking man, who, from a certain air and manner which he had, could be detected not to be a Londoner. He rather resembled some substantial yeoman, who had come to town to pay or to receive money, and, as he came near to Sweeney Todd's shop he might have been observed to stroke his chin, as debating in his mind the necessity or otherwise of a shave. The debate, if it were taking place in his mind, ended by the ayes having it, for he walked into Todd's shop, being most unquestionably the first customer which he had had that morning. Situated as the colonel and his friend were, they could not see into Todd's shop, even if the door had been opened, but they saw that after the customer had been in for a few moments, it was closed, so that, had they been close to it, all the interior of the shaving establishment would have been concealed. They felt no great degree of interest in this man, who was a commonplace personage enough, who had entered Sweeney Todd's shop; but when an unreasonable time had elapsed, and he did not come out, they did begin to feel a little uneasy. And when another man, went in and was only about five minutes before he emerged, shaved, and yet the first man did not come, they knew not what to make of it, and looked at each other for some few moments in silence. At length the colonel spoke — and he did so in a tone of excitement, saying —

"My friend, have we waited here for nothing now? What can have become of that man whom we saw go into the barber's shop; but who, I suppose, we feel ourselves to be in a condition to take our oaths never came out?"

"I could take my oath; and what conclusion can we come to?"

"None, but that he met his death there; and that, let his fate be what it may, it is the same which poor Thornhill has suffered. I can endure this no longer. Do you stay here, and let me go alone."

"Not for worlds — you would rush into an unknown danger; you cannot know what may be the powers of mischief that man possesses. You shall not go alone, colonel, you shall not indeed; but something must be done."

"Agreed; and yet that something surely need not be of the desperate character you meditate."

"Desperate emergencies require desperate remedies; and yet I think that in this case everything is to be lost by precipitation, and nothing is to be gained. We have to do with one who, to all appearance, is keen and subtle, and if anything is to be accomplished contrary to his wishes, it is not to be done by that open career, which for its own sake, under ordinary circumstances, both you and I would gladly embrace."

"Well, well," said the colonel, "I do not and will not say but you are right."

"I know I am — I am certain I am; and now hear me: I think we have gone quite far enough unaided in this transaction, and that it is time we drew some others into the plot."

"I do not understand what you mean."

"I will soon explain. I mean, that if in the pursuit of this enterprise, which grows each moment to my mind more serious, anything should happen to you and me, it is absolutely frightful to think that there would then be an end of it."

"True, true; and as for poor Johanna and her friend Arabella, what could they do?"

"Nothing, but expose themselves to great danger. Come, now, colonel, I am glad to see that we understand each other better about this business; you have heard, of course, of Sir Richard Blunt?"

"Sir Richard Blunt — Blunt — oh, you mean the magistrate?"

"I do; and what I propose is that we have a private and confidential interview with him about the matter — that we make him possessed of all the circumstances, and take his advice what to do. The result of placing the affair in such hands will, at all events, be that if, in anything we may attempt, we may by force or fraud be overpowered, we shall not fall wholly unavenged."

"Reason backs your proposition."

"I knew it would, when you came to reflect. Oh, Colonel Jeffery, you are too much a creature of impulse."

"Well," said the colonel, half jestingly, "I must say that I do not think the accusation comes well from you, for I have certainly seen you do some rather impulsive things, I think."

"We won't dispute about that; but since you think with me upon the matter, you will have no objection to accompany me at once to Sir Richard Blunt's?"

"None in the least; on the contrary, if anything is to be done at all, for Heaven's sake let it be done quickly. I am quite convinced that some fearful tragedy is in progress, and that, if we are not most prompt in our measures, we shall be too late to counteract its dire influence upon the fortunes of those in whom we have become deeply interested."

"Agreed, agreed! Come this way, and let us now for a brief space, at all events, leave Mr. Todd and his shop to take care of each other, while we take an effectual means of circumventing him. Why do you linger?"

"I do linger. Some mysterious influence seems to chain me to the spot."

"Some mysterious fiddlestick! Why, you are getting superstitious, colonel."

"No, no! Well, I suppose I must come with you. Lead the way, lead the way; and believe me that it requires all my reason to induce me to give up a hope of making some important discovery by going to Sweeney Todd's shop."

"Yes, you might make an important discovery; and only suppose now that the discovery you did make was that he murdered some of his customers. If he does so, you may depend that such a man takes good care to do the deed effectually, and you might make the discovery just a little too late. You understand that?"

"I do, I do. Come along, for I positively declare, that if we see anybody else go into the barber's, I shall not be able to resist rushing forward at once, and giving an alarm."

It was certainly a good thing that the colonel's friend was not quite so enthusiastic as he was, or from what we happen actually to know of Sweeney Todd, and from what we suspect, the greatest amount of danger might have befallen Jeffery, and instead of being in a position to help others in unravelling the mysteries connected with Sweeney Todd's establishment, he might himself have been past all help, and most absolutely one of the mysteries. But such was not to be.

CHAPTER XXV.

TOBIAS MAKES AN ATTEMPT TO ESCAPE FROM THE MADHOUSE.

WE CANNOT FIND IT IN OUR HEARTS to force upon the mind of the reader the terrible condition of poor Tobias. No one, certainly, of all the *dramatis personæ* of our tale, is suffering so much as he; and, consequently, we feel it to be a sort of duty to come to a consideration of his thoughts and feelings as he lay in that dismal cell, in the madhouse at Peckham Rye. Certainly Tobias Ragg was as sane as any ordinary Christian need wish to be, when the scoundrel, Sweeney Todd, put him into the coach to take him to Mr. Fogg's establishment; but if by any ingenious process the human intellect can be toppled from its throne, certainly that process must consist in putting a sane person into a lunatic asylum. To the imagination of a boy, too, and that boy one of vivid imagination, as was poor Tobias, a madhouse must be invested with a world of terrors. That enlarged experience which enables persons of more advanced age to shake off much of the unreal, which seemed so strangely to take up its abode in the mind of the young Tobias, had not reached him; and no wonder, therefore, that to him his present situation was one of acute and horrible misery and suffering.

HE LAY FOR A LONG TIME IN THE GLOOMY dungeon-like cell into which he had been thrust, in a kind of stupour, which might or might not be the actual precursor of insanity, although, certainly, the chances were all in favour of being so. For many hours he neither moved hand nor foot, and as it was a part of the policy of Mr. Fogg to leave well alone, as he said, he never interfered, by any intrusive offers of refreshment, with the quiet or the repose of his patients. Tobias, therefore, if he had chosen to remain as still as an Indian fakir, might have died in one position, without any remonstrances from any one. It would be quite an impossibility to describe the strange visionary thoughts and scenes that passed through the mind of Tobias during this period. It seemed as if his intellect was engulfed in the charmed waters of some whirlpool, and that all the different scenes and actions which, under ordinary circumstances, would have been clear and distinct, were mingled together in inextricable confusion.

In the midst of all this, at length, he began to be conscious of one particular impression or feeling, and that was, that some one was singing in a low, soft voice, very near to him. This feeling, strange as it was in such a place, momentarily increased in volume, until at length it began in its intensity to absorb almost every other; and he gradually awakened from the sort of stupor that had come over him.

Yes, some one was singing. It was a female voice, he was sure of that, and as his mind became more occupied with that one subject of thought, and his perceptive faculties became properly exercised, his intellect altogether assumed a healthier tone. He could not distinguish the words that were sung, but the voice itself was very sweet and musical; and as Tobias listened, he felt as if the fever of his blood was abating, and that healthier thoughts were taking the place of those disordered fancies that had held sway within the chambers of his brain.

"What sweet sounds!" he said. "Oh! I do hope that singing will go on. I feel happier to hear it; I do so hope it will continue. What sweet music! Oh, mother, mother, if you could but see me now!"

He pressed his hands over his eyes, but he could not stop the gush of tears that came from them, and which would trickle through his fingers. Tobias did not wish to weep; but those tears, after all the horrors of the night, did him a world of good, and he felt wonderfully better after they had been shed. Moreover, the voice kept singing without intermission.

"Who can it be," thought Tobias, "that don't tire with so much of it."

Still the singer continued; but now and then Tobias felt certain that a very wild note or two was mingled with the ordinary melody; and that bred a suspicion in his mind, which gave him a shudder to think of, namely, that the singer was mad.

"It must be so," said he. "No one in their senses could or would continue for so long a period of time such strange snatches of song. Alas! alas! it is some one who is really mad, and confined for life in this dreadful place; for life do I say, am not I too confined for life here? Oh! help! help! help!"

Tobias called out in so loud a tone, that the singer of the sweet strains that had for a time lulled him to composure, heard him, and the strains which had before been redolent of the softest and sweetest melody, suddenly changed to the most terrific shrieks that can be imagined. In vain did Tobias place his hands over his ears, to shut out the horrible sounds. They would not be shut out, but ran, as it were, into every crevice of his brain, nearly driving him distracted by their vehemence. But hoarser tones soon came upon his ears, and he heard the loud, rough voice of a man say —

"What, do you want the whip so early this morning? The whip — do you understand that?"

These words were followed by the lashing of what must have been a heavy carter's whip, and then the shrieks died away in deep groans, every one of which went to the heart of poor Tobias.

"I can never live amid all these horrors," he said. "Oh, why don't you kill me at once? it would be much better, and much more merciful. I can never live long here. Help! help! help!"

When he shouted this word "help," it was certainly not with the most distant idea of getting any help, but it was a word that came at once uppermost to his tongue; and so he called it out with all his might, that he should attract the attention of some one; for the solitude, and the almost total darkness of the place he was in, was beginning to fill him with new dismay. There was a faint light in the cell, which made him know the difference between day and night; but where that faint light came from he could not tell, for he could see no grating or opening whatever; but yet that was in consequence of his eyes not being fully accustomed to the obscurity of the place; otherwise he would have seen that close up to the roof there was a narrow aperture, certainly not larger than any one could have passed a hand through, although of some four or five feet in length; and from a passage beyond that, there came the dim borrowed light which made darkness visible in Tobias's cell. With a kind of desperation, heedless of what might be the result, Tobias continued to call aloud for help; and after about a quarter of an hour, he heard the sound of a heavy footstep. Some one was coming; yes, surely some one was coming, and he was not to be left to starve to death. Oh, how intently he now listened to every sound, indicative of the near approach of whoever it was who was coming to his prison-house. Now he heard the lock move, and a heavy bar of iron was let down with a clanging sound.

"Help! help!" he cried again, "help! help!" for he feared that whoever it was they might even yet go away again after making so much progress to get at him. The cell door was flung open, and the first intimation that poor Tobias got of the fact of his cries having been heard, consisted in a lash with a whip, which, if it had struck him as fully as it was intended to do, would have done him serious injury.

"So, do you want it already?" said the same voice he had before heard.

"Oh no — mercy! mercy!" said Tobias.

"Oh, that's it now, is it? I tell you what it is, if we have any disturbance here, this is the persuader to silence that we always use: what do you think of that for an argument, eh?"

As he spoke, the man gave the whip a loud smack in the air, and confirmed the truth of the argument, by inducing poor Tobias to absolute silence; indeed the boy trembled so that he could not speak.

"Well, now, my man," added the fellow, "I think we understand each other. What do you want?"

"Oh, let me go," said Tobias, "let me go. I will tell nothing. Say to Mr. Todd that I will do what he pleases, and tell nothing, only let me go out of this dreadful place. Have mercy upon me — I am not at all mad — indeed I am not."

The man closed the door, as he whistled a lively tune.

CHAPTER XXVI.

THE MADHOUSE YARD, AND TOBIAS'S NEW FRIEND.

THIS SUDDEN RETREAT OF THE MAN was unexpected by Tobias, who at least thought it was the practice to feed people, even if they were confined to such a place; but the unceremonious departure of the keeper, without so much as mentioning anything about breakfast, began to make Tobias think that the plan by which he was to be got rid of was starvation; and yet that was impossible, for how easy it was to kill him if they felt so disposed.

"Oh, no, no," he repeated to himself, "surely they will not starve me to death."

As he uttered these words, he heard the plaintive singing commence again; and he could not help thinking that it sounded like some requiem for the dead, and that it was a sort of signal that his hours were numbered. Despair again began to take possession of him, and despite the savage threats of the keeper, he would again have loudly called for help, had he not become conscious that there were footsteps close at hand. By dint of listening most intently he heard a number of doors opened and shut, and sometimes when one was opened there was a shriek, and the lashing of the whips, which very soon succeeded in drowning all other noises. It occurred to Tobias, and correctly too, for such was the fact, that the inmates of that most horrible abode were living, like so many wild beasts, in cages fed. Then he thought how strange it was that even for any amount of money human beings could be got to do the work of such an establishment. And by the time Tobias had made this reflection to himself, his own door was once more opened upon its rusty hinges. There was the flash of a light, and then a man came in with a water-can in his hand, to which there was a long spout, and this he placed to the mouth of Tobias, who fearing that if he did not drink then he might be a long time without, swallowed some not over-savoury ditch water, as it seemed to him, which was thus brought to him. A coarse, brown-looking, hard loaf was then thrown at his feet, and the party was about to leave his cell, but he could not forbear speaking, and in a voice of the most supplicating earnestness he said —

"Oh, do not keep me here. Let me go, and I will say nothing of Todd. I will go to sea at once if you will let me out of this place, indeed I will; but I shall really go mad here!"

"Good that, Watson, ain't it?" said Mr. Fogg, who happened to be one of the party.

"Very good, sir. Lord bless you, the cunning of 'em is beyond anything in the world, sir; you'd be surprised at what they say to me sometimes."

"But I'm not mad — indeed I'm not mad!" cried Tobias.

"Oh," said Fogg, "it's a bad case I'm afraid; the strongest proof of insanity in my opinion, Watson, is the constant reiteration of the statement that he is not mad on the part of a lunatic. Don't you think it is so, Mr. Watson?"

"Oh, of course, sir, of course."

"Ah! I thought you would be of that opinion; but I suppose as this is a mere lad, we may do without chaining him up; and, besides, you know that to-day is inspection day, when we get an old fool of a superannuated physician to make us a visit."*

"Yes, sir," said Watson, with a grin, "and a report that all is well conducted."

"Exactly. Who shall we have this time, do you think? I always give a ten guinea fee."

"Why, sir, there's old Dr. Popplejoy, he's 84 years old, they say, and sand blind; he'll take it as a great compliment, he will, and no doubt we can humbug him easily."

"I dare say we may; I'll see to it; and we will have him at twelve o'clock, Watson. You will take care to have everything ready, of course, you know; make all the usual preparations."

Tobias was astonished that before him they chose thus to speak so freely, but despairing as he was, he little knew how completely he was in the power of Mr. Fogg, and how utterly he was shut out from all human sympathy. Tobias said nothing; but he could not help thinking that, however old and stupid the physician whom they mentioned might be, surely there was a hope that he would be able to discover Tobias's perfect sanity.

But the wily Mr. Fogg knew perfectly well what he was about, and when he retired to his own room, he wrote the following note to Dr. Popplejoy, who was a retired physician, who had purchased a country house in the neighbour-hood. The note will speak for itself, being as fine a specimen of hypocrisy as we can ever expect to lay before our readers —

The Asylum, Peckham.
Sir, —
Probably you may recognise my name as that of the keeper of a lunatic asylum in this neighbourhood. Consistent with a due regard for the safety of that most unhappy class of the community submitted to my care, I am most anxious, with the blessing of Divine Providence, to ameliorate as far as possible, by kindness, that most shocking of all calamities — insanity. Once a year it is my custom to call in some experienced, able,

---

* *These inspections were required by an Act of Parliament passed in 1774 in response to growing public outrage over abuses in madhouses reported in the press.*

and enlightened physician to see my patients (I enclose a fee) — a physician who has
nothing to do with the establishment, and therefore cannot be biassed. If you, sir, would
do me the favour at about twelve o'clock to-day, to make a short visit of inspection, I
shall esteem it a great honour, as well as a great favour.

Believe me to be, sir, with the most profound respect, your most obedient and humble
servant,

O. D. FOGG.

To Dr. Popplejoy, *&c.*

This note, as might be expected, brought the old purblind, superannuated Dr. Popplejoy to the asylum, and Mr. Fogg received him in due form, and with great gravity, saying, almost with tears in his eyes —

"My dear sir, the whole aim of my existence now, is to endeavour to soften the rigours of the necessary confinement of the insane, and I wish this inspection of my establishment to be made by you in order that I may thus for a time stand clear with the world — with my own conscience I am, of course, always clear; and if your report be satisfactory about the treatment of the unhappy persons I have here, not the slightest breath of slander can touch me."

"Oh yes, yes," said the old garrulous physician; "I — I — very good — eugh, eugh — I have a slight cough."

"A very slight one, sir. Will you, first of all, take a look at one of the sleeping chambers of the insane?"

The doctor agreed, and Mr. Fogg led him into a very comfortable sleeping-room, which the old gentleman declared was very satisfactory indeed, and when they returned to the apartment into which they had already been, Mr. Fogg said —

"Well then, sir, all we have to do is to bring in the patients, one by one, to you as fast as we can, so as not to occupy more of your valuable time than necessary; and any questions you ask will, no doubt, be answered, and I, being by, can give you the heads of any case that may excite your especial notice."

"Exactly, exactly. I — I — quite correct. Eugh — eugh!"

The old man was placed in a chair of state, reposing on some very comfortable cushions; and take him altogether, he was so pleased with the ten guineas and the flattery of Mr. Fogg — for nobody had given him a fee for the last fifteen years — that he was quite ready to be the foolish tool of the madhouse-keeper in almost any way that he chose to dictate to him.

We need not pursue the examination of the various unfortunates who were brought before old Dr. Popplejoy; it will suffice for us if we carry the reader through the examination of Tobias, who is our principal care, without, at the same time, detracting from the genial sympathy we must feel for all who, at that time, were subject to the tender mercies of Mr. Fogg. At about half-past twelve the door of Tobias's cell was opened by Mr. Watson, who, walking in, laid hold of the boy by the collar, and said —

"Hark you, my lad! you are going before a physician, and the less you say the better. I speak to you for your own sake; you can do yourself no good, but you can do yourself a great deal of harm. You know we keep a cart-whip here. Come along."

Tobias said not a word in answer to this piece of altogether gratuitous advice, but he made up his mind that, if the physician was not absolutely deaf, he should hear him. Before, however, the unhappy boy was taken into the room where old Dr. Popplejoy was waiting, he was washed and brushed down generally, so that he presented a much more respectable appearance than he would have done had he been ushered in in his soiled state, as he was taken from the dirty mad-house cell.

"Surely, surely," thought Tobias, "the extent of cool impudence can go no further than this; but I will speak to the physician, if my life should be sacrificed for so doing. Yes, of that I am determined."

In another minute he was in the room, face to face with Mr. Fogg and Dr. Popplejoy.

"What — what? — eugh! eugh!" coughed the old doctor; "a boy, Mr. Fogg, a mere boy. Dear me! I — I — eugh! eugh! eugh! My cough is a little troublesome I think, to-day — eugh! eugh!"

"Yes, sir," said Fogg, with a deep sigh, and making a pretence to dash a tear from his eye; "here you have a mere boy. I am always affected when I look upon him, doctor. We were boys ourselves once, you know, and to think that the divine spark of intelligence has gone out in one so young, is enough to make any feeling heart throb with agony. This lad though, sir, is only a monomaniac. He has a fancy that some one named Sweeney Todd is a murderer, and that he can discover his bad practices. On all other subjects he is sane enough; but upon that, and upon his presumed freedom from mental derangement, he is furious."

"It is false, sir, it is false!" said Tobias, stepping up. "Oh, sir, if you are not one of the creatures of this horrible place, I beg that you will hear me, and let justice be done."

"Oh, yes — I — I — eugh! Of course — I — eugh!"

"Sir, I am not mad, but I am placed here because I have become dangerous to the safety of criminal persons."

"Oh, indeed! Ah — oh — yes."

"I am a poor lad, sir, but I hate wickedness; and because I found out that Sweeney Todd was a murderer, I am placed here."

"You hear him, sir," said Fogg; "just as I said."

"Oh, yes, yes. Who is Sweeney Todd, Mr. Fogg?"

"Oh, sir, there is no such person in the world."

"Ah, I thought as much — I thought as much — a sad case, a very sad case, indeed. Be calm, my little lad, and Mr. Fogg will do all that can be done for you, I'm sure."

"Oh! how can you be so foolish, sir," cried Tobias, "as to be deceived by that man, who is making a mere instrument of you to cover his own villany? What I say to you is true, and I am not mad!"

"I think, Dr. Popplejoy," said Fogg, with a smile, "it would take rather a cleverer fellow than I am to make a fool of you; but you perceive, sir, that in a little while the boy would get quite furious, that he would. Shall I take him away?"

"Yes, yes — poor fellow!"

"Hear me — oh, hear me," shrieked Tobias. "Sir, on your death-bed you may repent this day's work — I am not mad — Sweeney Todd is a murderer — he is a barber in Fleet-street — I am not mad!"

"It's melancholy, sir, is it not?" said Fogg, as he again made an effort to wipe away a tear from his eyes. "It's very melancholy."

"Oh! very, very."

"Watson, take away poor Tobias Ragg, but take him very gently, and stay with him a little, in his nice comfortable room, and try to soothe him; speak to him of his mother, Watson, and get him round if you can. Alas, poor child! my heart quite bleeds to see him. I am not fit exactly for this life, doctor, I ought to be made of sterner stuff, indeed I ought."

"WELL," SAID MR. WATSON, AS HE SALUTED poor Tobias with a kick outside the door, "what a deal of good you have done!"

The boy's patience was exhausted; he had borne all that he could bear, and this last insult maddened him. He turned with the quickness of thought, and sprang at Mr. Watson's throat. So sudden was the attack, and so completely unprepared for it was that gentleman, that down he fell in the passage, with such a blow of his head against the stone floor that he was nearly insensible; and, before anybody could get to his assistance, Tobias had so pommelled and clawed his face, that there was scarcely a feature discernible, and one of his eyes seemed to be in fearful jeopardy. The noise of this assault soon brought Mr. Fogg to the spot, as well as old Dr. Popplejoy, and the former tore Tobias from his victim, whom he seemed intent upon murdering.

CHAPTER XXVII.

THE CONSULTATION OF COLONEL JEFFERY WITH THE MAGISTRATE.

THE ADVICE WHICH HIS FRIEND had given to Colonel Jeffery was certainly the very best that could have been tendered to him; and, under the whole of these circumstances, it would have been something little short of absolute folly to have ventured into the shop of Sweeney Todd without previously taking every possible precaution to ensure the safety of so doing. Sir Richard was within when they reached his house, and, with the acuteness of a man of business, he at once entered into the affair. As the colonel, who was the spokesman, proceeded, it was evident that the magistrate became deeply interested. Colonel Jeffery concluded by saying —

"You will thus, at all events, perceive that there is great mystery somewhere."

"And guilt, I should say," replied the magistrate.

"You are of that opinion, Sir Richard?"

"I am, most decidedly."

"Then what would you propose to do? Believe me, I do not ask out of any idle curiosity, but from a firm faith, that what you set about will be accomplished in a satisfactory manner."

"Why, in the first place, I shall certainly go and get shaved at Todd's shop."

"You will venture that?"

"Oh, yes; but do not fancy that I am so headstrong and foolish as to run any unnecessary risks in the matter — I shall do no such thing: you may be assured that I will do all in my power to provide for my own safety; and if I did not think I could do that most effectually, I should not be at all in love with the adventure; but, on the contrary, carefully avoid it to the best of my ability. We have before heard something of Mr. Todd."

"Indeed! — and of a criminal character?"

"Yes; a lady once in the street took a fancy to a pair of shoe-buckles of imitation diamonds that Todd had on, when he was going to some city entertainment; she screamed out, and declared that they had belonged to her husband, who had gone out one morning, from his house in Fetter-lane, to get himself shaved. The case came before me, but the buckles were of too common a kind to enable the lady to persevere in her statement; and Todd, who preserved the most imperturbable coolness throughout the affair, was, of course, discharged."

"But the matter left a suspicion upon your mind?"

"It did; and more than once I have resolved in my own mind what means could be adopted of coming at the truth: other affairs, however, of more immediate urgency have occupied me, but the circumstances you detail revive all my former feelings upon the subject; and I shall now feel that the matter has come before me in a shape to merit immediate attention."

This was gratifying to Colonel Jeffery, because it not only took a great weight off his shoulders, but it led him to think, from the well-known tact of the magistrate, that something certainly would be accomplished, and that very shortly too, towards unravelling the secret that had as yet only appeared to be more complicated and intricate the more it was inquired into. He made the warmest acknowledgments to the magistrate for the courtesy of his reception, and then took his leave. As soon as the magistrate was alone, he rang a small hand-bell that was upon the table, and the summons was answered by a man, to whom he said —

"Is Crotchet here?"

"Yes, your worship."

"Then, tell him I want him at once, will you?"

The messenger retired, but he presently returned, bringing with him about as rough a specimen of humanity as the world could have produced. He was tall and stout, and his face looked as if, by repeated injuries, it had been knocked out of all shape, for the features were most strangely jumbled together indeed, and an obliquity of vision, which rendered it always a matter of doubt who and what he was looking at, by no means added to his personal charms.

"Sit down, Crotchet," said the magistrate, "and listen to me without a word of interruption."

If Mr. Crotchet had no other good quality on earth, he still had that of listening attentively, and he never opened his mouth while the magistrate related to him what had just formed the subject matter of Mr. Jeffery's communication; indeed, Crotchet seemed to be looking out of the window all the while; but then Sir Richard knew the little peculiarities of his visual organs. When he concluded his statement, Sir Richard said —

"Well, Crotchet, what do you think of all that? What does Sweeney Todd do with his customers?"

Mr. Crotchet gave a singular and peculiar kind of grin, as he said, still looking apparently out of the window, although his eyes were really fixed upon the magistrate —

"He *smugs*'em."

"What?"

"Uses 'em up, yer worship; it's as clear to me as mud in a wine-glass, that it is. Lor' bless you! I've been thinking he did that 'ere sort of thing a deuce of a while, but I didn't like to interfere too soon, you see."

"What do you advise, Crotchet? I know I can trust to your sagacity in such a case."

"Why, your worship, I'll think it over a bit in the course of the day, and let your worship know what I think. It's a awkward job rather, for a wariety of reasons, but howsomdever there's always a something to be done, and if we don't do it, I'll be hung if I know who can, that's all!"

"True, true, you are right there; and, perhaps, before you see me again, you will walk down Fleet-street, and see if you can make any observations that will be of advantage in the matter. It is an affair which requires great caution indeed."

"Trust me, yer worship: I'll do it, and no mistake. Lor' bless you, it's easy for anybody now to go lounging about Fleet-street, without being taken much notice of; for the fact is, the whole place is agog about the horrid smell as has been for never so long in the old church of St. Dunstan."

"Smell — smell — in St. Dunstan's church! I never heard of that before, Crotchet."

"Oh, Lor' yes, it's enough to p'ison the devil himself, Sir Richard; and t'other day when the blessed bishop went to 'firm a lot of people, he as good as told 'em they might all be damned first, afore he 'firm nobody in such a place."

The magistrate was in a deep thought for a few minutes, and then he said suddenly —

"Well, well, Crotchet, you turn the matter over in your mind and see what you can make of it; I will think it over likewise. Do you hear? — mind you are with me at six this evening punctually; I do not intend to let the matter rest, and you may depend, that from this moment I will give it my greatest attention."

"Wery good, yer worship; wery good indeed; I'll be here, and something seems to strike me uncommon forcible that we shall unearth this fox very soon, yer worship."

"I sincerely hope so."

Mr. Crotchet took his leave, and when he was alone the magistrate rose and paced his apartment for some time with rapid strides, as if he was much agitated by the reflections that were passing through his mind. At length he flung himself into a chair with something like a groan, as he said —

"A horrible idea forces itself upon my consideration — most horrible! most horrible! most horrible! Well, well, we shall see — we shall see. It may not be so: and yet what a hideous probability stares me in the face! I will go down at once to St. Dunstan's and see what they are really about. Yes, yes, I shall not get much sleep I think now, until some of these mysteries are developed. A most horrible idea, truly!"

The magistrate left some directions at home concerning some business calls which he fully expected in the course of the next two hours, and then he put on a plain, sad-coloured cloak and a hat destitute of all ornament, and left his house with a rapid step. He took the most direct route towards St. Dunstan's church, and finding the door of the sacred edifice yielded to the touch, he at once entered it; but he had not advanced many steps before he was met and accosted by the beadle, who said, in a tone of great dignity and authority —

"This ain't Sunday, sir; there ain't no service here to-day."

"I don't suppose there is," replied the magistrate; "but I see you have workmen here. What is it you are about?"

"Well, of all the impudence that ever I came near, this is the worstest — to ask a beadle what he is about; I beg to say, sir, this is quite private, and there's the door."

"Yes, I see it, and you may go out at it just as soon as you think proper."

"Oh, *conwulsions!* oh, *conwulsions!* This to a beadle."

"What is all this about?" said a gentlemanly-looking man, stepping forward from a part of the church where several masons were employed in raising some of the huge flag-stones with which it was paved. "What disturbance is this?"

"I believe, Mr. Antrobus, you know me," said the magistrate.

"Oh, Sir Richard, certainly. How do you do?"

"Gracious," said the beadle, "I've put my blessed foot in it. Lor' bless us, sir, how should I know as you was Sir Richard? I begs as you won't think nothing o' what I said. If I had a knowed you, in course I shouldn't have said it, you may depend, Sir Richard — I humbly begs your pardon."

"It's of no consequence — I ought to have announced myself; and you are perfectly justified in keeping strangers out of the church, my friend."

The magistrate walked up the aisle with Mr. Antrobus, who was one of the churchwardens; and as he did so, he said, in a low, confidential tone of voice —

"I have heard some strange reports about a terrible stench in the church. What does it mean? I suppose you know all about it, and what it arises from?"

"Indeed I do not. If you have heard that there is a horrible smell in the church after it has been shut up for some time, and upon the least change in the weather, from dry or wet, or cold or warm, you know as much as we know upon the subject. It is a most serious nuisance, and, in fact, my presence here to-day is to try and make some discovery of the cause of the stench; and you see we are going to work our way into some of the old vaults that have not been opened for some time, with a hope of finding out the cause of this disagreeable odour."

"Have you any objection to my being a spectator?"

"None in the least."

"I thank you. Let us now join the workmen, and I can only now tell you that I feel the strongest possible curiosity to ascertain what can be the meaning of all this, and shall watch the proceedings with the greatest amount of interest."

"Come along then; I can only say, for my part, that, as an individual, I am glad you are here, and as a magistrate, likewise, it gives me great satisfaction to have you."

———————

CHAPTER XXVIII.

TOBIAS'S ESCAPE FROM MR. FOGG'S ESTABLISHMENT.

THE RAGE INTO WHICH MR. FOGG was thrown by the attack which the desperate Tobias had made upon his representative, Mr. Watson, was so great, that, had it not been for the presence of stupid old Dr. Popplejoy in the house, no doubt he would have taken some most exemplary vengeance upon him. As it was, however, Tobias was thrown into his cell with a promise of vengeance as soon as the coast was clear. These were a kind of promises which Mr. Fogg was pretty sure to keep, and when the first impulse of his passion had passed away, poor Tobias, as well indeed he might, gave himself up to despair.

"Now all is over," he said; "I shall be half murdered! Oh, why do they not kill me at once? There would be some mercy in that. Come and murder me at once, you wretches! You villains, murder me at once!"

In his new excitement, he rushed to the door of the cell, and banged at it with his fists, when to his surprise it opened, and he found himself nearly falling into the stone corridor from which the various cell doors opened. It was evident that Mr. Watson thought he had locked him in, for the bolt of the lock was shot back, but had missed its hold — a circumstance probably arising from the state of rage and confusion Mr. Watson was in, as a consequence of Tobias's daring attack upon him. It almost seemed to the boy as if he had already made some advance towards his freedom, when he found himself in the narrow passage beyond his cell door, but his heart for some minutes beat so tumultuously with the throng of blissful associations connected with freedom, that it was quite impossible for him to proceed. A slight noise, however, in another part of the building roused him again, and he felt that it was only now by a great coolness and self-possession, as well as great courage, that he could at all hope to turn to account the fortunate incident which had enabled him, at all events, to make that first step towards liberty.

"Oh, if I could but get out of this dreadful place," he thought; "if I could but once again breathe the pure fresh air of heaven, and see the deep blue sky, I think I should ask for no other blessings."

Never do the charms of nature present themselves to the imagination in more lovely guise than when some one with an imagination full of such beauties, and a mind to appreciate the glories of the world, is shut up from real, actual contemplation. To Tobias now the thought of green fields, sunshine and flowers, was at once rapture and agony.

"I must," he said, "I must — I will be free."

A thorough determination to do anything, we are well convinced, always goes a long way towards its accomplishment; and certainly Tobias now would cheerfully have faced death in any shape, rather than he would again have been condemned to the solitary horrors of the cell, from which he had by such a chance got free. He conjectured the stupid old Dr. Popplejoy had not left the house, by the unusual quiet that reigned in it, and he began to wonder if, while that quiet subsisted, there was the remotest chance of his getting into the garden, and then scaling the wall, and so reaching the open common.

While this thought was establishing itself in his mind, and he was thinking that he would pursue the passage in which he was until he saw where it led to, he heard the sound of footsteps, and he shrank back. For a few seconds they appeared as if they were approaching where he was; and he began to dread that the cell would be searched, and his absence discovered, in which case there would be no chance for him but death.

Suddenly, however, the approaching footsteps paused, and then he heard a door banged shut. It was still, even now, some minutes before Tobias could bring himself to traverse the passage again, and when he did, it was with a slow and stealthy step. He had not, however, gone above thirty paces, before he heard the indistinct murmur of voices, and being guided by the sound, he paused at a door on his right hand, which he thought must be the one he had heard closed but a few minutes previously. It was from the interior of the room which that was the door of, that the sound of voices came, and as it was a matter of the very first importance to Tobias to ascertain in what part of the house his enemies were, he placed his ear against the panel, and listened attentively.

He recognised both the voices: they were those of Watson and Fogg. It was a very doubtful and ticklish situation that poor Tobias was now in, but it was wonderful how, by dint of strong resolution, he had stilled the beating of his heart and the general nervousness of his disposition. There was but a frail door between him and his enemies, and yet he stood profoundly still and listened. Mr. Fogg was speaking.

"You quite understand me, Watson, I think," he said, "as concerns that little viper, Tobias Ragg; he is too cunning, and much too dangerous to live long. He almost staggered old superannuated Popplejoy."

"Oh, confound him!" replied Watson, "and he's quite staggered me."

"Why, certainly your face is rather scratched."

"Yes, the little devil! but it's all in the way of business, that, Mr. Fogg, and you never heard me grumble at such little matters yet; and I'll be bound never will, that's more."

"I give you credit for that, Watson; but between you and I, I think the disease of that boy is of a nature that will carry him off very suddenly."

"I think so too," said Watson, with a chuckle.

"It strikes me forcibly that he will be found dead in his bed some morning, and I should not in the least wonder if that were to-morrow morning: what's your opinion, Watson?"

"Oh, damn it, what's the use of all this round-about nonsense between us? the boy is to die, and there's an end of it, and die he shall during the night — I owe him a personal grudge, of course, now."

"Of course you do — he has disfigured you."

"Has he? Well, I can return the compliment; and I say, Mr. Fogg, my opinion is, that it's very dangerous having these medical inspections you have such a fancy for."

"My dear fellow, it is dangerous, that I know as well as you can tell me, but it is from that danger we gather safety. If anything in the shape of a disturbance should arise about any patient, you don't know of what vast importance a report from such a man as old Dr. Popplejoy might be."

"Well, well, have it your own way. I shall not go near Master Tobias for the whole day, and shall see what starvation and solitude does towards taming him down a bit."

"As you please; but it is time you went your regular rounds."

"Yes, of course."

Tobias heard Watson rise. The crisis was a serious one. His eye fell upon a bolt that was outside the door, and, with the quickness of thought, he shot it into its socket, and then made his way down the passage towards his cell, the door of which he shut close. His next movement was to run to the end of the passage and descend some stairs. A door opposed him, but a push opened it, and he found himself in a small, dimly-lighted room, in one corner of which, upon a heap of straw, lay a woman, apparently sleeping. The noise which Tobias made in entering the cell, for such it was, roused her up, and she said —

"Oh! no, no; not the lash! not the lash! I am quiet. God, how quiet I am, although the heart within is breaking. Have mercy upon me!"

"Have mercy upon me," said Tobias, "and hide me if you can."

"Hide you! hide you! God of Heaven, who are you?"

"A poor victim, who has escaped from one of the cells, and I —"

"Hush!" said the woman; and she made Tobias shrink down in the corner of the cell, cleverly covering him up with the straw, and then lying down herself in such a position that he was completely screened. The precaution was not taken a moment too soon, for, by the time it was completed, Watson had burst open the door of the room which Tobias had bolted, and stood in the narrow passage.

"How the devil," he said, "came that door shut, I wonder?"

"Oh! save me," whispered Tobias.

"Hush! hush! He will only look in," was the answer. "You are safe. I have been only waiting for some one who could assist me, in order to attempt an escape. You must remain here until night, and then I will show you how it may be done. Hush! — he comes." Watson did come, and looked into the cell, muttering an oath, as he said —

"Oh, you have enough bread and water till to-morrow morning, I should say; so you need not expect to see me again till then."

"Oh! we are saved! we shall escape," said the poor creature, after Watson had been gone some minutes.

"Do you think so?"

"Yes, yes! Oh, boy, I do not know what brought you here, but if you have suffered one-tenth part of the cruelty and oppression that I have suffered, you are indeed to be pitied."

"If we are to stay here," said Tobias, "till night, before making any attempt to escape, it will, perhaps, ease your mind, and beguile the time, if you were to tell me how you came here."

"God knows! it might — it might."

Tobias was very urgent upon the poor creature to tell her story, to beguile the tedium of the time of waiting, and after some amount of persuasion she consented to do so.

"You shall now hear," she said to Tobias, "if you will listen, such a catalogue of wrongs, unredressed and still enduring, that would indeed drive any human being mad; but I have been able to preserve so much of my mental faculties as will enable me to recollect and understand the many acts of cruelty and injustice that I have endured here for many a long and weary day. My persecutions began when I was very young — so young that I could not comprehend their cause, and used to wonder why I should be treated with greater rigour or with greater cruelty than people used to treat those who were really disobedient and wayward children. I was scarcely seven years old when a maiden aunt died; she was the old person whom I remember as having been uniformly kind to me; though I can only remember her indistinctly, yet I know she was kind to me; I know also I used to visit her, and she used to look upon me as her favourite, for I used to sit at her feet upon a stool, watching her as she sat amusing herself by embroidering, silent and motionless sometimes, and then I asked her some questions which she answered. This is the chief feature of my recollection of my aunt: she soon after died, but while she lived, I had no unkindness from anybody; it was only after that that I felt the cruelty and coolness of my family. It appeared that I was a favourite with my aunt above all others, either in our family or any other; she loved me, and promised that when she died, she would leave me provided for, and that I should not be dependent upon any one.

"Well, I was, from the day after the funeral, an altered being. I was neglected, and no one paid any attention to me whatsoever; I was thrust about, and nobody appeared to care even if I had the necessaries of life. Such a change I could not understand. I could not believe the evidence of my own senses; I thought it must be something that I did not understand; perhaps my poor aunt's death had caused this distress and alteration in people's demeanour to me. However, I was a child, and though I was quick enough at noting all this, yet I was too young to feel acutely the conduct of my friends. My father and mother were careless of me, and let me run where I would; they cared not when I was hurt, they cared not when I was in danger. Come what would, I was left to take my chance. I recollect one day when I had fallen from the top to the bottom of some stairs and hurt myself very much; but no one comforted me; I was thrust out of the drawing-room, because I cried. I then went to the top of the stairs, where I sat weeping bitterly for some time. At length, an old servant came out of one of the attics, and said —

"'Oh! Miss Mary, what has happened to you, that you sit crying so bitterly on the stair head? Come in here!'

"I arose and went into the attic with her, when she set me on a chair, and busied herself with my bruises, and said to me —

"'Now, tell me what are you crying about, and why did they turn you out of the drawing-room — tell me now?'

"'Ay,' said I, 'they turned me out because I cried when I was hurt. I fell all the way down stairs, but they don't mind.'

"'No, they do not, and yet in many families they would have taken more care of you than they do here!'

"'And why do you think they would have done so?' I inquired.

"'Don't you know what good fortune has lately fallen into your lap? I thought you knew all about it.'

"'I don't know anything, save they are very unkind to me lately.'

"'They have been very unkind to you, child, and I am sure I don't know why, nor can I tell you why they have not told you of your fortune.'

"'My fortune,' said I; 'what fortune?'

"'Why, don't you know that when your poor aunt died you were her favourite?'

"'I know my aunt loved me,' I said; 'she loved me, and was kind to me; but since she has been dead, nobody cares for me.'

"'Well, my child, she has left a will behind her which says that all her fortune shall be yours; when you are old enough you shall have all her fine things; you shall have all her money and her house.'

" 'Indeed!' said I; 'who told you so?'

" 'Oh, I have heard it from those who were present at the reading of the will, that you are, when you are old enough, to have all. Think what a great lady you will be then! You will have servants of your own.'

" 'I don't think I shall live till then.'

" 'Oh yes, you will — or at least I hope so.'

" 'And if I should not, what will become of all those fine things that you have told me of? Who'll have them?'

" 'Why, if you do not live till you are of age, your fortune will go to your father and mother, who take all.'

" 'Then they would sooner I should die than live?'

" 'What makes you think so?' she inquired.

" 'Why,' said I, 'they don't care anything for me now, and they will have my fortune if I were dead — so they don't want me.'

" 'Ah, my child!' said the old woman, 'I have thought of that more than once; and now you can see it. I believe that it will be so. There has many a word been spoken truly enough by a child before now, and I am sure you are right — but do you be a good child, and be careful of yourself, and you will always find that Providence will keep you out of any trouble.'

" 'I hope so,' I said.

" 'And be sure you don't say who told you about this.'

" 'Why not,' I inquired; 'why may I not tell who told me about it?'

" 'Because,' she replied, 'if it were known that I told you anything about it, as you have not been told by them, they might discharge me, and I should be turned out.'

" 'I will not do that,' I replied; 'they shall not learn who told me, though I should like to hear them say the same thing.'

" 'You may hear them do so one of these days,' she replied, 'if you are not impatient: it will come out one of these days — two may know of it.'

" 'More than my father and mother?'

" 'Yes, more — several.'

"No more was said then about the matter; but I treasured it up in my mind. I resolved that I would act differently, and not have anything to do with them — that is, I would not be more in their sight than I could help — I would not be in their sight at all, save at meal times — and when there was any company there I always appeared. I cannot tell why; but I think it was because I sometimes attracted the attention of others, and I hoped to be able to hear something respecting my fortune; and in the end I succeeded in doing so, and then I was satisfied — not that it made any alteration in my conduct, but I felt I was entitled to a fortune. How such an impression became imprinted upon a girl of eight years of age, I know not: but it took hold of me, and I had some kind of notion that I was entitled to more consideration than I was treated to.

"'Mother,' said I one day to her.

"'Well, Mary, what do you want to tease me about now?'

"'Didn't Mrs. Carter the other day say that my aunt left me a fortune?'

"'What is the child dreaming about?' said my mother. 'Do you know what you are talking about, child? — you can't comprehend.'

"'I don't know, mother, but you said it was so to Mrs. Carter.'

"'Well, then, what if I did, child?'

"'Why, you must have told the truth or a falsehood.'

"'Well, Miss Impudence! — I told the truth, what then?'

"'Why, then I am to have a fortune when I grow up, that's all I mean, mother, and then people will take care of me. I shall not be forgotten, but everything will be done for me, and I shall be thought of first.'

"My mother looked at me very hard for a moment or two, and then, as if she was actuated by remorse, she made an attempt to speak, but checked herself, and then anger came to her aid, and she said —

"'Upon my word, miss! what thoughts have you taken into your fancy now? I suppose we shall be compelled to be so many servants to you! I am sure you ought to be ashamed of yourself — you ought, indeed!'

"'I didn't know I had done wrong,' I said.

"'Hold your tongue, will you, or I shall be obliged to flog you!' said my mother, giving me a sound box on the ears that threw me down. 'Now, hold your tongue and go up stairs, and give me no more insolence.'

"I arose and went up stairs, sobbing as if my heart would break. I cannot recollect how many bitter hours I spent there, crying by myself — how many tears I shed upon this matter, and how I compared myself to other children, and how much my situation was worse than theirs by a great deal. They, I thought, had their companions — they had their hours of play. But what companions had I? and what had I in the way of relaxation? What had I to do save to pine over the past, the present, and the future? My infantile thoughts and hours were alike occupied by the sad reflections that belonged to a more mature age than mine; and yet I was so. Days, weeks, and months passed on — there was no change, and I grew apace; but I was always regarded by my family with dislike, and always neglected. I could not account for it in any other way than they wished me dead. It may appear very dreadful — very dreadful indeed — but what else was I to think? The old servant's words came upon my mind full of their meaning — if I died before I was one-and-twenty, they would have all my aunt's money.

"'They wish me to die,' I thought, 'they wish me to die; and I shall die — I am sure I shall die! But they will kill me — they have tried it by neglecting me, and making me sad. What can I do — what can I do?'

"These thoughts were the current matter of my mind, and how often do they recur to my recollection now I am in this dull, dreadful place! I can never forget the past. I am here because I have rights elsewhere, which others can enjoy, and do enjoy. However, that is an old evil. I have thus suffered long. But to return. After a year had gone by — two, I think, must have passed over my head — before I met with anything that was at all calculated to injure me. I must have been near ten years old, when, one evening, I had no sooner got into bed, than I found I had been put into damp — I may say wet sheets. They were so damp that I could not doubt but this was done on purpose. I am sure no negligence ever came to anything so positive and so abominable in all my life. I got out of bed and took them off, and then wrapped myself up in the blankets and slept till morning, without awaking any one. When morning came, I inquired who put the sheets there?

" 'What do you mean, minx?' said my mother.

" 'Only that somebody was bad and wicked enough to put positively wet sheets in the bed; it could not have been done through carelessness — it must have been done through sheer wilfulness. I'm quite convinced of that.'

" 'You will get yourself well thrashed if you talk like that,' said my mother. 'The sheets are not damp; there are none in the house that are damp.'

" 'These are wet.'

"This reply brought her hand down heavily upon my shoulder, and I was forced upon my knees. I could not help myself, so violent was the blow.

" 'There,' added my mother, 'take that, and that, and answer me if you dare.'

"As she said this she struck me to the ground, and my head came in violent contact with the table, and I was rendered insensible. How long I continued so I cannot tell. What I first saw when I awoke was the dreariness of one of the attics into which I had been thrust, and thrown upon a small bed without any furniture. I looked around and saw nothing that indicated comfort, and upon looking at my clothes there were traces of blood. This, I had no doubt, came from myself. I was hurt, and upon putting my hand to my head, found that I was much hurt, as my head was bound up. At that moment the door was opened, and the old servant came in.

" 'Well, Miss Mary,' she said, 'and so you have come round again? I really began to be afraid you were killed. What a fall you must have had!'

" 'Fall,' said I; 'who said it was a fall?'

" 'They told me so.'

" 'I was struck down.'

" 'Struck, Miss Mary! Who could strike you? And what did you do to deserve such a severe chastisement? Who did it?'

" 'I spoke to my mother about the wet sheets.'

" 'Ah! what a mercy you were not killed! If you had slept in them, your life would not have been worth a farthing. You would have caught cold, and you would have died of inflammation, I am sure of it. If anybody wants to commit murder without being found out, they have only to put them into damp sheets.'

"'So I thought, and I took them out.'

"'You did quite right—quite right.'

"'What have you heard about them?' said I.

"'Oh! I only went into the room in which you sleep, and I at once found how damp they were, and how dangerous it was; and I was going to tell your mamma, when I met her, and she told me to hold my tongue, but to go down and take you away, as you had fallen down in a fit, and she could not bear to see you lying there.'

"'And she didn't do anything for me?'

"'Oh, no, not as I know of, because you were lying on the floor bleeding. I picked you up, and brought you here.'

"'And has she not inquired after me since?'

"'Not once.'

"'And don't know whether I am yet sensible or not?'

"'She does not yet know that.'

"'Well,' I replied, 'I think they don't care much for me, I think not at all, but the time may come when they will act differently.'

"'No, miss, they think, or affect to think, that you have injured them; but that cannot be, because you could not be cunning enough to dispose your aunt to leave you all, and so deprive them of what they think they are entitled to.'

"'I never could have believed half so much.'

"'Such, however, is the case.'

"'What can I do?'

"'Nothing, my dear, but lie still till you get better, and don't say any more; but sleep, if you can sleep, will do you more good than anything else now for an hour or so, so lie down and sleep.'

"THE OLD WOMAN LEFT THE ROOM, and I endeavoured to compose myself to sleep; but could not do so for some time, my mind being too actively engaged in considering what I had better do, and I determined upon a course of conduct by which I thought to escape much of my present persecution. It was some days, however, before I could put it in practice, and one day I found my father and mother together, and I said to her—

"'Mother, why do you not send me to school?'

"'You—send you to school! did you mean you, miss?'

"'Yes, I meant myself, because other people go to school to learn something, but I have not been sent at all.'

"'Are you not contented?'

"'I am not,' I answered, 'because other people learn something; but at the same time, I should be more out of your way, since I am more trouble to you, as you complain of me; it would not cost more than living at home.'

"'What is the matter with the child?' asked my father.

"'I cannot tell,' said my mother.

"'The better way will be to take care of her, and confine her to some part of the house, if she does not behave better.'

"'The little minx will be very troublesome.'

"'Do you think so?'

"'Yes, decidedly.'

"'Then we must adopt some more active measures, or we shall have to do what we do not wish. I am amused at her asking to be sent to school! Was ever there heard of such wickedness? Well, I could not have believed such ingratitude could have existed in human nature.'

"'Go out of the room, you hussy,' said my mother; 'go out of the room, and don't let me hear a word from you more.'

"'I left the room terrified at the storm I had raised up against me. I knew not that I had done wrong, and went up crying to my attic alone, and found the old servant, who asked what was the matter. I told her all I had said, and what had been the result, and how I had been abused.

"'Why, you should let things take their own course, my dear.'

"'Yes, but I can learn nothing.'

"'Never mind; you will have plenty of money when you grow older, and that will cure many defects; people who have money never want for friends.'

"'But I have them not, and yet I have money.'

"'Most certainly — most certainly, but you have it not in your power, and you are not old enough to make use of it, if you had it.'

"'Who has it?' I inquired.

"'Your father and mother.'

"No more was said at that time, and the old woman left me to myself, and I recollect I long and deeply pondered over this matter, and yet could see no way out of it, and resolved that I would take things as easily as I could; but I feared that I was not likely to have a very quiet life; indeed, active cruelty was exercised against me. They would lock me up in a room a whole day at a time, so that I was debarred the use of my limbs. I was even kept without food, and on every occasion I was knocked about, from one to the other, without remorse — every one took a delight in tormenting me, and in showing me how much they dared do. Of course servants and all would not treat me with neglect and harshness if they did not see it was agreeable to my parents. This was shocking cruelty; but yet I found that this was not all. Many were the little contrivances made and invented to cause me to fall down stairs — to slip — to trip, or do anything that might have ended in some fatal accident, which would have left them at liberty to enjoy my legacy, and no blame would be attached to them for the accident, and I should most likely get blamed for what was done, and from which I had been the sufferer — indeed, I should have been deemed to have suffered justly. On one occasion, after I had been in bed some time, I found it was very damp, and upon examination I found the bed itself had been made quite wet, with the sheets put over it to hide it. This I did not discover until it was too late, for I caught a violent cold, and it took me some weeks to get over it, and yet I escaped eventually, though after some months' illness. I recovered, and it evidently made them angry because I did live. They must have believed me to be very obstinate; they thought me obdurate in the extreme — they called me all the names they could imagine, and treated me with every indignity they could heap upon me.

"Well, time ran on, and in my twelfth year I obtained the notice of one or two of our friends, who made some inquiries about me. I always remarked that my parents disliked any one to speak to, or take any notice of me. They did not permit me to say much — they did not like my speaking; and on one occasion, when I made some remark respecting school, she replied —

"'Her health is so bad that I have not yet sent her, but shall do so by and by, when she grows stronger.'

"There was a look bent upon me that told me at once what I must expect, if I persisted in my half-formed resolve of contradicting all that had been said. When the visitor went I was well aware of what kind of a life I should have had, if I did not absolutely receive some serious injury. I was terrified, and held my tongue. Soon after that I was seized with violent pains and vomiting. I was very ill, and the servant being at home only, a doctor was sent for, who at once said I had been poisoned, and ordered me to be taken care of.

"I know how it was done: I had some cake given me — it was left out for me; and that was the only thing I had eaten, and it astonished me, for I had not had such a thing given me for years, and that is why I believe the poison was put in the cake, and I think others thought so too.

"However, I got over that after a time, though I was a long while before I did so; but at the same time I was very weak, and the surgeon said that had I been a little longer without assistance, or had I not thrown it up, I must have sunk beneath the effects of a violent poison. He advised my parents to take some measures to ascertain who it was that had administered the poison to me; but though they promised compliance, they never troubled themselves about it — but I was for a long time very cautious of what I took, and was in great fear of the food that was given to me.

"However, nothing more of that character took place, and at length I quite recovered, and began to think in my own mind that I ought to take some active steps in the matter, and that I ought to seek an asylum elsewhere. I was now nearly fifteen years of age, and could well see how inveterate was the dislike with which I was regarded by my family: I thought that they ought to use me better, for I could remember no cause for it. I had given no deadly offence, nor was there any motive why I should be treated thus with neglect and disdain. It was, then, a matter of serious consideration with me, as to whether I should not go and throw myself upon the protection of some friend, and beg their inter-ference in my behalf; but then there was no one whom I felt that would do so much for me — no one from whom I expected so great an act of friendship. It was hardly to be expected from any one that they should interfere between me and my parents; they would have had their first say, and I should have contra-dicted all they said, and should have appeared in a very bad light indeed. I could not say they had neglected my education — I could not say that, because there I had been careful myself, and I had assiduously striven when alone to remedy this defect, and had actually succeeded; so that, if I were examined, I should have denied my own assertions by contrary facts, which would injure me.

"Then again, if I were neglected I could not prove any injury, because I had all the means of existence; and all I could say would either be attributed to some evil source, or it was entirely false — but at the same time I felt that I had great cause of complaint, and none of gratitude. I could hold no communion with any one — all alike deserted me, and I knew none who could say aught for me if I requested their good-will. I had serious thoughts of possessing myself of some money, and then leaving home, and staying away until I had arrived at age; but this I deferred doing, seeing that there were no means, and I could not do more than I then did — that is, to live on without any mischief happening, and wait for a few years more.

"I contracted an acquaintance with a young man who came to visit my father — he came several times, and paid me more civility and attention than any one else ever did, and I felt that he was the only friend I possessed. It is no wonder I looked upon him as being my best and my only friend. I thought him the best and the handsomest man I ever beheld. This put other thoughts into my head. I did not dress as others did, much less had I the opportunity of becoming possessed of many of those little trinkets that most young women of my age had. But this made no alteration in the good opinion of the young gentleman, who took no notice of that, but made me several pretty presents. These were treasures to me, and I must say I gloated over them, and often, when alone, I have spent hours in admiring them; trifling as they were, they made me happier. I knew now one person who cared for me, and a delightful feeling it was too. I shall never know it again — it is quite impossible. Here, among the dark walls and unwholesome cells, we have no cheering ray of life or hope — all is dreary and cold; a long and horrible punishment takes place, to which there is no end save with life, and in which there is no one mitigating circumstance — all is bad and dark. God help me!"

"However, my dream of happiness was soon disturbed. By some means my parents had got an idea of this, and the young man was dismissed the house, and forbidden to come to it again. This he determined to do, and more than once we met, and then in secret I told him all my woes. When he had heard all I said, he expressed the deepest commiseration, and declared I had been most unjustly and harshly treated, and thought that there was not a harder or harsher treatment than that which I had received. He then advised me to leave home.

"'Leave home,' I said; 'where shall I fly? I have no friend.'

"'Come to me, I will protect you; I will stand between you and all the world; they shall not stir hand or foot to your injury.'

"'But I cannot, dare not to do that; if they found me out, they would force me back with all the ignominy and shame that could be felt from having done a bad act; not any pity would they show me.'

"'Nor need you; you would be my wife — I mean to make you my wife.'

"'You?'

"'Yes! I dreamed not of anything else. You shall be my wife; we will hide ourselves, and remain unknown to all until the time shall have arrived when you are of age — when you can claim all your property, and run no risk of being poisoned or killed by any other means.'

"'This is a matter,' said I, 'that ought to be considered well before adopting anything so violent and so sudden.'

"'It does; and it is not one that I think will injure by being reflected upon by those who are the principal actors; for my own part my mind is made up, and I am ready to perform my share of the engagement.'

"I resolved to consider the matter well in my own mind, and felt every inclination to do what he proposed, because it took me away from home, and because it would give me one of my own. My parents had become utterly estranged from me: they did not act as parents, they did not act as friends, they had steeled my heart against them; they never could have borne any love to me, I am sure of it, who could have committed such great crimes against me.

"As the hour drew near, that in which I was likely to become an object of still greater hatred and dislike to them, I thought I was often the subject of their private thoughts, and often when I entered the room my mother and father, and the rest, would suddenly leave off speaking, and look at me, as if to ascertain if I had overheard them say anything. On one occasion I remember very well I heard them conversing in a low tone. The door happened to have opened of itself, the hasp not having been allowed to enter the mortise. I heard my name mentioned: I paused and listened.

"'We must soon get rid of her,' said my mother.

"'Undoubtedly,' he replied; 'if we do not, we shall have her about our ears: she'll get married, or some infernal thing, and then we shall have to refund.'

"'We could prevent that.'

"'Not if her husband were to insist upon it, we could not; but the only plan I can now form is, what I told you of already.'

"'Putting her into a madhouse?'

"'Yes: there, you see, she will be secured, and cannot get away. Besides, those who go there die in a natural way before many years.'

"'But she can speak.'

"'So she may; but who attends to the ravings of a mad woman? No, no; depend upon it, that is the best plan: send her to a lunatic asylum — a private madhouse. I can obtain all that is requisite in a day or two.'

"'Then we will consider that settled?'

"'Certainly.'

"'In a few days, then?'

"'Before next Sunday; because we can enjoy ourselves on that day without any restraint, or without any uncomfortable feelings of uncertainty about us.'

"I WAITED TO HEAR NO MORE: I had heard enough to tell me what I had to expect. I went back to my own room, and having put on my bonnet and shawl I went out to see the individual to whom I have alluded, and saw him. I then informed him of all that had taken place, and heard him exclaim against them in terms of rising indignation.

"'Come to me,' he said; 'come to me at once.'

"'Not at once.'

"'Don't stop a day.'

"'Hush!' said I, 'there's no danger; I will come the day after to-morrow; and then I will bid adieu to all these unhappy moments, to all these persecutions; and in three years' time I shall be able to demand my fortune, which will be yours.'

"WE WERE TO MEET THE NEXT day but one, early in the morning; there was not, in fact, to be more than thirty hours elapse before I was to leave home — if home I could call it — however, there was no time to be lost. I made up a small bundle and had all in readiness before I went to bed, and placed in security, intending to rise early, and let myself out and leave the house. That, however, was never to happen. While I slept, at a late hour of the night, I was awakened by two men standing by my bedside, who desired me to get up and follow them. I refused, and they pulled me rudely out of bed. I called out for aid, and exclaimed against the barbarity of their proceedings.

"'It is useless to listen to her,' said my father, 'you know what a mad woman will say!'

"'Ay, we do,' replied the men, 'they are the cunningest devils we ever heard. We have seen enough of them to know that.'

"To make the matter plain, I was seized, gagged, and thrust into a coach, and brought here, where I have remained ever since."

CHAPTER XXIX.

TOBIAS'S RAPID JOURNEY TO LONDON.

THERE WAS SOMETHING EXTREMELY TOUCHING in the tone, and apparently in the manner in which the poor persecuted one detailed the story of her wrongs, and she had a tribute of a willing tear from Tobias.

"After the generous confidence you have had in me," he said, "I ought to tell you something of myself."

"Do so," she replied, "we are companions in misfortune."

"We are indeed."

Tobias then related to her at large all about Sweeney Todd's villanies, and how at length he, Tobias, had been placed where he was for the purpose of silencing his testimony of the evil and desperate practices of the barber. After that, he related to her what he had overheard about the intention to murder him that very night, and he concluded by saying —

"If you have any plan of escape from this horrible place, let me implore you to tell it to me, and let us put it into practice to-night, and if we fail, death is at any time preferable to continued existence here."

"It is — it is — listen to me."

"I will indeed," said Tobias: "you will say you never had such attention as I will now pay to you."

"You must know, then, that this cell is paved with flag-stones, as you see, and that the wall here at the back forms likewise part of the wall of an old wood-house in the garden, which is never visited."

"Yes, I understand."

"Well, as I have been here so long, I managed to get up one of the flag-stones that forms the flooring here, and to work under the wall with my hands — a slow labour, and one of pain, until I made a regular kind of excavation, one end of which is here, and the other in the wood-house."

"Glorious!" said Tobias. "I see — I see — go on."

"I should have made my escape if I could, but the height of the garden wall has always been the obstacle. I thought of tearing this miserable quilt into strips, and making a sort of rope of it; but then how was I to get it on the wall? you, perhaps will, with your activity and youth, be able to accomplish that."

"Oh, yes, yes! you're right enough there; it is not a wall shall stop me."

THEY WAITED UNTIL, from a church clock in the vicinity, they heard ten strike, and they began operations. Tobias assisted his new friend to raise the stone in the cell, and there, immediately beneath, appeared the excavation leading to the wood-house, just sufficiently wide for one person to creep through. It did not take long to do that, and Tobias took with him a piece of work, upon which he had been occupied for the last two hours, namely the quilt torn up into long pieces, twisted and tied together, so that it formed a very tolerable rope, which Tobias thought would sustain the weight of his companion. The wood-house was a miserable-looking hole enough, and Tobias at once thought that the door of it was fastened, but by a little pressure it came open; it had only stuck through the dampness of the woodwork at that low point of the garden. And now they were certainly both of them at liberty, with the exception of surmounting the wall, which rose frowningly before him in all its terrors.

There was a fine cool fresh air in the garden, which was indeed most grateful to the senses of Tobias, and he seemed doubly nerved for anything that might be required of him after inhaling that delicious, cool fresh breeze. There grew close to the wall one of those beautiful mountain-ash trees, which bend over into such graceful foliage, and which are so useful in the formation of pretty summer-houses. Tobias saw that if he ascended to the top of this tree there would not be much trouble in getting from there to the wall.

"We shall do it," he said, "we shall succeed."

"Thank God, I hear you say so," replied his companion.

Tobias tied one end of the long rope they had made of the quilt to his waist, so that he might carry it up with him, and yet leave him free use of his hands and feet, and then he commenced ascending the tree. In three minutes he was on the wall. The moon shone sweetly. There was not a tree or house in the vicinity that was not made beautiful now, in some portions of it, by the sweet, soft light that poured down upon them, Tobias could not resist pausing a moment to look around him on the glorious scene; but the voice of her for whom he was bound to do all that was possible, aroused him.

"Oh, Tobias!" she said, "quick, quick — lower the rope; oh, quick!"

"In a moment — in a moment," he cried.

The top of the wall was here and there armed with iron spikes, and some of these formed an excellent grappling place for the torn quilt. In the course of another minute Tobias had his end of it secure.

"Now," he said, "can you climb up by it, do you think? Don't hurry about it. Remember, there is no alarm, and for all we know we have hours to ourselves yet."

"Yes, yes — oh, yes — thank God!" he heard her say.

Tobias was not where he could, by any exertion of strength, render her now the least assistance, and he watched the tightening of the frail support by which she was gradually climbing to the top of the wall with the most intense and painful interest that can be imagined.

"I come — I come," she said, "I am saved."

"Come slowly — for God's sake, do not hurry."

"No, no."

At this moment Tobias heard the frail rope giving way; there was a tearing sound — it broke, and she fell. Lights, too, at that unlucky moment, flashed from the house, and it was now evident an alarm had been given. What could he do? if two could not be saved he might himself be saved. He turned, and flung his feet over the wall; he hung by his hands as low as he could, and then he dropped the remainder of the distance. He was hurt, but in a moment he sprang to his feet, for he felt that safety could only lie in instant and rapid flight. The terror of pursuit was so strong upon him that he forgot his bruises.

"THANK HEAVEN," EXCLAIMED TOBIAS, "I am at last free from that horrible place. Oh, if I can but reach London now, I shall be safe; and as for Sweeney Todd, let him beware, for a day of retribution for him cannot be far off."

So saying, Tobias turned his steps towards the city, and at a hard trot, soon left Peckham Rye far behind him as he pursued his route.

CHAPTER XXX.

MRS. LOVETT'S COOK MAKES A DESPERATE ATTEMPT.

THERE ARE FOLKS WHO CAN and who will bow like reeds to the decrees of evil fortune, and with a patient, ass-like placidity, go on bearing the ruffles of a thankless world without complaining; but Mrs. Lovett's new cook was not one of those. The more destiny seemed to say to him — "Be quiet!" the more he writhed, and wriggled, and fumed, and could not be quiet. The more fate whispered in his ears — "You can do nothing," the more intent he was upon doing something, let it be what it might. And he had a little something, in the shape of a respite too, now, for had he not baked a batch of pies, and sent them up to the devouring fangs of the lawyers' clerks, in all their gelatinous beauty and gushing sweetness, to be devoured? To be sure he had, and therefore having, for a space, obeyed the behests of his task-mistress, he could sit with his head resting upon his hands and think. Thought! What a luxury! Where is the Indian satrap — where the arch-Inquisitor — where the grasping, dishonest, scheming employer who can stop a man from thinking? — and as Shakespeare, says of sleep,

> *"From that sleep, what dreams may come?"**

— so might he have said of thought,

> *"From that thought what acts may come?"*

NOW WE ARE AFRAID THAT, in the first place, the cook, in spite of himself, uttered some expression concerning Mrs. Lovett of neither an evangelical or a polite character, and with these we need not trouble the reader. They acted as a sort of safety-valve to his feelings, and after consigning that fascinating female to a certain warm place, where we may fancy everybody's pie might be cooked on the very shortest notice, he got a little more calm.

"What shall I do? — what shall I do?"

Such was the rather vague question he asked of himself. Alas! how often are those four simple words linked together, finding but a vain echo in the over-charged heart. "What shall I do?" Aye, what! — small power had he to do anything, except the quietest thing of all — that one thing which Heaven in its mercy has left for every wretch to do if it so pleases him — to die!

But, somehow or another, a man upon the up-hill side of life is apt to think he may do something rather than that, and our cook, although he was about as desperate a cook as the world ever saw, did not like yet to say die.

Now, in that curious combination of passions, impulses, and prejudices in the mind of this man it would be a hard case if some scheme of action did not present itself, even in circumstances of the greatest possible seeming depression, and so, after a time, the cook did think of something to do.

"Many of these pies," he said to himself, "are not eaten in the shop, ergo they are eaten out of the shop, and possibly at the respective houses of the purchasers — what more feasible mode of disclosing my position, and 'the secrets of my prison-house,' can there be than the enclosing a note in one of Mrs. Lovett's pies?"

After reviewing all the pros and cons of this scheme, there only appeared a few little difficulties in the way, but, although they were rather serious, they were not insurmountable. In the first place, it was possible enough that the unfortunate pie in which the note might be enclosed might be eaten in the shop, in which event the note might go down the throat of some hungry lawyer's clerk, and it might be handed to Mrs. Lovett, with a "God bless me, ma'am, what's this in the pie?" and then Mrs. Lovett might, by a not very remote possibility, say to herself — "This cook is a scheming, long-headed sort of a cook, and notwithstanding he does his duty by the pies, he shall be sent upon

---

* *Somewhat imprecisely quoted from Hamlet's "to be, or not to be" soliloquy (Act III, Scene I).*

an errand to another and a better world," and in that case the delectable scheme of the note could only end in the total destruction of the unfortunate who conceived it. Objection the second was, that, although nothing is so easy as to say — "Oh, write a note all about it," nothing is so difficult as to write a note about anything without paper, ink, and a pen. The cook rubbed his forehead, and cried —

"D—n it!"

This seemed to have the desired effect, for he at once recollected that he was supplied with a thin piece of paper for the purpose of laying over the pies if the oven should by chance be over heated, and so subject them to an over-browning process.

"Surely," he thought, "I shall be able to make a substitute for a pen, and as for ink, a little coal and water, or — ah, I have it, black from my lights, of course. Ha — ha! How difficulties vanish when a man has thoroughly made up his mind to overcome them. Ha — ha! I write a note — I post it in a pie — some lawyer sends his clerk for a pie, and he gets that pie. He opens it and sees the note — he reads it — he flies to a police-office, and gets a private interview with a magistrate — a couple of Bow-street runners walk down to Bell-yard, and seize Mrs. Lovett — I hear a row in the shop, and cry — 'Here I am — I am here — make haste — here I am — here I am!' Ha — ha — ha — ha — ha — ha!"

"Are you mad?"

The cook started to his feet —

"Who spoke — who spoke?"

"I," said Mrs. Lovett, looking through the ingenious little wicket at the top of the door. "What do you mean by that laughing? If you have gone mad, as one cook once did, death will be a relief to you. Only convince me of that fact, and in two hours you sleep the long sleep."

"I beg your pardon, ma'am, I am not at all mad."

"Then why did you laugh in such a way that it reached even my ears above?"

"Why, ma'am, are you not a widow?"

"Well?"

"Well then, you could not have possibly looked at me as you ought to have done, or you would have seen that I am anything but a bad looking fellow, and as I am decidedly single, what do you say to taking me for better or for worse? The pie business is a thriving one, and, of course, if I had an interest in it, I should say nothing of affairs down below here."

"Fool!"

"Thank you, madam, for the compliment, but I assure you, the idea of such an arrangement made me laugh, and at all events, provided I do my duty, you don't mind my laughing a little at it?"

Mrs. Lovett disdained any further conversation with the cook, and closed the little wicket. When she was gone he took himself seriously to task for being so foolish as to utter his thoughts aloud, but yet he did not think he had gone so far as to speak loud enough about the plan of putting the letter in a pie for her to hear that.

"Oh, no — no, I am safe enough. It was the laughing that made her come. I am safe as yet!"

Having satisfied himself fully upon this point, he at once set to work to manufacture his note. The paper, as he had said, was ready at hand. To be sure, it was of a thin and flimsy texture, and decidedly brown, but a man in his situation could be hardly supposed to stand upon punctilios. After some trouble he succeeded in making an apology for a pen by the aid of a piece of stick, and he manufactured some very tolerable ink, at least, as good as the soot and water commonly sold in London for the best "japan," and then he set about writing his note. As we have an opportunity of looking over his shoulder, we give the note verbatim.

> SIR — *(or Madam)* —
> *I am a prisoner beneath the shop of Mrs. Lovett, the pie female, in Bell-yard. I am threatened with death if I attempt to escape from my now enforced employment. Moreover, I am convinced that there is some dreadful secret connected with the pies, which I can hardly trust my imagination to dwell upon, much less here set it down. Pray instantly, upon receipt of this, go to the nearest police-office and procure me immediate aid, or I shall soon be numbered with the dead. In the sacred names of justice and humanity, I charge you to do this.*

The cook did not, for fear of accidents, put his name to this epistle. It was sufficient, he thought, that he designated his condition, and pointed out where he was. This note he folded into a close flat shape, and pressed it with his hands, so that it would take up a very small portion of room in a pie, and yet, from its size and nature, if the pie fell into the hands of some gourmand who commenced eating it violently, he could not fail to feel that there was a something in his mouth more indigestible than the delicate mutton or veal and the flaky crust of which Mrs. Lovett's delicacies were composed. Having proceeded thus far, he concluded that the only real risk he ran was, that the pie might be eaten in the shop, and the enclosure, without examination, handed over to Mrs. Lovett merely as a piece of paper which had insinuated itself where it had no right to be. But as no design whatever can be carried out without some risk or another, he was not disposed to give up his, because some contingency of that character was attached to it. The prospect of deliverance from the horrible condition to which he was reduced, now spread over his mind a pleasing calm, and he set about the manufacture of a batch of pies, so as to have it ready for the oven when the bell should ring. — Into one of them he carefully introduced his note.

Oh, what an eye he kept upon that individual pie. How often he carefully lifted the upper crust, to have a peep at the little missive which was about to go upon an errand of life or death. — How he tried to picture to his mind's eye the sort of person into whose hands it might fall, and then how he thought he would listen for any sounds during the next few hours, which should be indicative of the arrest of Mrs. Lovett, and the presence of the police in the place. He thought, then, that if his laugh had been sufficiently loud when merely uttered to himself, to reach the ears of Mrs. Lovett, surely his shout to the police would be heard above all other sounds, and at once bring them to his aid.

Tingle! tingle! tingle! went a bell. It was the signal for him to get a batch of pies ready for the oven.

"Good," he said, "it is done."

He waited until the signal was given to him to put them in to be cooked, and then, after casting one more look at the pie that contained his note, in went the batch to the hot air of the oven, which came out upon his face like the breath of some giant in a highly febrile state.

" 'Tis done," he said. " 'Tis done, and I am saved!"

He sat down and covered his face with his hands, while delicious dreamy thoughts of freedom came across his brain. Green fields, trees, meadows and uplands, and the sweet blue sky, all appeared before him in bright and beautiful array.

"Yes," he said. "Yes, I shall see them all once again. — Once again I shall look, perchance, upon the bounding deep blue sea. Once again I shall feel the sun of a happier clime than this fanning my cheek. Oh, liberty, liberty, what a precious boon art thou!"

Tingle! tingle! tingle! He started from his dream of joy. The pies are wanted; Mrs. Lovett knew well enough how long they took in doing, and that by this time they should be ready to be placed upon the ascending trap. Down it came. Open went the oven door, and in another minute the note was in the shop. The cook placed his hand upon his heart to still its tumultuous beating as he listened intently. He could hear the sound of feet above — only dimly though, through that double roof. Once he thought he heard high words, but all died away again, and nothing came of it. — All was profoundly still. The batch of pies surely were sold now, and in a paper bag he told himself his pie, par excellence, had gone perhaps to the chambers of some attorney, who would be rejoiced to have a finger in it; or to some briefless barrister, who would be rejoiced to get his name in the papers, even if it were only connected with a story of a pie. Yes, the dream of freedom still clung to the imagination of the cook, and he waited, with every nerve thrilling with expectation, the result of his plan.

One, two, three hours had passed away, and nothing came of the pie or the letter. All was as quiet and as calm as though the malignant fates had determined that there he was to spend his days for ever, and gradually as in a frigid situation the narrow column of mercury in a thermometer will sink, sank his spirits — down — down — down!

"No — no," he said. "No hope. Timidity or incredulity has consigned my letter to the flames, perhaps, or some wide-mouthed, stupid idiot has actually swallowed it. Oh that it had choked him by the way. Oh that it had actually stuck in his throat. — It is over, I have lost hope again. This horrible place will be my charnel-house — my family vault! Curses! — No — no. What is the use of swearing? My despair is past that — far past that —"

"Cook!" said a voice.

He sprang up, and looked to the wicket. There was Mrs. Lovett gazing in at him.

"Cook!"

"Well — well. — Fiend in female shape, what would you with me? Did you not expect to find me dead?"

"Certainly not. Here is a letter for you."

"A — a — letter?"

"Yes. Perhaps it is an answer to the one you sent in the pie, you know."

The unfortunate grasped his head, and gave a yell of despair. The letter — for indeed Mrs. Lovett had one — was dropped upon the ground floor from the opening through which she conversed with her prisoner, and then, without another word, she withdrew from the little orifice, and left him to his meditation.

"Lost! — lost! — lost!" he cried. "All is lost. God, is this enchantment? Or am I mad, and the inmate of some cell in an abode of lunacy, and all this about pies and letters merely the delusion of my overwrought fancy? Is there really a pie — a Mrs. Lovett — a Bell-yard — a letter — a — a — a — damn it, is there such a wretch as I myself, in this vast bustling world, or is all a wild and fathomless delusion?"

He cast himself upon the ground, as though from that moment he gave up all hope and desire to save himself. It seemed as though he could have said —

"Let death come in any shape he may, he will find me an unresisting victim. I have fought with fate, and am, like thousands who have preceded me in such a contest — beaten!"

A kind of stupor came over him, and there he lay for more than two hours; but youth will overcome much, and the mind, like some depressed spring, will, in the spring of life, soon recover its rebound; so it was with the unhappy cook. After a time he rose and looked about him.

"No," he said, "it is no dream. It is no dream!"

He then saw the letter lying upon the ground, which Mrs. Lovett had with such irony cast unto him.

"Surely," he said, "she might have been content to tell me she had discovered my plans, without adding this practical sneer to it."

He lifted the letter from the floor, and found it was addressed "To Mrs. Lovett's Cook, Bell-yard, Temple Bar;" and what made it all the more provoking was, that it seemed to have come regularly through the post, for there were the official seal and blue stamp upon it. Curiosity tempted him to open it, and he read as follows: —

Sir —

Having, in a most delicious pie, received the extraordinary communication which you inserted in it, I take the earliest opportunity of replying to you. The character of a highly respectable and pious woman is not, sir, to be whispered away in a pie by a cook. When the whole bench of bishops were proved, in black and white, to be the greatest thieves and speculators in the known world, it was their character that saved them, for, as people justly enough reasoned, bishops should be pious and just — therefore, a bishop cannot be a thief and a liar! Now, sir, apply this little mandate to Mrs. Lovett, and assure yourself; but no one will believe anything you can allege against a female with so fascinating a smile, and who attends to her religious duties so regularly. Reflect, young man, on the evil that you have tried to do, and for the future learn to be satisfied with the excellent situation you have. The pie was very good.

I am, you bad young man,
A Parishioner of St. Dunstan's,
Sweeney TODD."

"Now was there ever such a piece of cool rascality as this?" cried the cook, "Sweeney Todd — Todd — Todd. Who the devil is he? This is some scheme of Mrs. Lovett's to drive me mad."

He dashed the letter upon the floor.

"Not another pie will I make! No — no — no. Welcome death — welcome that dissolution which may be my lot, rather than the continued endurance of this terrible imprisonment. Am I, at my time of life, to be made the slave of such a demon in human shape as this woman? Am I to grow old and grey here, a mere pie machine? No — no, death a thousand times rather!"

Tears! yes, bitter scalding tears came to his relief, and he wept abundantly, but those tears were blessed, for as they flowed, the worst bitterness of his heart flowed with them, and he suddenly looked up, saying —

"I am only twenty-four."

There was magic in the sound of those words. They seemed in themselves to contain a volume of philosophy. Only twenty-four. Should he, at that green and unripe age, get rid of hope? Should he, at twenty-four only, lie down and say — "Let me die!" just because things had gone a little adverse, and he was the enforced cook of Mrs. Lovett?

"No — no," he said. "No, I will endure much, and I will hope much. Hitherto, it is true, I have been unsuccessful in what I have attempted for my release, but the diabolical cunning, even of this woman, may fail her at some moment, and I may have my time of revenge. No — no, I need not ask for revenge, justice will do — common justice. I will keep myself alive. Hope shall be my guiding star. They shall not subdue the proud spirit they have succeeded in caging, quite so easily, I will not give up, I live and have youthful blood in my veins, I will not despair. Despair? No — Hence, fiend! — I am as yet only twenty-four. Ha — ha! Only twenty-four."

CHAPTER XXXI.

SHOWS HOW TOBIAS GOT TO LONDON.

WE WILL NOW TAKE A PEEP AT TOBIAS. On — on — on, like the wind, went the poor belated boy from the vicinity of that frightful prison-house at Peckham. Terror was behind him — terror with dishevelled locks was upon his right hand, and terror shrieking in his ear was upon his left. On — on, he flew like a whirl-wind. Alas, poor Tobias, will your young intellects yet stand these trials? We shall see! Through the deep mud of the Surrey roads — past pedestrians — past horsemen, and past coaches flew poor Tobias, on — on. He had but one thought, and that was to place miles and miles of space between him and Mr. Fogg's establishment. The perspiration poured down his face — his knees shook under him — his heart beat as though in some wild pulsation it would burst, but he passed on until he saw afar off the old Bridge of London. The route to Blackfriars he had by some chance avoided. Many, who for the last two miles of Tobias's progress, had seen him, had tried to stop him. They had called after him, but he had heeded them not. Some fast runners had pursued him for a short distance, and then given up the chase in despair. He reached the bridge.

"Stop that boy!" cried a man, "he looks mad!"

"No — no," shrieked Tobias, "I am not mad! I am not mad!"

A man held out his arms to stop him, but Tobias dashed past him like a flash of lightning, and was off again.

"Stop him!" cried twenty voices. "Stop thief!" shouted some who could not conceive that anybody was to be stopped on any other account.

"No, no," gasped Tobias, as he flew onwards — "not mad, not mad!"

His feet failed him. He reeled a few more paces like a drunken man, and then fell heavily upon some stone steps, where he lay bathed in perspiration. Blood too gushed from his mouth. A gentleman's horse was standing at the door, and the man came out to mount him at that moment, and he saw the

THE FLIGHT OF TOBIAS FROM PECKHAM MAD-HOUSE.

rapidly collecting crowd. With the reins of his steed in his hand, he pushed his way through the mob, saying —

"What is it? what is it?"

"A mad boy, sir," said some. "Only look at him. Did you ever see the like. He looks as if he had run a hundred miles."

"Good God!" cried the gentleman. "It is he! It is he!"

"Who, sir? who, sir?"

"A poor lad that I know, I will take charge of him. My name is Jeffery, I am Colonel Jeffery. A couple of guineas to any strong man who will carry him to the nearest surgeon's. Alas! poor boy, what a state is this to meet him in."

It was quite astonishing the numbers of strong men that there were all of a sudden in the crowd, who were each anxious and willing to earn the colonel's two guineas. There was danger of a fight arising upon the subject, when one man, after knocking down two others and threatening the remainder, stepped up, and lifting Tobias as though he had been an infant, exclaimed —

"Ale does it! ale does it! Come on, my little 'un."

All gave way before the gigantic proportions of no other than our old friend Big Ben the Beef Eater, who, as chance would have it, was upon the spot, and who, without a thought of the colonel's two guineas, only heard that a poor sick boy had to be carried to the nearest medical man.

Tobias could not be in better hands than Ben's, for the latter carried him much more carefully than ever nursemaid carried a child out of sight of its mother.

"Follow me," said Colonel Jeffery, as he saw in the distance a parti-coloured lamp, which hung over a door appertaining to a chemist. "Follow, and I will reward you."

"Doesn't want it," said Ben. "It's ale as does it."

"What?"

"Ale does it. Here you is. Come on."

Colonel Jeffery was rather surprised at the droll customer he had picked up in the street, but provided he carried Tobias in safety, which by-the-bye he (the colonel) would not have scrupled to do himself, had he not been encumbered by his horse, it was all one to him, and that he saw Ben was effectually doing. Tobias had shown some slight symptoms of vitality before being lifted from the step of the door close to which he had fallen, but by the time they all reached the chemist's shop, he was in a complete state of insensibility. Of course the usual crowd that collects on such occasions followed them, and during the walk the colonel had time to think, and the result of those thoughts was, that it would be a most desirable thing to keep the knowledge to himself that Tobias was Tobias. He had, in order to awe the mob from any interference with him, announced who he was, but had not announced Tobias. At least if he had uttered his name, he felt certain that it was in an interjectional sort of way, and not calculated to awaken any suspicion.

"I will keep it to myself," he thought, "that Tobias is in my possession, otherwise if such a fact should travel round to Sweeney Todd, there's no saying to what extent it might put that scoundrel upon his guard."

By the time the colonel had arrived at this conclusion the whole party had reached the chemist's, and Big Ben walked in with Tobias, and placed him at once upon the top of a plate-glass counter, which had upon it a large collection of trumpery scent bottles and wonderful specifics for everything, through which Tobias went with a crash.

"There he is!" said Ben — "ale does it."

"Fire! murder! my glass case!" cried the chemist, "Oh, you monster!"

"Ale does it. What do you mean, eh?"

Big Ben backed a pace or two and went head and shoulders through a glass case of similar varieties that was against the wall.

"Gracious bless the beasteses," said Ben, "is your house made of glass? What do you mean by it, eh? A fellow can't turn round here without going through something. You ought to be persecuted according to law, that you ought."

Now this learned chemist had in the glass case against which Big Ben had tumbled a skeleton, which, from the stunning and terrible look it had in his shop, brought him many customers, and it was against this remnant of humanity that Big Ben's head met, after going through the glass as a preparatory step. By some means or another Ben caught his head under the skeleton's ribs, and the consequence was that out he hooked him from the glass case, and the first intimation Ben had of anything unusual, consisted of seeing a pair of bony legs dangling down on each side of him. So unexpected a phenomenon gave Ben what he called a "blessed turn," and out he bounced from the shop, carrying the skeleton for all the world like what is called pick-a-back, for the wires that supplied the place of cartilages held it erect, and so awful a sight surely was never seen in the streets of London as Big Ben with a skeleton upon his back. People fled before — some turned in at shop doors; and an old lady with a large umbrella and a pair of gigantic pattens went clean through a silversmith's window. But we must leave Ben and the skeleton to get on as well as they can en route to the Tower, while we turn our attention to Tobias.

"Are you a surgeon?" cried Colonel Jeffery.

"A — a surgeon? No, I'm only a druggist; but is that any reason why a second Goliath should come into my shop and destroy everything?"

Colonel Jeffery did not wait for anything more, but snatching Tobias from the remnants of the plate glass, he ran to the door with him, and handing him to the first person he saw there, he cried —

"When I am mounted give me the boy."

"Yes, sir."

He sprang upon his horse; Tobias was handed to him like a bale of goods, and laying him comfortably as he could upon the saddle before him, off set the colonel at a good round trot through Finsbury to his own house. Colonel Jeffery had no sort of intention that the chemist should be a sufferer, but in his hurry to be off with Tobias, and speedily get medical advice for him, he forgot to say so, and accordingly there stood the man of physic then fairly bewildered by the events of the last few moments, during which his stock in trade had been materially damaged and a valuable amount of glass broken, to say nothing of the singular and most unexpected abduction of his friend the skeleton.

"Here's a pretty day's work!" he said. "Here's a pretty day's work! More mischief done than enough, and the worst of it is, my wife will hear of it, and then there will be a deal of peace in the house. Oh, dear — oh, dear — was there ever such an unfort — I knew it —"

A good rap upon his head from a pair of bellows wielded by a little meagre-faced woman, that he was big enough to have swallowed, confirmed his words.

WHILE ALL THIS WAS GOING ON, Colonel Jeffery had ridden fast, and passing through Finsbury and up the City-road, had reached his house in the fashion-able — but now quite the reverse, as the man says in the play — district of Pentonville.

"This is a prize," thought the colonel, "worth the taking. It will go hard with me but I will extract from this boy all that he knows of Sweeney Todd, and we shall see how far that knowledge will go towards the confirmation of my suspicions regarding him."

He carried Tobias himself to a comfortable bed-room, and immediately sent for a medical practitioner of good repute in the neighbourhood, who, happening fortunately to be at home, obeyed the summons immediately. He sent likewise for his friend the captain, whom he knew would be overjoyed to hear of what he would call the capture of Tobias Ragg. The medical man made his appearance first, as being much closer at hand, and the colonel led him to the apartment of the invalid boy, saying to him as he went —

"I know nothing of what is the matter with this lad — I have been very anxious to see him on account of certain information that he possesses, and only found him this morning upon a door step in the street, in the state you see him."

"Is he very ill?"

"I am afraid he is."

The medical man followed the colonel to the room in which poor Tobias lay, and after gazing upon him for a few moments, and opening with his fingers the closed eyelids of Tobias, he shook his head.

"I wish I knew," he said, "what has produced this state. Can you not inform me, sir?"

"Indeed I cannot, but I suspect that the boy's imagination has been cruelly acted upon by a man, whom you will excuse me from naming just at present, but whom I sincerely hope to bring to justice shortly."

"The boy's brain, no doubt, is in a bad condition. I do not take upon myself to say that, as an organ, it is diseased, but fractionally it is damaged. However, we must do the best we can to recover him from this condition of collapse in which he is."

"Can you form any opinion as to his probable recovery?"

"Indeed I cannot, but he is young, and youth is a great thing. The best that can be done shall be done."

"I thank you. Spare nothing for the lad, and pay him every attention, as though he were a son or a brother of my own; I long to hear him speak, and to convince him that he is really among friends, who are not only willing to protect him, but have likewise the power to do so."

The medical man bowed, as he said —

"May I ask his name, sir?"

He had his tablets in his hand ready to book the name of Tobias, but the colonel was so very much afraid that Sweeney Todd might by some means learn that Tobias was in his house, and so take an alarm, that he would not trust even the medical man, who, no doubt, had no other motive in asking the name than merely to place it in his list of calls.

"Smith," said the colonel.

The medical man gave a short dry sort of cough, as he wrote "Master Smith" upon his tablets, and then promising to return in half an hour, he took his leave.

At the expiration of half an hour Tobias was put under a course of treatment. His head was shaved, and a blister clapped upon the back of his neck. The room was darkened, and strict quiet was enjoined.

"As soon as he betrays any signs of consciousness, pray send for me, sir," said the surgeon.

"Certainly."

In the course of the day the captain made his appearance, and Colonel Jeffery detailed to him all that had taken place, only lamenting that, after so happily getting possession of Tobias, he should be in so sorry a condition. The captain expressed a wish to see him, and they both went to the chamber, where a woman had been hired to sit with Tobias, in order to give the first intimation of his stirring. Of course, as it was her duty, and what she was specially hired for, to keep wide awake, she was fast asleep, and snoring loud enough to awaken any one much worse than poor Tobias. But that was to to be expected.

"Oh," said the captain, "this is a professional nurse."[*]

"A professional devil!" said the colonel. "How did you know that?"

"By her dropping off so comfortably to sleep, and her utter neglect of her charge. I never knew one that did not do so, and, in good truth, I am inclined to think it is the very best thing they can do, for if they are not asleep they are obnoxiously awake."

---

[*] *In pre-Florence Nightingale England, nursing was not a respected or well-paid profession.*

The colonel took a pin from his cravat, and rather roughly inserted its point into the fat arm of the nurse. She started up, exclaiming—

"Drat the fleas, can't a mortal sleep in peace for them?"

"Madam," said the colonel, "how much is owing to you for sleeping here a few hours?"

"Lord bless me, sir, is this you? The poor soul has never so much as stirred. How my heart bleeds continually for him, to be sure. Ah, dear me, we are all born like sparks, and keep continually flying upward, as the psalm says."

"How much do I owe you?"

"Here to-day, and gone to-morrow. Bless his innocent face."

The colonel rung the bell, and a strapping footman made his appearance.

"You will see this woman to the door, John," he said, "and pay her for being here about three hours."

"Why, you mangy skin-flint," cried the woman. "What do you —"

She was cut short in her vituperative eloquence by John, who handed her down stairs with such dispatch that a pint bottle of gin rolled out of her pocket and was smashed, filling the house with an odour that was quite unmistakeable.*

"What do you propose to do?" said the captain.

"Why, as we have dined, if you have no objection we will sit here and keep this poor benighted one company for awhile. He is better with no one than such as she whom I have dislodged; but before night he shall have a more tender and less professional nurse. You know more of the world, after all, than I do, captain."

CHAPTER XXII.

TOBIAS HAS A MIND DISEASED.

WITH A BOTTLE OF CLARET UPON the table between them, Colonel Jeffery and his old friend sat over the fire in the bed-room devoted to the use of poor Tobias Ragg. Alas! poor boy, kindness and wealth that now surrounded him came late in the day. Before he first crossed the threshold of Sweeney Todd's odious abode, what human heart could have more acutely felt genuine kindness

---

* *Gin, in the early 1800s, was coarse and cheap, and considered a very low-class drink (unless it was Hollands gin, a.k.a. jenever). In Rymer's work, it's almost exclusively drunk by debauched urban middle-aged women.*

than Tobias's, but his destiny had been an evil one. Guilt has its victims, and Tobias was in all senses one of the victims of Sweeney Todd.

"I am sufficiently, perhaps superstitious, you will call it," said Colonel Jeffery in a low tone of voice, "to think that my meeting with this boy was not altogether accidental."

"Indeed?"

"No. Many things have happened to me during life — although I admit that they may be all accounted for as natural coincidences, curious only at the best but still suggestive of something very different, and make me at times a convert to the belief in an interfering special Providence, and this is one of them."

"It is a dangerous doctrine, my friend."

"Think you so?"

"Yes. It is much better and much safer both for the judgment and imagination to account naturally for all those things which admit of a natural explanation, than to fall back upon a special Providence, and fancy that it is continually interfering with the great and immutable laws that govern the world. I do not — mark me — deny such a thing, but I would not be hasty in asserting it. No man's experience can have been without numerous instances such as you mention."

"Certainly not."

"Then I should say to you, as St. Paul said to the Athenians — 'In all things I find you superstitious.' What's that?"

A faint moan had come upon both their ears, and after listening for a few moments another made itself heard, and they fancied, by the direction of the sound, that Tobias's lips must have uttered it. Placing his finger against his mouth to indicate silence, the colonel stepped up to the bedside, and hiding behind the curtains, he said, in the softest and kindest voice he could assume —

"Tobias! Tobias! fear nothing now; you are with friends, Tobias; and, above all, you are perfectly free from the power of Sweeney Todd."

"I am not mad! I am not mad!" shouted Tobias with a shrill vehemence that made both the colonel and his friend start.

"Nay, who says you are mad, Tobias? We know you are not mad, my lad. Don't alarm yourself about that, we know you are not mad."

"Mercy! mercy! I will say nothing — nothing. How fiend-like he looks. Oh, Mr. Todd, spare me, and I will go far, far away, and die somewhere else, but do not kill me now, I am yet such — such a boy only, and my poor father is dead — dead — dead!"

"Ring the bell," said Jeffery to his friend, "and tell John to go for Mr. Chisolm, the surgeon. Come — come, Tobias, you still fancy you are under the power of Todd, but it is not so — you are quite safe here."

"Hush! hush! mother — oh, where are you, mother — did you leave me here, mother? Say you took, in a moment of thoughtlessness, the silver candle-stick! Is Todd to be a devil, because you were thoughtless once? Hide me from him — hide me — hide! hide! I am not mad. Hark! I hear him — one — two — three — four — five — six steps, and all Todd's. Each one leaves blood in its track. Look at him now! His face changes — 'tis a fox's — a serpent's — hideous — hideous — God — God! I am mad — mad — mad!"

The boy dashed his head from side to side, and would have flung himself from the bed had not Colonel Jeffery advanced and held him.

"Poor fellow," he said, "this is very shocking. Tobias! Tobias!"

"Hush! I hear — poor thing, did they say you was mad too? — Hide me in the straw! There — there — what a strange thing it is for all the air to be so full of blood. Do we breathe blood, and only fancy it air? Hush! not a word — he comes with a serpent's face — oh, tell me why does God let such beings ever riot upon the beautiful earth — one — two — three — four — five — six — Hiss — hiss! Off — off! I am not mad — not mad. Ha! ha! ha!"

An appalling shriek concluded this paroxysm, and for a few moments Tobias was still. The medical man at this time entered the room.

"Oh," he said, "we have roused him up again, have we." (Medical men are rather fond of the plural identifying style of talking.)

"Yes," said Colonel Jeffery, "but he had better have slept the sleep of death than have awakened to be what he is, poor fellow."

"A little — eh?"

The doctor tapped his forehead.

"Not a little."

"Far away over the sea!" said Tobias, "oh, yes — in any ship, only do not kill me, Mr. Todd — let me go and I will say nothing, I will work and send my poor mother hard-earned gold, and your name shall never pass our lips. Oh, no — no — no, do not say that I am mad. Do you see these tears? I have — I have not cried so since my poor father called me to him and held me in a last embrace of his wasted arms, saying, 'Tobias, my darling, I am going — going far from you. God's blessing be upon you, poor child.' I thought my heart would break then, but it did not, I saw him put from the face of the living into the grave, and I did not quite break my heart then, but it is broken — broken now! Mad! mad! oh, no, not mad — no — no, but the last — but the last. I tell you, sir, that I am — am — am not mad. Why do you look at me, I am not mad — one — two — three — four — five — six. God — God — God! I am mad — mad. Ha! ha! ha! There they come, all the serpents, and Todd is their king. How the shadows fly about — they shrink — I cannot shrink. Help! God! God! God!"

"This is horrible," said Colonel Jeffery.

"It is appalling, from the lips of one so young," said the captain.

The medical man rubbed his hands together as he said —

"Why, a-hem! it certainly is strangely indicative of a considerable amount of mental derangement, but we shall be able, I dare say, to subdue that. I think, if he could be persuaded to swallow a little draught I have here, it would be beneficial, and allay this irritation, which is partly nervous."

"There cannot be much difficulty," said the colonel, "in making him swallow anything, I should think."

"Let us try."

They held Tobias up while the doctor poured the contents of a small phial into his mouth. Nature preferred performing the office of deglutition to choking, and it was taken. The effect of the opiate was rapid, and after some inarticulate moans and vain attempts to spring from the bed, a deep sleep came over poor Tobias.

"Now, gentlemen," said Mr. Chisolm, "I beg to inform you that this is a bad case."

"I feared as much."

"A very bad case. Some very serious shock indeed has been given to the lad's brain, and if he at all recovers from it, he will be a long time doing so. I do not think those violent paroxysms will continue, but they may leave a kind of fatuity behind them which may be exceedingly difficult to grapple with."

"In that case, he will not be able to give me the information I desire, and all I can do is to take care that he is kindly treated somewhere, poor lad. Poor fellow, his has been a hard lot. He evidently has a mind of uncommon sensibility, as is manifest from his ravings."

"Yes, and that makes the case worse. However, we must hope for the best, and I will call again in the morning."

"Will he awake soon?"

"Not for six or eight hours at least, and when he does, it is very unlikely that those paroxysms will again ensue. He will be quiet enough."

"Then it will be scarcely necessary, during that time, to watch him, poor fellow?"

"Not at all. Of course, when he awakens it will be very desirable that some one should be here to speak to him; for, finding himself in a strange place, he will otherwise naturally be terrified."

All this was promised by the colonel, and the medical man left the house, evidently with very slender hopes in his own mind of the recovery of Tobias. The colonel and his friend retired to another room, and then, after a consultation, they agreed that it was highly proper they should inform Sir Richard Blunt of what had taken place, for although poor Tobias was in no present condition to give any information, yet his capture, if it might be called by such a term, was so important an event that it would be unpardonable to keep it from the magistrate. They accordingly went together to his house, and luckily finding him at home, they at once communicated to him their errand. He listened to them with the most profound attention, and when they had concluded, he said —

"Gentlemen, it will be everything, if this lad recovers sufficiently to be a witness against his rascal of a master, for that is just what we want. However, from the account you give me of him, I am very much afraid the poor fellow's mind is too severely affected."

"That, too, is our fear."

"Well, we must do the best we can, and I should advise that when he awakens some one should be by him with whose voice, as a friendly sound, he will be familiar."

"Who can we get?"

"His poor mother."

"Ah, yes, I will set about that at once."

"Leave it to me," said Sir Richard Blunt, "leave that to me — I know where to find Mrs. Ragg, and what's best to say to her in the case. Let me see, in about four hours from now probably Tobias may be upon the point of recovery."

"Most probably."

"Then, sir, expect me at your house in that time with Mrs. Ragg. I will take care that the old lady's mind is put completely at ease, so that she will aid us in any respect to bring about the recovery of her son, who no doubt has suffered severely from some plan of Todd's to put him out of the way. That seems to me to be the most likely solution to the mystery of his present condition."

"Todd, I am convinced," said Colonel Jeffery, "would stop at no villany."

"Certainly not. My own belief is, that he is so steeped to the lips in crime, that he sees no other mode of covering his misdeeds already done than by the commission of new ones. But his career is nearly at an end, gentlemen."

The colonel and the captain took the rising of the magistrate from his chair as a polite hint that he had something else to do than to gossip with them any longer, and they took their leave, after expressing again to him how much they appreciated his exertions.

"If the mystery of the fate of my unhappy friend," said the colonel, "is ever cleared up, it will be by your exertion, Sir Richard, and he and I, and society at large, will owe to you a heavy debt of gratitude for unmasking so horrible a villain as Sweeney Todd, for that he is such no one can doubt."

CHAPTER XXXIII.

JOHANNA WALKS ABROAD IN DISGUISE.

BUT, AMID ALL THE TRIALS, AND PERPLEXITIES, and anxieties that beset the *dramatis personæ* of our story, who suffered like Johanna? What heart bled as hers bled? What heart heaved with sad emotion as hers heaved? Alas! poor Johanna, let the fate of Mark Ingestrie be what it might, he could not feel the pangs that tore thy gentle heart. Truly might she have said —

> *"Man's love is of his life a thing apart*
> *'Tis woman's whole existence,"**

— for she felt that her joy — her life itself, was bartered for the remembrance of how she had been loved by him whose fate was involved in one of the most painful and most inscrutable of mysteries. Where could she seek for consolation, where for hope? The horizon of her young life seemed ever darkening, and the more she gazed upon it with the fond hope of singing —

> *"The first faint star of coming joy,"†*

— the more confounded her gentle spirit became by the blackness of despair. It is sad indeed that the young, the good, and the gentle, should be the grand sufferers in this world, but so it is. The exquisite capacity to feel acutely is certain to find ample food for agony. If human nature could wrap itself up in the chill mantle of selfishness, and be perfectly insensible to all human feeling, it might escape, but such cannot be done by those who, like the fine and noble-minded Johanna Oakley, sympathise with all that is beautiful and great in creation. Already the pangs of hope deferred were feeding upon the damask of her cheeks. The lily had usurped the rose, and although still exquisitely beautiful, it was the pale beauty of a statue that she began to show to those who loved her. In the street people would turn to gaze after her with admiration blended with pity. They already looked upon her as half an angel, for already it seemed as though she had shaken off much of her earthly lurements, and was hastening to —

---

* *From* Don Juan *by Lord Byron (1819).*

† *Probably a reference to* The Forest Sanctuary, *a long poem by Felicia Hemans (1825)*

"Rejoin the stars."

Let us look at her as she lies weeping upon the breast of her friend Arabella Wilmot. The tears of the two young girls are mingling together, but the one is playing the part of comforter, while the other mourns over much.

"Now, Johanna," sobbed Arabella, "you talk of doing something to save Mark Ingestrie, if he be living, or to bring to justice the man whom you suspect to be his murderer. Let me ask you what you can hope to do, if you give way to such an amount of distress as this?"

"Nothing — nothing."

"And are you really to do nothing? Have you not agreed, Johanna, to make an attempt, in the character of a boy, to find out the secret of Ingestrie's disappearance, and have not I provided for you all that you require to support the character? Courage, courage, courage. — Oh, I could tell you such stories of fine ladies dressing as pages, and following gallant knights to the field of battle, that you would feel as though you could go through anything."

"But the age of chivalry is gone."

"Yes, and why — because folks will not be chivalric. To those who will, the age of chivalry comes back again in all its glory."

"Listen to me, Arabella: if I really thought that Mark was no more, and lost to me for ever, I could lie down and die, leaving to Heaven the punishment of those who have taken his life, but in the midst of all my grief — in the moments of my deepest depression, the thought clings to me, that he lives yet. I do not know how it is, but the thought of Mark Ingestrie dead, is but a vague one, compared to the thought of Mark Ingestrie suffering."

"Indeed?"

"Yes, and at times it seems as if a voice whispered to me, that he was yet to be saved, if there existed a heart fair enough and loving enough in its strength to undertake the task. It is for that reason, and not from any romantic love of adventure, or hope of visiting with punishment a bad man, that my imagination clings to the idea of going in boy's apparel to Fleet-street, to watch, and perchance to enter that house to which he last went, and from which, according to all evidence, he never emerged."

"And you are really bold enough?"

"I hope so — I think, if I am not, God will help me."

A sob that followed these words, sufficiently testified how much in need of God's help poor Johanna was, but after a few minutes she succeeded in recovering herself from her emotion, and she said more cheerfully —

"Come, Arabella, we talked of a rehearsal of my part; but I shall be more at ease when I go to act it in reality, and with danger. I shall be able to comport myself well, with only you for a companion, and such chance passengers as the streets of the city may afford for my audience."

JOHANNA'S ALARM AT THE SIGHT OF SWEENEY TODD.

"I am glad," said Arabella, "that you keep in this mind. Now come and dress yourself, and we will go out together. You will be taken for my brother, you know."

In the course of a quarter of an hour, Johanna presented the appearance of as good-looking a lad of about fourteen as the world ever saw, and if she could but have imparted a little more confidence and boyish bustle to her gait and manner, she would have passed muster under the most vigilant scrutiny. But as it was, nothing could be more unlikely than that any one should penetrate her disguise, for what is not suspected, is seldom seen very readily.

"You will do capitally," said Arabella, "I must take your arm, you know. We will not go far."

"Only to Fleet-street."

"Fleet-street. You surely will not go so far as that?"

"Yes, Arabella. Now that I have attired myself in these garments for a special purpose, let me do a something towards the carrying it out. By walking that distance I shall accustom myself to the road; and, moreover, a dreadful kind of fascination drags me to that man's shop."

Arabella, if the truth must be told, shook a little as they, after watching an opportunity, emerged into the street, for although the spirit of romantic adventure had induced her to give the advice to Johanna that she had, her own natural feminine sensibilities shrunk from the carrying of it out. Ashamed, however, of being the first to condemn her own suggestion, she took the arm of Johanna, and those two young creatures were in the tide of human life that ebbs and flows in the great city. The modest walk and gentle demeanour of the seeming young boy won Johanna many a passing glance as she and Arabella proceeded down Ludgate Hill towards Fleet-street, but it was quite clear that no one suspected the disguise which, to do Arabella justice, in its general arrangement was very perfect, and as Johanna wore a cap, which concealed much of the upper part of her face, and into which was gathered all her hair, she might have really deceived those who were the most intimate with her, so that it was no wonder she passed unobserved with mere strangers. In this way, then, they reached Fleet-street without obstruction, and Johanna's heart beat rapidly as they approached the shop of Sweeney Todd.

"It will be imprudent to stop for even a moment at his door or window," said Arabella, "for, remember, you have no opportunity of varying your disguise."

"I will not stop. We will pass rapidly on, but — but it is something to look upon the doorstep over which the shadow of Mark has last passed."

In another moment they were on a level with the shop. Johanna cast a glance at the window, and then shrunk back with affright as she saw, occupying one of the upper panes of glass, the hideous face of Todd. He was not looking at her though, for with an awful squint that revealed all the whites of his eyes — we were going to say, but the dirty yellows would have been much nearer the truth — he seemed to be observing something up the street.

"Come on — come on," whispered Johanna.

Arabella had not happened to observe this apparition of Todd in the window, and she looked round to see what occasioned Johanna's sudden terror, when a young Temple clerk, who chanced to be a few paces behind them, immediately, with the modesty peculiar to his class, imagined the glance of the blooming girl to be a tribute to his attractions. He kissed the end of a faded glove, and put on what he considered a first-class fascinating aspect.

"Come on — come on," said Arabella now in her turn.

Johanna, of course, thought that Arabella too had caught sight of the hideous and revolting countenance of Sweeney Todd, and so they both hastened on together.

"Don't look back," said Arabella.

"Is he following?"

"Oh, yes — yes."

Johanna thought she meant Todd, while Arabella really meant the Temple gent, but, notwithstanding the mutual mistake, they hurried on, and the clerk taking that as quite sufficient encouragement, pursued them, putting his cravat to rights as he did so, in order that when he came up to them, he should present the most fascinating aspect possible.

"No — no." said Johanna, as she glanced behind. "You must have been mistaken, Arabella. He is not pursuing us."

"Oh, I am so glad."

Arabella looked back, and the Temple gent kissed his dilapidated glove.

"Oh, Johanna," she said, "how could you tell me he was not following, when there he is."

"What, Todd?"

"No. That impertinent ugly puppy with the soiled cravat."

"And you meant him?"

"To be sure."

"Oh, what a relief, I was flying on, fancying that Todd was in pursuit of us, and yet my judgment ought at once to have told me that that could not be the case, knowing nothing of us. How our fears overcome all reason. Do you know that strange-looking young man?"

"Know him? Not I."

"Well, my darling," said the gent, reaching to within a couple of paces of Arabella, "how do you do to-day? — a-hem! Are you going far? Ain't you afraid that somebody will run away with such a pretty gal as you — 'pon soul, you are a charmer."

"Cross," whispered Arabella, and the two young girls at once crossed Fleet-street. It was not then so difficult an operation to get from one side of that thoroughfare to the other as it is now. The gent was by no means disconcerted at this evident wish to get out of his way, but he crossed likewise, and commenced a series of persecution, which such animals call gallantry, and which, to any respectable young female, are specially revolting.

"Now, my dear," he said, "St. Dunstan's is just going to strike the hour, and you will see the clubs hit the bells if you look, and I shall expect a kiss when it's all over."

"You are impertinent," said Johanna.

"Come, that's a good joke — why, you little whipper snapper, I suppose you came out to take care of your sister. Here's a penny to go and buy yourself a cold pie at Mrs. Lovett's. I'll see to your sister while you are gone. Oh, you need not look so wild about it. Did you never hear of a gent talking to a pretty gal in the street?"

"Often," said Johanna, "but I never heard of a gentleman doing so."

"Upon my word, you are as sharp as a needle, so I'll just pull your ears to teach you better manners, you young rascal — come — come, it's no use your kicking."

"Help — help!" cried Arabella.

They were now just opposite the principal entrance to the Temple, and as Arabella cried "help," who should emerge from under the gateway but Ben the Beef Eater. The fact is, that he was on his way to the Tower just previous to the meeting with Colonel Jeffery and Tobias. Arabella, who had twice or thrice seen him at the Oakley's, knew him at once.

"Oh, sir," she cried, "I am Johanna's friend, Miss Wilmot, and this — this gent won't leave me and my cousin here alone."

The gent made an effort to escape, but Ben caught him by the hinder part of his apparel, and held him tight.

"Is this him?"

"Yes — yes."

"Oh dear no — oh dear no, my good sir. It's that fellow there, with the white hat. There he goes, up Chancery Lane. My dear sir, you are quite mistaken; I wanted to protect the young lady, and as for the lad, bless his heart. I — oh dear, it wasn't me."

Still holding the gent by the first grasp he had taken of him, Ben suddenly crossed the road to where a parish pump stood, at the corner of Bell-yard, and holding him under the spout with one hand, he worked the handle with the other, despite the shrieks and groans of his victim, who in a few moments was rendered so limp and wet, that when Ben let him go, he fell into the sink below the pump, and there lay, until some small boys began pelting him.

During the confusion and laughter of the bystanders, Arabella and Johanna rapidly retreated towards the City again, for they thought Ben might insist upon escorting them, and that, in such a case, it was possible enough the disguise of Johanna, good as it was, might not suffice to save her from the knowledge of one so well acquainted with her.

"Let us cross, Arabella," she said. "Let us cross, if it be but for one moment, to hear what the subject of the conversation between Todd and that man is."

"If you wish it, Johanna."

"I do, I do."

They crossed, and once again passed the shop of Todd, when they heard the man say—

"Well, if he has gone he has gone, but I think it is the strangest thing I ever heard of."

"So do I," said Todd.

Without lingering, and so perhaps exciting Todd's attention and suspicion, they could hear no more, but Johanna had heard enough to give the spur to imagination, and when they had again crossed Fleet-street, and were making their way rapidly up Ludgate-hill, she whispered to Arabella—

"Another! another!"

"Another what, Johanna? You terrify me by that tone. Oh, be calm. Be calm, I pray you. Some one will observe your agitation."

"Another victim," continued Johanna. "Another victim—another victim. Did you not hear what the man said? Was it not suggestive of another murder? Oh, Heaven preserve my reason, for each day, each hour, brings to me such accumulating proof of horrors, that I fear I shall go mad."

"Hush! hush! Johanna—Johanna!"

"My poor, poor Mark—"

"Remember that you are in the street, Johanna, and for my sake, I pray you to be calm. Those tears and that flushed cheek will betray you. Oh, why did I ever advise you to come upon such an enterprise as this? It is my fault, all my fault."

The terror and the self-accusation of Arabella Wilmot did more to bring Johanna to a reasonable state than anything else, and she made an effort to overcome her feelings, saying—

"Forgive me—forgive me, my dear friend—I, only, am to blame. But at the moment I was overcome by the thought that, in the heart of London, such a system of cold-blooded murder—"

She was unable to proceed, and Arabella, holding her arm tightly within her own, said—

"Do not attempt to say another word until we get home. There, in my chamber, you can give free vent to your feelings, but let the danger, as well as the impropriety of doing so in the open street, be present to your mind. Say no more now, I implore you; say no more."

This was prudent advice, and Johanna had sufficient command of herself to take it, for she uttered not one other word until they were both almost breathless with the haste they had made to Arabella's chamber. Then, being no longer under the restraint of locality or circumstances, the tears of Johanna burst forth, and she wept abundantly. Arabella's romantic reading did sometimes, as it would appear, stand her in good stead, and upon this occasion she did not attempt to stem the torrent of grief that was making its way from the eyes of her fair young friend. She told herself that with those tears a load of oppressive grief would be washed from Johanna's spirit, and the result fully justified her prognostications. The tears subsided into sobs, and the sobs to sighs.

"Ah, my dear friend," she said, "how much have you to put up with from me. What a world of trouble I am to you."

"No," said Arabella, "that you are not, Johanna; I am only troubled when I see you overcome with too excessive grief, and then, I confess, my heart is heavy."

"It shall not be so again. Forgive me this once, dear Arabella."

Johanna flung herself into her friend's arms, and while they kissed each other, and Arabella was about commencing a hopeful kind of speech, a servant girl, with open mouth and eyes, looked into the room, transfixed with amazement.

"Well, Miss Bella," she cried at last, "you is fond of boys!"

Arabella started, and so did Johanna.

"Is that you, Susan?"

"Yes, Miss Bella, it is me. Well I never! The idea! I shall never get the better of this here! Only to think of you, Miss Bella, having a boy at your time of life."

"What do you mean, Susan? How dare you use such language to me? Get you gone!"

"Oh, yes, I'm a-going in course; but if I had anybody in the house, it shouldn't be a little impudent looking boy with no whiskers."

"She must know all," whispered Johanna.

"No, no," said Arabella, "I will not, feeling my innocence, be forced into making a confidant of a servant. Let her go."

"But she will speak."

"Let her speak."

Susan left the room, and went direct to the kitchen, holding up her hands all the way, and giving free expression to her feelings as she did so —

"Well, the *idea* now, of a little stumpy looking boy, when there's sich a lot of nice young men with whiskers to be had just for the wagging of one's little finger. Only to think of it. Sitting in her lap too, and them a kissing one another like — like — coach horses. Well I never. Now there's Lines's, the cheesemonger's, young man as I has in of a night, he is somebody, and such loves of whiskers I never seed in my born days afore; but I is surprised at Miss Bella, that I is — a shrimp of a boy in her lap! Oh dear, oh dear!"

CHAPTER XXXIV.

MR. FOGG FINDS THAT ALL IS NOT GOLD THAT GLITTERS.

WE FEEL THAT WE OUGHT NOT ENTIRELY to take leave of that unfortunate, who failed in escaping with Tobias Ragg, from Mr. Fogg's establishment at Peckham, without a passing notice. It will be recollected that Tobias had enough to do to get away himself, and that he was in such a state of mind that it was quite a matter of new mechanical movement of his limbs that enabled him to fly from the madhouse. Horror of the place, and dread of the people who called it theirs, had lighted up the glare of a partial insanity in his brain, and he flew to London, we admit, without casting another thought upon the wretched creature who had fallen in the attempt to free herself from those fiends in human shape who made a frightful speculation in the misery of their fellow creatures. The alarm was already spread in the madhouse, and Mr. Fogg himself arrived at the spot where the poor creature lay stunned and wounded by her fall.

"Watson! Watson!" he cried.

"Here," said that official, as he presented himself.

"Take this carcase up, Watson. I'm afraid Todd's boy is gone."

"Ha! ha!"

"Why do you laugh?"

"Why where's the odds if he has. I tell you what it is, Fogg, I haven't been here so long without knowing what's what. If that boy ever recovers his senses enough to tell a rational tale, I'll eat him. However, I'll soon go and hunt him up. We'll have him again."

"Well, Watson, you give me hopes, for you have upon two different occasions brought back runaways. Bring the woman in and — and, Watson?"

"Aye, aye."

"I think I would put her in No. 10."

"Ho! ho! — No. 10. Then she's booked. Well, well, come on Fogg, come on, it's all one. I suppose the story will be 'An attempt to escape owing to too much indulgence;' and some hints consequent on that, and then brought back to her own warm comfortable bed, where she went asleep so comfortably that we all thought she was as happy as an Emperor, and then —"

"She never woke again," put in Fogg. "But in this case you are wrong, Watson. It is true that twice or thrice I have thought, for the look of the thing, it would be desirable to have an inquest upon somebody, but in this case I will not. The well is not full!"

"Full?"

"No, I say the well is not full, Watson; and it tells no tales."

"It would hold a hundred bodies one upon another yet," said Watson, "and tell no tales. Ha! ha!"

"Good!"

"It is good. She is to go there, is she? well, so be it."

Watson carried the miserable female in his arms to the house.

"By-the-bye, it is a second thought," he said, "about No. 10."

"Yes, yes, there's no occasion. Watson, could you not at once — eh? It is a good hour. Could you not go right through the house, my good Watson, and at once — eh?"

"At once what?"

"Oh, you know. Ha! ha! You are not the dull fellow at comprehending a meaning you would fain make out; but you, Watson — you understand me well enough, you know you do. We understand each other, and always shall."

"I hope so, but if you want anything done I'll trouble you to speak out. What do you mean by 'couldn't you go through the house at once' — eh?"

"Pho! pho! Put her down the well at once. Humanity calls upon us to do it. Why should she awaken to a sense of her disappointment, Watson? Put her down at once, and she will never awaken at all to a sense of anything."

"Very well. Come on, business is business."

"You — you don't want me?"

"Don't I," said Watson, bending his shaggy brows upon him, and looking extra hideous on account of a large black patch over one eye, which he bore as a relict of his encounter with Tobias. "Don't I? Hark you, Fogg; if you won't come and help me to do it, you shall have it to do by yourself, without me at all."

"Why — why, Watson, Watson. This language —"

"Is nothing new, Fogg."

"Well, well, come on. — Come on — if it must be so, it must. — I — I will hold a lantern for you, of course; and you know, Watson, I make things easy to you, in the shape of salary, and all that sort of thing."

Watson made no reply to all this, but went through the house to the back part of the grounds, carrying with him his insensible burthen, and Fogg followed him, trembling in every limb. The fact was, that he, Fogg, had not for some time had a refresher in the shape of some brandy. The old deserted well to which they were bound was at a distance of about fifty yards from the back of the house; towards it the athletic Watson hastened with speed, closely followed by Fogg, who was truly one of those who did not mind holding a candle to the devil. The walls of that building were high, and it was not likely that any intruder from the outside could see what was going on, so Watson took no precaution. — The well was reached, and Fogg cried to him —

THE MURDER AT THE WELL BY FOGG AND WATSON.

"Now — now — quick about it, lest she recovers."

Another moment and she would have been gone in her insensibility, but as if Fogg's words were prophetic, she did recover, and clinging convulsively to Watson, she shrieked —

"Mercy! mercy! Oh, have mercy upon me! Help! help!"

"Ah, she recovers!" cried Fogg, "I was afraid of that. Throw her in. Throw her in, Watson."

"Confound her!"

"Why don't you throw her in?"

"She clings to me like a vice. I cannot — Give me a knife, Fogg. You will find one in my coat pocket — a knife — a knife!"

"Mercy! mercy! Have mercy upon me! No — no — no, — Help! Oh God! God!"

"The knife! The knife, I say!"

"Here, here," cried Fogg, as he hastily took it from Watson's pocket and opened it. "Here! Finish her, and quickly too, Watson!"

The scene that followed is too horrible for description. The hands of the wretched victim were hacked from their hold by Watson, and in the course of another minute, with one last appalling shriek, down she went like a flash of lightning to the bottom of the well.

"Gone!" said Watson.

Another shriek and Fogg, even, stopped his ears, so appalling was that cry, coming as it did so strangely from the bottom of the well.

"Throw something upon her," said Fogg. "Here's a brick —"

"Bah!" cried Watson, "bah! there's no occasion to throw anything on her. She'll soon get sick of such squealing."

Another shriek, mingled with a strange frothy cry, as though some one had managed to utter it under water, arose. The perspiration stood in large drops upon the face of Fogg. — He seized the brick he had spoken of, and cast it into the well. All was still as the grave before it reached the bottom, and then he wiped his face and looked at Watson.

"This is the worst job," he said, "that ever we have had —"

"Not a whit. — Brandy — give me a tumbler of brandy, Fogg. Some of our own particular, for I have something to say to you now, that a better opportunity than this for saying is not likely to occur."

"Come into my room then," said Fogg, "and we can talk quietly. — Do you think — that — that —"

"What?"

"That she is quite dead?"

"What do I care. — Let her crawl out of that, if she can."

With a jerk of his thumb, Watson intimated that the well was the "that" he referred to, and then he followed Fogg into the house, whistling as he went the same lively air with which he had frequently solaced his feelings in the hearing of poor Tobias Ragg.

Never had Fogg been in such a state of agitation, except once, and that was long ago, upon the occasion of his first crime. Then he had trembled as he now trembled, but the —

"Dull custom of iniquity"

— had effectually blunted soon the keen edge of his conscience, and he had for years carried on a career of infamy without any other feeling than exultation at his success. — Why then did he suffer now? Had the well in the garden ever before received a victim? Was he getting alive to the excellence of youth and beauty? — Oh no — no. Fogg was getting old. He could not stand what he once stood in the way of conscience. When he reached his room — that room in which he had held the conference with Todd — he sank into a chair with a deep groan.

"What's the matter now?" cried Watson, who got insolent in proportion as Fogg's physical powers appeared to be upon the wane.

"Nothing, nothing."

"Nothing? — Well, I never knew anybody look so white with nothing the matter. Come, I want a drop of brandy; where is it?"

"In that cupboard; I want some myself likewise. Get it out, Watson. You will find glasses there."

Watson was not slow in obeying this order. The brandy was duly produced, and, after Fogg had drank as much as would have produced intoxication in any one not so used to the ardent spirit as himself, he spoke more calmly, for it only acted upon him as a gentle sedative.

"You wished to say something to me, Watson."

"Yes."

"What is it?"

"I am tired, completely tired, Fogg."

"Tired? Then why don't you retire to rest at once, Watson? There is, I am sure, nothing to keep you up now; I am going myself in a minute."

"You don't understand me, or you won't, which is much the same thing. I did not mean that I was tired of the day, but I am tired of doing all the work, Fogg, while you — while you —"

"Well — while I —"

"Pocket all the profit. Do you understand that? Now hark you. We will go partners, Fogg, not only in the present and the future, but in the past. I will have half of your hoarded up gains, or —"

"Or what?"

Mr. Watson made a peculiar movement, supposed to indicate the last kick of a culprit executed at the Old Bailey.

"You mean you will hang yourself," said Fogg. "My dear Watson, pray do so as soon as you think proper. Don't let me hinder you."

"Hark you, Fogg. You may be a fox, but I am a badger. I mean that I will

---

* *Probably a reference from Frederick Marryat's novel "Mr. Midshipman Easy" (1836).*

hang you, and this is the way to do it. My wife — "

"Your what?"

"My wife," cried Watson, "has, in writing, the full particulars of all your crimes. She don't live far off, but still far enough to make it a puzzle for you to find her. If she don't see me once in every forty-eight hours, she is to conclude something has happened to me, and then she is to go at once to Bow-street with the statement, and lay it before a magistrate. You understand. Now I have contrived, with what I got from you by fair means as well as by foul, and by robbing the patients besides, to save some money, and if you and I don't agree, Mrs. Watson and I will start for New Zealand, or some such place, but — but, Fogg — "

"Well?"

"We will denounce you before we go."

"And what is to be the end of all this? The law has a long as well as a strong arm, Watson."

"I know it. You would say it might be long enough to strike me."

Fogg nodded.

"Leave me to take care of that. But as you want to know the result of all this, it is just this. I want to have my share, and I will have it. Give me a couple of thousand down, and half for the future."

Fogg was silent for a moment or two, and then he said —

"Too much, Watson, too much. I have not so much."

"Bah! At your banker's now you have exactly £11,267."

Fogg writhed.

"You have been prying. Well, you shall have the two thousand."

"On account."

Fogg writhed again. "I say you shall have so much, Watson, and you shall keep the books, and have your clear half of all future proceeds. Is there anything else you have set your mind upon, because if you have, while we are talking about business, you may as well state it, you know."

"No, there's nothing else — I am satisfied. All I have to add is, that you had better put your head into the fire than attempt to play any tricks with me. You understand?"

"Perfectly."

Watson was not altogether satisfied. He would have been better pleased if Fogg had made more resistance. The easy compliance of such a man with anything that touched his pocket looked suspicious, and filled the mind of Watson with a thousand vague conjectures. Already — aye, even before he left Fogg's room, Watson began to feel the uneasiness of his new position, and to pay dearly for the money he was to have. Even money may be given an exorbitant price for. When he was by himself, as he traversed the passage leading to his own sleeping room, Watson could not forbear looking cautiously around him at times, as though gaunt murder stalked behind him, and he fastened his bed-room door with more than his usual caution. The wish to sleep came not to him, and sitting down upon his bed-side he rested his chin upon his hand and said to himself in a low anxious shrinking kind of whisper —

"What does Fogg mean to do?"

Nor was the recent interview without its after effects upon the mad-house keeper himself. When the door closed upon Watson he shook his clenched hand in the direction he had taken, and muttered curses, —

"Not loud, but deep."*

"The time will come," he said, "Master Watson, and that quickly too, when I will let you see that I am still the master spirit. You shall be satisfied for the present, but your death-warrant is preparing. You will not live long to triumph over me by threats of what your low cunning can accomplish."

He rose and drank more raw brandy, after which, still muttering maledictions upon Watson, he returned to his bed-room, where, if he did not sleep, and if during the still hours of the night his brain was not too much vexed, he hoped to be able to concoct some scheme which should present him with a prospect of exemplary vengeance upon Watson.

CHAPTER XXXV.

MRS. LOVETT'S NEW LOVER.

MRS. LOVETT WAS A WOMAN OF luxurious habits. Perhaps the constant savoury hot pie atmosphere in which she dwelt contributed a something to the development of her tastes, but certainly that lady, in dress, jewellery, and men, had her fancies. Did the reader think that she saw anything attractive in the satyr-like visage of Todd, with its eccentricities of vision? Did the reader think that the lawyers' clerks frequenting her shop suited her taste, varying, as all the world knows that class of bipeds does, between the fat and flabby, and the white and candle-looking, if we may be allowed the expression? Ah, no, — Mrs. Lovett's

---

**A Shakespeare reference, from Macbeth, Act V, Scene II, as Macbeth's sins are finally catching up with him: "As honour, love, obedience, troops of friends, I must not look to have; but, in their stead, curses, not loud but deep, mouth-honor, breath, which the poor heart would fain deny, and dare not."*

dreams of man had a loftier range, but we must not anticipate. Facts will speak trumpet-tongued for themselves.

> IT IS THE HOUR *when lawyers' clerks*
> *From many a gloomy chamber stalk;*
> *It is the hour when lovers' vows*
> *Are heard in every Temple walk.*

Mrs. Lovett was behind her counter all alone, but the loneliness continued but for a very brief period, for from Carey-street, with a nervousness of gait highly suggestive of a fear of bailiffs — bailiffs were there in all their glory — comes a — a what shall we say? Truly there are some varieties of the genus *homo* that defy minute classification, but perhaps this individual who hastened down Bell-yard was the nearest in approximation to what used to be called "a swaggering companion,"* that can be found. He was a gent upon town — that is to say, according to his own phraseology, he lived upon his wits; and if the reader will substitute dishonesty for wits, he will have a much clearer notion of what the swaggering companion of modern days lived upon.

He was tall, burly, forty years of age, and his bloated countenance and sleepy eyes betrayed the effects of a long course of intemperance. He wore mock jewellery of an outrageous size; his attire was flashy and gaudy — his linen … the less we say about that the better — enormous black whiskers (false) shaded his cheeks, and mangey-looking moustache (real) covered his upper lip — add to all this, such a stock of ignorance and impudence as may be supposed to thoroughly saturate one individual, and the reader has the swaggering companion before him. At a rapid pace he neared Mrs. Lovett's, muttering to himself as he went —

"I wonder if I can gammon her out of a couple of guineas."

Yes, reader, this compound of vulgarity, ignorance, impudence and debauchery was Mrs. Lovett's gentle fancy — her taste — her — her, what shall we say? — her personification of all that a man should be. Do not start; Mrs. Lovett has many imitators, for, without libelling the fairer, better, and more gentle of that sex, who can be such angels as well as such — a-hem! — there are thousands who would be quite smitten with the "swaggering companion." When he reached the shop-window, he placed his nose against it for a moment

---

* *A reference from Shakespeare, from* Henry IV Part II, *Act II Scene IV, a London tavern scene in which Mistress Quickly says to Sir John Falstaff, quoting from the Rev. Dumbe, " 'Neighbor Quickly,' says he, 'receive those that are civil; for,' said he, 'you are in an ill name:' now a' said so, I can tell whereupon; 'for,' says he, 'you are an honest woman, and well thought on; therefore take heed what guests you receive: Receive,' says he, 'no swaggering companions.' "*

to reconnoitre who was in the shop, and seeing the fair one alone, he at once crossed the threshold.

"Ah, charmer, how do the fates get on with you?"

"Sir —"

A smile upon the face of Mrs. Lovett was a practical contradiction to the rebuff which her reception of him by words of mouth seemed to carry.

"Oh, you bewitching — a — a —"

The remainder of the sentence was lost in the devouring a pie, which the "swaggering companion" took from the shop counter.

"Really, sir," said Mrs. Lovett — "I wish you would not come here, I am all alone, and —"

"Alone? You beautiful female. — Oh you nice creature. — Allow me."

The "swaggering companion" lifted up that portion of the counter which enabled Mrs. Lovett to pass from one side of it to the other, and as coolly as possible walked into the parlour. Mrs. Lovett followed him, protesting at what she called his impudence. But for all that, a bottle of spirits and some biscuits were procured. The "swaggering companion," however, pushed the biscuits aside, saying —

"Pies for me. Pies for me."

Mrs. Lovett looked at him scrutinisingly as she said —

"And do you really like the pies, or do you only eat them out of compliment to me?"

"Really like them? I tell you what it is; out of compliment to you, of course, I could eat anything, but the pies are delicacies. — Where *do* you get your veal?"

"Well, if you will have pies you shall, Major Bounce." * — That was the name which the "swaggering companion" appended to his disgusting corporealty.

"Certainly, my dear, certainly. As I was saying, I could freely, to compliment you, eat old Tomkins, the tailor, of Fleet-street."

"Really. How do you think he would taste?"

"Tough!"

"Ha! Ha!"

It was an odd laugh that of Mrs. Lovett's. Had she borrowed it from Todd?

"My dear Mrs. L.," said the major, "what made you laugh in that sort of way? Ah, if I could only persuade you to go from L to B —"

"Sir?"

"Now, my charmer, seriously speaking: — Here am I, Major Bounce, a

---

* *"Bounce" had a number of definitions in the slang of the 1840s, none of them good. A "bouncer" was an audacious lie — a "whopper" in modern lingo. Also, thieves and highwaymen used "give it to 'em on the bounce" to mean "to steal or embezzle something by assuming the appearance of respectability and importance."*

gentleman with immense expectations, ready and willing to wed the most charming woman under the sun, if she will only say 'yes.'"

"Have you any objection to America?"

"America? None in the least.—With you for a companion, America would be a Paradise. A regular garden of, what do you call it, my dear? Only say the word, my darling."

The major's arm was gently insinuated round the lady's waist, and after a few moments she spoke.

"Major Bounce, I—I have made money."

"The devil!—so have I, but the police one day—a-hem!—a-hem!—what a cough I have."

"What on earth do you mean?"

"Oh, nothing—nothing—only a joke. You said you had made money, and that put me in mind of what I read in the 'Chronicle' to-day of some coiners, that's all. Ha-ha!"

"When I spoke of making money, I meant in the way of trade, but having made it, I should not like to spend it in London, and be pointed out as the well-known pie-woman."

"Pie-woman! Oh, the wretches—only let—"

"Peace. Hold your tongue, and hear me out. If I marry and retire, it will be far from here—very far indeed."

"Ah, any land, with you." The major absolutely saluted the lady.

"Be quiet. Pray, in what service are you a major?"

"The South American, my love. A much higher service than the British."

"Indeed."

"Lord bless you, yes. If I was now to go to my estates in South America, there would be a jubilee of ten days at the very least, and the people as well as the government would not know how to make enough of me, I can assure you. In fact, I have as much right to take the rank of general as of major, but the natural modesty of a military man, and of myself in particular, steps in and says 'A major be it.'"

"Then you have property?"

"Property—property? I believe you, I have. Lots!"

The major dealt his forehead a slap as he spoke, which might be taken as an indication that that was where his property was situated, and that it consisted of his ignorance and impudence—very good trading capitals in this world for, strange to say, the parties solely possessing such qualifications get on much better than education, probity, and genius can push forward their unhappy victims.

Mrs. Lovett was silent for some minutes, during which the major saluted her again. Then, suddenly rising, she said—

"I will give you an answer to-morrow. Go away now. We shall be soon interrupted. If I do consent to be yours, there will be something to do before we leave England."

"By Jove, only mention it to me, and it is as good as done. By-the-bye, there is something to do before I leave here, and that is, my charmer, to pay you for the pies."

"Oh, no — no."

"Yes, yes — my honour. Touch my honour, even in regard of a pie, and touch my life. — I put two guineas in one end of my purse, to pay my glover in the Strand, and at the other end are some small coins — where the deuce — can — I — have — put — it."

The major made an affectation of feeling in all his pockets for his lost purse, and then, with a serio-comic look, he said —

"By Jove, some rascal has picked my pocket."

"Never mind me," said Mrs. Lovett, "I don't want payment for the pies."

"Well, but — the — the glover. Poor devil, and I promised him his money this morning. For a soldier and a man of honour to break his word is death. What shall I do? — Mrs. L., could you lend me a couple of guineas until I have the happiness of seeing you again?"

"Certainly, major, certainly I can."

The gallant son of Mars pocketed the coins, and after saluting Mrs. Lovett some half score of times — and she, the beast, liked it — he left the shop and went chuckling into the Strand, where in a few minutes he was in a pot-house, from whence he emerged not until he had liquidated one of the guineas.

Was Mrs. Lovett taken in by the major? Did she believe his title, or his wealth, and his common honesty? Did she believe in the story of the purse and of the two guineas that were to be paid to the poor glover because he wanted them? No — no — certainly not. But for all that, she admired the major. — He was her *beau ideal* of a fine man! That was sufficient. Moreover, being what he was — a rogue, cheat, and common swindler — she could exercise, so she thought, a species of control over him which no decent man would put up with, and so in her own mind she had determined to marry the major and fly; but as she said — "There was a little something to be done first." Did that relate to the disposal of Todd? We shall see. If she calculated upon the major putting Sweeney Todd out of the way, she sadly miscalculated; but the wisest heads will blunder. Compared to Todd, the major was indeed a poor creature; but Mrs. Lovett, in the stern courage of her own intellect, could not conceive the possibility of the great, puffy, bloated, fierce Major Bounce being as arrant a coward as ever was kicked. He was so, though, for all that.

After he had left her, Mrs. Lovett sat for a long time in a profound reverie, and as it happened that no one came into the shop; the current of her evil thoughts was uninterrupted.

"I have sufficient," she said; "and before it gets too late, I will leave this mode of life. Why did I — tempted by the fiend Todd — undertake it, but that I might make wealth by it, and so assume a position that my heart panted for. I will not delay until it is too late, or I may lose the enjoyment that I have sacrificed so much to find the means of getting. I live in this world but for the gratification of the senses, and finding that I could not gratify them without abundant means, I fell upon this plan. I — ah — that is he —"

Suddenly the swaggering companion, the redoubtable Major Bounce, rushed past the shop-window, without so much as looking in for a single moment, and made his way towards Carey-street. Mrs. Lovett started up and made her way into the front shop. Major Bounce was out of sight, but from Fleet-street came a poor, draggled, miserable looking woman, making vain efforts at a speed which her weakness prevented her from keeping up. — She called aloud —

"Stop! stop! — only a moment, Flukes! Only a moment, John. Stop! — stop!"

Her strength failed her, and she fell exhausted upon Mrs. Lovett's door-step.

"Heartless! — heartless ever!" she cried. "May the judgment of the Almighty reach him — may he suffer — yes — may he suffer only what I have suffered."

"Who and what are you?" said Mrs. Lovett.

"Poor, and therefore everything that is abject and despicable in London."

"What a truth," said Mrs. Lovett. "What a truth that is. Who would not do even as I do to avoid poverty in a widowed life! — It is too horrible. Amid savages it is nothing, but here it is indeed criminality of the deepest dye. Whom did you call after, woman?"

"My husband."

"Husband. Describe him."

"A sottish-looking man, with moustache. Once seen, he is not easily mistaken — ruffian and villain are stamped by nature upon his face."

Mrs. Lovett winced a little.

"Come in," she said, "I will relieve you for the present. Come in."

The woman by a great effort succeeded in rising and crossing the threshold. Mrs. Lovett gave her a seat, and having presented her with a glass of cordial and a pie, she waited until the poor creature should be sufficiently recovered to speak composedly, and then she said to her with perfect calmness, as though she was by no manner of means personally interested in the matter —

"Now tell me — Is the man with moustache and the braided coat, who passed hastily up Bell-yard a few moments only before you, really your husband?"

"Yes, madam, that is Flukes —"

"Who?"

"Flukes, madam."

"And pray who and what is Flukes?"

"He was a tailor, and he might have been as respectable a man, and earned as honest and good a living as any one in the trade, but a love of idleness and dissipation undid him."

"Flukes — a tailor?"

"Yes, madam; and now that I am utterly destitute, and in want of the common necessaries of life, if I chance to meet him in the streets and ask him for the merest trifle to relieve my necessities, he flies from me in the manner he has done to-day."

"Indeed!"

"Yes, madam. If we were in a lonely place he would strike me, so that I should, from the injury he would do me, be unable to follow him, but that in the public streets he dare-not do, for he fears some man would interfere and put a stop to his cruelty."

"There, my good woman," said Mrs. Lovett, "there are five shillings for you. Go now, for I expect to be busy very shortly."

With a profusion of thanks, that while they lasted were quite stunning, poor Mrs. Flukes left the pie-shop and hobbled homewards. When she was gone the colour went and came several times upon the face of Mrs. Lovett, and then she repeated to herself — "Flukes — a tailor!"

"Pies ready?" said a voice at the door.

"Not quite."

"How long, mum; we want half a dozen of the muttons to-day."

"In about ten minutes."

"Thank you, I'll look in again."

"Flukes — a tailor? Indeed! — Flukes — a tailor? Well I ought to have expected something like this. What a glorious thing it is really to care for no one but oneself after all. I shall lose my faith in — in — fine men."

CHAPTER XXXVI.

TOBIAS'S MOTHER AWAKENS OLD RECOLLECTIONS.

POOR TOBIAS STILL REMAINS UPON his bed of sickness. The number of hours at the expiration of which the medical man had expected him to recover were nearly gone. In Colonel Jeffery's parlour three persons, besides himself, were assembled. These three were his friend the captain, Sir Richard Blunt, and Mrs. Ragg. The lady was sitting with a not over clean handkerchief at her eyes, and keeping up a perpetual motion with her knee, as though she were nursing some fractious baby, and Mrs. Ragg had been used of late to go out as a monthly nurse occasionally, which, perhaps, accounted for this little peculiarity.

"Now, madam," said the colonel, "you quite understand, I hope, that you are not to mention to any living soul the fact of your son Tobias being with me."

"Oh, dear me, no, sir. Who should I mention it to?"

"That we can't tell," interrupted the captain, "you are simply desired not to tell it."

"I'm sure I don't see anybody once in a week, sir."

"Good God! woman," cried the colonel, "does that mean that when you do see any one you will tell it?"

"Lord love you, sir, it's few people as comes to see you when you are down in the world. I'm sure it's seldom enough a soul taps at my door with a 'Mrs. Ragg, how are you?'"

"Now was there ever such an incorrigible woman as this?"

"If you were to talk to her for a month," said Sir Robert Blunt, "you would not get a direct answer from her. Allow me to try something else — Mrs. Ragg."

"Yes, sir — humbly at your service, sir."

"If you tell any one that Tobias is here, or indeed anywhere within your knowledge, I will apprehend you about a certain candlestick."

"Goodness gracious, deliver us."

"Do you understand that, Mrs. Ragg? You keep silence about Tobias, and I keep silence about the candlestick. You speak about Tobias, and I speak about the candlestick."

Mrs. Ragg shook her head and let fall a torrent of tears, which the magistrate took as sufficient evidence that she did understand him and would act accordingly, so he added —

"Shall we all proceed up stairs? for a great deal will depend upon the boy's first impression when he awakens — and in this case we should not lose a chance."

In pursuance of this sound advice they all proceeded to poor Tobias's bed-room, and there he lay in that profound repose which the powerful opiate administered to him had had the effect of producing. It did not seem as though he had moved head or foot since they had left him. His face was very pale, and when Mrs. Ragg saw him she burst into tears, exclaiming —

"He is dead — he is dead!"

"No such thing, madam," said Colonel Jeffery. "He only sleeps."

"But, oh deary me, what makes him look so old and so strange now? He was bad enough when I saw him last, poor fellow, but not like this."

"He has received ill-usage from someone, and that is precisely what we want to find out. If you can get from him the particulars of what he has suffered, we will take care those who have made him suffer shall not escape."

"Bless you, gentlemen, what's the use of that if my poor boy is killed?"

There was a good home truth in these words from Mrs. Ragg, although, upon the score of general social policy, they might well be answered. An argument with Mrs. Ragg, however, upon such a subject was not very a-propos. The colonel made her sit down by Tobias's bed-side, and he was then upon the point of remarking to his friend, the captain, that it would be as well, since so many hours had passed, to send for the medical man, when that personage made his appearance.

"Has he awakened?" he asked.

"No — not yet."

"Oh, I see you have a nurse."

"It is his mother. We hope that she, by talking to him familiarly, may produce a good effect, and possibly rid him of that bewilderment of intellect under which he now labours. What think you, sir?"

"That it is a good thought. Let us darken the room as much as possible, as twilight will be most grateful to him upon awakening, which he must do shortly."

The curtains of the window were so arranged that the room was in a state of semi-darkness, and then they all waited with no small anxiety for Tobias to recover from the deep and death-like sleep that had come over him. After about five minutes he moved uneasily and uttered a low moan.

"Speak to him, Mrs. a — a — what's your name?"

"Ragg, sir."

"Aye, Ragg, just speak to him; of course he is well acquainted with your voice, and it may have the effect of greatly rousing him from his lethargic condition."

Poor Mrs. Ragg considered that she had some very extraordinary post to perform, and accordingly she collected to her aid all her learning, which, interrupted by her tears, and now and then by a sob, which she had to gulp down like a large globule of castor oil, had certainly rather a droll effect.

"My dear Tobias — my dear — lie a bed, sluggard, you know — well, I never — Put the kettle on, Polly, and let's all have tea. Tobias, my dear — bless us and save us, are you going to stay in bed all day?"

Another groan from Tobias.

"Well, my dear, perhaps you won't mind getting up and just running towards the corner for a bunch of water cresses? Dear heart alive, there goes the muffin-man like a lamplighter!"

It was by such domestic themes that Mrs. Ragg sought to recall the wandering senses of poor Tobias to a cognizance of the present. But alas! his thoughts were still in the dim and misty land of visions. Suddenly he spoke —

"Hush — hush! There they come! — elephants! — elephants! — on — on

— on. Now for the soldiers, and all mad — mad — mad! Hide me in the straw — deep in a world of straw. Hush! He comes. Sing, oh sing again! — and he — he will not suspect."

The surgeon made a sign to Mrs. Ragg to speak again.

"Why, Tobias, my dear, what are you talking about? Do you mean the Elephant and Castle?"

"Call to his remembrance," said the surgeon, "some old scenes."

"Yes, sir, but when one's heart and all that sort of thing is in one's mouth it's very difficult to recollect things oneself. Tobias!"

"Yes — yes. Ha-ha!"

It was a low, plaintive, strange laugh that, that came from the poor boy whose mind had been so overthrown, and it jarred upon the feelings of all who heard it.

"Tobias, do you recollect the little cottage down the lane at Holloway, where we lived, and the cock roaches, and the strange cat, you know, Tobias, that would not go away? Don't you recollect, Tobias, how the coals there were all slates, and how your poor father, as is dead and gone —"

"Yes, I see him now."

Mrs. Ragg gave a faint scream.

"Father! — father!" said Tobias, as he held out his arms, and the big tears rolled down his cheeks. "Father — father, Todd has not got me now. Don't cry so, father. Stand out of the way of the elephants."

"My dear! my dear!" cried Mrs. Ragg, "do you want to break my heart?"

Tobias rose to a sitting position in the bed, and looked his mother in the face —

"Are you, too, mad?" he said. "Are you, too, mad? Did you tell of Todd?"

"Yes, the only way," said Colonel Jeffery, "for people not to be mad, is to tell of Todd."

"Yes — yes."

"And so you, Tobias, will tell us all you know. That is what we want you to do, and then you will be quite happy and comfortable for the remainder of your days, and live with your mother again far from any apprehension from Todd. Do you understand me?"

Tobias opened his mouth several times in an eager, gasping sort of manner, as though he would have said something rapidly, but he could not. He placed his hands upon his brain, and rocked to and fro for a few moments, and then he broke out into the same low, peculiar laugh that had before so strangely affected Colonel Jeffery and the others who were there present in that room. The surgeon shook his head as he said, mournfully —

"It is of no use!"

"Do you really think so?" said the colonel.

"For the present, I am convinced that it is of no use to attempt to recall

TOBIAS'S DELIRIUM.

his wandering senses. Time will do wonders, and he has the one grand element of youth in his favour. That, as well as time, will do wonders. The case is a bad one, and the shock the brain of this lad has received must be a most fearful one."

"Do not," said Sir Richard Blunt, "give up so readily, Mrs. Ragg; I would have you try him again. Speak to him again of his father — that seemed to be the topic that most moved him."

Mrs. Ragg could hardly do so for her tears, but she managed to stammer out —

"Tobias, do you recollect when your father bought you the rabbit, and out of vexation, the creature eat its way out of a willow-work cage in the night? Do you remember your poor father's funeral, Tobias, and how we went, you and I, my poor boy, to take the last look at the only one who — who — who —"

Mrs. Ragg could get no further.

"Ha — ha — ha!" laughed Tobias, "who told of Todd?"

"Who is this Todd," said the surgeon, "that he continually speaks of, and shudders at the very name of?"

Colonel Jeffery glanced at Sir Richard Blunt, and the latter, who wished the affair by no means to transpire, merely said —

"We are quite as much in the dark as you, sir. It is just what we should like to know, who this Todd is, whose very name seems to hold the imagination of this poor boy in a grasp of iron. I begin to think that nothing more can be done now."

"Nothing, gentlemen, you may depend," said the surgeon. "How old is the lad?"

"Sixteen as never was," replied Mrs. Ragg, "and a hard time I had of it, sir, as you may suppose."

The surgeon did not exactly see how he was called upon to suppose anything of the sort; however he made no further remark to Mrs. Ragg, but continued in conversation for some time with Colonel Jeffery, who informed him that Tobias should remain for a time where he was, so that there should be every possible chance given for his recovery.

"I wish you to continue attending upon him, sir," he added, "for I would spare nothing that medical advice can suggest to restore him. He has, I am convinced, been a great sufferer."

"That is sufficiently clear, sir. You may rely upon my utmost attention."

"Mrs. Ragg," said the colonel, "can you cook?"

"Cook, sir? Lord bless you, sir. I can cook as well as here and there a one, though I say it that oughtn't, and if poor Tobias was but all right, I should not go to be after making myself miserable now about bygones. What's to be cured must be endured — it's a long lane as hasn't a turning. As poor Mr. Ragg often used to say when he was alive — 'Grizzling ain't fattening.'"

"I should think it was not. It so happens, Mrs. Ragg, that there is a vacancy in my house for a cook, and if you like to come and take the place, you can look after Tobias as well, you know, for I intend him to remain here for the present. Only remember, you tell this to no one."

"Me, sir! Lord bless you, sir, who do I see?"

The colonel was by no means anxious to convince himself a second time of the impossibility of bringing Mrs. Ragg to a precise answer, so he changed the subject, and it was finally arranged that without a word to any one upon the subject, that very night Mrs. Ragg was to take up her abode with Tobias. After this had been all arranged, the three gentlemen proceeded to the dining room, and held a consultation.

"Of the guilt of Todd," said the magistrate, "I entertain no doubt, but I own that I am extremely anxious to bring the crime legally home to him."

"Exactly," said the colonel, "and I can only say that every plan you can suggest will be cheerfully acquiesced in by me and my friend here."

The captain signified his assent.

"Be assured, gentlemen," added Sir Richard Blunt, "that something shall be done of a decisive character before many days are past. I have seen the higher powers upon the subject, and have full authority, and you may rest satisfied that I shall not mind running a little personal risk to unravel the mysteries that surround the career of Sweeney Todd. I think one thing may be done conveniently."

"What is that, sir?"

"Why, It seems to be pretty well understood that no one resides in Todd's house but himself, and as now he has no boy — unless he has provided himself with one already — he must go out sometimes and leave the place to itself, and upon one of those occasions an opportunity might be found of thoroughly searching the upper part, at all events, of his house."

"Could that be done with safety?"

"I think so. At all events, I feel inclined to try it. If I do so, and make any discovery, you may depend upon my letting you know without an hour's delay, and I sincerely hope that all that will take place may have the effect of setting your mind at rest regarding your friend, Mr. Ingestrie."

"But not of restoring him to us?"

The magistrate shook his head.

"I think, sir," he said, "that you ought to consider that he has, if any one has, fallen a victim to Sweeney Todd."

"Alas! I fear so."

"All the evidence points that way, and we can only take measures in the best way possible to bring his murderer to justice — that that murderer is Sweeney Todd, I cannot for one moment of time bring myself to doubt."

Sir Richard Blunt shortly afterwards left Colonel Jeffery's house and proceeded to the execution of a plan of proceeding, with the particulars of which he had not thought proper to entrust to the colonel, and his friend the captain. Long habits of caution had led the magistrate — who was not one of the fancy magistrates of the present day, but a real police officer — active, cool, and determined — to trust no one but himself with his secrets, and so he kept to himself what he meant to do that night.

When he was gone, Colonel Jeffery had a long talk with his friend, and the subject gradually turned to Johanna, whom the colonel yet hoped, he said, to be able one day to call his own.

"No one," he remarked, "would be more truly rejoiced than I to restore Mark Ingestrie to her whom he loves, and whose affection for him is of so enduring and remarkable a character, but if, as Sir Richard Blunt supposes, he is really no more, I think Johanna, by being mine, would stand a better chance of recovering her serenity, if not of enjoying all the happiness in this world that she deserves."

"Hope for the best," said the captain, "and recollect what the surgeon said as regarded Tobias, that time works wonders."

CHAPTER XXXVII.

THE SEARCH AT TODD'S.

THE HOUSE IN FLEET-STREET, next door to Todd's, was kept by a shoemaker, named Whittle, and in this shoemaker's window was a bill, only put up on the very day of poor Tobias's escape from Peckham, announcing—"An Attic to Let." This was rather an alluring announcement to Sir Richard Blunt. At about half an hour after sunset on the same evening that had witnessed the utter discomfiture of the attempt to restore poor Tobias Ragg to his senses, two men stood in the deep recess of a doorway immediately opposite to the house of Sweeney Todd. These two men were none other than Sir Richard and his esteemed but rather eccentric officer, Mr. Crotchet. After some few moments' silence, Sir Richard spoke, saying—

"Well, Crotchet—what do you think of the affair now?"

"Nothink."

"Nothing? You do not mean that, Crotchet?"

"Says what I means—means what I says, and then leaves it alone."

"But you have some opinion, Crotchet?"

"Had, master—had—"

"Well, Crotchet; I think we can now cross over the way, and endeavour to get possession of the shoemaker's attic, from which we can get into Todd's house."

"And find nothink criminatory."

"You think not; but do you know, Crotchet, I am of opinion that the greatest and cleverest rogues not unfrequently leave themselves open to detection, in some little particular, which they have most strangely and unaccountably neglected. I am not without a hope that we shall find the man, Sweeney Todd, to be one of that class, and if so, we shall not fail to do some good by our visit to the house.—You remain here and watch for his going out, and when he is gone, come over the way and ask for Mr. Smith. Have you seen Fletcher?"

"No, but he will be here presently, and will wait till that 'ere fellow goes away, if so be as he goes out, and then when you and me hears two notes on the key-bugle*, it will be time all for us to go for to come to mizzle."

"Very good," said Sir Richard Blunt, and he crossed over to the shoemaker's shop, leaving Crotchet on the watch in the deep doorway.

The fact is, they had been waiting there for some time, in the hope that Todd would go out, but he had not stirred, so that the magistrate thought it would be as well to let Crotchet remain while he secured the shoemaker's attic, with a view to ulterior proceedings. The magistrate was dressed as a respectable, staid clerk, and he walked into the shoemaker's shop with a gravity of gait that was quite imposing.

"You have an attic to let," he said. "Is it furnished?"

"Oh yes, sir, and comfortably too. My missus looks after all that, I can tell you."

"Very well, I want just such a place; for, do you know, since I have left a widower, I like to live in some lively situation, and as all my friends are at Cambridge, and not a soul that I know in London, I don't half fancy going into an out-of-the-way place to live; though, I dare say, for all that, London is safe enough."

"Why, I don't know that," said the shoemaker. "However, you'll be safe enough here, sir, never doubt. The rent is four shillings a week."

"Very good. I think, if you will show it to me, we shall suit each other. The great object with me is to find myself in the house of a respectable man, and one look at you, sir, is quite sufficient to show me that you are one."

This was all highly flattering to the shoemaker, and he was so well pleased to get such a respectable, civil-spoken, middle aged gentleman into his house, that he was prepared, upon half a word to that effect, to come down a whole sixpence a week in the rent, if needs were. Of course, the would-be-lodger was well enough pleased with the attic, and turning to the shoemaker, he handed him four shillings, saying—

"As my friends are all so far off, I ought to give you a week's rent in advance, instead of a reference, and there it is."

After this, who could ask any further questions? The magistrate, just, of his own accord, added that his name was Smith, and that he would stay a short time in his room if the shoemaker could oblige him with a light, which was

---

* A military bugle with seven keys fitted to it so that it could play regular songs. The key-bugle was the direct precursor to the modern cornet or trumpet.

done accordingly, and when the shoemaker's wife came home — that lady having been out to gossip with no less a personage than Mrs. Lovett — he was quite elated to tell her what a lodger they had, and as he handed her the four shillings, saying "My dear, that will buy you the ribbon at Mrs. Keating's, the mercer, that you had set your mind upon," how could she be other than quite amiable?

"Well, John," she said, "for once in a way, I must say that you have shown great judgment, and if I had been at home myself, I could not have managed better."

This, we are quite sure our lady readers will agree with us, was as much as any married female ought to say.

Sir Richard Blunt ascended to the attic, of which he was now, by virtue of a weekly tenancy, lord and master, with a light; and, closing the door, he cast his eyes around the apartment. Its appointments were decidedly not luxurious. In one corner a stump-bedstead awakened anything but lively associations, while the miserable little grate, the front of which was decidedly composed of some portions of an old iron hoop from a barrel, did not look redolent of comforts. The rest of the apartments were what the auctioneers call *en suite*, the said auctioneers having but a dreamy notion of what *en suite* means.

But the appointments or disappointments of his attic were of little conse-quence to Sir Richard Blunt. It was the window that offered attractions to him. Softly opening it, he looked out, and found that there was a leaden gutter, with only the average amount of filth in it, the drain being, of course, stopped up by a dishclout and a cracked flower-pot, which is perfectly according to custom in London. He saw enough at a glance, however, to convince him that there would be no difficulty whatever in getting to the attic of Todd's house, and that fact once ascertained, he waited with exemplary and placid patience the return of Crotchet.

Now, SWEENEY TODD WAS, DURING much of that day, in what is denominated a brown study. He could not make up his mind in what way he was to make up for the loss of the senses of Tobias. It was with him an equal choice of disagreeables. To have a boy, or not to have a boy, which to do became an anxious question.

"A boy is a spy," muttered Todd to himself — "a spy upon all my actions — a perpetual police-officer in a small way, constantly at my elbow — an alarum continually crying to me 'Todd! Todd! beware!' Curses on them all, and yet what a slave am I to this place without a lad; and, after all, when they do become too troublesome and inquisitive, I can but dispose of them as I have disposed of him."

Todd patrolled his shop for some time, thus communing with himself; but as yet he could not make up his mind which to do. — A boy or not a boy? — that was the question.

He remained in this unsatisfactory state of mind until sunset had passed away and the dim twilight was wrapping all things in obscurity. Then, without deciding upon either course, he suddenly, in a very hurried manner, shut up his shop, and closing the outer door carefully, he walked rapidly towards Bell-yard.

He was going to Mrs. Lovett's, whither we shall follow him at a more convenient opportunity; but just now we have Sir Richard Blunt's enterprise to treat of. Todd had no sooner got fairly out of sight, than Mr. Crotchet emerged from the doorway in which he was concealed, and went a few paces down Fleet-street, towards the Temple. — He soon met a man genteelly dressed, who seemed to be sauntering along in an idle fashion.

"All's right, Fletcher," said Crotchet.

"Oh, is it?"

"Yes. Have you got that ere little article with you?"

"The bugle? Oh, yes."

"Mind you blows it then, if you sees Todd come home, and no gammon."

"Trust to me, old fellow."

Without another word, Mr. Crotchet crossed over the road, and opened the shop-door of the shoemaker. Now the face of Mr. Crotchet was not the most engaging in the world, and when he looked in upon the shoemaker, that industrious workman felt a momentary pang of alarm, and particularly when Mr. Crotchet, imparting a horrible obliquity to his vision, said —

"How is yer, old un?"

"Sir?" said the shoemaker.

"You couldn't show a fellow the way up to Smith's *hattic*, I supposes?"

"Smith — Smith? — Oh, dear me, that's the new lodger. I'll call him down if you wait here."

"No occasion. I'll toddle up, my tulip. He's a relation o' mine, don't you see the likeness atween us? — We was considered the handsomest pair o' men as was in London at one time, and it sticks to us now, I can tell you."

"If you wish, sir, to go up, instead of having Mr. Smith called down, of course, sir, you can, as you are an old friend. Allow me to light you, sir."

"Not the least occasion. Only tell me where it isn't, and I'll find out where it is, old chap."

"It's the front attic."

"All's right. Don't be sich a hass as to be flaring away arter me, with that 'ere double dip, I can find my way in *worserer* places than this here. All's right — easy does it."

To the surprise of the shoemaker, his mysterious visitor opened the little door at the back of the shop, which led to the staircase, and in a moment disappeared up them.

"Upon my life, this Mr. Smith," thought the shoemaker, "seems to have some very strange connexions. He told me he knew nobody in London, and then here comes one of the ugliest fellows, I think, I ever saw in all my life, and claims acquaintance with him. What ought I to do? — Ought I to tell Mrs. W. of it?"

At this moment Mrs. W. made her appearance from the mercer's, with the ribbon that had tickled her feminine fancy — all smiles and sweetness. The heart of the shoemaker died within him, for well he knew what visitation he was likely to come in for, if anything connected with the lodger turned out wrong.

"A-hem! a-hem! Well, my dear, have you got the ribbon?"

"Oh yes, to be sure, and a love it is —"

"Ah! — ah!"

"What's the matter?"

"Nothing, my dove. I was only thinking that it wasn't the ribbon that makes folks look lovely, but the person who wears it. You would look beautiful in any ribbon."

"Why, my dear, that may be very true, but still one ought to look as well as one can, you know, for the credit of one's maker."

"Oh, yes, yes, but I was only thinking —"

"Thinking of what? Bless me, Mr. Wheeler, how mystifying you are to-night, to be sure. What do you mean by this conduct? Was ever a woman so pestered and tormented with a fool of a man, who looks like an owl in an ivy bush for all the world, or a crow peeping into a marrowbone."

"My duck, how can you say so?"

"Duck indeed? Keep your ducks to yourself. Hoity toity. Duck, indeed. You low good-for-nothing —"

"My dear, my dear. I was only thinking, and not in the least wishing to offend."

"But you do offend me, you nasty insinuating, sneering wretch. — What were you thinking about? Tell me this moment."

"Why, that a pretty silver-grey satin mantle would set off your figure so well, that —"

"Oh, John!"

"That, though quarter-day is near at hand, I think you ought to have one."

"Really, Jackey."

"Yes, my dear."

"What a man you are. Ah, Jackey, after all, though we have, like all people, our little tiffs and wiffs and sniffs — after all, I say it, perhaps, that should not say it, you are a dear, good, obliging —"

"Don't mention it."

"Yes, but —"

"No, don't. By-the-bye, do you know, Susey, that I begin to have my suspicions — mind, I may be wrong, but I begin to have my suspicions, do you know, that our attic lodger is, after all, no better than he should be."

"Gracious!"

"Hush! hush! There has been a man here; so ugly — so — so — squintified, if I may say so, that between you and me and the post, my dear, it's enough to frighten any one to look at him, it is indeed. — But as for the silver-grey satin, don't stint the quality for a sixpence or so."

"The wretch!"

"And take care to have plenty of rich trimming to it."

"The monster!"

"And have something pretty to match it, so that when you go to St. Dunstan's next Sunday, all the folks will ask what fine lady from court has come into the city out of curiosity to see the old church."

"Oh, Jackey."

"That's what I call," muttered Mr. Wheeler, "pouring oil upon the troubled waters." He then spoke aloud, saying — "Now, my dear, it is your judgment and advice I want. What shall we do in this case? for you see — first of all, the new lodger denies knowing a soul, and then, in half an hour, an old acquaintance calls upon him here."

The silver-grey satin — the flattering allusion to the probable opinion of the people in St. Dunstan's Church on the next Sunday — the obscure allusion to a something else to match it, and the appeal to her judgment, all had the effect desired upon Mrs. Wheeler, who, dropping entirely the hectoring tone, fell into her husband's views, and began calmly and dispassionately, without abuse or crimination, to discuss the merits, or rather the probable demerits, of the new lodger.

"I tell you, my dear, my opinion," said the lady. "As for stopping in the house and not knowing who and what he is, I won't."

"Certainly not, my love."

"Then, Mr. W., the only thing to do, is for you and I to go up stairs, and say that as I was out you did not know a Mr. Jones had spoken about the lodging, but that, if he could give a reference in London, we would still have him for a lodger."

"Very well. That will be only civil, and if he says he can't, but must send to Cambridge —"

"Why then, my dear, you must say that he may stay till he writes, and I'll be guided by his looks. If I give you a nudge, so, with my elbow, you may consider that it's pretty right."

"Very well, my dove."

CHAPTER XXXVIII.

SIR RICHARD PRIES INTO TODD'S SECRETS.

CROTCHET SOON REACHED THE ATTIC FLOOR of the shoemaker's house, and although in profound darkness, he managed, as he thought, to touch the right door. Tap! tap! went Crotchet's knuckles, and as he did so he followed a habit very general, when the knock is only a matter of ceremony, and opened the door at the same moment. He popped his head into a room where there was a light, and said —

"Here yer is."

A scream was the reply to him, and then Crotchet saw, by the state of affairs there, that he had made a little mistake in the topography of the attic landing. The attic in which he found himself, for he had crossed the threshold, was in the occupation of an elderly gaunt-looking female, who was comforting her toes by keeping them immersed in a pan of water by the side of a little miserable fire, which was feebly pretending to look cheerful in the little grate.

"Lor, mum!" said Crotchet. "Who'd a thought o' seeing of you?"

"Oh, you monster. You base man, what do you want here?"

"Nothink!"

"Be off with you, or else I'll call the *perlice*."

"Oh, I'm a going, mum. How do you bring it in, mum, in a general way?"

"Help! Murder!"

"Lord bless us, what a racket. Don't you go for to fancy, mum, that I comed up these here attic stairs for to see you. Quite the rewerse, mum."

"Then, pray who did you come to see, you big ugly monster you? The other attic is empty. Oh, you base infidel. I believe I knows what men are by this time."

"No doubt on it, mum. Howsomedever this here's the wrong door, I take it. No harm done, mum. I wish you and your toes, mum, a remarkably good evening."

"Crotchet," said a voice.

"Here yer is."

Sir Richard Blunt had been attentively listening for Crotchet, and when he heard the screams of the old lady in the next attic, he opened the door of his apartment, and looked out. He soon discovered what was amiss, and called out accordingly.

"Bless us, who's that?"

"The Emperor o' Russia, mum," said Crotchet. "He's took that 'ere attic next to you, cos he's heard so much o' the London chumbley pots, and he wants to have a good look at them at his leisure."

With these words Mr. Crotchet left the old lady's attic, and closed the door carefully, leaving her, no doubt, in a considerable state of bewilderment. In another moment he was with the magistrate.

"Crotchet," said Sir Richard, "I thought I told you to do this thing as quietly as you possibly could."

"Down as a hammer, sir."

"I think it is anything but down."

"Right as a trivet, sir, with a hextra leg. Lots o' fear, but no danger. Now for it, Sir Richard. What lay is we to go on?"

It certainly never occurred to Sir Richard Blunt to hold any argument with Mr. Crotchet. He had long since found out that he must, if he would avail himself of his services — and for courage and fidelity he was unequalled — put up with his eccentricities; so upon this occasion he said no more about Crotchet's mistake, but, after a few moments' pause, pointing to the attic door, he said —

"Secure it."

"All's right."

Crotchet took a curious little iron instrument from his pocket, and secured it into the wall by the side of the door. It did not take him more than a moment to do so, and then, fully satisfied of the efficacy of his work, he said —

"Let 'em get over that if they can."

While he was so occupied. Sir Richard Blunt himself had opened the window, and fastened it open securely.

"Now, Crotchet," he said, "look to your pistols."

"All's right, sir."

The magistrate carefully examined the priming of his own arms, and seeing that all was right, he at once emerged from the attic through the window on to the parapet of the house. He might have crept along the gutter just within the parapet, but the gutter aforesaid was not exactly in the most salubrious condition. Indeed, from its filthy state, one might have fancied it to be peculiarly under the direction of the city commissioners of sewers. Crotchet followed Sir Richard closely, and in a moment or two they had traversed a sufficient portion of the parapet to find themselves at the attic window of Todd's house. It would have been next thing to a miracle if they had been seen in their progress, for the roof was very dark coloured, and the night had fairly enough set in, so that if any one had by chance looked up from the street below, they would scarcely have discovered that there was anybody creeping along the parapet.

Now there was a slight creaking noise for about half a minute, and then the window of Sweeney Todd's attic swung open.

"Come on," said Sir Richard, and he softly alighted in the apartment.

Crotchet followed him, and then the magistrate carefully closed the window again, and left it in such a way, that a touch from within would open it. Then they were in profound darkness, and as it was no part of the policy of Sir Richard Blunt to run any unnecessary risks, he did not move one inch from the place upon which he stood until he had lighted a small hand lantern, which had a powerful reflector and a tin shade, which in a moment could be passed over the glass, so as to hide the light upon an emergency.

"Now, Crotchet," he said, "we shall see where we are."

"Reether," said Crotchet.

By holding the light some height up, they were able to command a good view of the attic. It was a miserable looking room: the walls were in a state of premature decay, and in several places lumps of mortar had fallen from the ceiling, making a litter of broken plaster upon the floor. It was entirely destitute of furniture, with the exception of an old stump bedstead, upon which there lay what looked like a quantity of old clothes.

"Safe enough," said Sir Richard.

"Stop!" said Crotchet.

"What's the matter?"

"There's something odd on the floor here. Don't you see as the dust has got into a crevice as is bigger nor all the other crevices, and goes right along this ways and then along that ways? Don't you move, sir. I'll be down upon it in a minute."

Mr. Crotchet laid himself down flat upon the floor, and then crept on until he came to that part of the flooring which had excited his suspicions. As soon as he pressed upon it with both his hands it gave way under them plainly, by the elevation of the other end of the three boards of which this trap was composed, proclaiming that it was a moveable portion of the floor, revolving or turning upon one of the joists as a centre.

"Oh dear, how clever!" said Crotchet. "If Mr. Todd goes on a cutting away his joists in this here way he'll bring his blessed old house down with a run some day. How nice and handy, now, if any one was to step upon here — they'd go down into the room below, and perhaps break their blessed legs as they went."

"Escape the first for us!" said Sir Richard.

"Oh, lor, yes. Now this here Todd thinks, by putting this here man-trap here, as he has *perwided* again any accidents; but we ain't them 'ere sort o' birds as is catched by chaff, not we. Why he must have spilted his blessed ceiling down below to make this here sort of a jigamaree concern."

"It's not a bad contrivance though, Crotchet. Its own weight, you see, restores it to its place again, and so there's no trouble with it."

"Oh dear, no. It's a what I calls a self-acting catch-'em-who-can sort o' machine. Yes, Sir Richard, I never did think that 'ere Todd was wery green. He

THE SECRET TRAP DISCOVERED IN TODD'S HOUSE.

don't know quite so much as we know; but yet he's a rum 'un."

"No doubt of it. Do you think, Crotchet, there is anything else in this attic to beware of?"

"Not likely; when he'd finished this here nice little piece of handywork, I dare say he said to himself—'This will catch 'em,' and so down stairs he toddled, and grinned like a monkey as has swallowed a whole nut by haccident, and gived himself a pain in the side in consekence. 'That'll catch 'em,' says he."

Mr. Crotchet seemed so much amused at the picture he drew to himself of the supposed exultation of Todd, that for some moments he did nothing but laugh. The reader must not suppose, however, that in the circumstances of peril in which they were, he indulged in a regular "Ha! ha!"— quite the contrary. He had a mode of laughing under such circumstances that was entirely his own, and which, while it made no noise, shook his huge frame as though some commotion had taken sudden possession of it, and the most ridiculous part of the process was the alarming suddenness with which he would become preter-naturally serious again. But Sir Richard Blunt knew his peculiarities, and paid no attention to them, unless they very much interfered with business.

"We must not waste time. Come on, Crotchet."

Sir Richard walked to the door of the attic and tried it. It was as fast as though it had been part of the wall itself.

"So — so," he said. "Master Todd has taken some precautions against being surprised from the top of his house. He has nailed up this door as surely as any door was ever nailed up."

"Has he really, though?"

"Yes. Quick, Crotchet. You have your tools about you, I suppose."

"Never fear," said Crotchet. "I'm the *indiwedal* as never forgets nothink, and if I don't have the middle panel out o' this door a'most as soon as look at it, it's only cos it takes more time."

With this philosophical and indisputable remark, Mr. Crotchet stooped down before the door, and taking various exquisitely made tools from his pocket, he began to work at the door. He knocked nearly noiselessly, and it looked like something little short of magic to see how the panel was forced out of the door without any of the hammering and flustering which a carpenter would have made of it.

"All's right," he said. "If we can't creep through here, we are bigger than I think we is."

"That will do. Hush!"

They both listened attentively, for Sir Richard thought he heard a faint noise from the lower part of the house. As, however, five minutes of attentive listening passed away, and no repetition of it occurred, they thought it was only some one of those accidental sounds which will at times be heard in all houses whether occupied or not. Crotchet took the lead by creeping clearly enough through the opening that he had made in the door of the attic, and Sir Richard followed him.

They were both, now, at the head of the staircase, and Sir Richard held up the lantern so as to have a good look around him. The walls looked damp and neglected. There were two other doors opening from that landing, but neither of them was fastened, so that they entered the rooms easily. They took care, though, not to go beyond the threshold for fear of accidents, although it was very unlikely that Todd would take the trouble to construct a trap-door in any other attic than the one which was so easily accessible from the parapet.

"Old clothes — old clothes!" said Crotchet. "There seems to be nothing else in these rooms."

"So it would appear," said Sir Richard.

He lifted up some of the topmost of a heap of garments upon the floor, and a cloud of moths flew upwards in confusion.

"There's the toggery," said Mr. Crotchet, "of the *smugged 'uns!*"

"You really think so."

"Knows it."

"Well, Crotchet, I don't think from what I know myself that we shall disagree about Todd's guilt. The grand thing is to discover how, and in what way he is guilty."

"Just so. I'm quite sure we have seed all as there is to see up here, so suppose we toddle down stairs now, sir. There's, perhaps, quite a lot o' wonders and natur', and art, down below."

"Stop a bit. Hold the lamp."

Crotchet did so, while Sir Richard took from his pocket a pair of thick linsey-woolsey* stockings, and carefully drew them on over his boots, for the purpose of deadening the sound of his footsteps; and then he held the light, while Mr. Crotchet, who was similarly provided with linsey-woolseys, went through the same process.

After this, they moved like spectres, so perfectly noiseless were their footsteps upon the stairs. Sir Richard went first, while Crotchet now carried the light, holding it sufficiently high that the magistrate could see the stairs before him very well, as he proceeded. It was quite evident, from the state of those stairs, as regarded undisturbed dust, that they had not been ascended for a considerable time; and indeed, Todd, considering the top of his house as perfectly safe after the precautions he had taken, did not trouble himself to visit it. Our adventurers reached the landing upon the second floor in perfect safety; and after giving a few minutes more to the precautionary measure of listening, they opened the first door that presented itself to the observation, and entered the room.

They both paused in astonishment, for such a miscellaneous collection of matters as was in this room, could only have been expected to be met with in the shop of a general dealer. Several chairs and tables were loaded with wearing apparel of all kinds and conditions. The corners of the room were literally crowded with mobs of swords, walking sticks, and umbrellas; while a countless heap of hats lay upon the floor in disorder. You could not have stepped into that room for miscellaneous personal appointments of one sort or another; and

---

* A thick, coarse, warm–but–ugly fabric made of linen and wool.

Mr. Crotchet and Sir Richard Blunt trod upon the hats as they walked across the floor, from sheer inability to get out of the way.

"Well," said Crotchet, "if so be as shaving should go out of fashion, Todd could set up a clothier's shop, and not want for stock to begin with."

"I can imagine," muttered the magistrate to himself, "what a trouble and anxiety all these things must be to Todd, and woollen goods are so difficult to burn. Crotchet, select some of the swords, and look if there are maker's names upon the blades."

While Crotchet was preparing this order, Sir Richard was making a hasty but sufficiently precise examination of the room.

CHAPTER XXXIX.

THE MYSTERIOUS CUPBOARD.

"HERE THEY ARE," SAID CROTCHET. "Some of these are worth something."

"Get a cane or two, likewise."

"All's right, sir. I tell you what it is, sir. If there's such things as ghosts in the world, I wonder how this Todd can sleep o' nights, for he must have a plaguy lot of 'em about his bed of a night."

"Perhaps he satisfied himself upon that head, Crotchet, before he began his evil practices, for all we know; but let us make our way into another room, for I think we have seen all there is to see in this one."

"Not a doubt of it. It's only a kind of store-room, this, and from the size of it, I should say it ain't the largest on this floor."

Sir Richard walked out of the room on to the landing place. All was perfectly still in the barber's house, and as he had heard nothing of the bugle sound in Fleet-street, he felt quite satisfied that Todd had not returned. It was a great thing, in all his daring exploits in discovering criminals, and successfully ferreting out their haunts, that he (Sir Richard) could thoroughly depend upon his subordinates. He knew they were not only faithful but brave. He knew that, let what might happen, they would never leave him in the lurch. Hence, in the present instance, he felt quite at his ease in the house of Todd, so long as he did not hear the sound of the bugle. Of course, personal danger he did not consider, for he knew he was, if even he had been alone, more than a match for Todd; but what he wanted was, not to overcome Sweeney Todd, but to find out exactly what were his practices. He could, upon the information he already had, have walked into Todd's shop at any time, and have apprehended him, but that would not have answered. What he wanted to do was to —

"Pluck out the heart of his mystery," *

— and, in order to do that, it was not only necessary that Todd should be at large, but that he should have no hint that such a person as he, Sir Richard Blunt, had his eyes wide open to his actions and manoeuvres. Hence was it that, in this examination of the house, he wished to keep himself so secret, and free from any observation.

There were three rooms upon the second floor of Todd's house, and the very next one they met with, was the one immediately beneath the trap in the floor of the attic. A glance at the ceiling enabled them easily to perceive it. This room was larger than the other considerably, and in it were many boxes and chests, as well as in the centre an immense old-fashioned counting-house desk, with six immense flaps to it, three upon each side, while a brass railing went along the middle.

"Ah!" said Sir Richard, "here will be something worth the examining, I hope."

"Let's take the cupboards first," said Crotchet. "There are two here, and as they are the first we have seen, let's look at 'em, Sir Richard. I never likes to be in a strange room long, without a peep in the cupboard."

"Very well, Crotchet. Look in that one to the left, while I look in this one to the right."

Sir Richard opened a cupboard door to the right of the fire-place in this room, while Crotchet opened one to the left.

"More clothes," said Sir Richard. "What's in yours, Crotchet?"

"Nothing at all. Yet stay. There's a something high up here. I don't know what it is, but I'll try and reach it if I can."

Crotchet went completely into the cupboard, but he had no sooner done so, than Sir Richard Blunt heard a strange crushing sound, and then all was still.

"Hilloa! What's that, Crotchet?"

He hastily stepped to the cupboard. The door had swung close. It was evidently hung upon its hinges in a manner to do so. With his disengaged hand, the magistrate at once pulled it open. Crotchet was gone.

The astonishment of Sir Richard Blunt for a moment was excessive. There was the flooring of the cupboard perfectly safe, but no Crotchet. Nothing to his eyes had looked so like a magical disappearance as this, and with the trap

---

* *A reference from Shakespeare's* Hamlet, *Act III Scene II, in which Hamlet says to Guildenstern, the friend he is about to betray, "You would play upon me; you would seem to know my stops; you would pluck out the heart of my mystery."*

in his hand, he stood while any one might have counted twenty, completely motionless and transfixed by astonishment. Starting then from this lethargic condition, he drew a pistol from his pocket, and rushed to the door of the room. At this instant, he heard the bugle sound clearly and distinctly in the street. Before the echo of the sound had died away, the magistrate was upon the landing-place outside the door of the second floor. He listened intently, and heard some one below coughing. It was not the cough of Crotchet. What was he to do? If he did not make a signal to the officers in the street that all was safe, the house would soon be stormed, and, for all he knew, that might ensure the destruction of Crotchet, instead of saving him. For a moment, the resolution to go down the staircase at all hazards and face Todd — for he had no doubt but that he had come home — possessed him, but a moment's reflection turned the scale of thought in another direction. If the officers, not finding him make a signal that he was safe, did attack the house, they would not do so for some minutes. It was their duty not to be precipitate. He leant on the balustrade, and listened with an intentness that was perfectly painful. He heard the cough again from quite the lower part of the house, and then he became aware that some one was slowly creeping up the stairs. He had placed the slide over the bull's eye of his little lamp, so that all was darkness, but he heard the breathing of the person who was coming up towards him. He shrunk back close to the wall, determined to seize, and with an iron hand, any one who should reach the landing. Suddenly, from quite the lower part of the building, he heard the cough again. The thought, then, that it must be Crotchet who was coming up, impressed itself upon him, but he would not speak. In a few moments some one reached the landing, and stretching out his right arm, Sir Richard caught whoever it was, and said in a whisper —

"Any resistance will cost you your life."

"Crotchet it is," said the new comer.

"Ah, how glad I am it is you!"

"Reether. Hush. The old 'un is below. Ain't I shook a bit. It's a precious good thing as my bones is in the blessed habit o' holding on, one of 'em to the rest and all the rest to one, or else I should have tumbled to bits."

"Hush! hush!"

"Oh, he's a good way off. That 'ere cupboard has got a descending floor with ropes and pullies, so down I went and was rolled out into a room below and up went the bit of flooring again. I was very nearly startled a little."

"Nearly?"

"Reether, but here I is. I got out and crept up stairs as soon as I could, cos, says I, the governor will wonder what the deuce has become of me."

"I did, indeed."

"Just as I thought. Sir Richard, just listen to me! I've got a fancy for Todd."

"A fancy for Todd?"

"Yes, and I want to stay here a few hours — yes, go and let them as is outside know all's right, and leave me here, I think somehow I shall like to be in this crib alone with Todd for an hour or two. You have got other business to see to, you know, so just leave me here; and mind yer, if I don't get here by six in the morning, just consider as he's got the better of me."

"No, Crotchet, I cannot."

"Can't what?"

"Consent to leave you here alone."

"Bother! what's the row, and where's the danger, I should like to know? Who's Todd? Who am I? Gammon!"

Sir Richard shook his head, although Crotchet could not very well see him shake it, and after a pause he added —

"I don't suppose exactly that there is much danger, Crotchet, but, at all events, I don't like it said that I brought you into this place and then left you here."

"Bother!"

"You go and leave me."

"A likely joke that. No, I tell yer what it is, Sir Richard. You knows me and I knows you, so what does it matter what other folks say? Business is business I hope, and don't you believe that I'm going to be such a flat as to throw away my life upon such a fellow as Todd. I think I can do some good by staying here; if I can't I'll come away, but I don't think, in either case, that Todd will see me. If he does I shall, perhaps, be forced to nab him, and that, after all, is the worst that can come of it."

"Well, Crotchet, you shall have your own way."

"Good."

"I will return to the attic as soon as I conveniently can, and, let what will happen to you, remember that you are not deserted."

"I knows it."

"Good bye. Take care of yourself, old friend."

"I means it."

"I should be indeed afflicted if anything were to happen to you."

"Gammon."

Sir Richard left him his own pistols, in addition to the pair which he, Crotchet, always had about him, so that he was certainly well-armed, let what would happen to him in that house of Sweeney Todd's, which had now become something more than a mere object of suspicion to the police. Well, they knew Todd's guilt — it was the mode in which he was guilty only that still remained a mystery.

The moment Sir Richard Blunt reached the attic again, he held his arm out at full length from the window, and waved to and fro the little lantern as a signal to the officers in the street that he was safe. This done, he would not return to the room he had hired of the bootmaker, but he resolved to wait about ten minutes longer in case anything should happen in the house below that might sound alarming. After that period of time, he resolved upon leaving for an hour or two, but he, of course, would not do so without apprising his officers of Crotchet's situation.

DURING THE TIME THAT HAD BEEN PASSED by Crotchet and Sir Richard Blunt in Sweeney Todd's house, the shoemaker and his wife had had an adventure which created in their minds abundance of surprise. It will be recollected that the shoemaker's wife had decided upon what was to be done regarding the new lodger — namely, that under the pretence that a Mr. Jones was a more satisfactory lodger, he was to be asked to be so good as to quit the attic he had so strangely taken. The arrival of Mr. Crotchet with so different a story from that told by Sir Richard Blunt certainly had the effect of engendering many suspicions in the minds of Sir Richard's new landlord and landlady.

"Well, my dear," said the shoemaker, "if you are willing to come up stairs, I will say what you wish to this man, particularly as his pretended friend don't seem to be coming down stairs again."

"Very well, my dear; I'll take the kitchen poker and follow you, and while I am behind you, if I think he is a pleasant man, you know, and we had better let him stay, I will give you a slight poke."

"A-hem! Thank you — yes."

Armed with the poker, the lady of the mansion followed her husband up the staircase, and perhaps we may fairly say that curiosity was as strong a feeling with her as any other in the business. To tell the truth, the shoemaker did not half like the job; but what will a man, who is under proper control at home, not do to keep up the shallow treaty of peace which his compliance produces between him and his better half? Is there anything which a hen-pecked husband dares say he will not do, when the autocrat of his domestic hearth bids him do it?

Up — up the long dark staircase they went! Our ancestors, as one of their pieces of wisdom, had a knack of making steep dark staircases; and, to tell the truth, there are many modern architects equally ingenious.

At length the attic landing was reached. The shoemaker knew the localities of his house better than to make such a mistake as Crotchet had done; so the old lady, with her feet in the pan of water, was saved such another interruption as had already taken place into her peaceful domains.

"Now, my dear, knock boldly," said the lady of the mansion. "Knock like a man."

"Yes, my love."

The shoemaker tapped at the door with about the energy of a fly. The soft appeal produced no effect whatever, and the lady growing impatient, then poised the poker, and dealt the door a blow which induced her husband to start aside, lest the lodger should open it quickly, and rush out in great wrath. All was profoundly still, however; and then they tried the lock, and found it fast.

"He's gone to bed," said the shoemaker.

"He can't," said the lady, "for there are no sheets on the bed. Besides, they have not both gone to bed. I tell you what it is. There's some mystery in this that I should like to find out. Now, all the keys of all the attics are alike. Just wait here, and I'll borrow Mrs. MacConikie's."

The shoemaker waited in no small amount of trepidation, while this process of key-borrowing from the old lady who enjoyed a pan of water, took place upon the part of his wife.

CHAPTER XL.

CROTCHET ASTONISHES MR. TODD.

THE KEY WAS SOON PROCURED, but it will be recollected that Crotchet had fastened the door rather too securely for it to be opened by any such ordinary implement as a key, and so disappointment was the portion of the shoemaker's wife.

"Don't you think, my love," said the shoemaker, "that it will be just as well to leave this affair until the morning, before taking any further notice of it?"

"And pray, then, am I to sleep all night, if I don't know the rights of it, I should like to know? Perhaps, if you can tell me that, you are a little wiser than I think you. Marry, come up!"

"Oh, well, I only —"

"You only! Then only don't. That's the only favour I ask of you, sir, is to only don't."

What extraordinary favour this was, the lady did not condescend to explain any more particulars, but it was quite enough for the husband to understand that a storm was brewing, and to become humble and submissive accordingly.

"Well, my dear, I'm sure I only wish you to do just what you like; that's all, my dear, I'm sure."

"Very good."

After this, she made the most vigorous efforts to get into the attic, and if any one had been there — which at that juncture there was not — they might truly have asked "Who's that knocking at the door?" Finding that all her efforts were ineffectual, she took to peeping through the key-hole, but nothing was to be seen; and then, for the first time, the idea struck her that there was something supernatural about the business, and in a few moments this notion gained sufficient strength to engender some lively apprehensions.

"I tell you what," she said to her husband, "if you don't fetch a constable at once, and have the door opened, and see all about, I'm afraid — indeed I'm quite sure — I shall be very ill."

"Oh, dear — oh, dear."

"It's of no use your standing here and saying 'Oh, dear,' like a great stupid as you are — always was and always will be. Go for a constable, at once."

"A constable?"

"Yes, There's Mr. Otton, the beadle of St. Dunstan's, lives opposite, as you well know, and he's a constable. Run over the way and fetch him, this minute."

She began hastily to descend the stairs, and the shoemaker followed her, remonstrating, for the idea of fetching a constable, and making him and his house the talk of the whole neighbourhood, was by no means a proposition that met with his approval. The lady was positive, however, and Mr. Otton, the beadle of St. Dunstan's, was brought from over the way, and the case stated to him at length.

"*Conwulsions!*" exclaimed Otton, "what can I do?"

"*Burst* open the door," said the lady.

"*Burst* a door open, mum! What is you a thinking on? Why, that's contrary to *Habus Corpus*, mum, and all that sort of thing. Conwulsions, mum! you mustn't do it. But I tell you what, now, will be the thing."

Here Mr. Otton put his finger to the side of his nose, and looked so cunning that you would hardly have believed it possible.

"What? — what?"

"Why, suppose, mum, we ask Mr. Todd, next door, to give us leave to go up into his attic, and get out at the window and look in at yours, mum?"

"That'll do. Run in —"

"Me!" cried the shoemaker. "Oh, M — Mr. Todd is a strange man — a very strange man — not at all a neighbourly sort of man, and I don't like to go to him. — I won't go, that's flat — unless, my love, you particularly wish it."

"Conwulsions!" cried the beadle. "Ain't I a-going with you? Ain't I a constabulary force, I should like to know? Conwulsions! What is yer afeard on? Come on. Lor, what's the meaning o' that, I wonders, now; I should just like to take that ere fellow up. Whoever heard of a horn being blowed at such a rate, in the middle o' Fleet-street, afore, unless it was somethin' as consarned the parish? Conwulsions! it's contrary to *Habus Corpus*, it is. Is me a constabulary force, or is me not?"

This was the bugle sound which warned Sir Richard Blunt and his friend

Crotchet that Sweeney Todd had returned to his shop; and, in fact, while this very conversation was going on at the shoemaker's, Todd had lit the lamp in his shop, and actually opened it for business again, as the evening was by no means very far advanced. Mr. Otton went to the door, and looked about for the audacious bugle player, but he was not to be seen; so he returned to the back parlour of the shoemaker, uttering his favourite expletive of "Conwulsions" very frequently.

"Now, if you is ready," he said, "I is; so let's come at once, and speak to Mr. Todd. He may be a strange man, but for all that, he knows, I dessay, what's proper respect to a *beetle*."

With this strange transformation of his own title upon his lips, Mr. Otton stalked on rather majestically, as he thought, to the street, and thence to Todd's shop door, with the shoemaker following him. The gait of the latter expressed reluctance, and there was a dubious expression upon his face, which was quite amusing to behold.

"Really, Mr. Otton," he said, "don't you think, after all, it would be better to leave this affair alone till the morning? We can easily tell my wife, you know, that Mr. Todd won't let us into his attic. That must satisfy her, for what can she say to it?"

"Sir," said the beadle, "when you call in the *constabullary* force, you must do just what they say, or lasteways you acts contrary to *Habus Corpuses*. Come on. Conwulsions! is we to be brought over the street, and then is we to do nothing to go down to prosperity?"

The beadle uttered these words with such an air of pomposity and importance that the shoemaker, who had a vague idea that *Habus Corpus* was some fearful engine of the law at the command of all its administrators, no longer offered any opposition, but, as meekly as any lamb, followed Mr. Otton into Sweeney Todd's shop. The door yielded to a touch, and Mr. Otton presented his full rubicund countenance to the gaze of Sweeney Todd, who was at the further end of the shop, as though he had just come from the parlour at the back of it, or was just going there. He did not at first see the shoemaker, who was rather obscured by the portly person of the beadle, and Todd's first idea was, the most natural one in the world, namely, that the beadle came upon an emergency to be shaved. Giving him an hideous leer, Todd said —

"A fine night for a clean shave."

"Werry. In course, Mr. T., you is the best judge o' that 'ere, but I does for myself."

As he spoke, Mr. Otton rubbed his chin, to intimate that it was to his shaving himself that he alluded just then.

"Hair cut?" said Todd, giving a snap to the blades of a large pair of scissors, that made Mr. Otton jump again, and nearly induced the shoemaker to run out of the shop into the street.

"No," said the beadle; and taking off his hat, he felt his hair, as though to satisfy himself that it was all there, just as usual. "No."

Todd looked as though he would have shaved him with extreme pleasure, and advancing a few steps, he added —

"Then what is it that you bring your wieldy carcase here for, you gross lump of stupidity? Ha! ha! ha!"

"What? Conwulsions!"

"Pho! — Pho! Can't you take a joke, Mr. Otton? I know you well enough. It's my funny way to call people, whom I admire very much, all the hard names I can think of."

"Is it?"

"Oh, dear, yes. I thought you and all my neighbours knew that well enough. I'm one of the drollest dogs alive. That I am. Won't you sit down?"

"Well, Mr. Todd, a joke may be a joke." The beadle looked very sententious at this discovery. "But you have the oddest way of poking your fun at any one that ever I heard of; but, I comes to you now as a respectable parishioner, to —"

"Oh," said Todd, putting his hands, very deliberately into his pockets, "how much?"

"It ain't anything to pay. It's a mere trifle. I just want to go up to your front attic, and —"

"What?"

"Your front attic, and get out of the window to look into the front attic next door. We won't trouble you if you will oblige us with a candle. That's all."

Todd advanced two steps further towards the beadle and looked peeringly in his face. All the suspicious qualities of his nature rose up in alarm. Every feeling of terror regarding the instability of his position, and the danger by which he was surrounded, rushed upon him. At once he conjectured that danger was approaching him, and that in this covert manner the beadle was intent upon getting into the house, for the purpose of searching it to his detriment. As the footpad sees in each bush an officer, so, in the most trivial circumstances, even the acute intellect of Sweeney Todd saw dangers, and rumours of dangers, which no one but himself could have had the remotest idea of. He glared upon the beadle with positive ferocity, and so much affected was Otton by that lynx-like observation of Sweeney Todd's, that he stepped aside and disclosed that he was not alone.

If anything could have confirmed Todd in his suspicions that there was a dead-set at him, it was finding that the beadle was not alone. And yet the shoemaker was well known to him. But what will lull such suspicion as Sweeney Todd had in his mind? Once engendered, it was like the jealousy that —

"Makes the meat it feeds on!" *

He advanced, step by step, glaring upon the beadle and upon the shoemaker. Reaching up his hand, he suddenly turned the lamp that hung from the ceiling clear round, so that, in lieu of its principal light falling upon him, it fell upon the faces of those who had paid him so unceremonious a visit.

"Lawks!" said the beadle.

"Excuse us, Mr. Todd," said the shoemaker, "I assure you we only meant —"

"What?" thundered Todd. Then suddenly softening his voice, he added — "You are very welcome here indeed. Pray what do you want?"

"Why, sir," said Otton, "you must know that this gentleman has a lodger."

"A what?"

"A lodger, sir, and so you see that's just the case. You understand that this lodger — lor, Mr. Todd, this is your neighbour the shoemaker, you know. The front attic, you know, and all that sort of thing. After this explanation, I hope you'll lend us a candle at once, Mr. Todd, and let us up to the attic."

Todd shaded his eyes with his hands, and looked yet more earnestly at the beadle.

"Why, Mr. Otton," he said, "indeed you do want a shave."

"A shave?"

"Yes, Mr. Otton, I have a good razor here that will go over your chin like a piece of butter. Only take a seat, sir, and if you, neighbour, will go home comfortably to your own fireside, I will send for you when Mr. Otton is shaved."

"But really," said the beadle, rubbing his chin, "I was shaved this morning, and as I do for myself always, you see, why I don't think I require. Conwulsions! Mr. Todd, why do you look at a man so? Remember the *Habus Corpus*. That's what we call the *paladermius* of the British Constitution, you know."

By this time the beadle had satisfied himself that he did not at all require shaving, and turning to the shoemaker, he said —

"Why don't you be shaved?"

"Well, I don't care if I do, and perhaps, in the meantime you, Mr. Otton, will go up to the attic, and take a peep into the next one, and see if my lodger is up or in bed, or what the deuce has become of him. It's a very odd thing, Mr. Todd, that a man should take one's attic, and then disappear without coming down stairs."

"Disappear without coming down stairs?" said Todd.

"Yes, and my wife says —"

Todd made an impatient gesture.

"Gentlemen, I will look in my attic myself. The fact is, that the flooring is

---

* *A line from Shakespeare's Othello, Act III Scene III, tweaked a bit to better fit the situation. In it, Iago says to Othello, "Beware, my lord, of jealousy; it is the green-eyed monster which doth mock the meat it feeds on."*

rather out of order, and unless you know exactly where to step you will be apt to fall through a hole into the second floor."

"The deuce you are!" said Otton.

"Yes; so I would not advise either of you to make the attempt. Just remain there, and I'll go at once."

The proposition suited both parties, and Mr. Todd immediately passed through a door at the back of his shop, which he immediately closed behind him again. Instead of going up stairs, however, he slid aside a small opening in the panel of this door, and placed his ear to it. "If people say anything impudent, it is the moment they are free from the company that has held them in check," was one of Sweeney Todd's maxims. His first notion that the beadle and the shoemaker had come covertly to search his house, had given way a little, and he wanted to convince himself of the innocency or the reverse of their intentions, before he put himself to any further trouble.

"I don't like it," said the shoemaker.

"Like what? Conwulsions! what don't you like?"

"Intruding upon Mr. Todd. What does he care about my lodgers? It ain't as if he let any of his own house, and had a fellow feeling with us."

"Werry good," said the beadle, "but you send for me, and you ask me what's best, and I tell yer that *Habus Corpus*, and one thing and another, what I advised was the only thing, that was to get into Mr. Todd's attic, and then get on the parapet and into yours. But if so be as there's holes in Mr. Todd's attic, that will alter the affair, you know."

"Fool — fool!" muttered Todd. "After all, they only come upon their own twaddling affairs, and I was idiot enough to suspect such muddy pated rascals."

In an instant he was in the shop again.

"Nobody there, gentlemen; I have looked into the attic, and there's nobody there."

"Well, I'm very much obliged to you, Mr. Todd," said the shoemaker, "for taking so much trouble. I'll go, and rather astonish my wife, I think."

"Conwulsions!" said the beadle. "It's an odd thing, but you know, Mr. Todd, *Habus Corpus* must have his way."

CHAPTER XLI.

TODD'S VISION.

WHEN THEY HAD LEFT, TODD remained for some minutes in an attitude of thought.

"Is this an accident?" he said, "or is it but the elaboration of some deep design to entrap me. What am I to think?"

Todd was an imaginative man quite. He was just the individual to think, and think over the affair until he made something of it, very different from what it really was, and yet there was some hope that the matter was no more than what it appeared to be, by the character of the parties who had come upon the mission. If anything serious had come to the ears of the authorities, he thought, that surely two such people as the beadle of St. Dunstan's, and his neighbour the shoemaker, would not be employed to unravel such a mystery. He sat down in an arm chair and rested his head upon his hand, and while he was in that attitude the door of his shop opened, and a man in the dress of a carter made his appearance.

"Be this Mister Todd's?"

"Well," said Todd, "what then?"

"Why, then, this be for him like. It's a letter, but larning waren't much i' the fashion in my young days, so I can't read what's on it."

Todd stretched out his hand. An instant examination showed him it bore the Peckham post-mark.

"Ah!" he muttered, "from Fogg. Thank you, my man, that will do. That will do. What do you wait for?"

"Please to remember the carter, your honour!"

Todd looked daggers at him, and slowly handed out twopence, which the man took with a very ill grace.

"What," said Todd, "would you charge me more for carrying a letter than King George the Third does, you extortionate rascal?"

The carter gave a nod.

"Get out with you, or by—"

Todd snatched up a razor, and the carter was off like a shot, for he really believed, from the awful looks of Todd, that his life was not worth a minute's purchase. Todd opened the letter with great gravity.—It contained the following words:—

Dear Sir:—

*The lad, T. R., I grieve to say, is no more. Let us hope he is gone where the weary
are at rest, and where there is neither sin nor sorrow.*

I am, dear Sir,

Yours faithfully,

Jacob B. FOGG.

"Humph!" said Todd.

He held the letter in the flame of the lamp until it fell a piece of airy tinder
at his feet.

"Humph!" he repeated, and that humph was all that he condescended to
say of poor Tobias Ragg, whom the madhouse-keeper had thought proper to
say was dead; hoping that Todd might never be undeceived, for the barber was
a good customer.

If, however, Tobias should turn up to the confusion of Fogg and of Todd,
what could the latter do for the deceit that had been practised upon him? — literally nothing.

"No sooner," said Todd, "does one cloud disappear from my route than
another takes its place. What can that story mean about the attic next door?
It sounds to my ears strange and portentous. What am I to think of it?"

He rose and paced his shop with rapid strides. At length he paused as
though he had come to a determination.

"The want of a boy is troublesome to me," he said. "I must get one, but for
the present this must suffice."

He wrote upon a small slip of paper the words — "Gone to the Temple — will
return shortly." He then, by the aid of a wafer, affixed this announcement to
the upper part of the half-glass door leading into his shop. Locking this door
securely on the inside, and starting a couple of bolts into their sockets, he lit a
candle and left his shop.

With a stealthy, cat-like movement, Todd passed through the room immediately behind his business apartment, and opening another door he made his
way towards the staircase. Then he paused a moment. He thought some sound
from above had come upon his ears, but he was not quite sure. To suspect,
however, was with such a man as Todd to be prepared for the worst, and
accordingly he went back to the room behind his shop again, and from a table-
drawer he took a knife, such as is used by butchers in their trade, and firmly
clutching it in his right hand, while he carried the candle in his left, he once
more approached the staircase.

"I do not think," he said, "that for nine years now any mortal footsteps,
but my own, have trod upon these stairs or upon the flooring of the rooms
above. Woe be to those who may now attempt to do so. Woe, I say, be to them,
for their death is at hand."

These words were spoken in a deep hollow voice, that sounded like tones from a sepulchre, as they came from the lips of that man of many crimes. To give Todd his due, he did not seem to shrink from the unknown and dimly appreciated danger that might be up stairs in his house. He was courageous, but it was not the high-souled courage that nerves a man to noble deeds. No, Sweeney Todd's courage was that of hate — hatred to the whole human race, which he considered, with a strange inconsistency, had conspired against him; whereas he had been the one to place an impassable barrier between himself and the amenities of society. He ascended the stairs with great deliberation. When he reached the landing upon the first floor, he cast his eyes suspiciously about him, shading the light as he did so with his hand — that same hand that held the knife, the shadow of which fell upon the wall in frightful proportions.

"All is still," he said. "Is fancy, after all, only playing me such tricks as she might have played me twenty years ago? I thought I was too old for such freaks of the imagination."

Todd did not suspect that there was a second period in his life, when the mental infirmities of his green youth might come back to him, with many superadded horrors accumulated, with a consciousness of guilt. He slowly approached a door and pushed it open, saying as he did so —

"No — no — no. Above all things, I must not be superstitious. If I were so, into what a world of horrors might I not plunge. No — no, I will not people the darkness with horrible phantasies, I will not think that it is possible that men with —

'Twenty murders on their heads,' *

— can revisit this world to drive those who have done them to death with shrieking madness — this world do I say? There is no other. Bah! Priests may talk, and the weak-brained fools who gape at what they do not understand, may believe them, but when man dies — when the electric condition that has imputed to his humanity what is called life, flies, he is indeed —

'Dust to dust!'

"Ha! ha! I have lived as I will die, fearing nothing and believing nothing."

As he uttered those words — words which found no real echo in his heart, for at the bottom of it lay a trembling belief in, and a dread of the great God that rules all things, and who is manifest in the meanest seeming thing that

---

* *A reference from Shakespeare's* Macbeth, *Act III Scene IV. Macbeth, after seeing the ghost of Banquo, remarks, "The times have been that, when the brains were out, the man would die, and there an end; but now they rise again, with twenty mortal murders on their crowns, and push us from our stools."*

crawls upon the earth — he entered one of the rooms upon that floor, and glanced uneasily around him.

All was still. There were trunks — clothes upon chairs, and a vast amount of miscellaneous property in this room, but nothing in the shape of a human being. Todd's spirits rose, and he held the long knife more carelessly than he had done.

"Pho! pho!" he said. "I do, indeed, at times make myself the slave of a disturbed fancy. Pho! pho! I will no more listen to vague sounds, meaning nothing; but wrapping myself up in my consciousness of having nothing to fear, I will pursue my course, hideous though it may be."

He turned and took his way towards the landing place of the staircase again. He was now carrying both the light and the knife rather carelessly, and everybody knows that when a candle is held before a person's face, that but little indeed can be seen in the hazy vapour that surrounds it. So it was with Todd. He had got about two paces from the door, when a strange consciousness of something being in his way came over him. He immediately raised his hand — that hand that still carried the knife, to shade the light, and then, horror! horror! He saw standing upon the landing a figure attired in faded apparel, whose face was dabbled in blood, and the stony eyes which were fixed upon the face of Todd, with so awful an expression, that had the barber's heart been made of much more flinty materials than it was, he could not have resisted the terrors of that awful moment. With a shriek that echoed through the house, Todd fell upon the landing. The light rolled from stair to stair until it was finally extinguished, and all was darkness.

"Good," said Crotchet, for it was he who had enacted the ghost. "Good! I'm blessed if I didn't think that ere would nail him. These sort o' chaps are always on the look-out for something or another to be frightened at, and you have only to show yourself to put 'em almost out of their seven senses. It was a capital idea that of me to cut my finger a little, and get some blood to smear over my face. It's astonishing what a long way a little drop will go, to be sure. I dare say it makes me look precious rum."

Mr. Crotchet was quite right regarding the appearance which the blood, smeared over his face, gave to him. It made him look perfectly hideous, and any one whose conscience was not —

> *"With injustice corrupted!"**

— might well have been excused for a cold chill, and, perchance, even a swoon, like Sweeney Todd's, at his appearance.

---

* *A reference from Shakespeare's* Henry VI Part II, *Act III Scene II, in which the king says,* "Thrice is he armed that hath his quarrel just, and he but naked, though lock'd up in steel, whose conscience with injustice corrupted."

SWEENEY TODD ASTONISHED BY CROTCHET, THE BOW-STREET OFFICER.

"I rather think," added Crotchet, "that's a settler; so I'll just take the liberty, old fellow, of lighting your candle again, and then mizzling, for I don't somehow think much good is to be done in this crib just now."

By the aid of his phosphorus match Crotchet soon succeeded in re-illumining the candle, which he found on a mat in the passage; but notwithstanding his opinion that he had seen about as much as there was to see in Todd's house, he, when he had the candle alight, thought he might just as well peep into the parlour immediately behind the shop, before going up-stairs again.

The door offered no opposition, for Todd had certainly not expected any one down stairs, and Mr. Crotchet found himself in the parlour about as soon as he had formed the wish to be there. This parlour was perfectly crammed with furniture, and all of the bureau kind, that is to say, large shapeless looking pieces of mahogany, with no end of drawers. Crotchet made an attempt at several before he found one that yielded to his efforts to open it, and that only did so because the hasp into which the lock was shot had given way, and no longer held it close. This drawer was full of watches.

"Humph!" said Crotchet, "Todd ought to know the time of day certainly, and no mistake. Ah, these ere machines, if they had tongues now, I rather think, could tell a tale or two. Howsomedever, I'll pocket some of 'em."

Mr. Crotchet put about a dozen watches in his pocket forthwith, and then he began to think that, as he did not wish to take Mr. Todd just then into custody, it would be just as well if he left the house. Besides, the barber had only fell into a swoon through fright, so that his recovery was a matter that could be calculated upon with something like certainty in a short time.

"It would be a world of pities if he was to find out as the ghost was only me," said Crotchet, "so I'll be off before he comes to himself."

Extinguishing the light, Crotchet wound his way up the staircase again, but when he got to the landing he stopped, and said —

"Bless us! I've not got them canes and swords as Sir Richard wanted me to bring away with me. Well, the watches will answer better than them, for all he wants is to compare 'em with the descriptions of some folks as has been missed by their blessed relations in London, so that's all right. Hilloa!"

This latter ejaculation arose from Crotchet having trodden upon Todd.

"The deuce!" he added, "I thought I had got clear of him."

He paused, and heard Todd utter a deep groan. Mr. Crotchet took this as a signal that he had better be off; and accordingly he ascended the next staircase quickly, and in a very few minutes reached the attic of Todd's house. When there, he quickly made his appearance in the shoemaker's attic, and found that Sir Richard Blunt had left the door of it just upon the latch for him. He was upon the point of passing out of the room, and going down stairs, when he heard a confused sound approaching the attic, and he paused instantly. The sound came nearer and nearer, until Crotchet found that some half dozen people were upon the landing, and all talking together in anxious whispers.

"What the deuce is up now?" he thought.

He approached the door and listened.

"I tell you what it is, Mr. Otton," said a female voice. "It's now getting on for ten o'clock, and I positively can't sleep in my bed unless I know something more about this horrid attic."

"Well, but, mum —"

"Don't speak to me. Here's an attic, and two men go into it. Then all at once there's no men in it; and then all at once, one man comes down and walks out as cool as a cucumber, and says nothing at all; and then we know well enough as there was two men, and only one —"

"But, mum —"

"Don't speak to me, and only one has come down."

"And here's the t'other!" cried Crotchet, suddenly bouncing out of the attic.

The confusion that ensued baffles all description. A grand rush was made into the apartments of the lady who was fond of putting her feet into hot water; and in the midst of the confusion, Crotchet quickly enough went down stairs, and made his escape from the shoemaker's house.

CHAPTER XLII.

THE GREAT SACRIFICE.

WHILE ALL THESE THINGS WERE going on at Sweeney Todd's, in Fleet-street, Mrs. Lovett was not quite idle as regarded her own affairs and feelings. That lady's — what shall we say — certainly not affections, for she had none — passions is a better word — were inconceivably shocked by the discovery she had made of the perfidy of her flaunting and moustachied lover. It will be perceived, by this little affair of Mrs. Lovett's, how strong-minded women have their little weaknesses. The hour of the appointment, which she (Mrs. Lovett) had made with her military-looking beau, came round; and there she sat, looking rather disconsolate.

"Am I never to succeed," she muttered to herself, "in finding one with whom I can make my escape from this sea of horrors that surrounds me? Am I, notwithstanding I have so fully accomplished all I wished to accomplish, by — by"— she shuddered and paused. — "Well, well, the time will come — I must go alone. Let Todd go alone, and let me go alone. Why should he wish to trammel my actions? He cannot surely think, for a moment, that with him I will consent to pass the remainder of my life!"

The scornful curl of the lip, and the indignant toss of the head, which accompanied these words, would have been quite sufficient to convince Todd, had he seen them, of the hopelessness of any such notion.

"No," she added, after a pause, "I shall be alone in the world, or, if I make ties, they shall be made in another country. There it is possible I may be — oh, no, no — not happy; but I may be powerful, and have cringing slaves about me, who, finding that I am rich, will tell me that I am beautiful, and I shall be able to drink deeply of the intoxicating cup of pleasure, in some land where prudery, or what is called propriety, has not set up its banner as it has in this land of outward virtue. As for Todd — I — I will try to be assured that he is a corpse before I breathe freely; and if I fail in that, I will hope that we shall be thousands of leagues asunder."

A shadow passed the window. Mrs. Lovett started to her feet.

"Ah! who comes? 'Tis he — no — God! 'tis Todd."

For a moment she pressed her hands upon her face, as though she would squeeze out the traces of passion from the muscles, and then her old set smile came back again. Todd entered the shop. For a few moments they looked at each other in silence, and then Todd said —

"Alone?"

"Quite," she replied.

He gave one of his peculiar laughs, and then glided into the parlour behind the shop. Mrs. Lovett followed him.

"News?" he said.

"None."

"Hem! The time is coming."

"The time to leave off this —"

"Yes. The time to quit business, Mrs. Lovett. All goes well — swimmingly. Ha! ha!"

She shuddered as she said —

"Do not laugh."

"Let those laugh who win," replied Todd. "How old are you, Sarah?"

"Old?"

"Yes, or to shape the question perhaps more to a woman's liking, how young are you? Have you yet many years before you in which to enjoy the fruits of our labours? Have you the iron frame which will enable you to say — 'I shall revel for years in the soft enjoyments of luxury stolen from a world I hate?' Tell me."

Mrs. Lovett fell into a musing attitude, and Todd thought she was reflecting upon her age; but at length she said —

"I sometimes think I would give half of what is mine if I could forget how I became possessed of the whole."

"Indeed!"

"Yes, Todd. Has no such feeling ever crossed you?"

"Never! I am implacable. Fate made me a barber, but nature made me something else. In the formation of man there is a something that gives weakness to his resolves, and makes him pause upon the verge of enterprise with a shrinking horror. That is what the world calls conscience. It has no hold of me. I have but one feeling towards the human race, and that is hatred. I saw that while they pretended to bow down to God, they had in reality set up another idol in their heart of hearts. Gold! gold! Tell me — how many men there are in this great city who do not worship gold far more sincerely and heartily than they worship Heaven?"

"Few — few."

"Few? None, I say, none. No. The future is a dream — an *ignis fatuus* — a vapour. The present we can grasp — ha!"

"What is our wealth, Todd?"

"Hundreds of thousands."

He shaded his eyes with his hands, and peered from the parlour into the shop.

"Who is that keeps dodging past the window each moment, and peeping in at every convenient open space in the glass that he can find?"

Mrs. Lovett looked, and then, after an effort, she said —

"Todd, I was going to speak to you of that man."

"Ah!"

"Listen; I suspect him. For some days past he has haunted the shop, and makes endeavours to become acquainted with me. I did not think it sound policy wholly to shun him, but gave him such encouragement as might supply me with opportunities of judging if he were a spy or not."

"Humph!"

"I think him dangerous."

Todd's eyes glistened like burning coals.

"Should he come into your shop to be shaved, Todd —"

"Ha! ha!"

The horrible laugh rang through the place, and Mrs. Lovett's lover, with the moustache, sprung to the other side of Bell-yard, for the unearthly sound even reached his ears as he was peeping through the window to catch a glimpse of the charming widow.

"You understand me, Todd?"

"Perfectly — perfectly — I shall know him again. Ah, my dear Mrs. Lovett, how dangerous it is to be safe in this world. Even our virtue cannot escape detraction; but we will live in hopes of better times. You and I will show the world, yet, what wealth is."

"Yes — yes."

Todd crept close to her, and was about to place his arm round her waist, but she started from him, exclaiming —

"No — no, Todd — a thousand times no. Have we not before quarrelled upon this point. Do not approach me, or our compact, infernal as it is, is at an end. I have sold my soul to you, but I have not bartered myself."

The expression of Todd's countenance at this juncture was that of an incarnate fiend. He glared at Mrs. Lovett as though with the horrible fascination of his ugliness he would overcome her, and then slowly rising, he said —

"Her soul — ha! She has sold her soul to me — ha! I will call to-morrow."

He left the shop, and as he passed the gent who, by force of his moustache, hoped to win the affections of Mrs. Lovett, he gave him such a look that he terrified him and the gent found himself in the shop before he was aware.

"Bless me, what a horrid looking fellow! I swear by my courage and honour I never saw such a face. Ah, my charmer! Who was that left your charming presence just now?"

"Some one who came for a pie."

" 'Pon honour, he's enough to poison all the pies! Oh, you beauty, yo — ou — ou — ou —"

The gallant's mouth was so full of a veal pie that he had stuffed into it that for some few moments he could not produce an intelligible sound. When he had recovered, he walked into the parlour and sat down, saying —

"Now, Mrs. Lovett, here am I, 'pon honour, your humble servant, and stop my breath if I'd say as much to the commander-in-chief. When's the happy day to be?"

"Do you really love me?"

"Do I love you? Do I love fighting? Do I love honour — glory? Do I love eating and drinking? Do I love myself?"

"Ah, Major Bounce, you military men are so gallant."

" 'Pon honour we are. General Cavendish used to say to me — 'Bounce,' says he, 'if you don't make your fortune by war, which you ought to do, Bounce, 'pon honour, you will make it by love.' 'General,' says I — now I was always ready for a smart answer, Mrs. Lovett — so 'General,' says I, 'the same to you!'"

"Very smart."

"Yes, wasn't it. 'Pon honour it was, and 'pon soul you looks more and more charming every day that I see you."

"Oh you flatterer!"

"No — no. Bar flattering — bar flattering. His Majesty has often said, 'Talk of flattery. Oh dear, Bounce is the man for me. He is right down — straight up-off handed. And no sort of mistake, on — on — on.'"

Another pie converted the oratory of the major into something between a grunt and a sigh.

"But major, I'm afraid that you will regret marrying me. If I convert all I have into money"— the major pricked up his ears —"I could not make of it more than fifty thousand pounds."

The major's eyes opened to the size of pint saucers, as he said —

"Fifty — fift — fif. — Say it again!"

"Fifty thousand pounds."

The major rose and embraced Mrs. Lovett. Tears actually came into his eyes, and gulping down the pie, he cried —

"You have fifty thousand charms. Only let me be your slave, your dog, damme — your dog, Mrs. Lovett, and I shall consider myself the luckiest dog in the world, but not for the money — not for the money. No, as the Marquis of Cleveland once said, 'If you want a thoroughly disinterested man, go to Bounce.'"

"Well, major, since we understand each other so well, there are two little things that I must name as my conditions."

"Name 'em — name 'em. Do you want me to bring you the king's eye-tooth, or her majesty's wig and snuff-box — only say the word."

"One is, that I will leave England. I have a private reason for so doing."

"Damme, so have I. That is, *a-hem!* If you have a reason, that is a reason to me, you know."

"Exactly. In some other capital of Europe we may spend our money and enjoy all the delights of existence. Do you speak French?"

"A-hem! Oh, of course. I never tried particularly, but as Lord North said to the Duke of Bridgewater, 'Bounce is the man if you want anything done of an out of-the-way character.'"

"Very well, then. My next condition is, that you shave off your moustache."

"What?"

"Shave off your moustache; I have the greatest possible aversion to moustache, therefore I make that a positive condition without which I shall say no more to you."

"My charmer, do you think I hesitate? If you were to say to me, 'Bounce, off with your head,' in a moment it would roll at your feet."

"Go, then, to Mr. Todd's, the barber, in Fleet-street, and have them taken off at once, and then come back to me, for I declare I won't speak another word to you while you have them on."

"But, dear creature —"

Mrs. Lovett shook her head.

" 'Pon honour!"

She shook her head again.

"I'll go at once then, 'pon soul, and have 'em taken off. I'll be back in a jiffy, Mrs. Lovett. Oh, you duck, I adore you. Confound the cash! It's you I knuckle under to. Man doats on Venus, and I love Lovett. Bye, bye; I'll get it done and soon be back. Fifty thousand — fifty — fif. — Oh, lor' why Flukes, your fortune is made at last."

These last words did not reach the ear of Mrs. Lovett. That lady threw herself into a chair, where the gallant major had left her.

"Another!" she said. "Another! Why did he try to deceive me? The fool, to pitch upon me, of all persons, to make his victim. I must have found him out, and poisoned him, if I had married him. It is better that Todd should take vengeance for me, and then the time shall come when he shall fall. Yes, so soon as I can, by cajollery or scheming, get sufficient of the plunder into my own hands, Todd's hours are numbered."

After this, Mrs. Lovett fell into a train of musing, and her face assumed an expression so different from that with which she was wont to welcome her customers in the shop, that not one of them would have known her.

BUT WE MUST LOOK AT TODD. It was upon his return home from several calls, the last of which had been this recent visit to Mrs. Lovett, that he had heard the noise in his house, which had terminated in his going up stairs, and being so terrified by Crotchet. It will be recollected that he fell insensible upon the staircase, and that Crotchet took that opportunity of making good his retreat. How long he lay there, he, Todd, had no means of knowing, for all was profound darkness upon the staircase, but his first sensation consisted of a tingling in his feet and hands, similar to the sensation which is properly called "your limbs going to sleep." Then a knocking noise came upon his sense of hearing.

"What's that? Where am I?" he cried. "No — no. Don't hang me. Where's Mrs. Lovett? Hang her. She is guilty!"

Knock! — knock! — knock!

"Hush! hush! What is it? Who wants me? Good God — no — no. There is no good God for me!"

Knock! knock! knock! came again with increased violence at the door of the shop below.

―――――

CHAPTER XLIII.

AN OLD ACQUAINTANCE.

TODD SCRAMBLED TO HIS FEET. He held his head in his hand.

"What does it all mean? What does it all mean?"

Knock! knock! knock!

Todd's senses were slowly returning to him. He began to recollect events at first confusedly, and then the proper order of their occurrence — how he had come home, and then heard a noise, and gone up stairs and seen — what? There he paused in his catalogue of events. What had he seen?"

Knock! knock! knock!

"Curses!" he muttered. "Who can that be hammering with such devilish perseverance at my door? By all that's horrible they shall pay dearly for thus disturbing me. Who can it be? Not any one to arrest me? No — no! They would not knock so long. An enforced entrance long before this would have brought them to me. What did I see? What did I see? What did I see? Dare I give it a name?"

He slowly descended the stairs, and reaching the shop, he peeped through a place in the door which he had made for such a purpose. There stood the hero of the moustachios knocking away with all his might to get the behests of Mrs. Lovett obeyed. Todd suddenly flung open the door, and in fell Major Bounce, alias Flukes.

"The devil! What do you want?"

" 'Pon honour. Damn it. Is this the way to treat a military man?"

Todd turned to the side of the shop, and hastily put on a wig — by an adroit movement of his fingers, he pulled his cravat sufficiently out from his neck to be able to bury his chin in it, and when he turned to the mock major, the latter had no suspicion that he looked upon the same person who had so alarmed him by a look, in Bell-yard.

"Shaved or dressed sir?" said Todd.

"Confound you. Why did you open the door so quick?"

"Thought you knocked, sir."

"I did, but stop my breath, if you haven't given me an ugly fall. But no matter. None but the brave deserve the fair. You perceive I am a military man?"

"Oh, yes, sir, anybody may see that by your martial air."

"A-hem! You are right. Well then, Mr. Barber, I want my moustache shaved off. It's a fancy of a lady. One of the most charming of her sex. One with a fifty thousand pound charm. 'Pon my valour, she has. Ah! I am a lucky dog. Thirty-eight — handsome as Apollo, and beloved by the fairest of the fair.

> "Life is a jolly thing,
> Life is a jolly thing,
> While I drink deep and go frolicking,
> Fair maids, wives, and widows,
> Fair maids, wives, and widows
> Doat on the youth that goes frolicking."

"Ha! ha! ha! Life's a bumper. Upon my valour, Mr. Barber, I feel like a young colt, that I do."

"Really, sir. You don't say so?"

"Oh, yes, yes! Ha! ha! All's right. All's right. Now, Mr. What's-your-name. Off with the moustache. It's only in the cause of the fair that I would conde-scend to part with them, that's a fact, but when a lady's in the case — upon my valour, you are an ugly fellow."

"You don't say so," replied Todd, as he made a most hideous contortion. "Most people think me so fascinating that they stay with me."

"Ha! ha! A good joke."

Major Bounce — we may as well still call the poor wretch Major Bounce — placed his hat upon a chair, and his sword upon the top of it.

"Pray, sir, be seated," said Todd.

"Ah! Damme, is this seat a fixture?"

"Yes, sir, it's in the proper light, you see, sir."

"Oh, very well — I — pluff, pluff — puff, puff! Confound you, what have you filled my mouth with soap-suds for?"

"Quite an accident, sir. Quite an accident, for which I humbly beg your pardon, I assure you, sir. If you keep your mouth shut, and your eyes open, you will get on amazingly. Have you seen the paper to-day, sir?"

"No!"

"Sorry for that, sir. A very odd case, sir — a little on one side — a most remarkable case, I may say. A gentleman, sir, went into a barber's shop, and —"

"Eh! — puff! sleush! puff! Am I to be poisoned by your soap-suds? Upon my valour, I shall have to make an example of you to all barbers."

"You opened your mouth at the wrong time, sir."

"The wrong devil. Don't keep me here all night."

"Certainly not, sir. But as I was saying about this curious case in the paper. A military gentleman went into a barber's shop to be shaved."

"Well. The devil — pluff, pluff! Good God! Am I to endure all this?"

"Certainly not, sir. I'll show you the paper itself. You must know, sir, that the paragraph is headed 'Mysterious disappearance of a gentleman.'"

"Damn it, what do I care about it? Get on with the shaving."

"Certainly, sir."

Todd gave a horrible scrape to Major Bounce's face with a blunt razor.

"Quite easy, sir?"

"Easy? Good gracious, do you want to skin me?"

"Oh, dear no, sir. What an idea. To skin a military gentleman. Certainly not, sir. I see you require one of my best keen razors — one of the Magnum Bonums. Ha! ha!"

"Eh? What was that?"

"Only me giving a slight smile, sir."

"The deuce it was. Don't do it again, then, that's all; and get your keen razor at once, and make an end of the business."

"I will — make an end of the business. Sit still, sir. I'll be back in a moment."

Todd went into the parlour.

"£50,000!" muttered Major Bounce. "I am a happy fellow. At last, after so many ups and downs, I light upon my feet. A charming widow! — and she wishes to leave England. How lucky. I wish the very same thing. £50,000! — 50,000 charms!"

"Good God! what's that?" said a man, who was passing Todd's window, in Fleet-street. "What a horrid shriek. Did you hear it, mum?"

"Oh dear, yes," said a woman. "I'm all of a tremble."

"It came from the barber's shop, here. Let's go in, and ask if anything is the matter?"

The man and woman crossed Todd's threshold, and opened the shop door. A glance showed them that a man's face was at a small opening of the parlour door. *The shaving chair was empty.*

"What's the matter?" said the man.

"With whom?" said Todd.

"Well, I don't know, but I thought somebody cried out."

Todd crept along the floor until he came close to the man, and then he said —

"My friend, have you anything to do?"

"Yes, thank God."

"Then, go and do it; and the next time you hear me cry out with the stomach-ache, ask yourself if it is your business to come in and ask me any questions about it. As for you, ma'am, unless you want to be shaved, I don't know, for the life of me, what you do here."

"Well, we only thought —"

Todd gave a hideous howl, which so terrified both the intruders, that they left the shop in a moment. His countenance then assumed that awful satanic expression which it sometimes bore, and he stood for the space of about five minutes in deep thought. Starting then suddenly, he took up the sword and hat of Major Bounce, and was in the act of putting both into a cupboard, when a smothered cry met his ears. Todd unsheathed the sword, and after fastening his shop door, he went into the parlour. He was absent about ten minutes, and when he returned he had not the sword, but he hastily washed his hands.

"Done!" he said.

Scratch! scratch! scratch! came something at his door, and Todd bent forward in an attitude of listening. Scratch! — scratch! — scratch! — His face turned ghastly pale, and his knees knocked together as he whispered to himself —

"What is that? — what is that?"

Todd was getting superstitious. Since his adventure with Mr. Crotchet, his nerves had been out of order, notwithstanding the exertions he had made to control himself, and to convince his judgment that it was all a matter of imagination. Yet now, somehow or another, although there was no visible connection between the two things, he could not help mentally connecting this scratching at the door with the vision on the staircase. It is strange how the fancy will play such tricks, but it is no less strange than true that she does so, yoking together matters most dissimilar, and leading the judgment into strange disorder.

Scratch! — scratch! — scratch!

"What — what is it?" gasped Todd.

But time works wonders, and after the first shock to his nerves, the barber began to think that some one must be playing him a trick, and, for all he knew, it might be the very man whom he had snubbed so for interfering with him, or it might be some boy — the boys would at times tease Sweeney Todd. This supposition gathered strength each moment.

"It is a trick — a trick," he said. "I will be revenged!"

He took a thick stick from a corner, and stealthily approached the door. The odd scratching noise continued, and he again paused for a few moments to listen to it.

"A boy — a boy," he growled. "It is one of the infernal boys."

Opening the door a little way with great quickness, Todd aimed a blow through the opening. There was a short angry bark, and his old enemy, the dog that had belonged to the mariner, thrust in his head, and glared at Todd.

"Help! — help! Murder!" cried Todd. "The dog again!"

He made a vain effort to shut the door; but Hector was too strong for him, and, as he had got his head in, he seemed to be determined to force in his whole body, which he fully succeeded in doing. Todd dropped the stick, and rushed into the back-parlour for safety, from whence, through a small square of glass near the top of the door, he glared at the proceedings of his four-footed foe. The dog went direct to the cupboard from which he had taken his master's hat, and, opening the door, he dragged out an assemblage of miscellaneous property, as though he hoped to find among it some other vestige of the dear master he had lost. When, however, after tossing the things about, he found that they were all strange to him, he gave a melancholy howl. Hector then appeared to be considering what he should do next, and, after a few moments' consideration, he made a general survey of the shop, and finally ended by leaping into the shaving-chair, where he sat and commenced such a series of melancholy howls, that Todd was nearly driven out of his mind at the conviction that the whole street must be soon in a state of alarm. Oh! how glad he would have been to have shot Hector; but then, although he had pistols in the parlour, he might miss him, and send the bullet into Fleet-street through his own window, and, perchance, hit somebody, and that would be a trouble. The report, too, would bring a crowd round his shop, and the old story of him and the accusing dog — for had not that dog accused him? — would be brought up again. But yet something must be done.

"Am I to be a prisoner here," said Todd, "while that infernal dog sits in the shaving chair, howling?"

Now and then, for the space of about half-a-minute, the dog would be quiet, but then the prolonged howl that he would give plainly showed that he had only been gathering breath to give it. Todd got desperate.

"I must and will shoot him," he said.

Going to a sideboard he opened a drawer, and took from it a large

SWEENEY TODD RE-VISITED BY THE DOG OF ONE OF HIS VICTIMS.

double-barrelled pistol. He looked carefully at the priming, and satisfying himself that all was right, he crept again to the parlour door.

"I must and will shoot him at any risk," he said. "This infernal dog will be else the bane and torment of my life. I thought I had been successful in poisoning the brute as he suddenly disappeared from my door, but he has been preserved by some sort of miracle on purpose to torment me."

Howl went the dog again. Sweeney Todd took a capital aim with the pistol. To be sure his nerves were not quite in such good order as they sometimes were, but then the distance was so short that how could he miss such an object as a Newfoundland dog?

"I have him — I have him," he muttered. "Ha! ha! I have him!"

He pulled the trigger of the pistol — snap went the lock, and the powder in the pan flashed up in Todd's face, but that was all. Before he could utter even an oath the shop door was opened, and a man's voice cried —

"Hasn't nobody seen nothing of never a great dog nowheres? Oh, there you is, my tulip. Come to your father, you rogue you. So you guved me the slip at last did you, you willain!"

CHAPTER XLIV.

TODD AND THE SILVERSMITH.

HECTOR WHINED A KIND OF RECOGNITION of this man, but he did not move from the chair in Todd's shop upon which he had seated himself.

"Come, old fellow," said the man, "you don't want to be shaved, do you?"

Hector gave a short bark, but he wagged his tail as much as to intimate — "Mind, I am not at all angry with you." And indeed it was quite evident, from the manner of the dog to this man, that there was a good understanding between them.

"Come now, Pison," said the man, "don't be making a fool of yourself here any more. You ain't on friendly terms here, my tulip."

"Hilloa!" cried Todd.

The man gave a start, and Hector uttered an angry growl.

"Hilloa! Who are you?"

"Why, I'm the ostler at the 'Bullfinch' *oppesite.*"

"Is that your dog?"

"Why in a manner o' speaking, for want of a better master, he's got me."

The ostler, by dint of shading his eyes with his hands, and looking very intently, at last saw Todd, and then he added —

"Oh, it's you, master, is it?"

"Take away that animal directly," cried Todd. "Take him away. I hate dogs. Curses on both you and him; how came he here?"

"Ah, Pison, Pison, why did you come here, you good for nothink feller you? You ought to have knowed better. Didn't I always say to you — leastways, since I've had you — didn't I say to you — 'Don't you go over the way, for that ere barber is your natural enemy, Pison,' and yet here yer is."

As he spoke, the ostler embraced Hector, who was not at all backward in returning the caress, although in the midst of it he turned his head in the direction of the back-parlour, and gave a furious bark at Todd.

"There is some mystery at the bottom of all this," muttered Todd; and then raising his voice, he added — "How did you come by the dog?"

"Why, I'll tell you, master. For a matter of two days, you know, he stuck at your door with a hat as belonged —"

"Well, well!"

"Yes, his master, folks said, was murdered."

"Ha! ha!"

"Eh? Oh, Lord, what was that?"

"Only me; I laughed at the idea of anybody being murdered in Fleet-street, that was all."

"Oh, ah! It don't seem very likely. Well, as I was a saying, arter you had finished off his master —"

"I?"

"Oh, I begs your pardon! Only, you see, the dog would have it that you had, and so folks say so as natural as possible; but, howsomdever, I comed by and seed this here dog in the agonies o' conwulsions all along o' pison. Now where I come from, the old man — that's my father as was — had lots o' dogs, and consekewently I knowed somethink about them 'ere creturs; so I takes up this one and carries him on my back over the way to the stables, and there I cures him and makes a pet of him, and I called him Pison, cos, you see, as he had been pisoned. Lor', sir, you should only have seed him, when he was a getting a little better, how he used to look at me and try to say — 'Bill, don't I love you neither!' It's affection — that it is, blow me!"

Todd gave an angry snarl of derision.

"I tell you what it is, my man," he said; "if you will hang that dog, I will give you a guinea."

"Hang Pison? No, old 'un, I'd much rather hang you for half that 'ere money. Come along, my daffydowndilly. Don't you stay here any more. Why, I do believe it was you as pisoned him, you old bloak."

The ostler seized Hector, or Pison, as he had fresh christened him, round the neck, and fairly dragged him away out of the shop. To be sure, if Hector had resisted, the ostler, with all the power of resistance he possessed, it would indeed have been no easy matter to remove him; but it was wonderful to see how nicely the grateful creature graduated his struggles, so that they fell short of doing the smallest hurt to his preserver, and yet showed how much he wished to remain as a terror and a reproach to Sweeney Todd. When they were both fairly gone, Todd emerged from his parlour again, and the horrible oaths and imprecations he uttered will not bear transcription. With eager haste he again bundled into the cupboard all the things that the dog had dragged out of it, and then stamping his foot, he said —

"Am I, after defeating the vigilance of heaven only knows who, and for so long preserving myself from almost suspicion, to live in dread of a dog? Am I to be tormented with the thought that that fiend of an animal is opposite to me, and ready at any moment to fly over here and chase me out of my own shop. Confound it! I cannot and will not put up with such a state of things. Oh, if I could but get one fair blow at him. Only one fair blow!"

As he spoke he took up a hammer that was in a corner of the shop, and made a swinging movement with it through the air. Some one at that moment opened the shop door, and narrowly escaped a blow upon the head, that would have finished their mortal career.

"Hilloa! Are you mad?"

"Mad!" said Todd.

"Yes: do you knock folks' brains out when they come to be shaved?"

"Mine's a sedentary employment," said Todd, "and when I am alone, I like exercise to open my chest. That's all. Ain't it rather late to be shaved? I was just about to shut up."

"Why it is rather late, Mr. Todd; but the fact is, I am going to York by the early coach from the Bullfinch Inn, opposite, and I want a shave before I get upon my journey, as I shan't have an opportunity you see, again, for some time."

"Very well, sir."

"Come in, Charley."

Todd started.

"What's that?" he said. He felt afraid that it was the dog again, under some new name. Truly, conscience was beginning to make a coward of Sweeney Todd, although he denied to himself the possession of such an article.

Charley came in the shape of a little boy, of about eight years of age.

"Now you sit down, and don't do any mischief," said the father, "while I get Mr. Todd to shave me. I am a late customer indeed. You see the coach goes in two hours, and as I have got to call the last thing upon Alderman Stantons, I thought I would be shaved first, and my little lad here would come with me."

"Oh, certainly, sir," said Todd; "I believe I have the pleasure of speaking to Mr. Brown, the silversmith."

"Yes — yes. The alderman gave me some jewels, worth about three thousand pounds, to re-set, and though they are not done, I really don't like to have them at home while I take such a journey, so I want to lodge them with him again until I come back."

Todd lathered away at Mr. Brown's chin, as he said with an air of innocence —

"Can you carry so many jewels about with you, sir?"

"So many? Aye, ten times as many. Why they are all in a little narrow case, that would not hold a pair of razors."

"Indeed!"

Todd began the shaving.

"And so this is your little boy? A sharp lad, no doubt."

"Tolerable."

"The whiskers as they are, sir?"

"Oh, yes — yes."

"I suppose you never trust him out alone in the streets?"

"Oh, yes; often."

"Is it possible. Well, now, I should hardly have thought it. What a sweet child he looks, and such a nice complexion, too. It's quite a pleasure to see him. I was considered myself a very fine child a good while ago."

Todd took care to lift the razor judiciously, so as to give Mr. Brown opportunities of replying; and the silversmith said —

"Oh, yes; he's a nice little fellow. He's got his mother's complexion."

"And he shan't lose it," said Todd, "if there's any virtue in *pearlometrical savonia*."

"In what?"

"Oh, that's the name I give to a soap that preserves the complexion in all its purity. I have only a small parcel of it, so I don't sell it, but I give it away now and then, to my lady customers. Excuse me for one moment."

"Oh, certainly."

Todd opened a glass case, and took out two pieces of soap, of a yellowish tint.

"There, Charley," he said as he handed them to the little fellow. "There's a piece for you, and a piece for mamma."

"Really you are very kind, Mr. Todd," said Brown.

"Oh, don't mention it. Run home at once, Charley, with them, and by the time you get back your father will be — finished. Run along."

"I won't," said Charley.

"Ah, come — come," said his father.

"I won't go, and I don't like soap."

"And why don't you like soap, my little man?" said Todd, as he recommenced operations upon the silversmith's face.

"Because I don't like to be washed at all, it scrubs so, and I don't like you, either, you are so dreadfully ugly — that I don't."

Todd smiled blandly.

"Now, Charley," said his father, "I am very angry with you. You are a very bad boy indeed. Why don't you do as Mr. Todd tells you?"

"Because I won't."

"Bless him," said Todd, "bless his heart. But don't you think, Mr. B." — here Todd's voice sank to a whisper — "don't you think that it's rather injudicious to encourage this obstinacy — if one may call it such — thus early in life? It may, you know, grow upon the dear little fellow."

"You are right, Mr. Todd; and I know that he is spoiled; but I have a more than ordinary affection for him, since, under most critical circumstances, once I saved his life. From that time, I confess that I have been weak enough to allow him too much of his own way. Thank you, Mr. Todd. A very clean comfortable shave indeed."

Mr. Brown rose from his chair and approached the little boy.

"Charley, my dear," he said; "you will save papa's life some day, won't you?"

"Yes," said Charley.

The father kissed him; as he added —

"How affected I feel to-night. I suppose it's the thought of the long journey I am going."

"No doubt," said Todd.

"Good night, Mr. Todd. Come along, Charley."

"Won't you give me a kiss, you darling, before you go?" said Todd.

"No, ugly, I won't."

"Oh, Charley — Charley, your behaviour to Mr. Todd is really anything but right. You are a very bad boy to-night. Come along."

Away they went, and Todd stood stropping the lately-used razor upon his hand, as he glared upon them, and muttered —

"Jewels worth three thousand pounds! And so you saved the child's life, did you? By all that's devilish he has returned the obligation."

He went to the door and looked after the retreating figures of the silversmith and his child. He saw with what tender care the father lifted the little one over the road-way, and again he muttered —

"Three thousand pounds gone! — gone, when it was almost within my grasp. All this is new. I used not to be the sport of such accidents and adverse circumstances. Time was, when by the seeming irresistible force of my will, I could bend circumstances to my purposes, but now I am the sport of dogs and children. What is the meaning of it all? Is my ancient cunning deserting me? Is my brain no longer active and full of daring?"

He crept back into his shop again. The hour was now getting late, and after sitting for some time in silent musing he rose, and without a word, commenced closing his establishment for the night.

"I must have another boy," he said, as he put up the last shutter and secured it in its place. "I must have another boy. This state of things will not do. I must certainly have another boy. Tobias Ragg would have suited me very well, if he had not been so — so — what shall I call it, confoundedly imaginative. But he is dead — dead! that is a comfort. He is dead, and I must have another boy."

Bang! went Sweeney Todd's shop door. The beautiful moon climbed over the house-tops in old Fleet-street. The clock of St. Dunstan's struck the hour of eleven. The streets began to be thin of pedestrians, and the din of carriages had almost entirely ceased. London then, although it was so not long ago, presented a very different aspect at the hour of eleven to what it does now. The old hackney-coaches had not been ousted from the streets by the cabs and the omnibuses, and the bustle of the city was indeed but a faint echo then, of what it is now. Time changes all things.

CHAPTER XLV.

JOHANNA'S NEW SITUATION.

"JOHANNA, ATTEND TO ME," SAID Mrs. Oakley, upon the morning after these events.

"Well, mother?"

"Your father is an idiot."

"Mother, mother! I dissent from the opinion, and if it were true, it comes with the worst possible grace from you, but I am sick at heart. I pray you to spare me reproaches or angry words, mother."

"Haity taity, one must not speak next, I suppose. Some people fancy that other people know nothing, but there is such a thing as overhearing what some people say to other people."

Johanna had not the most remote notion of what her mother meant, but Mrs. Oakley's tongue was like many pieces of machinery, that when once set in motion are not without considerable trouble brought to a standstill again, so on she went.

"Of course. I now know quite well why the godly man who would have made you a chosen vessel was refused. It was all owing to that scamp, Mark Ingestrie."

"Mother!"

"Marry come up! you need not look at me in such a way. We don't all of us see with the same eyes. A scamp he is, and a scamp he will be."

"Mother, he whom you so name is with his God. Mention him no more. The wild ocean rolls over his body — his soul is in heaven. Speak not irreverently of one whose sole crime was that he loved me. Oh, mother, mother, you —"

Johanna could say no more, she burst into tears.

"Well," said Mrs. Oakley, "if he is dead, pray what hinders you from listening to the chosen vessel, I should like to know?"

"Do not. Oh do not, mother, say any more to me — I cannot, dare not trust myself to speak to you upon such a subject."

"What is this?" said Mr. Oakley, stepping into the room. "Johanna in tears! What has happened?"

"Father — dear father!"

"And Mr. O.," cried Mrs. Oakley, "what business is it of yours, I should like to know? Be so good, sir, as to attend to your spectacles, and such like rubbish, and not to interfere with my daughter."

"Dear me! — ain't she my daughter likewise?"

"Oh yes, Mr. O.! Go on with your base, vile, wretched, contemptible, unmanly insinuations. Do go on, pray — I like it. Oh, you odious wretch! You spectacle-making monster!"

"Do not," cried Johanna, who saw the heightened colour of her father's cheek. "Oh, do not let me be the unhappy cause of any quarrelling. Father! father!"

"Hush, my dear, don't you say another word. Cousin Ben is coming to take a little bit of lunch with us to-day."

"I know it," cried Mrs. Oakley, clapping her hands together with a vengeance that made Oakley jump again. "I know it. Oh, you wretch. You couldn't have put on such airs if your bully had not been coming; I thought the last time he came here was enough for him. Aye, and for you too, Mr. O."

"It was nearly too much," said the spectacle-maker, shaking his head.

"Tow row, row, row, row!" cried Big Ben, popping his head into the parlour, "what do you all bring it in now? Wilful murder with the chill off or what? Ah, mother Oakley, what's the price of vinegar now, wholesale — pluck does it. Here you is. Ha, ha! Ain't we a united family. Couldn't stay away from you, Mother Oakley, no more nor I could from that 'ere laughing hyena we has in the Tower."

"Eugh! — wretch!"

"Sit down, Ben," said Mr. Oakley. "I am glad to see you, and I am quite sure Johanna is."

"Oh, yes, yes."

"That's it," said Ben. "It's on Johanna's account I came. Now, little one, just tell me —"

Johanna had just time to place her finger upon her lips, unobserved by any one, and shake her head at Ben.

"Ah — hem! How are you, eh?" he said, turning the conversation. "Come, Mother O., stir your old stumps and be alive, will you? I have come to lunch with your lord and master, so bustle — bustle."

Mrs. Oakley rose, and placing her hands upon her hips, she looked at Ben, as she said —

"You great, horrid, man-mountain of a wretch. I only wonder you ain't afraid, after the proper punishment you had on the occasion of your last visit,

MR. OAKLEY DEFENDS JOHANNA FROM THE VIOLENCE OF HER MOTHER.

to show your horrid face here again?"

"You *deludes* to the physicking, I suppose, mum. Lor' bless you, it did us no end of good; but, howsomedever, we provide agin' wice in animals when we knows on it aforehand, do you see. Oh, there you is."

A boy howled out from the shop — "Did a gentleman order two gallons of half-and-half here, please?"

"All's right," said Ben. "Now, Mother O., the only thing I'll trouble you for, is a knife and fork. As for the rest of the combustibles, here they is."

Ben took from one capacious pocket a huge parcel, containing about six pounds of boiled beef, and from the other he took as much ham.

"Hold hard!" he cried to the boy who brought the beer. "Take this half-crown*, my lad, and get three quartern loaves†."

"But, Ben," said old Mr. Oakley, "I really had no intention, when I asked you to come to lunch this morning, of making you provide it yourself. We have, or we ought to have, plenty of everything in the house."

"Old birds," said Ben, "isn't to be caught twice. A fellow, arter he has burnt his fingers, is afeard o' playing with the fire. No, Mrs. O., you gave us a benefit last time, and I ain't a-going to try my luck again. All's right — pitch into the grub. How is the chosen vessel, Mother O.? All right, eh?"

Mrs. Oakley waited until Ben had made an immense sandwich of ham and beef; and then in an instant, before he was aware of what she was about, she caught it up, and slapped it in his face with a vengeance that was quite staggering.

"Easy does it," said Ben.

"Take that, you great, fat elephant."

"Go it — go it."

Mrs. Oakley bounced out of the room. Johanna looked her with sorrow; and Mr. Oakley rose from his chair, but Ben made him sit down again, saying —

"Easy does it — easy does it. Never mind her, cousin Oakley. She must have her way sometimes. Let her kick and be off. There's no harm done — not a bit. Lord bless you. I'm used to all sorts of cantankerous animals."

Mr. Oakley shook his head.

"Forget it, father," said Johanna.

"I only wish, my dear, I could forget many things; and yet there are so many others, that I want to remember, mixed up with them, that I don't know how I should manage to separate them one from the other."

"You couldn't do it," said Ben. "Here's luck in a bag, and shake it out as you want it."

This sentiment was uttered while Ben's head was deep in the recesses of the two-gallon can of beer, so that it had a peculiar solemn and sonorous effect with it. After drinking about a quart, Ben withdrew the can, and drew a long breath.

"Has he brought yours?" he said.

"What? — who?"

"Why the other two gallons for you and Johanna."

---

* *Half a crown was a coin worth 2 shillings, sixpence — one-eighth of a pound sterling.*

† *A quartern loaf was an enormous loaf of bread, weighing four pounds.*

"Good gracious, Ben, you don't mean that?"

"Don't I, though. Oh, here he is. All's right. Now, my lad, get the little pint jug, with the silver top to it, and if we don't mull a drop, I'm a sinner. Now, you'll see if Mrs. O. don't come round quite handsome."

Ben, by the aid of some sugar, succeeded in making a very palatable drink, and just as the steam began to salute the nostrils of old Oakley and himself, the door of the parlour was opened, and who should heedlessly step into the room but the pious Mr. Lupin himself. Mr. Lupin was so transfixed by finding Ben there, that for a moment or two he could not gather strength to retreat; and during that brief period, Ben had shifted his chair, until he got quite behind the reverend gentleman, who, when he did step back, in consequence fell into Ben's lap.

"What do yer mean?" cried Ben, in a voice of thunder.

"Oh, murder — murder! Have mercy upon me! I only looked in as I was passing, to ask how all the family was."

"Yes," said Mr. Oakley, "and because you, no doubt, heard I was going to Tottenham, to Judge Merivale's, to fit him with a pair of spectacles."

"Oh, dear! Oh, dear! Let me go, sir."

"I don't want you," said Ben; "but as you are here, let's make an end of all differences, and have a pint together."

"A pint?"

"Yes, to be sure. By the look of your nose, I should say it knows pretty well what a pint is."

"Oh, dear — man is sinful alway. I bear no malice, and if the truly right-minded and pious Mrs. Oakley was only here, we might drink down all differences, Mr. a — a —"

"Ben."

"Mr. Ben. Thank you, sir."

"Oh, Mr. Lupin," cried Mrs. Oakley, at this moment bursting into the parlour. "Is it possible that you can give your mind in this way to the Philistines? Is not this backsliding?"

"Let us hope for the best, sister," said Mr. Lupin, with an evangelical twang. "Let us hope for the best. If people will drink, they had much better drink with the saints, who may take some favourable opportunity of converting them, than with sinners."

"Sit down, mum," said Ben, "and let's bury all animosities in the can. Easy does it. Don't you go, Johanna."

"Yes, but, Ben, I —"

"Now don't."

Ben saw by the direction of Johanna's eyes, that the reverend gentleman was resting one of his red raw-looking hands upon her arm, and, situated as she was, she could not get out of his way but by rising.

"Sit still," said Ben. "Easy does it."

Lifting up the can, then, he pretended to drink out of it, and then brought it with such a thundering crack upon Mr. Lupin's head, that it quite staggered him.

"Paws off," said Ben. "Just attend to that 'ere gentle hint, old friend."

Mr. Lupin sat down with a groan.

"Now, mum," said Ben, who all the while had held fast the stone mug of mulled porter. "Now, mum, here's some hot, that don't suit me so well as the cold, perhaps you and Mr. Lupin will take that, while I cuts a few more sandwiches."

He placed the jug before Mr. Lupin, who thereupon left off rubbing his head, and said —

"I'm sure it would be highly unchristian of me to bear any malice, so, with the Lord's leave, I will even partake of some of this worldly liquor, called mulled porter."

Now while Mr. Lupin drank the savoury stream from the jug, it assailed the senses of Mrs. Oakley, and when the porter was placed before her, she raised it to her lips, saying —

"If folks are civil to me, I'm civil to them, only I don't like my godly friends to be ill-treated. I'm sure nobody knows what I have gone through for my family, and nobody thinks what a mother and wife I have been. What would have become of Oakley if it hadn't been for me, is a question I often ask myself in the middle of the night?"

"She's a wonderful woman," sighed Lupin.

"Oh, uncommon," said Ben.

"Let me go," whispered Johanna to Ben.

"No, no! Wait for the fun."

"What fun?"

"Oh, you'll see. You don't know what a trouble it has cost me, to be sure. Only wait a bit, there's a duck, do."

Johanna did not like to say she would not, so she shrunk back in her chair in no small curiosity, to know what was about to happen. Mrs. Oakley lifted the jug to her lips and drunk deep. The aroma of the liquor must have been peculiarly grateful to the palate of Mrs. Oakley, for she certainly kept the jug at her mouth for a length of time, that, to judge by the look of impatience upon the countenance of Mr. Lupin, was something outrageous.

"Sister!" he said. "Mind your breath."

Down came the jug, and Mrs. Oakley, when she could draw breath, gasped —

"Very good indeed. A dash of allspice would make it delicious."

"Oh, sister," cried Lupin as he grasped the jug, that was gently pushed towards him by Ben after Mrs. Oakley had set it down. "Oh, sister, don't give your mind to carnal things, I beg of you. Why, she's drank it all."

Mr. Lupin peered into the jug. He shut the right eye and looked in with the left, and then he shut the left eye and looked in with the right, and then he moved the jug about until the silver lid came down with a clap, that nearly snapped his nose off.

"What's the matter?" said Ben.

"I — I — don't exactly —" Mr. Lupin raised the lid again and again, and peered into the jug in something of the fashion which popular belief supposes a crow to look into a marrow bone.

At length he turned the jug upside down, and struck the bottom of it with his pious knuckles. A huge toad fell sprawling upon the table. Mrs. Oakley gave a shriek, and rushed into the yard. Mr. Lupin gave a groan, and flew into the street, and the party in the parlour could hear them in a state of horrible sickness.

"Easy does it," said Ben, "it's only a piece of wood shaped like a toad and painted, that's all. Now I'm easy. I owed 'em one."

CHAPTER XLVI.

TOBIAS'S HEART IS TOUCHED.

TOBIAS IS NO WORSE ALL THIS TIME. But is he better? Has the godlike spirit of reason come back to the mind-benighted boy? Has that pure and gentle spirit recovered from its fearful thraldom, and once again opened its eyes to the world and the knowledge of the past? We shall see.

Accompany us, reader, once again to the house of Colonel Jeffery. You will not regret looking upon the pale face of poor Tobias again. The room is darkened, for the sun is shining brightly, and an almond tree in the front garden is not sufficiently umbrageous in its uncongenial soil to keep the bright rays from resting too strongly upon the face of the boy. There he lies! His eyes are closed, and the long lashes — for Tobias, poor fellow, was a pretty boy — hung upon his cheek, held down by the moisture of a tear. The face is pale, oh, so pale and thin, and the one arm and hand that lies outside the coverlet of the bed, show the blue veins through the thin transparent skin. And all this is the work of Sweeney Todd. Well, well! heaven is patient!

In the room is everything that can conduce to the comfort of the slumbering boy. Colonel Jeffery has kept his word.

And now that we have taken a look at Tobias, tread gently on tip-toe, reader, and come with us down stairs to the back drawing-room, where Colonel Jeffery, his friend Captain Rathbone, the surgeon, and Mrs. Ragg are assembled. Mrs. Ragg is "crying her eyes out," as the saying is.

"Sit down, Mrs. Ragg," said the colonel, "sit down and compose yourself. Come, now, there is no good done by this immoderate grief."

"But I can't help it."

"You can control it. Sit down."

"But I oughtn't to sit down. I'm the cook, you know, sir."

"Well, well; never mind that, if you are my cook. If I ask you to be seated, you may waive all ceremony. We want to ask you a few questions, Mrs. Ragg."

Upon this Tobias's mother did sit down, but it was upon the extreme edge of a chair, so that the slightest touch to it in the world would have knocked it from under her, and down she would have gone on to the floor.

"I'm sure, gentlemen, I'll answer anything I know, and more too, with all the pleasure in life, for, as I often said to poor Mr. Ragg, who is dead and gone, and buried accordingly in St. Martin's, as he naturally might, and a long illness he had, and what with one thing and —"

"Yes! yes! we know all that. Just attend to us for one moment, if you please, and do not speak until you thoroughly understand the nature of the question we are about to put to you."

"Certainly not, sir. Why should I speak, for as I often and often said, when —"

"Hush, hush!"

Mrs. Ragg was silent at last, and then the surgeon spoke to her calmly and deliberately, for he much wished her clearly to understand what he was saying to her.

"Mrs. Ragg, we still think that the faculties of your son Tobias are not permanently injured, and that they are only suffering from a frightful shock."

"Yes, sir, they is frightfully shook."

"Hush! We think that if anything that greatly interested him could be brought to bear upon the small amount of perception that remains to him he would recover. Do you now know of anything that might exercise a strong influence over him?"

"Lord bless you — no, sir."

"How old is he?"

"Fifteen, sir, and you would hardly believe what a time of it I had with Tobias. All the neighbours said — 'Well, if Mrs. Ragg gets over this, she's a woman of ten thousand;' and Mrs. Whistlesides, as lived next door, and had twins herself, owned she never —"

"Good God, will you be quiet, madam?"

"Quiet, sir? I'm sure I haven't said two words since I've been in the blessed room. I appeal to the kernel."

"Well! well! it appears then, Mrs. Ragg, you can think of nothing that is at all likely to aid us in this plan of awakening, by some strong impression, the dormant faculties of Tobias?"

"No, gentlemen, no! I only wish I could, poor boy; and there's somebody else wasting away for grief about him; poor little thing, when she heard that Tobias was mad, I'm sure I thought she'd have broke her heart, for if Tobias ever loved anybody in all the world, it was little Minna Gray. Ah! it's affecting to think how such children love each other, ain't it, sir? Lord bless you, the sound of her footstep was enough for him, and his eyes would get like two stars, as he'd clap his hands together, and cry — 'Ah! that's dear Minna.' That was before he went to Mr. Todd's, poor fellow."

"Indeed!"

"Yes, sir, oh, you haven't an idea."

"I think I have. Who is this Minna Gray, who so enthralled his boyish fancy?"

"Why, she's widow Gray's only child, and they live in Milford Lane, close to the Temple, you see, and even Tobias used to go with me to drink tea with Mrs. Gray, as we was both bequeathed women in a world of trouble."

"You were what?"

"Bequeathed."

"Bereaved you mean, I suppose, Mrs. Ragg; but how could you tell me that you knew of no means of moving Tobias's feelings. This Minna Gray, if he really loves her, is the very thing."

"Lor', sir. What do you mean?"

"Why, I mean that if you can get this Minna Gray here, the possibility is that it will be the recovery of Tobias. At all events, it is the only chance of that kind that presents itself. If that fails, we must only trust to time. How old is this girl?"

"About fourteen, sir, and though I say it —"

"Well, well. Do you now, as a woman of the world, Mrs. Ragg, think that she has an affection for poor Tobias?"

"Do I think? Lor' bless you, sir, she dotes on the ground he walks on, that she does — poor young thing. Hasn't she grizzled a bit. It puts me in mind of —"

"Yes, yes. Of course it does. Now, Mrs. Ragg, you understand it is an object with our friend the colonel here, that no one but yourself should know that Tobias is here. Could you get this young girl to come to tea, for instance, with you, without telling her what else she is wanted for?"

"Dear me, yes, sir; for, as I used to say to Mr. Ragg, who is dead and gone, and buried in St. Martin's —"

"Exactly. Now go and get her by all means, and when she comes here we will speak to her, but above all things be careful what you say."

"I think Mrs. Ragg is already aware," said Colonel Jeffery, "that her son's safety, as well as her own, depends upon her discretion in keeping his whereabouts a profound secret. We will instruct this young girl when she comes here."

Colonel Jeffery, when he heard that the medical man was of opinion that the experiment of awakening the feelings of Tobias, by bringing Minna Gray, was worth trying, at once acquiesced, and urged upon Mrs. Ragg to go and see Minna.

After many more speeches, about as much to the purpose as those which we have already formed, Mrs. Ragg got herself dressed and went upon her errand. She was instructed to say that she had found herself unequal to being a laundress in the Temple, and so had thought it was better to return to her own original occupation of cook in a gentleman's family, and that, as she had the liberty to do so, she wished Minna Gray to come and take tea with her.

Thus forewarned of the part she was to play, Mrs. Ragg started upon her mission, in which we need not follow her, for the result of it is all that we particularly care about, and that consisted in her bringing Minna in great triumph to the colonel's house.

Colonel Jeffery, and Captain Rathbone, who was staying to dine with him, saw the young girl as she came up the garden path. She was one of those small, delicately beautiful young creatures, who seem specially made to love and be loved. Her light auburn hair hung in dancing curls down her fair cheeks, and her beautifully shaped lips and pearly teeth were of themselves features that imparted much loveliness to her countenance. She had, too, about her face all the charm of childish beauty, which bespoke her so young as to have lost little of that springtide grace, which, alas! is so fleeting. Add to all this a manner so timid, so gentle, and so retiring, that she seemed to be an inhabitant of some quieter world than this, and you have Minna Gray, who had crept into the boyish heart of poor Tobias, before your eyes.

"What a gentle quiet looking little creature," said the captain.

"She is indeed; and what a contrast!"

"Between her and Mrs. Ragg, you mean? It does indeed look like an elephant escorting a fawn. But Mrs. Ragg has her good qualities."

"She has, and they are numerous. She is honest and candid as the day, and almost the only fault that can be laid to her charge is her garrulity."

"How do you mean to proceed?"

"Why, Rathbone, I mean to condescend to do what, under any other circumstances, would be most unjustifiable — that is, listen to the conversation of Mrs. Ragg with Minna Gray; I do so with the concurrence of the old lady, who is to lead her to speak of Tobias, and it is solely for the purpose of judging if she really loves the boy, and making a proper report to the surgeon, that I do so."

"You are right enough, Jeffery; the end in this case, at all events, sanctifies the means, however defective such a system of philosophy may be as a general thing. May I likewise be an auditor?"

"I was going to ask you to so far oblige me, for I shall then have the advantage of your opinion; so you will do me a favour."

There was a small pantry called a butler's pantry close to the kitchen, into which Mrs. Ragg had taken Minna Gray. A door opened from this pantry into the kitchen, and another on to the landing at the foot of the kitchen stairs. Now Mrs. Ragg was to take care that the door opening to the kitchen should be just ajar, and the colonel and his friend could get into the pantry by the other mode of entrance. Colonel Jeffery was a gentleman in the fullest sense of the term, and he kept no useless bloated menials about him, so the butler's pantry had no butler to interfere with him, the colonel, in his own house.

In the course of a few minutes Jeffery and Rathbone were in the pantry, from whence they could both see and hear what passed in the kitchen. To be sure there was a certain air of restraint about Mrs. Ragg at the thought that her master was listening to what passed, and that lady had a propensity to use hard words, of the meaning of which she was in the most delightful state of ignorance; but as it was to Minna Gray's conversation that the colonel wanted to listen, these little peculiarities of Mrs. Ragg upon the occasion did not much matter. Of course, Minna thought she had no other auditors than her old friend. Mrs. Ragg was quite busy over the tea.

"Well, my dear," she said to Minna, "this is a world we live in."

Mrs. Ragg, no doubt, intended this as a discursive sort of remark that might open any conversation very well, and lead to anything, and she was not disappointed, for it seemed to give to the young girl courage to utter that which was struggling to her lips.

"Mrs. — Mrs. Ragg," she began, hesitatingly.

"Yes. My dear, let me fill your cup."

"Thank you; but I was going to say —"

"A little more sugar?"

"No, no. But I cannot place a morsel in my lips, Mrs. Ragg, or think or speak to you of anything else, until you have told me if you have heard any news of poor — poor —"

"Tobias?"

"Yes — yes — yes!"

Minna Gray placed her two little hands upon her face and burst into tears. Mrs. Ragg made a snuffling sort of noise that, no doubt, was highly sympathetic, and after a pause of a few moments' duration, Minna gathered courage to speak again.

"You know, Mrs. Ragg, the last you told me of him was that — that Mr.

Todd had said he was mad, you know, and then you went to fetch somebody, and when you came back he was gone; and Mr. Todd told you the next day that poor Tobias ran off at great speed and disappeared. Has anything been heard of him since?"

"Ah, my dear, alas! alas!"

"Why do you cry alas? — Have you any more sad news to tell me?"

"He was my only son — and all the world and his wife, as the saying is, can't tell how much I loved him."

Minna Gray clasped her hands, and, while the tears coursed down her young fair cheeks, she said —

"And I, too, loved him!"

"I always thought you did, my dear, and I'm sure, if you had been an angel out of Heaven, my poor boy could not have thought more of you than he did. There was nothing that you said or did that was not excellent. He loved the ground you walked on; and a little old worsted mitten, that you left at our place once, he used to wear round his neck, and kiss it when he thought no one was nigh, and say — 'This was my Minna's!'"

The young girl let her head rest upon her hands, and sobbed convulsively.

"Lost — lost!" she said, "and poor, kind, good Tobias is lost!"

"No, my dear, it's a long lane that hasn't a turning. Pluck up your courage, and your courage will pluck up you. Keep sixpence in one pocket, and hope in another. When things are at the worst they mend. You can't get further down in a well than the bottom."

Minna sobbed on.

"And so, my dear," added Mrs. Ragg, "I do know something more of Tobias."

The young girl looked up.

"He lives! — he lives!"

"Lor' a mussy, don't lay hold of a body so. Of course he lives, and, what's more, the doctor says that you ought to see him — he's up stairs."

"Here? — here?"

"Yes, to be sure. That's why I brought you to tea."

Minna Gray took a fit of trembling, and then, making great efforts to compose herself, she said —

"Tell me all — tell me all!"

"Well, my dear, it's an ill wind that blows nobody good, and so here I am, cook in as good a place as mortal woman would wish to have. I can't tell you all the rights of the story, because I don't know it. But certainly Tobias is up stairs in bed like a gentleman, only they say as his brains is — is something or another that makes him not understand anything or anybody, and so you see the doctor says if you speak to him, who knows but what he may come to himself?"

With an intuitive tact that belongs to some minds, and which Minna Gray, despite the many disadvantages of her social position, possessed in an eminent degree, she understood at once the whole affair. Tobias was suffering from some aberration of intellect, which the voice and the presence of one whom he loved fondly might dissipate. Would she shrink from the trial? — would her delicacy take the alarm and overcome her great desire to recover Tobias? Oh, no; she loved him with a love that far outstripped all smaller feelings, and, if ever there was a time when that love took complete possession of her heart, it was at this affecting moment, when she was told that her voice might have the magic power of calling back to him the wandering reason that harshness and ill-usage had for a time toppled from its throne.

"Take me to him!" she cried — "take me to him! If all that is wanted to recover him be the voice of affection, he will soon be as he was once to us."

"Well, my dear, take your tea, and I'll go and speak to the kernel."

It was now time for Colonel Jeffery and his friend, the captain, to retire from the pantry, where we need not say that they had been pleased and affected listeners to what had passed between Mrs. Ragg and the fair and intelligent Minna Gray, who, in beauty and intelligence, far exceeded their utmost expectations.

CHAPTER XLVII.

TOBIAS RECOVERS HIS INTELLECT.

IN THE COURSE OF A QUARTER OF AN HOUR the surgeon was sent for, and then Mrs. Ragg tapped at the drawing-room door, to give the colonel an account of the success of her mission; but he at once said to her —

"We know all, Mrs. Ragg. We merely wish to see Tobias first, so that the medical gentleman may see exactly his condition, and then if you will bring Minna Gray here I will speak to her, and, I hope, put her quite at her ease as regards what she has to do."

"Certainly, sir, certainly. Hold fast, and good comes at last."

The surgeon and the two gentlemen went to Tobias's chamber, and there they found him in the same lethargic condition that, with only occasional interruptions, he had continued in since he had been in the colonel's house. These interruptions consisted in moaning appeals for mercy, and at times the name of Todd would pass his lips, in accents which showed what a name of terror it was to him. The surgeon placed his hand upon Tobias's head.

"Tobias!" he said, "Tobias!"

A deep sigh was his answer.

"Tobias! Tobias!"

"Oh, God! God!" cried Tobias, feebly. "Spare me — I will tell nothing. Oh, spare me, Mr. Todd. — Repent now. There, there — the blood! What a crowd of dead men. Dead — dead — dead — all dead!"

"No better?" said the colonel.

"Not a bit. On the contrary, the longer he remains in this condition, the less chance there will be of his recovery. I shall lose hope, if this last experiment produces no good results. Let us go and speak to the young girl."

They all descended to the drawing-room, and Minna Gray was summoned. Colonel Jeffery took her kindly by the hand and led her to a seat, and then he said to her —

"Now, Miss Gray, remember that all here are friends to you and to Tobias, and that we all feel deeply for him and for you. You are very young, both of you, but that is no reason on earth why you should not love each other."

Minna looked up at him through her tears, as she said —

"Is he very — very ill?"

"He is indeed. We suspect — indeed, I may say we know, that his mind has received so severe a shock that, for a time, it is deranged; but we hope that, as that derangement, you understand, has not arisen from any disease, pleasant and agreeable impressions may restore him. What we want you to do is to speak to him as you, no doubt, have been in the habit of doing in happier times."

"Yes, yes, sir."

"I think you know exactly what we mean?"

"I do, sir — indeed I do."

"Oh, bless you, sir, she understands," said Mrs. Ragg. "A nod is as good as a wink to a blind horse, you know, gentlemen. Handsome is as handsome does — as I used to say to the late Mr. Ragg, who is naturally dead and gone, and accordingly buried in St. Martin's —"

"You can tell us that another time, madam," said the surgeon. "At present, you see we are rather busy. Now, Miss Gray, if you will have the goodness to come with me, we will see what can be done for our young friend above stairs."

Poor Minna Gray! How her colour went and came like the sunlight of an April day, as she accompanied the three gentlemen and Mrs. Ragg up stairs to Tobias's chamber. How she trembled when they reached the landing; and what a faintness came over her when the door was opened, and she saw that dimly-lighted room.

"Courage," whispered Colonel Jeffery to her. "This is a holy errand you are upon."

"Yes, yes."

"Cut your coat according to your cloth," said Mrs. Ragg, who, provided she thought of a proverb, was not very particular with regard to its applicability to the circumstances under which she uttered it. "Keep your feet to the length of your sheet."

"Pray, madam," said the surgeon, who seemed to have quite a horror of Mrs. Ragg. "Pray, madam, oblige me by being silent."

"A still tongue makes a wise head."

"Good God, colonel! will you speak to her?"

"Hush, Mrs. Ragg!" said Colonel Jeffery. "Hush! You will perhaps be the means of spoiling this important effort for the recovery of your son if you are not perfectly quiet."

Thus admonished, Mrs. Ragg shrank into the background a little, and the colonel went to the window and let in a little more light. The surgeon conducted Minna Gray to the bed-side, and she looked upon the boy who had won her childish heart through a world of tears.

"It is — it is — Tobias!"

"Is he much altered?"

"Oh, yes; much — much. He — he used to look so happy. His — his face was like a piece of sunshine!"

She sank upon a chair that was by the bed-side, and sobbed.

"This will never do," said the surgeon.

"Wait — oh, wait a little," she whispered. "Only wait a little. — I shall be better soon."

The surgeon nodded; and then stepping back to the colonel and the captain, he said —

"This burst of grief must have its way, or it will mar all. We must have patience."

They all hid themselves behind the folds of the bed furniture, and Mrs. Ragg sat down in an obscure corner of the room, working her knee up and down, as though she were nursing an imaginary baby. Gradually the sobs of Minna Gray subsided, until all was still. She then gently took one of the thin wasted hands of poor Tobias in her own, and looked at it. Oh, how changed it was. She then bent over him, and looked in his face. What permeative lines of care were there, battling with rounded muscles of early youth! Then she summoned all her courage to speak. She placed her lips close to his ear, and in the soft sweet accents that had long before sank deep into his heart, she said —

"Tobias! — my Tobias!"

The boy started.

"Dear Tobias, it is I. Minna!"

He opened his eyes, which had been closed and seemingly cemented by tears.

"Tobias! Tobias, dear!"

A smile — a heavenly smile. It was the first that had played upon his lips since he set foot in the shop of Sweeney Todd, now broke like a sunbeam over his face.

"I am mad — mad!" he said, gently, "or that is the voice of my Minna."

"It is your Minna. It is — it is, Tobias; look at me."

He rose up in the bed — he cast one glance at the well-known and dearly remembered face, and then, with a gasping sob of joy, he clasped her in his arms.

"It's done," said the surgeon.

"Thank God!" said Colonel Jeffery.

Mrs. Ragg drew her breath so hard through her nose that she made a noise like some wild animal in the agonies of suffocation.

"You really know me, Tobias?"

"Know you, dear? Oh, why should I not know you, Minna? God bless you!"

"May He bless you, Tobias."

They wept together; Minna forgot that there was anybody in the world but herself and Tobias, and parting the long straggling masses of his hair from before his face, she kissed him.

"For my sake, Tobias, now you will take care of yourself, and recover quickly."

"Dear — dear Minna."

He seemed never tired of holding her hands and kissing them. Suddenly the surgeon stepped forward with a small vial in his hand.

"Now, Tobias," he said, "you are much better, but you must take this."

The look of surprise and consternation with which Tobias regarded him was beyond description. Then he glanced at the bedstead and the rich hangings, and he said —

"Oh, Minna, what is all this? Where am I? Is it a dream?"

"Give it to him," said the surgeon, handing the vial to Minna. She placed the neck of it to his lips.

"Drink, Tobias."

Had it been deadly poison she had offered him, Tobias would have taken it. The vial was drained. He looked in her face again with a smile.

"If this is indeed a dream, my Minna, may I never awaken — dear — dear — one — I — I —"

He fell back upon the pillow. The smile still lingered upon his face, but the narcotic which the surgeon had had administered to him had produced its effect, and the enfeebled Tobias fell into deep sleep. Minna Gray looked rather alarmed at this sudden falling off of Tobias from waking to sleeping, but the surgeon quieted her fears.

"All is right," he said. "He will awaken in some hours wonderfully refreshed, and I have the pleasure of now predicting his perfect cure."

"You do not know," said Colonel Jeffery, "what pleasure that assurance gives me."

TOBIAS RESTORED TO HIS SENSES BY MINNA'S ASSISTANCE..

"And me," said the captain.

Minna looked all that she thought, but she could not speak, and Mrs. Ragg, still kept up the mysterious noise she produced by hard breathing with her mouth close shut.

"Now, madam," said the surgeon to her, "our young friend must be left alone for some hours. It is now six o'clock, and I do not expect he will awaken until twelve. When he does so, I am very much mistaken if you do not all of you find him perfectly restored and composed, although very weak."

"I will take care to be at hand," said the colonel. "Miss Gray, perhaps you will call and see how he is to-morrow, and all I can say is, that you will be quite welcome to my house whenever you think proper, but let me impress upon you one thing."

"What is it, sir?"

"The absolute necessity of your keeping Tobias's place of abode and anything concerning him a most profound secret."

"I will do so."

"If you do not, you will not only endanger the cause of justice, but in all probability his life, for he has an enemy with great resources, and of the most unscrupulous disposition in the use of them: I say this much to you, because the least indiscretion might be fatal."

"I will guard the secret, sir, as I would guard his life."

"That will do — now come down stairs, and let us have a glass of wine to drink to the speedy restoration to perfect health of Tobias. Come, Rathbone, what do you think? Shall we be one too many yet for Todd?"

"I begin to think we shall."

"I feel certain of it. So soon as we see that Tobias is sufficiently well to make any statement, it will be necessary to send for Sir Richard Blunt."

"Certainly."

"And then I hope and trust that we shall get at something that will elucidate the mystery that is still attached to the fate of poor Thornhill."

"Ah, I fear he is gone!"

"Dead?"

"Yes. That fatal string of pearls has heralded him to death, I fear; but, perhaps we shall hear a something concerning that yet from Tobias."

They all sat down in the drawing-room, and with tearful pleasure Minna Gray drank a glass of wine to the health of Tobias, after which Mrs. Ragg saw her home again to Milford Lane, and no doubt all the road from this colonel's house to there did not want for a prolific subject of conversation. How happy Minna felt when she put up to Heaven her simple prayer that night, previous to seeking repose.

CHAPTER XLVIII.

JOHANNA MAKES A NEW CONFIDANT.

WE LEFT THE SPECTACLE-MAKER AND his family rather in a state of confusion. Big Ben the Beef-eater had had his revenge upon both Mrs. Oakley and the

Saint, and it was a revenge that really did them no harm, so that in that respect it had turned out well. The Rev. Josiah Lupin did not return to the house, but Mrs. Oakley, in a terrible state of prostration from the effects of the sickness that had come over her, staggered again into the parlour. She looked at Mr. Oakley, as she said—

"If you were half a man you would take the life of that villain for treating me in the way he has; I have no doubt but he meant to take the life of the pious Mr. Lupin, and so add him to the list of martyrs."

"My dear," said the spectacle-maker, "if Mr. Lupin intrudes himself into my house, and any friend of mine turns him out, I am very much obliged to him."

"Perhaps you would be equally obliged to this monster, whom you call your friend, if he would turn me out?"

Mr. Oakley shook his head as he said—

"My dear, there are some burthens which can be got rid of, and some that must be borne."

"Come — come, Mother Oakley," said Ben. "Don't bear malice. You played me a trick the last time I came here, and now I have played you one. That's all. It wasn't in human nature not to do it, so don't bear malice."

Mrs. Oakley, if she had been in a condition to do so, no doubt would have carried on the war with Big Ben, but she decidedly was not, and after a shudder or two, which looked as though she thought the toad was beginning again to oppress her, she rose to leave the room.

"Mother," said Johanna, "it was not a real toad."

"But you are!" said Mrs. Oakley, sharply. "You have no more feeling for your mother than as if she were a brickbat."

Feeling now that at all events she had had the last word at somebody, Mrs. Oakley made a precipitate retreat, and sought the consolations and solitude of her own chamber. Mr. Oakley was about to make some speech, which he prefaced with a sigh, when some one coming into the shop called his attention, and he left Johanna and Big Ben the Beef-eater together in the parlour. The moment they were alone, Ben began shaking his head and making some very mysterious signs, which completely mystified Johanna. Indeed she began to be afraid that Ben's intellects were not quite right, although an ordinary observer might have very well supposed there was something the matter with his nether garments, for he pointed to them repeatedly, and shook his head at Johanna.

"What is the matter, cousin?" she said.

"Oh, dear!—oh, dear!—oh—oh—oh!"

"Are you ill?"

"No, but I only wonder as you ain't. Didn't I see you in Fleet-street with these here on?—oh!—oh!—not these here exactly, but another pair. These would be a trifle too large for you. Oh, dear-a-me! my heart bled all for to see such a young and delicate little puss as you a taking to wear the thingamies so soon."

Johanna now began to understand what Ben meant, namely, that he had seen her in Fleet-street disguised in male attire, with her young friend Arabella Wilmot.

"Oh, Ben," she said, "you must not think ill of me on that account."

"But — but," said Ben, rather hesitatingly, as if he were only putting a doubtful proposition, "wasn't it rather unusual?"

"Yes, Ben, but there were reasons why I put on such garments. Surely it was better to do so than — than — to —"

"Than to go without any?" said Ben.

"No — no, I did not say that — I mean it was better for me to forget a little of that maiden delicacy which — which — than to let him —"

She burst into tears.

"Holloa!" cried Ben, as he immediately folded her in an immense embrace, that went very near to smothering her. "Don't you cry, and you may wear what you like, and I'll come and help you to put 'em on. Come, come, there's a nice little dear, don't you cry. Lord bless you! you know how fond I am of you, and always was since you was a little tottering thing, and couldn't say my name right. Don't you cry. You shall wear 'em as often as you like, and I'll go behind you in the street, and if anybody only so much as says half a word to you, I'll be down upon 'em. Fetch 'em now and put 'em on, my dear."

Johanna must have laughed if her life had depended upon her gravity, for all that Ben said upon the subject was uttered in the sheer simplicity of a kind heart, and well she knew that in his rough way he doted on her, and thought there was not such another being in the whole world as she. And yet he looked upon her as a child, and the imperceptible flight of time had made no difference in Ben's ideas concerning Johanna. She was still to him the sweet little child he had so often dandled upon his knee, and brought fruit and sweetmeats to, when such things were great treasures. After a few moments he let her go, and Johanna was able to draw breath again.

"Ben," she said, "I will tell you all."

"All what?"

"How I came to put on — the — the —"

"Oh, these here — very good. Cut on, and let's know all the particulars. I suppose you felt cold, my dear, eh?"

"No — no."

"No? Well then, tell it quick, for I was always a mortal bad hand at guessing. Your father is fitting an old gentleman with a pair of spectacles, and he seems hard to please, so we shall have lots of time. Go on."

"Your good opinion is of such moment to me," said Johanna, "for I have very few to love me; now that you have seen me in such a disguise, I should feel unhappy if I did not tell why I wore it."

Ben lent the most attentive ear to what she said, and then Johanna briefly and distinctly told him all the story of Mark Ingestrie, and how he had, as she thought, mysteriously disappeared at the barber's shop in Fleet-street. It will be seen that she still clung to the idea that the Thornhill of the arrived ship was no other than her lover. Ben heard her all out with the most fixed attention. His mouth and eyes gradually opened wider and wider as she proceeded, partly from wonder at the whole affair, and partly from intense admiration at the way in which she told it, which he thought was better than any book he had ever read. When she had concluded, Ben again folded her in his arms, and she had to struggle terribly to get away.

"My dear child," he said, "you are a prodigy. Why, there's not an animal as ever I knew comes near you; and so the poor fellow had his throat cut in the barber's for his string of pearls?"

"I fear he was murdered."

"Not a doubt of it."

"You really think so, Ben?"

The tone of agony with which this question was put to him, and the look of utter desolation which accompanied it, alarmed Ben, and he hastily said —

"Come, come, I didn't mean that. No doubt something has happened; but it will be all right some day or another, you may depend. Oh, dear! — oh, dear! The idea of your going to watch the barber with some boy's clothes on!"

"Tell me what I can do, for my heart and brain are nearly distracted by my sufferings?"

Ben looked all round the room, and then up at the ceiling, as though he had a hope and expectation of finding some startling suggestion written legibly before his eyes somewhere. At length he spoke, saying —

"I tell you what, Johanna, my dear, whatever you do, don't you put on them things again. You leave it all to me."

"But what will you do? — what can you do, Ben?"

"Well, I don't know exactly; but I'll let you know when it's done."

"But do not run into any danger for my sake."

"Danger? danger? I should like to see the barber that would interfere with me. No, my dear, no; I'm too well used to all sorts of animals for that. I'll see what I can do, and let you know all about it to-morrow, and in the meantime, you stick to the petticoats, and don't be putting on those thingamies again. You leave it to me — will you now?"

"Until to-morrow?"

"Yes, I'll be here to-morrow about this time, my dear, and I hope I shall have some news for you. Well, I declare, it's just like a book, it is. You are quite a prodigy."

Ben would have treated Johanna to another of the suffocating embraces, but she contrived to elude him; and, as by this time the old gentleman in the shop was suited with a pair of spectacles, Mr. Oakley returned to the parlour. Johanna placed her finger upon her lips as an indication to Ben that he was to say nothing to her father of what had passed between them, for, although Mr. Oakley knew generally the story of his daughter's attachment to Mark Ingestrie, as the reader is aware, he knew nothing of the expedition to Fleet-street in disguise. Ben, feeling that he had now an important secret to keep, shut his mouth hard, for fear it should escape, and looked so mysterious, that any one more sharp-sighted than the old spectacle-maker must have guessed that something very unusual was the matter. Mr. Oakley, however, had no suspicions; but as this state of things was very irksome to Ben, he soon rose to take his leave.

"I shall look in again to-morrow," he said, "Cousin Oakley."

"We shall be glad to see you," said Mr. Oakley.

"Yes," added Johanna, who felt it incumbent upon her to say something, "we shall be very glad to see you indeed."

"Ah," said her father, "you and Ben were always great friends."

"And we always shall be," said Ben. Then he thought that he would add something wonderfully clever, so as completely to ward off all suspicions of Oakley's, if he had any, and he added—"She ain't like some young creatures that think nothing of putting on what they shouldn't. Oh dear, no—not she. Bye, bye. I'll come to-morrow."

Ben was quite pleased when he got out of the house, for among the things that he (Ben) found it difficult to do, was to keep a secret.

"Well," he said, when he was fairly in the open air, "if I ain't rather nonplussed at all this. What shall I do?"

This was a question much easier asked than answered, as Ben found; but, however, he felt an irresistible desire to go and have a look at the shop of Sweeney Todd.

"I can easily," he said, "go to Fleet-street, and then, if I find myself late, I can take a boat at Blackfriars for the Tower-stairs, and after all get in to dinner comfortably enough."

With this conclusion, Ben set off at a good pace down Snow-hill, and was soon at the beginning of Fleet-street. He walked on until he came to Sweeney Todd's shop, and there he paused.

Now we have previously remarked that there was one great peculiarity in the shop-window of Todd, and that was that the articles in it were so well arranged that some one always was in the way of obtaining any view from the outside into the establishment. Todd was therefore secure against the dangers arising from peeping and prying. Big Ben placed himself close to the window, and made an attempt, by flattening his nose against the panes of glass, to peep in; but it was all in vain. He could not obtain the smallest glimpse into the inside.

"Confound it," he cried, "what a cunning sort of animal this is to be sure—he won't let one peep through the bars of his cage, that he won't."

Now Sweeney Todd became aware, by the additional darkness of his shop, that some one must be quite close to the window, and therefore, availing himself of a peep-hole that he had expressly for the purpose of reconnoitering the passing world without, he took a long look at Big Ben. It was some moments before Ben caught sight of a great eye in the window of Sweeney Todd glancing at him. This eye appeared as if it were set in the centre of a placard, which announced in glowing language the virtues of some condiment for the hair or the skin, and it had a most ferocious aspect. Big Ben looked fascinated and transfixed to the spot, and then he muttered to himself—

"Well, if that's his eye, it's a rum 'un. Howsomdever, it's no use staying outside: I'll pop in and get shaved, and then I shall be able to look about me. Who's afraid?"

As Ben turned round, he saw a plainly-attired man close to his elbow; but he took no notice of him, although from his close proximity to him it was quite impossible that the plain-looking man could have failed to overhear what Ben said. In another moment Big Ben was in Todd's shop.

"Shaved or dressed, sir?" said Todd.

"Shaved," said Ben, as he cast his eyes round the shop.

"Looking for anything, sir?" said Todd.

"Oh, no — nothing at all. Only a friend of mine, you see, said this was such a nice shop, you understand, to be shaved in."

"Was your friend finished off here, sir?"

"Well, I rather think he was."

"Pray sit down. Fine weather, sir, for the season. Now, pussy, my dear, get out of the way of the hot water." Todd was addressing an imaginary cat. "Are you fond of animals, sir? Lord bless me, I'm fond of all the world. God made us all, sir, from a creeping beetle to a beef-eater."

"Very likely," said Big Ben, as he seated himself in the barber's chair.

"And so," added Todd, as he mixed up a lather, and made the most horrible faces, "we ought to love each other in this world of care. How is your friend, sir, who was so kind as to recommend my shop?"

"I should like to know."

"What, is he in eternity? Dear me!"

"Well, I rather think he is."

"Was it the gentleman who was hung last Monday, sir?"

"Confound you, no. But there's somebody else who I think will be hung some Monday. I tell you what it is, Mr. Barber, my friend never got further than this infernal shop, so I'm come to enquire about him."

"What sort of man, sir?" said Todd, with the most imperturbable coolness.

"What kind of man?"

"Yes, sir. If you favour me with his description, perhaps I may be able to tell you something about him. By the bye, if you will excuse me for one moment, I'll bring you something that a gentleman left here one day."

"What is it?"

"I will satisfy you directly, sir, and I'm quite certain your mind will be at rest about your friend, sir, whoever he was. Remarkable weather, sir, for the time of year."

Todd had got only half way from the shop to the parlour, when the shop-door opened, and the plain-looking man walked in — the very same plain man who had stood so close to Big Ben at Todd's window.

"Shaved," he said.

Todd paused.

"If, sir, you will call again in a few minutes, or if you have any call to make and can conveniently look in as you come back —"

"No, I'll take a seat."

The plain-looking man sat down close to the door, and looked as calm and as unconcerned as any one possibly could. The look with which Todd regarded him for a moment, and only one moment, was truly horrible. He then quietly went into his back parlour. In a moment he entered with a common kid glove, and said to Ben —

"Did this belong to your friend? — a gentleman left it here one day."

Ben shook his head.

"I really don't know," he said. "Come, Mr. Barber, finish the shaving, for that gentleman is waiting."

Ben was duly shaved; while the plain-looking man sat quietly in the chair by the door, and when the operation was finished, Ben looked in Todd's face, and said, solemnly —

"A string of pearls."

"Sir," said Todd, without changing countenance in the least.

"A string of pearls. — Murder!"

"A what, sir?"

Ben looked staggered. He well knew that if he had cut any one's throat for a string of pearls, that such words said to him would have driven him frantic, but when he saw no change in Todd's face, he begun to think that, after all, the accusation must be unfounded, and muttering to himself —

"It must be nothing but the child's fancy after all," he hastily threw down twopence and left the shop.

"Now, sir," said Todd, to the plain-looking man.

"Thank you."

The plain-looking man rose, and as he did so he seemed just to glance through the door into the street as it was opened by Ben. Immediately his face was full of smiles, as he cried —

TODD AND THE BEEFEATER HAVE SOME WORDS.

"Ah, Jenkins, is that you? Ha, ha! I missed you this morning.— Excuse me, Mr. Barber, I'll look in again. My old friend Jenkins has just gone by."

With this, out he flew from Todd's shop like a shot, and was gone towards Temple Bar, before the barber could move or lay down the shaving cloth which he had in his hands all ready to tuck under his chin. Todd stood for a few moments in an attitude of irresolution. Then he spoke —

"What does all this mean?" he said. "Is there danger? Curses on them both, I would have —; but no matter, I must be wrong — very wrong. That string of pearls may yet destroy me. — Destroy! no — no — no. They must have yet more wit before they get the better of me, and yet how I calculated upon the destruction of that man. I must think — I must think."

Todd sat down in his own strong chair, and gave himself up to what is popularly denominated a "brown study."

CHAPTER XLIX.

THE VAULTS OF ST. DUNSTAN'S.

A PONDEROUS STONE WAS RAISED in the flooring of St. Dunstan's church. The beadle, the churchwarden, and the workmen shrunk back — back — back, until they could get no further.

"Ain't it a norrid smell," said the beadle.

Then the plain-looking man who had been at Sweeney Todd's advanced. He was no other than Sir Richard Blunt, and whispering to the churchwarden, he said —

"If what I expect be found here, we cannot have too few witnesses to it. Let the workmen be dismissed."

"As you please, Sir Richard. Faugh! what an awful — fuff! — stench there is. I have no doubt they won't be sorry to get away. Here, my men, here's half-a-crown for you. Go and get something to drink and come back in an hour."

"Thank yer honour!" cried one of the men. "An' sure, by St. Patrick's bones, we want something to drink, for the stench in the church sticks in my blessed throat like a marrow bone, so it does."

"Get out," said the beadle; "I hates low people, and Hirish. They thinks no more of beetles than nothink in the world."

The workmen retired, laughing; and when the church was clear of them, the churchwarden said to Sir Richard Blunt —

"Did you ever, Sir Richard, smell such a horrid charnel-house sort of stench as comes up from that opening in the floor of the old church?"

Sir Richard shook his head, and was about to say something, when the sound of a footstep upon the pavement of the church made him look round, and he saw a fat, pursy-looking individual approaching.

"Oh, it's Mr. Vickley, the overseer," said the beadle. "I hopes as yer is well, Mr. Vickley. Here's a horrid smell."

"God bless me!" cried the overseer, as with his fat finger and thumb he held his snub nose. "What's this? It's worse and worse."

"Yes, sir," said the beadle; "talking of the smell, we have let the cat out of the bag, I think."

"Good gracious! put her in again, then. It can't be a cat."

"Begging your pardon, Mr. Vickley, I only spoke anatomically. If you comes here, sir, you'll find that all the smell comes out of this here opening."

"What! An opening close to my pew! My family pew, where I every Sunday enjoy my repose — I mean my hopes of everlasting glory? Upon my life, I think it's a piece of — of d — d impudence to open the floor of the church, close to my pew. If there was to be anything of the sort done, couldn't it have been done somewhere among the free sittings, I should like to know?"

"Mr. Vickley," said Sir Richard, "pray be satisfied that I have sufficient authority for what I do here; and if I had thought it necessary to take up the flooring of your pew while you had been in it, I should have done it."

"And pray, sir," said Mr. Vickley, swelling himself out to as large a size as possible, and glancing at his watch chain, to see that all the seals hung upon the convexity of his paunch as usual — "who are you?"

"Oh, dear — oh, dear," said the beadle. "Conwulsions! — conwulsions! What a thing it is to see authorities a-going it at each other. Gentlemen — gentlemen. Conwulsions! — ain't there lots of poor people in the world? Don't you be a-going it at each other."

"I am a magistrate," said Sir Richard.

"And I am an overseer. Ah!"

"You may be an overseer or an underseer, if you like. I am going to search the vaults of St. Dunstan's."

The churchwarden now took the overseer aside, and after a while succeeded in calming down his irascibility.

"Oh, well — well," said Mr. Vickley. "Authorities is authorities; and if so be as the horrid smell in the church can be got rid of, I'm as willing as possible. It has often prevented me sleeping — I mean listening to the sermon. Your servant, sir — I shall, of course, be very happy to assist you."

The beadle wiped his face with his large yellow handkerchief as he said —

"Now this here is delightful and affecting, to see authorities agreeing together. Lord, why should authorities snap each other's noses off, when there's lots o' poor people as can be said anything to and done anything to, and they may snap themselves?"

"Well, well," added Mr. Vickley. "I am quite satisfied. Of course, if there's anything disagreeable to be done in a church, and it can be done among the free seats, it's all the better; and indeed, if the smell in St. Dunstan's could have been kept away from the respectable part of the congregation, I don't know that it would have mattered much."

"Conwulsions!" cried the beadle. "It wouldn't have mattered at all, gentlemen. But only think o' the bishop smelling it. Upon my life, gentlemen, I did think, when I saw the Right Rev. Father in God's nose a looking up and down, like a cat when she smells a bunch o' lights, and knowed as it was all owing to the smell in the church, I did think as I could have gone down through the floor, cocked hat and all, that I did. Conwulsions — that was a moment."

"It was," said the churchwarden.

"Mercy — mercy," said Mr. Vickley.

The beadle was so affected at the remembrance of what had happened at the confirmation, that he was forced to blow his nose with an energy that produced a trumpet-like sound in the empty church, and echoed again from nave to gallery. Sir Richard Blunt had let all the discourse go on without paying the least attention to it. He was quietly waiting for the foul vapours that arose from the vaults beneath the church to dissipate a little before he ventured upon exploring them. Now, however, he advanced and spoke.

"Gentlemen, I hope I shall be able to rid St. Dunstan's of the stench which for a long time has given it so unenviable a reputation."

"If you can do that," said the churchwarden, "you will delight the whole parish. It has been a puzzle to us all where the stench could come from."

"Where is the puzzle now?" said Sir Richard Blunt, as he pointed to the opening in the floor of the church, from whence issued like a steamy vapour such horrible exhalations.

"Why, certainly it must come from the vaults."

"But," said the overseer, "the parish books show that there has not been any one buried in any of the vaults directly beneath the church for thirty years."

"Then," said the beadle, "it's a very wrong thing of respectable parishioners — for, of course, them as has waults is respectable — to keep quiet for thirty years and then begin stinking like blazes. It's uncommon wrong — conwulsions!"

Sir Richard Blunt took a paper from his pocket and unfolded it.

"From this plan," he said, "that I have procured of the vaults of St. Dunstan's, it appears that the stone we have raised, and which was numbered thirty, discloses a stone staircase communicating with two passages, from which all the vaults can be reached. I propose searching them; and now, gentlemen, and you, Mr. Beadle, listen to me."

They all three looked at him with surprise as he took another letter from his pocket.

"Here," he said, "are a few words from the Secretary of State. Pray read them, Mr. Vickley."

The overseer read as follows —

"The Secretary of State presents his compliments to Sir Richard Blunt, and begs to say that as regards the affair at St. Dunstan's, Sir Richard is to consider himself armed with any extraordinary powers he may consider necessary."

"Now, gentlemen," added Sir Richard Blunt, "if you will descend with me into the vaults, all I require of you is the most profound secrecy with regard to what you may see there. Do you fully understand?"

"Yes," stammered Mr. Vickley, "but I rather think I — I would as soon not go."

"Then, sir, be silent regarding the going of others. Will you go, sir?" to the churchwarden.

"Why yes, I — I think I ought."

"I shall be obliged to you. I may feel the want of a witness. We will take you with us, Mr. Beadle, of course."

"Me — me? Conwulsions!"

"Yes — yes. You go, you know, *ex officio.*"

"Ex, the deuce, I don't want to go. Oh conwulsions! conwulsions!"

"We cannot dispense with your services," said the churchwarden. "If you refuse to go, it will be my duty to lay your conduct before the vestry."

"Oh — oh — oh!"

"Get a torch," said Sir Richard Blunt, "and I will lower it down the opening in the floor. If the air is not so bad as to extinguish the light, it will not be too bad for us to breathe for a short space of time."

Most reluctantly, and with terrible misgivings of what might be the result of the frightful adventure into which he was about to be dragged, the beadle fetched a link from the vestry. It was lighted, and Sir Richard Blunt tying a string to it, let it down into the passage beneath the church. The light was not extinguished, but it burnt feebly and with but a wan and sickly lustre.

"It will do," said Sir Richard. "We can live in that place, although a protracted stay might be fatal. Follow me; I will go first, and I hope we shall not have our trouble only for our pains."

CHAPTER L.

THE DESCENT TO THE VAULTS.

SIR RICHARD COMMENCED the descent.

"Come on," he said. "Come on."

He got down about half a dozen steps, but finding that no one followed him he paused, and called out —

"Remember that time is precious. Come on!"

"Why don't you go?" said the churchwarden to the beadle.

"What! Me go afore a blessed churchwarden? Conwulsions — no! I thinks and I hopes as I knows my place better."

"Well, but upon this occasion, if I don't mind it —"

"No — no, I could not. Conwulsions — no!"

"Ah!" said Sir Richard Blunt. "I see how it is; I shall have to do all this business alone, and a pretty report I shall have to make to the Secretary of State about the proceedings of the authorities of St. Dunstan's."

The churchwarden groaned.

"I'm a coming, Sir Richard — I'm a coming. Oh dear, I tell you what it is, Mr. Beadle, if you don't follow me, and close too, I'll have you dismissed as sure as eggs is eggs."

"Conwulsions! conwulsions! I'm a-coming."

The churchwarden descended the stairs, and the beadle followed him. Down — down they went, guided by the dim light of the torch carried by Sir Richard, who had not waited for them after the last words he had spoken.

"Can you fetch your blessed breath, sir?" said the beadle.

"Hardly," said the churchwarden, gasping. "It is a dreadful place."

"Oh, yes — yes."

"Stop — Stop. Sir Richard — Sir Richard!"

There was no reply. The light from the torch grew more and more indistinct as Sir Richard Blunt increased his distance from them, and at length they were in profound darkness.

"I can't stand this," cried the churchwarden; and he faced about to ascend to the church again. In his effort to do so quickly, he stretched out his hand, and seized the beadle by the ankle, and as that personage was not quite so firm upon his legs as might be desired, the effort of this sudden assault was to upset him, and he rolled over upon the churchwarden, with a force that brought them both sprawling to the bottom of the little staircase together. Luckily they had not far to fall, for they had not been more than six or eight steps from the foot of the little flight. Terror and consternation for a few moments deprived each of them of the power of speech. The beadle, however, was the first to recover, and he in a stentorian voice called —

"Murder! Murder!"

Then the churchwarden joined in the cries, and they buffeted each other in vain efforts to rise, each impeding the other to a degree that rendered it a matter of impossibility for either of them to get to their feet. Mr. Vickley, who was waiting in the church above, with no small degree of anxiety, the report from below, heard these sounds of contention and calls for help with mingled horror. He at once made a rush to the door of the church, and, no doubt, would have endangered the success of all Sir Richard Blunt's plans, if he had not been caught in the arms of a tall stout man upon the very threshold of the church door.

"Help! murder! Who are you?"

"Crotchet they calls me, and Crotchet's my name. London my birth place, is your'n the same? What's the row?"

"Call a constable. There's blue murder going on in the vaults below."

"The devil there is. Just you get in there, will you, and don't you stir for your life, old fellow."

So saying, Mr. Crotchet, who knew the importance of secrecy in the whole transaction, and who had been purposely awaiting for Sir Richard Blunt, thrust Vickley into a pew, and slammed the door of it shut. Down fell the overseer to the floor, paralysed with terror; and then Mr. Crotchet at once proceeded to the opening in the floor of the church, and descended without a moment's hesitation.

"Hilloa!" he cried, as he alighted at the bottom of the stairs upon the churchwarden's back. "Hilloa, Sir Richard, where are you?"

"Here," said a voice, and with the torch nearly extinguished, Sir Richard Blunt made his appearance from the passage. "Who is there?"

"Crotchet, it is."

"Indeed. Why, what brought you here?"

"What a row."

"Why — why, what's all this? You are standing upon somebody. Why bless my heart it's —"

Out went the torch.

"Fire! — help! — murder!" shouted the beadle, "I'm being suffocated. Oh, conwulsions! Here's a death for a beadle. Murder! robbery. Fire — oh — oh — oh."

The churchwarden groaned awfully.

"Ascend, and get a light," said Sir Richard. "Quick, Crotchet, quick! God only knows what is the matter with all these people."

Both Crotchet and Sir Richard Blunt scrambled over the bodies of the churchwarden and the beadle, and soon reached the church. The churchwarden made a desperate effort, and, shaking himself free of the beadle, he ascended likewise, and rolled into a pew, upon the floor of which he sat, looking a little deranged.

"If you don't come up," said Sir Richard Blunt, directing his voice down the staircase, "we will replace the stone, and you may bid adieu to the world."

"Conwulsions!" roared the beadle. "Oh, don't — conwulsions!"

Up he tumbled, with the most marvellous celerity, and rolled into the church, never stopping until he was brought up by the steps in front of the communion-table, and there he lay, panting and glaring around him, having left his cocked hat in the regions below. Sir Richard Blunt looked ghastly pale, which Crotchet observing, induced him to take a small flask from his pocket, filled with choice brandy, which he handed to his chief.

"Thank you," said Sir Richard.

The magistrate took a draught, and then he handed it to the churchwarden, as he said —

"I'll fill it again."

"All's right."

The churchwarden took a pull at the brandy, and then the beadle was allowed to finish it. They were both wonderfully recovered.

"Oh, Sir Richard," said the churchwarden, "what have you seen?"

"Nothing particular."

"Indeed!"

"No. You can have the stone replaced as soon as you like, over the opening to the vaults."

"And you have seen nothing?" said the beadle.

"Nothing to speak of. If you have any doubts or any curiosity, you can easily satisfy yourself. There's the opening. Pray descend. You see I have escaped, so it cannot be very dangerous to do so. I will not myself go again, but I will wait for either of you, if you please. Now, gentlemen, go, and you will be able to make your own discoveries."

"Me?" cried the beadle. "Me? Oh, conwulsions! I thinks I sees me."

"Not I," said the churchwarden. "Cover it up — cover it up. I don't want to go down. I would not do so for a thousand pounds."

A covert smile was upon the lips of Sir Richard Blunt as he heard this, and he added —

"Very well; I have no objection, of course, to its being at once covered up; and I think the least that is said about it, will be the better."

"No doubt of that," said the churchwarden.

"Conwulsions! yes," said the beadle. "If I was only quite sure as all my ribs was whole, I shouldn't mind; but somebody stood a-top of me for a good quarter of an hour, I'm sure."

Some of the workmen now began to arrive, and Sir Richard Blunt pointed to them, as he said to the churchwarden —

"Then the stone can be replaced without any difficulty, now; and, sir, let me again caution you to say nothing about what has passed here to-day."

"Not a word — not a word. If you fancy somebody stood upon your ribs, Mr. Beadle, I am quite sure somebody did upon mine."

The workmen were now directed to replace the stone in its former position; and when that was completely done, and some mortar pressed into the crevices, Sir Richard Blunt gave a signal to Crotchet to follow him, and they both left the church together.

"Now, Crotchet, understand me."

"I'll try," said Crotchet.

"No one, for the future, is to be shaved in Sweeney Todd's shop alone."

"Alone?"

"Yes. You will associate with King, Morgan, and Godfrey; I will stand all necessary expenses, and one or the other of you will always follow whoever goes into the shop, and there wait until he comes out again. Make what excuses you like. Manage it how you will; but only remember, Todd is never again to have a customer all to himself."

"Humph!"

"Why do you say humph?"

"Oh, nothing partickler; only hadn't we better grab him at once?"

"No; he has an accomplice or accomplices, and their discovery is most important. I don't like to do things by halves, Crotchet; and so long as I know that no mischief will result from a little delay, and it will not, if you obey my instructions, I think it better to wait."

"Very good."

"Go at once, then, and get your brother officers, and remember that nothing is to withdraw your and their attention from this piece of business."

"All's right. You know, Sir Richard, you have only to say what's to be done, and it's as good as done. Todd may shave now as many people as he likes, but I don't think he'll polish 'em off in his old way quite so easy."

"That's right. Good day."

"When shall we see you, Sir Richard?"

"About sunset."

By the time this little conversation was over, Sir Richard Blunt and Crotchet had got through Temple Bar, and then they parted, Crotchet taking his way back to Fleet-street, and Sir Richard Blunt walking hastily to Downing-street. When he got there he entered the official residence of the Secretary of State for the Home Department, and being well known to the clerk, he was at once conducted into a little room carefully hung round with crimson cloth, so as to deaden the sound of any voices that might be raised in it. In the course of a few minutes a small door was opened, and a shabby looking man entered, with a hesitating expression upon his face.

"Ah, Sir Richard Blunt," he said, "is that you?"

"Yes, your lordship, and if you are disengaged for a few minutes, I have something to communicate."

"Ah, some new plot. Confound those Jacobin rascals!" *

"No, my lord, the affair is quite domestic and social. It has no shade of politics about it."

The look of interest which the face of the secretary had assumed was gone in a moment, but still he could not very well refuse now to hear what Sir Richard Blunt had to say, and the conference lasted a quarter of an hour. At its termi-

---

* Apparently an error. The Jacobins, and the French Revolution in which they played so prominent a part, were still several years in the future in 1785, when this story was set.

nation, as Sir Richard was leaving the room, the secretary said —

"Oh, yes, of course, take full discretionary powers, and the Home-office will pay all expenses. I never heard of such a thing in all my life."

"Nor I, my lord."

"It's really horrible."

"It is even so far as we know already, and yet I think there is much to learn. I shall, of course, communicate to your lordship anything that transpires."

"Certainly — certainly. Good day."

Sir Richard Blunt left the Secretary of State, and proceeded to his own residence, and while he is there, making some alteration in his dress, we may as well take a glance at Crotchet, and see what that energetic but somewhat eccentric individual is about. After parting with Sir Richard Blunt at Temple Bar, he walked up Fleet-street, upon Sweeney Todd's side of the way, until he overtook a man with a pair of spectacles on, and a stoop in his gait, as though age had crept upon him.

"King," said Crotchet.

"All right," said the spectacled old gentleman in a firm voice. "What's the news?"

"A long job, I think. Where's Morgan?"

"On the other side of the way."

"Well, just listen to me as we walk along, and if you see him, beckon him over to us."

As they walked along Crotchet told King what were the orders of Sir Richard Blunt, and they were soon joined by Morgan. The other officer, Godfrey, who had been mentioned by the magistrate, was sent for.

"Now," said Crotchet, "here we are, four of us, and so you see we can take it two and two for four hours at a stretch as long as this confounded barber's shop keeps open."

"But," said Morgan, "he will suspect something."

"Well, we can't help that. It's quite clear he smugs the people, and all we have got to do is to prevent him smugging any more of 'em, you see."

"Well, well, we must do the best we can."

"Exactly; so now keep a bright look out, and hang it all, we have been in enough rum adventures to be able to get the better of a rascally barber, I should think. Look out — look out; there's somebody going in now."

CHAPTER LI.

JOHANNA RUSHES TO HER DESTINY.

JOHANNA HAD ENOUGH CONFIDANTS NOW. Her father — Colonel Jeffery — Big Ben — and Arabella Wilmot, all knew —

> "*The sad story of her love.*"

It will be a hard case if, among so many councillors, she hits upon the worst — a most truly hazardous course of proceeding; but then it is a fault of the young to mistake daring for ability, and to fancy that that course of proceeding which involves the most personal risk is necessarily the most likely to be successful. Colonel Jeffery was, of all Johanna Oakley's advisers, the one who was most likely to advise her well, but unfortunately he had told her that he loved her, and from that time, with an instinctive delicacy of feeling which no one could have to greater perfection than Johanna, she had shunned him. And yet the reader, who knows the colonel well, knows that, quite irrespective of the attachment that had sprung up in his bosom for the beautiful and heart-stricken girl, he would have played the part of a sincere friend to her and stood manfully between her and all danger. But it was not to be. From the moment that he had breathed to her the secret of his attachment, a barrier was, in her imagination, raised between them. Her father evidently was not one who could or who would advise anything at all energetic; and as for Big Ben, the conversation she had had with him upon the subject had quite been sufficient to convince her that to take him out of the ordinary routine of his thoughts and habits was thoroughly to bewilder him, and that he was as little calculated to plot and to plan in any emergency as a child. She would indeed have trembled at the result of the confidential communication to Big Ben, if she had been aware of the frightfully imprudent manner in which he had thrown himself into communication and collision with Todd, the consequences of which glaring act of indiscretion he was only saved from by Sir Richard Blunt entering the shop, and remaining there until he (Ben) was shaved.

Under all these circumstances, then, Johanna found herself thrown back upon her old friend Arabella Wilmot.

Now, Arabella was the worst adviser of all, for the romantic notions she had received from her novel reading, imparted so strong a tone to her character, that she might be said in imagination to live in a world of the mind. It was, as the reader will recollect, to Arabella Wilmot that Johanna owed the idea of going to Todd in boy's apparel — a measure fraught with frightful danger, and yet, to the fancy of the young girl, fascinating upon that very account, because it had the appearance as though she were doing something really serious for Mark Ingestrie. To Arabella, then, Johanna went, after Ben had left her, and finding her young friend within, she told her all that had occurred since they last met.

"What shall I do?" she said. "I tell my tale of woe, and people look kind upon me, but no one helps me."

"Oh, Johanna, can you say that of me?"

"No, no. Not of you, Arabella, for you see I have come to you again; but of all others, I can and may say it."

"Comfort yourself, my dear Johanna. Comfort yourself, my dear friend. Come, now — you will make me weep too, if I see those tears."

"What shall I do? — what shall I do?"

"There, now, I am putting on my things; and as you are dressed, we will go out for a walk, and as we go along we can talk of the affair, and you will find your spirits improve by exercise. Come, my dear Johanna. Don't you give way so."

"I cannot help it. Let us go."

"We will walk round St. Paul's Churchyard."

"No — no. To Fleet-street — to Fleet-street!"

"Why would you wish to add to your sorrows, by again looking upon that shop?"

"I do not know, I cannot tell you; but a horrible species of fascination draws me there, and if I come from home, I seem as though I were drawn from all other places towards that one by an irresistible attraction. It seems as though the blood of Mark Ingestrie called aloud to me to revenge his murder, by bringing the perpetrators of it to justice. Oh, my friend — my Arabella, I think I shall go mad."

Johanna sunk upon her knees by a chair, and hid her fair face in her hands, as she trembled with excess of emotion. Arabella Wilmot began to be really alarmed at the consequences of her friend's excited and overwrought feelings.

"Oh, Johanna — Johanna!" she cried, "cheer up. You shall go when you please, so that you will not give way to this sorrow. You do not know how much you terrify me. Rise — rise, I implore you. We will go to Fleet-street, since such is your wish."

After a time, Johanna recovered from the burst of emotion that had taken such certain possession of her, and she was able to speak more calmly and composedly to her friend than she had yet done during that visit. The tears she had shed, and the show of feeling that had crept over her, had been a great relief in reality.

"Can you pardon me for thus tormenting you with my grief?" said Johanna.

"Do not talk so. Rather wonder how I should pardon you if you tell your griefs elsewhere. To whom should you bring them but to the bosom of one who, however she may err in judgment regarding you, cannot err in feeling."

Johanna could only press her friend's hand in her own, and look the gratitude which she had not the language to give utterance to.

It being then settled that they were to go to Fleet-street, it next became a matter of rather grave debate between them whether they were to go as they were, or Johanna was to again equip herself in the disguise of a boy.

"This is merely a visit of observation, Johanna; I will go as I am."

"Very well, dear."

They accordingly set out, and as the distance from the house of Arabella Wilmot's father was but short to the shop of Sweeney Todd, they soon caught sight of the projecting pole that was his sign.

"Now be satisfied," said Arabella, "by passing twice; once up Fleet-street, and once down it."

"I will," said Johanna.

Todd's shop was closed as usual. There was never an open door to that establishment, so that it was, after all, but a barren satisfaction for poor Johanna to pass the place where her imagination, strengthened by many circumstantial pieces of evidence, told her Mark Ingestrie had met with his death; still, as she had said to Arabella before starting, a horrible sort of fascination drew her to the spot, and she could not resist the fearful attraction that the outside of Todd's shop had for her. They passed rather rapidly, for Arabella Wilmot did not wish Johanna to pause, for fear she should be unable to combat her feelings, and make some sort of exhibition of them in the open street.

"Are you content, Johanna?" she said. "Must we pass again?"

"Oh, yes — yes. Again and again; I can almost fancy that by continued looking at that place I could see what has been the fate of Mark."

"But this is imagination and folly."

"It may be so, but when the realities of life have become so hideously full of horrors, one may be excused for seeking some consolation from the fairy cave. Arabella, let us turn again."

They had got as far as Temple Bar, when they again turned, and this time Johanna would not pass the shop so abruptly as she had done before, and any one, to see the marked interest with which she paused at the window, would have imagined that she must have some lover there whom she could see, notwithstanding the interior of the shop was so completely impervious to all ordinary gazers.

"There is nothing to see," said Arabella.

"No. But yet — ha! — look — look!"

Johanna pointed to one particular spot of the window, and there was the eye of Sweeney Todd glaring upon them.

"We are observed," whispered Arabella; "it will be much better to leave the window at once. Come away — oh, come away, Johanna."

"Not yet — not yet. Oh, if I could look well at that man's face, I think I ought to be able to judge if he were likely to be the murderer of Mark Ingestrie."

Todd came to his door.

"Good God, he is here!" said Arabella. "Come away. Come!"

"Never. No! Perhaps this is providential. I will, I must look at this man, happen what may."

Todd glared at the two young girls like some ogre intent upon their destruction, and as Johanna looked at him, a painter who loved contrast, might have indeed found a study, from the wonderful difference between those two human countenances. They neither spoke for some few moments, and it was reserved for Todd to break the silence.

"What do you want here?" he cried, in a hoarse rough voice. "Be off with you. What do you mean by knocking at the window of an honest tradesman? I don't want to have anything to say to such as you."

"He — he did it!" gasped Johanna.

"Did what?" said Todd, advancing in a menacing attitude, while his face assumed a most diabolical expression of concealed hatred. "Did what?"

"Stop him! Stop him!" cried a voice from the other side of the street. "Stop Pison, he's given me the slip, and I'm blessed if he won't pitch into that ere barber. Stop him. Pison! Pison! Come here, boy. Come here! Oh, lor, he's nabbed him. I knew'd he would, as sure as a horse's hind leg ain't a gammon o' bacon. My eyes, won't there be a row — he's nabbed the barber, like ninepence."

Before the ostler at the Bullfinch, for it was from his lips this speech came, could get one half of it uttered, the dog — who is known to the readers by the name of Hector, as well as his new name of Pison — dashed over the road, apparently infuriated at the sight of Todd, and rushing upon him, seized him with his teeth. Todd gave a howl of rage and pain, and fell to the ground. The whole street was in an uproar in a moment, but the ostler rushing over the way, seized the dog by the throat, and made him release Todd, who crawled upon all fours into his own shop. In another moment he rushed out with a razor in his hand.

"Where's the dog?" he cried. "Where's the fiend in the shape of a dog?"

"Hold hard!" said the ostler, who held Hector between his knees. "Hold hard. I have got him, old chap."

"Get out of the way. I'll have his life."

"No you won't."

"Humph!" cried a butcher's boy who was passing. "Why that's the same dog as said the barber had done for his master, and collected never such a lot of halfpence in his hat to pay the expenses of burying of him."

"You villain!" cried Todd.

HECTOR'S ATTACK ON SWEENEY TODD.

"Go to blazes!" said the boy. "Who killed the dog's master? Ah, ah! Who did it? Ah, ah!"

The people began to laugh.

"I insist upon killing that dog!" cried Todd.

"Do you?" said the ostler; "now, this here dog is a partickler friend of mine, so you see I can't have it done. What do you say to that now, old stick-in-the-mud? If you walk into him, you must walk through me first. Only just put down that razor, and I'll give you such a wolloping, big as you are, that you'll recollect for some time."

"Down with the razor! Down with the razor!" cried the mob, who was now every moment increasing.

Johanna stood like one transfixed for a few moments in the middle of all this tumult, and then she said with a shudder —

"What ought I to do?"

"Come away at once, I implore you," said Arabella Wilmot. "Come away, I implore you, Johanna, for my sake as well as for your own. You have already done all that can be done. Oh, Johanna, are you distracted?"

"No — no. I will come — I will come."

They hastily left the spot and hurried away in the direction of Ludgate Hill, but the confusion at the shop door of the barber did not terminate for some time. The people took the part of the dog and his new master, and it was in vain that Sweeney Todd exhibited his rent garments to show where he had been attacked by the animal. Shouts of laughter and various satirical allusions to his beauty were the only response. Suddenly, without a word, Todd then gave up the contest and retired into his shop, upon which the ostler conveyed Pison over the way and shut him up in one of the stables of the Bullfinch.

Todd, it is true, retired to his shop with an appearance of equanimity, but it was like most appearances in this world — rather deceitful. The moment the door was closed between him and observation he ground his teeth together and positively howled with rage.

"The time will come — the time will come," he said, "when I shall have the joy of seeing Fleet-street in a blaze, and of hearing the shrieks of those who are frying in the flames. Oh, that I could with one torch ignite London, and sweep it and all its inhabitants from the face of the earth. Oh, that all those who are now without my shop had but one throat. Ha! ha! how I would cut it."

He caught up a razor as he spoke, and threw himself into a ferocious attitude at the moment that the door opened, and a gentleman neatly dressed looked in, saying —

"Do you dress artificial hair?"

CHAPTER LII.

TODD'S ANNOUNCEMENT.

"YES," SAID TODD, AS HE COMMENCED stropping the razor upon his hand as though nothing at all was the matter. "I do anything in an honest and religious sort of way for a living in these bad times."

"Oh, very well. A gentleman is ill in bed and wants his peruke properly dressed, as he has an important visit to make. Can you come to his house?"

"Yes, of course. But can't the peruke be brought here, sir?"

"Yes. But he wants a shave as well, and although he can go in a sedan chair to pay his visit, he is too ill to come to your shop."

Todd looked a little suspicious, but only a little, and then he said—

"It's an awkward thing that I have no boy at present, but I must get one—I must get one, and in the meantime, when I am called out I have no resource but to shut up my shop."

At this moment a stout man came in, saying—

"Shaved—oh, you are busy. I can wait, Mr. Todd—I can wait," and down he sat.

Todd looked at the new-comer with a strange sort of scowl, as he said—

"My friend, have not I seen you here before, or somewhere else?"

"Very likely," said the man.

"Humph, I am busy and cannot shave you just now, as I have to go out with this gentleman."

"Very well, I can wait here and amuse myself until you come back."

Todd fairly staggered for a moment, and then he said—

"Wait here—in my shop—and amuse yourself until I come back? No, sir, I don't suffer any one. But it don't matter. Ha! ha! Come in, I am ready to attend you. But stop, are you in a very great hurry for two minutes, sir?"

"Oh, dear no, not for two minutes."

"Then it will only just take me that time to polish off this gentleman; and if you will give the address I am to come to, I will be with you almost as soon, sir, as you can get home, I assure you."

"Oh, dear no," cried the stranger, who had come in to be shaved, suddenly starting up, "I really could not think of such a thing. I will call again."

"It's only in Norfolk-street," said the applicant for the dressing of the artificial hair, "and two minutes can't make any difference to my friend, at all."

"Do you think," said the other, "that I would really interrupt business in this way? No, may I perish if I would do anything so unhandsome — not I. I will look in again, Mr. Todd, you may depend, when you are not going out. I shall be passing again, I know, in the course of the day. Pray attend to this gentleman's orders, I beg of you."

So saying, the shaving customer bounced out of the shop without another word; and as he crossed the threshold, he gave a wink to Crotchet, who was close at hand, and when that gentleman followed him, he said —

"Crotchet, Todd very nearly got me into a line. He was going out with the person we saw go to the shop, but I got away, or else, as he said, he would have polished me off."

"Not a doubt of it, in this here world, Foster," said Crotchet. "Ah, he's a rum 'un, he is. We haven't come across sich a one as he for one while, and it will be a jolly lot o' Sundays afore we meets with sich another."

"It will, indeed. Is Fletcher keeping an eye on the shop?"

"Oh, yes, right as a trivet. He's there, and so is Godfrey."

While this brief conversation was going on between the officers who had been left to watch Sweeney Todd's shop, that individual himself accompanied the customer, whom he had been conversing with, to Norfolk-street, Strand. The well-dressed personage stopped at a good-looking house, and said —

"Mr. Mundell only lodges here for the present. His state of mind, in consequence of a heavy loss he has sustained, would not permit him to stay in his own house at Kensington."

"Mr. Mundell?" said Todd.

"Yes. That is the gentleman you are to shave and dress."

"May I presume to ask, sir, what he is?"

"Oh, he is a — a — kind of merchant, you understand, and makes what use of his money he thinks proper."

"The same!" gasped Todd.

The door of the house was opened, and there was no retreat, although, at the moment, Todd felt as though he would much rather not shave and dress the man of whom he had procured the £8,000 upon the string of pearls; but to show any hesitation now might beget enquiry and enquiry might be awkward, so summoning all his natural audacity to his aid, Todd followed his guide into the house. He was a little puzzled to know who this person could be, until a woman made her appearance from one of the rooms upon the ground floor, and cried —

"There now, go out, do. We don't want you any more; you have got your pocket money, so be off with you, and don't let me see your face again till night."

"No, my dear," said the well-dressed personage. "Certainly not. This is the barber."

"Good God, Blisset, do you think I am blind, that I can't see the barber. Will you go? The captain is waiting for me to pour out his coffee, and attend to his other concerns, which nobody knows better than you, and yet you will be perpetually in the way."

"No, my dear. I — I only —"

"Hoity toity, are we going to have a disturbance, Mr. B? Recollect, sir, that I dress you well and give you money, and expect you to make yourself agreeable while I attend to the gentlemen lodgers, so be off with you; I'm sure, of all the troublesome husbands for a woman to have, you are about the worst, for you have neither the spirit to act like a man, nor the sense to keep out of the way."

"Ha!" said Todd.

Both the lodging-house keeper and his wife started at the odd sound.

"What was that?" said the woman.

"Only me, madam," said Todd, "I laughed slightly at that blue-bottle walking on the ceiling, that's all."

"What a laugh," said Blisset, as he left the house; and then the lady of the mansion turning to Todd, said —

"You are to attend to Mr. Mundell, poor man. You will find him in the front room on the second floor, poor man."

"Is he ill, madam?"

"Oh, I don't know, I rather think he's grizzling about some of his money, that's all, but it don't matter one way or the other. They say he is as rich as a Jew, and I'll take good care he pays enough here."

"Mrs. B — Mrs. B," cried a voice from the parlour.

"Yes, captain, I'm coming. — I'm coming, captain."

The lady bounced into the breakfast-parlour and closed the door, leaving Todd to find his way up stairs as he best could. After a hideous chuckle at the thought of Mr. Blisset's singular position in society, he commenced ascending the stairs. He accomplished the first flight without meeting with any one, but upon the second he encountered a servant girl with a pail, and Todd gave her such a hideous glance, accompanied by such a frightful contortion of his visage, that down went the pail, and the girl flew up stairs again, and locked herself in one of the attics. Without waiting to ascertain what effect the descent of the pail might have upon the nerves of the captain and the landlady, Todd pursued his course to the room whither he had been directed, and tapped at the door.

"Come in," said a meek, tremulous voice. "Come in."

Todd opened the door, and stood in the presence of the man over whose long tried skill and habitual cunning he had obtained such a triumph in the affair of the pearls at Mundell Villa. John Mundell now, though, was far from looking like the John Mundell of the villa. He sat by the fire, wrapped up in a flannel dressing-gown, with a beard of portentous length. His cheeks had fallen in. His brow was corrugated by premature wrinkles, and the corners of his mouth were drawn down as though a look of mental distress had become quite a thing of habit with him now.

"Who are you?" he growled out, as Todd came into the room, and with a show of carefulness closed the door after him. "Who are you, eh?"

"Come to shave you, sir, and dress your hair."

"Ah!" cried Mundell, as he gave a start. "Where have I heard that voice before? Why does it put me in mind of my loss? My £8000! My money — my money. Am I to lose another £8000? That will make £16,000. Oh, dear. Oh, dear. Oh dear! Who are you? Speak, friend. Who are you?"

"Only a barber, sir," said Todd, "come to shave you, and dress your hair. Ain't you well, sir? Shall I call again?"

"No — no — no! My losses distracts me. Only the barber? Ah, yes to be sure — only the barber. I must go to court, and ask for the duke of something. Good God, yes! I will see all the dukes, until I find out my duke. He who had my £8000, and has left me so poor and so wretched. Oh, dear! Oh, dear, my money — my hard-earned money. Oh, gracious, if I were to lose another £8000, I should go mad — mad — mad!"

"Shall I begin, sir?" said Todd.

"Begin? Begin what? Oh, yes, my hair; and I must be shaved too, or they won't let me in at all. I will have the pearls or my money. I will see all the dukes, and pounce upon my duke. Oh, yes, I will have the pearls or the money."

"Pearls, sir?" said Todd, as he began to arrange the shaving apparatus he had brought with him. "Did you say pearls?"

"Bah! what do you know about pearls, who, I dare say, never saw one. Bah! You — a poor beggarly barber. But I will have them back, or my money. I will raise London, but I will find them. I will see the queen herself, and know what duke she gave the pearls to, and then I will find him and have my money."

"Now, sir. A little this way." "Oh, dear — oh, dear! What do you charge?"

"Anything you please, sir. When I come to a gentleman, I always leave it to his generosity to pay me what he pleases."

"Ah! more expense. More expense. That means that I am to pay for the service done me, and something else besides for the sake of a compliment upon my liberality. But I ain't liberal. I won't be generous. Where's my money, my pearls; and now to go to all sorts of expense to go to court, and see dukes. Oh, the devil. Eh? Eh?"

"Sir?"

"Stop. What an odd thing. Why, you are very — very —"

"Very what, sir?" said Todd, making a hideous face.

"Like the duke, or my fancy leads me astray. Wait a bit. Don't move."

Mundell placed his hands over his eyes for a moment, and then suddenly withdrawing them he looked at Todd again.

"Yes, you are like the duke. How came you to be like a duke, the villain. Oh, if I could but see my pearls."

"What duke, sir?"

"I would give £500 — no, I mean £100, that is £50, to know what duke," screamed Mundell with vehemence. Then suddenly lapsing into quietness, he added — "Shave me. Shave me, I will go to court, and St. James's shall ring again with the story of my pearls. Lost! lost! lost! Did he abscond from his wife with them, or was he murdered? I wonder? I wonder? — £8000 gone all at once. I might have borne such a loss by degrees, but d — n it —"

"Really, sir, if you will go on talking about pearls and dukes, the shaving brush will go into your mouth, and there's no such thing as avoiding it."

"Confound you. Go on. Shave me and have done with it. Oh, dear! Oh, dear!"

John Mundell now contented himself by uttering drawn sighs, with now and then the accompaniment of a hideous groan, while Todd lathered his face with great affected care. The sighs and the groans both, however, ceased soon, and Todd became aware that the eyes of John Mundell were fixed upon him with a steady stare. No doubt, the usurer was recalling bit by bit to his memory the features of the sham duke, and comparing them with Todd's. To be sure, upon the occasion of his visit to Mundell Villa, Todd had taken every precaution to disguise his features; but then it must be admitted that the features of the barber were rather peculiar, and that John Mundell was professionally a more than ordinary keen observer, and thus it was that, as Todd lathered away, he became more and more impressed by the fact that there was a startling resemblance between Todd and the nobleman who had borrowed £8000 upon the string of pearls.

"What's your name?" he said.

"Todd."

"Humph! a well-to-do man?"

"Poor as Job."

"How very like you are to a great man. Do you ever go to court? I think — I am sure I have seen you somewhere."

"Very likely," said Todd, "for I often go there."

"What, to court?"

"Nay, sir, not to court, but somewhere. Will you have the whiskers left just as they are, or taken off entirely, sir?"

Tap! tap! came at the chamber door, and a boy peeped in, saying —

"Please, sir, the tailor has brought the things."

CHAPTER LIII.

THE MURDER OF THE USURER.

"COME IN! COME IN! MORE EXPENSE. More losses. As if an honest man, who only does what he can with his own, could not come to the court with a hope of meeting with a civil reception, unless he were decked out like a buffoon. Come in. Well, who are you?"

"Augustus Snipes, sir, at your service. Brought home the clothes, sir. The full dress suit you were so good as to order to be ready to-day, sir."

"Oh, you are a tailor?"

"Oh, dear no, sir. We are not tailors now-a-days. We are artists."

"Curse you, whatever you are. I don't care. Some artist I'm afraid has done me out of £8000. Oh, dear. Put down the things. What do they come to?"

"Eighteen pounds ten shillings and threepence, sir."

John Mundell gave a deep groan, and the tailor brushed past Todd to place the clothes upon a side table. As he returned he caught sight of Todd's face, and in an instant his face lighting up, he cried —

"Ah! how do? How do?"

"Eh!" said Todd.

"How did the Pompadour-coloured* coat and the velvet smalls do, eh? — Fit well? Lord, what a rum start for a barber to have a suit of clothes fit for a duke."

"Duke!" cried Mundell.

Todd lifted one of his huge feet and gave the "artist" a kick that sent him sprawling to the door of the room.

"That," he said, "will teach you to make game of a poor man with a large family, you scoundrel. What, you won't go, won't you? The —"

The artist shot out at the door like lightning, and flew down the stairs as though the devil himself was at his heels. Todd carefully closed the door again, and fastened it by a little bolt that was upon it. A strange expression was upon the countenance of John Mundell. His face looked perfectly convulsed, and he slowly rose from his chair. Todd placed one of his huge hands upon his breast and pushed him back again.

"What's the matter?" said Todd.

"He — he — knows you."

"Well."

---

* *Pompadour, in fabric, was a dark pinkish-purple color.*

"The Pompadour-coloured coat! Ah, I recollect the Pompadour-coloured coat, too. I thought I knew your face. There was a something, too, about your voice that haunted me like the remembrance of a dream. You — you — are —"

"What?"

"Help — help! Tell me if I be mad, or if you are a duke in the disguise of a barber, or a barber in the likeness of a duke. Ah, that Pompadour coloured coat, it sticks — sticks in my throat."

"I wish it did," growled Todd. "What do you mean, Mr. Mundell? — Pray express yourself. What do you mean by those incoherent expressions?"

"Are you human?"

"Dear me, I hope so. Really, sir, you look quite wild."

"Stop — stop — let me think — the face — the voice — the Pompadour coat — the costume fit for a duke. It must be so. — Man or devil, I will grapple with you, for you have got my pearls and my money. My £8000 — my gold that I have lived, that I have toiled for — that I have schemed, and cheated to keep up — that I have shut my eyes to all sights for — and my heart to all tender emotions. You have my money, and I will denounce you!"

"Stop," said Todd.

The usurer paused in what he was saying, but he still glared at Todd fiercely, and his eyes protruded from their orbits, while the muscles of his mouth worked as though he were still trying to utter audible sounds, but by some power was denied the capacity to utter them.

"You say you have lost pearls?"

"Yes — yes. — Orient pearls."

Todd dived his hand into the breast of his apparel and produced the string of pearls. He held them before the ravished and dazzled eyes of John Mundell, as he said —

"Were they like these?"

With a cry of joy Mundell grasped at the pearls. Tears of gratified avarice gushed from his eyes.

"My own — my own pearls — my beautiful pearls! — Oh, blessed chance — my pearls back again. Ha! ha! ha!"

"Ha!" echoed Todd, as he stepped behind the chair on which John Mundell was sitting.

With his left hand he took one vigorous grasp of the remaining hair upon the head of the usurer, and forced his back against the chair. In another instant there was a sickening gushing sound. Todd, with the razor he held in his right hand, had nearly cut John Mundell's head off. Then he held him still by the hair. Gasp — gasp — gasp — bubble — gasp — bubble. — Ah! ah! ah! — Goggle — goggle. A slight convulsive movement of the lashes, and the eyes set, and became opaquely dim. The warm blood still bubbled, but John

Mundell was dead. Todd picked up the pearls and carefully replaced them in his bosom again.

"How many strange events," he said, "hang upon these baubles. Ah, it's only one more — a dirty job rather — but business is business!"

He stood in the room as silent as a statue, and listened intently. Not the slightest sound indicative of the proximity of any one came upon his ears. He felt quite convinced that the deed of blood had been done in perfect secrecy. But then there he was. — Who but he could be accused? There he stood, the self-convicted murderer. Had he not done the deed with the weapon of his handicraft that he had brought to the house? How was Todd to escape the seeming inevitable cold-blooded murder?

We shall see. Huddled up in the chair, was the dead body. Mundell had not fallen out of the capacious easy seat in which he sat when he breathed his last. The blood rolled to the floor, where it lay in a steaming mass. Todd was careful — very careful not to tread in it, and he looked down his garments to see if there were any tell-tale spots of gore; but standing behind the chair to do the deed, as he had done, he had been saved from anything of the sort. There he stood, externally spotless, like many a seeming and smirking sinner in this world — but oh, how black and stained within!

"Humph!" said Todd; "John Mundell was half distracted by a heavy loss. He was ill, and his mind was evidently affected. He could not even shave himself. Oh, it is quite evident that John Mundell, unable to bear his miseries, real or ideal, any longer, in a fit of partial insanity, cut his throat. Yes, that will do."

Todd still kept the razor in his grasp. What is he going to do? — Murder again the murdered? — Is he afraid that a man, —

"With twenty murders on his head!"

— will jostle him from his perilous pinnacle of guilty safety? — No. He takes one of the clammy dead hands in his own — he clasps the half rigid fingers over the handle of the razor, and then he holds them until, in the course of a minute or so, they have assumed the grasp he wishes, and the razor, with which he, Todd, did the deed of blood, is held listlessly, but most significantly, in the hand of the dead.

"That will do," said Todd.

The door is reached and unfastened, and the barber slips out of the room. He closes the door again upon the fetid hot aroma of the blood that is there, fresh from the veins of a human being like himself — no — no — not like himself. — No one can be like Sweeney Todd. He is a being of his own species — distinct, alone, an incarnation of evil!

Todd was in no particular hurry to descend the stairs. He gained the passage with tolerable deliberation, and then he heard voices in the parlour.

THE MURDER OF THE USURER.

"What a man you are!" said Mrs. Blisset.

"Ah, my dear, I am indeed. Who would not be a man for your sake? As for Mr. Blisset, I don't think him worth attention."

"Nor I," said the lady, snapping her fingers, "I don't value him that. The poor mean-spirited wretch — he's not to be compared to you, captain."

"I should think not, my love. Have you got any change in your pocket?"

"Yes. I — I-think I have about seven shillings or so."

"That will do. Much obliged to you, madam — I mean, my dear Mrs. B.

Ah, if you would but smother Blisset, so that I might have the joy of making you Mrs. Captain Coggan, what a happy man I should be."

Todd tapped at the door.

"What was that?" cried the captain in evident alarm; "Is it Blisset?"

"No, captain — oh, no; I should like to see him interrupt me, indeed. A pretty thing that I cannot do what I like in the house I keep. Come in."

Todd just opened the door far enough to introduce his hideous head; and having done so, stared at the pair with such a selection of frightful physiognomical changes, that they both sat transfixed with horror. At length Todd broke the silence by saying —

"He's frightfully nervous."

"What? — what? — who?" gasped the captain.

"What?" repeated Mrs. Blisset.

"What's his name, upstairs, that I was sent for to shave just now."

"What, Mr. Mundell. Ah, poor man, he has been in a very nervous state ever since he has been here. He continually talks of a heavy loss he has had."

"Yes," said Todd, "I suppose he means you to pay me."

"Me?"

"Yes, ma'am. He says he is too nervous and excited for me to shave him just now, but he has borrowed a razor from me and says he will shave himself in the course of an hour or so, and send it back to me."

"Oh, very well. Your money will be sent with the razor, no doubt; for although Mr. Mundell is so continually talking of his losses, they tell me he is as rich as a Jew."

"Thank you, ma'am. Good morning; good morning, sir."

The captain cast a supercilious glance upon Todd, but did not deign to make the remotest reply to the mock civility with which he was bidden good morning. No one stands so much upon his dignity, as he whose title to any at all is exceedingly doubtful. The female heart, however, is mollified by devotion, and Mrs. Blisset returned the adieu of Todd. When he got into the passage, he uttered one of his extraordinary laughs, and then opening the street door, he let himself out.

Todd by no means hurried back to Fleet-street, but as he walked along he now and then shrugged his shoulders and shook his huge hands, which, to those acquainted with his peculiarities, would have been sufficient indications of the fact that he was enjoying himself greatly. At length he spoke —

"So — so — what a Providence we have, after all, watching over us. The moment I am in any real danger as regards the string of pearls, up starts some circumstance that enables me to ward it off. Well, well, some day I almost think I shall turn religious and build a church, and endow it. Ha!"

Todd was so tickled at the idea of his building a church and endowing it, that he stopped at the corner of Milford Lane, to enjoy an unusual amount of laughter; as he did so he saw no other than Mrs. Ragg, slowly coming towards him.

"Ah," he said, "Tobias's mother. The mother of the Tobias that was! — I will avoid her."

He darted on, and was through Temple Bar before Mrs. Ragg could make up her mind which way to run, for run she fully intended to do, when she saw Todd standing at the corner of Milford Lane. But she had no occasion for hurrying from him, as he walked in the direction of his shop as speedily as possible. Although he was perfectly satisfied with the clever manner he had ridded himself of the usurer, who probably might have been a source of annoyance to him, and who might eventually have been the means of bringing him to justice, he thought that he might be losing opportunities of making more victims for the accumulation of his ill-gotten wealth.

CHAPTER LIV.

SIR RICHARD BLUNT'S PROGRESS.

WE WILL NOW RETURN, AND SEE with what zeal Sir Richard Blunt and his active co-operators are at work, and how that persevering gentleman has taken the cause of humanity in hand, with a determined will to bring the atrocious criminals to a just tribunal. Sir Richard and his men continued to pass and repass Todd's window, and one or other had an eye upon the door, so that it was almost impossible for any one to go in without the officers seeing them; and as some one of the officers followed each customer into the shop, under some pretence, and did not return till the strangers had been shaved, it was impossible that he could continue his murderous trade. The barouet, however, could not continue to remain long in the vicinity of Todd's shop without exciting the suspicions of that crafty demon in human form. Todd seemed very ill at ease, and his eye was more frequently at the hole which commanded a view of everything within range of his window, and in spite of the various guises the officers assumed, he seemed to take a more close survey of their features than he had done when they had first visited his shop. It was rarely that his customers came in pairs, otherwise it would have continually prevented his schemes; but now none came alone, each one had his companion or attendant. One morning, almost as soon as the barber had opened his shutters, a seafaring man entered his shop in haste, and throwing himself on a chair, requested to be shaved immediately. He appeared to have but lately returned from India, or some other hot climate, for his features were well bronzed, and from his general aspect and conversation, he appeared to be a man of superior station in life. However, in this manner, the barber reasoned and came to the conclusion that he should have a good morning's work if none of his tormentors came to avert his intentions.

"A fine morning, sir," said Todd.

"Very," said the stranger; "but make haste and accomplish your task; I have a payment to make to a merchant in the city this morning by nine o'clock, and it is now more than half-past eight."

"I will polish you off in no time," said the barber, with a grin; "then you can proceed and transact your business in good time. Sit a little nearer this way, sir, the chair will only stand firmly in one position, and it is exceedingly uncomfortable for gentlemen to remain, even for a few moments, on an unsteady chair."

Todd adjusted the chair, by dint of what appeared to the stranger to be a deal of unnecessary trouble, and he said—

"You seem remarkably anxious to put the chair in what you call a comfortable position, but we sailors are rather rough, therefore you need not make so much fuss about my comfort for so short a time, but proceed with the business."

Todd seemed rather disconcerted at the stranger's remarks, and could not understand whether his words were uttered by chance, or imported more than Todd liked.

"It is a maxim of mine, sir," said Todd, "to make everybody that comes to my shop as comfortable as possible during the short time they remain with me. One half-inch further this way, sir, and you will be in a better position."

As he spoke he drew the chair to the spot he wished it, which circumstance seemed to please him, for he looked around him, and indulged in one of those hideous grins he executed just when he was on the point of committing some diabolical act. The gurgling noise he made in his throat caused the seaman to give a sudden start, which Todd perceiving, said—

"Did you hear the noise my poor old cat made, sir? she often does so when strangers come in, sir."

"It did not sound much like a cat; but if I had an animal that made such a demoniacal noise, I should soon send her to rest. Every one to their taste, though; I suppose you term the noise, that almost startled me, agreeable."

"Yes, sir," said the barber; "I like to hear her, because I think she is enjoying herself; and you know men and beasts require a something to stimulate the system."

By this time the lather was over the seaman's face. He could not speak, except at the imminent risk of swallowing a considerable quantity of the soap that Todd had covered his face with. The barber seemed dexterously to ply a razor on the seaman's face, which caused him to make wry faces, indicating that the operation was painful; the grimaces grew more fantastic to the beholder, but evidently less able to be withstood by the person operated upon.

"Good God, barber," he at length ejaculated, "why the devil don't you keep better materials? — I cannot stand this. The razor you are attempting to shave me with has not been ground, I should think, for a twelvemonth. Get another and finish me off, as you term it, in no time."

"Exactly, sir — I will get one more suited to your beard, and will return in one minute, when you will be polished off to my satisfaction."

He entered the little parlour at the back of the shop, but previously he took the precaution of putting his eye to the hole that gave a sight into the street; turning round, apparently satisfied with his scrutiny, he went in search of the superior razor he spoke of.

A low grating sound, like that of a ragged cord commencing the moving of pullies, was to be heard, when Sir Richard Blunt threw the door open, and took a seat in the shop near where the stranger was sitting. He was so disguised that Todd could not recognise him as the same person that had been in his shop so many times before. The barber's face was purple with rage and disappointment; but he restrained it by an immense effort, and spoke to Sir Richard in a tolerably calm tone —

"Hair cut, sir, or shaved, sir? I shall not be long before I have finished this gentleman off — perhaps you would like to call in again in a few minutes?"

"Thank you; I am not in a particular hurry, and being rather tired I will rest myself in your shop, if you have no objection."

"My shop is but just open, and our ventilation being bad, it is much more pleasant to inhale the street air for a few minutes, than the vitiated air of houses in this neighbourhood."

"I am not much afraid of my health for a few minutes, therefore would rather take rest."

Todd turned his face away and ground his teeth, when he found that all his arguments were unavailing in moving the will of his new customer; therefore he soon finished shaving the first customer.

"At your service, sir," said Todd to Sir Richard, who seemed absorbed in reading a newspaper he took from his pocket. He looked up, and saw that the stranger was nearly ready to leave, therefore he continued reading till the stranger was in the act of passing out of the shop, when he said —

"What time do the royal family pass through Temple-bar to the City this morning?"

"Half-past nine," said Todd.

"Then I have not time to be shaved now — I will call in again. Good morning." Saying which he also left the shop.

In a few minutes after leaving the shop of Todd, Sir Richard and the men employed by him were in consultation; and he urged strongly that the men should remain nearer to the shop than they had hitherto done, for if Sir Richard had been two minutes later, most likely he who had escaped the angry billows, would have been launched into eternity by the villanous barber.

For the remainder of the day Todd was more closely besieged than ever, and when night came on, Sir Richard Blunt, with two of his men, set watch upon the house of Mrs. Lovett. Sir Richard had provided himself with skeleton keys, candles, and other housebreaking implements, for the purpose of entering Mrs. Lovett's house after that lady had retired, as he had the full sanction of the law to use every means he could think of in bringing the culprits to justice.

About eleven o'clock Mrs. Lovett was seen in her bedroom, with a candle in her hand, and making every preparation for retiring; in a few minutes the light was put out, and everything seemed still as death. Nothing was to be heard in the adjoining streets but the monotonous tread of the watchmen, with an occasional drawling forth of the hour of the night.

This was the time Sir Richard had waited for — it was the time for him to act. He approached the street door and applied his implements with success, for the door yielded to the baronet's tools, and he soon was in the shop of the piemaker. As complete a silence reigned within as was maintained without.

He waited for some time yet, though, before he moved. Finding, at length, that all was profoundly still, and feeling quite convinced that Mrs. Lovett had really retired for the night, the magistrate set about procuring a light. By the aid of some chemical matches that he had with him, this was soon accomplished, and a faint blue light shone upon the various articles in the pie-shop of Mrs. Lovett. He then took a small piece of wax taper from his pocket, and lit it. This gave him sufficient light to enable him to distinguish with accuracy any object in the place.

Once again he listened, in order to be quite sure that Mrs. Lovett was not stirring, and then, finding himself perfectly satisfied upon that head, he fearlessly commenced an examination of the shop. There was nothing to excite any very particular attention, except the apparatus for lowering the platform upon which the pies were sent up from the ovens below, and in a few moments the whole attention of Sir Richard Blunt was concentrated upon that contrivance. He did not meddle with it further, than looking at it sufficiently to fully comprehend it, for he had other views just then.

After, then, making himself quite master of the details of that piece of machinery, he turned his whole attention to the parlour. By the aid of a skeleton-key which he took from his pocket, he opened the door with ease, and at once entered that room, where lay the remains of the supper which Mrs. Lovett had so liberally provided for Sweeney Todd. This parlour was rather a large rambling-room, with a number of snug, handy looking cupboards in various corners. It was towards those cupboards that Sir Richard Blunt directed his attention. They were all locked, but with the means he had with him, ordinary locks presented no impediment to the prosecution of his research.

CHAPTER LV.

MRS. LOVETT'S WALK.

SUDDENLY HE HEARD, OR FANCIED he heard a noise above in the house, like the sudden shutting of a door.

"Oh," thought Sir Richard, "all is safe. She is shutting herself in for the night, I suppose. Well, Mrs. Lovett, we will see what we can find in your cupboards."

The little bit of wax light, which Sir Richard had lighted, gave but a weak kind of twilight while he moved about with it in his hand, but when he stuck it on a corner of the mantel-shelf it burnt much clearer, and was sufficient to enable him just to see what he was about. So thoroughly impressed was he with the idea that Mrs. Lovett had retired to rest, that he paid no sort of attention to the house, and may be said, in a manner of speaking, to have negligently shut his ears to all sounds that did not violently attack them. He opened a cupboard, in which were some books, and on the top-shelf, lying in a confused kind of heap, were some watches, and several sets of very rich buckles for shoes. There were, likewise, several snuff-boxes in the lot. Were these little trifles presented to Mrs. Lovett, by Todd, as proofs of the thriving business he was carrying on? Sir Richard put two of the watches in his pocket.

"These may be identified," he said. "And now, if I can but find the door by which she descends to the oven below, I —"

At this moment he was startled by a sudden accession of light in the room. His first idea, and a natural enough one too, was, that the little wax light was playing some vagaries incidental to all lights, and he turned rapidly from the cupboard to look at it. What was his astonishment to see the door that led to the upper part of the house open, and Mrs. Lovett, partially undressed, standing upon the threshold with a chamber-candlestick in her hand in which was a rushlight*, the dim and dubious rays from which had produced the extra illumination that had first startled Sir Richard Blunt. No wonder that, with amazement upon his countenance, he now glanced upon this vision, for such

---

* A rushlight was a cheap candle, or rather miniature torch, made by soaking the pith of a rush stem in tallow or grease.

it looked like at the moment; and yet he saw that Mrs. Lovett it was to all intents and purposes, and that he was discovered in his exploring expedition in her parlour appeared to be one of those facts it would have required no small share of moral hardihood to dispute. Seeing, however, should not always be believing, despite the venerable saying which asserts as much.

"I must apprehend her, now," thought Sir Richard Blunt; "I have no resource but to apprehend her at once."

With this object he was about to dart forward, when something strange about the appearance of Mrs. Lovett arrested his attention, and stayed his progress. He paused and remained leaning partly upon the back of a chair, while she slowly advanced into the room, and then as she came nearer to him he became convinced of what he had begun to suspect, namely — that she was walking in her sleep.

There is something awful in this wandering of the mortal frame when its senses seem to be locked up in death. It looks like a resurrection from the grave — as though a corpse was again revisiting —

"The glimpses of the pale moon;" *

— and even Sir Richard Blunt, with all his constitutional and acquired indifference to what would be expected to startle any one else, could not help shrinking back a little, and feeling an unusual sort of terror. This transient nervousness of his, though, soon passed away, and then he set himself to watch the actions of Mrs. Lovett with all the keenness of intense interest and vividly awakened curiosity.

She did not disappoint him. Moving forward into the room with a slow and stately action, so that the little flame of the rushlight was by no means disturbed, she reached the middle of the parlour and then she paused. She assumed such a natural attitude of listening, that Sir Richard Blunt voluntarily shrunk down behind the chair, for it seemed to him at the moment that she must have heard him. Then, in a low and slightly indistinct tone, she spoke —

"Hush! hush! So still. The poison! Where is the poison? — Will he take it? Ah, that is the question, and yet how clear it is. But he is fiend-like in his suspicions. When will he come?"

She moved on towards the cupboard, in which the decanter of poisoned wine had been placed, and opening it, she felt in vain upon the shelf for it. It was still upon the table, and if anything more than another could have been a convincing proof of the mere mechanical actions of the somnambulist, this fact, that she passed the wine where it was, and only recollected where it had

---

* *Probably an imperfectly quoted line from Shakespeare's* Hamlet, *Act I Scene IV, "What may this mean/ That thou, dead corpse, again in complete steel,/ Revisits thus the glimpses of the moon")*

MRS. LOVETT IN A STATE OF SOMNAMBULISM.

been, would have been amply sufficient. After finding that her search was ineffectual, she turned from the cupboard, and stood for a few moments in silence. Then a horror shook her frame, and she said—

"They must all die. Bandage your eyes, and you will shut out the death shrieks. Yes, that will be something, to get rid of those frightful echoes. Bandage after bandage will, and shall do it."

Sir Richard stood silently watching; but such was the horror of the tones in which she spoke, that even his heart felt cold, as though the blood flowed but sluggishly through its accustomed channels.

"Who," he thought to himself, "for the world's wealth, would have this woman's memory of the past?"

She still held the light, and it appeared to him as though she were about to go into the shop, but she paused before she reached the half-glass door of communication between it and the parlour, and shook like one in an ague.

"Another! — another!" she said. "How strange it is that I always know. The air seems full of floating particles of blood, and they all fall upon me! Off, off. Oh, horror! horror! I choke — I choke. Off, I say. How the hot blood steams up in a sickly vapour. There — there, now! Why does Todd let them shriek in such a fashion?"

She now shook so, that Sir Richard Blunt made sure she would either drop the light she carried, or, at all events, shake it out, but neither of these contingencies took place; and, after a few moments, she got more calm. The violent agitation of her nerves gradually subsided. She spoke horrors, but it was in a different tone; and abandoning, apparently, the intention of going into the shop, she approached a portion of the parlour which had not yet been subjected to the scrutiny of Sir Richard Blunt, although it would not ultimately have escaped him. The appearance of this part of the room was simply that there was there a cupboard, but the back of this seeming cupboard formed, in reality, the door that led down the flight of stairs to the other strong iron door that effectually shut in the captive cook to his duties among the ovens. This was just the place that Sir Richard Blunt wanted to find out; and here we may as well state, that Sir Richard had an erroneous, but very natural idea, under the circumstances, that the cook or cooks were accomplices of Mrs. Lovett in her nefarious transactions. Had he been at all aware of the real state of affairs below, our friend, who had become so thoroughly disgusted with the pies, would not have been left for so long in so precarious a situation. Mrs. Lovett paused, after opening the lock of the cupboard, and in a strange, sepulchral sort of voice, she said —

"Has he done it?"

"Done what?" Sir Richard would fain have asked; but, although he had heard that people, when walking in their sleep, will answer questions put to them under such circumstances, he was doubtful of the fact, and by no means wished to break the trance of Mrs. Lovett.

"Has he done it?" she again repeated. "Is he no more? How many does it make? One — two — three — four — five — six — seven. Yes, seven, it must be the seventh, and I have heard all. Hush! hush! Todd — Todd — Todd, I say. Are you dead? No — no. He would not drink the wine. The devil, his master, whispered to him that it had in it the potent drug that would send his spirits howling to its Maker, and he would not drink. God! he would not drink! No — no — no!"

She pronounced these words in such a tone of agony, that her awakening from the strange sleep she was in, seemed to be a natural event from such a strong emotion, but it did not take place. No doubt Mrs. Lovett had been long habituated to these nocturnal rambles. She now began slowly and carefully the descent of the stairs leading to the oven; but she had not got many paces, when a current of air from below, and which, no doubt, came through the small grating in the iron door, extinguished her light. This circumstance, however, appeared to be perfectly unnoticed by her, and she proceeded in the profound darkness with the same ease as though she had had a light. Sir Richard would have followed her as he was, but in the dark he did not feel sufficient confidence in her as a guide to do so; and with as noiseless a tread as possible, he went back, and fetched from the chimney-piece shelf his own little wax light, which was still burning, and carefully guarding its flame from a similar catastrophe to what had happened to Mrs. Lovett's light, he descended the staircase, slowly and cautiously, after her.

She went with great deliberation, and it was not until being rather surprised at the total absence of sound from her tread, that upon looking down to her feet, he found that they were bare. After this, he could have no doubt but that, almost immediately upon her lying down in bed, this somnambulistic trance had come over her, and she had risen to creep below, and go through the singular scene we are describing. Step by step they both descended, until Mrs. Lovett came to the iron door. She did not attempt to open it. If she had, Heaven only knows what might have resulted from the desperate risk the captive cook might have made to escape. But even in the madness of Mrs. Lovett — for a sort of madness the scene she was enacting might be called — there was a kind of method, and she had no idea of opening the iron door that shut the cook from the upper world. Pausing, then, at the door leading to the ovens, she, with as much facility as though she had had broad daylight to do it in, unfastened the small square wicket in the top part of the window. A dull reddish glare of light came through it from the furnaces, which night nor day were extinguished.

"Hist! hist!" said Mrs. Lovett.

"Who speaks?" said a dull hollow voice, which sounded as if coming from the tomb. "Who speaks to me?"

Mrs. Lovett shut the small wicket in a moment.

"He has not done it, yet," she said. "He has not done it yet. No — no — no. But blood will flow — yes. It must be so. One — two — three — four — five — six — seven. The seventh, and not the last. Horrible! horrible! — most horrible! If, now, I could forget —"

She began rapidly to ascend the stairs, so that Sir Richard Blunt had to take two at a step, and once three, in order to be up before her, and even then she reached the parlour so close upon him, that it was a wonder she did not touch him; but he succeeded in evading her by a hair's breadth, and then she stood profoundly still for a few moments with her hands clasped. This quiescent state, however, did not last long, for suddenly, with eagerness, she leaned forward, and spoke again.

"No suspicion!" she said; "all is well! — Dear me, heap up thousands more. Oh, Todd, have we not enough? — There, clean up that blood! — Here is a cloth! — Stop it up — don't you see where it is running to, like a live thing? — He is not dead yet. — How clumsy. — Another blow with the hammer! — There — there — on the forehead! — What a crash! — Did the bone go that time? — Why the eyes have started out! — Horror! horror! — Oh, God, no — no — no — I cannot come here again. — Oh, God! — Oh, God!"

She sunk down upon the floor in a huddled up mass, and Sir Richard Blunt, who could not forbear shuddering at the last words that had come from her lips now he thought that her trance was over, rapidly approaching her, said —

"Wretched woman, your career is over."

She suddenly rose, and with the same stately movement as before, she made her way from the parlour by the door leading to the staircase. During all the strange scenes she had gone through, she had not abandoned the light, and although the air in the narrow passage of the staircase had extinguished it, she still continued to carry it with the same care as though it lit her on her way. Seeing that she still walked in that strange and hideous sleep, the magistrate let her pass him, nor did he make any attempt to follow her.

"Be it so," he said. "Let her awaken once again in the fancied security of her guilt. The doom of the murderess is hanging over her, and she shall not escape. But there is time yet."

He watched her until, by the turn of the stairs, she disappeared from his sight, and then he sat down to think. And there, for a brief space, we leave Sir Richard, while we take a peep at Tobias.

CHAPTER LVI.

TOBIAS UNBOSOMS HIMSELF.

MRS. RAGG, WHEN SHE MET SWEENEY TODD, after he had so comfortably put out of this world of care, John Mundell, the usurer, was really upon a mission to Minna Gray, to tell her that Tobias was, to use her own expressive phraseology — "Never so much better." Together with this news, Mrs. Ragg, at the colonel's suggestion, sought the company of Minna to tea upon that afternoon; and the consent of all parties whom it might concern being duly obtained to that arrangement, we will suppose Minna upon her way to Colonel Jeffery's.

Timidly, and with a bashful boldness, if we may use the expression, did the fair young girl ring the area bell at the colonel's. But he and his friend, Captain Rathbone, were both in the parlour, and saw her advance, so that she was at once welcomed into that portion of the house. The colonel, like most gentlemen, had the happy knack of making those with whom he spoke at their ease, so that Minna in a very short time recovered her first agitation — for if she had gone a thousand times to that house, agitated she would have been at first — and was able to discourse with all that gentle fervour and candid simplicity which belongs to such minds as hers.

"A most favourable change," said the colonel, "has taken place in Tobias — a change which I attribute to the strong influence which your visit had upon him; such an opinion is not a mere fancy of mine, for the medical gentleman who is in attendance upon him fully concurs in that view of the case."

Minna had no need to say that she was pleased, for she looked all the delight that such a communication was calculated to give her.

"Under these circumstances, then," continued the colonel, "that which was only a faint hope of his recovery, has become a certainty."

Minna's eyes filled with tears.

"Yes," added Captain Rathbone, "and we expect that to you he will make such revelations as shall bring proper punishment upon all those who have in any way been the cause of this calamity."

"Oh, forgive them all, now," said Minna. "Since he recovers, we can forgive them all, you know, now."

"That cannot be, for the persecution that Tobias has endured is but part of a system which he will be the means of exposing. Will you come up stairs at once now, Miss Gray, and see him?"

"Oh, yes — yes."

How her heart beat as she ascended the staircase, and how quickly she inspired and respired when she actually got to the door of Tobias's room. But then she heard the kind, although not very musical voice of Mrs. Ragg from within, say —

"But, my dear, you will give her time to come?"

"A long time, mother," said Tobias.

Ah, how well Minna knew that voice. It was the voice of Tobias as of old. The same voice, in tone perhaps only a little weakened, and rendered more soft by sickness than it had been, but to her it was like the soft memory of some well remembered tone that she had heard, and wept with joy to hear in happier days.

"I am here, Tobias! I am here."

"Minna — Minna!"

She entered the room radiant and beautiful as some fairy come to breathe joy by the magic of some spell; Tobias stretched out his arms towards her. She paused a moment, and then with a soft and gentle movement, embraced him. It was but for an instant she held him in her arms, and then she stepped back a pace or two and looked at him.

"Quite well," said Tobias, understanding the look.

"Quite?"

"Oh, yes, Minna, and as happy — as — as — fifty kings."

"Are kings happy?"

"Well, I don't know that they are, Minna, but at all events if they are, they can't possibly be happier than I am."

"Bless the boy," said Mrs. Ragg, "how he does talk, to be sure."

"Why, Tobias," said Colonel Jeffery, "you are wonderfully improved within this last hour."

"Yes, sir, and still more wonderfully since the best physician in the world has come to see me."

The direction of his eyes towards Minna Gray let them know, if they had not guessed it before, who Tobias considered the best physician in the world to him. Minna shook her head, and said —

"But, Tobias, it is to this gentleman that you owe your life."

"Yes," replied Tobias, "and if ever I forget to be grateful to him for all that he has done for me, I shall consider myself the worst person in the world. Aye, as bad, quite as — as Sweeney Todd."

Tobias shuddered perceptibly as he pronounced Todd's name, and it was quite evident that even in safety, as he could not but feel himself, and profoundly protected from the deadly malice of his late master, he could not divest himself of the absolute horror which even a mere remembrance of him engendered.

"Well, Tobias," said the colonel, as he drew a chair close to him, "since you have named Todd, pray tell us all about him."

"All?"

"Yes, all, Tobias."

"I will tell all I know. Come closer to me, Minna; I feel, when you are near me, as though God had sent one of his angels to keep Todd from me. Oh, yes, I will tell all I know. How can he harm me now?"

"How indeed, Tobias?" said Minna.

Tobias still trembled. What a shock that bold, bad, unscrupulous man had given to the nerves of that boy. His bodily health might be restored, and his mind once more be brought back to sanity, but if Tobias Ragg were to live to the age of a patriarch, the name of Todd would be to him a something yet to shrink from, and the tone of his nervous system could never be what it once was. Minna looked up in his face, and the colonel, too, gazed fully upon him, so that Tobias found he was absolutely called upon to say something.

"Yes," he began, "I remember that people came to the shop, and — and that they never went out of it again."

"Can you particularise any instance?"

"Yes, the gentleman with the dog."

Colonel Jeffery showed by his countenance how much he was interested.

"Go on," he said. "What about the gentleman with the dog?"

"I don't know how it was," added Tobias, "but that circumstance seemed to tell more upon my fancy than any other. I suppose it was the conduct of the dog."

"What sort of a dog was it?"

"A large handsome dog, and Todd would not let it remain in the shop, so his master made him wait outside."

"Did he name the dog?"

Tobias passed his hand across his brow several times, and then his countenance suddenly brightening up, he said —

"Hector! Yes, Hector!"

Colonel Jeffery nodded.

"What then happened, Tobias?" said Minna.

"Why, I think Todd sent me out upon some message, and when I came back the gentleman was gone, but not the dog."

"Now, Tobias, can you tell us what sort of a man the man with the dog was?"

"Yes, fresh-coloured, and good-looking rather, with hair that curled. I should know him again."

"Ah, Tobias," said the colonel, "I am afraid we shall none of us ever see him again in this world."

"Never!" said Tobias. "Todd killed him. How he did it, or what he did with the body, I know not; but he did kill him, and many more, I am certain as that I am now here. Many people came into the shop that never left it again."

"No doubt; and now, Tobias, how came you in the street by London Bridge so utterly overcome and destitute?"

"The madhouse."

"Madhouse?"

"Yes, I shall recollect it all. Where are you, mother?"

"Bless us and save us! — here, to be sure," said Mrs. Ragg.

"Did I not come to you at your room and find you ironing, and did I not tell you that I had something to say about Todd, and ask you to fetch somebody?"

"To be sure."

"Well, when you left, Todd came, and after once looking in his face, I almost forgot what happened, except that there was a madhouse and a man named Watson."

"Watson?" said Colonel Jeffery, as he made a note of the name.

"Yes," added Tobias, "and Fogg."

"Good! Fogg, I have it. Now, Tobias, where did you encounter this Fogg and Watson?"

"That I cannot tell. I recollect trees, and a large house, and rooms, and a kind of garden, and some dark and dismal cells, and then my mind seems, when I think of all those things, like some large room full of horrors, and anything comes before me just like some dreadful dream. I recollect falling, I think, from some wall, and then running at my utmost speed until I fell, and then the next thing that I remember was hearing the voice of Minna in this house."

"One thing," said Captain Rathbone, "is pretty certain, and that is, that this madhouse, if it were one in reality, must be in the immediate vicinity of London, or else the strength of Tobias would not have enabled him to run so far as to London from it."

"Mrs. Ragg, I believe Todd told you that he had placed Tobias in a madhouse, did he not?" said the colonel.

"Yes, sir, he did, the wagabone!"

"Well, I am inclined to think that it was a madhouse — one of those private dens of iniquity which are, and have been for many years, a disgrace to the jurisprudence of this country."

"If so, then," said the captain, "there will be no great difficulty in finding it with the clue that Tobias has given us respecting the names."

"I will not be satisfied until I have rooted out that den," said the colonel, "but at present all our exertions must be directed to ascertain the fate of poor Ingestrie. Every circumstance appears really to combine in favour of the opinion of Johanna Oakley, to the effect that this Thornhill and Mark Ingestrie were the same."

"It does look marvellously probable," said the captain.

"Do you recollect any more, Tobias?" said Minna.

"Not clearly, Minna, and I am afraid that what I have recollected is not very clear, but it was the dog that made an impression upon my memory. Many things are, however, now each moment crowding to my mind, and I think that I shall soon be able to recollect much more."

"Not a doubt, Tobias. Do not attempt to strain your memory too far now. Things will come back to you gently, and by degrees."

"I have no doubt of that, sir, but — but —"

"But what, Tobias?"

"Oh, sir, you are quite sure —"

"Sure of what?"

"That when I least expect it, round the curtains of my bed, or from behind some chair, or from some cupboard about twilight, I shall not see the hideous face of Sweeney Todd, and feel his eyes glancing upon me?"

Poor Tobias covered his eyes with both his hands, as he gave almost frenzied utterance to these words, and both Colonel Jeffery and his friend, the captain, looked on with aspects of deep commiseration. The former, after the pause of a few moments, to allow the renewed excitement of Tobias fully to subside, spoke to him in a kind but firm voice.

"Tobias, listen to me. Do you hear me?"

"Yes, sir — oh, yes."

"Then I have to tell you that it is impossible Sweeney Todd can now come upon you in the way you mention, or in any other way."

"Impossible, sir?"

"Yes, quite. He is now watched by the officers of justice, day and night. His house door is never lost sight of for a moment while he is within it, and when he is abroad, he is closely followed and carefully watched by men, any one of whom is more than a match for him; so be at peace upon that head, for Sweeney Todd is more securely kept now than any wild beast in his den."

———

CHAPTER LVII.

SIR RICHARD BLUNT'S ADVENTURES CONTINUED.

ALL LEFT SIR RICHARD BLUNT, NOT in a critical situation, but in what may be called an embarrassing one, inasmuch as he could not very well make up his mind what to do next. He had heard much towards her enunciation from the lips of Mrs. Lovett, and he had possessed himself of some property, which he hoped would be authenticated as having belonged to some of Todd's victims. He had likewise found out the mode of secret communication with the ovens below, but whether or not to make any further use of that information just then was a question. While he was debating these matters in his mind, he saw that his little wax light was expiring. He accordingly produced another from his pocket, and lit it, and during the process of so doing, he made up his mind to risk a descent into the regions below, so far as the iron door. He at first took his light in his hand to take it with him, but a few moments' reflection decided him to go in the dark, and placing it upon a corner of the shelf, as he had done before, he opened the cupboard, at the back of which was the secret door, and soon found himself upon the little staircase. Of course, the object of Sir Richard

Blunt was to make what discovery he could, without betraying the fact of his own presence; and, accordingly with such a design, hastened lightly as foot could fall, so that he was some few minutes in reaching the iron door, which he felt with his left hand, which he kept during his progress outstretched before him. The next object was to get the little wicket open without noise, for he recollected that Mrs. Lovett had made a sharp sound by the sudden withdrawal of a bolt that secured it on the side next to the staircase. By carefully feeling over the door, he at last lit upon this bolt, and then, by taking his time over it, he succeeded in drawing it back without creating the least sound. When this was done, the wicket yielded easily, for it had no other fastening than that bolt, and when it opened, which it did towards the stairs, the same dull reddish glare came through the small aperture that he had noticed when Mrs. Lovett was there, but he found what he had not noticed upon that occasion, namely, that when the wicket was removed there were iron bars farther securing the opening, so that it was quite clear it was intended to be a thing of strength. When, however, the magistrate found that there was nothing between him and the region of the ovens but this grating, he placed his ear close to it, in order to listen if any one was stirring. After a few moments, he heard a deep groan. Somewhat startled at this sound — for it was certainly unexpected — he tried to pierce with his eyes the obscurity of the place, but the darkness, although not absolute, was of that puzzling character that the more he looked the more all sorts of odd images seemed to be conjured up before his eyes. He began, too, to think that the groan must have been only some accidental sound that he had mistaken, but he was quickly relieved from such an opinion by hearing it again, much more distinctly and unequivocally than it had before sounded upon his ears. There was no possibility of mistaking this groan now; but while the certainty that a groan it was came upon his ears, he became only the more puzzled to account for it; and this state of feeling in him certainly arose from the difficulty he naturally had in conceiving the possibility of any one being upon the premises, and engaged in the service of Mrs. Lovett, unless they were accomplices of that lady. The idea of the captive cook was not at all likely to cross the imagination of any one, and in her revelations upon that head, during her somnambulistic tour, Mrs. Lovett had not been sufficiently explicit to enable Sir Richard Blunt to come to a different conclusion.

"I will listen for it again," he thought.

After a few moments more he was rewarded for his patience by not only hearing another groan, but a voice, in accents of the most woe-begone character, said —

"I cannot sleep. It is of no avail. Alas! who dare sleep here! God help me, for I am past all human aid."

"Who on earth can this be?" said the magistrate to himself.

"It would be better for them to kill me at once," continued the voice. "Anything would be preferable to this continued horror; but I suppose they have not suited themselves yet with some one to take my place, so I am not to be sent to see my old friends. Oh, bitter — bitter fate. I would that I were dead!"

There was a heartiness in the pronunciation of the last word, that quite convinced Sir Richard Blunt of their sincerity; but yet he thought he ought to listen to a little more before he ran the risk of falling into any trap that might be laid for him by Mrs. Lovett or her satellites, if she had any. He had not to wait long, for whoever it was that was speaking had got into a good train of groaning, and did not seem inclined to leave off for some time.

"Is she a woman, or the devil in petticoats?" said the voice.

"Humph!" thought Sir Richard Blunt, "that would be rather a hard question to answer upon oath."

"How much longer am I to bear this load of misery?" continued the voice. "No sleep — no food, but just what will sustain nature in her continued sufferings. Oh, it is most horrible. Have I been preserved from death under many adventurous and fearful circumstances, at last to die here like a rat in a hole?"

"What on earth can be the matter with this man?" thought Sir Richard.

There was a pause in the lamentations of the man now for a few seconds, during which he only groaned once or twice, just as if by way of letting any one know, who might be listening, that he was not pacified. At length, with a sudden burst of passion, he cried —

"I can bear it no longer. Death of my own seeking, and by my own choice as to method, is far preferable to this state of existence. Farewell, all — farewell to you, fair and gentle girl, whom I loved and whose falseness first gave me a pang such as the assassin's dagger could not have inflicted. Farewell, dear companions of my youth, whom I had hoped to see again!"

"Stop!" said Sir Richard Blunt.

The captive cook was still.

"Stop!" cried Sir Richard Blunt again.

"Good God! who is that?" said the voice from the region of the oven.

"Your good genius, if I save you from doing anything rash; who and what are you? Tell me all."

"To be betrayed. Ah, you are some spy of Mrs. Lovett's of course, and you only wish to draw me into conversation for my destruction."

"What were you going to do just now?"

"Take my own life."

"Well, if you find I am an enemy instead of a friend, as I profess to be, you can but carry out your intention."

"That's true."

The captive cook pronounced these two words in such a solemn tone, that the magistrate was more than ever convinced of his sincerity, and that he was

THE CAPTIVE PIEMAKER CONTEMPLATES SUICIDE.

far more a victim of Mrs. Lovett and her associate, the barber, than an accomplice.

"Speak freely," said Sir Richard. "Who and what are you?"

"I am the most unhappy wretch that ever breathed. I am cribbed and cabined and confined, I live upon raw flour and water. I curse the hour that I was born, and wish I had been a blind kitten and drowned, rather than what I am."

"But what do you do here?"

"Make numberless pies."

"Well?"

"It's all very fine for you to say well, whoever you are, but it is anything but well with me. Where are you?"

"Upon the staircase, near an iron door."

"Ah, you are at the aperture through which that abominable Mrs. Lovett issues to me her commands and her threats. If you have any compassion in your nature, and the smallest desire to hear a story that will curdle your blood, you will find out the means of opening that door, and then I will climb up to it and make one effort for freedom."

"My good friend, I am very much afraid it would materially derange my plans to do so."

"Derange your what?"

"My plans."

"And are any plans to be placed in competition with my life and liberty? Oh, human nature — human nature, what a difference there is in you when you are upon the right side of the door from what you are when you are upon the wrong."

"My friend," said Sir Richard Blunt, "that is a very philosophical remark, and I compliment you upon it. But now answer me truly one question, and for your own sake, and for the sake of justice, I beg you to answer me truly."

"What is it?"

"Are you in present fear of death?"

"No. Not while I continue to make the pies."

"Very good!"

"Very good? Now by all that's abominable, I only wish you had but to make them here for one week, and at the same time know as much as I know — I rather suspect that you would never say very good again."

"One week?"

"Yes, only a week."

"Pray how long have you been here?"

"I have lost count of the long weary days and the anxious nights. Oh, sir, be you whom you may, do not sport with me, for I am very — very wretched!"

"If I could but be sure that you are a victim of the woman who lives above," said Sir Richard.

"Sure that I am a victim? Oh, God, you suspect me of being her accomplice. Well, well, it is but natural, finding me here — I ought to expect as much. What can I say — what can I do to convince you of the contrary?"

"Reveal all."

"Do you not know then that — that —"

"That what? I may suspect much, but I know nothing."

"Then — then —"

The man's voice sunk to a husky whisper, and when he had spoken a few words there was a death-like silence between him and Sir Richard Blunt. The latter at length said —

"And you affirm this?"

"I am willing to swear to it. Release me from here and take me to any court of justice you please, and I will affirm it. If you have any suspicion of my good faith, manacle me — bind me up in iron until I tell all."

"I am convinced."

"Oh, joy, I shall look upon the blessed sun again. I shall see the green fields — I shall hear the lark sing, and drink in the odour of sweet flowers. I — I am not quite desolate."

Sir Richard Blunt could hear him sobbing like a child. The magistrate did not interrupt this burst of feeling. He was, on the contrary, quite glad to be a witness of it, for it convinced him of the sincerity of the man. He could not think it possible he should find attending upon Mrs. Lovett's ovens so consummate an actor as it would have taken to play that part. After a few moments, however, he spoke, saying —

"Now, my friend, are you one who will listen to reason in preference to merely acting upon the feelings and suggestions of the moment?"

"I hope so."

"Well, then, I think I could set you free to-night, but to do so would materially interfere with the course of that justice which is about speedily to overtake Mrs. Lovett. By remaining here you will keep things as they are for the present, and that, I assure you, is a great object. You say that while you continue making pies, your life is not in positive peril; I ask of you, for the sake of justice, to put up with your present position a short time longer."

"Liberty is sweet."

"It is, but you would not like such a woman as Mrs. Lovett to take the alarm and escape the consequences of her crimes."

"Oh! no — no. I will remain. For how long will it be?"

"I cannot say exactly, but the time may be counted by hours, and not one shall be lost. Have but a little patience, and I will come to you again. When next you hear my voice at the grating, it will be to give the signal of liberty."

"How can I thank you?"

"Never mind that. Good night, and take care of yourself. All will be well."

"Good night. Good night."

CHAPTER LVII.

BIG BEN MAKES A DISCOVERY.

At seven o'clock on the morning following these strange events, there were early prayers at St. Dunstan's, and the bells called together the devout at half-past six. Todd was there! Is the reader surprised? Has he never yet in his mundane experience met with a case of sanctimonious villany? Does he think that going to prayer is incompatible with such a life as Todd's?

Pho — pho! Live and learn.

Todd met the beadle upon the steps of the church.

"Ah, Mr. T.," said that functionary. "It does one good to see you, that it does — a deal of good. I say that, of all the tradesmen in Fleet-street, you is the piousest."

"We owe a duty to our creator," said Todd, "which all the pomps and vanities of this world ought to make us neglect."

"Have you heard o' the suicide in Norfolk-street?"

Todd shook his head.

"Why, the beadle of St. Clement's was asking of me only last night, what sort of man you was."

"I?"

"Yes, to be sure. It's a gentleman as you went to shave, and as you lent a razor to, as has cut his blessed throat in Norfolk-street."

"God bless me," said Todd, "you don't mean that? Dear! dear! We are indeed here to-day and gone to-morrow. How true it is that flesh is grass; — and so the gentleman cut his throat with my razor, did he?"

"Above a bit."

"Well, well, it is to be hoped that the Lord will be merciful to the little frailties of his creatures."

"Conwulsions! Do you call that a little frailty?"

Todd had passed on into the body of the church, and any minute observer might have noticed, that when he got there, there was a manifest and peculiar twitching of his nose, strongly resembling the evolutions of a certain ex-chancellor.*

Then, in a low tone to himself, Todd muttered —

---

* *A reference to Lord Henry Brougham (1778-1868, in office as Lord High Chancellor 1830-1834), who was jocularly referred to as "Jemmy Twitcher" because of a tic in his nose.*

"They make a great fuss about the smell in St. Dunstan's, but I don't think it is so very bad after all."

Perhaps one of Todd's notions in going to early morning prayers was to satisfy himself upon the point of the stench in the church. The morning service was very short, so that Todd got back to his shop in ample time to open it for the business of the day. He gave a glance at the window, to be quite sure that the placard announcing the want of a pious lad was there, and then with all the calmness in the world he set about sharpening his razors.

Not many minutes elapsed ere a man came in, leading by the hand a boy of about thirteen years of age.

"Mr. Todd," he said, "you want a lad."

"Yes."

"You don't know me, but I am Cork, the greengrocer in the market."

"Oh," said Todd.

"You see this is Fred, by the first Mrs. C., and the second Mrs. C. thinks he'd better go out to something now; if you will take him 'prentice we will provide him, and he can run into our place for his meals and tell us all the gossip of the shop, which will amuse Mrs. C., as she's in a delicate condition, and I have no doubt you will find him just the lad for you."

"Dear! dear!" said Todd.

"What's the matter, Mr. T.?"

"I'm so aggravated. — Is he pious?"

"Decidedly."

"Does he know his catechism and his belief?"

"Oh, yes. Only ask him, Mr. Todd. Only ask him."

"Come here, my dear boy. Who was Shindrad, the great uncle of Joshua, and why did Nebuchadnezar call him Zichophobattezer the cousin of Neozobulcoxacride?"

"Eh?" said the boy. "Lor!"

"What learning!" said the greengrocer. "Ah, Mr. Todd, you are one too many for Fred, but he knows his catechiz."

"Well," said Todd, "if the boy that I have promised to think about don't suit me, I'll give you a call, Mr. Cork. But, you see, I am such a slave to my word, that if I promise to think about anything, I go on thinking until it would astonish you how I get through it."

"Well, I'm sure we are very much obliged to you, Mr. Todd. Come along, Fred."

"Indeed!" said Todd, when he was once more alone. "That would suit me certainly. A lying, gossiping boy, to be running home three or four times a day with all the news of the shop. Good — very good indeed."

Todd stropped away at the razors with great vehemence, until he suddenly became aware that some one must be blocking up nearly the whole of the window, for a sudden darkness, like an eclipse, had stolen over the shop. We have before had occasion to remark that Todd had a kind of peephole amid the multifarious articles which blocked up his windows, so that he was enabled to look out upon the passing world when he pleased. Upon this occasion he availed himself of this mode of ascertaining who it was that had stopped the light from making its way into the shop. It was no other than our old acquaintance, Big Ben from the Tower, who was on his way to Mr. Oakley's. The heart of Ben had been sensibly touched by the distress of Johanna, and he was going to give her a word or two of comfort and encouragement, which would wholly consist of advising her to "never mind." But still Ben's intention was good, however weak might be the means by which he carried it out. As for passing Todd's window without looking in, he could no more help having a good stare, than he could help doing justice to a flagon of old ale, if it were placed before him; and upon this occasion the little placard, announcing the want of a pious youth, fixed the whole of Ben's wonder and attraction.

"A pious lad!" said Ben. "Oh, the villain. Never mind. Easy does it — easy does it."

"Curses on that fellow!" muttered Todd. "What is he staring at?"

"A pious lad!" ejaculated Ben. "Pious — oh — oh. Pious!"

"Shaved this morning, sir?" said Todd, appearing at his door with a razor in his hand. "Shaved or dressed? Polish you off surprisingly, in no time, sir."

"Eh?"

"Walk in, sir — walk in. A nice comfortable shave makes a man feel quite another thing. Pray walk in, sir. I think I have had the pleasure of seeing you before."

Ben cast an indignant look at Sweeney Todd; and then, as upon the spur of the moment — for Ben was rather a shrewd thinker — he could not find anything strong enough to say, he wisely held his peace, and walked on. Todd looked after him with a savage scowl.

"Not much plunder," he muttered, "but suitable enough in another point of view. Well — well, we shall see — we shall see."

Ben continued his course towards the city, ever and anon repeating as he went — "A pious lad! — a pious lad. Oh, the rascal."

When he reached within a few doors of the spectacle-maker's, he saw a boy with a letter in his hand looking about him, and probably seeing that Ben had a good-humoured countenance, he said to him —

"If you please, sir, can you tell me which is Mr. Oakley's?"

"Yes, to be sure. Is that letter for him?"

"No, sir, it's for Miss Oakley."

Ben laid his finger upon the side of his nose, and tried to think.

"Miss Oakley," he said. "A letter for Miss Oakley;" and then, as nothing very alarming consequent upon that proposition presented itself to him, he said, "Easy does it."

"Do you know the house, sir?" asked the boy.

"Yes, to be sure. Come along, boy."

"Yes, sir."

"Who's the letter from?"

"A gentleman, sir, as is waiting at the Unicorn, in Addle-street."

"A gentleman as is waiting at the Addle in Unicorn-street," said Ben; and then, not being able still to hit upon anything very outrageous in all that, he contented himself once more with an "Easy does it."

The boy accompanied him to the door of Mr. Oakley's, and then Ben said to him —

"I'll give the letter to Miss Oakley if you like, and if you don't like, you can wait till I send her to you. Easy does it."

"Thank you, sir," said the boy, "I'd rather give it to the young lady myself."

"Very good," said Ben. "Rise betimes, and hear early chimes."

With this effort of proverbial lore, Ben marched into the shop, where old Oakley was, with a magnifying glass fitted to his eyes, performing some extraordinary operation upon a microscope. Ben merely said "How is you?" and then passed on to the back-room, having received from the old optician a slight nod by way of a return of the friendly salutation.

Ben always esteemed it a stroke of good fortune when he found Johanna alone, which, in the present instance, he did. She rose to receive him, and placed one of her small hands in his, where for a moment or two it was completely hidden.

"All right?" said Ben.

"Yes, as usual. No news."

"I saw a boy at the door with a letter from a unicorn."

"From a what?"

"No, an addle — no. Let me see. A unicorn, waiting with a gentleman in addle something. Easy does it. That ain't it, neither. Where is she?"

Guessing that it was some one with a communication from some friend to her, Johanna had glided to the door, and got the letter from the boy. She came with it to the parlour at once, and opened it. It was from Colonel Jeffery, and ran as follows: —

DEAR MISS OAKLEY, —

If you will oblige me with another meeting in the Temple-gardens this evening, at or about six, I have something to tell you, although I am afraid nothing cheering.

Believe me to be your sincere friend,

JOHN JEFFERY.

She read it aloud to Ben, and then said —

"It is from the gentleman who, I told you, Ben, had interested himself so much in the fate of poor Mark."

"Oh, ah," said Ben. "Easy does it. Tell him, if he'd like to see the beasts at the Tower any time, only to ask for me."

"Yes, Ben."

"Well, my dear, I came by the barber's, and what do you think?"

Johanna shook her head.

"Guess again."

"Spare me, Ben. If you have any news for me, pray tell me. Do not keep me in suspense."

Ben considered a little whether what he had to say was news or not; and then taking rather an enlarged view of the word, he added —

"Yes, I have. Todd wants a pious boy."

"A what?"

"A pious boy. He's got a bill in his window to say that he wants a pious boy. What do you think of that, now? Did you ever hear of such a villain? Easy does it. And he came out, too, and wanted to 'polish me off.'"

"Oh, Ben."

"Oh, Johanna. Take things easy."

"I mean that you should be very careful indeed not to go into that man's shop. Promise me that you will never do so."

"All's right. Never be afeard, or you'd never tame the beastesses. If I was only to go into that fellow's shop and fix a eye on him so — you'd see!"

Ben fixed one of his eyes upon Johanna in such a manner, that she was glad to escape from its glare, which was quite gratifying to him (Ben), inasmuch as it was a kind of tacit acknowledgment of the extraordinary powers of his vision.

"Easy does it," he said. "All's right. Do you mean to meet this colonel?"

"Yes, Ben."

"All's right. Only take care of yourself down Fleet-street, that's all."

"I will, indeed."

"What do you say to taking me with you?"

"Where, Ben?"

"Why, where you go to meet the colonel, my dear."

"Personally, I should not entertain the smallest objection; but there is no danger in the transaction. I know that Colonel Jeffery is a man of honour, and that in meeting him upon such an occasion I am perfectly safe."

"Good again," said Ben. "Easy does it. Hilloa! what's that in the shop?"

"Only my mother come home."

"Only? The deuce! Excuse me, my dear, I must be off. Somehow or another your mother and I don't agree, you see, and ever since I had that dreadful stomach ache one night here, it gives me a twinge to see her, so I'll be off. But remember — easy does it."

CHAPTER LVIII.

THE GRAND CONSULTATION IN THE TEMPLE.

WITH THIS SAGE APHORISM, BEN effected a hasty retreat from the optician's house by the private door, so that he should not run the risk of encountering Mrs. Oakley, who had made her appearance by the shop way. When Johanna was alone, she once again read the little missive from the colonel; and then, burying her face in her hands, she tried still to think that it was possible he might have some good news to tell her. And yet, if such had been the case, would he not have written it? Would he, feeling for her as she knew he did, have kept her in a state of suspense upon such a subject? Ah, no. He would rather have, in spite of all obstacles, made his way into the shop, and called to her — "Johanna, Mark Ingestrie lives," if he had really been in a position to say so much. As these thoughts chased each other through the mind of the young girl, she shed abundance of tears; and so absorbed was she in her grief, that she was not aware that any one was present, until she felt a light touch upon her shoulder, and upon starting round suddenly, she saw her friend Arabella Wilmot standing close to her.

"Johanna?"

"Yes — yes, Arabella. I am here."

"Yes, dear Johanna. But you are weeping."

"I am — I am. To you these tears shall be no secret, Arabella. Alas! alas! You, who know my heart, know how much I have to weep for. You can bear with me. You are the only one in all the world whom I would willingly let see these bitter — bitter tears."

At those words, Johanna wept afresh, and the heart of her young friend was melted; but recovering sooner than Johanna, Arabella was able to speak somewhat composedly to her, saying —

"Have you heard anything, Johanna, new?"

"No — no. Except that Mr. Jeffery wishes to see me again to tell me something, and as he has not said in his letter what it is, I can guess it is no good news."

"Nay; is not that assuming too much?"

"No — no. I know he would, if he had had any joyous intelligence for me, have written it. He would feel of what a suspense even a few hours would be upon such a subject. No, Arabella, I feel that what he has to say is some terrible confirmation of my worst fears."

Arabella found it no easy task to combat this course of reasoning upon the part of Johanna. She felt its force, and yet she felt at the same time that it was somewhat incumbent upon her to resist it, and to make at least the endeavour to ward off the deep depression that had seized upon Johanna.

"Now listen to me," she said. "Perhaps what Colonel Jeffery has to say to you is, after all, a something hopeful; but, at the same time, being only hopeful, and nothing positive, he may have felt how difficult it was to write it, without exciting undue effects in your mind, and so prefers saying it, when he can accompany it by all the little collateral circumstances which alone can give it its proper value."

There was something like a gleam of sunshine in this idea.

"Do you understand me, dear Johanna?"

"Yes — yes."

Johanna spoke more firmly than before. The last argument of her friend had had all its weight with her, and had chased away many of the gloomy thoughts that had but a few moments before possessed her. What a strange compound is the human mind, and how singularly does it take its texture, chameleon-like, from surrounding circumstances? But a few moments since, and to Johanna the brief epistle of the colonel was suggestive of nothing but despair. How different now was its aspect? Arabella Wilmot had, by a few simple words, placed it in a new light, so that it started to the imagination of Johanna symbols of life.

"Ah! you are hoping now," said Arabella.

"I am — I am. Perhaps it is as you say, Arabella. I will think it is."

Miss Wilmot was now almost afraid that she had gone too far, and conjured up too much hope; but she could not bear the idea of dashing down again the fairy fabric of expectation she had moved in the bosom of Johanna, and merely added —

"Well, Johanna, since you find that the letter will, at all events, bear two interpretations, I am sure that, until you may be convinced it owns to the worst, you will be as composed as possible."

"I will. And now, Arabella, will you, and can you accompany me this evening to the Temple-gardens, to meet Colonel Jeffery?"

"Yes, Johanna. I both can and will, if such is your wish."

"It is, Arabella, much my wish, for I feel that if what our friend, the colonel, has to say, should not be of a hopeful character, I should never be able to repeat it to you, so as to have your opinion of it."

"Then we will go together. But we will not pass that dreadful man's shop."

"Todd's?"

"Yes."

"Why not, Arabella? I feel, the moment that I leave this house, as though some irresistible fascination dragged me there, and I think I could no more pass down Fleet-street without directing my eyes to that building, which perchance has proved fatal to poor Mark, than I could fly."

"But — but, I shrink from that man recognising us again."

"We will pass upon the other side of the way, Arabella; but do not say nay to me, for pass I must."

There was such a frantic sort of earnestness in the manner in which Johanna urged this point, that Arabella no longer made any sort of opposition to it, and the two young girls soon arranged a time of meeting, when they would proceed together to the Temple-gardens, to give Colonel Jeffery the meeting he so much desired.

AS NOTHING OF A VERY PARTICULAR CHARACTER occurred that day, we will at once follow Arabella and Johanna upon the mission, premising that the hours have slipped away which intervened between the time of Johanna receiving the note from Colonel Jeffery, and the time when, if she kept the appointment with him, it would be necessary for her to start from home to do so. Both the young girls made as great alterations in their attire as they could upon this occasion, so that they should not be strikingly recognisable again by Todd; and then Arabella reminding Johanna that the bargain between them was to pass upon the other side of the way, they both set off from the old spectacle-maker's.

As they neared Fleet-street, the agitation of Johanna became more and more apparent, and Arabella was compelled to counsel her to calmness, lest the passers-by should notice how much she felt, from some cause to them unknown.

"My dear Johanna," she said. "Your arm trembles in mine. Oh! pray be calm."

"I will — I will. Are we near?"

"Yes. Let us cross."

They reached the other side of the way from that on which Todd's shop was situated, to the great relief of Arabella, who as yet knew not of the placard that Todd had exhibited in his window, announcing the want of a pious youth. The sight of the shop, however, seemed to bring that circumstance to the mind of Johanna, and she told her young friend of it at once.

"Oh! Johanna," said Arabella, "does it not seem as though —"

She paused, and Johanna looked enquiringly at her, saying —

"What would you say, Arabella? What would you say?"

"Nothing now, Johanna. Nothing now. A thought struck me, and when we return from this meeting with your friend, the colonel, I will communicate it to you. Oh! do not look opposite. Do not."

All such injunctions were thrown away upon Johanna. Look opposite she did, and as she herself had truly said, it would have been quite impossible for her to avoid the doing so, even if the greatest personal risk had been risked in the action. But Todd's shop, to look at from the other side of the way, presented no terrors. It simply presented the idea of a little barber's shop, of no very great pretensions, but of sufficient respectability, as barber's shops were in those days, not to make any decent person shrink from going into it. No doubt, in the crowd of Fleet-street — for Fleet-street was then crowded, although not to the extent it is now — Johanna and her friend passed quite unnoticed by Todd, even if he had been looking out. At all events, they reached Temple Bar without any obstruction or adventure.

Finding, then, that they had passed the main entrance to the Temple, they went down the nearest adjacent street, and pursuing a circuitous route through some curious-looking courts, they reached their destination yet a little before the appointed hour. Colonel Jeffery, however, was not likely to keep Johanna Oakley waiting.

"There," said Arabella. "Is that the colonel?"

Johanna looked up just as the colonel approached, and lifted his hat.

"Yes, yes."

In another moment he was with them. There was a look upon the countenance of Colonel Jeffery of deep concern, and that look, at one glance that was bestowed upon it by Johanna Oakley, was quite sufficient to banish all hidden hopes that she might yet have cherished regarding the character of the news that he had to impart to her. Arabella Wilmot, too, was of the same opinion regarding the physiognomical expression of the colonel, who bowed to her profoundly.

"I have brought my dearest friend with me," said Johanna, "from whom I have no secrets."

"Nor I," said the colonel, "now that I hear she stands in such an enviable relation to you, Miss Oakley."

Arabella slightly bowed; and Johanna fixing her eyes, in which tears were glistening, upon him, said —

"You have come to tell me that I may abandon all hope?"

"No — no; Heaven forbid!"

A bright flush came over the face of the young girl, and clasping her hands, she said —

"Oh, sir, do not play with feelings that perhaps you scarcely guess at. Do not tamper with a heart so near breaking as mine. It is cruel — cruel!"

"Do I deserve such a charge," said the colonel, "even by implication?"

"No — no," said Arabella. "Recollect yourself, Johanna. You are unjust to one who has shown himself to be your friend, and a friend to him whom you hope to see again."

Johanna held out her little child-like hand to the colonel, and looking appealingly in his face, she said —

"Can you forgive me? It was not I who spoke, but it was the agony of my heart that fashioned itself at the moment into words my better judgment and my better feelings will not own. Can you forgive me?"

"Can I, Miss Oakley! Oh, do not ask me. God grant that I could make you happy."

"I thank you, sir, deeply and truly thank you; and — and — now — now —"

"Now, you would say, tell me my news."

"Yes. Oh, yes."

"Then let us walk upon this broad path, by the river, while, in the first instance, I tell you that it was only from a deep sense of duty, and a feeling that I ought not, upon any consideration, to keep anything from you, that I came here to-day to give you some more information, and yet fresh information."

"You are very — very good to me, sir."

"No — no, do not say that, Miss Oakley. I am a friend. I am only very selfish; but, in brief, the lad who was in the barber's service at the time we think Mark Ingestrie called at the shop with the string of pearls in his possession, has told us all he knows upon the subject, freely."

"Yes — yes; and — and —"

"He knows very little."

"But that little?"

"Just amounts to this: — That such a person did come to the shop, and that he is quite clear that he never left it."

"Quite clear that he never left it!" repeated Johanna — "that he never left it. Quite clear that — that —"

She burst into tears, and clung to Arabella Wilmot for support. The colonel looked inexpressibly distressed, but he did not speak. He felt that any common-place topics of consolation would have been an insult; and he had seen enough of human feelings to know that such bursts of passionate grief cannot be stemmed, but must have their course, and that such tears will flow like irresistible torrents into the ocean of eternity.

Arabella was greatly distressed. She had not expected that Johanna would have given way in such a manner, and she looked at Colonel Jeffery as though she would have said — "Is it possible that you can say nothing to calm this grief?" He shook his head, but made no reply in words. In a few moments, however, Johanna was wonderfully recovered. She was able to speak more composedly than she had done since the commencement of the interview.

"Tell me all, now," she said. "I can bear to hear it all."

"You know all, Miss Oakley. The poor boy, in whose fate I have felt

JOHANNA AND ARABELLA MEET AND CONSULT COLONEL JEFFERY, IN TEMPLE GARDEN.

sufficiently interested to take him into my care, says that such a man as Thornhill did come to his master's shop. That he (the boy) was sent out upon some trivial errand, merely to get him out of the way, and that, pending his return, the visitor disappeared. He deposes to the fact of the dog watching the door."

"The dog?"

"Yes. Thornhill, it seems, had a faithful dog with him."

"Ah, Arabella, we must have seen that dog."

"Has not the creature, then, fallen a victim to Todd's malevolence?"

"We think not, sir," said Arabella.

"Go on — go on," said Johanna; "what more?"

"The boy states that he is certain he saw the hat of the visitor with the dog in Todd's house, after Todd had declared he had left, and proceeded to the city."

"The hat — the dog. Alas! alas!"

"Nay, Miss Oakley, do not forget one thing, and that is, that neither you nor any one else have as yet identified this Mr. Thornhill as Mr. Ingestrie."

"No, not positively; but my heart tells me —"

"Ah, Miss Oakley, the heart is the slave of the feelings and of the imagination. You must not always trust to its testimony or emotions upon cold fact."

"There is yet hope, then, Johanna," said Arabella. "A bright hope for you to cling to, for, as this gentleman says, there is nothing positive to prove that Mr. Thornhill was Mark Ingestrie. I would not, were I you, abandon that hope on any account, while I lived, and could still clutch it. Would it not be a great thing, sir, if any papers or documents which this Thornhill might have had about him, could be recovered?"

"It would indeed."

Arabella at first seemed upon the point of saying something contingent upon this remark of the colonel's, or rather this acquiescence of his in her remark, but she thought better of it, and was silent, upon which Johanna spoke, saying —

"And that is really all, sir?"

"It is, Miss Oakley."

"But will nothing be done? Will no steps be taken to bring this man Todd to justice?"

"Yes, everything will be done; and indeed, anything that can be done consistently with sound policy is actually now. Sir Richard Blunt, one of the most acute, active, and personally daring of the magistrates of London, has the affair in hand, and you may be quite assured that he will pursue it with zeal."

"And what is he doing?"

"Collecting such evidence against Todd, that at a moment the law will be enabled to come upon him with a certainty that by no ingenious quibble can he escape."

Johanna shuddered.

"I thank you, sir, from my heart," she said, "for all the kindness and — and — I need not again trespass upon your time or your patience."

"Ah, Miss Oakley, will you deny me your friendship?"

"Oh, no — no."

"Then why deny me the privilege of a friend to see you sometimes. If I cannot say to you anything positively of a consoling character regarding him whom you so much regret, I can at least share your sorrows, and sympathise with your feelings."

Johanna was silent, but after a few moments she began to feel that she was acting both with harshness and injustice towards one who had been all that the kindest and most generous friend could be to her. She held out her hand to the colonel, saying —

"Yes, sir, I shall be always happy to see you."

The colonel pressed her hand in his, and then turning to Arabella Wilmot, they parted at the garden.

CHAPTER LIX.

THE PROPOSAL OF ARABELLA.

"Johanna," said Arabella Wilmot, as they passed out of the Temple by the old gate at Whitefriars, "Johanna, if there had been no Mark Ingestrie in the world, could you not have loved some one else truly?"

"No, no — oh, no."

"Not such a one as Colonel Jeffery?"

"No, Arabella, I respect and admire Colonel Jeffery. He comes fully up to all my notions of what a gentleman should be, but I cannot love him."

Arabella sighed. The two young girls passed Todd's shop upon the other side of the way, and Johanna shuddered as she did so, and repeated in a low voice —

"He went there, but he never left."

"Nay, but you should remember that was Thornhill."

"Yes, Thornhill, alias Ingestrie."

"You will cling to that idea."

"I cannot help it, Arabella. Oh, that I could solve the dreadful doubt. You speak to me of finding consolation and hope from the possibility that this Thornhill might not have been Ingestrie; but I feel, Arabella, that the agony of that constant doubt, and the pangs of never ending thought and speculation upon that subject will drive me mad. I cannot endure them — I must be resolved one way or the other. It is suspense that will kill me. I might in the course of time reconcile myself to the fact that poor Mark had gone before me to that world where we shall assuredly meet again; but the doubt as to his fate is — is indeed madness!"

There was a manner about Johanna, as she pronounced these words, that was quite alarming to Arabella. Perhaps it was this alarm which went a long way towards inducing her, Arabella, to say what she now said to Johanna —

"Have you forgotten your idea of going disguised to Todd's, Johanna? And have you forgotten what Mr. Ben, your friend from the Tower, told you?"

"What? Oh, what, Arabella — what did he tell me that I should remember?"

"Why that Todd had placed a placard in his window, stating that he wanted a boy in his shop. Oh, Johanna, it would be so romantic; and to be sure, I have read of such things. Do you think you would have courage sufficient to dress yourself again in my cousin's clothes, and go to Todd's shop?"

"Yes, yes — I understand you — and apply for the vacant situation."

"Yes, Johanna; it might, you know, afford you an opportunity of searching the place, and then, if you found nothing which could assure you of the presence at one time there of Mark Ingestrie, you would come away with a heart more at ease."

"I should — I should. He could but kill me?"

"Who? who?"

"Sweeney Todd."

"Oh, no — no, Johanna, your stay would not exceed a few short hours."

"Oh, what long hours they would be."

"Well, Johanna, I almost dread the counsel I am giving to you. It is fraught probably with a thousand mischiefs and dangers, that neither you nor I have sufficient experience to see; and now that I have said what I have, I beg of you to think no further of it, and from my heart I wish it all unsaid."

"No, Arabella, why should you wish it unsaid? It is true that the course you suggest to me is out of the ordinary way, and most romantic, but, then, are not all the circumstances connected with this sad affair far out of the ordinary course?"

"Yes, yes — and yet —"

"Arabella, I will do it."

"Oh, Johanna, Johanna — if any harm should come to you —"

"Then absolve yourself, Arabella, from all reproach upon the subject. Remember always that I go upon my own responsibility, and against your wishes, feelings, and advice. All that I now ask of you is that you will once more lend me that disguise, and assist me in further making myself look like that I would represent myself, and I shall then, perhaps, ask no more of your friendship in this world."

Arabella was horrified. The plan she had proposed had, from her course of romantic reading, such charms for her imagination, that she could not have forborne mentioning it, but, now that in earnest Johanna talked of carrying it out, she became terrified at what might be the consequences. In the open streets she was afraid of making a scene by any further opposition to Johanna, whose feelings, she saw, were in a great state of excitement; but she hoped that she would be able yet to dissuade her from her purpose when she got her home.

"Say no more now of it, Johanna, and come home with me, when we will talk it over more at large."

"I am resolved," said Johanna. "The very resolution to do something bold and definite has given me already a world of ease. I am different quite in feeling to what I was. I am sure that God is, even now, giving me strength and calmness to do this much for him who would have risked anything for me."

To reason with any one impressed with such notions would have been folly indeed, and Arabella forbore doing so at that juncture. She could not but be amazed, however, at the firmness of manner of Johanna now, in comparison with the frantic burst of grief which she had so recently been indulging in. Her step was firm, her lips were compressed, and her countenance, although more than usually pale, was expressive in every feature of highly-wrought determination.

"She will do it or die," thought Arabella, "and if anything happens to her, I shall wish myself dead likewise."

In this state of feeling — not a very amiable one — the two young girls reached the abode of Arabella Wilmot. The strongly marked feeling of composure and determination by no means left Johanna, but, if anything, seemed to be rather upon the increase, while occasionally she would mutter to herself—

"Yes — yes; I will know all — I will know the worst."

When they were alone in the little chamber of Arabella — that little chamber which had witnessed so many of the mutual confidences of those two young girls — Arabella at once began to say something that might provoke a discussion about the propriety of the hazardous expedition to Todd's, but Johanna stopped her by saying as she laid her hands gently upon her arm —

"Arabella, will you do me two favours?"

"A hundred; but —"

"Nay, hear me out, dear friend, before you say another word. The first of those favours is, that you will not, by word or look, try to dissuade me from my purpose of going in disguise to Todd's. The second is, that you will keep my secret when I do go."

"Oh! Johanna! Johanna!"

"Promise me."

"Yes. I do — I do."

"I am satisfied. And now, my own dear Arabella, let me tell you that I do not think that there is any such danger as you suppose in the expedition. In the first place, I do not think Todd will easily discover me to be aught else than what I pretend to be, and if I should see that I am in any danger, Fleet-street, with all its living population, is close at hand, and such a cry for aid as I, being, as I am, forearmed by being forewarned, could raise, would soon bring me many defenders."

Arabella sobbed.

"And then, after all, I only want to stay until, by one absence of Todd's from the house, I shall be able to make a search for some memorial of the visit of Mark Ingestrie there. If I find it not, I return to you at once better satisfied, and with better hopes than I went forth. If I do find it, I will call upon the tardy law for justice."

"Johanna — Johanna, you are not the same creature that you were!"

"I know it. I am changed. I feel that I am."

Arabella looked at the sweet childish beauty of the face before her, and her eyes filled with tears again at the thought that something near akin to despair had implanted upon it that look of unnatural calmness and determination it wore.

"You doubt me?" said Johanna.

"Oh! no — no. I feel now that you will do it, and feeling that, I likewise feel that I ought not to drive you to seek assistance from another, in your enterprise. But something must be arranged between us."

"In what respect?"

"Such as, if I should not hear of you within a certain time, I — I — "

"You would feel bound to find me some help. Be it so, Arabella. If I do not come to you or send to you, before the midnight of to-morrow, do what you will, and I shall not think that you have committed any breach of faith."

"I am content, Johanna, to abide by those conditions; and now I will say nothing to you to bend you from your purpose, but I will pray to Heaven that you may become successful, not in finding any record of Mark Ingestrie, but in procuring peace to your mind by the utter absence of such record."

"I will go now."

"No — no, Johanna. Bethink you what pain your unexplained absence would give to your father. Something must be said or done to make him feel at ease during the, perhaps, many hours that you will be absent."

"It is well thought of, Arabella. Oh! how selfish we become when overwhelmed by our own strange emotions! I had forgotten that I had a father."

It was now agreed between the two young girls that Johanna should go home, and that Arabella Wilmot should call for her, and ask Mr. Oakley's permission for her (Johanna) to come to her upon a visit for two days. It was no very unusual thing for Johanna to pass a night with her friend, so that it was thought such a course now would have the effect of quieting all anxiety on account of the absence of the young girl from her parental home.

CHAPTER LX.

A SPIRITUAL QUARTERN LOAF FOR THE HUNGRY SINNER.

"TEMPORARY INSANITY, AND A DIVIDEND of one shilling upon the razor!"

Such was the enlightened verdict of twelve sapient shopkeepers in the Strand upon John Mundell — peace to his manes! He is gone where there are no discounts — no usury laws — no unredeemed pledges, and no strings of pearls! Good day to you, John Mundell!

"Ha! Ha! Ha!" laughed Sweeney Todd. "That affair is settled in an uncommonly satisfactory manner. What an odd thing it is, though, that nobody now comes into my shop, but somebody else, upon some shuffling excuse or another, comes in within two minutes afterwards. Now, if I were superstitious, which — I — I am not —"

Here Todd looked first over his right shoulder and then over his left, with two perceptible shudders.

"If, as I say, I were superstitious which — Hilloa! who's this?"

"Oh, I beg your pardon, Mr. Todd," said a woman in widow's weeds, as she entered the shop, "but they do say that — that —"

"What?" screamed Todd, "what?"

"That you are charitable to the poor."

"Oh, that's all. I — I. That's all. Very good. I am charitable to the poor. Very — very charitable to the poor. What may your business be, madam?"

"You don't know me, Mr. Todd, I dare say, but my name is Slick."

"Slick — Slick? No, madam, I have not the pleasure of knowing you; and may I again ask why I am honoured with the visit?"

"Why, sir, I have got up a little humble petition. You see, sir, my husband, Solomon Slick, is a watch-maker, and one day, about a month ago, he went out to go to the city with two chronometers, to take to Brown, Smuggins, Bugsby, and Podd, who employ him, and he was never afterwards heard of, leaving me with six children, and one at the breast. Now, Mr. Brown is a kind sort of man, and spoke to Podd about doing something, but Bugsby and Smuggins, they will have it that my husband ran away with the watches, and that we are only watching the best time to go to him; but my aunt, Mrs. Longfinch, in Bedfordshire, will do something for us if we go there; so I am trying to get up a pound or two to take me and the little ones."

Todd made a chuckling noise, like a hen in a farm-yard, and looked the picture of compassionate commiseration.

"Dear — dear, what a shocking thing."

"It is indeed, sir."

"And have you no idea of what has become of him, madam?"

"Not in the least, sir — not in the least. But I said to myself — 'I dare say Mr. Todd will be so good as to assist us in our necessities.'"

"Certainly, madam — certainly. Do you know what is the most nourishing thing you can give to your children?"

"Alas! sir, the poor things, since their poor father went, have had little choice of one thing or another. It was he who supported them. But what is it, sir?"

"Mrs. Lovett's pies."

"Ah, sir, they had one a-piece, poor things, the very day after poor Solomon Slick disappeared. A compassionate neighbour brought them, and all the while they ate them, they thought of their father that was gone."

"Very natural, that," said Todd. "Now, Mrs. Slick, I am but a poor man, but I will give you my advice, and something more substantial. The advice is, that if anybody is moved to compassion, and bestows upon you a few pence for your children, you go and lay it out in pies at Mrs. Lovett's; and as for the more substantial something, take that, and read it at your leisure."

Todd, as he spoke, took from a drawer a religious tract, entitled "The Spiritual Quartern Loaf for the Hungry Sinner," and handed it to Mrs. Slick. The poor woman received it with a look of disappointment, and said, with a slight shudder —

"And is this all you can do, Mr. Todd?"

"All!" cried Todd. "All? Good gracious, what more do you want? Recollect, my good woman, that there is another world where the poor will have their reward, provided that in this they are not too annoying to the rich and the comfortable. Go away. Dear — dear, and this is gratitude. I must go and pray for the hardness of heart and the Egyptian darkness of the common and the lower orders in general, and you in particular, Mrs. Slick."

The woman was terrified at the extraordinary faces that Todd made during the delivery of this harangue, and hastily left the shop, having dropped the "Spiritual Quartern Loaf for the Hungry Sinner" in the doorway.

"Ha! ha!" said Todd when she was gone. "They thought of their father, did they, while they ate Lovett's pies. Ha! ha!"

At this moment a man made his appearance in the shop, and looked with a sly twinkle at Sweeney Todd. The latter started, for in that man he imagined no other than an under attendant at the establishment of Mr. Fogg, at Peckham. That this man came with some message from Fogg, he did not for a moment doubt, but what could it possibly be, since he (Todd) fully believed that Tobias Ragg was no more.

"Do you know me?" said the man.

As a general proposition, Todd did not like to say yes to anything, so he looked dubious, and remarked that he thought it might rain soon, but if he (the man) wanted a clean shave, he (Todd) would soon do for him.

"But, really, Mr. Todd, don't you know me?"

"I know nobody," said Todd.

The man chuckled with a hideous grimace, that seemed habitual to him, for he at times indulged in it, when, to all appearance, no subject whatever of hilarity was on the topic, and then he said—

"I come from Fogg."

"Fogg's, not Fogg?"

The man did not at first seem to understand this nice distinction that Todd drew between coming from Fogg's establishment and coming from Fogg himself; but after knitting his brows, and considering a little, he said—

"Oh—ah—I see. No, I don't come from Fogg, confound him, he don't use me well, so I thought I'd come to tell you—"

The shop door opened, and a stout burly-looking man made his appearance. Todd turned upon him, with a face livid with passion, as he said—

"Well, sir, what now?"

"Eh?" said the stout burly man. "Ain't this a barber's shop?"

"To be sure it is; and, once for all, do you want to be shaved, or do you not?"

"Why, what else could I come in for?"

"I don't know; but you have been here more than once—more than twice—more than thrice, and yet you have never been shaved yet."

"Well, that is a good one."

"A good what?"

"Mistake, for I have only just come to London to-day; but I'll wait while you shave this gentleman. I am in no hurry."

"No, sir," said Todd; "this gentleman is a private friend of mine, and don't come to be shaved at all."

The stout burly-looking man seemed rather confused for a moment, and then he turned to the stranger, and said—

"Are you really a private friend of Mr. Todd's?"

"Very," said the other.

"Then I scorn to interrupt any one in their confidential discourse, just because my beard happens to be a day old. No; I trust that time, and old English politeness, will ever prevent me from doing such a thing; so, Mr. Todd, I will look in upon some other occasion, if you please."

"No—no," said Todd, "sit down: business is business. Pray sit down. You don't know how disappointed I shall feel if I don't polish you off, now that you are here, sir."

"Could not think of it," said the other, in whom the reader has, no doubt, recognised one of Sir Richard Blunt's officers. "Could not for a moment think of it. Good day."

Before Todd could utter another remonstrance, he was out of the shop, and when he got about twelve paces off, he met Crotchet, who said —

"Well, what do yer bring it in now?"

"I must cut it. Todd is beginning to recollect me, and to think there is something odd going on."

Mr. Crotchet gave a slight whistle, and then said —

"Wery good; but did you leave a hindevidel in the shaving crib, to be done for?"

"Yes; but he said he was a private friend of Todd's."

"Good agin, that will do. He's safe enough, I dare say, and if he isn't, why he ought to be more petikler in a-dressing of his acquaintances. Do you know where the governor is?"

"No. I have not seen him; but will you tell him, Crotchet, why I think it's better for me to be scarce for a day or two?"

"To be sure, old fellow. You can go on some other day."

"Surely — surely."

———

CHAPTER LXI.

TODD RECEIVES SOME STARTLING INTELLIGENCE.

It took Todd, master as he was, or used to be, in the art of dissimulation, some few minutes to recover his composure, after the officer had left the shop, and during that time, the gentleman from Fogg's looked at him with the quiet sniggering kind of laugh so peculiar to him. Todd was evidently, day by day, losing that amount of nerve which had at one time formed his principal characteristic. It was getting, in fact, clear to himself that he was not near so well fitted for the business he was carrying on as he had been. Turning to the man from Fogg's, he said, while he put on as bland a smile as he could —

"Well, my friend, I suppose you have sought me with some motive? Pray speak out, and tell me what it is."

The man laughed.

"I have had a row with Fogg," he said, "and we parted in anger. I told him I would split upon the den, but he is a deep one, and he only coughed. Fogg, though, somehow don't laugh as he used. However, as well as he could laugh, he did, and, says he, 'Peter, my lad,' says he, 'if you do split upon the old den, I'll get you transported, as safe as you think yourself.'"

"Well?"

"Well. I — I — didn't like that."

"Then you are probably," said Todd in a bland manner — "you are probably aware that you may be obnoxious to the law."

"A few!" said the fellow.

"And what followed?"

"'Why, Peter,' added Fogg, 'you may leave me if you like, and once a month there will be a couple of guineas here for you. There's the door, so away, I insist;' and it has struck me, that if Fogg gives me a couple of shiners a month to hold my tongue, other gentlemen might do as much, and through one and another, I might pick up a crust and something to moisten it with."

The man laughed again. Todd nodded his head, as much as to say — "You could not have explained yourself clearer," and then he said —

"Peter, in your way you have a certain sort of genius. I might just remark, however, that after paying Fogg handsomely for what he has done, it is rather hard that Fogg's cast-off officials should come upon Fogg's best customers, and threaten them out of any more."

"I know it's hard," said the man.

"Then why do you do it?"

"Because, to my thinking, it would be a deuced sight harder for me to want anything; and besides, I might get into trouble, and be in the hands of the police, when who knows but that in some soft moment some one might get hold of me, and get it all out of me. Wouldn't that be harder still for all?"

"It would."

"Ah! Mr. Todd, I always thought you were a man of judgment, that I did."

"You do me infinite honour."

"Not at all. I say what I think, you may take your oath of that. But when I saw you come about that last boy, I said to myself — 'Mr. Todd is carrying on some nice game, but what it is I don't know. Howsomdever he is a man with something more than would go into a small tea-spoon here-abouts.'"

Mr. Peter tapped his forehead with his finger as he spoke, to intimate that he alluded to the intellectual capacity of Todd.

"You are very obliging," said Todd.

"Not at all. Not at all. How much will you stand, now?"

"I suppose, if I say the same as Mr. Fogg, you will be satisfied, Mr. Peter. Times are very bad, you know."

Peter laughed again.

"No, no! Mr. Todd, times are not very bad, but I do think what you say is very fair, and that if you stand the same as Fogg, I ought not to say one word against it."

"How charming it is," said Todd, casting his eyes up to the ceiling, as though communing with himself or some higher intelligence supposed to be in that direction. "How charming it is to feel that you are at any time transacting business with one who is so very obliging and so very reasonable."

Somehow Peter winced a little before the look of Todd. The barber had come into his proposal a little too readily. It almost looked as though he saw his way too clearly out of it again. If he had declaimed loudly, and made a great fuss about the matter, Mr. Peter would have been better pleased, but as it was he felt, he scarcely knew why, wonderfully fidgetty.

"That boy," he said, "to change the conversation. That boy, used to say some odd things of you, Mr. Todd."

"Insanity," said Todd, "is a great calamity."

"Oh, very."

"And so clouds the faculties, that the poor boy no doubt said things of me, his best friend, that, if he had been restored to reason, he would have heard spoken of with a smile of incredulity."

"Ha! ha! By the bye — Ha! ha!"

"Well, sir?" said Todd, who did not in the smallest degree join in the odd laugh of Peter. "Well, sir?"

"I was merely going to say. Have you, by any chance, heard anything more of him?"

Todd walked close to Peter, and placed his two brawny hands upon his shoulders, as he slowly repeated —

"Have I by any chance heard anything more of him? What do you mean? Speak out, or by all that's powerful, this is the last moment of your existence. Speak out, I say."

"Murder!"

"Fool! Be more explicit, and you are safe. Be open and candid with me, and not a hair of your head shall suffer injury. What do you mean by asking me if I have heard anything more of him?"

"Don't throttle me."

"Speak."

"I — I can't while you hold me so tight. I — I — can — hardly — breathe."

Todd took his hands off him, and crossing his arms over his breast, he said in tones of most unnatural calmness —

"Now speak."

"Well, Mr. Todd — I — I — only — ."

"You only what?"

"Asked you naturally enough, if you had heard anything of the boy Tobias Ragg, you know, since he ran away from Fogg's. That's all."

"Since he what?"

"Ran away from Fogg's one night."

"Then he — he is not dead? The villain Fogg sent word to me that he was dead."

"Did he though? Well I never. That was so like Fogg. Only to think now. Lord bless you, Mr. Todd, he made his escape and ran away, and we never heard anything more of him from that time to this. The idea now of Fogg telling you he was dead. Well, I did wonder at your taking the thing so easy, and never coming down to enquire about it."

"Not dead? Not dead?"

"Not as I know on."

"Curses!"

"Ah! that will do you good, Mr. Todd. Whenever I am put out, I set to swearing like a good one, and that's the way I come round again. Don't mind me. You swear as long as you like. It was a shame for Fogg not to tell you he had bolted, but I suppose he thought he'd take his chance."

"The villain!"

"Worser! worser! nor a willain!" said Peter. "Who knows now what mischief may be done, all through that boy. Why, he may be now being gammoned by the police and a parson to tell all he knows. Oh, dear! Oh, dear!"

Todd sunk upon a chair — not the shaving one — and resting his hand upon his head, he uttered a sepulchral groan.

Peter shook himself.

"You don't seem well, Mr. Todd. I didn't think you was the sort of man to be down on your blessed luck in this sort of way. Cheer up. What's the use of grieving? as the old song says."

Todd groaned again.

"And if so be as the kid," continued Peter, "did run away, my opinion is as he'd seen enough and felt enough, while he was at Fogg's, to make him as mad as a March hare."

There was hope in that suggestion, and Todd looked up.

"You really think, then, Mr. Peter, that — that his intellects —"

"His what?"

"His mind, I mean, has not withstood the shock of what he went through while he was in Fogg's establishment?"

"How could it? Once or twice things very nigh infected me, and how should he stand up agin 'em? But arter all, Mr. Fogg, what was it all about? That's what used to bother me. Was there anything in what he said, or wasn't there?"

"My good fellow," said Todd, "I have only one question to ask you —"

"Fire away."

"And that is, if you would prefer to have a sum of money down, and not trouble me any more?"

"Down!"

"Yes, down."

"On the nail? Well, it's temptatious, I own. Let me see. Thus Fogg's riglar annuity, as a fellow may call it, and a good round sum down from you, Mr. T. I think you said a good round sum down on the nail, didn't you?"

"Yes — yes. Any sum in reason."

"Done, then. I'll do it. Honour bright and shining. Mr. T., when I says a thing, it's said, and no mistake, and if I takes something down, you won't hear no more of me; whatever you may think, Mr. T., I ain't one of them fellows as will spend their tin, and then come asking for more — not I. Oh, dear no! Only give me what's reasonable down, and the thing's settled."

"Very good," said Todd, in a voice which was calm and composed. "Just step this way, into the back parlour, and I'll satisfy you. As for troubling me any more, I am, I assure you, as perfectly easy upon that point as it is at all possible to be."

CHAPTER LXII.

TODD CLEARS OFF CIRCUMSTANCES.

The arrangement come to between Todd and his visitor seemed to give equal satisfaction to both, and Mr. Peter, if he had what the phrenologists[*] call an organ of caution at all developed, must have had acquisitiveness so large as completely to overpower its action at the present time. The idea of getting from Todd's fears a sum of money at once, and from Fogg's fears a regular small annuity, was to him a most felicitous combination of circumstances, and his reflections upon the pleasant consequences resulting therefrom had such full possession of him, that his scruples vanished, and as he followed Todd into the back parlour from the shop, he muttered to himself —

"I'll try and get enough out of him to open a public-house."

Todd heard the wish, and turning quickly with what he intended should be an engaging smile, he said —

"And why not, Peter — and why not? Nothing would give me more sincere gratification than seeing you in a public-house, for although a man may be a publican, he need not be a sinner, you know."

"Eh?"

---

[*] *Phrenology was a popular pseudoscience in which a person's aptitudes and personality traits were extrapolated from the shape of the skull.*

"I say he need not be a sinner; and there would be nothing in the world, Peter, to prevent you from having prayers night and morning, and I am sure I should be most happy to come now and then, if it were only to say 'Amen!'"

"Humph!" said Peter. "You are too good, you are. Much too good, really."

"Not at all, Peter. Let us be as good as we may, we cannot be too good. Human nature is a strange compound, you know, mixed up of several things opposite to each other, like a lather in a shaving dish."

With this sentiment Todd held open the door of the sanctum behind his shop, and by a cautious wave of his hand invited Mr. Peter to enter. That gentleman did so.

"Now," said Todd, in quite a confidential tone, "what is your peculiar affection in the —"

Here Mr. Todd went through the pantomimic action of draining a glass. Peter laughed, and then shaking his head waggishly, he said —

"What a rum 'un you are! Fogg had his funny ways, but I do think you beat him, that you do. Well, if I must say I have a partiality, it's to brandy. Do you know, I think, between you and me and the post, that a drop of good brandy is rather one of them things that makes human nature what it is."

"What a just remark," said Todd.

Peter looked as sage as possible. He was getting upon wonderfully good terms with his own sagacity — a certain sign that he was losing his ordinary discretion. Todd opened a small cupboard in the wall — what a number of small cupboards in the wall Todd had — and produced a long-necked bottle and a couple of glasses. He held the bottle up to the dim light, saying —

"That's the thing, rather."

"It looks like it," said Peter.

"And it is," said Todd, "what it looks. This bottle and the liquor within it have basked in the sun of a fairer clime than ours, Peter, and the laughing glades of the sweet south have capped it in beauty."

Peter looked puzzled.

"What a learned man you are, Mr. T.," he said. "You seem to know something of everything, and I dare say the brandy is to the full as good as it looks."

This was decidedly a quiet sort of hint to decant some of it without further loss of time, and Todd at once complied. He filled Peter's glass to the brim, and his own more moderately; and as the golden liquor came out with a pleasant bubble from the bottle, Peter's eyes glistened, and he sniffed up the aroma of that pure champaign brandy with the utmost complaisance.

"Beautiful! beautiful!" he exclaimed.

"Pretty well," said Todd.

"Pretty well? It's glorious!"

Mr. Peter raised the glass to his lips, and giving a nod to Todd over the rim of it, he said —

"I looks towards you."

Todd nodded, and then, in another moment Peter put down his empty glass.

"Out and out!" he gasped. "Out and out! Ah, that is the stuff."

Todd tossed off the glass, with the toast of "A long life, and a merry one!" which was duly acknowledged by Peter, who replied —

"The same to you, Mr. T., and lots of 'em."

"It's like milk," said Todd, as he filled Peter's glass again. "It's for all the world like milk, and never can do any one any harm."

"No — no. Enough. There — stop."

Todd did stop, when the glass was within a hair's breadth of running over, but not before; and then again he helped himself, and when he set the bottle upon the table, he said —

"A biscuit?"

"Not for me. No."

"Nay. You will find it pleasant with the brandy. I have one or two here. Rather hard, perhaps, but good."

"Well, I will, then. I was afraid you would have to go out for them, that was all, Mr. T., and I wouldn't give you any trouble for the world. I only hope we shall often meet in this quiet comfortable way, Mr. T. I always did respect you, for, as I often said to Fogg, of all the customers that come here, Mr. Todd for me. He takes things in an easy way, and if he is a thundering rogue, he is at all events a clever one."

"How kind!"

"No offence, I hope, Mr. Todd?"

"Offence, my dear fellow? Oh, dear me! How could you think of such a thing? Offence, indeed! You cannot possibly offend me!"

"I'm rejoiced to hear you say so, Mr. T., I am really; and this is — this is — the — very best — ah — brandy that ever I — where are you going, Mr. T.?"

"Only to get the biscuits. They are in the cupboard behind you; but don't stir, I beg. You are not at all in the way."

"Are you sure?"

"Quite."

Todd stepped easily between Peter's chair and the wall, and opening another of the mysterious small cupboards, he laid his hand upon a hammer, with a long handle, that was upon the shelf.

"If this," said Peter, "was the last word I had to say in the world, I would swear to the goodness of the brandy."

As he uttered the words he turned his head sharply, and faced Todd. The hammer was upraised, and would, if he had not so turned, have descended with fatal effect upon the top of his head. As it was, Peter had only time to utter one shriek, when down it came upon the lower part of his face. The crush was hideous. The lower jaw fell crushed and mangled, and, with a frightful oath, Todd again raised the hammer: but the victim closed with him, and face to face they grappled. The hammer was useless, and Todd cast it from him as he felt that he required all his strength to grapple with the man who, at that moment, fastened on him with the strength of madness. Over chair — over the table, to the destruction of all that was on it, they went, coiled up in each other's embrace — dashing here and there with a vehemence that threatened destruction to them both, and yet not a word spoken. The frightful injury that Peter had received effectually prevented him from articulating, and Todd had nothing to say. Down! down they both come; but Todd is uppermost. Yes; he has got his victim upon the floor, and his knee is upon his chest! He drags him a few inches further towards the fire-place — inches were sufficient, and then grappling him by the throat, he lifts his head and dashes it against the sharp edge of an iron fender! Crash! — crash! — crash! The man is dead! Crash again! That last crash was only an injury to a corpse!

Once more Todd raised the now lax and smashed skull, but he let it go again. It fell with a heavy blow upon the floor!

"That will do," said Todd.

He slowly rose, and left his cravat in the hands of the dead man. He shook himself, and again that awful oath, which cannot be transcribed, came from his lips. Rap! rap! rap! Todd listened. What's that? Somebody in the shop? Yes, it must be — or some one wanting to come in, rather, for he had taken the precaution to make the outer door fast. Rap! rap! rap!

"I must go," said Todd. "Stop. — Let me see."

He snatched a glass from the wall, and looked at himself. There was blood upon his face. With his hand, he hastily wiped it off, and then, walking as composedly as he could into the shop, he opened the door. A man stood upon the threshold with quite a smile upon his face, as he said —

"Busy, I suppose?"

"Yes, sir," said Todd. "I was just finishing off a gentleman. Shaved or dressed, sir?"

"Shaved, if you please. But don't let me hurry you, by any means. I can wait a little."

"Thank you, sir, if you will oblige me for a moment or two. You will find some amusements, sir, from the Evening Courant, I dare say."

As he spoke, he handed the then popular newspaper to his customer, and left him. Todd took good care to close the door leading into the parlour, and then proceeding up to the body of the murdered Peter, he, with his foot, turned it over and over, until it was under the table, where it was most completely hidden by a cover that hung down to within an inch of the floor. Before Todd had got this operation well completed, he heard his shop door open. That door creaked most villanously; by so doing, while he was otherwise engaged, he could always hear if it was opened or attempted to be opened. Todd was in the shop in a moment, and saw a respectable-looking personage, dressed in rather clerical costume, who said —

"You keep powder?"

"Certainly, sir."

"Then I wish my hair powdered; but do not let me interrupt this gentleman. I can wait."

"Perhaps, sir, if you could make it convenient to look in again," said Todd, "you will probably be more amused by looking at the shops, than by waiting here while this gentleman is shaved."

"Thank you, you are very kind; but I am rather tired, and glad of the opportunity of having a rest."

"Certainly, sir. As you please. The *Courant*, sir, at your service."

"Thank you — thank you."

The clerical looking old gentleman sat down to read the *Courant*, while Todd commenced the operation of shaving his first customer. When that operation was half completed, he said —

"They report, sir, that St. Dunstan's is giving way."

"Giving way," said the clerical looking gentleman. "How do you mean about giving way?"

"Why, sir," said Todd, with an air quite of reverential respect, "they say that the old church has a leaning towards Temple Bar, and that, if you stand at the opposite side of the way, you may just see it. I can't, but they do say so."

"Bless me," said the clerical looking gentleman. "That is a very sad thing indeed, and nobody can be more sorry than I am to hear such a tale of the old church."

"Well sir, it may not be true."

"I hope not, indeed. Nothing would give me greater pain than to be assured it was true. The stench in the body of the church that so much has been said about in the parish is nothing to what you say, for who ought to put his nose into competition with his eternal welfare?"

"Who, indeed, sir! What is your opinion of that alarming stench in old St. Dunstan's?"

"I am quite at a loss to make it out."

"And so am I, sir — so am I. But begging your pardon, sir, if I am not making too free, I thought as you were probably a clergyman, sir, you might have heard something more about it than we common folks."

"No — no. Not a word. But what you say of the church having a leaning to Temple Bar is grievous."

"Well, sir, if you were to go and look, you might find out that it was no such thing, and by the time you return I shall have completely finished off this gentleman."

SWEENEY TODD BUTCHERS THE TURNKEY.

"No — no. I make no sort of doubt in the world but that you would by that time have finished off the gentleman, but as for my going to look at the old church with any idea that it had a leaning to anything but itself, I can only say that my feelings as a man and a member of the glorious establishment will not permit me."

"But, my dear sir, you might satisfy yourself that such was really not the case."

"No — no. Imagination would make me think that the church had a leaning in all sorts of directions, until at last fancy might cheat me into a belief that it actually tottered."

The clerical-looking gentleman pronounced these words with so much feeling, that the person who was being shaved nearly got cut by twisting his head round in order to see him.

"True, sir," said Todd. "Very true — very true indeed, and very just; imagination does indeed play strange freaks with us at times, I well know."

The horrible face that Todd made as he spoke ought to have opened the eyes of any one to the fact that he was saying anything but what he thought, but no one saw it. When he pleased, Todd generally took care to keep his faces to himself.

"I don't wonder, Rev. sir," he said, "that your feelings prompt you to say what you do. I'm afraid I have taken off a little too much whisker, sir."

"Oh, never mind. It will grow again," said the person who was being shaved.

Todd suddenly struck his own head with the flat of his hand, as a man will do to whose mind some sudden thought has made itself apparent, and in a voice of doubt and some alarm, he pronounced the one word —

"Powder!"

"What's the matter? You are a long time shaving me."

"Powder!" said Todd again.

"Gunpowder," said the three-quarter shaved man, while the clerical-looking personage entirely hid his face, with the *Courant.*

"No," said Todd. "Hair powder. I told this gentleman, whose feelings regarding the church do him so much honour, that I had hair powder in the house, and it has just come over me like a wet blanket that I have not a particle."

The clerical-looking gentleman quickly laid down the *Courant,* and said wildly —

"Are you sure you have none?"

"Quite sure, sir."

"Then I won't occupy your shop and read your *Courant* for nothing, and as I am here I will have a shave."

"That's very kind of you, sir," said Todd. "Very kind."

"Not at all," said the gentleman, taking up the paper again with all the coolness in the world. "Not at all. Don't mention it, I always like to carry out the moral maxim of — Do unto others as you would that others should do unto you."

"How charming!" exclaimed Todd, lifting up his hands, in one of which was the razor. "How charming it is in this indifferent and selfish age to meet with any one who is so charitable as to do more than merely speak of such a sentiment as a curiosity in morals."

"You are above your condition as regards education," said the clerical-looking gentleman.

"Why, to tell the truth, sir —"

"Psha!" said he who was being or rather not being shaved — "psha! And all this while the very soap is drying upon my face."

"A thousand pardons," said Todd.

"Many apologies," said the clerical gentleman, hastily resuming the perusal of the *Courant*.

"Sir," added Todd, as he finished the shaving and whipped off the cloth from the patient. "Sir, I should have finished you five minutes ago, so that I am sure no one would have heard the slightest complaint from you, but for the truly engaging conversation of this gentleman here, whom I shall have great pleasure now in polishing off."

"Oh, don't name it," said the shaved customer, laying down a penny. "Don't name it, I said I was in no hurry, so I can hardly blame you for taking your time."

He went through the usual operation of a partial sloush of cold water from a pewter basin, and then dried himself upon a jack towel, and left the shop.

"Now, sir," said Todd.

The clerical-looking gentleman waved his hand as though he would have said —

"For goodness sake don't interrupt me until I have finished this paragraph."

Todd fixed his eyes upon him, and began slowly stropping the razor he had been recently using.

"Now, sir, if you please."

"One moment — one — mo — ment, I shall get through the deaths in an in — stant."

Todd continued stropping the razor, when suddenly the *Courant* dropped from the hands of the clerical-looking gentleman, and he uttered a groan that made Todd start.

"Hopkins — Hopkins — Gabriel Hopkins!"

"Sir."

"Hop — kins! my friend — my councillor — my fellow student — my companion — my Mentor — my — my Hopkins."

The clerical-looking gentleman shut up his face in his hands, and rocked to and fro in an agony of grief.

"Good God, sir," cried Todd, advancing. "What is the meaning of this?"

"In that paper you will find the death of Hopkins inserted, sir. Yes, in the obituary of that paper. Gabriel Hopkins — the true — the gentle — the affectionate — the christian — Hop — kins!"

"How sorry I am, sir," said Todd. "But, pray sit in this chair, sir, a shave will compose your feelings."

"A shave! You barbarian. Do you think I could think of being shaved within two minutes of hearing of the death of the oldest and best friend I ever had in the world. No — no. Oh, Hopkins — Hop — kins!"

The Rev. gentleman in a paroxysm of grief rushed from the house, and Todd himself sunk upon the shaving chair.

"It is, it must be so," cried Todd, as his face became livid with rage and apprehension. "There is more in these coincidences than mere chance will suffice to account for. Why is it that, if I have a customer here, some one else will be sure to come in, and then after waiting until he is gone himself, leave upon some frivolous excuse? Do I stand upon a mine? Am I suspected? — am I watched? or — or more terrible, ten times more terrible question still, am — am I at length, with all my care, discovered?"

CHAPTER LXIII.

JOHANNA STARTS FOR TODD'S.

WE WILL LEAVE TODD TO THE INDULGENCE of some of the most uncomfortable reflections that ever passed through his mind, while we once again seek the sweet companionship of the fair Johanna, and her dear romantic friend, Arabella Wilmot.

The project which these two young and inexperienced girls were bent upon, was one that might well appal the stoutest heart that ever beat in human bosom. It was one which, with a more enlarged experience of the world, they would not for one moment have entertained, but by long thought and much grief upon the subject of her hopeless love, Johanna had much observed that clearness of perception that otherwise would have saved her from what to all appearance is a piece of extravagance. As for Arabella, she had originally conceived the idea from her love for the romantic, and it was only when it came near to the execution of it that she started at the possible and indeed highly probable danger of the loss to one whom she loved so sincerely as she loved Johanna.

But all that has passed away. The remonstrances have been made, and made in vain; Arabella is silenced, and nothing remains but to detail to the reader the steps by which the courageous girl sought to carry out a plan so fraught with a thousand dangers.

Both Arabella and Johanna sought the abode of the latter's father, for the first step in the affair was to say something there which was to account seemingly satisfactorily for any lengthened stay of Johanna from home. This was by no manner of means a task of any difficulty, for in addition to the old spectacle maker being innocence itself as regarded the secreting of anything in the shape of a plot, Arabella Wilmot was the very last person in all the world he would have thought capable of joining in one. As for Mrs. Oakley, she was by far too intent, as she said herself frequently, upon things which are eternal, to trouble herself much about terrestrial affairs, always except they came to her in the shape of something enticing to the appetites. What a state of things, that a mother should forget the trust that is placed in her when she is given a child, and fancy she is really propitiating the Almighty by neglecting a stewardship which He has imposed upon her! But so it is. There are, we fear, in different ways, a great many Mrs. Oakleys in the world.

"Ah, my dear Miss Wilmot," said the old spectacle-maker to Arabella, when he saw her. "How glad I am to see you. How fresh you look."

Arabella's face was flushed with excitement, and some shame that the errand she came upon was to deceive. She had not heard yet of the spurious philosophy that the end sanctifies the means.

"I have come to — to — to —"

"Yes, my dear. To stay awhile, and let us look at your pretty face. Come, my dear Johanna, your mother is out. What can you get for your friend, Miss Wilmot? Here, my dear, take this half-crown and get some sweetmeats, and I will open for you a bottle of the old Malaga wine."

Johanna's eyes filled with tears, and she was compelled to turn aside to conceal those tell-tale traces of emotion from her father. Arabella saw that if anything was to be said or done in furtherance of the affair upon which Johanna had now set her heart, she must do it or say it. Summoning all her courage, she said —

"My dear sir —"

"Sir? — sir? Bless me, my child, when did you begin to call your old kind friend sir?"

"My dear Mr. Oakley —"

"Ah, that's nearer the old way. Well, my dear Arabella, what would you say to me?"

"Will you trust Johanna with me to-night, and perhaps to-morrow night?"

"I don't think Johanna can come to much harm with you, my dear," said Mr. Oakley. "You are older than she a little, and at your age a little goes a long way, so take her, Arabella, and bring her back to me when you like."

With what a shrill of agony did Arabella hear Johanna thus committed to her care. She was compelled to grasp the back of the old spectacle-maker's chair for support.

"Yes, yes, sir," she said. "Oh, yes, Mr. Oakley."

"Well, my dears, go, and God bless you both."

To both Arabella and Johanna's perception there was something ominous about this blessing, at such a time, and yet it had really about it nothing at all unusual, for Mr. Oakley was very much in the habit of saying to them "God bless you," when they left him; but feeling, as they did, the hazard that she (Johanna) might encounter before again she heard that voice say "God bless you," if, indeed, she ever again heard it, no wonder the words sank deep into their hearts, and called up the most painful emotions. Johanna certainly could not speak. Arabella tried to laugh, to hide an emotion that would not be hidden, and only succeeded in producing an hysterical sound, that surprised Mr. Oakley.

"What's the matter, my dear?" he said.

"Oh, nothing — nothing, dear Mr. Oakley, nothing."

"Well, I'm glad to hear it. Perhaps I only fancy it; but you both seem — seem —"

"What do we seem, father?" said Johanna, looking very pale, and speaking with a great effort.

"Not quite as usual, my darling."

"That — that," gasped Johanna, "can only be — be fancy."

"Of course not," said Oakley. "Fancy, I think I said it was, or if I did not, I meant to say so, my love."

"Come," said Arabella.

"Yes — yes. Father — father. Good day."

She kissed his cheek; and then, before the old man could say another word, she rushed to the door.

"Farewell!" said Arabella. "Good day, Mr. Oakley. I — I thank you, sir. Good day, sir."

"Dear, dear," said the old man, "what is the matter with the girls? How odd they both seem to-day. What can be the cause of it? I never before saw them so strange in their manner. Ah! I have it. My wife has met them, I dare say, and has said some unkind things to them about hats or ribbons, or some harmless little piece of girlish pride. Well — well. All that will pass away. I'm glad I hit upon it, for —"

At this moment old Oakley was astounded by the sudden entrance of Johanna, who, clasping him in her arms, cried in a voice, half choked with tears —

"Good bye, father — good bye. God help me!"

Without, then, waiting for a word from the spectacle-maker, she again rushed from the shop, and joining Arabella a few doors off, they both hurried to the house of the latter. Old Oakley tottered back until he came to a seat, upon which he sank, with an air of abstraction and confusion, that threatened to last him for some time; and in that, for the present, we must leave him, while we look narrowly at the conduct of the two young creatures, who have, in the

JOHANNA'S FAREWELL OF HER FATHER PRIOR TO HER ENCOUNTER WITH TODD.

pride of their virtue and their nobleness of purpose, presumed to set up their innocence against the deep craft of such a man as Sweeney Todd. Well might Johanna say "God help me!"

"It is done!" said Johanna, as she clutched her friend by the arm. "It is done now. The worst is over."

"Oh, Johanna — Johanna —"

"Well, Arabella, why do you pause? What would you say?"

"I scarcely know, and yet I feel that it ought to be something that I have promised you. I would not say."

"Let your lips be sealed, then, dear friend; and be assured that now nothing but the visible interposition of God shall turn me from my purpose. I am calm and resolved."

These words, few as they were, were too significant, and spoken with too evident sincerity to permit a doubt of their deep intensity and truth, and from that moment Arabella Wilmot looked upon the scheme of Johanna going in disguise to Todd's as quite settled so far as regarded the attempt. It was the result now only that had to be looked to.

"I will say no more, Johanna, except as regards detail. In that I may offer you advice."

"Oh, yes — yes, Arabella. Thankfully received advice, as well you know. What is it you would say?"

"That you ought to wait until the morning."

"And so perhaps lose precious hours. Oh, no — no. Do not ask me now to submit to any delays, Arabella."

"But if there be reason, Johanna?"

"Well, the reason, then — the reason?"

"I think that, if possible, it would be well to avoid the necessity of remaining a night at Todd's; and so if you go in the morning, you see, Johanna, you may have an opportunity before nightfall of making all the discoveries you wish, or of satisfying yourself that they are not to be made at all."

"It might be so, and yet — yet I almost think night will be the best time of all."

"But by waiting until to-morrow morning, Johanna, you will have both day and night."

"Yes, yes. I wish I knew what would be the best, Arabella. My feelings are wound up to this enterprise, and I am altogether in such a frightful state of excitement concerning it, that — that I know not how I should be able to support myself under the delay of the remainder of to-day and the whole of the ensuing night."

"In the night you will have repose, and to-morrow morning, with much more calmness and effect, you will be able to start upon your errand. Believe me, Johanna, I don't counsel this delay with any hope, or wish, or expectation, that it will turn you from your purpose, but simply because I think it will the better ensure its successful termination."

"Successful! What will you call successful, Arabella?"

"Your coming back to me uninjured, Johanna."

"Ah, that speaks your love for me, while I — I love him for whose sake I am about to undergo so much, sufficiently to feel that were I sure he was no more, my own death at the hands of Sweeney Todd would be success."

"Johanna — Johanna, don't speak in such a strain. Have you no thought for me? have you no thought for your poor father, to whom, as you well know, you are the dearest tie that he has in the world? Oh, Johanna, do not be so selfish."

"Selfish?"

"Yes, it is selfish, when you know what others must suffer because they love you, to speak as though it were a thing to be desired that you should die by violence."

"Arabella, can you forgive me? can you make sufficient allowances for this poor distracted heart, to forgive its ravings?"

"I can — I do, Johanna, and in the words of your father, I am ever ready to say 'God bless you!' You will not go till to-morrow?"

After the pause of a few moments, Johanna said faintly —

"I will not — I will not."

"Oh that is much. Then at least for another night we shall enjoy our old sweet companionship."

They by this time had reached the home of Arabella, and as it was an understood thing that Johanna was not expected home, the two young girls retired to converse in unrestrained freedom upon all their hopes and fears.

CHAPTER LXIV.

TODD COMMENCES PACKING UP.

"Yes," said Todd, as he suddenly with a spring rose from the shaving-chair, upon which we left him enjoying reflections of no very pleasant character. "Yes, the game is up."

He stood for a few moments now in silence, confronting a small piece of looking glass that hung upon the wall exactly opposite to him, and it would appear that he was struck very much by the appearance of his own face, for he suddenly said —

"How old and worn I look."

No one could have looked upon the countenance of Todd for one moment without fully concurring in this opinion. In truth, he did look old and worn. But a comparatively short time has elapsed since we first presented him to the readers of this most veracious narrative. Then he was a man whose hideous ugliness was combined with such a look of cool triumphant villany, that one did not know which most to ponder upon. Now his face had lost its colour; a yellowish whiteness was the predominating tint, and his cheeks had fallen. There was a wild and an earnest restlessness about his eyes that made him look very much like some famished wolf, with a touch of hydrophobia to set him off; and certainly, take him for all in all, one would not be over anxious —

"To see his like again!" *

"Old and worn," he repeated, "and the game is up; I am decided. Off and away! is my game — off and away! — I have enough to be a prince anywhere where money is worshipped, and that of course must be the case in all civilised and religious communities. I must keep in some such. In the more savage wilds of nature man is prized for what he is, but, thank God, in highly cultivated and educated states he is only prized for what he has been. Ha! ha! If mankind had worshipped virtue, I would have been virtuous, for I love power."

A thought seemed suddenly to strike Todd; and he went into the parlour muttering to himself —

"My friend Peter must be effectually disposed of."

He raised the cover which was upon the table, and with a grunt of satisfaction, added —

"Gone! — that will do."

There was no trace of the body that he had kicked under the table. By some strange mysterious agency it had entirely disappeared, and then Todd went somehow to the back of the house and got a wet mop, by the aid of which he got rid of some stains of blood upon the floor and the fender.

"All's right," he said, "I have done some service to Fogg, and I will, when I am far enough off for any sting not to recoil upon myself, take good care that the law pays him a visit. The villain as well as the fool, to deceive me regarding the boy Tobias. What can have become of him?"

This was a question that gave Todd some uneasiness, but at length he came to the conclusion that the dreadful treatment he, Tobias, had received at the asylum had really driven him mad, and that in all human probability he had fallen or cast himself into the river, or gone into some field to die.

"Were it otherwise," he said, "I should and must have heard something of him before now."

Todd then fairly began packing up. From beneath several tables in the room he dragged out large trunks, and opening then some of the drawers and cupboards that abounded in his parlour, he began placing their valuable contents in the boxes.

"My course is simple enough," he said — "very simple; I must and will, by violence — for she is by far too wily and artful to allow me to do so by any other means — get rid of Mrs. Lovett. Then I must and will possess myself of all that she calls her share of the proceeds of business. Then, at night — the dead hour of the night — after having previously sent all my boxes full of such valuables as from their likelihood to be identified I dare not attempt to dispose of in England, to Hamburgh, I will set the whole house in a flame."

---

* *A reference to Shakespeare's* Hamlet, *Act I Scene II, in which Hamlet describes his late father to Horatio:* "He was a man; take him for all in all, I shall not look upon his like again."

The idea of burning down his house, and if possible involving a great portion of Fleet-street in the conflagration, always seemed to be delightful enough to Todd to raise his spirits a little.

"Yes," he added, with a demoniac grin. "There is no knowing what amount of mischief I may do to society at large upon that one night, besides destroying amid the roar of the flames a mass of accumulated evidence against myself that would brand my memory with horrors, and, for aught I know, cause a European search after me."

As he spoke, watches — rings — shoe buckles — brooches — silver heads of walking canes — snuff boxes, and various articles of bijouterie were placed row upon row in the box he was packing.

"Yes," he added, "I know — I feel that there is danger; I know now that I have spies upon me — that I am watched; but it is from that very circumstance that I ground my belief that as yet I am safe. They fancy there is something to find out, and they are trying to find it out. If they really knew anything, of course it would be — Todd, you are wanted."

Having placed in one of the boxes as many articles of gold and silver as made up a considerable weight, Todd lifted it at one end, and feeling satisfied that if he were to place any more metal in the box it would be too heavy for carriage, he opened a cupboard which was full of hats, and filled up the box with them. By this means he filled up the box, so that the really valuable articles within it would not shake about, and then he securely locked it.

"One," he said. "Some half-dozen of such will be sufficient to carry all that I shall think worth the taking. As for my money, that will be safest about me. Ah, I will outwit them yet, I will be off and away — only just in time. Suspicion will take a long time to ripen into certainty, and before it does, the flaming embers of this house will be making the night sky as fair and magnificent as the most golden sunset of summer."

Another box was now opened, and in that, as it was of considerable length, he began to pack swords of a valuable character. He went to the rooms above stairs, which, as the reader is already aware, contained much valuable property, and brought down troops of things, which with complacent looks he carefully placed in the chest. Ever and anon, as he went through this process, he kept muttering to himself his hopes and fears. "What is to hinder me, in some principality of Germany,* from purchasing a title which shall smother all remembrance of what I now am, and as the Baron Something, I shall commence a new life, for I am not old; no — no, I am not old — far from old, although late anxieties have made me look so. I am not so nervous and fearful of slight things as I was, although my imagination has played me some tricks of late."

Before Napoleon's conquests, Germany was made up of more than 200 individual sovereign states.

Some slight noise, that sounded as if in the house, although it was in all probability in the next one, came upon his ears, and with a howl of terror he shrunk down by the side of the box he had been packing.

"Help! mercy! What is that?"

The noise was not repeated, but for the space of about ten minutes or so, Todd was perfectly incapable of moving except a violent attack of trembling, which kept every limb in motion, and terribly distorted his countenance, if it might be called so.

"What — what was it?" he at length gasped. "I thought I heard something, nay, I am sure I heard something — a slight noise, but yet slight noises are to me awfully suggestive of something that may follow. Am I really getting superstitious now?"

He slowly rose and looked fearfully round him. All was still. True, he had heard a voice, but that was all. No consequences had resulted from it, and the fit of trembling that had seized him was passing away.

He went to the cupboard where he kept that strong stimulant that had so much excited the admiration of Peter. He did not go through the ceremony of procuring a glass, but placing the neck of the bottle to his throat, he took a draught of the contents which would have been amply sufficient to confound the faculties of any ordinary person. Upon Todd, however, it had only a sort of sedative effect, and he gradually recovered his former diabolical coolness.

"It was nothing," he said. "It was nothing. My fears and my imaginations are beginning now to play the fool with me. If there were none others, such would be sufficient warnings to me to be off and away."

He continued the packing of the box which had been temporarily suspended, but ever and anon he would pause, and lifting up one of his huge hands, placed it at his ear to listen more acutely, and when nothing in the shape of alarm reached him he would say with a tone of greater calmness and contentment —

"All is still — all is still. I shall be off and away soon — off and away!"

The dusky twilight had crept on while Todd was thus engaged, and he was thinking of going out, when he heard the creaking noise of his shop door opening. As he was but in the parlour, he made his way to the shop at once, and saw a young man, who spoke with an affected lisp, as he said —

"Mr. Todd, can you give my locks a little twirl? I'm going to a party to-night, and want to look fascinating."

"Allow me," said Todd, as he rapidly passed him and bolted the door. "I am annoyed by a drunken man, so, while I am dressing your hair, I wish to shut him out, or else I might scorch you with the tongs."

"Oh, certainly. If there's anything, do you know, Mr. Todd, that I really dislike more than another, it's a drunken man."

TODD ALARMED AT STRANGE SOUNDS WHILST PACKING HIS PLUNDER.

"There's only one thing in society," said Todd, "can come near it. — Sit here, sir."

"What's that?"

"Why, a drunken woman, sir."

"Werry good — Werry good."

Some one made an effort to enter the shop, but the bolt which Todd had shot into its place effectually resisted anything short of violence sufficient to break the door completely down.

"Mr. Todd — Mr. Todd," cried a voice.

"In a moment, sir," said Todd. "In a moment."

He darted into the parlour. There was a loud bang in the shop as though something had fallen, and then a half-stifled shriek. Todd reappeared. The shaving chair in which the young man had been sitting was empty. Todd took up his hat, and threw it into the parlour. He then unbolted the door, and admitted a man who glanced around him, and then, without a word, backed out again, looking rather pale. Todd did not hear him mutter to himself, as he reached the street —

"Sir Richard will be frantic at this. I must post off to him at once, and let him know that it was none of our faults. What an awkward affair to be sure."

CHAPTER LXV.

A MOONLIGHT VISIT TO ST. DUNSTAN'S VAULTS.

For the remainder of that day Todd was scarcely visible, so we will leave him to his occupation, which was that of packing up valuables, while we take a peep at a very solemn hour indeed at old St. Dunstan's Church. The two figures on the outside of the ancient edifice had struck with their clubs the sonorous metal, and the hour of two had been proclaimed to such of the inhabitants of the vicinity who had the misfortune to be awake to hear it. The watchman at the gate of the Temple woke up and said "past six," while another watchman, who was snugly ensconced in a box at the corner of Chancery Lane, answered that it was "four o'clock and a rainy morning." Now it was neither four o'clock nor a rainy morning — for the sky, although by no means entirely destitute of clouds, was of that speckled clearness which allows the little stars to pass out at all sorts of odd crevices, like young beauties through the jalousies of some Spanish Castle. The moon, too, had, considering all things, a pretty good time of it, for the clouds were not dense enough to hide her face, and when behind them, she only looked like some young bride, with the faint covering of bashful blonde before her radiant countenance. And at times, too, she would peep out at some break in that veil with such a blaze of silvery beauty as was dazzling to behold, and quite stopped the few passengers who were in the streets at that lone hour.

"Look," said one of four gentlemen, who were walking towards Temple Bar from the Strand. "Look! Is not that lovely?"

"Yes," said another. "A million fires are out in London now, and one can see the blue sky as it was seen when —

*'Wild in the woods the painted savage ran.'" ***

"But, after all," said another, "I prefer good broadcloth to red ochre. What say you, Sir Richard?"

"I am of your lordship's opinion," said Sir Richard Blunt, who was one of the party of four: "I certainly think we have gained something by not being Ancient Britons any longer than was absolutely necessary. This is, in truth, a most splendid night."

"It is — it is," they all said.

By this time, strolling along in an independent sort of fashion, they had reached Temple Bar, and then Sir Richard, bowing to the one who had not yet made any sort of remark, said —

"Mr. Villimay, you have not forgotten the keys?"

"Oh no, Sir Richard; oh no."

"Then, gentlemen, we are very near our place of destination. It will be advisable that we look about us, and use the utmost precaution, to be sure that we are not watched by any one."

"Yes — yes," said the other. "You will be the best judge of that Sir Richard; with your tact, you will be able to come to a conclusion upon that subject much better than we can."

Sir Richard Blunt made a slight kind of bow in acknowledgment of the compliment to his tact, and then, while what we may call the main body waited under the arch of Temple Bar, he advanced alone into Fleet-street. After advancing for a short distance, he took from his pocket a small silver whistle, and produced upon it a peculiar thrilling note. In a moment a tall man, with a great coat on him, merged from behind a column that lent its support to a door-way.

"Here you is," said the man.

"Is all right, Crotchet?" said Sir Richard.

"Yes; everything is quiet enough. Not a blessed mouse hasn't wagged his tail or smoothened his whiskers for the last half hour or so."

"Very good, Crotchet. I'm afraid, though, I cannot dismiss you just yet, as the business is very important."

"What's the odds," said Crotchet, "as long as you are happy?"

Sir Richard Blunt smiled, as he added —

"Well, Crotchet, you deserve, and you shall have an ample reward for the

---

* Probably a reference to John Dryden's 1672 play. The Conquest of Granada: *"I am as free as Nature first made man/ Ere the base laws of servitude began/ When wild in the woods the noble savage ran."*

services you are doing and have done, in this affair. I and some gentlemen will go into the church, and I wish you to remain at the porch, and if you find occasion to give any warning, I think your whistle will be quite shrill enough to reach my ears."

"Not a doubt on it, Sir Richard. If what they calls the last trumpet is only half as loud as my last whistle, it will wake up the coves, and no mistake."

"Very good, Crotchet. Only don't make any profane allusions in the hearing of the gentlemen with me, for one of them is the Under Secretary of State, and the other two are men of account. We have to meet some one else in the church."

"Then he hasn't come."

"That's awkward. The Lord Mayor was to meet us. Ah! who is this?"

A private carriage stopped on the other side of the way, and some one alighted, and a voice cried —

"Go home now, Samuel, and put up the horses. I shall not want you any more to-night. Go home."

"Shan't we call anywhere for you, my lord?" said Samuel, the coachman.

"No — no, I say. Go away at once."

"That's the Lord Mayor," said Sir Richard. "He is pretty true to his time."

As he spoke, Sir Richard crossed the road, and addressed the chief magistrate of the city, saying —

"A fine night, my lord."

"Oh, Sir Richard, is that you? Well, I am very glad to meet with you so soon. If I were to tell you the difficulty I have had to get here, you would not believe me. Indeed you could not."

"Really, my lord."

"Yes. You must know, Sir Richard, between you and I, and — and" — Here the Lord Mayor, who did not like to say post, looked about him, and his eyes falling upon Temple Bar, added — "Bar, I say; between you and me and the Bar, the Lady Mayoress, although a most excellent woman — indeed I may say an admirable woman — has at times her little faults of temper. You understand?"

"Who is without?" said Sir Richard.

"Ah, who indeed — who indeed, Sir Richard. That is a very sensible remark of yours. Who is without? as you justly enough say."

"The Lord Mayor!" said Sir Richard, who had been gradually leading his lordship to Temple Bar, and now announced his arrival to the three gentlemen who were there in waiting.

The three gentlemen professed themselves to be quite delighted to see the Lord Mayor, and the Lord Mayor professed to be quite in raptures to see the three gentlemen, so that a pleasanter party than they all made, could not have been imagined.

"Now," said Sir Richard Blunt, "I think, with all deference, gentlemen, that the sooner we proceed to business the better."

"Yes, yes," said Mr. Villimay, who was the senior churchwarden. "Oh, yes — certainly."

"And yet," said the Lord Mayor, "we must be very cautious."

"Oh, very — very cautious," cried Villimay.

"But a bold front is the best," remarked Sir Richard.

"Yes. As you say, sir, there's nothing like a bold front," cried Villimay.

Sir Richard, with a quiet smile, said to the under secretary —

"A very obliging person, you perceive, Mr. Villimay is."

"Oh, very," laughed the secretary.

Preceded now by the churchwarden, they all made their way towards the church, but the watchman at the corner of Chancery Lane must have had something upon his mind, he was so very wakeful, for after they had all passed but Crotchet, he looked out of his box, and said — "Thieves!"

"What's that to you?" said Crotchet, facing him with a look of defiance, "eh? Can't you be quiet when you is told?"

"Murder!" said the watchman, as he began to fumble for his rattle.

"Hark ye, old pump," said Crotchet. "I've settled eight watchmen atween this here and Charing Cross, and you'll make nine, if you opens your mouth again."

The appalled watchman shrank back into his box.

"Eight, did you say?"

"Yes."

Crotchet took the lantern off its hook in front of the box, and smashed it upon the head of the guardian of the night, whereupon the aforesaid guardian shrank completely down to the bottom of the box, with the fragments of the lantern hanging about him, and said not another word.

"I rather think," said Mr. Crotchet to himself, "as I've settled that old fellow comfortable."

With this conviction upon his mind — the amiability or the non-amiability of which we shall not stop to discuss — Mr. Crotchet ran hastily after the rest of the party, and stationed himself by the church porch, according to orders. By this time, Mr. Villimay, the churchwarden, had produced a little gothic-looking key, and proceeding to a small side door, he, after some rattling, partly consequent upon the lock being in a state of desuetude, and partly from personal nervousness, he did succeed in turning the rusty wards, and then, with an ominous groan, the door yielded. Sir Richard Blunt had quite satisfied himself that there were no eaves-droppers at hand, so he was anxious to get the party housed — perhaps in this instance "churched" would be a more appropriate expression.

"Gentlemen," he said, "the night is stealing past, and we have much to do."

"That is true, Sir Richard," said the secretary. "Come on, Donkin, and let us get through it."

The Lord Mayor shook a little as he passed through the little door, last, having, although king of the city, given the pass to every one of his companions, upon that most mysterious mission to old St. Dunstan's church at such an hour. Perhaps he had a faint hope that they might leave him entirely behind, and shut the door precipitately, so that he could not get in. If he had any such hope, however, it was doomed, like too many human hopes, to bitter disappointment, for Sir Richard Blunt held the door open for him, saying blandly —

"Now, my lord. We could not get on without you."

"Oh, thank you — thank you. You are very good."

The Lord Mayor crossed the threshold, and then Mr. Villimay, who had occupied a remote and mysterious position at the back of the door, closed it, and locked it on the inside.

"If — if you were to lose the key, Mr. Villimay?" said the Lord Mayor.

"Why, then," interposed Sir Richard Blunt, "I'm afraid we should have to stay there until Sunday, unless some couple kindly got married in the meantime."

The Lord Mayor gave a very odd kind of cough, as he said —

"What would the Lady Mayoress say?"

The air without had been cold, but what was that compared with the coldness within? At least, the street breeze had been dry, but in the church there was such a fearful dampness pervading the narrow passage in which the party found itself, that every one felt as though his very marrow was cold.

"This passage," said Mr. Villimay, "hasn't been opened for many a long day."

"Indeed!" said the secretary.

"No, my lord, it has not: and it's only a wonder that, after a good hunt in the vestry cupboard, I at all found the key of it."

"Fortunate that you did," said Sir Richard Blunt, who was all this time making exertions to procure a light, which were as often defeated by the dampness of the air. At length he was successful in igniting a piece of wax candle, and he said —

"Gentlemen, this will show us our way through the church to the vestry, where we can get lanthorns."

"Yes," said the Lord Mayor, who was getting so nervous that he thought himself called upon to make some reply to anything and anybody. "Yes, lanthorns in the vestry."

"Well," said the secretary, "my Lord Mayor, your mayoralty will be distinguished by this dreadful affair for all time to come."

"Many thanks to your lordship, it will."

The secretary smiled as he whispered to his friend Donkin —

"The city magistrate don't seem happy, Donkin."

"Far from it."

At the end of the little narrow, damp, gloomy, cobwebby passage in which they were, was another little door, the upper half of which was of highly ornamented iron fret work, the side of which next to the church interior being gilt. This door likewise yielded to a key which Mr. Villimay produced, and then they found themselves at once in the western aisle of the church.

"The stench don't seem so bad," said Sir Richard.

"No, sir," said Villimay. "We have got all the windows open far up above there, and there's quite a current of air, too, right up the belfry."

CHAPTER LXVI.

THE COOK'S VISITORS.

SIR RICHARD SHADED WITH HIS HAND the little light that he carried as he walked solemnly across the nave towards the chancel, where the vestry room was situated. He was followed closely by the whole party, and the audible breathing of the Lord Mayor sufficiently proclaimed the uneasy state of his lordship's nerves.

"How strange it is," said the secretary, "that men will pile up stones and timber until they make something to enter, which then terrifies their weak natures, and they become the slaves of the very materials that they have made to enclose and roof in a certain space upon which otherwise they would stand unmoved."

"It is so," said Donkin.

"Why the fact is, I suppose," said Sir Richard Blunt, "that it is what is called original sin that sticks to us, and so —

'Conscience doth make cowards of us all!' *

— whether we are personally or not obnoxious to the pangs of the still small voice."

"Upon my word, Sir Richard," said the secretary, "you are quite a free-thinker — indeed you are."

---

* *A line from Shakespeare's* Hamlet.*, Act III Scene I, from the "To be or not to be" soliloquy, meaning that awareness of guilt causes us to fear death.*

Suddenly the whole party paused, for something resembling a moan was heard from among the pews in the centre of the church, and every one was anxious to listen for a repetition of the sound.

"Did you hear it?" whispered the secretary.

"In faith, I did," said Mr. Donkin.

"And I," said Sir Richard Blunt.

"And we," said the Lord Mayor, in defiance of grammar. "I — I — feel rather unwell, gentlemen, do you know."

"Hush! let us listen," said the secretary.

They all stood profoundly still for a few minutes, and then, just as they were one and all beginning to think that after all it must be a mere thing of fancy, the same mournful moan came once more upon their ears.

"There can be no mistake," said Sir Richard. "We all hear that; is it not so, gentlemen?"

"Yes — yes!" said everybody.

"I'm getting worser," said the Lord Mayor.

"This mystery must be cleared up," said the secretary. "Is it a trick upon us, do you think, Sir Richard?"

"No, my lord, certainly not."

"Then we cannot go on until this is cleared up. You are armed, of course, Sir Richard?"

"Yes, my lord."

Sir Richard Blunt took from his pocket a double-barrelled pistol. There was now a sort of pause, as though each of those present expected the others to say or to do something which should have the effect of discovering what the singular noise portended. Of course, Sir Richard Blunt felt that in such an emergency he would be the man naturally looked to.

"It is absolutely necessary," he said, "that we should find out what this means before proceeding farther."

"Yes, yes," said the Lord Mayor, "no doubt of it; and in the meantime I'll run to the Mansion House and get some assistance, gentlemen."

"Oh, no, my lord — oh, no," said the secretary to the chief magistrate of the city. "We cannot think of sparing you."

"But — but —"

"Certainly not," said Sir Richard Blunt, who was keenly alive to the tone of irony in which the secretary spoke. "Certainly not; and as I fancy the sound which has excited our curiosity comes from about the centre of the pews, you and I, my lord, will go and find out who it is. Come, if you please, at once."

"I — I —" stammered the Lord Mayor, "I really — humph! If I felt quite well, do you know, Sir Richard, I should not hesitate a moment."

"Pho! pho!" said Sir Richard, taking his arm, and leading him unwillingly forward. "Remember that the eyes of those are upon you whose opinions are to you of importance."

With a groan the unfortunate Lord Mayor, who from the first had shrunk from the enterprise altogether, being fearful that it might possibly involve dangerous consequences, allowed himself to be dragged by Sir Richard Blunt in the direction of the pews.

"If you have a pistol," said the magistrate, "you had better keep it in your hand ready for service."

"Lord bless you," said the Lord Mayor, in a nervous whisper, "I never fired off a pistol in all my life."

"Is that possible?"

"I don't know about being possible, but it's true."

"Well, you do surprise me."

"So — so you see, Sir Richard," added his temporary lordship, suddenly popping into the churchwarden's pew, which they had just reached — "so I'll stay here and keep an eye upon you."

Sir Richard Blunt was not at all sorry to get rid of such a companion as the Lord Mayor, so with a cough, he left him in the pew, and went forward alone, determined to find out what it was that made the extraordinary noise. As he went forward, towards the spot from whence it had come, he heard it once again, and in such close proximity to him, that albeit, unaccustomed to allow anything to affect his nerves, he started back a pace. Shading, then, the little bit of wax candle that he had in his hand, he looked steadily in the direction of the low moaning sound.

In an instant he found a solution of the mystery. A couple of pigeons stood upon the hand rail of one of the pews, and it was the peculiar sound made by these birds, that, by the aid of echo in the silent empty church, had seemed to be of a very different character from its ordinary one.

"And from such simple causes," said Sir Richard, "arise all the well-authenticated stories of superstition which fancy and cowardice give credence to."

He looked up, and saw that in the wish to ventilate the church, the windows had been liberally opened, which had afforded the means of ingress to the pigeons, who, no doubt, would have slumbered soundly enough until morning, if not disturbed by the arrival of the party at the church.

As Sir Richard Blunt retraced his steps, he passed the pew where the Lord Mayor was; and willing to punish that functionary for his cowardice, he said, in a well-affected voice of alarm —

"Gracious Heaven! what will become of us?"

With a groan, the Lord Mayor flopped down to the floor of the pew, and there he lay, crouching under one of the seats in such an agony of terror, that Sir Richard felt certain he and the others would be able to transact all the business they came about, before he would venture to move from that place of concealment. The magistrate speedily informed the rest of the party what was the cause of the alarm, and likewise hinted the position of the Lord Mayor, upon which the secretary said —

"Let him be. Of course, as a matter of courtesy, I was obliged to write to him upon the subject; but we are as well, and perhaps better without him."

"I am of the same opinion," said Sir Richard.

They now went at once to the vestry, and two good lanterns were then procured, and lit. The magistrate at once led the way to the stone that had been raised by the workmen, in the floor of the church, and which had never been effectually fastened down again. In a corner, where no one was likely to look, Sir Richard placed his hand for a crow-bar which he knew to be there, and, having found it, he quickly raised the stone on one side. The other gentlemen lent their assistance, and it was turned fairly over, having exposed the steps that led down to the vaults of old St. Dunstan's church.

"Let us descend at once," said the secretary, who, to tell the truth, in the whole affair, showed no lack of personal courage.

"Allow me to precede you, gentlemen," said Sir Richard Blunt; "and you, Mr. Villimay, will, perhaps, bring up the rear."

"Yes, oh, yes," said the churchwarden, with some degree of nervousness, but he was quite a hero compared to the Lord Mayor.

Sir Richard handed one of the lanterns, then, to Mr. Villimay, and took the other himself. Without another moment's delay, then, he began the descent. They could all, as they went, feel conscious that there was certainly a most unearthly smell in the vaults — a smell which, considering the number of years that had elapsed since any interments had taken place in them, was perfectly unaccountable. As they proceeded, this stench became more and more sickening, and the secretary said, as he held a handkerchief to his mouth and nose —

"The Bishop of London spoke to me of this, but I really thought he was exaggerating."

"It would be difficult to do that," said Sir Richard. "It is as bad almost as it can very well be, and the measures taken for the purpose of ventilation, have not as yet had a very great effect upon it."

"I should say not."

With tolerable speed the magistrate led the party on through a vast number of vaults, and through several narrow and rather tortuous passages, after which he came to an iron door. It was locked, but placing the lantern for a few moments upon the floor, he soon succeeded in opening it with a skeleton key. The moment he had done so, the secretary exclaimed —

"Hey day! This is something different."

"In what respect, my lord?"

"Why, if my senses don't deceive me, the horrible charnel-house smell, which we have been enduring for some time past, has given way to one much more grateful."

"What is it like, my lord?"

"Well, I should say some delicious cooking was going on."

"You are right. There is cooking going on. We are not very far from Mrs. Lovett's pie manufactory."

"Indeed!"

"Yes; and the smell, or rather I ought to say the odour of which the air is full, comes from the bakehouse."

The secretary gave a perceptible shudder, and Mr. Villimay uttered a groan. The gentleman who was with the secretary was about to say something, but the magistrate, in a low voice, interrupted him, saying —

"Pardon me, but now we are in close proximity to the place of our destination, I would recommend the profoundest caution and silence."

"Certainly — certainly. We will only be silent spectators."

"It is better, I think," added Sir Richard Blunt, "to allow me to carry on the whole of the conversation that is to ensue; and at the same time, any of you gentlemen can suggest to me a question to ask, and I will at once put it to the man we come to speak to."

"That will do, Sir Richard, that will do."

The magistrate now hurried on as though those savoury steams that scented the air from the bakehouse of Mrs. Lovett's pies were to him more disagreeable than the horrible smell in the vaults that made everybody shake again. In a few minutes he arrived at a room, for it could not be called a vault. It had a floor of rough stone flags, which seemed as though they had originally belonged to some of the vaults, and had been pulled up and carried to this place to make a rude flooring. There was nothing very remarkable about the walls of this place, save at one part, and there there was evidently a door, across which was placed a heavy iron bar.

"It is through there," said Sir Richard.

"But — but you do not intend to open it?"

"Certainly not. There is a small crevice through which there will be no difficulty in maintaining a conversation with the imprisoned cook, if I can only make him hear me from this spot."

CHAPTER LXVII.

THE REVELATIONS IN THE VAULTS.

THE OBJECT OF SIR RICHARD BLUNT WAS, of course, to make the cook hear him, but no one else. With this aim he took a crown-piece from his pocket and tapped with the edge of it upon the stone-work which at that place protruded from the wall to the extent of nearly a foot. The stone shelves upon the other side were let into the wall in that fashion. The monotonous ringing sound of the coin against the stone was likely enough to reverberate through the wall, and that the cook was rather a light sleeper, or did not sleep at all, was soon sufficiently manifest, for a voice, which the magistrate recognised as his, cried from the other side —

"Who is there? If a friend, speak quickly, for God knows I have need of such. If an enemy, your utmost malice cannot make my situation worse than it is."

Sir Richard placed his mouth close to a crevice, and said —

"A friend, and the same who has spoken to you before."

"Ah! I know that voice. Do you bring me freedom?"

"Soon. But I have much to ask of you."

"Let me look at the daylight, and then ask what you will, I shall not tire of answering."

"Nay, the principal thing I have to ask of you is yet a little more patience."

"Patience! patience! It seems that I have been years in this place, and yet you ask me to have more patience. Oh, blessed liberty, am I not to hail you yet?"

"Can you forget that you have another object — namely, to bring to the just punishment of the law those who have placed you and others in this awful position?"

"Yes — yes. But —"

"But you would forego all that to be free, a few short hours before you would be free with the accomplishment of all that justice and society required?"

"No — no. God help me! I will have patience. What is it that you demand of me now? Speak."

"Your name?"

"Alas! — alas!"

"Surely you cannot hesitate to tell one, who has run some risks to befriend you, who you are?"

"If, by my telling that, I saw that those risks were made less, I would not hesitate; but, as it is, London, and all that it contains now, is so hateful to me, that I shall leave it the instant I can. Falsehood, where I most expected truth, has sunk deeply, like a barbed arrow, into my heart."

"Well, I certainly had hoped you would have placed in me that amount of confidence."

"No. I dare not."

"Dare not?"

"Yes, that is the word. The knowledge of my name spread abroad — that is to say, my real name, would inflict much misery for all, I can just now say to the contrary, upon one whom I yet wish all the happiness that God can give his creatures in this world. Let it be thought that I and the world have parted company."

"You are a strange man."

"I am. But the story I have to tell of the doings in this den of infamy, will come as well from a Mr. Smith as from any one else."

"I wish you now, in a few words, to relate to me what you know, fully and freely."

"Anticipating that a statement would be wanted, I have, with no small amount of trouble, manufactured for myself pens and ink, and have written all that I have to say. How can I give you the document?"

"There is a chink here in the wall, through which I am addressing you. Can you pass it through?"

"I will try. I see the chink now for the first time since my long and painful residence here. Your light upon the other side has made it quite apparent to me. I think, by folding my paper close, I can pass it through to you."

"Try it."

In about half a minute Sir Richard Blunt got hold of a piece of folded paper, which was pushed partly through the chink. He pulled it quite through, and handed it to the secretary, who, with a nod, at once put it in his pocket.

"And now for how long," said the cook, "am I to pine for freedom from this dreadful place? Recollect that each hour here has upon its passing wings a load of anxieties and miseries, such as I only can appreciate."

"I have brought a letter for you," said Sir Richard, "which will contain all the intelligence you wish, and give you such instructions as shall not only ensure your safety, but enable you to aid materially in bringing your persecutors to justice. Place your hand to the crevice and take it."

"I have it."

"Well, read it at your leisure. Have you any means of knowing the time of day in your prison?"

"Oh yes. There is a clock in the bakehouse, by which I am forced to regulate the different batches of pies."

"That will do. Have you had any more threats from Mrs. Lovett?"

"None. As long as I perform my loathsome duty here, I see no one and hear of no one."

"Be of good cheer, your desolate condition will not last long. It is not easy under present circumstances to enter at large into matters which might induce you to declare who you really are, but when you and I meet in the bright sunshine from which you have been debarred for so long, you will think very differently from what you do now upon many things."

"Well, sir, perhaps I shall."

"Good night to you. Take what rest and refreshment you can, my good friend, and believe that there are better days in store for you."

"I will strive to think so. — Good night."

There was such a mournful cadence in the voice of the imprisoned young man, as he said "Good night," that the secretary remarked in a low voice to Sir Richard —

"Would it not be a mercy now to let him free, and take him away with us?"

"I don't like his concealing his name, my lord."

"Well, it is not the thing exactly."

"His imprisonment now will be of very short duration indeed, and his liberation is certain, unless by some glaring act of imprudence he mars his own fortune. But now, gentlemen, I have a sight to show you in these vaults that you have come to see, and yet, that I think it would have been wise if you had left unseen."

"Indeed!"

"Yes. You will soon agree with me in opinion."

Sir Richard, bearing the lantern in his hand, led the way for a considerable distance back again, until they were fairly under the church, and then he said —

"A large vault belonging to a family named Weston, which is extinct I fancy, for we can find no one to claim it, has been opened near this spot."

"By whom?"

"That you will have no difficulty in guessing. It is that vault that I wish to show you. There are others in the same condition, but one will be enough to satiate your appetites for such sights. This way, gentlemen, if you please."

As the light from the two lanterns fell upon the faces of Sir Richard Blunt's companions, curiosity and excitement could be seen paramount upon their features. They followed him as their guide without a word, but they could not but see that he trod slowly, and that now and then a shudder crossed his frame.

"Even you are affected," said the secretary, when the silence had lasted some minutes.

"I were something more or less than human," replied Sir Richard Blunt "if I could go unmoved into the presence of that sight, that I feel it to be my duty to show to you."

"It must be horrible indeed."

"It is more horrible than all the horrors your imagination can suggest. Let us go quicker."

Apparently with a desperate feeling of resolution, such as might actuate a man who had some great danger to encounter, and who after shrinking from it for a time, should cry "Well, the sooner it is over the better," did the magistrate now quicken his steps, nor paused he until he arrived at the door of the vault of which he had spoken.

"Now, Mr. Villimay," he said. "Be so good as to hold up your lantern as high as you can, at the same time not to get it above the doorway, and I will do the same by mine. All that we want is a brief but clear view."

"Yes, yes. Quite brief," said the secretary.

Sir Richard Blunt laid his hand upon the door of the vault, which was unfastened, and flung it open.

"Behold!" he said, "one of the vaults of old St. Dunstan's."

For the space of about a minute and a half no one uttered a word, so it behoves us to state what that vault contained, to strike such horror into the hearts of bold educated men. Piled one upon each other on the floor, and reaching half way up to the ceiling lay, a decomposing mass of human remains. Heaped up one upon another, heedlessly tossed into the disgusting heap any way, lay the gaunt skeletons with pieces of flesh here and there only adhering to the bones. A steam — a foetid steam rose up from the dead, and upon the floor was a pool of corruption, creeping along as the declivities warranted. Eyes, teeth, hands half denuded of flesh — glistening vermin, shiny and sleek with the luxurious feeding they there got, slipped glibly in and out of the heaped-up horror.

"No more — no more!" cried the secretary.

"I sicken," said his friend, "I am faint."

Sir Richard Blunt let go the door, and it slammed shut with a hollow sound.

"Thank God!" he said.

"For — for what?" gasped Mr. Villimay.

"That you and I, my friend, need not look upon this sight again. We are all sufficient evidence upon our oaths that it is here to see."

"Yes — yes."

"Come away," said the secretary. "You told me something of what was to see, Sir Richard Blunt, but my imagination did not picture it to be what it is."

"I told you that likewise, my lord."

"You did — you did."

With hurried steps they now followed the magistrate; and it was with a feeling of exquisite relief that they all found themselves, after a few minutes, fairly in the body of the church, and some distance from that frightful spectacle

TODD'S VICTIMS IN THE VAULTS OF OLD ST. DUNSTAN'S CHURCH.

they had each thought it to be their duty to look upon.

"Let us go to the vestry," said the secretary, "and take something. I am sick at heart and stomach both."

"And I am everything, and hungry too," cried a voice, and the Lord Mayor popped his head up from the churchwardens' pew.

No one could help laughing at this, although, to tell the truth, those men, after what they had seen, were in no laughing mood, as the reader may well imagine.

"Is that our friend, the King of the City?" said the secretary.

"It is," said Sir Richard.

"Well, I must say that he has set a good example of bravery in his dominions."

"He has indeed."

"Gentlemen — gentlemen," added the Lord Mayor, as he rolled out of the churchwardens' pew, "don't think of going into the vestry without me, for it was I who gave a hint to have refreshments put there, and I have been dying for some of them for this last half-hour, I assure you."

CHAPTER LXVIII.

RETURNS TO JOHANNA.

WE RETURN to Johanna Oakley.

"WHAT IS THE MEANING OF ALL THIS?" SAID Sweeney Todd, as he sat in his shop about the hour of twelve on the morning following that upon which Johanna Oakley and her friend Arabella had concerted so romantic a plan of operations regarding him. "What is the meaning of all this? Am I going mad?"

Now Todd's question was no doubt a result of some peculiar sensations that had come over him; but, propounded as it was to silence and to vacancy, it of course got no answer. A cold perspiration had suddenly broke out upon his brow, and, for the space of about ten minutes, he was subject to one of those strange foreshadowings of coming ills to him, which of late had begun to make his waking hours anything but joyous, and his dreams hideous.

"What can it mean?" he said. "What can it mean?"

He wiped his face with a miserable looking handkerchief, and then, with a deep sigh, he said — "It is that fiend in the shape of a woman!"

No doubt he meant his dear friend, Mrs. Lovett. Alas! what a thorn she was in the side of Sweeney Todd. How poor a thing, by way of recompense for the dark and terrible suspicions he had of her, was his heaped up wealth? Todd — yes, Sweeney Todd, who had waded knee-deep — knee-deep do we say? — lip-deep in blood for gold, had begun to find that there was something more precious still which he had bartered for it — peace! That peace of mind — that sweet serenity of soul, which, like the love of God, is beautiful, and yet passeth understanding. Yes, Todd was beginning to find out that he had bartered the jewel for the setting! What a common mistake. Does not all the world do it? They do; but the difference between Todd and common people merely was that he played the game with high stakes.

"Yes," added Todd, after a pause, "curses on her, it is that fiend in the shape of a woman, who —

'*Cows my better part of man,*' *

— and she or I must fall. That is settled; yes — she or I. There was a time when I used to say she and I could not live in the same country; but now I feel that we cannot both live in the same world. She must go — she must lapse into the sleep of death."

Todd rose, and stalked to and fro in his shop. He felt as if something was going to happen: that undefinable fidgetty feeling which will attack all persons at times, came over him, and yet it was not a feeling of deep apprehension that was at his heart.

"Oh," he muttered, "it is the recollection of that dreadful woman — that fiend, who, with a seeming prescience, knows when there is poison in her glass, and baffles me. It is the dim and shadowy thought of what I must do with her that shatters me. If poison will not do the deed, steel or a bullet must. Ah!"

Some one was trying the handle of the shop door, and so timidly was it tried, that Todd stood still to listen, without saying "Come in," or otherwise encouraging the visitor.

"Who is it?" he gasped.

Still the handle of the door-lock only shook. To be sure, it was a difficult door to open to all who did not know it well. Todd had taken care of that, for if there was anything more than another which such a man as he might be fairly enough presumed to dislike, it would be to be glided in upon by the sudden opening of an easy-going door.

"Come in," he now cried.

The person without was evidently anxious to obey the invitation, and a more strenuous effort was made to unfasten the door. It yielded at length. A young and pretty looking lad, apparently of about thirteen or fourteen years of age, stood upon the threshold.

He and Sweeney Todd looked at each other in silence for a few moments. If a painter or a sculptor could have caught them as they stood, and transferred them to canvas or to marble, he might have called them an idea of Guilt and Innocence. There was Todd, with evil passions and wickedness written upon every feature of his face. There was the boy, with the rosy gentleness and innocence of Heaven upon his brow. God made both these creatures! It was Todd

---

* *A line from Shakespeare's* Macbeth, *Act V Scene VIII. It's Macbeth's response after learning that Macduff was "from my mother's womb untimely ripp'd," and therefore not subject to the prophecy that Macbeth would never be killed by any man "born."*

who broke the silence. A gathering flush was upon the face of the boy, and he could not speak.

"What do you want?" said Todd.

He rattled his chair as he spoke, as though he would have said, "It is not to be shaved." The boy was too much engaged with his own thoughts to pay much attention to Todd's pantomime. He evidently, though, wished to say something, which he could not command breath to give utterance to. Like the "Amen" of Macbeth, something he would fain have uttered, seemed to stick in his throat.

"What is it?" again demanded Todd, eagerly.

This roused the boy. The boy, do we say. Ah, our readers have already recognised in that boy the beautiful and enthusiastic Johanna Oakley.

"There is a bill in your window —"

"A what?"

Todd had forgotten the announcement regarding the youth he wanted, with a taste for piety.

"A bill. You want a boy, sir."

"Oh," said Todd, as the object of the visit at once thus became clear and apparent to him. "Oh, that's it."

"Yes, sir."

Todd held up his hand to his eyes, as though he were shading them from sunlight, as he gazed upon Johanna, and then, in an abrupt tone of voice, he said —

"You won't do."

"Thank you, sir."

She moved towards the door. Her hand touched the handle. It was not fast. The door opened. Another moment, and she would have been gone.

"Stop!" cried Todd.

She returned at once.

"You don't look like a lad in want of a situation. Your clothes are good — your whole appearance is that of a young gentleman. What do you mean by coming here to ask to be an errand boy in a barber's shop? I don't understand it. You had different expectations."

"Yes, sir. But Mrs. Green —"

"Mrs. who?"

"Green, sir, my mother-in-law, don't use me well, and I would rather go to sea, or seek my living in any way, than go back again to her; and if I were to come into your service, all I would ask would be, that you did not let her know where I was."

"Humph! Your mother-in-law, you say?"

"Yes, sir. I have been far happier since I ran away from her, than I have been for a long time past."

"Ah, you ran away? Where lives she?"

"At Oxford. I came to London in the wagon, and at every step the lazy horses took, I felt a degree of pleasure that I was placing a greater distance between me and oppression."

"Your own name?"

"Charley Green. It was all very well as long as my father lived; but when he was no more, my mother-in-law began her ill-usage of me. I bore it as long as I could, and then I ran away. If you can take me, sir, I hope you will."

"Go along with you. You won't suit me at all. I wonder at your impudence in coming."

"No harm done, sir. I will try my fortune elsewhere."

Todd began sharpening a razor, as the boy went to the door again.

"Shall I take him?" he said to himself. "I do want some one for the short time I shall be here. Humph! An orphan — strange in London. No one to care for him. The very thing for me. No prying friends — nowhere to run, the moment he is sent of an errand, with open mouth, proclaiming this and that has happened in the shop. I will have him."

He darted to the door.

"Hoi! — hoi!"

Johanna turned round, and came back in a minute. Todd had caught at the bait at last. She got close to the door.

"Upon consideration," said Todd, "I will speak to you again. But just run and see what the time is by St. Dunstan's Church."

"St. — St. who?" said Johanna, looking around her with a bewildered, confused sort of air. "St. who?"

"St. Dunstan's, in Fleet-street."

"Fleet-street? If you will direct me, sir, I dare say I shall find it — oh, yes. I am good at finding places."

"He is strange in London," muttered Todd. "I am satisfied of that. He is strange. Come in — come in, and shut the door after you."

With a heart beating with violence, that was positively fearful, Johanna followed Todd into the shop, carefully closing the door behind her, as she had been ordered to do.

"Now," said Todd, "nothing in the world but my consideration for your orphan and desolate condition, could possibly induce me to think of taking you in; but the fact is, being an orphan myself — (here Todd made a hideous grimace) — I say, being an orphan myself, with little to distress me amid the oceans and quicksands of this wicked world, some very strong sense of religion — (another hideous grimace) — I naturally feel for you."

"Thank you, sir."

"Are you decidedly pious?"

"I hope so, sir."

JOHANNA APPLIES TO TODD TO BECOME HIS ERRAND BOY.

"Humph! Well, we will say more upon that all-important subject another time, and if I consent to be your master, a — a — a —"

"Charley Green, sir."

"Ay, Charley Green. If I consent to take you for a week upon trial, you must wholly attribute it to my feelings."

"Certainly, sir."

"Have you any idea yourself as to terms?"

"None in the least, sir."

"Very good. Then you will not be disappointed. I shall give you sixpence a week, and your board wages of threepence a day, besides perquisites. The threepence I advise you to spend in three penny pies, at Mrs. Lovett's, in Bell-yard. They are the most nutritious and appetizing things you can buy; and in the Temple you will find an excellent pump, so that the half hour you will be allowed for dinner will be admirably consumed in your walk to the pie shop, and from thence to the pump, and then home here again."

"Yes, sir."

"You will sleep under the counter, here, of a night, and the perquisites I mention will consist of the use of the pewter wash-hand basin, the soap, and the end of a towel."

"Yes, sir."

"You will hear and see much in this place. Perhaps now and then you will be surprised at something; but — but, master Charley, if you go and gossip about me or my affairs, or what you see, or what you hear, or what you think you would like to see or hear, I'll cut your throat!"

"Charley" started.

"Oh! sir," he said, "you may rely upon me. I will be quite discreet. I am a fortunate lad to get so soon into the employment of such an exemplary master."

"Ha!"

Todd, for a space of two minutes made the most hideous and extraordinary grimaces.

"Fortunate lad," he said. "Exemplary master! How true. Ha!"— Poor Johanna shuddered at that dreadful charnel-house sort of laugh.

"My God," she thought, "was that the last sound that rung in the ears of my poor Mark, ere he bade adieu to this world for ever?" Then she could not but utter a sort of groan.

"What's that?" said Todd.

"What, sir?"

"I — I thought some one groaned, or — or sighed. Was it you? No.— Well, it was nothing. See if that water on the fire is hot. Do you hear me? Well — well don't be alarmed. Is it hot?"

"I think."

"Think! Put your hand in it."

"Quite hot, sir."

"Well, then, master Charley — Ah! A customer! Come in, sir; come in, if you please, sir. A remarkably fine day, sir. Cloudy, though. Pray be seated, sir. A-hem! Now, Charley, bustle — bustle. Shaved, sir, I presume? D — n the door!"

Todd was making exertions to shut the door after the entrance of a stout-built man, in an ample white coat and a broad brimmed farmer looking hat; but he could not get it close, and then the stout-built man cried out—

"Why don't you come in, Bob — leave off your tricks. Why you is old enough to know better."

"It's only me," said another stout-built man, in another white coat, as he came in with a broad grin upon his face. "It's only me, Mr. Barber — ha! ha! ha!"

Todd looked quite bland, as he said —

"Well, it was a good joke. I could not for the moment think what it was kept the door from shutting, and I always close it, because there's a mad dog in the neighbourhood, you see, gentlemen."

Crack went something to the floor.

"It's this mug, sir," said Charley. "I dropped it."

"Well — well, my dear, don't mind that. Accidents, you know, will happen; bless you."

Todd, as he said this, caught up a small piece of Charley's hair in his finger and thumb, and gave it a terrific pinch. Poor Johanna with difficulty controlled her tears.

"Now, sir, be seated if you please. From the country, I suppose, sir?"

"Yes. A clean shave, if you please. We comed up from Barkshire, both on us, with beasts."

"You and your brother, sir?"

"My cousin, t'other'un is; ain't you Bill?"

"Yes, to be sure."

"Now, Charley, the soap dish. Look alive — look alive, my little man, will you?"

"Yes, sir."

"You must excuse him being rather slow, gentlemen, but he's not used to the business yet, poor boy — no father, no mother, no friend in all the world but me, sir."

"Really!"

"Yes, poor lad, but thank God I have a heart — Leave the whiskers as they are, sir? — Yes, and I can feel for the distresses of a fellow creature. Many's the — Your brother — I beg pardon, cousin, will be shaved likewise, sir? — pound I have given away in the name of the Lord. Charley, will you look alive with that soap dish. A pretty boy, sir; is he not?"

"Very. His complexion is like — like a pearl."

Johanna dropped the soap dish, and clasped her hands over her eyes. That word "pearl" had for the moment got the better of her.

CHAPTER LXIX.

TAKES A PEEP AT ARABELLA.

WE REGRET TO LEAVE JOHANNA in such a predicament, but the progress and due understanding of our tale compel us briefly to revert to some proceedings of Arabella Wilmot, a short detail of which can nowhere come in so well as at this juncture. Up to the moment of parting with Johanna, when the latter went upon her perilous interprise, Arabella had kept up pretty well, but from that moment her spirits began to fail. All the romantic feelings which had at first prompted the advice that concentrated Johanna's expedition to Todd's, evaporated before the hard truthful fact that she, Arabella, had led her young friend into a situation of the greatest peril. Each moment added to the mental agony of the young girl; and at length her sufferings became too acute for further dallying with, and wringing her hands, all she could ask herself was —

"What shall I do to save her? — What shall I do to save her?"

Arabella felt that it would kill her to endure the suspense of one hour instead of four-and-twenty; but to whom was she to turn in this sad condition of her feelings? If she went to old Mr. Oakley, what could she expect but the greatest reproaches for leading one so dear to him into such a path of danger; and those reproaches would not be the less stinging on account, probably, of their being only implied, and not spoken. If she appealed to her own friends, it would only be a kind of second-hand mode of appealing to Mr. Oakley, for they, of courses, would go to him.

"Oh, wretched girl that I am," she cried, as she wrung her hands. "What shall I do? — What ought I to do?"

It was very improbable that, in the midst of such a state of feeling as this, Arabella Wilmot should think of the wisest and best thing to do; and yet strange to say, she did. By mere accident the name of Sir Richard Blunt came to her mind. She had heard Colonel Jeffery speak of him; and from common report, too, she knew he was a man who, of all others, was likely, from inclination as well as power and duty, to aid her. The idea of going to him gained strength and consistency each moment in her mind, as good ideas will.

"Yes — yes!" she exclaimed, as with frantic eagerness she arrayed herself for the event, for she had gone home after seeing Johanna on her way; "yes — yes! I will go to him — I will tell him all. He shall know what a silly, foolish, wicked girl I have been, and how by my mad — mad council, I have perhaps destroyed

Johanna. But he will save her — oh, yes, he will save her from the consequences of the visit to Todd, and save me from madness."

Now, a more decidedly prudent resolve than this could not possibly have been aimed at by Arabella, had she been as cool and collected; as, on the contrary, she was nervous and excited, and it had all the effect upon her mind; for it was astonishing how the mere feeling that she was about to take a good course calmed her down. She had the prudence to interpose no delays by speaking to any one of her intention; but hastily getting into the street, she ran on for some time without reflecting that she had but a very vague idea of where Sir Richard Blunt was to be found. It is astonishing how, under the passions of extraordinary circumstances, people will boldly do things which ordinarily they would shrink from. It was so with Arabella Wilmot. She walked into a shop, and at once asked if they could tell her the exact address of Sir Richard Blunt, the magistrate.

"Yes, it is at No. 6, Essex-street, Strand."

Off she went again. Fleet-street was passed. True, she lingered a little opposite to Todd's shop, and the idea came across her of rushing in, and saying, "Johanna, come away." But she controlled that feeling, from a conviction that she was doing better by going to the magistrate, who, if it were necessary to take that course, could take it much more effectually than she could. Essex-street was gained, and Arabella's trembling hand sounded an alarm upon the knocker.

"Is Sir Richard within?"

"No. But if you particularly want him, he is at his private office in Craven-street."

To Craven-street then she sped. The number she had been told was 10, and upon the door of that house being opened, she asked a man who was big enough to block up all the passage, and who did so, for the magistrate.

"Yes, but you can't see him. He's busy."

"I must."

"But you can't, my dear."

"I will."

The man whistled.

"Will is a short word, my dear, for you to use. How do you mean to do it, eh?"

A door opened, and with his hat on, ready to go out, Sir Richard Blunt himself appeared. Another minute and Arabella would have missed him, and then God knows where, for the next twelve hours, he would be.

"What is this, Davis?" he said.

"Here's a little 'un, says she will see you, Sir Richard."

"Ah, thank God!" cried Arabella, rushing forward and catching a tight hold of the magistrate by the arm. "Yes, I will see you, sir; I have a matter of life and death to speak to you of."

"Walk in," said Sir Richard. "Don't hurry yourself in the least, Miss. Pray be composed; I am quite at your disposal."

Arabella followed him into a small room. She still kept close to him, and in her eagerness she placed her hand upon her breast, as she said —

"Sir — sir. You — and you only. Todd, Todd — oh, God! he will kill her, and I am more her murderer than he. Johanna — Johanna, my poor Johanna!"

Sir Richard slightly changed colour at the sound of those names; and then he said, calmly and slowly —

"I don't think, unless you can assume a greater command of your feelings, that you will ever be able to tell me what you came about."

"Oh, yes — yes."

"Be seated, I pray you."

"Yes — yes. In a moment. Oh, how calm and unimpassioned you are, sir."

"It would not do for us both to lose our judgment."

Arabella began to feel a little piqued, and that feeling restored her powers to her, probably quicker than any other could have possibly done. She spoke rapidly, but distinctly.

"Sir, Miss Johanna Oakley has gone to Sweeney Todd's to find out what has become of Mr. Mark Ingestrie, and I advised her to do so; but now the knowledge that I did so advise her has driven me nearly mad. It will drive me quite mad!"

Sir Richard rose from the arm chair into which he had thrown himself, and said —

"'Miss Oakley?' said you? Why — why — what folly. But she has gone home again."

"No, she is disguised as a boy, and has taken the situation that Todd put a placard in his window about, and she will be found out of course, and murdered."

"No doubt of it."

"Oh, God! Oh, God! Is there no lightning to strike me dead?"

"I hope not," said Sir Richard Blunt; "I don't want a thunder storm in my parlour."

"But, sir —"

"But, Miss Wilmot. Is she there now?"

"She is — she is."

"When did she go?"

"About two hours since. Oh, sir — you must do something — you shall do something to save her, or I will run into the streets, and call upon any passenger I meet, that has the form of a man, to aid me; I will raise the town, sir, but I will save her."

"That course would be about as wise as the original advice to Miss Oakley to go upon the expedition at all. Now answer me calmly what I shall ask of you."

"I will — I will."

"What is the prime cause of action that Miss Oakley projects as the result of this disguised entrance into Todd's shop, provided he be deceived by it?"

"To search the place upon the first opportunity for some relic of Mark Ingestrie, and so put an end to the torturing suspense regarding his fate."

Sir Richard Blunt shook his head.

"Do you think that Sweeney Todd would leave such relics within such easy acquisition and inspection? Is he the sort of man, think you, to expose himself to such danger? Oh, Miss Wilmot, this is indeed a hair-brained scheme."

"It is — it is, and I have come to you for aid, and —"

"Hush! Is the secret of this expedition entirely confined to you and to Miss Oakley?"

"It is — it is."

"Will her friends not miss her?"

"No — no. All has been arranged with what now I cannot help calling a horrible ingenuity. She is like one led to slaughter, and she will pass away from the world, leaving the secret of her disappearance to you and to me only. Sir, I am young, and there are those in this great city who love me, but if Johanna be not saved, I will no longer live to be the most wretched of beings. If there can be found a poison that will let me leave the world, to cast myself at the feet of God, and of Johanna in another, I will take it."

Sir Richard looked at his watch.

"An hour and a half, you say?"

"More than that. Let me think. It was twelve — yes, it was twelve. More you see, sir, than that. Tell me, sir. Tell me at once what can be done. Speak — oh speak to me. What will you do?"

"I don't know, Miss Wilmot."

With a deep sigh Arabella fainted.

It was seldom indeed that, even amid his adventurous life, the magistrate found a circumstance that affected him so strongly as that which Arabella Wilmot had related to him. For a short time, even he, with all his powers of rapid thought, and with all the means and appliances which natural skill and practice had given him to meet any emergency, could not think of any mode of escape from the peculiarly awkward position into which this frightfully imprudent step of Johanna had plunged him.

"My good girl," he said. "Oh, she has fainted."

He rung a hand-bell, and, when a man appeared in answer to the summons, he said —

"Is Mrs. Long within?"

"Yes, Sir Richard."

"Then bring her here, and tell her to pay every attention to this young lady, who is a friend of mine; and when she recovers, say to her that I shall return in an hour."

"Certainly, Sir Richard."

In a few moments a matronly-looking woman, who acted in that house as a sort of general manager, made her appearance, and had Arabella removed to a chamber. Before that, the magistrate had hastily put on his hat, and at a quick pace was walking towards Fleet-street. What he intended to do in the emergency — for emergency he evidently thought it was — we shall see quickly. Certain it is that, even by that time, he had made up his mind to some plan of proceeding, and our readers have sufficient knowledge of him to feel that it is likely to be the very best that could be adopted under the circumstances. Certainly Johanna had, by the bold step she had taken, brought affairs to something like a crisis, much earlier than he, Sir Richard Blunt, expected. What the result will be remains to be seen.

CHAPTER LXX.

RETURNS TO JOHANNA.

We left Johanna in rather an awkward situation. The two graziers were in Todd's shop, and she — at the pronunciation of the word "pearl," which had too forcibly at the moment reminded her of the String of Pearls, which no doubt had been fatal to Mark Ingestrie — had dropped the soap-dish, and covered her face with her hands.

"What is this?" cried Todd.

"What, sir?"

"What is that, I say? What do you mean by that, you stupid hound? If I only —"

He advanced in a threatening attitude with a razor in his hand; but Johanna quickly saw what a fault she had committed, and felt that, if she were to hope to do any good by her visit to Todd's shop, she must leave all such manifestations of feelings outside the threshold.

"I have broken it," she said.

"To be sure you have; but —"

"And then, you see, sir, I was overcome at the moment by the thought that as this was my first day here, how stupid you would think me."

"Stupid, indeed."

"Poor little chap," said one of the graziers. "Let him off this once, Mr. Barber — he seems a delicate little lad."

Todd smiled. Yes, Todd admirably got up a smile, or a something that looked like a smile. It was a contortion of feature which did duty for a piece of amiability upon his face; and, in a voice that he no doubt fully intended should be dulcet and delightful, he spoke —

"I'm quite a fool to my feelings and to my good nature," he said. "Lord bless you, gentlemen, I could not hurt a fly — not I. I used at school to be called Affectionate Todd."

"In joke?" said one of the graziers.

"No, gentlemen, no; in earnest."

"You don't say so! Well, my boy, you see no harm will come to you, as your master forgives you about the soap-dish, and we are in no sort of hurry."

"Well," said Todd, as he bustled about for another article in which to mix the lather. "Well, do you know, sir, I'm so glad to hear that you are in no hurry."

"Indeed?"

"Yes, sir; because, if you are strangers in London both of you, it will give you an opportunity of seeing some of the curiosities, which will do for you to talk of when you get home, you know."

"Why, that would take too much time."

"Not at all, sir. Now, for example — Charley, my dear, whip up that lather — there's the church of St. Dunstan's, which, although I say it — Now, Charley, look sharp — is one of the greatest of London curiosities. The figures at the clock I allude to more particularly. I think you said the whiskers were to be left just as they are, sir?"

"Yes."

"Well then, gentlemen, if you have never seen the figures in the front of old St. Dunstan's strike the chimes, it's one of those things that it's quite a pity to leave London without watching narrowly. They may talk of the Tower, sir, or of the wild beasts at Exeter Change; but give me for a sight where there is real ingenuity, the figures striking the chimes at old St. Dunstan's."

"Indeed?"

"Yes. Let me see. Ah, it's just a half hour nearly now, and your friend can go, although you are being shaved, and then by the time you are comfortably finished off, the next quarter will be getting on. Charley?"

"Yes, sir."

"Put on your cap, and go with that gentleman to St. Dunstan's. You must cross over the way, and then you will soon see the old church and the two figures, as large as life, and five times as natural."

Johanna took up the cap she had worn in her disguise, and stood by the door.

"Why don't you go, Bill?" said the grazier who was being shaved.

"Why, the fact is," said the other, "I would not give a pin's head to see it without you. Do you know, Mr. Barber, he makes such comical remarks at anything, that it's worth one half the fun to hear him? Oh, no, I can't go without him."

"Very good," said Todd, "then I'll finish him off, and you shall both go together in a few moments, though I am afraid you will miss this time of the chimes striking."

There was now a silence of a few moments' duration in the shop; but nothing in the shape of rage or disappointment was visible in the manner of Todd, although both of those passions were struggling at his heart.

"Now, sir," he said at length, and with a whisk he took the cloth from under the grazier's chair. "That will do; I thank you, sir. Towel and plenty of water in that corner, sir."

"Thank you."

"No, I shall do," said the other grazier, in reply to a mute imitation from Todd to sit down in the shaving chair, "I shall do pretty well, I thank you, till to-morrow."

"Very good, sir. Hope I shall have the pleasure of your patronage another time, as well as your recommendation, gentlemen."

"You may depend," said the grazier, who had been shaved, "that we shall do all we can for you, and shall not lose sight of you."

Todd bowed like a Frenchman, and the graziers left the shop. No sooner was the door closed upon them, than his countenance altered, as if by magic, and the most wofully diabolical expression came over it, as with eyes flashing with rage, he cried — "Curses on you both! But I will have one of you, yet. May the bitterest curse of — but, no matter, I —"

"What, sir?" said Johanna. "What do you say, sir?"

"Hell's fury! what is that to you? Do dare you, you devil's cub, to ask me what I said? By all that's furious, I'll tear out your teeth with red-hot pincers, and scoop your eyes from their gory sockets with an old oyster knife. D — n you, I'll — I'll flay you!"

Johanna shrank back aghast. The pure spirit of the young girl, that had been used to little else but words of love and kindness, started at the furious and brutal abuse that was launched at it by Todd.

"Did I not tell you," he continued, "that I would have no prying — no peeping — no remarking about this or the other? I'll crush the life out of you, as I would that from a mad dog!"

A strange howling cry at the door at this moment came upon the ears of Todd. His countenance changed, and his lips moved as though he was still saying something, but he had not power to give it audibly. At length, somewhat mastering his emotion, he said —

"What — what's that?"

"A dog, sir."

"A dog! Confound all dogs."

Another howl, and a violent scratching at the door, was farther and most conclusive evidence of the canine character of the visitor.

"Charley," said Todd, in quite a soft tone — "Charley."

"Yes, sir."

"Take the poor dog something to eat — or — or to drink, rather I should say. You will find a saucer in yon cupboard, with some milk in it. If — if he only, bless him, takes one lick at it, I shall be satisfied. You know, Charley, God made all things, and we should be good to his creatures."

"Yes, sir," said Johanna, with a shudder.

She went to the cupboard, and found the saucer, in which there seemed to be a drop of fresh milk. She walked to the door, while Todd, as though he did not feel by any means sure of the pacific intentions of the dog, at once rushed into his back parlour, and locked himself in. Todd had a peep-hole from the back parlour into the shop, but he could not see further than the shop door. Moreover, Johanna's back was towards him, so he could only guess at what was going on if the dog did not actually come across the threshold. That the milk which Todd was so solicitous should be given to the dog was poisoned, occurred to Johanna in a moment; and just before opening the door, she threw it into a corner, upon some loose shavings, and odds and ends of waste paper, that were there. Johanna then opened the door. In an instant Hector, the large dog of the unfortunate Thornhill, whose identity with Mark Ingestrie appeared to be so established in the mind of Johanna, sprang upon her with an angry growl. It was only for one brief moment, however, that Hector made any such mistake as fancying Johanna to be Sweeney Todd; and then he, with an affectionate whine, licked the hands of the young girl.

"Pison! Pison!" cried a loud voice, and in another moment, the ostler, from the coach-office opposite, rushed to the door, and caught the dog around the neck.

"Ah, there ye is agin. Why, what a goose of a feller you is, to be sure, Pison. Don't you know, now, as well as I do, that that barber will do you a mischief yet, you great blockhead you? Come home, will yer? Come home, now. Come along wi' yer!"

"Yes — yes," said Johanna. "Take him away — take him away."

"Won't I, that's all. I suppose you are a young shaver? Only let me catch you a-interfering with Pison, that's all, and won't I let you know what's what, young feller."

The ostler having uttered this most uncalled-for threat to poor Johanna, took Pison in triumph over the way. Johanna closed the door.

"Is he gone?" said Todd.

"Yes, sir."

"And the milk? Is that gone, likewise?"

"Every drop of it."

"Ha! ha! ha! Well—well. Only to think, now. Ha! ha! I hope that milk won't disagree with the noble animal. How fond I am of him! How often he has been over here, in his little pretty playful way, to try and bite pieces out of my legs. Bless him. If now that milk should give him a stomach ache, what a pity it would be. Did I hear a man's voice?"

"Yes, sir; some man came and called the dog away."

"How good of him, and what a pity it would have been if he had called the noble animal away before the milk was all consumed. Dear me, some people would grudge a creature a drop of milk. A-hem—Charley?"

"Yes, sir."

"I am going out."

Johanna's heart beat rapidly.

"If any one should come, you can say it is of no use their waiting, for I am gone to shave and dress a whole family, at some distance off, and may not be back for some hours; but, Charley, for your own private information, let me tell you that I may look in at any moment, and that, although I shall be busy, I shall be able to come in for a minute or so, when I am least expected."

Todd gave an awful leer at Johanna as he spoke.

"Yes, sir," she said.

Todd carefully locked the parlour door.

"Charley. How do you like your place?"

"Very well, sir; and I think in a little time I shall like it better."

"Good lad! Good lad! Well, well. Perhaps I ought not to say too much so soon, but if you merit my esteem, Charley, I shall do as much for you as I did for the last lad I had. After some term of service with me, I provided him with an independent home. A large house, and a garden. Ha!"

"How very kind."

"Yes. Very."

"And is he happy?"

"Quite, in a manner of speaking, notwithstanding human nature is prone to be discontented, and there are persons, who would sigh, if in Paradise, for some change, even if it were to a region supposed to be its opposite zone. Charley, however, I think will be of a different mind; and when your time comes—which it certainly will—Ha!—to reap the fruits of your service with me, I am sure that no one will hear you complain."

"I will not be ungrateful sir."

"Well, well, we shall see; and now while I am gone let there be no peeping or prying about. No attempts to open doors or force locks. No scrambling to look upon shelves or raking in odd corners. If you do—I—Ha! ha! I will cut your throat, Charley, with the bluntest razor I have. Ha!"

Todd had got on his gloves by this time, and then he left the shop. Johanna was alone! Yes, there she was, at last, alone in that dreadful place, which now for days upon days had been food for her young imagination. There she was in that place, which her waking thoughts and her dreams had alike peopled with horrors. There she was between those walls, which had perchance echoed to the last despairing death cry of him whom she had loved better than life itself. There she was in the very atmosphere of murders. His blood might form part of the stains that were upon the dingy walls and the begrimed floor. Oh, it was horrible!

"God help me now! God help me now!" said Johanna, as she covered her face with her hands and wept convulsively.

She heard a faint sound. It was the chiming of St. Dunstan's clock, and she started. It put her in mind that time, her great ally, now was fleeting.

"Away tears!" she cried as she dashed the heavy moisture from her long eye-lashes. "Away tears! I have been strong in purpose. I have already waded through a sea of horrors, and I must be firm now. The time has come. The time that I looked forward to when I thus attired myself, and thought it possible to deceive this dreadful man. Courage! Courage! I have now much to do."

First she crept to the door and looked out into the street. A vague suspicion that Todd, after all, might only be watching near at hand, somewhere, took possession of her. She looked long and anxiously to the right and to the left, but she saw nothing of him. Then she fastened the door upon the inside.

"If he should return very suddenly," she said, "I shall have notice of it by his efforts to open the door. That will give me a moment for preparation possibly."

Then with such an anxious look as no language could do justice to in its delineation, Johanna looked round the shop. Where was she to begin her investigation? There were drawers, cupboards, chests, shelves. What was she to look at first? or was she in dread of some contrivances of Todd's to find out that she had looked at all, yet at this the last moment, forego the risk and rush into the street and so home?

"No, no! I am in God's hands," she said, "and I will not flinch."

And yet, although she felt that she was quite alone in that place, how cautiously she trod. How gently she touched one thing and then another, and with what a shudder she laid her hand for a moment to steady herself, upon the arm of the shaving chair. By so leaning upon it she found that it was a fixture; and upon a further examination of it, she found that it was nailed or screwed to the floor firmly. It was an old fashioned massive chair, with a wide deep reclining seat. A strange feeling of horror came over her as she regarded it.

CHAPTER LXXI.

THE MYSTERIOUS LETTER.

WHAT WAS THERE IN THE CHAIR that Johanna should for some few moments, now that she had begun to look at it, not be able to take her eyes off it? She tried to shake it, but it was as fast as a rock, and for all she knew it was quite usual to have a shaving chair fixed to the floor. In all likelihood it was in the best position for light which the dingy shop afforded.

She left the chair at last, and then a large cupboard in one corner of the room attracted her attention. It was locked. In vain did she try to force it open. It would not yield. She tried, too, the parlour door without effect. That was quite fast; but as she turned the handle of the lock, she fancied she heard, or she really did hear, something move in the room. A faint feeling came over her for a moment, and she was glad to hold by the wall, close at hand, to support herself.

"It must have been fancy," she said faintly. "I am learning nothing, and the time is flying fast."

A kind of counter ran parallel to the window, and beneath it was a space covered in by doors. Todd surely had forgotten that, for one of the doors was open. Johanna looked in and beheld quite a collection of sticks and umbrellas. Some clothing too lay upon the lowest shelf. With trembling hands, Johanna pulled at the sleeve of some article and found it to be a jacket, such as a sailor of the better sort might wear, for it was exquisitely fine, and had no end of silver buttons upon it. Her sight was dimmed by tears, as she said to herself—

"Oh, God! was this his?"

She held the jacket up to the light, and she found the breast portion of it stained, and all the buttons there tarnished. What was it but blood? The blood of the hapless wearer of that article of dress, that produced such an effect; but yet how was she to prove to herself that it had been Mark Ingestrie? Then it was that the thought struck her of how ill conceived had been that undertaking, which might, in the midst of all its frightful dangers, only end in furnishing her with more food for the most horrible surmises, without banishing one sad image of her imagination, or confirming one dreadful dream of the fate of her lover.

"'Tis all in vain!" she gasped. "All in vain! I shall know nothing, and only feel more desolate. It would be a mercy if that were to kill me! Ah! no. Not yet—not yet!"

JOHANNA RECEIVES A MYSTERIOUS LETTER IN TODD'S SHOP.

Some one was trying the handle of the shop door. With frightful energy Johanna hid the jacket, but not in its proper place, for she only thrust it beneath the cushion of a chair close at hand, and then shutting the door of the receptacle beneath the counter, she rose to her feet, and with a face pale as monumental marble, and her hands clasped rigidly, she said —

"Who — who is there?"

"Hilloa! Open the door!" said a voice.

Some one again tried the handle, and then kicked vigorously at the lower panel.

"Patience," said Johanna, "patience."

She opened the door.

"Is Mr. Todd at hand?" said a lad.

"No — no."

"You are his boy, are you not?"

"I am."

"Then take this."

The lad handed a sealed letter to Johanna, and in a moment left the door. She held the letter in her hand scarcely looking at it. Of course she thought it was for Todd, but after a few moments her eyes fell upon the superscription, and there, to her surprise, she read as follows —

To Miss Oakley, who is requested to read the enclosed quickly, and secretly, and then to destroy it.

To tear open the letter was the work of a moment. The sheet of paper tumbled in Johanna's hands as she read as follows —

From Sir Richard Blunt to Miss Oakley:—

Miss Oakley, the expedition upon which you are at present says much more for your courage and chivalrous spirit than it can ever say for your discretion or the discretion of her who permitted you so far to commit your life to such chances. You should, considering your youth and sex, have left it to others to carry out such schemes; and it is well that those others are aware of your position, and so, in a great measure, enabled to shield you from, perhaps, the worst consequences of your great indiscretion, for it cannot be called anything else.

Your young friend, Miss Wilmot, herself awakened, when, thank God, it was not too late, to the utter romantic character of the office, and communicated all to me. I blame both you and her very much indeed, and cannot speak in too strong language of the reprehensible character of your expedition; and now, my dear girl, do not be under any kind of apprehension, for you are well looked after, and Sweeney Todd shall not hurt a hair of your head.

If you should find yourself in any danger, seize the first small heavy article at hand and throw it, with all the strength you can, through the shop window. Assistance will immediately come to you.

And now, as you are where you are, I pray you to have confidence in me, and to remain until some one shall come to you and say 'St. Dunstan,' upon which you will know that he is a friend, and you will follow his directions.

God bless you. —

Richard Blunt.

Every word of this letter fell like sunshine upon the heart of Johanna, and she could not help mentally ejaculating —

"I am saved — I am saved! Yes — yes? I am not deserted. Strong, bold, good men will look to me. Oh! what kindness breathes in every sentence of this letter! Yes — yes; I am not forsaken — not forsaken!"

Tears came into the eyes of the young girl, and she wept abundantly. Her overcharged heart was relieving itself. After a few moments she began to be more composed, and had just crumpled up the letter and cast it into the fire for fear of accidents, when a shadow darkened the door-way, she saw Todd looking in above the curtain that was over the upper half of the door, and partially concealed some panes of glass that were let into it. As soon as Todd saw Johanna's eyes upon him, he entered the shop.

"What's that?" he said, pointing to the burning letter.

"Paper, sir."

"What paper?"

"A bill that a boy left. Something about Churchwardens, sir, and the parish of St. Brides, Fleet-street, and how things mean to — "

"Bah! any one else been?"

"No, sir."

Todd stood in the middle of the shop, and cast his eyes slowly round him, to see that all was as he had left. Then in a low growling tone, he added —

"No peeping and prying, eh? No rummaging in odd corners, and looking at things that don't concern you, eh?"

"Certainly not, sir."

Johanna crept close to the counter upon which lay a tolerably large piece of stone used for grinding razors upon. She thought that would do very well to throw through the window, and she kept an eye upon it with that intent, if such an act should by a trick of Todd's appear to be necessary. Todd took the key of the parlour-door from his pocket, and placed it in the lock. Before he opened the door, though, he turned the handle, and as he did so Johanna thought that he inclined his head and listened attentively. She threw down a chair, which made a lumbering noise.

"Confound you," roared Todd.

He passed into the parlour; but in a moment, with a glance of fury, he looked out, saying —

"You tried this door?"

"I, sir?" said Johanna, creeping closer still to the sharpening stone.

"Yes, villain, you. At least, I think so — I am pretty sure; but mark me, if I were quite sure, you should suffer for it."

He closed the door again; and then when he was alone, he placed his two hands upon his head for a few moments, and said —

"What does it mean? A boy brought him a letter; I saw him come and go. At least it looked like a letter. Could it be the bill he spoke of, and then the sudden upset of that chair, which prevented me from hearing if the piece of cat-gut I had fastened to the handle of the door had been moved, before I touched it or not. I will kill him. That is safe. It is the only plan; I will kill all who is now in my way. All — all. Yes, I will, if needs be, wade up to my neck in blood to the accomplishment of my wishes."

Todd went to a cupboard and got out a large knife, such as is used by slaughtermen in the shambles, and hid it under the table cover, but in such a place that he could lay hold of it and draw it out in a moment.

"Charley," he cried, "Charley."

"Yes, sir."

"Step in here a moment; I want you, my boy."

"Shall I or shall I not," thought Johanna. "Is this danger, or only the appearance of it? Heaven direct me now! Oh, what shall I do? What shall I do?"

"Charley? Are you coming, my boy?"

"Yes, sir, I — I am coming. God protect me!"

"The barber at home?" cried a voice at the door; and in another moment a man with a ruddy, jolly-looking countenance, made his appearance in the shop. "Barber at home, eh? my little lad?"

"Yes — yes."

Johanna heard a bitter execration come from the lips of Todd; and then with quite a serene smile upon his face, as though he were in the most unruffled mood possible, he made his appearance.

"Could you make me a wig?" said the man, taking off his hat, and showing that his hair was closely cropped.

"Certainly, sir. If you will sit down and allow me to measure your head, I shall have great pleasure — Charley!"

"Yes, Sir."

"You can go to Lovett's, in Bell-yard, and get your dinner now. There's two-pence for you, my lad, and if you have not yet tasted Mrs. Lovett's pies, you will say when you do, that they are the most delicious things in the whole world of cookery."

"Shaved, if you please," said another man, walking into the shop, and pouncing down upon a chair as though it were his own property. "Ah dear me, I'm tired rather. Don't hurry yourself, Mr. Todd, I can wait while you are doing what you have to do for that gentleman."

"Charley," said Todd, with quite a sweet expression of face. "You need not go just yet; I want the hot water. See to it."

"Yes, sir."

Todd then, in the most careful and business-like manner, proceeded to take the measure of the gentleman's head for a "real head of hair," and when he had finished, he said —

"Now, sir, if you will leave it all to me, I will match your hair to a shade."

"Match it?"

"Yes, sir."

"But that's just what I don't want. I have had my hair all cut off, and am going to wear a wig, for the sole reason that I have got tired of the old colour."

"Well then, sir, what colour do you propose now?"

"A few shades lighter than my own. But pray shave this gentleman, and I will tell you how I wish it to look at my leisure."

The man took a seat and crossed one leg over the other with the most home sort of look in the world; and the one who had come in to be shaved plumped into the shaving chair, and gave his chin a rub as though he would say "I don't care how soon you begin."

Todd smiled.

"Charley, the lather."

"Yes, sir. Here it is."

"Here, my little man," said the gentleman in want of a wig. "If you can tie a bow, just make one in front of my cravat. — A small one."

The gentleman slipped a small piece of paper into Johanna's jacket pocket.

CHAPTER LXXII.

ANOTHER VICTIM.

JOHANNA STARTED. "St. Dunstan's," said the stranger.

"What?" said Todd.

"St. Dunstan's last Sunday, I don't think was so highly-scented with the flavour of the grave as usual."

"Oh," said Todd.

Johanna trembled, for certainly Todd looked suspicious, and yet what could he have seen? Literally nothing, for he was so situated that the slight action of the stranger, in putting the slip of paper into her jacket-pocket, must have escaped him with all his watchfulness. She gathered courage.

Todd glanced at her, saying — "What is the matter, Charley? you don't look well at all, my lad."

"I am not very well, sir."

"How sorry I am; I think, do you know, Charley," — Todd was lathering the man's face as he spoke — "that one of Mrs. Lovett's hot pies would be the thing for you."

"Very likely, sir."

"Then, I think I can manage now to spare you."

As he said this, Todd bent an eagle glance upon the gentleman who had ordered the wig, and it seemed as if he doled out his words to Johanna with a kind of reference to the movements of that personage. The gentleman had found a hat-brush, and was carefully rubbing up his hat.

"I do hope," he said, "that the wig will be as natural as possible."

"Depend upon it, sir," said Todd. "I'll warrant if you look in here, and try it on some day when there's no one here but you and I to set you against it, you will never complain of it."

"No doubt. Good morning."

Todd made his best bow, accompanied by the flourish of his razor, that made the man who was being shaved shrink again, as the reflected light from its highly-polished blade flashed again in his eyes.

"Now, Charley, I think you may go for your pie," added Todd, "and don't hurry, for if anything is wrong with your stomach, that will only make it worse, you know."

"You are a good master to the lad," said the man who was lathered ready for shaving.

"I hope so, sir," said Todd. "With the help of Providence we all ought to do our best in this world, and yet what a deal of wickedness and suffering there is in it too."

"Ah, there is."

"I am sure, sir, it makes my heart bleed sometimes to think of the amount of suffering that only twenty-four hours of this sad work-a-day world sees. But I was always of a tender and sympathetic turn from my cradle — yes from my cradle."

Todd made here one of his specially horrible grimaces, which the man happened to see in a glass opposite to him, the reflective focus of which Todd had not calculated upon; and then as the sympathetic barber stropped his razor, the man looked at him as though he would have speculated upon how could such an article looked in a cradle.

"Now, sir, a little to this side. Are you going, Charley?"

"Yes, sir."

"That will do, sir. I'll polish you off very shortly, indeed, sir. Are you going, Charley?"

Johanna darted from the shop, and the moment she got clear of it, she by natural impulse drew the little slip of paper from her pocket, and read upon it —

"Miss O. do not if you can help it leave any one alone in Todd's shop, as circumstances may prevent us from always following his customers in; but if you should be forced to leave while any one is there, knock at No. 133 Fleet-street. This is from your friend R. B."

"133?" said Johanna, as she glanced around her, "133? Ah, it is close at hand. Here — here."

The number was only a short distance from Todd's, and Johanna was making her way to it, when some one stopped her.

"From Todd's," said a voice.

"Yes — yes. A man is there."

"Alone?"

"Yes, and —"

Before she could say another word the stranger darted from her, and made his way into Todd's shop. Johanna paused, and shrinking into a doorway, stood trembling like an aspen leaf.

"Oh, Heaven!" she ejaculated, "into what a sea of troubles have I plunged. Murder and I will become familiar, and I shall learn to breathe an atmosphere of blood. Oh, horror! horror! horror!"

The crowd in that dense thoroughfare passed on, and no one took heed of the seeming boy, as he wept and sobbed in that doorway. Some had no time to waste upon the sorrows of other people; — some buttoned up their pockets as though they feared that the tears that stood upon that pale face were but the preludes to some pecuniary demand; — others again passed on rapidly, for they were so comfortable and cosy that they really could not have their feelings lacerated by any tale of misery, not they. And so Johanna wept alone.

Ding dong! ding dong!

What is that? Oh, St. Dunstan's chimes. How long has she been from the shop? Shall she return to it, or fly at once and seek for refuge from all the sorrows and from all the horrors that surround her, in the arms of her father?

"Direct me, oh God!" she cried.

Some one suddenly clasps her arm.

"Johanna! Johanna!"

It was Arabella Wilmot.

"Johanna — dear, dear Johanna, you are safe — quite safe. Come home now — oh, come — oh, come — come."

"You here, Arabella?"

"Yes, I am mad — mad! — at least, I was going mad, Johanna; in my agony to know what had become of you, and notwithstanding I have told Sir Richard Blunt, I had no faith in the love and the courage of any one but myself. I was coming to Todd's."

"To Todd's?"

"Yes, dear, to Todd's. I could no longer exist unless I saw with my own eyes that you were safe."

"What a fatal step that might have been."

"It might. Perhaps it would; but God, in his goodness, has again, my dear Johanna, averted it by enabling me to meet you here. Come home now — come at once."

"Yes, I — I think —"

"Come — come; — you have done already much. Let, for the future, your

JOHANNA, DISGUISED AS A BOY, IS FOUND WEEPING BY ARABELLA,
NEAR ST. DUNSTAN'S.

feelings be, that for Mark Ingestrie you have adventured what not one girl in
a million would adventure."

At this mention of the name of Mark Ingestrie, a sharp cry of mental
agony burst from the lips of Johanna.

"Oh, I thank you, Arabella."

"Thank me?"

"Yes, you have recalled me to myself. You have, by the mention of that name, recalled me to my duty, from which I was shrinking and falling away. You have told me in the most eloquent language that could be used that as yet I have done nothing for him who is, dead or alive, my heart's best treasure."

"Oh, Johanna, you will kill me."

"No, Arabella — no. Good bye. Go home, love — go home, and — and pray for me — pray for me!"

"Johanna, for mercy's sake! what are you about to do? Speak to me. Do not look upon me in that way. What are you about to to do, Johanna?"

"Go to the shop."

"To Todds?"

"Yes. It is my place — I am in search of Mark Ingestrie. If he be living, it is I who must clear that man who is suspected of his murder. If he be no more, it is I, who weak and fragile as I am, must drag him to justice."

"No — no — no."

"I say yes. Do not stay me if you love me."

Arabella clasped the arm of Johanna, but with a strength that only the immense amount of mental excitement she was suffering from could have given her. Johanna freed herself from the hold of her friend, and dashing from the doorway, was in another moment lost to the sight of Arabella in the barber's shop.

"What now?" cried Todd, fiercely, as Johanna bounded into the shop so hurriedly.

"Nothing, sir — only the dog."

"Bolt the door — bolt the door."

"Yes, sir."

Todd wiped his brow.

"That infernal dog," he muttered, "will be the death of me yet; and so, Charley, the malignant beast flew at you, did he? the savage will attack you, will he?"

"Yes, sir, so it seems."

"We will kill it. I should like to cut its throat. It would be a pleasure, Charley. How strange that strong poisons have no effect upon that dog. Curses on it!"

"Indeed, sir."

"None whatever. It is very odd."

Todd remained in a musing attitude for some time, and then suddenly starting, he said —

"Charley, if that man come again after his wig, get him into talk, will you, and learn all you can about him. I have to go a little way into the city just now, and shall speedily return. I hoped you liked the pie?"

"Pie, sir?"

"Yes, Lovett's pie."

"Oh, yes — delicious."

"Ha! ha! he! he! ho!"

Drawing on a pair of huge worsted gloves, Todd walked out of the shop without saying another word. The moment he was gone, Johanna passed both her hands upon her breast, as if to stay the wild beating of her heart, as she whispered to herself—

"Alone—alone once more."

It was well that she had only whispered that much, for in the next moment Todd gently put his head into the shop. She started.

"Oh, sir—oh, sir, you frightened me."

"Beware!" was all he said. "Beware!"

The frightful head, more terrifying to Johanna than would have been the fabled Medusa's, was withdrawn again, and this time Johanna resolved to be certain that he was gone before she gave the smallest outbreak to her feelings, or permitted herself to glance around her in any way that could be construed into prying curiosity. She made a feint of clearing up the place a little, and, with a broom that had about six hairs only left in it, she swept the hobs of the little miserable grate in which a fire was kept for the shaving-water. This occupied some little time; but still not feeling sure that Todd was really gone, she then went to the door, and looked right and left. He was not to be seen; and so, when she went back, she bolted the shop-door upon the inside again, and really felt that she was alone once more in that dreadful place.

That poor Johanna was now in a great state of mental excitement is not a matter of surprise, for the events that had recently taken place were decidedly of a character to produce such a mental condition. The interview with Arabella had, no doubt, materially aided in such an effect. With trembling eagerness she now began again to look about her, and her great aim was by some means to get into the parlour, for if anywhere, she thought that surely there she should find some traces of that lost one who occupied, since the suspicions of the foul usage he had met with, a larger place in her affections than before. Feeling how surrounded she was by friends, probably Johanna was a little more reckless as regarded the means she adopted of carrying out her intention. The parlour-door was quite fast; but surely in the shop she thought she might find some weapon, by the aid of which it could be burst open; and even if Todd should suddenly return, it was but a rush, and she would reach the street; and if he intercepted her in that, as God knew he might, she could take the means of summoning assistance pointed out to her by Sir Richard Blunt, and cast some-thing through the window into the street.

Full of these thoughts and feelings, then, and only alive to the mad wish she had of discovering some traces of her lover, Johanna hunted the shop over for some weapon with which to attack the parlour-door. She opened a cupboard. A hat fell from within at her feet! One glance at that hat was sufficient; it was of a peculiar colour—she remembered it. It was the hat of the man whom she had left being shaved when she was sent ostensibly to purchase a pie at Mrs. Lovett's, in Bell-yard.

Johanna's hurry was over. A sickening feeling came over her as she asked herself what was the probable fate of the owner of the hat.

"Another victim! — another victim!" she gasped.

She tottered back overpowered by the thought that there had been a time when, opening that cupboard door, the carelessly cast-in hat of Mark Ingestrie would have fallen to her feet, even as did that of the stranger, who, no doubt, now was numbered with the dead. She sank almost in a state of fainting into the shaving-chair.

"Oh, yes, yes," she said. "This is horribly, frightfully condusive. My poor Mark. You have gone before me to that home where alone we may hope to meet again. Alas! alas! that I should live to feel such a truth."

She burst into tears, and sobbed so bitterly, that any one who had seen her would have truly thought her heart was breaking in that wild paroxysm of grief. What a mercy it was that Todd did not come in at such a moment as that, was it not? The sobs subsided into sighs. The tears no longer flowed in abundance; and after about five minutes Johanna arose, tottering and pale. She drenched her eyes and face with cold water, until the traces of the storm of emotion were no longer visible upon her face; and then she knelt by the shaving chair, and clasping her hands, she said —

"Great God, I ask for justice upon the murderer!"

She rose, and felt calmer than before; and then, sitting down by the little miserable fire, she buried her face in her hands, and tried to think — to think how she should bring to justice the man who had been the blight of her young existence — the canker in the rose-bud of her youth. You would have been shocked if you could just for a moment have looked into Sweeney Todd's shop, and seen that girl in such an attitude, without a sigh and without a tear, while all her dearest hopes lay about her heart in the very chaos of a frightful wreck.

CHAPTER LXXIII.

STARTLING EVENTS.

BUSINESS AT MRS. LOVETT'S WAS BRISK. During the whole of that day — that most eventful day upon which the fair Johanna Oakley had gone upon her desperate errand to Sweeney Todd's — the shop in Bell-yard had been besieged by customers. Truly it was a pity to give up such an excellent business. The tills groaned with money, and Mrs. Lovett's smiles and pies never appeared so perfect as upon that day. At about half-past twelve o'clock, when the Lord Chancellor suddenly got up from his chair, in the great hall of Lincoln's Inn, and put on his furry-looking hat, and when the curtain which shuts in his lordship from invidious blasts was withdrawn with a screaming jerk, and a gentleman was stopped in the middle of an argument, what a rush of lawyer's clerks there was to the pie-shop in Bell-yard.

Then was it that the anxious solicitor's fag, who must know something, and have some brains, smiled at the prospect of the luxurious repast he was about to have, and jingled the twopence he had kept in a side pocket for only one pie, and grudged it not out of his hard-earned pittance. Then was it that the bloated barrister's clerk, who had grown shining and obese upon fares, and who is not required to know anything but the complete art of insolence to his brothers, nor to have any more brains than will suffice him to make up his book in the long vacation, smacks his lips at the thought of Lovett's pies, and sends the expectant boy of the chamber — the snob of a snob — for three twopennies. Lean and hungry-looking young men start into Bell-yard from the Strand, producing crumbled pieces of paper, bag their twopenny, and retire to eat it in some corner of the old Temple. All is bustle — all is animation, and the side counter — that one, you know, which ran parallel to the window — was lined by clerks, who sat eating and driving their heels against the boarding, and joking, and laughing "Ha! ha!" — how they did laugh! And then what stories they told of their "Governors;" and how such an one was going out of practice; and how such another one was a screw, and so on, to the great delight of the mere boys, who hoped one day to wear their hair long and grey, and to dress in an outrageous caricature of the mode!

As the machine that let down at the back of the counter, to bring up the pies, went down for the one o'clock batch, it was noticed that Mrs. Lovett looked a little anxious. The fact was, that the cook had been so prompt upon that day in his movements, that she began to think there must be, as folks say, "Something in it," and she was beginning to terrify herself with the idea that he had some scheme of redemption for himself in view, that might most unseasonably develop itself before the customers.

"Ah, Mrs. Lovett," said one young gent, while the gravy ran down the sides of his mouth from the pie he was consuming. "You don't seem at all yourself to-day. Indeed you don't."

"Who do I seem, then?"

"Ha! ha! Upon my life that's good!" roared another.

A small amount of wit did for Lovett's pie shop. It was like the House of Commons in that particular, and "loud laughter" was sure to welcome the smallest joke. Mrs. Lovett's eyes were bent upon the abyss, down which the trap had descended but a moment before.

"Ain't they a-coming, mum?" said one.

"Oh, don't I sniff'em," said another, working his nose like an ex-chancellor. "Don't I sniff'em."

"De — licious!" cried another.

A feeling of relief was visible upon the face of Mrs. Lovett as the trap slowly ascended, bringing with it the one o'clock batch, in all their steaming glory. The whole shop was in a moment filled with the fresh appetite-giving aroma of those bubbling hot pies; and as the French newspapers say, when a member of the extreme right, or half way to the left, or two degrees from the centre, swerves, there was "a sensation." Five minutes — only five minutes — and the whole batch was cleared off, not one was left!

"Another batch of one hundred, gentlemen, at two," said Mrs. Lovett, with a bland look.

"At two, mum?" cried a customer. "Why, what's to become of the half-past one batch?"

"We are rather short of — of meat," said Mrs. Lovett, with one of her strange metallic smiles.

"The devil you are! Ain't there butchers enough?"

"Oh, dear, yes; but we could not get such meat as we put in our pies, at the butcher's."

"You kill your own, mum, then, I suppose?"

"We do," replied Mrs. Lovett, with another smile, more metallic than the former.

"And where is your farm, mum?"

"Really, sir, you want to know too much. I appeal to those gentlemen if any of them know where my farm is."

"No — no. D — n it, no, nor don't care," said all the lawyer's clerks. "Don't know anything about it."

"And don't care," said another. "Sufficient for the day is the pie thereof."

"Very good — Ha! ha! — Very good."

The crowd gradually dispersed. Mrs. Lovett put a placard in the window, announcing —

"A hot batch at two o'clock."

She then closed the shop door, and retired to the parlour. She cast herself upon a sofa, and hiding the light from her eyes with one of her arms, she gave herself up to thought.

Yes, that bold bad woman was beginning to have her moments of thought, during which it appeared to be as though a thousand mocking fiends were thronging around her. No holy thoughts or impulses crossed her mind. Solitude, that best of company to the good and just, was to her peopled with countless horrors; and yet there must have been a time when that woman was pure, and her soul spotless — a time when it was free from —

"The black engraved spots" *

—which now deformed it. And yet who, to look upon her now, could fancy that she was ever other than what she seemed? Who could bring themselves to think that she had not been placed at once by the arch-fiend as she was upon the beautiful world, to make in the small circle around her a pestilence, a blight, and a desolation? There are persons in the world that it would be the greatest violence to our feelings ever to attempt to picture to our imaginations as children; and as such, surely were Sweeney Todd and Mrs. Lovett. Was she ever some gentle little girl, fondly clinging to a mother's arms? Was he ever a smiling infant, with pretty dimples? Was there at his or her birth much joy? Did a mother's tears ever fall upon his or her cheek, in sweet gratitude to God for such a glorious gift? No — no. We cannot — we will not believe that such persons as Sweeney Todd and Mrs. Lovett ever came into this world otherwise than ready-made man and woman! Any other belief, concerning such fiends in human shape is too repugnant.

But we are forgetting that Mrs. Lovett is upon the sofa all this while, and that her metallic smile has quite vanished, giving way to such a look of utter abandonment of spirit, that you would have shuddered to have cast but one glance upon her. She could bear the quietude of the attitude she had assumed but for a very short time, and then she sprang to her feet.

"Yes," she said, "it must, and it shall come to an end!"

She stood for some few moments trembling, as though the dim echo of that word end, as she had jerked it forth, had awakened in her mind a world of horrifying thoughts. Again she sank upon the couch, and speaking in a low, plaintive voice, she said —

"Yes. I have need of the waters of oblivion, one draught of which shuts out for ever all memory of the past. Oh, that I had but a cup of such nectar at my lips!"

Not a doubt of it, Mrs. Lovett. It is the memory of the wicked that constitutes that retribution, which is assuredly to be found in this world as day follows night.

"I — I must have this," she muttered. "Let Todd be dead or alive, I must have it. I am going mad — I feel certain. That I am going mad, and the only way to save myself, is to flee. I must collect as much money as I can and then flee far away. If I cannot quite obliterate the past from my memory, I can at least leave it as it is, and add nothing to it. Yes, that man may live. He seems to bear a charmed life. But I must flee."

She rested her head upon her hands, and in a softer voice, said —

---

* *A probable reference to Shakespeare's* Hamlet, *Act III Scene IV, in which Queen Gertrude says to Hamlet: "Thou turn'st my eyes into my very soul, and there I see such black and grained spots as will not leave their tinct."*

"Let me think—let me think of the means, now that I have yet a little time. What do I dread most? The man below? Yes. He is at work for his deliverance. I feel that he is, and if he succeed before I flee from here, all is lost—all is lost! I must speak to him."

Filled with this idea, and with an unknown dread of what the discontented cook might do, Mrs. Lovett stepped into the shop first, and made the door fast by slipping a bolt at the back of it. It was not very often that immediately after the disposal of a batch of pies any customers came in, and if they should attempt to do so for the purpose of purchasing any stale pies, she was by far too intent upon what she was come about, and considered it by far too important to heed what they might think or say upon finding the door fast. She then opened the seeming cupboard in the parlour, which conducted to the strong iron door, with the small grating at the top of it. She reached that point of observation with great rapidity, and peered into the cavernous dungeon-like bakehouse. At first she could see nothing by the uncertain light that was there, but as her eyes got accustomed to the absence of daylight, she could just see the figure of the cook sitting upon a stool, and apparently watching one of the fires.

"It is a long—long time."

"What is a long time?" cried Mrs. Lovett.

The captive cook sprang to his feet in a moment, and in a voice of alarm, he said—

"Who spoke? Who is that?"

"I," replied Mrs. Lovett. "Do you not know me?"

"Ah," said the cook, directing his eyes to the grating above the door, "I know you too well. What do you want with me? Have I failed in doing your bidding here? Have I disappointed you of a single batch of those execrable pies?"

"Certainly not, but I have come to see—if—if you are quite comfortable."

"Comfortable! What an insult!"

"Nay, you wrong me."

"That is impossible. This is the commencement only of some new misery. Speak on, madam. Speak on. I am helpless here, and condemned to suffer."

Notwithstanding these words of the cook there was a certain tone of hilarity about him, that Mrs. Lovett might well be surprised at, and she asked herself what does he hope. The fact is that much as he wished still to enact the character of a man full of despair, the cook could not get out of his head and heart the promises of Sir Richard Blunt—promises which still rung in his ears, like a peal of joy bells.

"Come, come," said Mrs. Lovett, "you are getting reconciled to your fate. Confess as much."

"I reconciled? Never."

"But you are not so unhappy?"

"Worse — worse. This apathetic condition that I am now in, and which to you may look like the composure of resignation, will end, in all likelihood, in raging madness."

"Indeed?"

"Yes, madam, I feel already the fire in my brain."

"Be calm."

"Calm — calm! Ha! — ha! Calm. It is all very well for you upon that side of the iron door to talk of calmness, madam, but upon this side the words sound strange."

"It will not sound so strange when I tell you that I have absolute compassion upon you, and that the cause of my present visit was to talk to you of some means by which the worst portion of your fate here might be in some measure ameliorated, and your existence rendered tolerable."

CHAPTER LXXIV.

BIG BEN CREATES A SENSATION.

THE COOK WAS SO SURPRISED AT these words from Mrs. Lovett that for some moments he made no answer to them.

"Pray, speak again," he said at length, when he could find words in which to express himself.

"I repeat," she said, "that I am desirous, as far as lies in my power, to ameliorate your condition, of which you so much complain."

"Indeed!"

"Ah, you are too suspicious."

"Humph! I think, madam, when you come to consider all things, you will hardly think it possible for me to be too suspicious."

"You are wrong again. I dare say now, in your mind, you attribute most of your evils to me."

"Well, madam, candidly speaking, should I be far wrong by so doing?"

"You would be quite wrong. Alas! alas! I —"

"You what, madam? Pray, speak up."

"I am the victim of another. You cannot suppose that, of my own free will, I should shut up in these gloomy places a person of your age, and by no means ill-looking." — "I have him there," thought Mrs. Lovett; "what human heart is proof against the seductions of flattery? Oh, I have him there."

The cook was silent for some few moments, and then he said, quite calmly, as though the tribute to his personal appearance had not had the smallest effect —

"Pray go on, madam, I am quite anxious to hear all that you may have to say to me."

This composed manner of meeting her compliments rather discomposed Mrs. Lovett; but after all, she thought — "He is only acting an indifference he is far from feeling." With this impression she resolved to persevere, and she added, in a kind and conciliating tone of voice —

"I grant that circumstances are such that you may well be excused for any amount of doubt that you may feel regarding the honesty of my words and intentions towards you."

"I quite agree with you there, madam," said the cook.

"Then all I have to do is, by deeds, to convince you that I am sincere in my feelings towards you. As I have before said, I am in the power of another, and therefore is it that, contrary to my nature, I may seem to do cruel things at which my heart revolts."

"I cannot conceive anything so distressing," said the cook, "except being the unfortunate victim as I am of such a train of circumstances."

"That is what I am coming to."

"Are you? I wish you were."

There was a tone of irony about the enforced cook which Mrs. Lovett did not at all like; but she had an object to gain, and that was to fully persuade him that the shortest way to his freedom would be to remain profoundly quiet for a day or two, and then she would be able to make her own arrangements and be off without troubling either him or Todd with any news of her departure or her whereabouts.

"You still doubt me," she said. "But listen, and I think you will soon be of opinion that although I have wronged you as yet, I can do something to repair that wrong."

"I am all attention, madam."

"Then, in the first place, you are quite tired of eating pies, and must have some other kind of food."

"You never said a truer thing in all your life, madam."

"That other food, then, I will provide for you. You shall, within an hour from now, have anything to eat or to drink that you may please to name. Speak, what is it to be?"

"Well," he said, "that is kind indeed. But I can do without food further than I have here, for I have hit upon a mode of making cakes that please me. Nevertheless, if you can bring me a bottle of brandy, in order that I may slightly qualify the water that I drink, I shall be obliged to you."

"You shall have it; and now I hope you will be convinced of the sincerity of my desire to be of service to you."

"But my liberty, madam, my liberty. That is the grand thing after all that I must ever pant for."

"True, and that is what you shall have at my hands. In the course of two, or it may be three days, I shall have perfected some arrangements which will enable me to throw open your prison for you, and then —"

"Then what?"

"May I hope that you will not think so harshly of me as you have done?"

"Certainly not."

"Then I shall be repaid for all I do. You must believe me to be the victim of the most cruel circumstances, of which some day you may be informed. At present, to do so, would only be to involve both you and myself in one common destruction."

"Then don't mention it."

"I will not. But beware of one thing."

"What is that?"

"Simply this, that any attempts upon your own part to escape from here previous to the time when I shall have completed my arrangements to set you free, will not only derange all that I am planning for you, but end in your utter destruction; for he who has forced me into my present cruel situation will not for one moment hesitate at the murder of us both; so if you wish to be free in a few days you will try nothing, but if on the contrary you wish to destroy both yourself and me, you will make some attempts to rescue yourself from here."

Mrs. Lovett waited rather anxiously for his answer to this speech.

"I dare say you are right," he said at length.

"You may be assured I am."

"Then I consent."

Mrs. Lovett drew a long breath of relief, as she muttered to herself—

"It will do — I have him in the toils; and come what may, I am free from the torturing thought that he may achieve something that may have the effect of delivering me up to the hands of justice. When I am gone, he may remain where he is, and rot for all I care."— "You have done wisely," she said aloud, "and if anything could more powerfully than another incite me to the greatest exertions to liberate you, it would be the handsome manner in which you have placed confidence in me."

"Oh, don't mention it."

Again there was that tone of sarcasm about the cook's voice, which created a doubt in the mind of Mrs. Lovett if, after all, he was not merely playing with her, and in his heart utterly disregarding all that she said to him. It is quite questionable if this doubt was not in its bitterness worse than the former anxieties that had preyed upon the mind of the lady; but she found she could do nothing to put an end to it, so she merely said —

"Well, I feel much happier now; so I will go at once and get you the brandy that you ask for." — "I hope he will drink it freely — it will aid him in drowning reflection."

"Thank you," said the cook, "I shall expect it with impatience." — "Confound her, she can't very well put anything queer in the brandy. I will take care to taste a very small portion of it first; for Sir Richard Blunt has cautioned me particularly to be careful of poison."

"I am going," said Mrs. Lovett.

"Good-bye, madam; I only hope you will be able to carry your benevolent intentions into effect" — "and," added the cook to himself, "that I may some fine morning have the pleasure of seeing you hanged."

"Farewell," said Mrs. Lovett; and she, too, had her aside as she ascended the stairs, for she muttered — "If I were only a little better assured than I am that you meditated something dangerous, I would steal upon you while you slept, and with a knife soon put an end to all trouble regarding you."

Now, it happened that when Mrs. Lovett reached her shop, she saw three people outside the window. The actions of these people attracted her observation. One was a big stout man, of such a size as was rarely seen in the streets of London. The other was a young girl, nicely attired, but with a look of great grief and agitation upon her countenance. The third person of the group was a gentlemanly-looking man, attired in a great coat which was buttoned up to his chin. The big stout man was making a kind of movement towards the door of the pie-shop, and the gentleman with the great-coat was holding up his hand and shaking his head, as though forbidding him. The big stout man then looked angry; and then Mrs. Lovett saw the young girl cling to him, and heard her say —

"Oh, no — no; I said I wanted nothing. — Come away."

Then the gentleman with the great-coat pulled his collar down a little; upon which the young girl sprang towards him, and, clasping his arm, cried in tones of intense interest —

"Ah, sir, is it indeed you? Tell me is she saved — oh, is she saved?"

"She will be," was the reply of the gentleman in the great-coat. "Come away."

The big stout man appeared to be getting rather furious at the idea of the gentleman with the great-coat dictating what he and the young girl should do; but she by a few words pacified him; and then, as if they were the best friends in the world, they all walked away towards the Strand, conversing very seriously and rapidly.

"What does this mean?" said Mrs. Lovett.

Terror overspread her countenance. Oh, conscience! conscience! how truly dost thou make —

"Cowards of us all!"

What could compensate Mrs. Lovett for the abject terrors that came over her now? What could recompense her for the pang that shot across her heart, at the thought that something was amiss in the fine-drawn web of subtlety that she and Sweeney Todd had drawn? Alas! was the money in the Bank of England, upon which she expected to enjoy herself in a foreign land, now any set-off against that shuddering agony of soul with which she said to herself—

"Is all discovered?"

Her strength forsook her. She quite forgot all about the cook, and the brandy she had promised him — she forgot even how necessary it was, in case any one should come, for her to keep up the appearance of composure; and tottering into the back-parlour, she sunk upon her knees on the floor, and shook as though the spirit of twenty agues possessed her.

So it will be seen that Todd was not quite alone in his sufferings from those compunctious visitations, which we have seen at times come over him in his shop. But we will leave Mrs. Lovett to her reflections, hoping that even she may be made a little wiser and a little better by those soft —

"Whisperings of awakened sense;"

— and that she may find some one among the invisible hosts of spirits of another world who may whisper to her—

"Repent! repent! — it is not yet too late." *

Let us look at those three persons whose mysterious conduct at the shop windows had, like a match applied to gunpowder, at once awakened a fever in the breast of Mrs. Lovett, which she was scarcely aware slumbered there. These folks made their way, then, into Fleet-street; and as the reader has probably guessed already who they are, we may as well make a merit of saying that the big one was our old friend Ben, the beef-eater — the gentlemanly-looking man was Sir Richard Blunt, and the young lady was no other than Arabella Wilmot.

Poor Arabella! Of all the personages concerned in our *dramatis personæ*, we have no hesitation in saying that your sufferings are the greatest. From the moment that Johanna had started upon that desperate expedition to Sweeney Todd's, peace left the bosom of her young friend. We have already traced the progress of Arabella to Sir Richard Blunt's office, and we have seen what was the result of that decidedly judicious movement; but notwithstanding she was assured over and over again subsequently by Sir Richard that Johanna was now well protected, she could not bring herself to think so, or to leave the street.

---

* *A line from Lady Caroline Lamb's sensational 1816 novel,* Glenarvon.

MRS. LOVETT ALARMED AT THE STRANGE FACES AT HER WINDOW IN HER PIE-SHOP.

It was by her lingering about in this way that she became in the company of our friend Ben.

The fact was, that the kind of statement or confession that Johanna had made to Ben on that occasion of his visit to her father's house, when she found herself alone with him in the parlour, had made such an impression upon the poor fellow, that he described it himself in the most forcible possible language, by saying —

"It interferes with my meals."

Now, everything that had such an effect as that, must to Ben be a matter for the most serious consideration indeed. He accordingly, finding that —

"The peace of the Tower was fled,"*

— so far as he was concerned, had come into the City upon a sort of voyage of discovery, to see how matters were going on. As he was proceeding along Fleet-street, he chanced to cast his eyes into the entrance of a court, nearly opposite Sweeney Todd's, and there he saw a female form crouching. There was something about this female form which Ben thought was familiar to him, and upon a close look, he felt certain it was Johanna's friend, Arabella Wilmot. Full of surprise at finding her there, Ben paused, and stared at her so long, that she at last looked at him, and recognising him, immediately flew to his side, and grasping his arm, cried —

"Oh, pity me, Mr. Ben. Pity me!"

"Hold!" said Ben, who was not, as the reader is aware, the fastest thinker in the world. "Hold. Easy does it."

Ben tried to look very wise then.

"Oh, you will hate me, Ben."

"Eh?"

"I say you will hate me, Ben, when you know all."

Ben shook his head.

"Shan't do any such thing," he said. "Lord bless your pretty eyes, I hate you? I couldn't."

"But — but —"

"Come, come," added Ben, "just take your little bit of an arm under mine. Easy does it, you know. Always think of that, if anything goes amiss. Easy does it; and then you will find things come right in the long run. You may take my word for it."

CHAPTER LXXV.

COLONEL JEFFERY OPENS HIS EYES.

ARABELLA WAS WEEPING, SO THAT for some little time she could say nothing more to Ben; and he did not, in the profundity of his imagination, very well

---

* *A reference to a song from the popular opera "Joan of Arc," by M.W. Balfe and Edward Fitzball, which premiered at Drury Lane in 1837. The actual line in the song is "The peace of the valley is fled."*

know what to say to her, except now and then muttering the maxim of "Easy does it," which Ben thought singularly applicable to all human affairs. But this was a state of things which could not last; and Arabella Wilmot, nerving herself sufficiently to speak in a few minutes, said to Ben in a low self-deprecatory tone —

"Oh, sir, I — I — have done something very wrong."

"Eh?" said Ben, opening his eyes to their utmost.

"Yes," added Arabella, "very wrong, indeed."

"Humph!"

"You would not probably have expected it of me, Mr. Ben, would you now?"

"Well, a-hem!" said Ben. "Easy does it."

"I am a wicked — wicked girl."

"Oh, dear — oh, dear!" said Ben.

"You cannot guess, Mr. Ben, what I have done; but I feel I ought to tell you, and it will be quite a relief to me to do so."

Ben shook his head.

"I tell you what it is, my dear," he said. "Your best plan is to go and tell your mother, my dear. That's the proper person to tell. She is sure to find it out somehow or another; and you had better tell her at once, and then — Easy does it."

"My mother? Tell my mother? Oh, no — no — no!"

"Well, if you have got any respectable old aunt now, who is a good, kind old soul, and would not make too much fuss, you had better tell her; but goodness gracious, my dear, what puts it into your head to tell me?"

"Because I think you are kind-hearted."

"Well, but — well, but —"

"And, then, of course, as you are mixed up, you know, Mr. Ben, in the whole transaction, it is only proper that you should know what has happened at last."

Ben turned fairly round, and looked down into the face of Arabella Wilmot with such a coarse expression of alarm upon his face, that at any other than so serious a time she must have laughed.

"Me?" he cried. "Me?"

"Yes, Mr. Ben."

"Me mixed up in the — the — Oh dear!"

"Ah, Mr. Ben, you know you are by far too kind not to be; and so I feel as though it would be quite a relief to me to tell you everything."

"Everything?"

"Yes, all — all."

"Not all the particulars, surely. Come — come. I ain't an old woman, you know, my dear."

"An old woman, Ben?"

"No, my dear, I say I ain't an elderly female, so I don't think I ought to listen to all the particulars, do you know. Come — come, you go home now, and say no more about it to me. Easy does it, you know; and keep your own counsel. I won't say a word; but don't you, because you are in such a state of mind as you hardly know what you are about, go on blubbering to me about all the particulars, when perhaps to-morrow you'll give one of your pretty little ears that you had not said a word to me about it."

"Alas! — Alas!"

"Pho! Pho! Easy does it."

"Who am I to cling to but you?"

"Cling to me? Perhaps you'll say it's me?"

"What's you, Mr. Ben? Explain yourself. How strange you talk. What do you mean, Mr. Ben?"

"Well, that's cool," said Ben.

"What's cool?"

"I tell you what it is, Miss Arabella W., I'm disappointed in you; ain't you ashamed to look me in the face?"

"Ashamed?"

"Yes, positively ashamed?"

"No, Mr. Ben. I may regret the indiscretion that is past; but I cannot see in it anything to be ashamed of."

"You don't?"

"Indeed, Mr. Ben, I do not."

"Then, Miss A. W., you are about the coolest little piece of goods I have met with for some time. Come — come, easy does it; but haven't you been telling me all this time about something you have been about, that — that — was rather improper, in a manner of speaking?"

It might have been the tone in which Ben pronounced the word improper, or it might have been the sagacious shake of the head which Ben accompanied his words with, or it might have been that Arabella was drawing a conclusion from the whole transaction; but certain it is, that she began to have a glimmering perception that Mr. Ben was making a great mistake.

"Oh, heaven!" she said. "What are you saying Mr. Ben? I am speaking of the advice I was foolish enough to give Johanna."

"Advice?"

"Yes, that is all. Into what mischief could you have tortured my meaning? I am much mistaken in you, sir."

"What? Then, it isn't — a-hem! That is to say, you haven't — dear me, I shall put my foot in it directly. What a fool I am."

"You are, indeed," said the now indignant Arabella, and a slight flush upon her cheeks showed how deeply wronged she was by the unworthy construction Ben had put upon her innocent words.

"Good-bye, Miss A. W.," added Ben. "Good-bye; I see I am out of your books; but if you fancy I meant any harm, you don't know me. God bless you.

Take care of yourself my dear, and go home. I won't stay to plague you any longer. Good-bye."

"Stop! Stop!"

Ben paused.

"I am sure, Mr. Ben, you did not mean to say a single word that could be offensive to a friendless girl in the street."

"Then, then? — Easy does it."

"Let us be friends again then, Mr. Ben, and I will tell you all, and you will then blame me for being so romantic as to give Johanna advice which has induced her to take a step which, although my reason tells me she is now well protected in, my imagination still peoples with horror."

Ben's eyes opened to an alarming width.

"You recollect meeting us in this street, Ben?"

"Oh, yes."

"When Johanna was disguised?"

"Yes, Miss A. When she had on them, a-hem! You may depend upon it, my dear, there's no good comes of young girls putting on pairs of thingamys. Don't you ever do it."

"But, Mr. Ben, hear me."

"Well — well. I was only saying. You stick to the petticoats, my dear. They become you, and you become them, and don't you be trusting your nice little legs into what-do-you-call-'ems."

"Mr. Ben?"

"I've done. Easy does it. Now go on and tell us what happened, my dear. Don't mind me. Go on."

"Then Johanna, in boy's cloathes, is now —"

"Now? Oh, the little vixen. Didn't I tell her not."

"Is now filling the situation of errand boy at Sweeney Todd's, opposite. Can I be otherwise than wretched, most wretched!"

"Arrant boy?"

"No, not arrant boy. Errand boy."

"At Todd's — opposite — in — boys — clothes? Oh — oh — just you wait here, and I'll soon put that to rights. I'll — I'll. Only you wait in this door-way, Miss A. W., just a moment or two, and I'll teach her to go and do such things. I'll — I'll —"

"No — no Ben. You will ruin all, you will, indeed. I implore you to stay with me. Let me tell you all that has happened, and how Johanna is protected. In the first place, Ben, you must know that Sir Richard Blunt the Magistrate has her under his special protection now, and he says that he has made such arrangements that it is quite impossible she can come to any harm."

"But —"

"Nay, listen me out. He says that nothing can now expose her to any danger, but some injudicious interference. I ought not, you see, to have told you, Mr. Ben; but since I have, I only ask of you, for Johanna's sake, for her life's sake, to do nothing."

Ben looked aghast.

"And — and how long is the little lamb to be left there?" he asked.

"Only a few hours I think now, Ben — only a few hours. Where are we now, Mr. Ben?"

"Why, this, my dear, is Bell-yard we have strolled into; and that is the famous pie-shop of which they talk so much. They say the woman has made an immense fortune by selling them."

As Ben made a kind of movement towards Mrs. Lovett's window, it was then that Sir Richard Blunt, who had followed him and Arabella Wilmot from Fleet-street, and who had, in fact, overheard some portion of their conversation, stepped up in the manner that Mrs. Lovett had remarked from within the shop.

WE HAVE BEFORE STATED THAT the three personages, consisting of the magistrate, big Ben the beef-eater, and Arabella Wilmot, walked to Fleet-street together from Bell-yard. Sir Richard Blunt shook his head at Arabella Wilmot, as he said —

"Miss Wilmot, I cannot help saying that it would have been better in every respect, and possibly much more conducive to the safety of Miss Oakley, if you had gone home quietly, and not lingered about Fleet-street."

"I could not go, sir."

"But yet a consideration for Miss Oakley's safety should have induced you to put that violence upon your own feelings."

"I felt that when once you, sir, had pledged yourself for her safety, that safe she was; and that my weeping perchance in a doorway in Fleet-street could not be so important as to compromise her."

"I am fairly enough answered," said Sir Richard Blunt, with a slight smile. "But what say you to coming with me to the Temple?"

"The Temple?"

Arabella cast a lingering look towards Todd's shop, which Sir Richard at once translated, and replied to it by saying —

"Fear nothing for your young friend. She knows she is protected; but even she does not know the extent to which she is so protected. I tell you, Miss Wilmot, that I pledge my own life for her safety — and that, although to all seeming she is in the power of Todd, such is not the case."

"Indeed?"

"I have a force of no less than twenty-five men in Fleet-street now — one half of whom have their eyes upon Todd's shop. By Heaven! I would not have a hair of that young and noble girl's head injured for the worth of this great kingdom!"

"Bravo!" cried Ben, as he seized Sir Richard by the hand, and gave it a squeeze that nearly brought the tears into the eyes of the magistrate; "bravo! that's what I like to hear. All's right. Bless you, sir, easy does it. You are the man for my money!"

"Will you both come with me, then?"

"To be sure," said Ben; "to be sure; and as we go along, I'll tell you what a sad mistake I made about Miss Arabella here. You must know that I met her crying in Fleet-street, and she —"

Arabella shook her head, and frowned.

"And — and — and — she — nothing."

"Well," said Sir Richard, "I must confess I have heard anecdotes with a little more point to them."

"You don't say so!" said Ben.

"I think I will go home," said Arabella, gently.

"If you will," replied the magistrate, "of course, I cannot say anything to stay you; but I think it will be a great disappointment to Colonel Jeffery not to meet with you to-day."

"Colonel Jeffery!" exclaimed Arabella, while her face became of the colour of a rose-bud; "Colonel Jeffery?"

There was just the ghost of a smile upon the face of Sir Richard Blunt, as he calmly replied —

"Yes; I am on my way to meet that gentleman in the garden of the Temple; and I am sure he would be glad to see you."

"Glad to see me?"

"Yes, as so true a friend of Johanna's, he will be more than glad; he will be delighted."

"Delighted?"

"Do you doubt the Colonel's friendly feeling towards you?"

"Oh no — no. I — no — certainly not."

"Then let me beg of you to come."

"No. Not now; I will go home. It will look particular for me to go to the garden to meet him."

"It will look much more particular to refuse, I think, Miss Wilmot. You are with me, and with your old friend, and Johanna's relative, Mr. a — a —"

"They calls me Ben."

"Mr. Ben; and so you cannot refuse," he said, "to go to meet Colonel Jeffery, you know. Come, come, I pray you come. Indeed, I know the Colonel wishes to speak to you; and as it would be obviously out of order for him to call upon you, I think you ought, seeing that you're not alone, to give him, as a gentleman of wealth and honour, this opportunity of doing so."

"You say, he wishes to speak to me?"

"He does, indeed. What do you say, Mr. Ben? Don't you think Miss Wilmot might as well come with us?"

"Easy does it," said Ben, "and that's my opinion all the world over."

"Then allow me to look upon it that we have prevailed with you, Miss Wilmot. Pray do me the favour to take my arm."

Arabella trembled, but she did take the arm of Sir Richard Blunt, and made no further opposition to proceeding to that Temple-gardens, where already such affecting interviews had taken place between the Colonel and poor Johanna. The gardens appeared to be empty when they reached it, but from behind some shrubs Colonel Jeffery in a moment made his appearance, for Sir Richard, in consequence of his meeting with Ben and Arabella, was considerably behind his time.

CHAPTER LXXVI.

ARABELLA AND THE COLONEL.

IF ANY ONE HAD BEEN LOOKING at the face of Arabella Wilmot at this particular juncture, and if the party so looking had chanced to be learned in reading the various emotions of the heart from the expression of the features, they might have chanced upon some curious revelations. It was only one glance that Arabella gave to the Colonel, but that was sufficient. A word slightly spoken, and in due season, may say more than a volume of preaching; and so one transient glance, fleeting as a sun-beam in an English April, may, with most eloquent meaning, preach a sermon that would puzzle many a divine. But we have become so familiar with the reader, and put ourselves upon such a cordial shake-hands sort of feeling, in particular with you, Miss, who are now reading this passage, that we will whisper a secret in your ear, and the more readily, too, as to whisper we must come particularly close to that soft downy cheek, and almost be able to look askance into those eyes in which the light of Heaven seems dancing, — Arabella Wilmot is in love!

Yes, Arabella Wilmot is in love with Colonel Jeffery; and small blame to her, as they say in Ireland, for is he not a gentleman in the true acceptation of the term? Not a manufactured gentleman, but one of nature's gentlemen.

You will have promised, my dear what's-your-name, that Arabella, to herself even, has hardly confessed her feelings; but still they are creeping upon her most insidiously as such feelings somehow or other will and do creep.

To be sure, if any one were to stop her in the street or any where else to say, "Arabella, you are in love with Colonel Jeffery," she would say—"No, no, no!" many times over.

But yet it is true:—

You read it in her glistening eyes,
And thus alone should love be read:
She says it in her gentle sighs,
And thus alone should love be said.

After this, who will be hardy enough, my dear, to dispute the fact with you and I?

And now we will watch her, aye, that we will, and see how she will behave herself under such trying circumstances.

Colonel Jeffery advanced, and as in duty and gallantry called upon, he, after slightly bowing to the gentlemen, spoke to Arabella.

"This is an unexpected pleasure, Miss Wilmot," he said. "I hope I see you well. Here is a seat close at hand. May I have the pleasure of conducting you to it?"

"Johanna is—is—is—" stammered Arabella.

"Well, I hope," interposed the colonel.

"Oh, no—no—that is, yes."

The colonel looked puzzled. He was not a conjurer, and so might look puzzled, if he looked like any ordinary man, who hears any one say no, and yes in the same breath, without any injury to his reputation.

"Mr. Ben," said Sir Richard Blunt, "I have something for your private ear, if you will just step on with me."

"My private ear?" said Ben with a confused look, as if he would have liked to add, "which is that?"

"Yes. This way if you please."

Ben walked on with the magistrate, and Colonel Jeffery was alone with Arabella Wilmot. Yes, alone with the one person who insensibly had crept into her affections. Alas! Is the pure love of that young creature scattered to the winds? Is she one of those who drag about them in this world the heavy chain of unrequited affection? We shall see.

Arabella had permitted the colonel to hand her to one of the garden-seats near at hand. How could she prevent him? If he had chosen instead to hand her into the river it would have been just the same, and she would have gone. He led her by that wreath of flowers which in old Arcadia was first linked by Cupid, and which, in all time since, has wound itself around the hearts of all the boy-god's victims.

"Miss Wilmot," said the colonel, and now his voice faltered a little, "I have much wished to see you."

"Very fine, indeed," said Arabella. "You said something about the weather, did you not?"

"Not exactly," he said; "I had much wished to see you."

"Me?"

"Yes, and to begin at the beginning, you know I — I — loved Johanna Oakley. Yes, I loved her."

"Yes — yes."

"I loved her for her beauty, and for the gentle and the chivalrous devotion of her character, you understand. I loved her for the very tears she shed for another, and for the very constancy with which she clung to the memory of his affection for her. I saw in her such child-like purity of mind, such generosity of disposition, such enchanting humanity of soul, that I could not but love her."

"Yes, yes," gasped Arabella. "Yes."

"Will you pardon me for saying all this to you?"

"Oh yes. Go on — go on, unless you have said all?"

"I have not."

"Then, then you have only to add that you love her still?"

"Yes, but —"

Arabella's heart beat painfully.

"Ah," she said, "has true love any reservations? You love her, and yet you have something else to say."

"I have. I love her still. But it is not as I loved her. She has convinced me of her constancy to her first affection, that — that —"

"Yes, yes."

"That being so convinced, I now love her, but with that love a brother might feel for a dear sister, and I almost think it was a kind of preparation to try to awaken in the smouldering fires of her lost love a new passion. She has made me feel that the love of woman once truly awakened is an undying passion and can know no change — no extinction."

"True. Oh, how true!"

"I have learnt from her that when once the heart of a young and gentle girl — one in whom there are no evil passions, no world-wise failings nor earthly varieties — is touched by the holy flame of affection, it may consume her being, but it never can be extinguished."

Arabella burst into tears.

"Love," added the colonel, "may be trodden down, but like truth it can never be trodden out!"

"Never! never!" sobbed Arabella. "Let me go now! Oh, sir, let me go home now?"

"One moment!"

She trembled, but she sat still.

COLONEL JEFFERY DECLARES HIS LOVE FOR ARABELLA.

"Only a moment, Arabella, while I tell you that man's love is different from this. That man can reason upon his affections, and that when the first beauty and excellence upon which he may cast his eyes is denied to his arms, he can look for equal beauty — equal excellence — equal charms of mind and person in another, and —"

Arabella tried to go, but somehow she felt spell-bound and could not rise from that garden seat.

"And," added the colonel, "with as pure a passion, man can make an idol of her who can be his, as he approached her who could not. — Miss Wilmot, I love you!"

"Oh, no, no — Johanna."

"I do not shrink from the pronunciation of that name; I have said that I loved Johanna. If she had been fancy-free and would have looked upon me with eyes of favour, I would have made her my wife; but such was not to be, and for the same qualities that I loved her I love you. I am afraid I have not explained my feelings well."

"Oh, yes. That is, I don't know."

"And now, Miss Wilmot, will you allow me to hope that what I have said to you may not be all in vain? That —"

"No, no."

"No?"

"Allow me to go, now. My mind is too full of the fate of Johanna even to permit me to reject in the language taught —"

"Reject?"

"Yes," she said, "reject. I wish you all the happiness this world can afford to you, Colonel Jeffery."

"Then you will be mine?"

"No, no, no. Farewell."

She rose, and this time the colonel did not attempt to detain her. He stepped back a pace or two, and bowed, and then rose and walked a pace or two away. Then she turned, and holding out her hand, she cried —

"We may — may be friends."

The colonel took the little hand in silence, but the expression of his face was one of deep chagrin.

"Good-bye," said Arabella.

How courageous she had become all of a sudden, as it were.

"And is this all?" said Jeffery.

"Yes, all. When I see Johanna I will remember you to her."

The colonel bowed again, as he replied —

"I shall be much beholden to you, Miss Wilmot, for that kindness."

"And — and I hope you will find — find — that is, meet with some one, who — who don't chance to know that your love is a kind of second-hand — that is, I don't mean that, but a — a — Yes, that is all."

Arabella was saying too much. The colonel replied gently —

"I am truly obliged for the highly explanatory speech just uttered by Arabella Wilmot, whom I have the honour to wish a very good-day."

Arabella trembled.

"No, no. Not thus, Colonel Jeffery. We are friends, indeed."

"Remarkable good acquaintans," said the colonel, as he walked away towards Sir Richard Blunt and Ben. Arabella walked hastily on, having but one idea at the moment, and that was to leave the garden, but she could not find the gate, and Ben ran after her as well as he could, calling —

"Miss A. W. — Miss A. W., where are you a-going? Don't you go yet. I'll take care of you and see you all right, you know, or perhaps you'd like to take a wherry here at the Temple stairs, and go to the Tower, and see the animals fed?"

"Yes, no — that is, anything," replied Arabella. "I will go home now, I am so very — very wretched!"

"What, wretched? Here, Colonel thingumy, she says she —"

"If you dare!" said Arabella, as she placed her hand upon the arm of Ben. "If you dare!"

"Lor!" said Ben, as he looked down from his altitude upon the frail and beautiful young creature. "Lor! easy does it!"

The voice of Ben, however, had brought both the colonel and Sir Richard Blunt to the spot. During that brief time that had elapsed since the colonel had last spoken to Arabella, Sir Richard had told him of the perilous position of Johanna, and the look of anxiety upon his face was most marked. Arabella heard him say —

"Make use of me in any way you please, Sir Richard. Regard my safety or even my life as nothing compared to her preservation."

Arabella knew what he meant.

"Ben," she said, "will you come with me, and see me a part of my way home?"

"Yes, my dear, to be sure. Then you won't come and see the criturs fed to-day, I supposes?"

"No, no."

"Very well. Easy does it. Come along, my dear — come along. Lord love you! I'll take care of you. I should only like to see anybody look at you while you are with me, my duck. Bless your little bits of twinkling eyes!"

"Thank you — thank you."

"Lor! it's enough to make a fellow go mad in love, to see such criturs as you, my dear; but whenever I thinks of such things, I says to myself — 'I'll just pop in and see Mother Oakley,' and that soon puts it all out of my head, I can tell you."

"Indeed?"

"Yes. You should go in at feeding time some day, and see her a-coming it strong with fried ingins."

"Fried what?"

"Ingins — ingins; round things. Ingions — ah! that's it."

"Onions?"

"Very like — very like. But come on, my dear — come on. Easy does it!

Always remember that whenever you gets into any fix. Easy does it!"

Did Arabella think the colonel would run after her and say something? Yes she did; but he came not. Did she think he would be loath to part with her upon such terms as they had seemed to part? Yes, yes. Surely he could not let her go without some kinder, softer, word that he had last spoken to her? But he did. He only watched her with his eyes; and when Sir Richard Blunt, who, it would appear, knew something of the colonel's feelings, said to him —

"All right, I suppose, Colonel Jeffery?"

He only shook his head.

"What, anything amiss?"

"She has rejected me!"

"Oh, is that all?"

"All? And enough too."

"Phoo! She was sure to do that. Don't you know the old adage, that —

> *'Woman's nay still stands for nought.'* *

"Why, man, 'No' comes as naturally to the tip of a young girl's tongue when she means 'Yes,' as 'Don't' when she expects to be kissed. I tell you, she loves you. She adores the very ground you walk on."

"And yet she taunted me with my passion for Johanna, and called me a second-hand lover."

"Did she, though? Ha! ha! ha! ha! Upon my life that was good — was it not?"

———

CHAPTER LXXVII.

MRS. LOVETT VISITS THE BANK.

MRS. LOVETT, MRS. LOVETT, we are neglecting you! Excuse us, fascinating piece of wickedness. We are now in Bell-yard again. It will be recollected what a mental ferment the appearance of Ben, and Arabella, and Sir Richard Blunt, at the window of her shop had put her in. Not that she knew any of those parties — nor that she connected any of them in any way with her feelings,

---

* *Possibly quoting a popular maxim, or possibly a line from Poem 19 of* The Passionate Pilgrim, *a sequence of poems published in 1599 and attributed, possibly spuriously, to Shakespeare.*

except so far as their attitudes might at that moment lead her to suppose. The attitudes certainly were such as to create suspicion. All this, joined to the previous state of mind of Mrs. Lovett, did not tend to produce that heavenly calm, which philosophers tell us is such a remarkably nice thing. On the contrary, the mind of Mrs. Lovett rather resembled a raging torrent, boiling and bubbling to some destruction which was afar off, and which could only be reached through the perils and dangers of some stormy passage.

She was sighing for peace. She had begun to sicken for the results of her life of iniquity — not those results which an indignant and outraged public would have visited her with, but those results which she and all persons, who deliberately and systematically commence a career of guilt, picture to themselves. Criminality is never engaged in for its own sake. There is always some ultimate object in view, which makes the retrospect less horrible, and the prospect dim and dubious, though it may be yet a thing of pleasurable anticipation. Of course, we are only reasoning upon those minds that reflect. There are many who lead a life of criminality, who do so as the manifestation of an intellect that can picture nothing else. But the reader knows that Mrs. Lovett was not of such an order. She was to some extent an educated, and to a considerable extent a clever woman. Hence, then, she had always pictured to herself wealth and retirement, respect and power, as the ends for which she was striving with such unscrupulous means. But of late, with a shuddering horror, she had begun to dread that all she had hoped for was getting only more distant. She had contracted a strong notion of the bad faith of Todd, and if such were really the case, all was indeed lost. If he allowed his cupidity just to induce him to commit the crime that would be one too many, destruction must fall upon them both. If likewise he instantly made an effort to take to himself all the profits of the unholy traffic that they were mutually engaged in, all would be lost to both; for was she a likely woman to crouch down in silence under such a blow? No! the scaffold prepared by her instrumentality for Todd, would be scarcely less a triumph to her that she herself would share it with him. He ought to have known better than he did.

How clear and long-sighted we find people upon subjects that from this distance may be supposed to present difficulties, and yet how shallow they are upon what is close to them. One would have thought that such a man as Todd could easily have said to himself, with regard to Mrs. Lovett, "I dare not tamper with the objects of that woman," and he would have said it with truth; but on the contrary, he only looked upon her as a convenient tool, which was to be thrown aside when it had served all the purposes for which he intended it. There could not have been a more fatal mistake upon the part of Todd as concerned his safety.

But to return to Mrs. Lovett. The brandy she had promised to the prisoner was quite forgotten. She sat revolving in her mind, how she could put an end to the state of horrible doubt and perplexity in which she was. There were some little difficulties in the way of Mrs. Lovett emerging from her present condition.

It has been before hinted at, that Todd and the fair lady of the pie-shop had between them accumulated a large sum of money, and that the money was duly deposited in the hands of a stock-broker, who was by no means to part with it to either of them, except upon an order signed by both. So far all looked fair enough; and as they were likewise bound together by such a bond of mutual guilt, it did not look likely that either would make an endeavour to get the better of the other. Suppose there was £40,000 in the hands of the stock-broker, it did not seem, we say, under all the circumstances likely that Todd — being fairly entitled as between them, to £20,000 — would peril the safety of both their necks, by getting up a quarrel about the division equitably of the spoil. The same reasoning will apply to Mrs. Lovett.

But these unlikely things are the very things that do come to pass to upset the finest plans. Todd never from the first — whenever that was — meant that Mrs. Lovett should share with him; no, he thought that he, as the superior genius, the greater villain, would manage to cheat her, and that she would, for her own safety's sake, be obliged to put up with what he chose to give her. That would have been only such a pittance, as to keep her constantly in a state of dependance upon him.

Now, to do Mrs. Lovett justice upon the old equitable principle of giving the devil his due, she never had any intention, until she saw symptoms of bad faith in Todd, of attempting to act otherwise than fairly by him. She loathed him; and all she meant to do, was when the division of the spoil should take place, to ascertain where he was going, and then to get as far off him as possible. Of late, however, finding that Todd was getting lucky, and feeling quite convinced that he aimed at her life, other views had dawned upon her, as we are already well aware. She did not so much care for all the money as she would have liked in her retirement, wherever it was, to have felt sure that Todd was not —

"An inhabitant of the earth;" *

— and hence she had taken the pains, all of which had been frustrated, to put him into another world. But a feeling, superstitiously consequent upon her failure, had started up in her mind that he bore a charmed life; and hence she bethought herself of flying from England; but the money — how was she to get the money to do so? How was she, without his cognisance, to get her share of the funds which had been placed in the hands of a stock-broker?

---

* *A line from Shakespeare's* Macbeth, *spoken by Banquo in description of the three witches:* "What are these, so wither'd and so wild in their attire, that look not like the inhabitants o' the earth, and yet are on't?" *(Act I Scene III)*

Now, since she had begun to feel uncomfortable regarding the faith of Todd, Mrs. Lovett had kept what cash she saved at home; therefore some weeks had elapsed since she had paid a monetary visit to the city. If she had gone as usual, she might have got some news. To a woman of lively and discursive imagination like Mrs. Lovett, a plan of operation was not long in suggesting itself. Why, she asked herself, should she hesitate to put Todd's name to the document necessary to get her half of the money from the stock-broker? What a natural consequence from this question it was to ask herself another, which was — If I am forging Todd's signature at all, might I not do it for the whole amount as for half, and so take the only revenge upon him which he would feel, or which I dare offer myself the gratification of exacting from him?

When such a question as this is asked, it is practically answered in the affirmative. Mrs. Lovett felt quite decided upon it. She was a woman of courage. No faint-hearted scruple interposed between the thought and the execution of a project with her. The recent scene that had taken place in front of her window decided her. Now or never! she told herself. Now or never is the time to escape. I have nothing to encumber myself with. Let Todd keep his jewels and trinkets. All I want is the money which is in the hands of Mr. Anthony Brown, the stock-broker, and that I will have forthwith.

Mrs. Lovett did not know the exact amount; but as it was a joint account, such an amount of ignorance need not appear at all surprising to the stock-broker; so she drew up an order for the money, and signed it with both Todd's name and her own, leaving a blank for the amount. She then carefully locked up all doors but that of the outer shop, and having procured the services of a young girl from a greengrocer's shop in the vicinity, to mind the place for an hour, as she said, she considered she was all right. The girl had attended to the shop before for Mrs. Lovett at times when no batches of pies were expected from the regions below, so she did not feel at all surprised at the call upon her services.

"I shall be an hour," said Mrs. Lovett. "You can take a pie or two for yourself if you feel at all hungry; and if Mr. Todd should come in, say I'm gone to call upon a dress-maker in Bond-street."

"Yes, mum!"

Mrs. Lovett left the shop. At the corner of Bell-yard she turned and cast a glance at it. She hoped it was a farewell one — She shuddered and passed on; and then she muttered to herself —

"If I am — which assuredly I shall be — successful in the city, I will take post-horses there at once for some sea-port, and from thence reach the Continent, before Todd can dream of pursuit, or find out what I have done, or where bestowed myself."

She was not so impudent as to pass Todd's shop, but she went down one of the streets upon the opposite side of Fleet-street, and came up another, which was considerably past the house which was so full of horrors. A lumbering old hackney coach met her gaze. It was disengaged, and Mrs. Lovett got into it.

"To Lothbury," she said; and after swaying to and fro for a few moments, the machine was set in action, and duly steering up Ludgate Hill.

The impatience of Mrs. Lovett was so great, that she would gladly have done anything to induce the horses to go at a faster rate than the safe two miles and a half an hour to which they were accustomed, but she dreaded that if she exhibited any signs of extreme impatience she might excite suspicion. To the guilty, any observation of a more than ordinary character is a thing to dread. They would fain glide through life gently, and not at all do they sigh to be —

"The observed of all observers." *

But the longest journey even in the slowest hackney coach must come to an end. As Ben the beef-eater would have said — "Easy does it;" and as Mrs. Lovett's journey was anything but a long one, the gloomy precincts of Lothbury soon loomed upon her gaze. After the customary oscillations, and wheezing and creaking of all its joints and springs, the coach stopped.

"Wait," said Mrs. Lovett with commendable brevity; and alighting, she entered a dark door-way upon the side of which was painted, in letters that had contracted so much the colour of the wood-work that they were nearly illegible, "Mr. Anthony Brown."

This was the stock-broker, who held charge of the ill-gotten gains of that pair of un-worthies, Mrs. Lovett and Sweeney Todd. A small door, covered with what had been green baize, but which was now of some perfectly original brown, opened into the outer office of the man of business, and there a spruce clerk held dominion.

At the sound of the rustling silks of Mrs. Lovett, he raised his head from poring over the cumbrous ledger; and then seeing, to use his own vernacular, it was "a monstrous fine woman," he condescended to alight from his high stool, and he demanded the lady's pleasure.

"Mr. Brown."

"Yes, madam. Certainly. Mr. B. is in his private room. What name shall I have the pleasure of saying?"

"Lovett."

"Lovett? Yes, madam. Certainly — a-hem! Pray be seated, madam, if you please."

Mrs. Lovett made a gesture of dissent, and the clerk went upon his errand.

---

* *A line from Shakespeare's* Hamlet, *from Ophelia's "O what a mind is here o'erthrown!" soliloquy.*

He was scarcely absent a moment, and then holding open a door, he said, with quite a chivalric air —

"This way, if you please, madam."—"A monstrous fine woman," he added to himself.

The door closed after Mrs. Lovett, and she was in the private room of Mr. Anthony Brown.

"Ah, Mrs. Lovett. Pray be seated, madam. I am truly glad to see you well. Well, to be sure, you do look younger, and younger, and younger, every time I have the pleasure of a visit from you."

"Thank you, Mr. Brown, for the compliment. My visits have not been so numerous as usual of late."

"Why, no ma'am, they have not; but I hope we are going to resume business again in the old way?"

"Not exactly."

"Well, my dear madam, whatever it is that has procured me the honour and the pleasure of this visit, I am sure I am very glad of it, and shall not quarrel with it. He! he! Nice weather, Mrs. Lovett."

"Very."

"Ah, madam — ah, it was a world of pities to disturb the investments. It was indeed. But ladies will be ladies."

"Sir?"

"I — I merely said ladies will be ladies you know. And indeed — he! he! — I fully expected the interesting ceremony had come off before now, I did indeed; and I should have wagered a new hat."

"Mr. Brown, what are you talking about?"

"About?"

"Yes, what do you mean?"

"Why, a — a — that is — the — a — a — about — concerning — the — my dear madam, if I have inadvertently trodden upon your sensibilities, I — I really —"

"You really what?"

Mr. Brown looked perplexed. Mrs. Lovett looked a little furious.

"Sir," she said. "Before I explain the cause of my visit to you, I insist upon knowing to what all your mysterious hints and remarks allude. Speak freely and plainly, sir."

"Well then, madam, when Mr. Todd was last here, he said that you had at last consented to reward years of devotion to you by becoming his, and that the ceremony which was to make him a happy man by uniting him to so much excellence and beauty, was to come off almost immediately, and that that was the reason you had both agreed to withdraw all the money I had in such snug and comfortable safe investments for you both. He! he! he!"

CHAPTER LXXVIII.

MUTUAL DEFIANCE.

BE SO GOOD, READER, AS TO PICTURE to yourself the look of Mrs. Lovett. We feel that one brief moment of imagination will do more to enable you to feel and to see with —

"Your mind's eye"

— her aspect, than as if we were to try a paragraph upon the subject. How that "he! he! he!" of Mr. Brown's rung in her ears. It was at any time almost enough to provoke a saint, and we need not say that this time of all others was not one at which Mrs. Lovett's feelings were attuned to gentleness and patience. Besides, she certainly was no saint. A rather heavy inkstand stood upon the table between Mrs. Lovett and the stock-broker. The next moment it narrowly escaped his head, leaving in its progress over his frontispiece a long streak of ink down his visage.

"Wretch!" said Mrs. Lovett. "It is not true."

"Murder!" cried Mr. Brown.

Mrs. Lovett covered her face with both her hands for a moment, as though, to enable her to think clearly, it were necessary to shut out the external world; and then starting up, she advanced to the door of the room.

"Murder!" said the stock-broker again.

"Silence!"

"A constable."

"If you dare to say one word of this interview, I will return, and tear you limb from limb."

Mrs. Lovett opened the door of the private room with such a vengeance that the nose of the clerk, who had been listening upon the other side, was seriously damaged thereby. He started back with a howl of pain.

"Fool!" said Mrs. Lovett, as she passed him, and that was all she conde-scended to say to him; — not by any means an agreeable reminiscence of his last words with a lady to a gentleman who prided himself upon his looks — rather!

Mrs. Lovett reached the street, and walked for some distance as though street it was not. She was only roused to a sense of the world in which she was, by hearing the sound of a voice calling —

"Mum — mum! Here yer is — mum — mum! woo!"

She turned and saw the coach in which she had come to the stock-broker.

"Going back, mum?" said the man.

"Yes, yes."

She stepped into the vehicle, looking more like an animated statue than aught human. The man stood touching what was once the brim of a hat, as he said—

"Where to, mum?"

Mrs. Lovett looked at him with an air of such abstraction that it was quite clear she did not see him, but she heard the question, that came to her like an echo in the air.

"Where to, mum?"

"To Fleet-street!"

Wheeze — creak — wheeze — creak — sway — sway, and the coach moved on again.

Mrs. Lovett sunk down among the straw with which the lower part of the vehicle was plentifully strewed; and then, with her head resting upon the seat, her throbbing temples clasped in her hands, she tried to think. Yes — she called upon all that calmness — that decision — that talent or tact, call it which you will that had saved her for so long, not to desert her now in this hour of her dire extremity. She called upon everything for aid but upon Heaven! and then, to ease her mind, she cursed a little. Somebody says—

> "Swearing when the passions are at war,
> And light the chambers of the brain with anger's flash.
> Has an effect quite moral — a kind of safety valve,
> Sparing what might be a tremendous crash!"

— and so Mrs. Lovett got cooler, but not a whit the less determined, as the crazy vehicle conveyed her to Fleet-street. She fully intended now to measure conclusions with Todd. The distance was so short that even a hackney-coach performed it with tolerable promptitude. Mrs. Lovett did not wish to alight exactly at the door of Todd's shop; so she was rather glad upon finding the coach stop at the corner of Fleet-street by the old Market, and the driver demanded what number?

"This will do."

She was in the street in another minute. It took a minute to get out of a hackney-coach. It was like watching the moment to spring from a boat to the shore in a heavy surf. And yet, oh much vilified old hackney-coach! how much superior wert thou to thy bastard son, the present odious rattling, bumping, angular, bone-dislocating, horrid cab!

The driver received about double his fare, and a cab-man of the present day would have gathered a mob by his vociferations, and blackguarded you into a shop, if you had treated him in such a way. Nothing less than three times what he's entitled to ever lights up the smallest spark of civility in the soul of a modern cab-driver, but the old hackney-coach-man was always content with double; so upon this occasion Mrs. Lovett got a "thank ye, mum;" and a long straw that had taken an affection for the skirt of her dress was arrested by jarvey and restored to the coach again.

Mrs. Lovett walked to all appearance composedly up Fleet-street. Alas! in this world who can trust to appearances? She had time, before reaching the shop of Sweeney Todd, to arrange slightly what she should say to that worthy. Of course, he could know nothing of her visit to the City — of her interview with Mr. Brown, and she need not blurt that out too soon. She would argue with him a little, and then she would be down upon him with the knowledge of his knavery and treachery. She reached the shop. No wonder she paused there a moment or two to draw breath. You would have done the same; and after all, Mrs. Lovett was mortal. But she did not hesitate for long. The threshold was crossed — the handle of the door was in her hand — it was turned, and she stood in Todd's shop. Todd was looking at something in a bottle, which he was holding up to the light; and Mrs. Lovett saw, too, that a pretty genteel-looking lad was poking about the fire, as if to rouse it.

"Ah, Mrs. Lovett!" said Todd, "how do you do? Some more of that fine grease for the hair, I suppose, madam?" Todd winked towards the lad (our dear friend Johanna), as though he would have said — "Don't appear to know me too well before this boy. Be careful, if you please."

"I have something to say to you, Mr. Todd."

"Oh, certainly, madam. Pray walk in — this way, if you please, madam — to my humble bachelor-parlour, madam. It is not fit exactly to ask a lady into; but we poor miserable single men, you know, madam, can only do the best we can. Ha! ha! This way."

"No."

"Eh? Not come in?"

"No. I have something to say to you, Mr. Todd; but I will say it here."

And now Mrs. Lovett gave a sidelong glance at the seeming boy, as much as to say — "You can easily send him away if you don't want him to listen to our discourse."

Todd saw the glance; and the diabolical look that he sent to Mrs. Lovett in return would indeed have appalled any one of less nerve than she was possessed of. But she had come to that place wound up firmly to a resolution, and she would not shrink. Todd had no resource.

"Charley," he said, "you can go and take a little turn — here is a penny to spend; get yourself something in the market. But be sure you are back within half an hour, for we shall have some customers, no doubt."

"Yes, sir."

Johanna did not exactly know whether to think that Mrs. Lovett came in anger or friendship; but, at all events, she felt that it would be hazardous to remain after so marked a dismissal from Todd, although she would gladly have heard what the subject of the conversation between those two was to be. Neither Mrs. Lovett nor Todd now spoke until Johanna had fairly gone and closed the door after her. Then Todd, as he folded his arms, and looked Mrs. Lovett fully in the face, said —

"Well?"

"The time has come."

"What time?"

"For the end of our partnership — the dissolution of our agreement. I will go on no further. You can do as you please; but I am content."

"Humph!" said Todd.

"After much thought, I have come to this conclusion, Todd. Of course, let me be where I may, the secret of our road to fortune remains hidden here (she struck her breast as she spoke). All I want is my half of the proceeds, and then we part, I hope, for ever."

"Humph!" said Todd.

"And — and the sooner we can forget, if that be possible, the past, the better it will be for us both — only tell me where you purpose going, and I will take care to avoid you."

"Humph!"

Passion was boiling in the heart of Mrs. Lovett; and that was just what Todd wanted; for well he knew that something had gone amiss, and that as long as Mrs. Lovett could keep herself calm and reasonable, he should stand but a poor chance of finding out what it was, unless she chose, as part of her arrangement, to tell it; but if he could but rouse her passion, he should know all. Therefore was it that he kept on replying to what she said with that cold insulting sort of "humph!"

"Man, do you hear me?"

"Humph!"

"You villain!"

"Humph!"

Mrs. Lovett took from a side-table an iron, which, in the mystery of hair-dressing, was used for some purpose, and in a cool, calm voice, she said —

"If you do not answer me as you ought, I will throw this through your window, into the street; and the first person who comes in, in consequence, I will ask to seize Todd, the murderer! and offer myself as evidence of his numerous atrocities — contrite evidence — myself repenting of my share in them, and relying upon the mercy of the crown, which, in recompense for my denouncing you may graciously pardon me."

"And so it has come to this?" said Todd.

"You see and hear that it has."

It was rather a curious coincidence, that Mrs. Lovett had threatened Todd that she would awaken public attention to his shop by the same means that Sir Richard Blunt had recommended to Johanna to use in case of any emergency — namely, throwing something through the window into the street. If Mrs. Lovett had been goaded by Todd to throw the iron through a pane of his glass, the officers of Sir Richard would quickly have made their appearance to hear her denunciation of the barber. Unhappy woman! If she had but known what the future had in store for her, that act which she threatened Todd with, and which to her imagination seemed such a piece of pure desperation, would have been the most prudent thing she could have done.

But it was not to be! There was a few moments silence now between them. It was broken by Todd.

"Are you mad?" he said.

"No."

"Then, what, in the name of all that is devilish, has got possession of you?"

"I have told you my determination. Give me twenty thousand pounds — you may profit by the odd sum — give me that amount, and I will go in peace. You know I am entitled to more; but there is no occasion for us to reckon closely. Give me the sum I seek, and you will see me no more."

"You take me by surprise. Just step into the parlour, and —"

"No — no."

"Why not? Do you suspect —"

"I suspect nothing; but I am sure of much. Now, for me to set foot within your parlour would be tantamount to the commission of suicide, and I am not yet come to that — you understand me?"

Todd understood her. His hand strayed to a razor that lay partially open close to him. Mrs. Lovett raised the iron.

"Beware!" she said.

Todd shrunk back.

"Pho! pho! this is child's play," he said. "You and I, Mrs. Lovett, ought to be above all this — far above it. You want your half of the proceeds of our joint business, and I must confess, at the moment, that the demand rather staggered and distressed me; but the more I think of it, the more reasonable it appears."

"Very well. Give it to me, then."

"Why, really now, my dear Mrs. Lovett, you quite forget that all our joint savings are in the hands of Mr. Brown."

Todd glared at her as though he would read her very soul. She felt that he more than suspected she knew all, and she adopted at once the bold policy of avowing it.

"I do not forget anything that it is essential should be remembered," she said; "and among other things, I know that, by forging my name, you have withdrawn the whole of the money from the hands of Brown. It is not worth our while to dispute concerning your motives for such an act. Let it suffice that I know it, and that I am here to demand my due."

"Ha! ha!"

"You laugh?"

"I do, indeed. Why, really now — ha! ha! — this is good; and so it is this withdrawal of the money from Brown that has made all this riot in your brain? Why, I withdrew it from him simply because I had certain secret information that his affairs were not in the best order; and from a fear, grounded upon that information, that he might be tempted to put his hand into our purse, if he found nothing in his own."

"Well, well; it matters not what were your reasons. Give me my half. It will be then out of your custody, and you will have no anxiety concerning it, while I can have no suspicions."

"In a moment —"

"You will?"

"If I had it here; but I have re-invested the whole, you see, and cannot get it at a moment's notice. I have moved it from the hands of Brown to those of Black."

CHAPTER LXXIX.

MRS. LOVETT FINDS THAT IN THIS WORLD THERE IS RETRIBUTION.

"Black?" said Mrs. Lovett.

"Yes, Black."

"Do you think me so —" green, she was going to say, but the accidental conjunction of the colours — brown, black, and green — suddenly struck her as ludicrous, and she altered it to foolish. "Do you think me so foolish as for one moment to credit you?"

"Hark you, Mrs. Lovett," pursued Todd, suddenly assuming quite a different tone. "You have come here full of passion, because you thought I was deceiving you."

"You are."

"Allow me to proceed. It is, I believe, one of the penalties of all associations for — for — why do I hesitate about a word? — guilty purposes that there should be mutual distrust. I tell you again, that if I had not moved the money from Brown, we should have lost it all."

"But why not come to me and get my signature?"

"There — really — was — not — time," said Todd, dropping his words out one by one, with a staccato expression.

"That is too absurd."

Todd shrugged his shoulders, as though he would have said — "Well, if you will have it so, I cannot help it;" and then he said —

"I was in the City. I heard the rumour of the instability of Brown. I flew into a shop. I wrote the order like a flash of lightning. I went to Brown's like an avalanche, and I brought away the money, as if Heaven and earth were coming together."

There was not the ghost of a smile upon Todd's face as he made use of these superlatives. Mrs. Lovett began to be staggered.

"Then you have it here?"

"No, no!"

"You have. Tell me that you have, and that this Mr. Black you mentioned is a mere delusion."

"Black may be no colour, but it is not a delusion."

"You trifle with me. Beware!"

"In a word then, my charming Mrs. Lovett, I dreaded to bring the money here. I thought my house the most unsafe place in the world for it. I and you stand upon the brink of a precipice — a slumbering volcano is beneath our feet. Pshaw! Where is your old acuteness, that you do not see at once how truly foolish it would have been to bring the money here?"

"Juggler! Fiend!"

"Hard words, Mrs. Lovett."

She dashed her hand across her brow, as though by that physical effort she could brush from her intellect the sophistical cobwebs that Todd had endeavoured to move before it, and then she said —

"I know not. I care not. All I ask — all I demand — is my share of the money. Give it to me, and let me go."

"I will."

"When?"

"This day. Stay, the day is fast going, but I will say this night, if you really, in your cool judgment, insist upon it."

"I do. I do!"

"Well, you shall have. This night after business was over and the shop was closed, I intended to have come to you, and fully planned all this that you have unfortunately tortured yourself by finding out. I regret that you think of so quickly leaving the profits of a partnership which, in a short time longer, would have made us rich as monarchs. Of course, if you leave, I am compelled."

TODD AND MRS. LOVETT QUARREL.

"You compelled?"

"Yes. How can I carry on business without you? How could I, without your aid, dispose of the —"

"Hush, hush!"

Mrs. Lovett shuddered.

"As you please," said Todd. "I only say, I regret that a co-partnership that promised such happy results should now be broken up. However, that is a matter for your personal consideration merely. If I had thought of leaving, and being content with what I had already got, of course it would have compelled you to do so. Therefore I cannot complain, although I may regret your excuse of a right of action that equally belonged to me."

"If I only thought you sincere —"

"And why not?"

"If I could only bring myself to believe that the money was once more rightly invested —"

"You shall come with me yourself, if you like, in the morning to Mr. Black the broker in Abchurch Lane, No. 3, and ascertain that all is right. You shall there sign your name in his book, so that he may know it, and then you will be satisfied, I presume?"

"Yes, I should then."

"And this dream of leaving off business would vanish?"

"Perhaps it would. But — but —"

"But what?"

"Why did you say to Brown that our union was to take place?"

"Because it was necessary to say something, to account for the sudden withdrawal of the money; and surely I may be pardoned, charming Mrs. Lovett, for even in imagination dreaming, that so much beauty was mine."

The horrible leer with which Todd looked upon her at this moment made her shudder again; and the expression of palpable hatred and disgust that her countenance wore, added yet another, and not the least considerable, link to the chain of revenge which Todd cherished against her in his cruel and most secret heart. While he was philosophising about guilty associations producing a feeling of mutual distrust, he should have likewise added that they soon produce mutual hatred. For a few moments they looked at each other — that guilty pair — with expressions that sought to read each other's souls; but they were both tolerable adepts in the art of dissimulation. The silence was the most awkward for Todd, so he broke it first by saying —

"You are satisfied, let me hope?"

"I will be."

"You shall be."

"Yes, when I have my money. Henceforward, Todd, we will have much shorter reckonings, so shall we keep much longer friends. If you keep, in some secret place, your half of the proceeds of our — our —"

"Business," said Todd.

Mrs. Lovett made a sort of gulph of the word, but she adopted it.

"If you, I say, keep your half of the proceeds of our business, and I keep mine, I don't see how it is possible for us to quarrel."

"Quite impossible."

He began to strop a razor diligently, and to try its edge across his thumb nail. Mrs. Lovett's passion — that overwhelming passion which had induced her to enter Todd's shop, and defy him to a species of single combat of wits — had in a great measure subsided, giving place to a calmer and more reflective feeling. One of the results of that feeling was a self-question to the effect of, "What will be the result of an open quarrel with Todd?" Mrs. Lovett shook a little at the answer she felt forced to give herself to this question. That answer was continued in two words — mutual destruction! Yes, that would be the consequence.

"Todd," she said in a softened tone, "if I had forged your name, and gone to the city and possessed myself of all the money, what would you have thought? Tell me that."

"Just what you thought — that it was the most scandalous breach of faith that could possibly be; but an explanation ought to put that right."

"It has."

"Then you are satisfied?"

"I am. At what time shall we go together, to-morrow morning, to Mr. Black's in Abchurch Lane?"

"Name your own time," said Todd with the most assumed air in the world. "Black lives at Ballam Hill, and don't get to business until ten; but any time after that will do."

"I will come here at ten, then."

"So be it. Ah, Mrs. Lovett, how charming it is to be able to explain away these little difficulties of sentiment. Never trust to appearances. How very deceitful they are apt to be."

There was an air of candour about Todd, that might have deceived the devil himself. Notwithstanding all his hideous ugliness — notwithstanding his voice was of the lowest order, and notwithstanding that frightful laugh, and that obliquity of vision that seemed peculiar to himself in its terrible malignancy, there was a plausibility about his manner, when he pleased, that was truly astonishing. Even Mrs. Lovett, with all her knowledge of the man, felt that it was a hard struggle to disbelieve his representations. What must it have been to those who knew him not?

"No," said Mrs. Lovett, "it don't do to trust to appearances."

She still held the iron in her hand.

"Nor," added Todd, giving the razor he had been putting an edge to, a flourish, "nor will it do to listen always to the dictates of compassion; for if we did, what miseries might we inflict upon ourselves. Now, here is a cure in point."

"Where?"

"I allude to this little affair between us. If you had flown to Bow-street, and there, to spite me, made a full disclosure of certain little facts, why, the result would have been that we might both have slept in Newgate to-night."

"Yes, yes."

"And then there would have been no recall. You could not have freed us by telling the police that you had made a mistake. Then the gallows would have risen up in our dreams."

"Horrible!"

"And it being easily discovered that it was no love of public justice or feeling of remorse, that induced you to the betrayal, they would have shown you no mercy, but you would have swung from the halter amid the shouts and execrations of—"

"No, no!"

"I say yes."

"No more of this—no more of this. Can you bear to paint such a picture—does it not seem to you as though you stood upon that scaffold, and heard those shouts? Oh, horror, horror!"

"You don't like the picture?"

"No, no!"

"Ha! ha! Well, Mrs. Lovett, you and I had far better be friends than foes; and above all, you ought by this time to feel that you could trust me. The very fact that to all the world else I am false, ought to prove to you that to you I am true. No human being can exist purely isolated, and I am not an exception."

"Say no more—say no more. We will meet to-morrow."

"To-morrow be it, then."

"At ten."

"At ten be it, and then we will go to Black. Come now, since all this is settled, take a glass of wine to our—"

"No, no. Not that. I—I am not very well, A throbbing head-ache—a—a. That is, no!"

"As you please—as you please. By-the-by, did Black give me a receipt, or did he say it was not usual? Stay a moment, I will look in my secretaire. Sit down a moment in the shaving chair; I will be with you again directly."

"We will settle that to-morrow," said Mrs. Lovett; "I feel convinced that Black did not give you a receipt. Good-day."

She left the shop, unceremoniously carrying the iron with her. Todd breathed more freely when Mrs. Lovett was gone. He gave one of his horrible laughs as he watched her through the opening in his window.

"Ha! ha! Curses on her; but I will have her life first, ere she sees one guinea of my hoard!"

He saw Charley Green crossing the road.

"Ah, the boy comes back. 'Tis well. I don't know how or why it is, but the sight of that boy makes me uneasy. I think it will be better to cut his throat and have done with him. I—"

Todd was suddenly silent. He saw two women pass, and as they did so, one pointed to his shop and said something to the other, who lifted up her hands as though in pious horror. One of these women was Mrs. Ragg, poor Tobias's mother. The other was a stranger to Todd, but she looked like what Mrs. Ragg had been, namely, a laundress in the temple.

"Curses," he muttered.

Johanna entered the shop. Todd caught up his hat.

"Charley?"

"Yes, sir."

"I shall be gone five minutes. Be vigilant. If any one should come, you can say I have stepped a few doors off to trim Mr. Pentwheezle's whiskers."

"Yes, sir."

Todd darted from the shop. Mrs. Ragg and her friend were in that deep and earnest course that is a foe to rapid locomotion, so they had not got many yards from Todd's door. He was rarely seen, however, for either to —

"Paint a moral or adorn a tale." *

Mrs. Ragg turned suddenly and pointed to the shop, and then both the ladies lifted up their hands as though in horror, after which they resumed their deep and all-absorbing discourse as before. Todd followed them closely, and yet with abundance of caution.

CHAPTER LXXX.

TODD TAKES A JOURNEY TO THE TEMPLE.

THE TWO FEMALES TOOK THEIR WAY to the Temple. Todd had been quite right in his conjectures. The friend of Mrs. Ragg was one of the old compatriots of the laundress tribe; and that good lady herself, although, while there was no temptation to do otherwise, she had kept well the secret of her son's residence at Colonel Jeffery's, broke down like a frail and weak vessel as she was with the weight of the secret the moment she got into a gossip with an old friend. Now Mrs. Ragg had only come into that neighbourhood upon some little errand of her own, and with a positive promise of returning to the colonel's house as soon as possible. She would have kept this promise, but that amid the purlieus of Fetter-lane she encountered Martha Jones, her old acquaintance. One word begot another, and at last as they walked up Fleet-street, Mrs. Ragg

---

* *A line from Dr. Samuel Johnson's 1749 poem,* The Vanity of Human Wishes.

could not help, with many head-shakings and muttered interjectional phrases, letting Martha Jones know that she had a secret. Nay, as she passed Todd's shop, she could not help intimating that she fully believed certain persons, not a hundred miles off, who might be barbers or who might not, would some day come to a bad end in front of Newgate, in the Old Bailey. It was at this insinuation that Martha Jones lifted up her hands, and Mrs. Ragg lifted up hers in sympathy. Todd had seen this action upon the part of the ladies. To overhear what they were saying was to Todd a great object. That it in some measure concerned him he could not for a moment doubt, since the head-shaking and hand-uplifting reference that had been made to his shop by them both as they passed, could not mean anything else. And so, as we have said, he followed them cautiously, dodging behind bulky passengers, so that they should not see him by any sudden glance backwards. One corpulent old lady served him for a shield half up Fleet-street, until, indeed, she turned into a religious bookseller's shop, and left him nothing but thin passengers to interfere between him and the possibility of observation.

But Mrs. Ragg and her friend Martha Jones were much too fully engaged to look behind them. In due course, they arrived opposite to the Temple; and then, after much flurrying, in consequence of real and supposed danger from the passing vehicles, they got across the way. They at once dived into the recesses of the legally-learned Temple. Todd dashed after them.

"Now, my dear Mrs. Ragg," said Martha Jones, "you must not say No. It's got a beautiful head upon it, and will do you good."

"No — no. Really."

"Like cream."

"But, really, I — I —"

"Come, come, it ain't often you is in the Temple, and I knew very well he don't miss a bottle now and then; and 'twix you and me and the pump, I think we has as much a right to that beautiful bottled ale as Mr. Juggas has, for I'd take my bible oath, he don't mean to pay for it, Mrs. Ragg."

"You don't say so?"

"Yes, I does, Mrs. Ragg. Oh, he's a bad 'un, he is. Ah, Mrs. Ragg, you don't know, nor nobody else, what takes place in his chambers of a night."

"Is it possible?"

"Yes. I often say to myself what universal profundity he must be possessed with, for he was once intended, he says, for the church, and I heard him say he'd have stuck to it like bricks, if he could have heard of any church that was intended for him."

"Shocking!"

"Yes, Mrs. Ragg. There's profundity for you."

Did Martha Jones mean profanity?

"Ah," interposed Mrs. Ragg, "we live in a world."

"Yes, Mrs. Ragg, we does; but as you was a saying?"

"Eh?"

"As you was a saying about somebody being hung, if rights was rights, you know."

"Oh, dear, really you must not ask me. Indeed you must not."

"Well, I won't; but here we are, in Pump Court."

Todd darted into a door-way, and watched them up the staircase of No. 6, in that highly classic locality. He slunk into the door-way, and by taking a perspective glance up the staircase, he saw them stop upon the first floor. He saw that they turned to the right. He darted up a few stairs, and just caught sight of a black door. Then there was a sharp sound, as of some small latch closing suddenly, after which all was still. Todd ascended the stairs.

"Curses on them!" he muttered. "What can they mean by looking in such a manner at my shop? I thought the last time I saw that woman, Ragg, that she was cognizant of something. If now she, in her babbling, would give me any news of Tobias — Pho! he is — he must be dead."

By this time Todd had got to the top of the first flight of stairs, and stood upon the landing, close to several open doors — that is to say, outer black heavy-looking doors — and within them were smaller ones, armed with knockers.

"To the right," he muttered. "They went to the right — this must be the door."

He paused at one and listened. Not a sound met his ears, and his impatience began to get extreme. That these two women were going to have a conference about him he fully believed; and that he should be so near at hand, and yet not near enough to listen to it, was indeed galling. In a few moments it became insupportable.

"I must and will know what they mean," he said. "My threats may wring the truth from them; and if necessary, I should not scruple to silence them both. Dead men tell no tales, so goes the proverb, and it applies equally well to dead women."

Todd smiled. He was always fond of a conceit.

"Yes," he muttered, "every circumstance says to me now in audible language, 'Go — go — go!' and go I will, far away from England. I feel that I have not now many hours to spare. This fracas with Mrs. Lovett expedites my departure wonderfully, and to-morrow's dawn shall not see me in London. But I will — I must ascertain what these women are about. Yes, and I will do so at all risks."

A glance showed him that the act of temerity was a safe one. The door opened upon a dingy sort of passage, in which were some mops, pails, and brooms. At its further extremity there was another door, but it was not quite shut, and from the room into which it opened, came the murmur of voices. There were other doors right and left, but Todd heeded only that one which conducted to the room inhabited. He crept along the passage at a snail's pace;

and then having achieved a station exactly outside the door, he placed one of his hands behind one of his elephantine-looking ears, and while his countenance looked like that of some malignant demon, he listened to what was going on within that apartment. Martha Jones was speaking.

"It is good, indeed, Mrs. Ragg, as you may well say, and the glasses sticks to the table, when they is left over-night, showing, as Mr. Juggus says, as it's a gluetenious quality this ale is."

"Sticks to the table?" said Mrs. Ragg.

"Yes, mum, sticks. But as you was a saying?"

"Well, Martha, in course I know that what goes to you goes no farther."

"Not a step."

"And you won't mention it to no one?"

"Not a soul. Another glass?"

"No, no."

"Only one. Nonsense! it don't get into your head. It's as harmless as milk, Mr. Juggus says."

"But ain't you afeard, Martha, he may come in?"

"Not he, Mrs. Ragg. Chambers won't see him agin till night. Oh, he's a shocking young man. Well, Mrs. Ragg, as you was a saying?"

"Well, it is good. As I was a saying, Martha, I don't feel uneasy now about Tobias, poor boy; for if ever a poor lad, as was a orphan in a half-and-half kind of way, seeing that I am his natural mother, and living, and thanking God for the same, and health, leastways, as far as it goes at this present moment of speakin, I — I — Bless me, where was I?"

"At Tobias."

"Oh, yes, I was at Tobias. As I was saying, if ever a poor body was well provided for, Tobias is. The colonel — "

"The who?"

"The colonel, Martha — the colonel as has took the care of him, and who, sooner or later, will have all the truth out of him about the Toddey Sween."

"Who? Who?"

"Bless my poor head, I mean Sweeney Todd. Dear me, what am I thinking of?"

"The barber?"

"Yes, Martha; that horrid barber in Fleet-street; and between you and me, there isn't in all the mortal world a more horrid wretch living than he is."

"I'm all of a shake."

"He — he — "

"Yes, yes. What — "

"He takes folks in and does for 'em."

"Kills 'em?"

"Kills 'em."

TODD LISTENS AND LEARNS A DANGEROUS SECRET.

"What — why — what — ? You don't mean to say — why — ? Take another glass Mrs. Ragg. You don't mean to say that Tobias says, that Todd the barber is a murderer? — My dear Mrs. Ragg, take another glass, and tell us all about it; only look at the cream on the top of it."

"You'll excuse me, Mrs. Jones, but the truth is, I aught not to say more than I have said; and if the colonel only knew I'd said as much, I can tell you, I think he'd be like a roaring lion. But Tobias is quite a gentleman now, you see, and sleeps in as fine a bed as a nobleman could have for love or money. The colonel is very good to him; and there never was such a kind good — good — ."

Mrs. Ragg began to run over with tears of ale.

"Bless me, and where does he live?"

"Who?"

"The colonel. The good, kind, colonel — colonel — a — a dear me, I forget what you said his name was."

"Jeffery, and may his end be peace. He will get the reward of all his good actions in another world than this, Martha. Ah, Martha, such men as he can afford to smile at their latter ends. — No — no, I couldn't."

"Only half a glass; look at the —"

"No — no —"

"Cream on it."

"I must go, indeed. In course the colonel, since I have been his cook, knows what cooking is, for though I say it, perhaps as should not, I am a cook, and not a spiler of folks' victuals. Of course what's said, goes no further. I know I can trust you, Martha."

"Oh dear, yes, in course. I'll just put on my shawl and walk a little way with you, Mrs. Ragg. Dear me — dear me!"

"What is it, Martha?"

"Its a raining like cats and dogs, it is. Well, I never; what shall you do, Mrs. Ragg? What shall you do?"

"Call a coach, I shall, Martha. The last words the colonel said to me was, 'Mrs. Ragg, rather than there should be any delay in your return,' says he, 'as Tobias may want you, call a coach, and I will pay for it.'"

Todd had only just time to dart down the staircase before the two ladies made their appearance; and then hiding sometimes in doorways, and sometimes behind columns and corners, he dodged them into Fleet-street. A coach was duly called, and Mrs. Ragg by the assistance of Martha Jones, was safely bestowed inside it. Todd heard distinctly the colonel's address given to the coachman, who would have it twice over, so that he should be sure he had it all right.

"That will do," said Todd.

He darted across the street, and made the best of his way to his shop again. He listened at the door for a few moments before he entered, and he thought he heard the sound of weeping. He listened more attentively, and then he was sure. Some one was sobbing bitterly within the shop.

"It must be Charley," thought Todd.

He placed his ear quite close to the panel of the door, in the hope that the boy would speak. Todd was quite an adept at listening, but this time he was disappointed, for the sham Charley Green spoke not one word. Yet the deep sobs continued. Todd was not in the best of tempers. He could stand the delay no longer, and bouncing into the shop, he cried —

"What the devil is the meaning of all this? What is the meaning of it, you young rascal? I suspect—"

"Yes, sir," said Johanna, looking Todd full in the face, "and so do I."

"You—you? suspect what?"

"That I shall have to have it out, for its aching distracts me. Did you ever have the tooth-ache, sir?"

"The tooth-ache?"

"Yes, sir. It's—it's worse than the heart-ache, and that I have had."

"Ah!—humph! Any one been?"

"One gentleman, sir, to be shaved; he says he will call again."

"Very good—very good."

Todd took from his pocket the key of the back-parlour—that key without which in his own possession he never left the shop; and then, after casting upon Johanna a somewhat sinister and threatening look, he muttered to himself—

"I suspect that boy. If he refuse to come into the parlour, I will cut his throat in the shop; but if he come in I shall be better satisfied. Charley? Come here."

"Yes, sir," said Johanna, and she walked boldly into the parlour.

"Shut the door."

She closed it.

"Humph," said Todd. "It is no matter. I will call you again when I want you."

CHAPTER LXXXI.

JOHANNA IS ENCOURAGED.

Was Todd satisfied with Johanna's excuse about the toothache? Was he satisfied of the good foible of the supposed Charley Green, by the readiness with which she had come into the parlour? We shall see. If he were not satisfied, he was staggered in his suspicions sufficiently to delay—and delay just then was to Sweeney Todd—one of the most fatal things that could be imagined. There are crumbs of consolation under all circumstances. When Johanna was best sent out of the shop, upon the occasion of the visit of Mrs. Lovett to Todd, she had scarcely got a half dozen steps from the door of the barber's, when a man in passing her, and without pausing a moment, said—

"Miss Oakley, be so good as to follow me."

Johanna at once obeyed the mandate. The man walked rapidly on until a fruiterer's shop was gained, into which he at once walked.

"Mr. Oston," he said to a man behind the counter, "is your parlour vacant?"

"Yes, Sir Richard, and quite at your service," said the fruiterer.

By this Johanna found that she had made no mistake, and that the person she had followed was no other than Sir Richard Blunt, the magistrate, who was interesting himself so much for her safety, as well as for the discovery of what had befallen Mark Ingestrie. The fruiterer's parlour was a prettily fitted up place, where a couple of lovers might in a very romantic manner, if they chose, eat strawberries and cream, and quite enjoy each other's blissful society, in whispered nothing the while. Sir Richard handed Johanna a seat as he said — "Miss Oakley, I am very much pleased, indeed, to have this opportunity of seeing you, and of saying a few words to you."

"Ah, Sir, how much do I owe you."

"Nay, Miss Oakley, you owe me nothing. When once I happily become aware of your situation, it becomes my duty as well as my inclination to protect you in every way against what, I am sure you will forgive me, for calling your rashness."

"Call it what you will, sir."

"Well, Miss Oakley, we will dismiss that part of the subject. Are you going upon any errand, or have you a little time to spare."

"I have some time."

"Then it is a very proper thing that you should enjoy it in taking some proper refreshment."

"I want nothing."

"Nay, but you shall have something whether you want it or not, before I say any more to you about Todd and his affairs."

Johanna, whose mental excitement had prevented her completely from feeling the amount of exhaustion, which otherwise must by that time have come over her, would still have protested that she wanted nothing, but Sir Richard Blunt opened the door of the parlour, and called out —

"Mr. Orton, is your daughter at home?"

"Yes, Sir Richard, Ann is up stairs."

"Very good. My young friend here can find the way, I dare say. Is it the first floor?"

"Yes, don't you hear her practising upon her spinet."

The tinkling sounds of a spinet, then all the fashion; came upon their ears, and Sir Richard, said to Johanna —

"Go up stairs, now, to that young lady. She is about your own age, and her father's housekeeper. She will find you something to eat and drink, and then come down to me, as soon as you can."

Sir Richard nodded to Mr. Orton, who nodded in return, and then Johanna seeing that it was all right, ascended the staircase, and guided by the sound of the spinet, soon found herself in a tolerably handsome room, upon the first floor.

A young girl with a profusion of chestnut curls hanging down her back, was seated at the spinet. Johanna made up to her at once, and throwing her arms round her neck, said —

"And will you say a kind word to me?"

The girl gave a slight scream, and rose.

"Well, I'm sure, you impertinant — handsome —"

"Girl," said Johanna.

"Boy," faltered Miss Orton.

"No, girl," added Johanna. "Your father sent me to you, and Sir Richard Blunt suggested it. Shall I leave you again."

"Oh, no — no," said Ann Orton, as she sprang towards Johanna, and kissed her on both cheeks, "you are Miss Johanna Oakley."

"How is it that you know me?"

"My father is an old friend of Sir Richard's, and he has told us all your story. How truly delighted I am to see you. And so you have escaped from that odious Todd, and —"

"Immediate refreshment, my dear, and all the attention you can cram into a very short space of time to Miss Oakley, my dear," said Mr. Orton, just putting his head so far into the room as to make himself plainly and distinctly heard.

"Yes, father, yes."

"How kind you all are," said Johanna.

"No — no — at least we wish to be, but what I mean is that we are no kinder than we ought to be. My father is so good, I have no mother."

"And I, too, am motherless."

"Yes, I — I heard that Mrs. Oakley —"

"Lived, you would say; and yet am I motherless."

Johanna burst into tears. The sense of desolation that came over the young girl's heart whenever she thought how little of a mother the fanatical personage who owned that title was to her, generally overcame all her firmness, as upon the present occasion. Ann flung her arms around Johanna, and the two young creatures wept in unison. We will leave them to their sacred intercourse.

SIR RICHARD BLUNT REMAINED in conversation with Mr. Orton for about a quarter of an hour, and then both Johanna and Ann came down stairs. Johanna looked calmer and happier. Ann had said some kind things to her — such as none but a young girl can say to a young girl.

"I am ready," said Johanna.

"Ready for what?" enquired Sir Richard Blunt, with a look of earnest affection in the face of the beautiful heroine — for if ever there were a heroine, we really think Johanna Oakley was one, and we are quite sure that you agree with us.

"For my mission," said Johanna, "I am ready."

"And can you really find courage to go again to that—that—"

Sir Richard could not find a fitting name for Todd's home, but Johanna understood him, and she replied gently—

"I may not pause now. It is my duty."

"Your duty?"

"Yes. Oh, Mark—Mark, I cannot restore you from the dead, but in the sacred cause of justice I may bring your murderer to the light of day. It is my duty to do so much for your memory."

Ann turned aside to hide her tears. Mr. Orton, too, was much affected, and there was an unwonted jar, as though some false note had had been struck in voice of Sir Richard Blunt as he spoke, saying—

"Miss Oakley, I will not—I cannot deny that by your going back to Todd's house, you may materially assist in the cause of justice. But yet I advise you not to do so."

"I know you are all careful of my safety, while I—"

"Ah, Johanna," said Ann, "you do not know yet that you are so desolate as to wish to die."

"Yes, yes—I am desolate."

"And so," added Sir Richard, "because you loved one who has been, according to your judgment upon the circumstances that have come to your knowledge, torn from you by death, you will admit no other ties which could bind you to the world. Is that right? Is it like you?"

The tones of voice in which these words were uttered, as well as the sentiment embodied in them, sunk deeply into Johanna's heart. Clasping her hands together, she cried—

"Oh, no, no! Do no think me so inhuman. Do not think me so very ungrateful."

"Had you forgotten, Arabella Wilmot? Had you forgotten your father? Nay, had you forgotten the brave Colonel Jeffery?"

"No, no! I ought not to forget any, when so many have so kindly remembered me, and you too, sir, I ought not, and will not forget you, for you have been a kind friend to me."

"Nay, I am nothing."

"Seek not, sir, to disparage what you have done, you have been all kindness to me."

Before he was aware of what she was about, Johanna had seized the hand of Sir Richard Blunt, and for one brief moment touched it with her lips. The good magistrate was sensibly affected.

"God bless me!" said Mr. Orton, "something very big keeps blocking up the whole of my window."

They all looked, and as they were silent at that moment, they heard a voice from the street, say —

"Come! Come, my dear! Don't set the water-works a-going. Always remember, that easy does it. You come in here, and have something to eat, if you won't go home. Lor bless me! what will they think has become of me at the tower?"

"Why, it is Ben!" cried Johanna.

"Ben?" said Ann. "Who is Ben?"

"Hush! Stop," said Sir Richard, "I pray you, stop."

Johanna would have rushed out to speak to Ben, who certainly was at the window of the fruiterer's shop, with Arabella Wilmot upon his arm, endeavouring to persuade her to enter, and partake of some refreshment.

"I will bring him in," said Sir Richard. "Retire into the parlour, I beg of you, Miss Oakley, for he will make quite a scene in the shop if you do not."

Johanna knew well Ben's affection for her, and doubted not, but that as Sir Richard said, he would not scruple to show it, even in the open shop, probably to the great edification of the passers by. She accordingly retired to the parlour with Ann. In a few moments, Sir Richard Blunt ushered in both Ben and Arabella Wilmot. Arabella with a shriek of joy, rushed into Johanna's arms, and then with excess of emotion she fainted. Ben caught up Johanna fairly off her feet, as though he had been dancing some little child, and holding her in a sitting posture upon one arm, he said —

"Bless you! Easy does it. Easy I say — does — it. Don't you think I'm a crying. It's a tea-chest has flew in my eye from that grocer's shop opposite. Oh, you little rogue, you. Easy does it. What you have got them what do you call 'ems on, have you?"

The kiss that Ben gave her might have been heard at Sweeney Todd's, and then when prevailed upon to sit down, he would insist upon holding her fast upon his knee.

"I must go," said Johanna, and then looking at Arabella, she added — "Let me go, before she awakens from her transient forgetfulness to beg me to stay."

Ben was furious at the idea of Johanna going back to Todd's, but Sir Richard, overruled him, and after some trouble, got him to consent. Then turning to Johanna, he said —

"The moment night comes on, you will have some visitors, and remember, Miss Oakley, that St. Dunstan's is the watch-word. Whoever comes to you with that in his mouth, is a friend."

"I will remember, and now farewell and God bless and reward you for all your goodness to me. I will live for the many who love me yet, and whom I love in this world."

WAS IT NOT A WORLD OF WONDERS that amid all this, Johanna did not go mad? Surely something more than mortal strength must have sustained that young and innocent girl in the midst of all these strange events. No human power that she possessed, could have possibly prevented her mind from sinking, and the hideous fascinations of an overcharged fancy from breeding

"Rude riot in her brain."

But there was a power who supported her — a power which from the commencement of the world has supported many — a power which while the world continues, will support many more, strengthening the weak and trampling on the strong. The power of love in all the magic of its deep and full intensity. Yes, this was the power which armed that frail and delicate-looking girl with strength to cope with such a man — man shall we call him? no, we may say such a fiend as Sweeney Todd. If it required no small amount of moral courage to go in the first instance upon that expedition — so fraught with danger, to Todd's shop — what did it require now to enable her to return after having passed through much peril, and tasting the sweets of friendship and sympathy? Surely any heart but Johanna's must have shrunk aghast from ever again even in thought, approaching that dreadful place. And yet she went. Yes upon her mission of justice she went. To be sure, she was told that as far as human means went, she would be upheld and supported from those without; but what could that assure to her further than that if she fell she should not fall unavenged? Truly, if some higher, some far nobler impulse than that derived from any consciousness that she was looked after, had not strengthened her, the girl's spirit, must have sunk beneath the weight of many terrors. With a sad smile she once again crossed the threshold of that house, which she now no longer suspected to be the murderer's haunt. She knew it.

CHAPTER LXXXII.

TODD PLANS.

HOW SHE SPED WITH TODD we are already aware. Let us take a peep at the arch-demon in that parlour, which he considered his sanctuary, his city of refuge as it were. At least Todd considered it to be such, whether it was or not. He sits at a table, the table beneath which there was no floor, and covering up his face with his huge hands, he sets about thinking. Yes, that man now abandons himself to thought, as to how he is, with a blaze of wickedness, to disappear from the scene of his iniquities. It was not remorse that now filled his brain. It was not any feeling of bitter heart-felt regret for what he had done that oppressed him now. No such feeling might possibly find a home in his heart at the hour of success, but now when he saw and felt that he was surrounded by many difficulties, it had no home in his brain. But yet he thought that they were only difficulties that now surrounded; he did not as yet dream of positive danger. He still reasoned, as you have heard him reason before, namely, that if anything beyond mere suspicion were entertained regarding his mode of life, he would be at once apprehended. He thought that some-body — most likely Colonel Jeffery — was trying to find out something, and the fact that he, Todd, was there in his own parlour, a free man, appeared to him proof-sufficient that nothing was found out.

"How fallacious!"

If he had but known that he was virtually in custody even then, as he, indeed, really was, for Fleet-street was alive with officers and the emissaries of the police. If he had but guessed so much for a moment what a wild tumult would have been raised in his brain. But he knew nothing and suspected little.

After a time from generalizing upon his condition, Todd began to be particular, and then he laid down, as it were, one proposition or fact which he intended should be the groundwork of all in other proceedings. That propo-sition was contained in the words —

"Before the dawn of to-morrow I must be off!"

"That's settled," said Todd, and he gave the table a blow with his hand. "Yes, that's settled."

The table creaked ominously, and Todd rose to peep into the shop to see what his boy was doing. Charley Green, alias, Johanna Oakley, was sitting upon a low stool reading a bill that some one had thrown into the shop, and which detailed the merits of some merchandise. How far away from the contents of that bill which she held before her face, were her thoughts?

"Good," said Todd. "That boy, at all events, suspects nothing, and yet his death is one of the things which had better not be left to chance. He shall fall in the general way of this place. What proper feeling errand-boy would wish to survive his master's absence. Ha!"

Of late Todd had not been very profuse in his laughs, but now he came out with one quite of the old sort.

The sound startled himself, and he retired to the table again.

By the dim light he opened a desk and supplied himself with writing materials; the twilight was creeping on, and he could only just see. Spreading a piece of paper before him, he proceeded to make a memoranda of what he had to do.

It was no bad plan this of Todd's, and the paper, when it was finished was quite a curiosity in its way. It ran thus —

Mem. — To go to Colonel Jeffery's, and by some means get into the house and murder Tobias.

Mem. — To pack off goods to the wharf where the Hamburg vessel, called the Dianna, sails from.

Mem. — To arrange combustibles for setting fire to the house.

Mem. — To cut Charley Green's throat, if any suspicion arise — if not to let him be smothered in the fire.

Mem. — To have a letter ready to post to Sir Richard Blunt, the magistrate, accusing Mrs. Lovett of her own crimes, and mine likewise.

"I think that is all," said Todd.

He folded the paper and placed it in his bosom, after which he came out of the parlour into the shop, and called to Johanna.

"Charles?"

"Yes, sir."

"Go to the market, and get me a couple of stout porters — I want something carried a short distance."

"Yes, sir."

Away went Johanna, but before she got half way down to Fleet Market she met Sir Richard, who said —

"What is it?"

"He wants a couple of porters to carry something."

"Very well, get them. Depend upon me."

"I do, sir. I feel now in good heart to go through with anything, for you are near to me, and I know that I am safe."

"You are safe. It will need to be some very extraordinary circumstances, indeed, that could compromise you. But go at once for these porters; I, and my men will take good care to find where they go to."

There was no difficulty in finding parties in abundance at the end of Fleet Market, and Johanna speedily returned, followed by two sturdy fellows. Todd had quite a smile upon his face, as he received them.

"This way," he said — "This way. I hope you have been lucky to day, and have had plenty of work."

"No, master," said one, "we haven't, I'm sorry to say."

"Indeed," added Todd. "Well, I am very glad I have a little job for you. You see these two little boxes. You can carry one each of you, and I will go with you and show you where to."

One of the porters raised one of the boxes, and then he gave a long whistle, as he said —

"I say, master is there penny pieces or paving stones in this here, its deuced heavy, that it is."

"And so is this, Bill," said the other. "Oh, my eyes ain't it. There must be a quarter of a pound of goose feathers in here."

"Ha! ha!" said Todd, "How funny you both are."

"Funny?"

"Yes, to be sure, but come. This will put strength into you if you had none before."

He took a bottle and glass from a cupboard, and gave each of the men a full measure of such frightfully strong spirits, that they winked again, and the tears came into their eyes, as they drank it.

"Now shoulder the little boxes, and come along," he said, "and I tell you what I'll do. If you step in here in the evening, and I should happen to be at home, I'll give each of you a shave for nothing, and polish you off in such a manner, that you will recollect it as long you live."

"Thank you, master — thank you. We'll come."

One of the porters helped his companion with the chest on to his back and head, and Todd then lent a helping hand with the other.

"Charley," he said. "I shall be back in a quarter of an hour."

Away he went, preceding the porter by some half dozen steps only, but yet ever and anon keeping a wary eye upon the two chests, which contained cash, and jewels, sufficient to found a little kingdom. If he got clear off with those two chests only, he felt that he would not give himself much uneasiness about what was left behind. But was Todd going to trust these two porters from out his own immediate neighbourhood, with the secret of the destination of the boxes? No. He was by far too crafty for that. After proceeding some distance, he took them round the unfrequented side of St. Paul's Church yard, and stopping suddenly at the door of a house that was to let, he said —

"This will do."

"In here, master."

"This will do. Put them down."

The porters complied, and Todd set down upon one of the boxes, as he said —

"How much?"

"A shilling each of us, master."

"There's double the money, and now be off, both of you, about your business."

The porters were rather surprised, but as they considered themselves sufficiently paid, they made no objection, and walked off with considerable alacrity, leaving Todd, and his treasure in the street.

"Now for a coach," he muttered. "Now for a coach. Here boy" — to a ragged boy who was creeping on at some short distance. "Earn a penny by fetching me a coach directly."

The boy darted off, and in a very few minutes brought Todd a hackney coach. The boxes, too, were got upon it by the united efforts of Todd, the coachman, and the boy, and then, and not till then did Todd give the correct address of the wharf in Thames-street from which the Hamburg ship was going, and in which he fully intended to embark that night. The ship was advertised to sail at the turn of the tide, which would be about four o'clock in the morning.

All this did not take long to do. The coach rumbled along Thames-street, but Todd was not aware that Mr. Crotchet had got up behind the vehicle, but such was the fact, and when the lumbering old machine stopped at the wharf, that gentleman got down, and felt quite satisfied with the discovery he had made. "He's a trying of it on," soliloquised Mr. Crotchet in the bolting line, "but it ain't no manner of a go. He'll swing, and he can't help it, if he were to book himself to the moon, and there was a coach or a ship as went all the way, and no stoppages."

"Mem," said Todd to himself. "To go to Colonel Jeffery's and murder Tobias — Ha!"

"Lor!" said the coachman, "was that you, sir?"

"What do you mean?"

"Why as made that horrid sort of noise."

"Mind your business, my friend, and tell me if you can take me quickly to Islington, for I have no time to lose."

"Like the wind, sir, you can go with these here osses," replied the coachman, "did you ever see sich bits o' blood, sir, one on 'em's blind, and' t'other on 'em is deaf, which is advantages as you don't get in one pair."

"Advantages?"

"Lor bless you, yes, sir. The blind 'un goes unknown quick, cos you sees, sir, he thinks he's only in some dark place, and in course he wants to get out on it as soon as he can."

"Indeed?"

"Yes, sir, and the deaf 'un, he goes quick too, cos as he hears nothink, he thinks as there never was sich a quiet place as he's go's, and he does it out o' feeling and gratitude, sir, yer sees."

"Be quick then, and charge your own price."

Todd sprang into the vehicle, and stimulated by the idea of charging his own price, the coachman certainly did make the bits of blood do wonders, and in quite an incredibly short space of time, Todd found himself in the immediate neighbourhood of the Colonel's house. It was now getting dark, but that was what he wished. He dismissed the coach, and took from the angle of a wall, near at hand, a long and earnest look at the Colonel's house, and as he did so dark and hideous thoughts concerning Tobias passed through his mind.

CHAPTER LXXXII.

TODD VISITS THE COLONEL

"WELL, TOBIAS," SAID COLONEL JEFFERY, as he entered the pretty, cheerful room into which the now convalescent boy had been removed. "Well, Tobias, how are you now?"

"Much better, sir. Oh, sir, — I — I —"

"What would you say?"

"I feel that when I see you, sir, I ought to say so much to convince you of how truly, and deeply grateful I am to you, and yet I can scarcely ever say a word about it. I pray for your happiness, sir, indeed I do. Your name and my mother's, and — and Minna Gray's, are always uttered to God by me."

"Now, Tobias," said Colonel Jeffery gravely. "I am quite satisfied that as regards all that has passed, you feel as you ought to feel, and for my own part, I beg you to feel and to know that your saying anything about it only distresses me."

"Distresses you, sir?"

"Yes, it does, indeed. I see your eyes are upon the door. You expect Minna, to day, I am sure."

"Yes, sir, — she — she — my mother was to bring her, sir."

A ringing at a bell now came upon Tobias's ear, and his colour went and came fitfully.

"You are still very weak, my poor boy," said the colonel, "but you are certainly much improved. Do you feel any confusion in your head now?"

"None at all, only when I think of Todd suddenly, ever it makes me feel cold and sick, and something seems to rush through my heart."

"Oh, that will go away. That is nothing. There, I will draw up the blind for you. The evening is coming, and the sky is overclouded. You can see better now, and there is one coming whom I know you wish to lose no sight of."

"I hear her foot upon the stairs," said Tobias.

"Do you? — It is more than I do."

"Ah, sir, the senses are sharpened, I think, by illness."

"Not so much as by love. Tobias! do you hear her footstep now?"

"Yes, and it is like music."

He had his head on one side in an attitude of listening; and then with joy sparkling from every feature of his face, he spoke again —

"She comes — she comes. Ah, she comes fast. My own — my beautiful. She come — she comes."

"This is real love," said the colonel, and he stepped from the room. Nearly on the landing at the head of the stairs, he met Minna Gray.

"Welcome," he said as he held out his hand to her. "You will find your young friend up and much better."

Minna could only look her thanks. Mrs. Ragg was following her, and as the ascent of stairs was always rather a task to that good Lady, she was making a noise like a stranded grampus in breathing.

"Ah, colonel," she said, "young legs get up stairs faster than old ones, sir, as you see. Well — well, there was a time when first I knew poor dear Ragg, who is of course dead and gone, quite premature."

"Exactly, Mrs. Ragg," said the colonel, as he rapidly descended the stairs.

"Did you ever, my dear, know such a strange man?" said Mrs. Ragg to Minna.

"Who?"

"The colonel, to be sure. So soon as I begin to tell him any little what do you call it. No it ain't nannygoat — that's ridiculous. It's — it's — what is it?"

"Anecdote do you mean, Mrs. Ragg?"

"Yes, to be sure. Well, as I was a saying, no sooner do I begin telling him a little nannygoat — no, I mean anecdote, than off he is like a shot."

Minna smiled to herself, and she was far from wondering that the colonel was off like a shot, for well she knew, that when Mrs. Ragg did begin anything concerning the late Mr. Ragg, it usually lasted three quarters of an hour at the very least.

"Minna, Minna!" called Tobias.

"I am here, Tobias."

In another moment she was in the room. Truly it was a pleasant thing to see the face of Tobias, when, his sunshine, as he called Minna, came close to him, and in her soft voice asked him if he was better.

"Don't mind me," said Mrs. Ragg, "I am going to darn a stocking or two. that's all. Just say what you both like. Young folks will be young folks. Bless me, I recollect just as if it were only yesterday, when I used to speak to poor departed Mr. Ragg, who is, premature, dead and gone, in a manner of speaking. Ah, dear me! How the world goes round and round — round and round, continually."

Tobias and Minna were so well accustomed to the garrulity of Mrs. Ragg, and so well aware that she required no answer, that they let her talk on, and did not mind her, as she requested they would not; and so the evening grew apace, and the light gradually began to wane, as those two young loving hearts spoke together of the future, and indulged in that day dream of happiness which can only belong to youth and love.

TODD HORRIFIES MRS. RAGG.

TODD IS SKULKING ROUND THE ANGLE of the garden wall, from which he can get a view of the colonel's house, and yet not be seen himself.

The more he looked the more the desire grew upon him, notwithstanding the immense risk he ran of personal detection, by so doing, to get into the house, and finish the career of poor Tobias. He would have had no particular objection rather to have taken the life of Mrs. Ragg, if it could be easily and comfortably done.

It has been said that there are folks in the world who never forgive any one for doing them a kindness; and such paradoxical views of human nature have been attempted to be laid down as truths; but whether this be so or not, is still to be proved, although it is certain that nothing stirs the evil passions of men who will inflict injury upon the innocent, as to find themselves baffled in their villany. From that moment the matter becomes a personal affair of vengeance.

Hence, since Todd had become thoroughly aware that Tobias had escaped from the death he had intended for him at the mad-house, his rage against the boy knew no bounds.

Indeed, the reader will conclude that it must have been a feeling of no ordinary strength, that, at such a busy and ticklish time, would take Todd to the colonel's house at all.

It was revenge — bitter, uncompromising revenge!

Now, you must know the colonel's house was one of those half-villa, half-mansion-like residences, that are so common in the neighbourhood of London. There was a kind of terrace in the front, and a garden with flowering shrubs, that had a pretty enough appearance, and which at night afforded abundance of shelter.

It was by this front garden that Todd hoped to reach the house.

When it was nearly dark, he slunk in, crouching down among the trees and shrubs, and crawling along like a serpent as he was. He soon came to a flight of stone steps that led to the kitchens.

By the time Todd had got thus far, some of her domestic duties had called Mrs. Ragg to the lower part of the house. He saw by the fire-light that some one was going about the kitchen, close to the foot of the stone steps; but he could not exactly, by that dim and uncertain radiance, take upon himself to say that it was Mrs. Ragg.

She soon lit a candle, though, and then all was clear. He saw the good lady preparing divers lights for the upper rooms.

While Todd was half-way down the stone steps, peeping into the kitchen, one of the other servants of the house came into that receptacle for culinary articles, and commenced putting on a bonnet and shawl. Todd could not hear one word of what was said by Mrs. Ragg and this young woman who was getting ready to go out; but he saw them talk, and by their manner he felt convinced that it was only upon ordinary topics.

If the young woman left the house by the steps upon which Todd was, and which it was more than likely she would do, his situation would be anything but a pleasant one, and discovery would be certain.

To obviate the chance of this, he stepped back, and crouched down in among the shrubs in the garden.

He was not wrong in his conjectures, for in a few moments the servant, who was going out, ascended the steps, and passed him so closely, that by stretching out his hand, he could, if he had been so minded, have touched her dress. In a short time she was out of ear-shot.

Todd emerged from his concealment again, and crept down the steps, and once more peeped into the kitchen.

Mrs. Ragg was still busy with the candles.

He was just considering what he should do, when he heard the tramp of horses' feet in the road above. He ascended sufficient of the steps to enable himself to get a peep at what was going on. He saw a groom well mounted, and leading another horse. Then no other than Colonel Jeffrey himself, although he did not of his own knowledge, feel assured that it was him, come out at the front door of the house and mounted.

"Now, William," said the colonel, "we must ride sharply."

"Yes, sir," said the groom.

Another moment and they were gone.

"This is lucky," said Todd. "It is not likely that there is any other room in the house; and if not, I have the game in my own hands."

He crept down the remainder of the stone steps, and placed his ear quite close to the kitchen window.

Mrs. Ragg was enjoying a little conversation to herself.

"Ah!" she said, "it's always the way — girls will be girls; but what I blame her for is, that she don't ask the colonel's leave at once, and say — 'Sir, your disorderly has won my infections, and may he come here and take a cup of tea?'"

This was Greek to Todd.

"What is the old fool talking about," he muttered. "But I will soon give her a subject that will last for her life."

He now arrived at the door of the kitchen. It was very unlikely to be locked or otherwise fastened, so immediately after the young woman, who had left the house, and passed so close to him, Todd. Yet he listened for a few moments more, as Mrs. Ragg kept making observations to herself.

"Listeners hear no good of themselves, says the proverb, and at all events it was verified in this instance."

"Lor' a mussy," ejaculated Mrs. Ragg, "how my mind do run upon that horrid old ugly monster of a Todd to-day. Well, I do hope I shall never look upon his frightful face again, and how awful he did squint, too. Dear me, what did the colonel say he had with his vision — could it be — a something afixity? No that isn't it."

"Obliquity!" said Todd, popping his head in at the kitchen door. "It was obliquity, and if you scream or make the least alarm, I'll skin you, and strew this kitchen with your mangled remains!"

Mrs. Ragg sank into a chair with a melo-dramatic groan, that would have made her fortune over the water in domestic tragedy if she could have done it so naturally. Todd kept his eye upon her. That basilisk-like eye, which had fascinated the good woman often, and this time it acted as a kind of spell, for truly might he have said, or rather might some one have said for him,—

"He held her with his glittering eye." *

Todd's first care now was to get between Mrs. Ragg and the kitchen door, lest upon some sudden impulse she should rise and flee. Then he folded his arms, and looked at her calmly, and with such a devilish smile as might have become Mephistopheles himself, while contemplating the ruin of a soul. He took from his pocket a razor.

"Mercy," gasped Mrs. Ragg.

"Where is Tobias?"

"Up stairs. Back room, second floor, looking into the garden."

"Alone?"

"No, Minna Grey is with him."

"Listen to me. If you stir from here until I come to you again, I will not only murder you, but Tobias likewise, and every one whom I meet with in this house. You know me, and can come to some opinion as to whether or not I am a man likely to keep my word. Remain where you are; move not, speak not, and all will be well."

Mrs. Ragg slowly slid off her chair, and fell to the floor of the kitchen, where she lay, in what seemed a swoon.

"That will do as well," said Todd as he glanced at her, "and yet as I return." He made a movement with his hand across his throat to indicate what he would do, and then feeling assured that he had little or, indeed, no opposition to expect in the house, he left the kitchen, and walked up stairs.

When he reached the top of the kitchen stairs he paused to listen. All was very still in the house.

" 'Tis well," he said " 'tis well. This deed of blood shall be done, and long before it can be thought that it was I who struck the blow, I shall be gone."

Alas! After passing through so much! After being pursued in so almost a miraculous manner from the murderous intentions of Todd, backed by the cupidity of Fogg, and his subordinate Watson, was poor Tobias yet to die a terrible death as a victim to the cruel passions of his relentless persecutor?

No, we will not yet believe that such is to be the fate of poor honest Tobias, although at the present time, his prospects look gloomy. Todd may have, and no doubt has, taken as worthy lives, but we will hope that the hand of Providence will prevent him from taking this one.

He reached the landing of the first floor, and he paused to listen again. He thought this time, that he heard the faint sound of voices above, but he was not quite sure. Otherwise all was quiet.

---

* *A line from Samuel Taylor Coleridge's* The Rime of the Ancient Mariner *(1834).*

This was a critical situation for Todd. If any one who was a painter of pictures or of morals had but seen him, Sweeney Todd, as he there stood, they would no longer have doubted either that there was a devil, or that some persons in this world were actuated by a devilish fiend. He looked the incarnate fiend! — the Mephistopheles of the imagination, such as he is painted by the German enthusiast. His laugh too? Was not that satanic?

He set himself to listen to the voices that he heard in that quiet rooms and the sounds, holy and full of affection as they were, awakened no chord of answering feeling in that bold, bad man's breast. He stood apart from human nature, a solitary being. A wreck upon the ocean of society

"None loving, and by none beloved." *

Who would be Sweeney Todd, for all the wealth, real or fabled, of a million Californias?

"He is here," he said, "I know his voice. Tobias is here. Ah! he mentions the name of God. Ha! He is more fitting to go to that heaven he can talk of so glibly, but there is none. There is none! No, no! all that is a fable."

Of course Todd could not believe in a divinity of goodness and mercy. If he had, what on earth could have saved him from absolute madness?

CHAPTER LXXXIII.

TOBIAS IN JEOPARDY.

"AND SO YOU DO LOVE ME, MINNA?" said Tobias.

How his voice shook like a reed swayed by the wind, and yet what a world of melody was in it.

"Can you ask me to say yes?" was the reply of the fair young creature by his side. "Can you ask me to say yes, Tobias?"

"It seems to me," said Tobias, "as though it would be such a joy to hear you say so, Minna, and yet I will not ask you."

"How well you have got, Tobias. Your cheek has got its old colour back again. The colour it had long before you knew there was such a man as Sweeney Todd in the world. Your eyes are bright too, and your voice has its old pleasant sound."

"Used it to be pleasant to you, Minna?"

* *A line from the ancient Roman poet Juvenal, written circa 100 C.E.*

She held up her hand, and shook her head laughingly.

"No questions, Tobias! No questions. I will confess nothing."

"Stop!" said Tobias, as he put himself into an attitude of listening, "what was that, I thought I heard something? It was like a suppressed growl. I wish the colonel would come home. Did you not hear it, Minna?"

Minna had heard it, but she did not say she had.

"Where did it come from, Tobias?"

"From the stair-head, Minna."

"Oh, it is some accidental noise, such as is common to all houses, and such as always defy conjecture and explanation, and being nothing and meaning nothing, always comes to nothing. Yet I will go and see. Perhaps a door has been left open, and is banging to and fro by the wind, and if so it will only vex you to hear it again, Tobias."

It was Todd, who upon hearing the soft and tender speeches from the young lovers, had not been able to suppress a growl, and now that he had heard Minna Grey talk of coming to look what it was, he felt the necessity of instantly concealing himself somewhere.

It was not likely she would come down the stairs, so Todd adopted an original mode of keeping himself out of sight.

He descended steps sufficient, that by laying at full length along them, his head did not reach the top, and in the darkness he then considered that he should be quite safe from the casual glance, that in all likelihood, merely to satisfy Tobias, Minna would give outside the room door.

Todd thought by her manner she had heard nothing.

"No, no, Minna," said Tobias, "there is no occasion. It is nothing, I dare say, and I don't like you to be out of my sight a moment."

"It is only a moment."

She rose, and proceeded to the door.

An unknown feeling of dread, she knew not why, was at the heart of Minna. Certainly the slight sound she had heard, and that too in the house of Colonel Jeffery, was not sufficient to warrant such a feeling, and yet there, at her heart, it sat brooding.

She stood for a moment at the door.

It was only for a moment.

"How foolish I am," she thought, and then she passed out on to the landing, where she stood for a moment glancing round her.

"It is nothing, Minna," called out Tobias, "or shall I try and come. I feel quite strong enough to do so."

"Oh, no — no! It is nothing."

Minna stepped lightly back and sat down. She clasped her hands very tight indeed together, and then placed both upon her breast.

She had seen Todd.

HEROIC CONDUCT OF MINNA GRAY.

Yes, Minna Grey had seen the man that had been, and who was for all she knew to the contrary still to be, the bane of Tobias's existence. The clear eyes of youth had noticed the lumbering figure as it lay upon the stairs before them.

And she did not scream — she did not cry for help — she did not faint, she only crept back as we have seen, and held her hands upon her heart, and looked at Tobias.

There was no mistaking Todd. Once seen he was known for ever. Like some hideous picture, there dwelt the memory of Sweeney Todd upon the young imagination of the fair Minna Grey.

Once before, a long time ago, so it seemed to her, she had seen him in the

Temple skulking up an old staircase. From that moment the face was Daguerreotyped upon her brain.

It was never to be forgotten, and with the face comes the figure too. That she saw upon the stairs.

Alas! Poor Minna!

"And so it was nothing but one of those odd accidents that will occur in defiance of all experience, and calculation," said Tobias.

"Just that," replied Minna.

"Ah, my dear Minna. We are so safe here. It always seems to me as though the very air of this house, belonging as it does to such a man, so full of goodness as the colonel is, such that nothing very bad could live in it for long."

"I — I hope so — I think so. — What a calm and pleasant evening it is, Tobias, did you see the new book of the seasons, so full of pretty engravings in the shape of birds and trees, and flowers, that the colonel has purchased."

"New book?"

"Yes, it lies in his small study, upon this floor. I will fetch it for you, if you wish it, Tobias?"

"Nay, I will go."

"You are still weak. Remain in peace upon the couch, dear Tobias, and I will go for you."

Before she left the room, she kissed the forehead of the boy. A tear, too, fell upon his hand.

"Who knows," she thought, "that I shall ever see him in life again?"

"Minna, you weep."

"Weep? No — no — I am so — so happy."

She hastily left the room. Todd had heard what had passed, and had turned to hide himself again. The young girl knew that she passed the murderer within a hair's breadth. She knew that he had but to stretch out his right hand and say — "Minna Gray, you are my victim!" and his victim she would have become. Was not that dreadful? And she so young and so fair — so upon the threshold, as it were, of the garden of her existence — so loving, and so well-beloved. She felt for a moment, as she crossed the landing — just for a moment as though she were going mad. But the eye of the Omnipotent was upon that house. She staggered on. She made her way into a bed-room. It was the colonel's. Above the mantel-shelf, supported on a small bracket, was a pair of pistols. They were of a large size, and she had heard from the current gossip of the house, how they were always loaded, and how the servants feared to touch them, and how even they shrank from making the bed, lest the pistol from some malice afore-thought, or from something incidental to such watching, should go off at once of their own accord, and inevitably shoot whoever chanced to be in the room. Minna Gray laid her hand upon the dreaded weapons.

"For Tobias! for Tobias!" she gasped.

Then she paused to listen. All was still as the grave. Todd was not yet ready for the murder, or he wished to take their lives both together, and in the one room. That was more probable. Then she began to think that he must have some suspicion, and that it was necessary upon her part to do something more than merely make no alarm. The idea of singing occurred to her. It was a childish song that she had been taught, when a pretty child, that she now warbled forth a few lines of—

> *If I were a forest bird,*
>   *I'd shun the noisy town;*
> *I'd seek the verdure of the spring*
>   *The dear autumnal brown.*
> *And even when the winter came,*
>   *By sunny skies bereft,*
> *I'd sleep in some deep distant cave,*
>   *Which wanton winds had left.*

She crossed the landing.

"Minna," said Tobias. "My Minna!"

"I come."

She passed into the room, and the moment she crossed the threshold — she turned her face to it and presented both the pistols before her. Then as she wound, inch by inch, into the centre of the room, all her power of further concealment of her feelings deserted her, and she could only say, in a strange choking tone—

"Todd! — Todd! — Todd!"

"No — no — no! Oh, God, no!" cried Tobias.

"Todd! — Todd! — Todd!"

"No — no! Help! help!"

"D — n!" said Sweeney Todd, as he dashed open the door of the chamber, and stood upon the threshold with a glittering knife in his right hand.

"Hold!" shrieked Minna Gray. "Another step, murderer, and I send you to your God!"

Todd waited. He could almost see down the barrels of the large pistols, which a touch of the young girl's finger would explode in his face. With a sharp convulsive cry, Tobias fell to the floor. The blood gushed from his mouth, and he lay bereft of sensation.

"Away!" cried Minna. "Monster, away! Another moment, and as Heaven hears me, I will fire; once — twice —"

Todd darted to the stair head, but he darted away again quicker than he had gone there; for who, to his horror, should he meet, advancing with great speed up the steps, but Mrs. Ragg, who had managed to get out of the kitchen, and who bore, as a weapon of offence and defence, the large kitchen poker, which was of a glowing red heat. Todd caught a touch of it on his face.

"Oh, you villain of the world!" cried Mrs. Ragg, "I'll teach you to come here murdering people. My poor Tobias is no more, I know; but I'll take the law of you, I will. Murder! murder! Police! Colonel!"

With an alacrity, that was far beyond to all appearance Mrs. Ragg's powers, that good lady pursued Todd with the red-hot poker. He dared not take refuge in Tobias's room, for there stood Minna with the pistols in her hand, so he darted up the first flight of stairs he saw, which led to the top of the house. Mrs. Ragg pursued him; but when she got to the head of the stairs, Minna pressed too hard upon the hair-trigger of one of the pistols, and off it went. Mrs. Ragg fully believed herself shot, and rolled down the stairs, poker included; while Todd, labouring under the impression that the shot was at him, became still more anxious to find some place of refuge. Upon the landing, which he was not a moment in reaching, he found a great show of doors; for he was, in fact, upon the floor from which all the sleeping rooms of the servants opened. It was quite a chance that the first one he bounced into was one that had in the roof a little square trap-door, facetiously called "a fire escape;" but which, in the event of a fire, would have acquired the agility of a harlequin, and the coolness of a tax-gatherer to get through. Todd dragged a bedstead beneath the trap; and then his great height enabled him to thrust it open, and project his head through it. He found that part of his corporality was in the roof as it were — that is to say, in the cavity, between the ceiling of the room and the house. A trap-door of somewhat larger size in the actual roof, opened to the air. Todd dragged himself through, and was fairly upon the top of the colonel's house. A slippery elevation! But surely that was better than facing a red-hot poker, and a pair of hair-trigger duelling pistols; and so, for a time, the desire to escape kept down every other feeling. Even his revengeful thoughts gave way to the great principle of self-preservation; and Todd was only intent upon safely getting away. He glared round him upon the night sky, and a gaudy assemblage of chimney tops. What was he to do? In a minute he uttered a string of such curses, as we cannot very well here set down, and he turned preternaturally calm and still.

"Shall I go back," he said, "or escape?"

He heard the tramp of horses' feet, and peeping carefully over the front parapet of the house, he saw Colonel Jeffery arrive on horseback, and dismount. His groom led the horse away, and the colonel ascended the steps. Then, and not until then, Todd made up his mind.

"Escape," he said, "and be off."

There was a long sloping part of the roof close to where he was, and he thought that if he slid down that very carefully he should be able to get on to the roof of the next house, and so perchance through their trap door, and by dint of violence or cunning, or both united, reach the street.

It was a desperate resource, but his only one.

The top part of the long sloping roof was easily gained, and then Todd began to let himself down very carefully, but the angle of the roof was greater than he had imagined, and by the time he got about half way down he found a dangerous and most uncomfortable acceleration of motion ensuing.

It was in vain he tried to stop himself: down he went with a speed into the gutter behind the copping-stone, that left him lying there for a few moments half stunned, and scarcely conscious if he were safe or not.

The colonel's house, however, was stoutly built, and Todd's weight had not displaced anything; so that there he lay safe enough, wedged into a narrow rain gutter, from which, when he did recover himself sufficiently to make the attempt, he found some difficulty in wrenching himself out of.

Sore and shaken, Todd now looked about him. He was close to the roof of the next-door house. To be sure there was a chasm of sixty feet; but its width was not as many inches, so Todd ought, with his long legs, to easily step it.

CHAPTER LXXXIV.

TODD'S WONDERFUL ESCAPE.

THE STEP WAS BUT A TRIFLE; and yet, shaken as Todd was by his fall, it really seemed to him to be one of the most hazardous and nervous things in the world to take it.

He made two feints before he succeeded. At length he stood fairly upon the roof of the adjoining house. He did not say "Thank God!"; such words were not exactly in the vocabulary of Sweeney Todd; but he wiped the perspiration from his brow, and seemed to think that he had effected something at last.

And yet how far was he from safety? It is some satisfaction to have got such a man as Todd upon the house-tops. Who pities him? Who would be violently afflicted if he made a false step and broke his neck? No one, we apprehend; but such men, somehow, do not make false steps; and if they do, they manage to escape the consequences.

Surely it was about as ticklish a thing to crawl up a sloping roof as to come down one. Todd did not think so, however, and he began to shuffle up the roof of the house he was now on, looking like some gigantic tortoise, slowly making its way.

Reasoning from his experience of the colonel's house, Todd thought he should very well be able to pitch upon the trap, in the roof of the domicile upon which he was, nor was he wrong. He found it in precisely the same relative position, and then he paused.

He drew a long breath.

"What a mad adventure this is," he said; "and yet what a satisfaction it would have been to me, before I left England, to be able to feel that I had had my revenge upon that brat Tobias. That he had not altogether failed me after I had paid so much money to be rid of him. But that is over. I have failed in that attempt; but they shall not say it cost me my life. They will be bold people who stop me in my passage to the street in this house."

He felt the trap-door. It was fast.

"Humph!" he said, "doors are but bonds; and the rains of a few winters rot them quickly enough. We shall see."

The knife, with which he would have been well pleased to give poor Tobias his quietus, was thick and strong. He slid it under the wooden trap, and by mere force lifted it up. The nails of the bolt easily withdrew themselves from the rotten wood.

Todd was right. The rains of a few winters had done their work.

It was not exactly a time in the evening, when, in such a class of house, any one might be expected to be found in the attics; so Todd made no scruple of at once removing the lower trap in the ceiling.

He dropped comfortably enough on to the floor.

And now, coming suddenly as he did from the light, faint as it was, of the open air in the room, which he found himself, seemed to be involved in profound darkness; but that he knew would wear away in a few moments, and he stood still for his eyes to get accustomed to the semi-obscurity of the place.

Gradually, then, as though out of chaos, there loomed a bedstead and all the necessary appointments of a bed-room. It was untenanted; and so Todd, after listening intently, and believing, from the marked stillness that there prevailed, that the upper part of the house was deserted, walked to the door, and opening it, stood upon the landing.

"If I can now but step down stairs noiselessly, and open the street door, all will be well. People don't sit upon the staircase, and I may be fortunate enough to encounter no one."

There was no time to lose. Affairs in Fleet-street required his presence; and, besides, the present moment might be the most propitious, for all he knew, for the enterprise.

Down he went, not clinging to the balustrades — for who should say they might not wheeze and creak? — not walking upon the middle of the stairs, for there was no saying what tell-tale sounds they might give vocality to; but sliding along close to the wall, and stepping so quietly, that it would have required attentive ears to have detected his silent and steady march.

And so, flight by flight of these stairs Todd descended in safety, until he reached the passage. Yes, he got to the passage without the shadow of an interruption.

Then he heard voices in one of the parlours.

"Confound them!" said Todd, "they will hear me open the street door to a certainty; but it must be done."

He crept up to the door. There was some complicated latch upon it that defied all his knowledge of latches, and all his perseverance; and yet, no doubt, it was something that only required a touch; but he might be hours in finding out in the dark where to apply that touch.

He still heard the voices in the parlour.

More than five minutes — precious minutes to him — had already been consumed in fumbling at the lock of the street door; and then Todd gave it up as useless, and he crept to the parlour-door to listen to the speakers, and so, perhaps, ascertain the force that was within.

A female voice was speaking.

"Oh, dear me, yes, I daresay," it said. "You no doubt think that house can be kept for nothing, and that a respectable female wants no clothes to her back; but I can tell you, Mr. Simmons, that you will find yourself wonderfully mistaken, sir."

"Pshaw!" said a man's voice. "Pshaw! I know what I mean, and so do you. You be quiet wife, and think yourself well off, that you are as you are."

"Well off?"

"Yes, to be sure, well off."

"Well off, when I was forced to go to Mr. Rickup's party, in the same dress they saw me in last Easter. Oh! you brute!"

"What's the matter with the dress?"

"The matter? Why I'll tell you what the matter is. The matter is, and the long and short of everything, that you are a brute."

"Very conclusive indeed. The deuce take me if it ain't."

"I suppose by the deuce, you mean the devil, Mr. Simmons; and if he don't take you some day, he won't have his own. Ha! ha! you may laugh, but there's many a true word spoken in jest, Mr. Simmons."

"Oh, you are in jest, are you?"

"No sir, I am not, and I should like to know what woman could jest with only one black silk, and, that turned. Yes, Mr. Simmons, you often call upon the deuce to take this, and to take that. Mind he don't come some day to you when you least expect it sir, and say —"

"Lend me a light!" said Todd, popping his awfully ugly face right over the top of the half open door, a feat which he was able to accomplish by standing on his tip toes.

There are things that can be described, but certainly the consternation of Mr. and Mrs. Simmons cannot be included in the list. They gazed upon the face of Todd in speechless horror, nor did he render himself a bit less attractive by several of his most hideous contortions of visage.

Finding then that both husband and wife appeared spell-bound, Todd stepped into the room, and taking a candle from the table, he stalked into the passage with it.

The light in his hand threw a light upon the mystery of the lock. Todd opened the street-door, and passed out in a moment. To hurl the candle and candlestick into the passage, and close the door, was the next movement of Todd, but then he saw two figures upon the steps leading to Colonel Jeffery's house, and he shrunk back a moment.

"Now William," said Colonel Jeffery himself, "you will take this letter to Sir Richard Blunt, and tell him to use his own discretion about it."

"Yes, sir."

"Be quick, and give it into no hands but his own."

"Certainly, sir."

"Remember, William, this is important."

The groom touched his hat, and went away at a good pace, and Colonel Jeffery himself closed the door.

"Indeed," muttered Todd. "Indeed. So, Sir Richard Blunt, who is called an active magistrate, is to know of my little adventure here? Well—well—we shall see."

He darted from the door of the house, through which he had made so highly successful and adventurous a progress, and pursued William with such strides as soon brought him close up to him. But the thoroughfare in which they were was too public a one for Todd to venture upon any overt act in it.

He followed William sufficiently closely however to be enabled to take advantage of any opportunity that might present itself to possess himself by violence of the letter.

Now William had been told the affair was urgent, so of course he took all the nearest cuts he could to the house of Sir Richard Blunt, and such a mode of progress soon brought him into a sufficiently quiet street for Todd's purpose.

The latter looked right and left. He turned completely round, and no one was coming—a more favourable opportunity could not be. Stepping lightly up to William he by one heavy blow upon the back of his neck felled him.

The groom lay insensible.

Todd had seen him place the colonel's letter in his breast-pocket, and at once he dived his huge hand into that receptacle to find it. He was successful—one glance at the epistle that he drew forth sufficed to assure him that it was the one he sought. It was duly addressed to Sir Richard Blunt—"With speed and private."

"Indeed, very private," said Todd.

"Wretch! Wretch!" cried some one from a window, and Todd knew then that the deed of violence had been witnessed by some one from one of the houses.

With an execration, he darted off at full speed, and soon placed a perfect labyrinth of streets between him and all pursuit. He thrust the letter all crumbled up into his pocket, and he would not pause to read it until he was much nearer to Fleet-street than to the colonel's house, or the scene of his attack upon the groom. Then, by the light of a more than usually brilliant lamp, which with its expiring energies was showing the world what an old oil lamp could do, he opened and read the brief letter.

It was as follows.

> *Dear Sir Richard:*
>
> *Todd has been here upon murderous thoughts intent. Poor Tobias has, I fear, broken a blood-vessel, and is in a most precarious condition. I leave all to you. The villain escaped, but is injured I think.*
>
> *Yours very faithfully,*
> *John JEFFERY.*
> *To Sir Richard Blunt.*

"Broken a blood-vessel," said Todd. "Ha! ha! Broken a blood-vessel. Ha! Then Tobias may yet be food for worms, and the meat of the pretty crawlers to the banquet. Ha!"

He walked on with quite a feeling of elation; and yet there was, as he came to think, a something — he could not exactly define what — about the tone of the letter, that began upon second thoughts to give him no small share of uneasiness.

The familiar way in which he was mentioned as Todd merely, without further description, argued some foregone conclusion. It seemed to say, Todd, the man whom we both know so well, and have our eyes upon.

Did it mean that? A cold perspiration broke out upon the forehead of the guilty wretch. What was he to think? What was he to do?

He read the letter again. It sounded much more unmeaning and strange now. He had at first been too much dazzled by the pleasant intelligence regarding Tobias, to comprehend fully the alarming tone of the epistle; but now it waked upon his imagination, and his brain soon became vexed and troubled.

"Off — off, and away," he muttered. "Yes, I must be off before the dawn. The interception of this letter saves me for some few hours. In the morning, the colonel will see Sir Richard Blunt, and then they will come to arrest me; but I shall be upon the German Ocean by then. Yes, the Hamburgh ship for me."

He was so near his home now that it was not worth while to call a coach. He could run to Fleet-street quicker, so off he set at a great pace till his breath failed him.

Then he held on to a post so faint and weak, that a little child might have apprehended him.

"Curse them all," he said. "I wish they all had but one throat, and I a knife at it. All who cross me, I mean."

Time was rather an important element now in Todd's affairs, and he felt that he could not allow himself a long period even to recover from the state of exhaustion in which he was.

After a few minutes rest, he pushed on.

One of those sudden changes that the climate of this country is subject to, now took place; and although the sky had looked serene and bright, and there had been twinkling stars in the blue firmament but a short time before, Todd began to find that his clothing was but little protection against the steady rain that commenced falling with a perseverance that threatened something lasting.

"All is against me," he said. "All is against me."

He struggled on with the rain dashing in his face, and trickling, despite all his exertions to the contrary, down his neck. Suddenly he paused, and laid his finger upon his forehead, as though a sudden thought of more than ordinary importance had come across his mind.

"The turpentine!" he said. "The turpentine. Confound it, I forget the turpentine."

What this might mean was one of Todd's own secrets; but before he went home, he ran down several streets until he came to a kind of wholesale drug warehouse.

He rang the bell violently.

"What is it?" said a voice.

"The small keg of turpentine that was to be sent to Mr. Todd's in Fleet-street, is particularly wanted."

"It was sent about half an hour ago."

"Oh, thank you — thank you. That will do. A wet night."

In a few minutes more he was at his own shop-door.

Made in the USA
Las Vegas, NV
25 November 2024

12530633R00295